Some Would Call This Living

by

Herman Bang

Translated from the Danish
by Janet Garton, Charlotte Barslund and Paul Russell Garrett

Norvik Press
2022

Norvik Press Series B: English Translations of Scandinavian Literature, no. 84.

A catalogue record for this book is available from the British Library.

ISBN: 978-1-909408-68-5

Norvik Press
Department of Scandinavian Studies
UCL
Gower Street
London WC1E 6BT
United Kingdom
Website: www.norvikpress.com
E-mail address: norvik.press@ucl.ac.uk

Layout: Essi Viitanen
Cover photograph of Herman Bang by Johan Georg Heinrich Ludwig Tönnies, Royal Danish Library.
Cover inside sketch of Herman Bang by P. S. Krøyer (1851-1909).

Norvik Press gratefully acknowledges grants from Statens Kunstfond, Augustinus Fonden, Konsul George Jorck og hustru Emma Jorck's Fond, and the University of Minnesota.

Acknowledgements

This volume would not have appeared without substantial help from a wide variety of people. We are indebted to *De Bangske Morgenmænd* (The Danish Bang Society) for taking the initiative and suggesting the list of contents; their intimate knowledge of Herman Bang's writings has been invaluable in guiding the editors and translators. They helped us with the location of elusive texts, and with information about possible sources of funding. Sonny Sahl was particularly helpful in chasing up obscure references, determining the meaning of some of Bang's more enigmatic expressions and generally giving us the benefit of his extensive bibliographical knowledge. Det Danske Sprog- og Litteraturselskab, through the good offices of Jesper Gehlert Nielsen, permitted us to make use of the texts, notes and information contained in their publications of Herman Bang's works, *Romaner og noveller* 1-10 (2008-10), *Vekslende Themaer* I-IV (2006), and *Ti Aar* (2013). Poul Houe, Emeritus Professor at the University of Minnesota, has contributed encouragement, assistance with grant applications and a scholarly introduction.

We are immensely grateful to the grant-awarding bodies who have made this publication possible. The ever-generous Statens Kunstfond, which has done so much to support translations of Danish authors, has again backed the translation of this Danish classic. Augustinus Fonden and Konsul George Jorck og hustru Emma Jorck's Fond have supported the project. And the University of Minnesota, through Poul Houe, has provided a grant towards the costs of publication. We hope that this volume will be worthy of the investment.

Janet Garton
Norvik Press
September 2021

CONTENTS

Journalism 351

Epilogue 423

Notes 431

Introduction

Introduction

by Poul Houe

When Danish critic Georg Brandes launched the so-called 'Modern Breakthrough' in Danish (and Nordic) literature some 150 years ago, he meant to animate literary artists to catch up with the times and debate current societal problems, embracing the progressive achievements of the natural sciences and democratic values such as women's rights – all parts of a secularized modernity. But not all of the best contemporary writers were in lockstep with Brandes's catch phrases, and when he published a volume on *Det moderne Gennembruds Mænd* (The Men of the Modern Breakthrough, 1883), it excluded 'such lesser militants as the eminent Realist Herman Bang, whose *Realisme og Realister* [Realism and Realists] (1879), a programmatic equivalent to Brandes's work, offered a far more generous treatment of its opponents, and a far more advanced Modernism than the traditional Romantic version espoused by Brandes'[1] – all of which suggests that the breakthrough Brandes envisioned was symptomatic of more complicated mental and social transformations.

Once the initial breakthrough had run its course, and Bang's younger generation of Danish realist prose writers emerged on the scene, subtler human sentiments came to the fore – whether in texts by Bang himself or by such contemporaries as Henrik Pontoppidan – and often with greater artistic strength, nuance and impact than their precursors had achieved. Born in 1857, incidentally the year free-trade competition became law and the modern liberal market economy took off in Danish society, Bang spent his earliest years in Southern Jutland, from where he and his parents moved further up the peninsula in 1864, the year their Schleswig home – along with two-fifths of Denmark's territory – was lost to Prussia. After high school graduation, Bang left this second Jutland home – and his mentally ill father, Pastor Bang – for Copenhagen, to begin a university course of study that would soon give way to his pursuit of a career as journalist and later writer of fiction.

What distinguished Bang from the outset was his feel for the conflicting sentiments that marked the modern era he inhabited; these later came to define his products of both journalistic and fictional prose, and the interplay between the two. A sense of stable provincial location and tradition never left him, but was early disrupted – directly or indirectly – by his equally alert attention to urban dynamics and restless vivacity. Always perceptive of mainstream culture's superficial features, Bang became a migratory spirit, notably targeted by homophobes. He stood out as a 'participant observer', displaying a variety of technical skills, whether in newspaper articles, novels or short stories, that revealed self-reflection and perceptions of the world in equal measure – and soon captured his readers' attention and liberated his own spirit in one gesture. A phrase used about the American historian Henry Adams as someone who 'climbed on the fence to watch himself go by', fits Bang as well.[2]

Although more than one hundred years have passed since Bang's death in 1912, the scale of technological progress and troubling disruptions that defined his phase of the modern era – and to which he bears striking witness – has not diminished. People's health and life expectancy have increased remarkably since those days, but so have the social inequities that repeatedly arrested Bang. Displacement remains both a social and geographical reality, and troubles as many now as it did then. And while many emigrants Bang watched leaving Denmark for the US were in more dire straits than some of today's refugees and asylum seekers, others were more hopeful. Criss-crossing Europe well before globalization's heyday, Bang may have been one of its trailblazers, but also one who ranked displacement as a major side-effect.

As for displacement overall, today's prospects of AI and machine learning both dwarf and magnify the cultural upheavals Bang encountered. Algorithms and robots will likely advance the well-being of some humans, but will as likely replace others, whether as workers or as members of a functioning democracy (a trend already on the rise in Bang's lifetime, now a worldwide siege). In his best work, Bang enables, or compels, his readers to witness and contemplate the increasingly delicate balance between the brightness of modern progress and the shadows it casts.

For these reasons alone he remains a moving stimulator, which is one justification for this anthology. Another is that Bang's century-old reputation as an important writer was limited to continental Europe and never took hold in the Anglophone world. During his lifetime, when most of his major works were translated across Europe – into German not least – hardly any appeared in English (which he didn't speak), and to this day such translations remain rare. All that has entered the English-speaking world is a small handful of his novels, less than twice that number of his many short stories, and not a single one of his countless journalistic pieces.

This anthology is meant to remedy this deplorable statistic by assembling some of Bang's best and most timely writings in the prose formats he is least known for in the English-speaking world, where only four of the selected texts have appeared before. To that end the editors have consulted with the Danish Bang Society (*De Bangske Morgenmænd*) and have largely followed its recommendations for the volume's contents, so that readers can rest assured that the first selection of the author's short prose in English translation is backed by scholarly consensus. What remains of this introduction will, first, point to some distinctive features of individual texts and, second, to the double-dealing just alluded to: Bang's negotiation of societal progress and its unintended human consequences. The theme unfolds in both his faction and fiction, but because its existential gravity is centered in the latter, texts from here (the volume's opening part) will be addressed last, to show the extent to which the same 'futurism' that upheld the Modern Breakthrough often undermined its humanism – and still does.

*

'Herman Bang the publicist delivered three to four thousand contributions to more than one hundred newspapers, magazines, and yearbooks,' writes John Chr. Jørgensen in his book about Bang's journalism.[3] Add to these numbers the multi-faceted portrait Jørgensen paints of the author and his craft – based on this elaborate source material – and it is clear that the eleven journalistic pieces selected for translation in the present anthology are but a small window on Bang's overall achievement. That said, his innovative force and means, tireless ability to capture the attention of readers within a rapidly changing public sphere, and unique artistic capacity, which he both invested in and separated from his journalism – all of these features are on view in the anthologized material.

In 'An Event', its second-to-last piece (no. 28), Bang celebrates the Danish automobile society for spotlighting the new technology, bypassing railway (im)mobility while new legislation submits to future speed and spirit. So, what's next, one wonders? The answer, both revealing and scary, comes from the same mouth that had just vented futuristic hyperbole. 'In a Flash' (no. 29), like a flash in the pan, is a short piece about an incident too shocking to be accidental. A person bumps into a car and gets decapitated, her head left behind in a pool of blood, 'like the face of a wax doll.' This is reportage, but shaped with theatrical means and self-reflection as its goal. The frenzy allowed to fuel 'An Event' is thus deflated into a shadow of the endless optimism it had failed to temper with afterthought. What got beheaded 'in a flash' was not progress but thoughtless progressivism – including Bang's own.

The Journalism section's opening salvo, a handful of texts written more than three decades earlier, reveals the same schism between modernity's upsides and downsides, but also the observer's different take on them. His piece about 'Magasin du Nord' (no. 20), modern Denmark's emblematic up-and-coming department store and corporation, lacks neither self-reflection nor self-criticism. What it points out, everyone could see for themselves – except those who have trouble seeing the forest for trees. For their sake – and with no ulterior motive – it lays out factual details that speak for the whole, no matter what thoughtless readers may think. Formally, it is Bang's impressionism incarnate, brimming with anecdotes and whimsical observations, now commented on, now mixed with data about the firm's business model and its large revenues allowing for low profits that in turn enable cheap consumer products. Neither these virtues nor the vices concern him as much as what he believes his audience should know about the future market economy's crankshaft, which he deems 'impressive', but whose inner workings he seeks to present as facts of life, rather than something good or evil.

Surrounding this neutral, if fairly upbeat, account are grimmer social reportages. 'A Poor Folks' Inn' (no. 19) features homeless lowlifes; 'Visiting the Poor Before Christmas' (no. 22), other deplorable adults; and 'The House with the Happy Faces' (no. 21), street children deposited in orphanages. A named person in the inn is lost in 'melancholy observation' while nameless others cunningly survive the chaos indoors, located near a snowy street that strikes the observer as 'deserted, empty and dark.'

In the Christmas piece, our witness, along with his police informant, tours entire city districts cursed by despair, hungry faces of women and children behind dirty windows in narrow alleys, bypassed by unaffected burghers. These are impressions of a reality beyond words that Bang deftly commits to – words. Even buildings and kitchens, as destitute as their paralyzed inhabitants, 'speak out', he recalls, because their testimony is unspeakable! Humanity dissolves before his eyes, and the policeman's stories sound like 'bad jokes at a funeral feast.' While adults float around like carrion, the children gulp vodka and would be lucky to drop off the cliff before *they* end up as adults. Too much to put into words, and Bang can hardly move the hand that holds his pen, yet succeeds in turning his verbal incapacity into a startling incentive. Empty stomachs cause this social evil, yet empty words are not lame bystanders but rather potential performatives that may incentivize readers to fill the empty stomachs that drained the writer's soul but moved his pen.

The Copenhagen orphanage and its young residents that Bang visited between his adult encounters are an offshoot of the blighted grown-up world. Yet calling it 'The House with the Happy Faces' is no misnomer. Though products of deprived adults, these little ones still harbor a zest for life, as when they mask their street-begging as sale of lottery tickets. Many elders turn a blind eye to this as an urban nuisance, but Bang does the opposite and nails what victimizes the children, wondering if the swamp they are stuck in cannot be drained, for instance, by heroic teachers socializing disadvantaged pupils into self-reliance and collaboration, or 'quiet existences' helping little apprentices turn their activities into an education for life.

Empathetic attention – not politics or religion, not preconceived optimism, pessimism, or cynicism – was Bang's most, if not entirely, reliable lodestar. Wouldn't, for instance, a child's secular work and deeds be worthy of religious praise? Isn't any virtue deserving of God's favor?

On balance, Bang claims no direct link between 'Magasin's' alluring marketplace and the sidelining of commoners, old and young, elsewhere in downtown Copenhagen. Lacking obvious cause-and-effect connections, like the one between the car and car accident, the juxtaposition of dystopian drunks and utopian shoppers at the same place and time instead invites readers' reflection, which Bang's inclusion of 'dark feuilletons' like nos. 19 and 21 among his social reportages in *Herhjemme og Derude* (At Home and Abroad, 1881) facilitates by highlighting decisive contrasts.[4] To expound this title's meaning Jørgensen maintains that for Bang, travel and places abroad are indispensable for grasping what is happening before your own eyes at home. The implication – that journalism always benefits from pointed comparisons – modifies Jørgensen's own conclusion that 'Bang's view of journalism was as fluctuating as his career'.[5] *Always* cannot be 'fluctuating'!

Another (double) text from *Herhjemme og derude* included in this anthology drives the point home. 'On "Thingvalla" I-II' has Bang onboard the America-liner from Copenhagen to Kristiania. In Part I he boards the ship, observes its passengers and digests his impressions. Unlike made-up fictional characters, these are victims of a reality that puts fiction to shame. Many, mostly farmers or farmhands, have been ousted from their homeland and homes – or rather houses, as Henrik Ibsen put it – either by poverty or by failures ignored by the selfish bourgeoisie. Empty-eyed, they bid farewell to the old country with 'something called a hurrah' before drifting in different directions. Some seem immoral skeptics or hotheaded thieves – at least that's what Bang figures as he tries to put himself in their shoes – others mere pragmatists just hoping for a better future abroad, including a schoolteacher doomed to spinsterhood in Denmark but anticipating an immigrant community short of women where she might yet get married.

In Part II of the article, on 'Thingvalla''s first day at sea, a more detailed image of the emigrant crowd shapes up as people calm down. Snooping around and peeping into trunks, recording ticket prices and passengers' constipation, meeting an unbearable American optimist – who deems him a worrier, reluctant to take chances – Bang also encounters chickens and pigs running around, even notes some urbanites whose fondness for luxury bodes ill for their survival. The atmosphere is idyllic, like a truce before battle. Disembarking in Kristiania, our reporter recalls the mood onboard as a feverish epidemic, crowned with noisy salutes to the future, teary goodbyes to the past and handshakes left and right. Soon dark smoke from the ship's chimney is the only trace that remains, and then not even that. Watching this load of countrymen moving on, Bang finds their hopes for the future as unrealistic as their dismissal of the past seems strained.

Bang's most revered journalistic piece is 'The Fire', his reportage from the conflagration that one night in 1884 consumed the Danish parliament building across from his editor's house, where he wrote his article. Earlier he had been directly on site, marginally participating in the rescue operation while amassing the nerve-wrecking impressions that fuel his article and throw the entire calamity into relief. To hold out such a finely-tuned antenna while life is at stake, and then to be able to process what was seen, heard, and smelled at that moment, takes sensitivity and writing skill all at once. Imparting 'chaos' and 'confusion' presupposes the ability to be personally shaken while staying unshakable enough to commit one's shakes to paper, so that they can shake the reader similarly. The opposites meeting here do not mitigate but illuminate each other – to the point of super-real transparency.

Other contradictions come together in Bang's remaining journalistic pieces. No. 25, 'Letter from Herman Bang', includes musings about travel and people from across Germany's class and gender divides: the imperial family's pettiness, the iron chancellor's concealed softness, the embarrassing uniformity of urban males, and females looking like numbers in double-entry book-keeping. In 'Smart', no. 27, Danish men of pleasure in cities large and small come across as empty shells heading for lucrative days in America.

Finally, in 'The Chinese', no. 26, Bang visits the sentiments Europeans and Americans alike harbor against far-Eastern migrants whose subservient labor force they see intruding on Western ways and norms. He criticizes both sides, but especially the hypocrisy of whites spewing venom at the 'others' while relishing the cheap consumer goods their presence enables; yet he concludes on a Eurocentric note – perhaps reflecting his constituents', perhaps his own stance – that the newcomers are 'souls, who dig like rats, who toil like ants, who cannot be held back by water or mountains … Is it possible that it is not only our linen cupboards we should be locking and bolting.' A prejudiced vision resonating to this day.

As others have pointed out, Bang's journalism is remarkably complex and multi-dimensional, and, we might add, in a timely way ahead of its time. Besides a variety of *issues*, his concern is about the *market* and the *sale* of his products – parts of *new journalism's* transition from opinion to news press.[6] But while he laments 'the screaming contradiction between the bourgeois ideas of equality and freedom and the actual miseries in society',[7] his primary focus remains the *human* condition, caught in the middle, with upsides he does not ignore, but downsides he prioritizes as he eyes the thin veil between utopia and dystopia. Probing these bright versus dark sides, Bang's fiction shows less concern for either than for the shadows cast by the bright side's inclination to self-congratulation.[8]

*

This interplay already marks the semi-fictional sections that surround his journalism, for instance his portrait of Sarah Bernhardt (no. 18), which features an artist as self-contradictory as the world itself, pursuing her own selfhood while enacting raging pessimism and larger fear of life than of death. Locked up in her art, this virtuosa, both a child of modernity and its slave, ends a signature performance with a hopeless dance – before 'troubled … stillness' descends as 'happiness' on stage. A borderliner like Shakespeare, Bernhardt feels both entitled and obligated to play Hamlet, torn between neurosis and insanity.

In no. 14, 'An Artist's Tour of Bornholm', the first of four autobiographical sketches, Bang travels with theater artists through an indifferent world and reflects their tragicomic plight with scathing irony. In 'Expelled from Germany' (no. 15), he himself is expelled as a dangerous revolutionary from one place and a nihilist from another, constantly chased, if not by bloodless authorities, then by a sneaky hostess looking for a spouse to provide for her. Finally, in 'A Christmas Eve on Foreign Soil' (no. 16), his experiences of hassle give way to more intimate scenes – still from Central Europe but more like his social reporting from Denmark.

Bang and another penniless artist visiting Prague have invited two neighbors to join them for Christmas. After an anxious start, quiet settles and holiday memories are shared that turn darker once the guests leave and Bang's co-host divulges his life before merciless audiences had rejected him, exactly what Bang had witnessed happen to others on Bornholm. Artists are outcasts, and unsentimental stories about their encounters with inhumanity are humanly gripping[9] – not just to them but to Bang, who has dark memories of his own. Parts of life are bright, but most are not, as brightness tends to breed darkness. For now, though, Christmas Eve is over, and while banality and reality reign supreme outside, the two hosts finally receive some money by mail that allows them to move on – to a better evening on the town.

The title of this anthology resonates directly with the concluding line of 'Irene Holm' (no. 6), and for good reason. Perhaps the best-known of all his short story fictions, this classical text is a model display of Bang's artistic craft and outlook. Frøken Holm is a humble spinster struggling for survival as an itinerant dance teacher for farm children. When asked at the end of a season by her pupils' parents to perform solo, she cannot resist the temptation but enacts the role she was never offered as a dance school student herself. But like Ibsen's Nora, ferociously dancing her tarantella, Irene goes overboard in her dance and arouses the laughter and scorn of the adults – except the pastor's daughter, whose empathy for the loser spells out an unsentimental respect for the human, not least when it borders on the pitiful.

Preceding the parents' reception of Irene's 'performance,' much small-scale inhumanity has come her way – what the story's finish line defines as the gap between life and what people *call* life. The solo dance she found climactic was socially – or more objectively – a low-point; even the narrative's display of her trivial life overall might be an embellishment, a *so-called* reality. An itinerant spinster traveling around in life, Irene is getting nowhere. Nor is humanity, shown in Bang's stagecraft to be caught between a verbal mask of life and nothingness behind the mask; or between empathy and pity. Entering the panoramic whole, most scenic elements are verbally stripped down. Bang's realism *makes* illusion – only to *break* it!

Even if this snapshot of his signature piece may capture his short story *oeuvre* in a nutshell, each nut has its own taste and texture. When 'A Poet's Wife' (no. 1) sees her husband return to poetry (inspired by another woman) after earlier expressing himself more straightforwardly, she feels betrayed and sets the relation between the human and the poetic on fire by nearly burning her wedding vows along with his poems. A more humble, lonely human, the eponymous protagonist of 'The Mistress' (no. 2), is rather devoted to other lonely people and to nature – and follows true morals instead of communal morality in the process. One more 'quiet existence' with no frills attached.

The title character of 'Charlot Dupont' (no. 4) is an unappreciated artist living what few would call a life. Once a child prodigy, both he and his mother were brutally exploited by his licentious father, assisted by a greedy impresario. Now Charlot performs for cynical audiences and reporters in an atmosphere of ruthless competition and deceit. Good in this world is exploitable, and once the youngster on stage no longer fits the bill, he is disposed of. Knocking about as best he can, by the age of twenty all he has left of life is a future on stage in empty theaters.

Both Charlot and the depravity around him remind one of 'Franz Pander' (no. 3). Lazy and decadent, a good-for-nothing addicted to surface aesthetics,

Franz is a boy obsessed with light but haunted by darkness, who ignores girls but relishes their attributes. Reified by self-destructive desires, he can find no meaningful place in the world, where the void of spectacle sucks all oxygen out of the air, so when you search, you shall find – death by suicide.

The world in which 'Her Highness' (no. 5) is trapped is no better, but one of tired youth, dispirited servility, suffocating formality – her mother's steely perfectionism not least – and pompous mediocrity, of which only she is aware! Bang's narrative is sarcastic, funny, over- and under-stating. Again, life is worth living only if you are not part of it. Her Highness sees no future, only a past lost in the now. Given the story's humor, her *lack* of it is tragi-comic. Only in nature may she briefly escape the shade of bygone times – before her own story, like a firework, 'was extinguished, little by little'. Another case of what is called living. 'The Last Ballgown' (no. 7), published a year later, is both different and similar. No highfalutin dystopia here, but an idyllic, provincial life, it seems, yet one of lifeless banality. Time ticks away – until another life is left behind, wasted, to watch a new generation indulge *its* appetite for so-called life.

The title of 'A Lovely Day' (no. 8), seems to strike a different tone. But as an upper-class celebrity and her entourage exploit a lower-class family's hospitality, these underlings' stressed life and lost souls are laid bare, and the 'lovely day' they try to provide is proven a sham. Similarly, the title character of 'Frøken Caja' (no. 9) is an underdog laboring for an ice-cold, guesthouse-owning mother, whose self-centered customers Caja unselfishly serves (even advising one not to let life pass her by – as it does Caja!). This farcical mess of humans buzzing around and acting happy in their splendid isolation could be a prelude to 'A Tale of Happiness' (no. 11), which would then be happiness' postmortem: pleasure-seeking young nobility killing time – and a protagonist's vitality – under heaps of platitudes.

Spleen lurks in most of Bang's stories, and 'Les Quatres Diables' (no. 10) is no exception. Four children, brought up together by a ruthless showman training them to become circus artists, turn successful adults as the 'Four Devils' – until one's erotic deception of another triggers (self-)destructive instincts. The urge for sexual satisfaction ignites a struggle that effaces all morality and empathy and humiliates even the humiliator. The team loses self-control and heads for the abyss, with only a pack of castrated dogs suggesting a peaceful end to the madness. The devils are on a suicidal roller coaster, whose driver's single source of joy is the havoc in his path. Still, the ride goes unnoticed, and the marketplace is especially lively on the day of death![10] As so often, Bang sees humans casting the darkest shadows – on the values they supposedly hold most dear.

Rock bottom is hit in 'The Ravens' (no. 12), one of his later and longest short stories. When wealthy turn-of-the-century hunchback Viktoria, after hosting a family gathering of older and younger civil servants, questions herself about what life has brought her, the answer is nothing – nothing but the conviction that her guests, falsely praising while de facto mocking her, will remember her after her death because of the inheritance she has left them. Associations to death are as many as the shades of sarcasm and irony cast during the narrative's dance of death around its central figure. Her family's microcosm of tragi-comic modernity is interconnected by the lowest common denominator of greed and envy, indirectly aimed at one another, and directly at Viktoria, who, they agree, deserves the madhouse because the cost of her party chips away at everyone else's inheritance.

Hollowness and falsehoods reign supreme within this group, in which sexuality, friendships, and family ties are all for sale to the highest bidder. Your money or your life is the law, or 'the dead are company for the dead', as one guest puts it. Besides consumption of people or news, appearances must be kept up at all cost – even Viktoria has a spider's eyes and an inside void. Meanwhile, as examples of moral decay pile up, the story repeats poetic lines about 'amour' and prosaic ones like: 'why don't you want to *do* anything, young man?' – which the young idler who answers the question wonders about himself: 'What is there to do?' Enhanced by ads and streetcars and other urban flavors, this is the world Bang's ravens swoop down upon and puncture.

Is there any light at the end of his short stories' tunnels? The anthology's last sample, '"Barchan is Dead"' (no. 13), seems to suggest there is, even as darkness here stems from the mystery of narration itself. The complicated storyline begins when the sole living character, a Russian, admits to the nameless epic narrator that he is a murderer. When he is not believed, he starts his lengthy story about another character, who tells about the death of Barchan, a third one – all the while absorbed in real and poetic lying and ghostly fantasies, fears and traumas. Doubtful as to who killed whom, the epic narrator interjects that 'all this is just fantasy', while his informant wonders '*how can you know what you don't know?*' and 'why can your willpower not control your dreams too?' Whatever the answers, the story ends with its fictitious teller 'looking out into the darkness', stating: '"I left Russia"' – after which Bang's narrator brings light to darkness by comforting him.

*

Two of the anthology's texts came about during Bang's last days alive. The vision of America he expressed thirty years earlier in his 'Thingvalla'-piece (no. 23) came to personal fruition when he finally went 'By Ship Across the Atlantic' (no. 17), as he called his autobiographical account of the trip that took him all the way to New York. Though comparable to the 'Thingvalla' scene, reactions, conversations, and emotions – from angst and fear to excited expectations – are now artfully depicted as a cacophony or mosaic of verbal tremors unfolding on a shaking deck. With Titanic fantasies about an unsinkable ship (the 'Imperator') as part of the mix, all served in spicy humanistic sauce, the whole world seems to be sailing with its life in the balance. Even a big loudmouth ends up next to Bang 'on the trembling sofa, silent, side by side, in front of the large mirror – in front of our own trembling reflections.'[11]

Bang the artist rarely loses his cool. Interviewed in the anthology's last entry, 'Herman Bang on America' (no. 30), he comes across as equally observant and open-minded – 'there isn't a spark of an idea in my books' – yet skeptical and fairly unimpressed by the new world, once he sets foot in New York. A more technically advanced modernity than one finds in Europe's big cities, perhaps, but as much for ill as for good, judging from the gadgets he must master as a tourist. For all its ground-breaking boldness, modernity had a muted soundboard in Bang, one tempering impressions with will and skill. As 'participant observer' he staged himself close enough to get a penetrating view of his subjects and objects but not so close as to misunderstand or be seduced by what he had in sight.

A restless traveler, Bang didn't belittle one place for the sake of another. Away and home are different and each may enlarge or diminish the other – and become a blessing or a curse. Travel between genres is no different, and while much separates Bang's short story fiction and journalism, border crossings allow elements from either side to assist the other in its grappling with the modern enterprise and its tendency to precipitate unintended consequences and make its utopian bent tilt towards dystopia.

There are many overriding – or underpinning – patterns to be found in the variety of texts in this volume, and while this introduction has been at pains to underscore some of them more than others, the purpose was never to minimize Bang's complexity but to suggest its scope by way of clarification. Especially when pursued for clarity, no single pattern should obscure the fact that Bang's richness exceeds any one trend or train of thought. Rather, such a pattern might inspire views of life beyond the pattern's own perimeter.

Though often castigated as a sissy by the prejudiced of his time, Bang is not a writer catering to sissies, which is to say, people discriminating against others. Instead, whether he crosses or upholds cultural demarcation lines as an artist or journalist, he never does so in disrespect for the underlying humanity. A timeless position that is now as timely as ever.[12]

Notes

1 Poul Houe: 'Georg Brandes', in *The Cambridge History of Literary Criticism*, Vol. VI. Ed. M.A.R. Habib (Cambridge, 2013), p. 472.

2 Cf. Carolyn Porter: *Seeing and Being: The Plight of the Participant Observer in Emerson, James, Adams, and Faulkner* (Middletown CT, 1981), p. 43, 168; my notion of 'participant observer' is also indebted to Porter, pp. 30-43, 47-53, 279-292, 300-2.

3 John Chr. Jørgensen: *Jeg der kender Pressens Melodier ...: Herman Bangs journalistik* (Copenhagen, 2003), p. 142.

4 Ibid., p. 41.

5 Ibid., pp. 119-120.

6 Claes Kastholm Hansen: 'Den professionelle', in Herman Bang: *Reportager*. Ed. Kastholm Hansen (Copenhagen, 1983), pp. 22, 24f.; Jørgensen, p. 10.

7 Kastholm Hansen, p. 21. Every so often Bang's social reportages call to mind the (Norwegian-)American economist and sociologist Thorstein Veblen (born the same year as Bang), who famously 'recast "economics as the cultural history of material life"' and with whose catchwords 'pecuniary culture' and 'conspicuous consumption' from his classical work on *The Theory of the Leisure Class* Bang's critical outlook and attitude seem remarkably in sync. This is not to say that Veblen, while of great import to many American literary figures, had any direct influence on Bang, but that his socio-cultural concerns have great affinity to Bang's journalistic agenda, e.g., the American's 'awareness that too much money was in the hands of too few people who had too limited a notion of what do with their barbaric booty'; his contempt for 'making money in ways that separate the haves from the have-nots'; and his scorn of discreet modern-day gluttony – all parts of his take on the new economic world order. (See Martha Banta: 'Introduction' to the Oxford World Classics edition of Veblen's work [Oxford, 2007], pp. vii, x, xiii, xix).

8 How fast the veil in question can get torn came across recently. In 2011 famed American journalist Thomas Friedman found his Minneapolis hometown breeding 'deep optimism about America and the notion that we really can act collectively for the common good', only to deem the same place 'a dangerous and dystopian ghost town' in 2021. Reversals like this were foregrounded in the era of Bang and his ilk – artistically emphasizing the human costs involved. (Quotes from *StarTribune* editorial, 06/29/21). Cf. also Jørgensen, p. 97.

9 Instead of unsentimental, the poet Johannes Jørgensen found Bang 'alternating between irony and sentimentality'; cf. (John Chr.) Jørgensen, p. 177, note 340.

10 The version of 'Les Quatre Diables' printed in *Værker i Mindeudgave* (1920) has a further sentence added which is not in the original version translated here: 'Der var netop den Aften meget livligt paa Markedet' ('That evening it was especially lively in the market').

11 Cf. also Jørgensen, pp. 115 f.

12 Jørgensen, p. 141.

Short Stories

1. A Poet's Wife

They had already been married for four years.

He was quite young when they first met, a young dark-eyed man who looked like a child. And his new renown as a poet, which he had won without struggle as if in a friendly tournament, where his finely-crafted sonnets singing the praises of the ladies had brought him the laurels of victory, had endowed him with a particular charm. There was something of the pampered child prodigy about this grown-up boy, who looked so childlike and yet sang so sweetly about Venetian nights and Neapolitan tarantellas. He was regarded as a precocious child.

Women always enjoy playing with such a child, in whom they can glimpse a future man. It is a woman's happiest dream to be a man's *first* love. So there were many who wanted to play with Viktor, and romantic and sensual as he was, he glided from one infatuation to the next. It rarely developed into anything very serious; he had become something of a troubadour – those troubadours of whom he sang so often – and sighs and fluttering hearts and stolen kisses had become for him the essentials of love.

And men indulged him as much as women did. It was as if they didn't regard him as their equal: he remained a strange luxury object with an aura of something foreign, an exotic nature. A child who made you smile, and with whom you could never get angry. Although he was not lacking in talent, he never seemed to stand in anyone's way; he was an exception who never challenged anyone else's ambition. And at the same time his helplessness was alluring, his attractive weakness appealing. Most men had something of the same feeling for Viktor as big dogs have for small ones. A superior sympathy, which is very satisfying because it involves such a secure awareness of one's own power.

But Viktor found nothing humiliating in this. He simply accepted the pampering, and the more he was pampered the more of a world-weary child prodigy he became, and the less of a man.

In this way Viktor could live under the protection of his fame as a young poet like a vulnerable boy.

She was not beautiful, her figure was too slender and her features too irregular. Only when she spoke did she sometimes appear good-looking; that was because of a peculiar lively mobility in her expression and a flash of intelligence in her eyes. The only intoxicating thing about her was her laughter; it began as a strange gurgle, and then gushed forth, clear as a bell, and you could feel that she was abandoning herself to it utterly. It made a remarkably refreshing impression, that laughter. Yet it was rare for her to laugh, and most of the time she seemed cool, very calm and self-possessed. She was very far from being sexily provocative; rather she was one of those unaware women who can die unmarried without having felt deprived.

Yet Martha had nevertheless loved, or rather she had been in love. One of those fleeting eighteen-year-old's infatuations, which are as fresh and tender as spring blossoms, of a purer colour than any other flowers and with a purer ethereal scent, which has nothing in common with the heavy sweetness of summer perfume. But it can happen that a late night frost destroys those tender early flowers.

That is what had happened to Martha. It was a straightforward and trivial event which she soon got over and later on only remembered with a slight feeling of shame. But if you were to examine it closely, you might find that this rapidly withering infatuation, which had wilted for lack of sunshine and sympathy, had left perceptible traces in her soul. You never forget your first love, and even in the most fleeting infatuation there is some love, something of the true spark, and we feel pain when it is extinguished.

When the first serious passion dies in a woman's heart like an early anemone mercilessly blighted by frost, there can still come a summer in her life, she can be happy in summer love. Nevertheless, she never forgets that frosty night in her early spring. Always in her innermost heart there grows the seed of an almost unnoticeable bitterness, there dwells a chilly breeze, a shade of the darkness of night.

Such women can forget and they can love. They rarely fall in love again.

Viktor had a strange effect on Martha. Her strength was indignant at the sight of his playful weakness, but his talent attracted her, captivated her constantly, ensnared her over and over again. She was bewitched, not by *him*, but by his talent, and her first feeling was one of pity, almost sorrow at the fact that so feeble a man should possess the capacity to become such a significant poet. His first overtures to her were driven by a whim; he was used to being flattered by all, and she had not flattered him. That was enough for him to want to force her to notice him.

Then on closer acquaintance she was suddenly seized by a kind of genuinely female enthusiasm for a mission which seemed to present itself to her, that of making a man of this poet, making him strong and watching him grow. And gradually he was possessed by a deep respect, which was something new and amazing to him, a respectful, not at all romantic attraction, which had more to do with friendship than with love and desire. She began to direct his life even before they became engaged.

When after three or four months he finally plucked up courage and proposed, she accepted.

So now they had been married for four years.

Their marriage had been unusually happy. Their sympathy had grown day by day, a deep, intimate sympathy, which encompassed their whole lives and completely filled Viktor's existence. He had grown under her hands, it was as if she had shared her strength, and by continually yielding she had adroitly made him strong. It was as if she became the weaker in their calm, harmonious marriage.

Martha relished her triumph. Yet some way into the third year of their marriage she was seized by a sudden anxiety, an inexplicable fear. She had brought her husband a not inconsiderable fortune, and he himself was in no way poor. Therefore he did not need to write in order to live. Shortly after his marriage he had published a large book of poetry, a collection of lyric poems principally from the period when he had been courting Martha. Since then he had written very little; he read a certain amount, and composed some critical articles for a weekly magazine, otherwise nothing. Martha mentioned the subject rarely, and when she did mention it he always complained about the lack of subjects. He saw nothing, he said.

And those three words: I see nothing, became her life's nightmare. She felt paralysed by a gnawing fear; it seemed that as the man in him grew, the poet faded away. So was he not able to live this life?

She sank into endless, oppressive reflection. She could sit for hours with her hands in her lap, going over and over the same thoughts, a long and laborious process which always ended in a question mark.

Was it necessary for a poet to be a weak or a bad person? She was watching the poet dying inch by inch, *withering away* in the existence she had dedicated her whole life to creating. And now she must destroy her work, she must pull down the spiritual edifice which she had built up so laboriously. Yes, she had to do it – her own heart would bleed as she did so, she was in effect pronouncing a death sentence on her own life – but the poet must not die, she had no right to kill the poet in him.

And how could that peaceful and bourgeois life they led be fruitful for the soul of a poet? He needs playful tenderness more than love, emotional turbulence more than happiness. Then she cursed her own cool nature and that night of frost which had placed its cold hand over her first tenderness, killing it off. She dressed herself up, restyled her hair, adopted an amorous tone of voice, tried painting her eyes and rouging her cheeks. But then she gave up again. Viktor didn't notice it, either that or he assumed it was one of those moods that often afflict women at certain times; he did not understand that she wanted to arouse his fantasy, that the man's wife wanted to become the poet's mistress.

This battle undermined Martha's health. And she realised with a fear approaching terror that if her husband were not to die as a poet, something new would have to enter their lives. Where was this new thing to come from? Where – *she* could not provide it. And yet perhaps ... Then all those old artifices started again, all those fruitless efforts to turn herself into someone else, all that dreary comedy which she found it so nauseating to play.

Viktor didn't see a great deal of these troubles. He was not much of a psychologist, and his very closeness, the role he himself was playing in his wife's struggle, made him even more blind. In addition to that, he had, half out of boredom, stumbled upon a little idyll, which he intended to turn into a drama; he was going to write the main role for a young artiste who was enjoying great success at that time, one of those many young women whose greatest talent is their liveliness, and who are admired as long as they are young. And as he started to get seriously involved in the work, Martha felt revived; perhaps it had just been a momentary apathy, an impasse in his poetic productivity, a transition from the lyricism of youth to the development of something greater, which she had created and helped bring forth. Once again she felt something which resembled the old triumphs from the happy days of certainty.

It was the lyrical poet who had died in their marriage, and the man she had created would become something greater, not a troubadour or a playful shepherd, but a man who wrote about life and told people about themselves. How she idealised that little idyll; for her it became a great work of art, a literary monument. She could recognise herself in every word, her work in every line, it was the beginning of the fruit her life would bear.

Her joy was silent and nameless.

Rehearsals began. Viktor led them himself and was out the whole morning, sometimes in the evening too. He was together with the theatre's actors, with the director, with the critics. Martha did not hold him back – she even encouraged him to go. This was something new in their lives, this was perhaps the 'something' he needed. But she herself had an unconquerable dread of footlights and wings, there was something in the whole of that painted existence which revolted her true nature, and when Viktor one day asked her to accompany him to a ball which the theatre was putting on for the director's wedding she refused adamantly to go along.

Viktor did not try to persuade her, but went alone.

Martha did not register the greater loneliness in her new life; she was far too happy to feel it. She read a great deal, as during the whole of their marriage she had studied not a little; foreign literature, criticism, and in addition a large part of the half-popular scientific theses reported by the larger journals. She was well aware that her husband was lacking in energy, and that it was against his nature to work. So she did the work, and let him benefit from it through conversations with her. In recent times her emotional state had prevented her from concentrating, and she had a lot to catch up on, so she applied herself with all the zest and perseverance which happiness can provide.

She was extremely happy. The drama had been a success, and her husband had already drafted the plan of a new one. She could not remember ever having had such sunshine in her life.

One day in spring Viktor was out, as he nearly always was in the mornings now. She was sitting in his room, a little dark green den with large bookcases and an oak writing desk, paintings, busts, statuettes and artfully arranged flowers.

Actually she was not very fond of that room; it was too much of a boudoir, it exuded too strong a sense of his coquettish approach to the craft of poetry. There was always a fragrance in there as if he had had a visit from a strongly-perfumed woman. It reminded her too much of that Viktor who was now dead, and she visited it rarely. But today it so happened that it was cold in the other rooms, so she had found a seat in here. She was sitting reading. Absent-mindedly she had picked up a blue notebook from the writing desk and doodled a little on the cover; she had no idea what was inside the book.

In the evening Viktor came in as usual.

'Is it you who's drawn these squiggles on this notebook?' he asked.

'Which notebook? Oh yes, it was this morning, when I was sitting in your room ... I'm sorry if I've done something I shouldn't.'

Viktor walked up and down the floor a couple of times with the notebook under his arm, then stopped by the window to look out and, with his back to the table where Martha was sitting in a rocking chair by the lamp, said: 'Did you read the poems?' There was a strange tone of deliberate casualness in the way he said it, an insecure glibness.

Martha raised her head. 'No – is it poems?' She felt some astonishment, and looked across at her husband, who was standing humming, beating time with his knuckles on the window ledge. 'When did you write them?'

He is still standing turned towards the window, his head slightly bowed. 'Oh, fairly recently,' he says quickly, cutting off the words to take a breath.

For a few moments it was quite silent ... . It seemed to Martha that something was slipping away from her, and she curled her fingers as if to hold on to the invisible presence. She felt all the blood leave her face and rush in a torrent to her heart. She waited for him to speak.

Perhaps it was meant as a surprise, she said to herself.

'Would you like to hear them?' he asked, turning round.

She made no answer, but just nodded and pointed to a chair. There was something strangely commanding about her gesture. She took in the room and him with one extended glance, saw how the light from the lamp played, glinting, on his dark curls, as they fell over his forehead when he bent his head, then leaned back in her chair, closed her eyes and waited.

He read. They were sonnets. His voice was a little thick, it sounded as if he were slurring the resonant lines, as if he wanted to erase their gleaming colours; his low-key recitation threw a veil over the love of which they sang.

She had heard the first song, her life was concentrated in a fearful receptiveness, she had breathlessly followed every slurred modulation in his voice, every emphasis, had noted every rhyme. He read the second, the third, the fourth ... the life in her soul was poised in a terrified, awful suspense, waiting for her name, for her picture in his song, for her place in his poems ... .

She waited ... her body turned to stone as the suspense filled her soul.

He continued reading. And as he read, he was lulled by the music of the words, bewitched by the songs he had sung. His voice grew warmer, his intonation more sincere, more passionate. He flew from line to line ... .

She sat motionless and silent – only her long eyelashes fluttered slightly.

He warmed to his reading. The poems became hymns of love, glowing, heated, pleading, begging, jubilant – he had forgotten who he was reading to.

She felt as if she was being hurled down from a high tower, far, far down, terribly far. And she fell and fell and fell. But his words pursued her ... it was such a slowly descending, endless, floating fall ... . And everything around became complete darkness.

She felt her husband's eyes on her and forced herself to smile. A frozen smile. It seemed to her that a heavy mask was covering her face, that her limbs were stiff and leaden. She lay there wondering whether she could lift her arm ... .

And there he sat, reading his love songs, with glowing warmth, to his wife.

Suddenly it seemed as if this humiliation brought her to life – this frightful humiliation. She wanted to hurl his words back at him, scream at the terrible insult, clench her fists. But she could not do so ... . Her willpower had deserted her, annihilated by the numbing pain. A sob threatened to escape from her breast, and her eyes burned. She felt as if a stabbing pain had dried up the source of her tears.

Finally he finished, and when he had read the final stanza and closed the book, he suddenly remembered who he was reading to. He looked across at her, and saw her leaning back, smiling.

He felt relieved.

'It's beautiful,' she said, getting up. 'You've not forgotten how to write sonnets.' She spoke calmly, in a flat voice. She had the feeling that her tongue would not obey her.

In the next few days Martha felt like a sleepwalker; she did everything mechanically, by instinct. Her whole life was concentrated on one thought which subsumed all others: that these poems were written to another, and her whole life was wasted. She had lost him, the poet in him needed someone other before he could sing. But she didn't ask who this other was. She was simply 'the other'.

After dinner they sat in the sitting room in the twilight. He was on a sofa by the window, his silhouette roughly outlined by the light from the street; she on a rocking stool by the stove, strangely hunched over, with her head on her knees and the harsh light and burning heat directly on her face.

Between them lay the darkness of the room.

They spoke little. And each time one of them said something, it was as if the brief words which they uttered mechanically *fell* into the darkness.

Every now and then Viktor cleared his throat and made himself more comfortable on the sofa. 'I have bought a ticket for the carnival, Martha,' he said.

'I see.'

The silence made Viktor feel awkward. He wished she would ask him something, say something … . But there was nothing but this ceaseless, irritating motion of the rockers on the carpet. It would be much easier if they could talk about it.

But this 'I see' was so mechanical, so indifferent … he did not know how to continue. The problem was that he had never actually asked Martha if she would like to go; she didn't feel at home in that circle and was not at all keen on the carnival. So she would only spoil the mood, and that was equally tiresome for all involved. But now that he was about to say that, he had a sudden indistinct awareness that what he was doing was somehow wrong … he felt like a schoolboy who has deserved a lecture.

'Yes, all the others are going,' he went on.

Martha raised her head a little from her knees. 'Who, all the others?' she asked.

'Rincks,' he said. And the moment he had said it he regretted it; he wished he had said a different name, Lunds, Dorfs, anyone, just not that particular name. Not that there was anything about it, but … he regretted it anyway!

Martha pushed the stool back across the floor. She felt a prickling sensation as her pulses raced, cold sweat started from all her pores, the stool shook beneath her … . She had guessed … suddenly, with a woman's instinct. So she was the one!

'And Bays,' he said.

She felt as if her heart was going to burst with her seething thoughts. Then everything disappeared as if in a thick fog. Everything else had gone, she thought of nothing but that one sound … . And her next thought was, how dare he mention her name.

Viktor shook himself, and walked up and down a little, urging himself to change the subject and begin a conversation. But he was confused, and felt bad without really knowing why. He felt that he was starting to freeze.

'It's cold in here,' he said, rubbing his hands.

'What is *she* going to be?' Martha asked from the darkness. The words were subdued, with a harsh stress on 'she', and a brittle tone.

'Karen,' he said. That was the female lead in his idyll.

'I see,' she whispered. She was rubbing the palms of her hands against her knees.

'Time's getting on,' he said. 'My ticket is for this evening.'

He was standing just next to her, and bent forward to kiss her on the cheek.

The kiss burnt. She rubbed her skin with her thumb where he had kissed her.

'You're so hot,' he said. She pushed him away with her hand.

'Yes, you shouldn't kiss me,' she said without expression, cold and distant.

Viktor laughed. 'You must be tired,' he said. 'Your voice sounds so odd and nasal.'

Then he went.

She got up and walked across the floor a couple of times, stopping by the window. She wasn't thinking, her thoughts were numbed, stultified, frozen. There was a rumbling sound inside her head, her gaze was unseeing. The lights in the house opposite were dancing in front of her eyes like will-o'-the-wisps. Her breast was laced tight by a thousand soundless screams.

Her whole being was paralyzed by the certainty.

Then her wifely indignation broke through her thoughts like a rushing flood. A thousand questions, fearful comparisons, crazy reproaches, accusations. A whirling tide of despair, indignation and resentment.

She lit the lamp and placed it on the writing desk. She became lost in thought and forgot to put the shade over it. Her eyes were red, feverishly red, dry, dull and staring. There was a long, dark red stripe down her cheeks, and her skin was shiny and dry with fever. She rummaged on the shelf, her hands shaking, the loose pages wafting around.

There they were – the poems, poems to her; the one he was writing comedies for, the one he loved … .

She rested her head on her hands and started to read. Slowly at first, then faster and faster. There was something horribly stiff and frozen about her features as she read. Now and then she let her hand slide from her hair down over her forehead, up and down, mechanically. Otherwise everything in her life was concentrated in her eyes, in her glance and in the sighs which at intervals convulsed her breast, like half-stifled screams … .

Yes – she could see her, it was her, every word was for her. The whole thing was a declaration of love, everything for her.

In the first poems it was dawning, vague and imprecise, like a fleeting erotic longing. But gradually it took form and grew; and the picture which the words celebrated became hers, entirely hers. Her hair, her eyes, her form … .

She read on, her soul tormented by fear, from verse to verse … every word was a blow to an open wound. She registered the comparisons, the reproaches, the accusations!

The verses became tender, playful, more aroused. She could not breathe, she rubbed her forehead hard with her hands, her hair was standing on end around her head; she slowly undid the buttons on her dress, all the while carrying on reading. She tore at her corset, suddenly noticed that there was no shade on the lamp, put it on, gave vent to one single meaningless, hoarse cry, read on … feverishly compelled, horrified at the frankness of these poems, which heaped derision upon derision.

But how beautiful they were! Rich images, colours, light, grandeur, passion … and each new image added a hundredweight to the stifling agony in her soul. With her: barren, impoverished, sluggish, with the other: rich, fiery, fertile … .

Her arm fell heavily onto the table, limp as a corpse, and her head, having lost its support, lolled onto her breast. Sometimes she went completely limp as if she were asleep, then sat up again, rocking, rocking. She had no thoughts, just saw constantly in front of her a wide, flat plain … an endless, flat plain.

Then she read more … no, it was too much, too much … .

No, no, it was too much!

She closed the book and stood up. She had become as white as a ghost. Her hair had come down, her bodice had come open, now and then her hands shook as if in spasm.

Then she seized the blue notebook, tore off the cover and walked across the floor to the stove. She sat down on the stool, opened the door and held out the white pages. The reflection of the fire made them gleam red – she saw *her* picture on every page.

Then she threw them away from her.

And with a choking sob she hurled herself backwards from the stool onto the carpet.

Her life's terrible struggle had begun.

Translated by Janet Garton

2. The Mistress

It is the smallest house in the whole street: the width of three sash windows and a green front door with three steps up and a railing which makes a delightful slide. And under the windows, the sloping doors to the cellar project onto the pavement – ancient and battered doors which all the town's street urchins climb up on their way to school and slide down again, whistling through their fingers. For 'the mistress's' cellar doors are the last ones left in the whole town.

The town clerk had conducted a campaign against both the cellar doors and the lime trees. It really was unacceptable to have three trees like that in the middle of a respectable street, blotting out the light from the gaslamps with their rebellious branches. But in the end the town clerk had to let the lime trees be, and now he just sends the constable over now and then in order to check on how the lamps and the branches are getting on together. Then the gardener generally comes along the following day and puts up his ladder in the street so that he can trim them 'on orders from above', because the mistress can hardly bear to do it herself; and she always thinks she can hoodwink the constable with a pastry and a large glass of blackcurrant liqueur.

Those are hard days for the mistress, when the gardener is chopping and chopping, and all those beautiful branches are falling, to lie side by side on the cellar doors. With every chop she seems to suffer real pain, and she pleads and pleads for each branch – surely he can let *that one* stay where it is.

Inside the garden things are different. *There* she is in charge, and there nothing is cut back. *There* everything grows just as it wishes: the grape vine climbing up the neighbour's high gable wall and the roses along the back of the house and all the lilies in the large flowerbed. There is only one bed, with a path around it which is quite narrow, so that if you want to get past it your sleeve is whitened by mortar from the neighbour's wall. But the bed is large, to make room for many flowers; though that is not easy to see, as the large white lilies have been allowed to grow unchecked, becoming a positive forest full of white crowns.

But there has to be room for both roses and harebells in the bed, because there are always roses in the mistress's wreaths. At times just some small pale ones, as the lilies do steal the sun, but roses there are. And the mistress makes many wreaths all summer long, for both acquaintances and strangers. If the mistress hears that someone has died in the workhouse, some poor creature with neither friends nor family, and perhaps not even a friendly hand to close their eyes, at once she plunders her large flowerbed and makes a wreath at the table beneath the old elder tree.

She says it is too sad to see a coffin with no flowers.

But there can also be merriment under the elder tree in the corner – when there are visitors for coffee, and the mistress bustles in and out with the silver coffee pot and pastries on a salver. The mistress herself gets little rest; she walks between the kitchen and the garden, fetches cream from the meat-safe and preserved strawberries from the outhouse, and is worried that not everyone has got to taste the elderflower cordial. But the young girls who are her visitors laugh and laugh, because they are sitting so squashed together that they can hardly move their arms. And the one sitting on the end gets pushed off the whole time – over into the lilies. The mistress always has so many visitors who have to join in, and she just says we'll make room. We'll manage, she says, and the young girls think it's such fun.

Yet most of all come at the time when 'the tree is ripe'. That means the cherry tree, which grows just by the boundary and over the smith's fence. Right there by its trunk is the garden's place of honour, where the dogs are buried; there is a whole cemetery with both names and dates: Ami and the new Ami and Pollux.* Ami became so old that he was blind and always had to lie on cushions; the new Ami was run over. The mistress looked after it and cared for it, but in the end the vet had to put it to sleep. Those were hard days for the mistress, for she cannot bear to see any living thing suffer; in the winter she brings all the frozen sparrows she can find into the living room, warms them up and feeds them bread.

It is when the tree is ripe that there are most visitors. Everyone has to taste the cherries – wonderful Spanish cherries, which the mistress counts along every branch. There aren't many for each one when such a large crowd has to share, but nevertheless it would not be proper cherry-time for the town's young girls if they hadn't been across to the mistress's and received their little bunch of cherries, tied in a red ribbon. Never would it be proper cherry-time … .

Later in the year the grapevine bears fruit, and the mistress harvests and preserves it. The grapes are eaten in sugar when winter arrives with its sleet, and the sparrows take up home in the empty nesting boxes; and the yard is covered in snow, so that it is difficult to make it over to the outhouse, and the whole garden is white, both the paths and the flower bed.

Then they stay in the living room.

It is quite dark in there, and warm from the peat fire, and the whole room smells of lavender and old potpourri. The mistress makes that in the summer. She gathers heaps of roses and spreads the petals out on newspapers and dries them on the bed and the living-room table. And when winter comes the dried petals lie on the old-fashioned stove tiles and give off the sweetest summer fragrance … .

The mistress has been reading. But since it has grown too dark, she has let the book of sermons fall into her lap and leaned her head back. Now she has dropped off, and is sleeping with hands folded. And over on the sofa the cat is purring softly, on the stove the water for tea is simmering … darkness is gathering in the house.

But then along comes the lamplighter out in the street, and he puts up his ladder and lights the lamps, and all at once there is bright light over all the old pictures on the walls, and the white antimacassars on the chairs, and on the carpet, which is divided into small pieces spread around.

But when the lamp is lit the mistress wakes up on her seat in the window and picks up her glasses and the book, and inserts the bookmark before closing it. Then she opens the door to the kitchen and calls. 'He's lighting up, Karen,' she says. The old maid has been waiting in the kitchen, and now she comes in, in her cap with pink ribbons, and sits down quietly on the chair by the door.

There in the lamplight sit those two old girls, each with her own thoughts, saying little. But every day when the lamp is lit the mistress calls at the door: 'Now he's lighting up, Karen,' and every day Karen comes in and sits down quietly on the same chair by the door. And when they've been sitting there for a while and it is getting on for teatime, she gets up and says 'Thank you, ma'am,' and goes out just as quietly as she came in. And it has been like that for many years.

For Karen has been in the house a long time. She used to work at the vicarage, and when the vicar died she stayed with 'the young mistress'. They were quite young then, both she and 'the young mistress', and Karen was engaged. But then things went wrong, and the boyfriend fled to America. Shortly afterwards the neighbours began to talk about Karen being in trouble, and one evening the smith's wife came over to have a word with the mistress: since she was all alone in the world, she ought to know who she had under her roof; she needed to protect her reputation.

But the mistress answered that *that* was her concern, and it would not damage *her* reputation to do what she ought. And she kept Karen and looked after her herself, and for as long as it lived the child had two mothers instead of one. But then the little creature died, and the mistress and Karen were alone again, and now they only have the grave over in the corner of the churchyard … .

The old maid sets out the things for tea. She places the tallow candle in the middle of the table and smooths out the cloth.

'I should think Line will be coming,' says the mistress.

Line has been coming every evening for ten years. At precisely seven o'clock there is a knock at the door, and Line comes in, stiff and old, and the mistress tries to speak loud enough for her friend to hear, but she fails, and when she takes her coat into the bedroom, she says to Karen: '*Really*, Karen, I think it's getting worse and worse – Line can hardly hear a thing these days.' And Karen shakes her head: 'We must thank the Lord that we have our faculties,' she says.

They have been saying that about Frøken Line for ten years.

So the two old maids sit there drinking their tea in silence, and every now and then they nod gently to one another, since they can't talk. Afterwards they play patience and then two-handed whist.

At ten o'clock Karen walks Frøken Line home. Then the mistress potters about on her own, rummages in an old drawer or reads letters. They are old yellowed papers, tied in large bundles with red silk ribbons … solid documents from the time when it was expensive to write, and you wanted to make sure you got value for money when you wrote.

She studies them, with their faded handwriting.

When Karen returns home, she creeps quietly into her bed, and the mistress is alone. She is still sitting bent over the old letters, and when she raises her head and trims the candle wick, there are often tears in her eyes. For they are dead, her old friends, and it is so very, very long ago, what she is reading from the time when she was young.

Sometimes she goes into the little closet which smells of orris root and apples, and she opens the bureau and pulls out the little drawer.

There she finds a couple of ancient flowers, dried and glued to paper, a verse from an album which doesn't scan properly, and inside a silver locket a little silhouette … .

She walks around the house, covering things up and shutting them away. Checks on the birds, which are sleeping in their cages, and gives the dog water.

And it is late in the night before the mistress falls asleep, with the cat on top of her quilt.

Translated by Janet Garton

3. Franz Pander

Franz Pander's mother took in people's washing. Her husband had been a joiner and had drunk himself to death.

It may be that this joiner was not Franz's father. Now and then Madam Pander would take Franz's childish hand between her chapped fists, spread out his remarkably slim fingers and admire their curved nails, which were a delicate shade of pink. Then Madam Pander said that that's what *his* fingers had been like and *his* nails. It was unlikely she was referring to the joiner.

It is possible that Franz was a bastard. He was an affectionate child, and ticklish, as a love child is often said to be. And he was more sensitive than any of the other boys in Kleine Dammstrasse.*

The boys called him 'girlie'. The class joker called out the name one day when the free school boys were bathing in the Elbe: Franz's body was *so* palely white and tender – and after that the name stuck.

It suited him well. Franz never played, never swore and did not smoke. The devil only knows what he did spend his time doing. He was never to be seen in the doorways in Kleine Dammstrasse, where the other boys were playing pitch and toss and turning cartwheels and falling out and getting into fights. He wasn't at home in the attic either. Mutter Pander could sit in the evening waiting anxiously for hours before Herr Franz came home.

'Where have you been, Franz?'

'Nowhere.'

'You never do anything.'

'Did the consul's wife give you anything?'

'Yes, they had guests yesterday. There's some titbits.'

Madam Pander fetched the pâté from the stove, where it was waiting between two plates. Franz ate it, smacking his lips like a gourmet.

'It's got mushrooms in it,' he said. He loved the leftovers which his mother was given when she visited the 'good' houses where she did washing, and asked for details about the names, and how you should eat each single thing. On normal days, when he had to make do with Dammstrasse food, Franz ate little, and what little he did eat he covered in so much pepper that it made Madam Pander sneeze just to look at it – what a way to ruin that good sausage.

All afternoon Franz would stroll around on Jungfernstieg.* He stood in front of the large shop windows of fancy goods for hours. He was most drawn to the gleaming gold-plated bronze objects, and to the displays of interior design, with their flowing silk draperies. *There* he stood open-mouthed. But longest of all he stood gaping in front of the bookshop windows. It was the coloured lithographs he loved. Pictures of velvet-clad men sitting at tables with women in silk, with red draperies and golden goblets on the table.

There was one picture which hung on the corner of Neuer Wall:* a dark woman dressed in yellow satin, deeply décolletée and with two rows of pearls in her hair, extending a round-fingered, diamond-studded hand to a page in white, who was bowing low – in front of that picture Franz could stand for hours, until he was burning hot and his cheeks were red. For now he was fourteen years old.

On winter evenings he read: all those novels in which a wild fantasy disgorges duchesses with flashing jewels around proud necks, and marchionesses languishing in orangeries full of roses.

Or he would sneak around the rich district along the River Alster, looking for those premises where lamps were being lit for a party. *There* he would wait at the gates until the carriages arrived, and his heart would beat faster when he was standing so close to the ladies as they swished out of the doors carrying their silken trains, and to the gentlemen, slim and elegant with their hair parted at the back and the scent of pomade.

Franz was crazy about anything that smelt good. Whatever Madam Pander could pilfer – when the occasion arose – in all innocence (what 'arm does it do, takin' from them wot 'as? as she said to Madam Fürst at the mangle) from some dressing table or other, Eau de Lubin or Ess Bouquet in a small bottle which she took pains (well, Good Lord, it's just for the lad) to bring along in her pocket, *that* Franz used liberally.

But that's what *he* did too – he whose hands and nails Franz had inherited.

And in fact his whole physique. For Franz had shot up and was in the process of becoming an attractive young chap. Blue eyes, it was difficult to say whether they were melancholy or listless, a small mouth – *too* small, really, for a man – with red lips and that aristocratic nose, straight and with nostrils which quivered so readily.

Slim, lithe body.

That was how he looked.

And that's why his mother wanted him to work in a draper's shop. Herr Schaltz had offered to take him on.

'Because nowadays you have to provide smooth faces,' said Herr Schaltz, 'and get them to dress up like princes to get the tills ringing. Otherwise – God help us, you don't see a single female coming through your doors all the live-long day.'

But Franz did not want to join the draper's trade. One evening the previous winter, when he was strolling along Jungfernstieg, he had stopped outside a large hotel. A club was giving a ball. He had seen carriage after carriage drawing up, and the ladies alighting, and inside in the vestibule the swarm of attendants in their black coats and white ties. How they leant over the ladies, how they slid the silken capes off their shoulders and whispered to them and preceded them through halls of blazing light.

That was what Franz wanted to do.

He was to learn his trade in a restaurant on Schaumburgerstrasse. A dismal backwater where a couple of dozen beery patrons came along to empty their tankards. Franz hated the work – rinsing all those greasy beer glasses in that dirty water, with *his* hands – and he hated the atmosphere with its stink of dark beer and its stink of tobacco.

But he knew that these years were necessary, and he waited. He was encouraged too, because he could see that he was growing more attractive by the day. In the evening, when he went up to his little garret, exhausted, he could sit for a long time in front of his bit of mirror with the lighted stump of a candle, looking happily at his face. He took tender care of all his attractive features, and spent all his tips on protecting his hands with hand lotion and suchlike.

The manager's son came home. He was travelling around as a waiter, and was on a visit home from London.

He was full of stories about splendid hotels with full-length mirrors and staircases of solid marble and door hangings of silk. And distinguished names and wines which cost more than Franz could ever have imagined, and long rows of *tables d'hôte* along tables festooned with flowers … .

Franz devoured every word of the descriptions.

And one morning, when the manager and his son were relaxing on a sofa – the inn was empty – the traveller was telling stories from over there. Franz was washing up in his corner.

'You have your lucky moments – over there in London – ' the waiter expelled cigarette smoke through his nose and pronounced 'London' with an

English accent – 'it's bloody amazing, the English aristocracy – all at once their eyes are boring into you, say a little golden-haired miss, sitting there straight-backed – they look you up and down three or four times, so that it sends shivers down your spine, and you can feel the electricity when you stand next to them with the dish … . Well – you've been there, you know the routine … .'

The manager and his son laughed familiarly, and the son talked about a couple of 'bloody lucky adventurers' –

'Of course, he was handsome, was John Jennings – striking chap … but the fact that Lady Haveland actually ran away with him and took the whole caboodle with her, so that his lordship had to whistle for it – that really was something – and Førner, he got *married* to a lass with millions – he's got his legs to thank for that … .'

Franz had emerged from his corner. He was standing with his sleeves rolled up a couple of paces from the counter, staring at the traveller.

So it did happen.

The colour came and went in his face as he listened. The son of the house turned suddenly and looked at him: 'Now then – my lad – are you dreaming?' he said, watching him. He laughed and muttered to his father: '*Der Bub' wird Glück haben*.'*

That morning the glasses in Franz's washing-up bowl clattered somewhat louder.

Franz was twenty years old when he applied to the Jungfernstieg hotel.

The manager turned to and fro on his chair, looking at Franz's hands with their pointed nails, whilst pretending to be reading his references.

'*Schön – eine dritte Stellung im Restaurant vacant.** You may start tomorrow.'

When Franz was out of the door – he had turned pale – the manager looked down at the book-keeper, who was alternately writing out invoices and picking his nose: '*Na – ein netter Zugvogel – nicht*?'*

For the first few days Franz was in a state of dazed happiness. He sneaked out of the restaurant onto the grand staircase, greedy to feel its carpets under his feet and let his hand slide down the black marble of the bannisters. He stationed himself on the landing, where the ladies passed close by him, smiling and carrying bouquets. And he followed their figures with his eyes, his heart thumping incessantly, until they disappeared around the turn of the stairs, and he observed their outfits and sensed the perfume of their garments more than he actually thought about them.

He returned to the restaurant and entered the large room where *table d'hôte* was served. This hall filled him with pleasurable satisfaction. The subdued light, which entered through impressive multicoloured window-panes; the high arches, borne upon marble pillars, and the candelabra, splendid enough for a church. He fell into a trance, until a colleague woke him: 'Are you earning a lot of money standing here, friend? – We have a full house.'

He began waiting again. Carrying the dishes from the menu to and fro to the restaurant tables, ordering wines and uncorking them. He breathed in the smells of the food eagerly, almost intoxicated, like a convalescent, and without differentiating or attributing it to any one thing, he walked around in something like a glow of love.

And in the evenings, when the lights in the halls were finally extinguished and the other waiters hurried upstairs to fall asleep at once, as tired as acrobats, he stayed behind in the darkened restaurant; he could not tear himself away from the darkness in there, where the fountain splashed so quietly into its pool among the large plants which reached up in the darkness towards the dome.

He wandered for a long time around the gloomy corridors, humming quietly to himself, and when he finally went up to where his room-mates were sleeping deeply with open mouths and burning heads, he lay awake for hours, feeling a rushing in his head as if he had been drinking wine. Despite that he was never tired during the day.

So the first period passed. Then Franz grew accustomed to his new life, and there came a time when he felt very tired and constantly sleepy.

His fellow workers were no fun either. They talked about their own things, about the positions they had had and how much they earned. They had girlfriends amongst the room maids or in the kitchen, and apart from that they spent most of their free time sleeping.

They seldom talked about the guests; but that was what interested Franz the most.

Johanne, the room maid from the first floor, a tall and buxom Viennese lass, had for a long time been lying in wait for Franz every time he went up in the mornings to 'groom himself', and she liked to give him a little push and tickle his neck or wrestle with him in one of the rooms she was cleaning.

One day she pushed him down onto the unmade bed where he was sitting on the edge, and tapped his head with her dusting brush.

Suddenly she bent down and kissed him on the side of the neck, as she held him down.

Franz jerked up, deathly pale. 'Let go,' he said, 'I don't want to.'

Johanne pushed him away angrily. 'Don't you get any funny ideas about me, stupid!' she said, then contemptuously: '*Louis – wie du bist – Louis*.'*

From that day on Johanne spread nasty rumours about Franz amongst all the maids. In fact they all nursed a silent rage against him. Really they all wanted to consort with him, but he didn't even *see* them. Never so much as a glance, the slightest push against the walls in the corridors, a pinch on the arm – nothing. Exactly as if they weren't women at all. That's how he was – it was really irritating.

Franz simply didn't notice them.

But on the evening of the day when Johanne had tumbled him onto the bed – that was when it happened, with Miss Ellinor from fifteen.

'Fifteen' was an aristocratic family, English, father, mother and daughter.

The family had been living there for a while. They always sat at Franz's table, even though there was a draught from the door, and Miss Ellinor had ten things to ask about and ten things to get him to bring, and first a bracelet and then a serviette were dropped at her feet.

Franz was bewitched. It was as if something chained him to that little serving table by the door. From there he could see her in profile. And it was as if he lingered over each thing he was called on to do at *that* table: when he passed a glass, when he brought a dish, when he spoke, when he leaned forwards. It was a struggle to walk away from her, and he itched just to touch her.

His eyes were on her figure incessantly, more often than he really dared, and every time he approached her his heart stood still. When she wasn't there he was restless; he couldn't stay in one place, and handled everything absent-mindedly; he saw no-one and nothing.

He would give a start when she stood in the doorway. He did not welcome them – though he welcomed all the others; she would smile, and ask slightly breathlessly for a soda, or a newspaper. And she always had a couple of words for him, and he had to brush a speck off her coat or help her with her parasol. It was always awkward, first it wouldn't open and then it wouldn't close.

It was hard for them to be apart.

Franz believed and did not believe; he expected and hoped for nothing. But he had to be near to her.

If she would just sit *there,* at his table, all day long, playing like that, stretching out her hands along the balustrade as she usually did, whilst humming in a low voice. If she would just do that.

But he became more and more restless. And he began to approach her stealthily – he just *had* to – in order to brush for a second the table edge where her hand so often rested; to gaze steadily, so that she became aware of it, at a particular place on her exposed white neck.

Miss Ellinor pursed her little mouth and looked at him and laughed; she caressed her bony father and looked at him; she placed her hand just beside his on the table and looked at him and laughed.

He thought of one thing only: to be able to touch her.

But gradually – for they stayed on day after day – he felt as if it was going to choke him. His whole being was swallowed up by her. Nothing existed except her. Just her, day and night: her hand, which had rested just *there*; and so many times she had spoken to him – and then she had looked at him – yes, definitely … .

At night he could not sleep, he tossed and turned in his blankets. Rehearsed the same thing over and over. *There* her hand had rested – did she want to touch him? She had laughed *then,* she had said *that* – he lay feverishly and crushed it to him, all of it, the whole night long.

And all at once, as he sat up in bed, he came to look over at his colleagues, who were lying there, flabby, stretching out in the gloom from the low gaslight. They seemed to him so repulsive, he could have struck them.

Miss Ellinor was always the same. She sparkled in the heat of his desire like a kitten in the glow from a coal fire.

Then came *that* evening. Franz was on duty on the first floor. *They* were out at a large gathering.

Franz wandered around, unable to keep still for a single instant. He walked in and out of the serving area, touching everything and doing nothing. He had to run up the stairs and down again constantly. Finally they arrived. He recognised her voice – she always had the habit of speaking a little loudly in the corridor – and his heart stood still.

He took a lamp and went out into the corridor.

'You're here,' she said.

'Yes – tonight.' His voice failed him.

She looked at him before she entered through the door he had opened. 'Why is that?' she said.

'My colleague is ill,' he said and lit the candles on the mantelpiece.

The old people came in and went into the next room. The door was half open.

Miss Ellinor took off her necklace in front of the mirror. Franz was about to leave, but stood still with the lamp in his hand.

Then their eyes met in the mirror. And in one second he had seized her arm and bent down and kissed her shoulder. He went out, conscious only of how her pulse had throbbed under his kiss.

Then he was overcome by a wild joy. He could not control himself; he laughed and sang. He joked with a half-asleep fellow-worker, chattering without being aware of what he was saying. In the corridors he wandered around kicking boots so they flew in the air.

At last he went upstairs; he undressed with particular ceremony, placing every item of clothing neatly by his bed, and climbed into bed. Then he lay there still, smiling.

But the next day Miss Ellinor left.

At breakfast, as he was bending over her, she suddenly looked him in the face and said: 'We're leaving today.'

'You're leaving – why?'

'Did you think I would stay here?' Miss Ellinor laughed.

No more was said, and they did not see each other again.

For days Franz registered nothing. Ceaselessly he replayed his scanty memories, mechanically carrying out his tasks in the same places where she no longer appeared.

A loud noise or a new face would suddenly rouse him, and for a moment he *saw* the room, the balustrade, the familiar tables and the people around him. Then he relapsed into apathy, sickened by everything and with a pain in his breast like a stab.

Some time passed like this, until one fine day he woke up, and suddenly it seemed to him that the whole thing was so far away and so long ago and almost like something which hadn't happened to *him,* or which was only a dream. And if he tried to recapture the memories, it was as if he had to walk a long distance to do so, and once he had captured them, he would stand there apathetically, lost in a reverie over his treasure.

He slipped into narcissism again. It was all over.

He carried out his tasks listlessly, wan and without a thought.

After a while he experienced the hunger familiar to waiters. It tortured him to carry the spicy food in and out. The smell of it tempted him so that he had to struggle not to reach suddenly into the dishes and satisfy his hunger urgently and gluttonously. He could be in a rage as with a lackey's smile he recommended to titillated guests the dishes he himself would never taste, and from over in his corner he followed greedily every bite they took.

But when he went down to the basement where the waiters ate, in the room over the wash cellar – the air was heavy with the odour of boiled washing, and his colleagues threw off their sweaty jackets and sat over their food with unbuttoned waistcoats – he put down his spoon, unable to eat in disgust. And the men sat dully along both sides of the table, unable to touch the thick gruel and the stringy meat from the bouillon.

But when Franz went back up into the restaurant, hunger tore at him. He carried the dishes to and fro, pale, whilst he tasted them on his dry tongue.

Behind the door, on the landing, he stuffed a roulette into his mouth, tore the leg off a chicken and slurped sauce from the dish, hasty and unseen.

On Tuesday evenings, when he had time off, he would get dressed up and visit a restaurant where he was not known. He would run nearly the whole way, and arrive overwrought and breathless with hunger. Then he forced himself to eat really slowly and taste each mouthful deliberately, until in a kind of intoxication he ordered more and more, eating quickly and gorging himself; until all at once he felt satiated, bloated, and sat there with many half-full glasses before him, slumped and half-drunk, sluggishly content.

Then he went home and slept, snoring, a heavy sleep.

One Tuesday evening he came home early and sat down on a bench under the lamps outside the hotel. He was replete and a little hazy.

It had rained recently, and there were plentiful puddles on the pavement. The ladies were tripping past with skirts lifted, teetering in and out of the puddles.

Franz watched all those feet, seeing *there* an ankle, *there* a calf, a clumsy flat foot in galoshes … . From the feet he looked up inquisitively at the swaying figures. The faces were so fresh beneath their veils. He tried to catch a glance. Was *she* not looking at him? He got up and walked after her. Restlessly he followed her, his eyes glued to the slim figure and the neck, shining under the upswept hair … but she turned along Neuer Wall and did not look back.

He returned, then set out again, hunting, pursuing an elegant outline, gliding forwards, rolling its hips … . She went into a doorway and disappeared from sight.

He roamed the streets.

A prostitute accosted him. 'Can I help you, sweetheart?' she said.

Franz gave a start and looked into her face. Then he took her arm, and they walked along the pavement towards the lights from the Alster Pavilion.

'So, my little pet is at a loose end, is he?' The girl spoke cloyingly.

Suddenly Franz dropped her arm and ran off.

'What – you making a fool of me?' the girl shrilled. 'What you think you're playing at, you lout … what a trick – making up to a lady – and then nothing … '

By then Franz was out of earshot.

He almost ran all the way home. Once there, he went to bed at once. But he tossed and turned all night long, and slept badly and restlessly. He dreamed continually about Ellinor.

Towards morning he got up. He couldn't stay in his bed any longer. He was uneasy, as if something was coming, something was going to happen. He went down to the corridors where the lighting was dim; there he wandered up and down, pausing in front of doors in order to pick up the ladies' shoes with careful hands and stare at them for a long time; he placed his hand inside them and believed that he could feel the gentle warmth from their feet.

That day he trembled if he came anywhere near a woman. The scent from a bowed neck wafted up to him, and drove the blood to his cheeks in a rush. And it was as if all at once he had a thousand eyes to see all that was beautiful. There were tender curls of hair at a temple; the easy rounding of a cheek, a hip or a waist to fit your arm around; or just the light on a satin-draped breast – that was enough to tempt him.

One day a buxom blonde came into the hotel. The first time she entered the restaurant she raised her gold lorgnette – Franz was watching – and inspected the waiters. Then she chose him.

Franz came over and waited for her to order. He had a particular way of standing, with his head slightly bent and his hands half folded in front of him.

The lady's husband came over and sat down. 'Well – shall we have the hotel's recommendation,' he said, turning round: 'Hm – hm –' and he laughed – 'there's a real Ganymede for you,' he said.* 'Erm, waiter, two set meals … .'

'Certainly …' Franz began to walk away. Then the lady said, without lowering her voice: 'His shirt front was the cleanest, you know.'

Franz spent three nights outside that lady's door; timid, flattened against the door panels like a thief, fearful of meeting the shoe-cleaners, who passed through the corridors with their baskets, his teeth chattering with cold.

He crept out of his bed, which was burning under him; he went to sit in a serving room and opened the window so that he could get enough air to breathe. He cursed himself, and had no other thoughts in his head than his desire.

He thought back to her indifferent glances, and tried to see some encouragement in them – it was so stupid that he laughed at it. He saw her figure and heard her voice and saw her fingers, as round as white slugs. And he went back to her door and stood there until daybreak. He knew it was completely crazy, yet he stayed.

When she left, someone else arrived. There was no let-up. What he loved was not really the women, it was a mouth, a neck, a beauty spot, a body.

He watched each woman keenly. Every single new one brought fresh hope. He knew that it was obvious that he was offering himself. All his beauty; how he measured it against other men's, their husbands' – he wanted to give it to them. But they never *saw* him. He stood there next to them – like a *thing*. Came and went with the dishes and the serviettes – a pure *object* – he could see himself clearly.

But at night there were sudden memories of a glance into his face, a warm hand giving him a tip. And he was aroused by this sip from a drink which only inflamed his thirst … .

Often Franz stole out of the restaurant to wander aimlessly through the corridors. He lurked outside doors. He peeped through the keyholes.

At the *table d'hôte*, where gentlemen and ladies sat in long rows, it sometimes happened that a man who had been leaning over towards the lady beside him with a smile would straighten up rather brusquely. He had such a strange feeling, seeing the pale face over the dish when Franz appeared. It was as if the lad's eyes were full of hatred.

After the meal, during coffee, it could happen that a gentleman, after lighting his cigar, would turn to his wife or his sister. 'Devilishly handsome chap,' he would say. Franz could hear it.

And she would raise her eyes and look at him as if at a clothes rack and say: 'Well, yes – up front driving the horses.'

So passed day after day.

He thought of nothing at all apart from *that*. Like a thief, he stole passing touches; they noticed nothing. His behaviour was almost insulting – they *felt* nothing.

And when a new day had passed with interminable slowness, and it was night and the restaurant was empty, Franz could stand for hours leaning on the balustrade; he was motionless, pale and staring under the electric lights. In his mind a hollow despair was forming, an impotent rage which was searching for an answer and finding nothing and had no idea which way to turn.

Sometimes he went home. It seemed to soothe him.

Madam Pander would sit there half-crying. 'He just sits there,' she would say to the woman who did the mangling, 'with a face like misery itself, not saying a peep. But I know what's wrong – oh yes – I know what's wrong … .'

He didn't want the lamp lit – it was best in the dark. Quietly he would take off his coat and sit down on the old sofa in the corner. Madam Pander fetched a chair and sat in front of him.

She took his hands between her own and patted them gently. And he smiled tiredly, without speaking, and leaned his head on her shoulder.

'What is it, my boy – my little boy – what's wrong with my boy?'

He gripped her hands tightly and did not answer. And Madam Pander could feel his forehead burning against her shoulder, and repeated in a voice almost choked with tears: 'What's wrong with my boy – my little boy – are they unkind to him?'

But when Franz had left, Madam Pander cursed the whole female sex to the mangle-woman: 'It's all their fault, the scum – dear Lord – and he didn't get *that* from strangers.'

One Tuesday evening Franz went to the theatre. Out to Carl Schulze's Theatre to see an operetta.*

It was a Turkish story about a princess. There was a fat eunuch with a padded stomach who parodied erotic gestures so that the whole house screamed with laughter. He took curtain call after curtain call, and he repeated his gestures more and more lewdly, singing his song over again:

Aber – es hat keinen Werth –

*Es hat keinen Werth.**

Franz was sitting up in a box in the darkness. He leaned his head back against the wall and wept.

When the play was over, he left. He crossed over towards Gänsemarkt and into one of the alleyways in that quarter.* He stayed there that night.

But when he woke up towards morning and saw her lying beside him in the half-light, he leapt up and ran from the place. He felt so sickened that he could vomit up his whole being. He was burning, and his head was aching. Disgust made him feel so nauseous that he groaned.

He went home, but he didn't want to go to bed. He crept down the back stairs to the restaurant. It was beginning to grow light, and a grey dawn was showing through the glass roof. Franz sat down on the stone steps with his head in his hands.

And as he sat there silently next to this room which had borne witness to his life, everything subsided into a deep, bottomless, unspeakable repugnance.

He looked along the balustrade. The chairs were stacked up on the tables, the soiled tablecloths were still spread … . The artificial palm trees poked up out of their majolica pots, dead.

Franz had no thoughts, felt no pain. But in his mind there surfaced a kind of numb amazement, that this was life.

The lamplighter had forgotten his long ladder after putting out the lamps. It was on the steps of this ladder that Franz stood as he strung himself up on the pole over the doorway.

The cleaners found him; there was a great fuss, and the night porter was summoned. He looked horrible, with his tongue sticking out of his mouth, and he was still warm. The manager came down in his nightwear, and swore so that the whole room echoed. A couple of colleagues hauled him up to the third floor, to a left luggage room. They cleared a table of rucksacks and hat boxes and laid him out there, in the midst of the suitcases. A couple of skivvies washed the body and covered it with a sheet.

Later that morning Johanne came in. She wanted to see him. Slowly she lifted the sheet, leaving only his head covered. She didn't cry, just looked quietly at him.

He was as white as marble – she had never seen anything so beautiful.

And as she was looking at that dead body, which had been tended with so much loving care, all in vain, Johanne clenched her fist and – without knowing why – shook it towards the heavens.

Translated by Janet Garton

4. Charlot Dupont

He was first put on the stage at the age of seven, wearing a velvet blouse with lace, at a charity concert at the Palais du Trocadéro.* He was a success; he could barely hold the violin.

After his performance of 'Herr Kakadu der Schneider', every member of the committee kissed him.*

Monsieur Theodor Franz sent for him the following morning. The great impresario wished to see him. Señor Emmanuelo de las Foresas brought his son there himself. Señor Emmanuelo de las Foresas was very emotional. He realised the moment had arrived.

Monsieur Theodor Franz was in his private office, sitting in front of a large desk in his favourite position, Napoleon after Leipzig.*

When he sat thus, one did not speak to Monsieur Theodor Franz; one waited. One knew that he was conquering the world, and one did not disturb him. Adelina Patti had waited for ten minutes a decade ago.*

Señor Emmanuelo de las Foresas waited without even twirling his moustache. The golden goose itself sensed the gravity of the situation and sucked its knuckles in silence.

It was very quiet in Monsieur Theodor Franz's private office, where photographic reproductions of famous people from across the world stared down from the walls.

'So – what's his name?'

Señor Emmanuelo de las Foresas was startled.

When Monsieur Theodor Franz spoke, his voice boomed as if he was trying to drown out an Erard piano.* Anyone hearing him for the first time was invariably startled, just like Señor Emmanuelo de las Foresas. Monsieur Theodor Franz was aware of this, but it served his purpose to startle people.

'So – what's his name?'

Señor Emmanuelo de las Foresas managed to utter: 'Carlo de las Foresas.'

'Hm – and where's he from?' Monsieur Theodor Franz indicated with a barely perceptible gesture that Señor Emmanuelo de las Foresas could sit down.

'Thank you.' Señor Emmanuelo de las Foresas felt better for sitting down. He positioned the golden goose between his legs and began to speak.

Señor Emmanuelo de las Foresas was very fond of speaking. He was from Chile. It might seem odd that a Spanish nobleman would settle in Chile. But that was what Señor Emmanuelo de las Foresas had done. It was an act of rebellion. This act was the secret in Señor Emmanuelo de las Foresas' story. It had happened in Mexico. What that had to do with Spain, no one knew. In fact whenever Señor Emmanuelo de las Foresas told his story, it never reached a point where it was relatively straightforward to follow him. The reason was that he travelled frequently between the two continents. You never knew on which side of the ocean you had him. But eventually he ended up in the Canaries.

And there he was when Monsieur Theodor Franz flung out his hand: 'Well – he's born in Provence.'

Señor Emmanuelo de las Foresas bridled: 'In Provence?'

'Yes, Monsieur, in Provence. You're middle-class, Monsieur, and from Provence.'

Monsieur Theodor Franz stood up.

'The public has tired of the exotic, Monsieur – the public doesn't believe in the aristocracy on stage, Monsieur – the public has tired of frauds. The public wants the real thing – the public doesn't want to be scammed.'

Monsieur Theodor Franz shouted out each sentence like an order. 'The public' came out like a trumpet blow. 'The public is tired. The public wants dignity. You must handle the public with care, Monsieur.'

Monsieur Theodor Franz began to sweat. The thought of the good sense of the audience excited him.

Señor Emmanuelo de las Foresas nodded at each sentence.

Monsieur Theodor Franz looked at the golden goose: 'He's seven years old?'

'Just turned.'

'We'll say six. He can pass for six.' Monsieur Theodor Franz bent down. 'What's this?' He pointed to a ten-franc diamond pin on Carlo de las Foresas' collar. 'Take it off.'

'It's an heirloom,' Señor Emmanuelo de las Foresas protested.

'Monsieur.' Monsieur Theodor Franz could face down an entire orchestra. 'The public doesn't believe in heirlooms.'

Señor Emmanuelo de las Foresas removed the pin.

'And now to the matter at hand – to *the performance*. What's the extent of his repertoire?'

'Three numbers.'

'And Schneider der Kakadu,' said the golden goose.

'Well, Monsieur. I will draw up my terms. You'll hear from me.'

Señor Emmanuelo de las Foresas and the golden goose left.

Monsieur Theodor Franz sat down in front of his desk. He chewed his nails. Monsieur Theodor Franz tended to bite his nails when he was deep in thought.

That was the last day the family was from Chile.

Monsieur Theodor Franz had lost faith in the tropics. The public had lost its taste for the exotic. Monsieur Theodor Franz promoted the idyllic. His artists all sprang from middle-class homes. His greatest success was an American lady he had discovered in a church and who never appeared in a theatre because it went against her religious beliefs. He had touched two continents when he had driven with her to church on Sundays.

That evening Monsieur Theodor Franz announced in the newspapers that the young violin prodigy, Charlot Dupont, was currently studying with Professor Dinelli.

'As you may know, the young prodigy from Provence is a member of the well-known family of civil servants, the Duponts, from Orléans.'

Monsieur Theodor Franz was pleased with the words 'family of civil servants, the Duponts, from Orléans'. It was excellent. It had tripped easily off his pen. But still it was excellent: 'a civil servant family, the Duponts, from Orléans.' It encompassed the full range of decency and middle-class respectability.

Monsieur Theodor Franz had stumbled across a success by accident.

The next day he visited the de las Foresas family. He wanted to see what he could offer it. He had to walk all the way up to the fifth floor; the coats in the hallway were threadbare, there was a great deal of children's clothing, all shop-bought.* He waited in a freezing cold salon where he could smell cooking.

Monsieur Theodor Franz offered 800 francs per month for six months. Señor Emmanuelo de las Foresas took half in advance and the bargain was struck.

Charlot got a teacher who rehearsed the three numbers with him. Monsieur Theodor Franz was present during the lessons. He noted every place where Charlot played out of tune. There he was to smile to the audience.

The time for the first concert approached. It would take place in Brussels.

The day before they were due to travel, Señor Emmanuelo de las Foresas paid Monsieur Theodor Franz a visit. Señor Emmanuelo de las Foresas had a pliable character, he was thoroughly Orléans: rather military, with a gold knob walking stick and a grey moustache.

'Monsieur,' Monsieur Theodor Franz said, 'why aren't you wearing crepe?'

'Crepe?'

'Yes, I'm sure I've read somewhere that Charlot has no mother, Monsieur.'

So when Monsieur Dupont travelled, he wore a crepe band around his hat. Monsieur Theodor Franz brought Charlot a present. It was a hoop with his name on it. He took it with him on the train.

Monsieur Theodor Franz remained in Paris. It was a point of principle. He always stayed away. 'An impresario frightens the press, Monsieur,' he said to Señor Emmanuelo de las Foresas. 'Those gentlemen think I turn up with my pockets full of humbug. The gentlemen of the press are so suspicious.'

The morning after the first concert, however, a telegram called him to Brussels. He waited yet another day, read the Brussels newspapers, and then set off. The young violin prodigy Charlot Dupont had pretty much flopped.

Señor Emmanuelo de las Foresas met him at the railway station. He was timid and rabbited on mournfully. 'Well, what can you expect from a child?' he said. 'What can you expect? He obviously can't play like Sarasate.'*

'Monsieur, be quiet, he played like an ass.'

Charlot was miserable. Señor Emmanuelo de las Foresas had beaten him black and blue across his back. He glanced up at Monsieur Theodor Franz, expecting more. Monsieur Theodor Franz, however, unpacked an entire warehouse of Parisian toys and scattered them across the living room. Charlot realised he would not be getting a beating.

Monsieur Theodor Franz found a new teacher, and they resumed practising the three numbers. They played for hours until Charlot was ready to drop with fatigue. Monsieur Theodor Franz added to the performance many smiles and childish gestures.

Charlot stood slumped over, playing, copying and smiling. Eventually he started sobbing. The violin dropped from his hands and he smeared tears across his face.

'Right – one more time … .'

'I'm so tired,' he wept, 'I don't want to.'

'Just one more time and you'll get a sweetie.'

Charlot sobbed. 'I don't want a sweetie,' he said.

'So what do you want – if you're a good boy and play it once more … .'

Charlot peeked out between his fingers. 'Cigarettes,' he said.

'Right, then play.'

'Three,' Charlot said.

'Very well, all right, three.'

Charlot removed his hands from his face. 'Show me,' he demanded.

Monsieur Theodor Franz placed three cigarettes on the table and Charlot played once more, shaking all over his body, he was so tired.

The lessons ended at two o'clock. Monsieur Theodor Franz would then stroll with Charlot on the boulevard. They had brought along the pretty hoop. Charlot would have preferred to sit on a bench; he was so sleepy he felt as if he had grit in his eyes. But Monsieur Theodor Franz would rap him with his knuckles until he woke up and ran with the hoop.

Monsieur Theodor Franz spoke amicably to all the well-dressed children and gave them sweets and candies. He also organised games. When their mothers were present, he would make conversation and introduce Charlot – when he could find him, that is. Because Charlot would often retreat and sleep curled up at the foot of a tree, his head resting on his knees.

Then he would be rapped again – Monsieur Theodor Franz could rap quite hard with his knuckles right against the collarbone – until he woke up and grabbed his whip and top, which lay beside him on the ground.

'He's so lively,' Monsieur Theodor Franz said, 'he's a real boy, he is.'

One time Charlot disappeared altogether. He could not be found on the boulevard. Señor Emmanuelo de las Foresas and Monsieur Theodor Franz competed to find him. Eventually they discovered Charlot in the park, behind a stone plinth. He was surrounded by a throng of urchins. He was putting a cigarette in their mouths and showing them how to smoke. The children pulled ugly faces and coughed from the smoke. That made Charlot sad. 'Idiots,' the boy said. He himself blew big clouds of smoke into the air with great pride.

When they returned home that day, Monsieur Theodor Franz beat Charlot for the first time.

When they had practised the three numbers for a further week, the violin prodigy Charlot Dupont was ready to oblige by performing one or two numbers for the pupils at Monsieur Rochebrune's school. Monsieur Rochebrune had invited a few of the pupils' mothers and aunts.

Charlot played two numbers and 'Der Schneider Kakadu'. There had never been such joy in Monsieur Rochebrune's school. The mothers were moved. Charlot was kissed by them in turn. Afterwards the ladies stood in the windows watching him play tag in the school playground.

Notices appeared in the newspapers. A couple of other schools invited the violin prodigy.

Monsieur Theodor Franz took Charlot to visit the critics. Charlot had become an incredibly sleepy child. No sooner had he been seated in the carriage than he fell asleep in his corner. And if they visited private homes – Monsieur Theodor Franz liked visiting people in their homes, he was fond of home visits

– he would stand gawping next to Monsieur Theodor Franz's chair, drawling a yes or a no.

They visited Monsieur Deslandes. Monsieur Deslandes was a correspondent for *The Times*. Monsieur Theodor Franz spoke in a low voice – Monsieur Theodor Franz always spoke to the authorities and the gentlemen of the press in a low voice – about his friend Monsieur Ambroise Thomas.

In the adjacent living room, Monsieur Deslandes' badly behaved children were making a racket. They could barely hear themselves speak. Monsieur Deslandes opened the door and told them off. Two seconds later the racket resumed.

'Monsieur – let them play, bless them.' Monsieur Theodor Franz spoke softly. 'Children will be children.'

He looked at Charlot, who was slumped in a chair. 'Charlot, I believe you're welcome to play with Monsieur Deslandes' children.'

He was of course more than welcome.

'Do you hear that, Charlot, you may go and play with Monsieur Deslandes' children.'

Charlot stayed where he was and didn't stir. He felt nothing but utter indifference to the offspring of the critic Monsieur Deslandes.

Monsieur Theodor Franz bent down and with a rap right on the collarbone, said in a gentle voice: 'Don't be shy, little Charlot. Monsieur Deslandes has just said you're welcome to play with his children.'

Charlot quickly got down from the chair and joined Monsieur Deslandes' children. They had red hair and amused themselves by sticking pins into the new arrival. Monsieur Theodor Franz and Monsieur Deslandes stood in the doorway, delighting in the children.

That was a few days before the young violin prodigy's second concert. This concert was a great success. The pupils from Monsieur Rochebrune's school had complimentary tickets and presented Charlot Dupont with a giant garland.

Charlot was photographed standing framed by the garland. It was a very great success.

After the third concert – by request the programme was the same as that of the second – Monsieur Theodor Franz personally toured Scandinavia with Charlot Dupont. Monsieur Theodor Franz prized Scandinavia highly. There the little prodigy had his baptism of fire. The way through Europe lay open. For two years, every corner was explored; they got as far as Baku.*

Charlot Dupont made Patti money all over Europe.*

Charlot celebrated his seventh birthday every time he gave a farewell concert. Señor Emmanuelo de las Foresas still wore a crepe band on his hat.

Señor Emmanuelo de las Foresas was very contented indeed. He earned a great deal of money and resumed certain passions from his youth. He had always been partial to blondes of a particular voluptuousness and had once broken the bank in Baden.* He was fond of a little baccarat in the evening after the concert, and travelling around Europe, he quite frequently found a blonde embonpoint in which to delight.

Thus passed a couple of years.

The company spent most of its time on the railway. There were concerts nearly every day. In the early morning they would leave for the train. Señor Emmanuelo de las Foresas would ruffle Charlot's curls eagerly. The boy was fast asleep, yet fought him in his sleep. Señor Emmanuelo de las Foresas then splashed his face with water to wake him up. Charlot would weep and put on his socks, whimpering as he sat on the edge of the bed. His limbs were leaden, so heavy.

Once dressed, he would stagger around in the gloom, half-asleep between the open suitcases which were packed haphazardly. He would fall asleep again sitting with a cup of lukewarm tea in his hand. They would rouse him yet again and, with their faces stiff and blue from the cold, the company would rattle along on the clammy omnibus to the railway station. It was never a quiet trip. Señor Emmanuelo de las Foresas and Monsieur Theodor Franz invariably argued in the morning.

Charlot curled up like a bundle of clothes in the corner of the train compartment and slept.

When Charlot woke up, he would see his father and Monsieur Theodor Franz. They were sprawled across the seats with their clothes loosened. Monsieur Theodor Franz was snoring. The carriage rocked from side to side, the locomotive rumbled along with its monotonous noise. The heat in the compartment made Charlot drowsy; he felt tired but was unable to sleep. He kept shifting, his body weary from sitting up as well as from lying down. He knelt on the seat and looked outside. It was always the same: trees and houses and fields. The only thing he cared about was little dogs. He always wanted to get out on the platform to pat them.

In the afternoon they would reach their destination, new porters would handle their luggage and Charlot would look eagerly across the platform, his arms filled with toys; they would wolf down some food in a rush, Charlot was then dressed in velvet, and they arrived at the concert venue. Once the excitement had died down after the first number, Charlot would often fall asleep in a corner of the dressing room where they would have to wake him when he was due to go back on.

They drove to their lodgings and had supper, and Monsieur Theodor Franz and Señor Emmanuelo de las Foresas grew loud over their bottles. Charlot, too, became animated late in the evening. He had cognac and water, and would listen with flushed cheeks.

Señor Emmanuelo de las Foresas knew many amusing stories about well-developed blondes from the two continents. Monsieur Theodor Franz, too, had tales to tell. Charlot learned a great deal about what life has to offer in this respect.

They also spoke about the profession.

Monsieur Theodor Franz stretched out his legs, stuffed his hands in his pockets and became confiding: 'The press, Monsieur, never feed it, the most stupid thing you can do is to feed it, I never feed it, food makes the press restless, Monsieur … . Call on them in their homes, Monsieur – eat thin soup in family circles, Monsieur, be unassuming – write many little notes, Monsieur. That's how it's done.'

'Yes – that's the way to do it,' Señor Emmanuelo de las Foresas said.

'And it's the cheapest,' Monsieur Theodor Franz said.

Señor Emmanuelo de las Foresas nodded.

'Miss Tisbyrs cost me less than a bottle of Bordeaux* … she was religious, she didn't drink alcohol – we all drank water, Monsieur … at the end she earned 5000 francs per night. Have you heard her sing?'

'Yes.'

'Then I don't have to tell you about her voice, Monsieur.' Monsieur Theodor Franz fell silent for a moment. 'Flowers – flowers are a mistake … . The public doesn't believe in flowers these days. Idiots throw flowers. Miss Tisbyrs cost me twenty-six crucifixes at three francs a piece – presented to her on the stage by a committee … that impresses. Crucifixes wreathed in dried flowers, Monsieur – Miss Tisbyrs wept … .'

They spoke about all kinds of virtuosi and artists. Señor Emmanuelo de las Foresas mostly said yes and amen.

'The audience is never extravagant, the audience is virtuous – you must address their hearts – their sentiments – appeal to their emotions. That's how it's done. I've saved ten singers with *Ave Maria* accompanied by a harp … I can make a fortune simply by putting a young woman next to a harp … .'

Monsieur Theodor Franz had no time for divas. They offended him outright: 'It's an insult,' he said. 'An insult to common sense.'

'Patti,' he said, 'Patti, my friend. A fraud, Monsieur. Patti has ruined twenty impresarios. I'm not King Midas, I'm a businessman – 12000 francs for two arias – I call that an insult. *Make* the stars – make them – I'm an impresario, Monsieur, not an elephant handler … .'

Charlot walked right up to Monsieur Theodor Franz; he listened as he rested his arms on the table. Monsieur Theodor Franz rattled with the jingling hundreds of thousands.

'Creation – the act of creation – now that's an art,' Monsieur Theodor Franz trailed off and the two gentlemen drank in silence for a while. A wide-eyed

Charlot continued to watch Monsieur Theodor Franz, who was sitting pensively in his chair.

Señor Emmanuelo de las Foresas was getting tired. Señor Emmanuelo de las Foresas' moustache tended to droop despondently when he grew sleepy.

'But it'll be over soon – it can't go on … . People want complimentary tickets, they'll only go if they get comps. There are too many world famous celebrities, celebrities everywhere you look, you trip over them … there are too many frauds … I've said it, I've said it to the gentlemen of the press: gentlemen, I've said, you're strangling the arts, gentlemen. You write too many articles, gentlemen, I've said. You exaggerate too much, gentlemen. But it's no use – what use is it … . They keep churning it out – they won't stop churning it out. They ruin it for us – they're not discriminating – it's the competition – one shouts louder than the other – the public can't hear themselves think.'

'Monsieur, the big money has already been made. In ten years I won't pay 100 Marks for a world-famous celebrity.' Monsieur Theodor Franz fell silent. His hands slipped limply out of his pockets. 'Not 100 Marks … .'

Señor Emmanuelo de las Foresas was startled by the silence and suddenly noticed Charlot, who was asleep with his head resting on the table.

'Charlot, are you still up, Charlot … . We've forgotten about the child.'

And Señor Emmanuelo de las Foresas put him to bed; Charlot was already half-asleep while he was being undressed. But suddenly he opened his eyes and, hoarse from sleep, he exclaimed: 'Father – do *we* have a lot of money?'

'Money?'

'Yes.'

'Well, yes – we have money.'

'Right.' And Charlot went back to sleep.

Charlot had started asking about this recently: about the money.

At times Monsieur Theodor Franz didn't accompany them on their travels. Instead he went on ahead. Then Señor Emmanuelo de las Foresas would play cards with Charlot in the train compartment. They played for pretend money. The gilded coins flowed between them on the seat. Señor Emmanuelo de las Foresas told lively stories. He talked about the bank in Baden he had broken.

'That was back when there still was a bank in Baden.' He spoke of gambling dens in Mexico where you could win big if you knew how. And Señor Emmanuelo de las Foresas dared say that he knew how. 'There were proper fortunes to be made, all that gold, gold worth talking about.'

Charlot listened and guarded his cards and gathered up the coins on the seat.

'And then there's Janeiro – Rio de Janeiro, that is – ' Señor Emmanuelo de las Foresas let his cards sink, '– in the morning when the gold ran out – diamonds would appear on the table – hundreds of diamonds would flow across the baize … . Or there's Peru – or Monaco, now there's a gambling den! No, they're worth a visit – if you know what you're doing … .'

And Señor Emmanuelo de las Foresas dared say that he had known what he was doing – in his youth. And he still had very nimble, very fast fingers.

There was the trick with the pin, the baize and the fine silk thread that swiped away the card right from under the dealer's nose. Señor Emmanuelo de las Foresas had pulled off this trick in Baden, in *Baden*, many times. He wanted to see if he still had it.

'Yes, try it, Father.'

Señor Emmanuelo de las Foresas still had it.

'It's a talent,' he said. 'Pure talent. It's all in the hands.' He repeated all his tricks, in front of Charlot, on the seat. The boy copied him many times. Señor Emmanuelo de las Foresas watched him. He livened up, he instructed, he corrected.

'Bravo – bravo. Now do it one more time.'

Charlot performed the trick.

'That's right – that's right – why, the boy has the gift. – But – bravo – bravo.' He really did have nimble fingers.

They continued to play. Charlot lost. He watched every card like a hawk and his hands holding the pretend money trembled with excitement. He lost again.

'You're cheating, Father,' he said, grabbing his father's hand. 'You have duplicate cards.'

Señor Emmanuelo de las Foresas grew angry. 'One doesn't cheat one's own children,' he said. He refused to play again.

Charlot, however, carried on; he played with himself as the partner and with the cards spread across the seat. The fake coins jingled in his hands.

When Señor Emmanuelo de las Foresas and Charlot were on their own, time passed easily. When there was just the two of them, a lady would always join them for supper after the concert. Charlot really liked those ladies. They kissed his ears and shared their cigarettes with him. They undressed him when it was time for him to go to bed and danced with him in his nightwear. They were so kind to him in every respect. He would squeal when they tickled him.

Charlot was given many presents. Señor Emmanuelo de las Foresas looked after them all for him.

Every now and then as they sat on a train, Charlot would say: 'Father – where's our money?'

'In Paris.'

'Hm. Is there a lot now?'

'Why – yes. But your mother also needs to eat, that costs a lot.'

There were days when Charlot was constantly troubled by thoughts of money. Then he would forget about it for a long time.

The third year passed. Monsieur Theodor Franz had Charlot learn a fourth number. It was the Radetzky March.* Charlot played it on a child's violin. He first performed it in Pesth.* Charlot wore a Magyar uniform and the students pulled his carriage home.

Monsieur Theodor Franz always had inspired ideas. He composed and published in the newspapers a letter of thanks to the students in which he announced that Charlot Dupont would give a charity concert in aid of flood victims.

Monsieur Theodor Franz and Señor Emmanuelo de las Foresas drafted the announcement jointly.

'But what flood victims?' Señor Emmanuelo de las Foresas wanted to know.

'Monsieur,' Monsieur Theodor Franz said, 'there are always flood victims in Hungary.'

Monsieur Theodor Franz knew how to write such letters. It was his speciality. He had had his greatest success through an open letter. It was with Miss Tisbyrs when, in an open letter to the public, he had requested there be no applause at a church concert in order to spare Miss Tisbyrs' sensitivities. The concert had made a gross profit of 26,000 francs – 'and do you know how much it costs to hire a church, Monsieur? Nothing – nothing at all, you can get them for nothing' – and the whole town had cheered her outside the church.

Monsieur Theodor Franz wrote that Monsieur Emmanuel Dupont, the father of the young artistic phenomenon – who had served his beloved France with honours and remained loyal to the Royal House of Orléans – was infinitely happy that his son was able to support a nation that had always maintained an unshakeable faith in the superiority and future of his precious home country.

Señor Emmanuelo de las Foresas had had tears in his eyes.

The concert in aid of flood victims was sold out before the ticket office even opened. The concert finished with 'Kakadu der Schneider'. When Charlot took his nineteenth curtain call, he performed the Radetzky March as his encore.

The next day their tour of Hungary began. Señor Emmanuelo de las Foresas took 200,000 guilders on that trip.

Charlot was growing awfully tall. A long stretch of skinny red leg stuck out from his short socks. Monsieur Theodor Franz had a lace border attached around the knee of his short trousers.

That evening when his glance landed upon Charlot who was, as always, slumped over a chair with a cigarette, Monsieur Theodor Franz started to fret.

'Monsieur – Charlot has to become eight,' he said. 'You can't be seven years old when you're nearly tall enough to join the Guards.'

At this point Charlot was coming up for his eleventh birthday.

They gave concerts in Berlin. Once they were over, Charlot would return home to Paris for a month's holiday before they made their way to America.

It happened during one of the first concerts. Charlot had played and was in his dressing room, listening to the applause coming from the auditorium. There were quite a few people in his dressing room.

'Go back on – go back,' Monsieur Theodor Franz said. Charlot went back. The applause erupted like a storm. Off and then back on and back on again.

He stood in his dressing room, warm and excited from the applause. The audience carried on clapping.

'Get back on – go back,' Monsieur Theodor Franz urged him from the door. And back on again.

Charlot returned. His arms were laden with flowers. Wearily he let them drop to the floor and slumped against the door frame.

He felt a hand through his hair and looked up. A mild, mournful face with large eyes was bent over him. Inside the auditorium the applause continued. He didn't know why, but suddenly he flung his arms around the neck of this young, unknown man, and clung to him. The young man continued to pat his hair.

'Pauvre enfant – mon pauvre enfant.'*

It was a critic from a major newspaper. He came every day to take Charlot for a walk. They walked down the avenues in Tiergarten. Charlot always held Hugo Becker's hand. He talked about his money and his travels like an old man.

'So where is your money?' Herr Becker asked.

'In Paris – with –' Charlot was about to say his mother, '– in Paris,' he then said again. 'Father sends it to Paris.'

'I see – your father has it.'

Charlot carried on chatting as they walked up and down the avenues.

Monsieur Theodor Franz travelled to Paris. A few days later Señor Emmanuelo de las Foresas also left.

'After all, I have to prepare his homecoming,' Señor Emmanuelo de las Foresas said. 'I'm going home to slaughter the fatted calf.' Señor Emmanuelo de las Foresas travelled discreetly to Potsdam with a blonde weighing two hundred and twenty pounds.

Charlot stayed behind with Herr Becker.

It was after the last concert. Herr Becker had come to help Charlot pack his suitcases.

'Charlot,' he said. 'I've saved you some money. It's something – Monsieur Theodor Franz and your father don't know about this, you understand – I managed to get the halls more cheaply, you see – here's 1000 Marks … .'

'1000 Marks – for me – just for me …' Charlot stared at the money. 'Is *that* for me? All that money just for me … .' Herr Becker gave it to him and

Charlot spread out the notes, one after the other, on the sofa, in a fan, then he smoothed them and stepped back to gaze at them. He couldn't stop talking. What he was going to buy, the presents he would give … with all that money. He divided the notes into piles – one for this and one for that.

'With that money I'm sure I can get Mother a dress … a silk dress.'

He prattled on for a long time about his mother and everyone at home, about how they were and where they lived – 'Because – you see – Mother – she spends most of her time crying … .'

And then he suddenly grew bright red and went quiet. 'Well – because it's just something …' he was verging on tears, '… it's not true that my mother is dead. It's just something Monsieur Theodor Franz insists on … . Mother is at home. That's why Father sends her all the money, so she can save it … .'

They gathered up the notes and stitched them into the lining of Charlot's blouse.

'Right, you should give the money to your aunt, Charlot, for safekeeping – so nobody knows anything about it – and then it'll be yours to spend whenever you want to, do you understand.'

'Yes – I'll give it to my aunt – then I can get it from her later – yes … .'

Charlot went up to Herr Becker and stood close to him. 'You're … kind to me,' he said.

'Do you think so, Charlot?' Herr Becker ran his white hand through Charlot's hair.

'Do you have any children?' Charlot wanted to know.

'No – I have no children.'

'Hm … you ought to have some … .'

'I'm not going to, Charlot.' Herr Becker let his arm glide onto Charlot's shoulder and pulled him close. 'But now we need to pack, my boy … .'

Charlot wept when he said goodbye to Herr Becker.

Señor Emmanuelo de las Foresas' family still lived on the fifth floor. Señora Emmanuelo de las Foresas' hair had turned white. Nothing else had changed.

Señor Emmanuelo de las Foresas had his first cup of chocolate brought to him in bed at two o'clock in the afternoon. Afterwards he got up. Señora Emmanuelo de las Foresas dressed him. She was terrified of Señor Emmanuelo de las Foresas during this process because he tended to be rather difficult in the morning. He used a curling tong, which he was wont to let touch Señora Emmanuelo de las Foresas' neck – when he was in a bad mood. The whole house would tremble while Señor Emmanuelo de las Foresas made his ablutions.

Once Señor Emmanuelo de las Foresas had finished getting dressed, he would go out.

While he was out, his wife would pace up and down, dreading his return.

And all nine kids grew taller and taller, half-starved in the same never-ending chaos.

Charlot slipped back into it. He never once asked about the money.

One day there wasn't a single coin left in the house. Señora Emmanuelo de las Foresas cried her eyes out. She had no supper for Señor Emmanuelo de las Foresas. Charlot went to his aunt and fetched the 1000 Marks. His mother hid nine hundred of them among the feathers in an old duvet.

Deep inside Charlot developed an enormous, slumbering hatred of his father, like a suffering animal.

As it happened, Señor Emmanuelo de las Foresas would often take Charlot with him when he went out. They went to the theatre and the opera. Monsieur Theodor Franz gifted them the boxes. For the final two weeks Charlot had driven to the Bois de Boulogne with two small ponies. He had worn a Scottish kilt. Monsieur Theodor Franz gave him everything. He was so kind.

Señora Emmanuelo de las Foresas would go outside, sit on a bench near the road and watch Charlot when he drove past in the parade of open carriages.

After four weeks they set off to 'do' America.

Deep down Monsieur Theodor Franz did not respect America. America offended his artistic sensitivity. He said that he wasn't a peddler.

He made a fortune.

Charlot did everything they told him to. Every night he was on the train, and he would often give two concerts a day. His eyes grew strangely sluggish and he took no interest in anything. He rarely spoke. *If* he thought anything at all, he inconvenienced no one with his thoughts.

He smoked constantly. For hours he would light one cigarette after another and gaze at the blue smoke. Eventually he was enveloped in a cloud. But otherwise, as previously mentioned, he would go wherever people wanted him to go and do exactly what they wanted him to do. He was always dog-tired.

In Chicago he was given a small gold violin encrusted with diamonds. It was presented to him at a concert. Señor Emmanuelo de las Foresas was prevented from attending that night – voluptuous Americans prevented him with increasing frequency from attending the concerts – and so he never saw the violin.

The next morning Charlot had the hotel porter sell the violin and send the money to his mother in Paris.

While drinking his chocolate, Señor Emmanuelo de las Foresas read the newspapers and learned about the violin. He wanted to see it.

'I've sold it,' Charlot said.

'What?' Señor Emmanuelo de las Foresas almost dropped his cup.

'Yes.'

Charlot looked hard at his father. 'And I've sent the money home,' he said.

Señor Emmanuelo de las Foresas sat with his cup, his arm frozen, in his bed and didn't utter a squeak.

Charlot's face had looked so strange.

The little violin prodigy was growing taller, so Monsieur Theodor Franz stated his age as ten on the posters. That was in California. They went on to Havana, Mexico and Brazil.

'Monsieur,' Monsieur Theodor Franz said to Señor Emmanuelo de las Foresas. 'I hate myself for it – but such are the times … Monsieur: we're going to Australia.'

Señor Emmanuelo de las Foresas judged that all currencies were equally attractive. They went to Australia.

Charlot was obliging and went along with it. Besides, no one had asked his opinion.

In the evenings, when Monsieur Theodor Franz happened to glance across the wine glasses at Charlot, who had nodded off in his chair, pale and with his arms hanging down, he would at times say to Señor Emmanuelo de las Foresas: 'I say – Charlot is a good boy really. You see, Monsieur, that's the advantage – children make no objections. They're not like tenors – they don't claim to be ill – they soldier on. You know where you have them … . I tell you honestly, I'm more than happy to "do" children.'

The violin prodigy Charlot Dupont allowed himself to be played like a fiddle. But he had fits of stubbornness.

One day when Charlot was packing his suitcase, he took his toys one by one and destroyed them. He smashed them to bits against the edges of chairs and stomped on them on the floor. With all his might he pressed the steel hoop against the wall so it warped – the sheer effort made him groan.

Señor Emmanuelo de las Foresas came in and saw the devastation. Charlot stood, his cheeks scarlet, among the wreckage.

'What's this about? What's happened to your toys – '

'I've broken them all,' Charlot said.

'Has the boy gone mad?'

Charlot clenched his fists: 'I'm not taking them with me.' He looked straight at his father. 'Let go of me. I'm not taking them with me.'

Señor Emmanuelo de las Foresas let him go. He had his moments of weakness. Señor Emmanuelo de las Foresas started picking up the pieces. –

People turned to stare at Charlot in the streets. He looked ridiculous in his blouse with his long, dangling arms, and his skinny legs, which were bare from the knee down. Monsieur Theodor Franz always bought such childish straw hats for him. Street urchins would often tease him.

One day Charlot passed a big group of boys on their way home from school. 'Oh – look at that big baby – hey – look at his blouse,' one of them called out. Their whistling and their laughing and their shouting turned into a concert:

'Ah – where's his nursemaid … '
'Who'll button up his trousers … '
'Do you think he's all there … '

'Cry, baby, cry,
Put your finger in your eye,
And tell your mother it wasn't I'

they jeered in unison.

'Put him in a nappy.'

'Where's his dummy?'

'Let's beat him up.'

Charlot picked up a stone and hurled it at them.

After that he refused to be seen in the street. Monsieur Theodor Franz had to impose his authority.

'I'm not doing it.' Charlot pressed himself up against the wall as if afraid they were going to drag him outside. 'I won't do it.'

Monsieur Theodor Franz was ready to rap him with his knuckles. Charlot pulled up his shoulders and gritted his teeth. His eyes were blazing. Monsieur Theodor Franz dropped his hand.

'And I *won't* wear a blouse any longer,' Charlot said.

'No blouse … have …' Monsieur Theodor Franz looked at Charlot, thin and gangly as he stood there in his blouse. He stopped himself. Monsieur Theodor Franz had realised that a blouse would no longer do. Charlot got a jacket.

He was almost fourteen years old.

The Charlot Dupont tour returned to Europe.

Monsieur Theodor Franz decided to assemble an artistic bouquet. He hoped to bring together six world-famous artistes on *one* poster. The public had become sluggish and needed wooing with an extravaganza. Monsieur Theodor Franz talked about a glittering segment of the Milky Way of European arts. The violin prodigy Charlot Dupont belonged to this segment. The other members of the company were an alto of Señor Emmanuelo de las Foresas' favourite proportions, a baritone, a virginal lyric tenor, a cellist and Madame Simonin, the pianist.

They rumbled through Europe with two programmes.

'Monsieur,' Monsieur Theodor Franz said, 'I'll take the smoking compartment.' Señor Emmanuelo de las Foresas also favoured the smoking compartment. The others travelled together.

Their compartment was littered with furs and filthy pillows. The alto travelled in a red blouse without a corset. She would bury her upper body in the pillows as if trying to stand on her head. The gentlemen turned their faces to the walls and snored.

Monsieur Theodor Franz's artistic segment became rather androgynous on its way through Europe and it lost its inhibitions. The pianist suffered from the heat. She took off half her clothes and curled up like a cat with her naked arms above her head.

Charlot woke up and looked about him. He could stare at the pianist's round arms for ages.

No one was able to sleep any more. They sat staring lethargically at one another, their heads empty. The pianist performed finger exercises on a practice keyboard. The tour acquired four jokes, which were told a few times every hour. Then everyone nodded off again.

Charlot crept closer and studied the pianist's childish face and soft eyelids. Charlot didn't sleep quite so much on the train these days. He would sit still for hours, his gaze resting on Madame Simonin as she lay there. He didn't move a muscle. He was afraid someone might wake up. It felt good to sit on his own in the corner, watching her sleep.

Whenever she practised, he was allowed to balance the silent keyboard on his knees.

They reached a venue for lunch. The ladies swirled a powder brush around their faces a few times and enveloped themselves in their coats. Charlot was always the first one out. He would stand by the best seat in the dining room, waiting for Madame Simonin.

Everyone laughed a great deal at the tall Charlot in his short trousers. He was the least successful performer in Monsieur Theodor Franz's artistic segment. He had grown so awkward with his long arms, and he would stand on the stage with his knees bent as if trying to hide his own legs.

'Don't slouch, don't slouch!' Señor Emmanuelo de las Foresas was outraged. 'Are you trying to play them all to sleep – is that what you're trying to do – idiot. Now go on … .'

Charlot stumbled onto the stage twice as clumsily.

Señor Emmanuelo de las Foresas stood behind the curtain. 'Come on, why aren't you smiling … straighten up – take a bow.'

Not a hand stirred in the auditorium.

'Take a bow – bow.'

The fragile notes emanating from Charlot's violin were as piercing as sewing needles. In anger Señor Emmanuelo de las Foresas pinched the prodigy with his nails until he bled.

During Charlot's last number, Monsieur Theodor Franz was standing next to Señor Emmanuelo de las Foresas behind the curtain. 'Have you seen his posture?' Señor Emmanuelo de las Foresas said. 'Or noticed how he has been standing recently… .'

'Monsieur – he's standing as if he had soiled himself.' Monsieur Theodor Franz left.

Monsieur Theodor Franz really said the most unpleasant things to Señor Emmanuelo de las Foresas.

Charlot received some sporadic applause from the gods.

'Go on – go on,' Señor Emmanuelo de las Foresas called out, 'on stage … smile, smile, God damn you.'

Señor Emmanuelo de las Foresas had taken to swearing rather viciously of late.

The violin prodigy was put on half pay. Charlot showed no surprise. If he had been expecting *anything* at all, then this was it.

But in the evenings after the concert when he sat on the floor close to Madame Simonin's instrument – it was his favourite position – he would often rest his head against the piano in tired anguish. It happened most often when he looked at her and when she played. Then Charlot felt at his most miserable.

The tour went from town to town. Monsieur Theodor Franz mostly travelled on ahead. On those occasions the alto would then join Señor Emmanuelo de las Foresas in the smoking compartment. Madame Simonin played a game of patience on the silent keyboard which Charlot balanced on his knees. The baritone would usually tell stories. He knew a scandal about every virtuoso in Europe. Madame Simonin's shiny eyes would widen and she laughed so hard that she dropped her playing cards. Charlot grew scarlet and felt very strange when she laughed like that.

'So what *did* she do?' Madame Simonin wanted to know.

'She dined for free in the evening – every evening – in all innocence.'

The virginal lyric tenor looked up from his newspaper. He was always looking at newspapers he couldn't read, searching for his own name. 'Do you know the story about the husband?' he said.

'No – which one is that?'

'Every time a new little Lizeski is born, he examines the baby closely to see which one of their friends it takes after … whereupon he borrows 1000 francs from the man in question.'

Charlot desperately wanted Madame Simonin not to laugh. It was best when she sat quietly with her hands in her lap. She would often smile to herself and her eyes were very bright. Charlot was so happy that he felt a surge of warm blood to his heart.

Charlot grew increasingly clumsy. He was still so busy trying to hide his arms that he invariably tripped over his own feet. He was embarrassed by his clothes. His baby clothes with lace trimmings – for a tall, growing boy. In hotel rooms he would always press himself into a corner. There he would hide with his head in his hands and not move for hours. He was happy as long as he didn't have to say anything.

Charlot always made a note of the time when the local boys came back from school. He would stand by the window watching groups of them saunter home with their piles of books. His eyes were sluggish as if they had been extinguished.

The other world-famous artists from Monsieur Theodor Franz's Milky Way drifted aimlessly around the hotel lounges and in and out of each other's rooms. They hated being alone with only the meagre company of their six-piece repertoire. They would pace up and down, tense and grumpy, and they were invariably too cold or too hot. They were always ill, and possessed an arsenal of medicine bottles. They spent most of their time with Madame Simonin, who intermittently went to her piano, playing scales all day long.

Charlot did not run around. He sat in his corner, immobile and tired, surrounded by the hubbub. Señor Emmanuelo de las Foresas had so much linen. There wasn't a single chair in the room without a filthy shirt on it.

In the evening before a concert they would gather in Madame Simonin's room while they waited for their carriages. They would weave and wander around the furniture like a flock of hens. *One* had aching fingers, *another* a sore throat.

During the concert Madame Simonin and the alto would sit in their dressing room and be courted by the gentlemen of the press. They conversed, in the cool words of worldly ladies, with the critics, who sat squirming with embarrassment in their voluminous black coats, distracted by the diamond necklace around Madame Simonin's neck, while they smiled sheepishly.

Madame Simonin wore a fortune in diamonds. She would casually rest her childlike head against her arm, which glittered with diamonds – a bracelet which never failed to impress wherever it was displayed – and smile with poised elegance. Charlot forgot everything. He stood in a corner without moving and just *stared*. His eyes loved this image like a dream.

He was commanded on and off stage for his numbers. He came back as if drawn to the light. Because now there was only *her*, radiant and beautiful.

Unknown women arrived with flowers. Madame Simonin took them, and thanked and kissed the unknown ladies on their cheeks.

After the concert the gentlemen of the press helped Madame Simonin and the alto into their long fur coats, and the ladies took the arms of the critics and allowed themselves to be escorted to their carriages. Holding their bouquets, they would smile behind the carriage windows as they drove off.

'Idiots,' Madame Simonin said.

The alto stuck out her tongue. And then they giggled like a couple of schoolgirls.

Charlot nearly burst into tears whenever Madame Simonin laughed like that. He sat in the darkness in the carriage, gripping his two laurel garlands until his hands hurt.

Señor Emmanuelo de las Foresas was the owner of the two garlands. They were thrown onto the stage for the violin prodigy after 'Kakadu der Schneider'.

After a concert everyone was merry. They would dine, casually dressed, in Madame Simonin's salon. They discussed virtuosi. They frequently mentioned money. The alto was rich; she had a couple of millions and a château in Normandy. Madame Simonin had a fortune. She would watch the pennies carefully, but would throw thousands out of the window. They talked about how much they were making. They got a cut. They could earn fifteen hundred francs a night. They spoke with unabashed greed about all this gold.

'The arts,' Madame Simonin said. 'Do even ten people understand them? The ladies can see I have good fingers, the gentleman stare at my arms – it's revolting. The arts – hah – hah – *I* want to be rich.'

At times they were overcome by intense frugality and would summon the waiter to complain about an expense of a few schillings. They refused to let themselves be robbed. They didn't travel for the fun of it. They didn't travel to make the hotels rich. They travelled to make money. Often they would depart without leaving a tip at all. And the waiter had been at their beck and call half the night.

'Why should I have to put up with common people all my life?' Madame Simonin said. 'I don't want to suffer – until I'm old. I travel to *make money* – '

Only that same morning Madame Simonin had squandered eleven hundred francs on a Damascene sword.

'Do those people think I *enjoy* watching them yawn?' Madame Simonin said.

They talked about all the wretches who sang without having a voice, who bashed the keyboard with their lame hands because they were poor and had to make a living. Charlot listened to them. Not out of fear – for that he felt too sluggish, as he did in everything. But he felt so tired that he couldn't lift his hand.

Once he got to bed, he would cry from despair. He cried over so many things. He cried about his clothes and about Madame Simonin and about the audience who didn't clap any more, and about Madame Simonin, who said so many ugly things.

One evening Charlot lay staring for a long time at the stove where a fire was burning. He got up from his bed and took Señor Emmanuelo de las Foresas' two dried laurel garlands and threw them onto the flames.

The morning after the concert newspapers were brought to the touring artists. They couldn't read them, but they could see how many lines each of them got and they guessed at the meaning of the words. Charlot never looked at the papers when anyone else was present. But in the afternoon when the others had forgotten all about the reviews, he would steal the newspapers and, in his room, in the corner, he would open one newspaper after the other on his knees and stare at the one miserable line about the 'phenomenon' Charlot Dupont.

One evening after dinner Madame Simonin was leafing through some sheet music. 'It's beautiful,' she said. 'If only we had a violinist on tour – but of course,' and she laughed, 'Charlot plays the violin. Charlot – fetch your violin.'

Charlot went to get his violin and they started to play together.

When they had been playing for some time, she nodded. 'Why, that's very – really – why it's – good. It's – good, Charlot.'

Charlot played as if in a dream. Only the notes and her face were clear.

'Good – Charlot … .'

Madame Simonin seemed to lead him with such confidence. He played with tears in his eyes. He thought he might start sobbing at any moment.

It was over.

'Goodness me, the boy has talent,' Madame Simonin said. 'Charlot – we'll play together.'

Charlot had never believed that this might actually happen. Madame Simonin played with him from morning till night. She aimed her bright eyes at him and laughed when he did well. She matched his pace and made her art readily available to him.

'Why it's a crying shame – the boy has talent … . We'll play together at a concert.'

They performed together. When, for the first time in a long time, Charlot heard the applause erupt once more, tears sprang from his eyes. At the curtain call Charlot took Madame Simonin's hands in his, kissed them, and whispered incomprehensible words which were choked by his sobs.

Their duet became the highlight of the concerts. Madame Simonin demanded that Charlot's former pay be reinstated.

Charlot was always with Madame Simonin now. He sat by the piano when she practised. She babbled like a child while her nimble fingers flew across the keys. She laughed with her tingling, girlish laughter, spoke her soft language and contorted her face into a hundred grimaces. She was as wild as a little cat, was Madame Simonin. Charlot knew only one joy – to sit close to her. And then later to be alone and relive it, many times, half the night, and kiss some flowers of hers that he wore in a medallion around his neck.

The tour came to an end. Everyone went their separate ways. Madame Simonin was going on tour in America.

It didn't worry Charlot that he didn't have another engagement or that he would be going back to Paris and the fifth floor. He was about to be parted from Madame Simonin and he thought he would die.

It was the final night. Charlot would be leaving the following morning. Madame Simonin had invited Señor Emmanuelo de las Foresas and Charlot to dine with her, just the three of them. Charlot didn't speak or touch the food.

'Eat up, Charlot,' Madame Simonin said. 'These are your favourite dishes.'

Charlot helped himself mechanically. 'Thank you,' he said. He sat like a mute, his eyes fixed on her, dumb and helpless. Charlot knew only one thing: his happiness was over. Now – tonight it was over. And there was nothing he could do, nothing at all.

Señor Emmanuelo de las Foresas was affronted. Monsieur Theodor Franz had been rude to Señor Emmanuelo de las Foresas.

'You're abandoning my Charlot at a critical time,' Señor Emmanuelo de las Foresas had said that morning.

'Monsieur,' Monsieur Theodor Franz had said, 'did you really think that scam could last for ever?'

Señor Emmanuelo de las Foresas had indeed suffered for a long time because of Monsieur Theodor Franz's lack of breeding. Monsieur Theodor Franz was a boorish person. It offended Señor Emmanuelo de las Foresas. 'He says *things* … .'

'As a member of society,' Señor Emmanuelo de las Foresas said.

They had finished eating. Madame Simonin was playing. Charlot sat on the floor, his head resting against the piano.

'So you're going to Paris?' Madame Simonin said.

'Yes – we're going to Paris.'

'You have a home there?'

'Yes,' Señor Emmanuelo de las Foresas said, 'we have a home *there*.'

'Where? Should I be able to visit you … .'

'On the Boulevard Haussmann.' Señor Emmanuelo de las Foresas' tone of voice installed the de las Foresas family on the first floor.

Suddenly Charlot burst into tears.

When they were about to leave, Madame Simonin said: 'Now you won't forget me, Charlot, will you?' Charlot looked at her with eyes as obedient and loyal as a dog's. Not a word crossed his trembling lips.

The next morning, just as Señor Emmanuelo de las Foresas was leaving, the waiter slipped Charlot a letter. 'It's for you,' he said.

Charlot hid the letter. There was a money order in the envelope. On a visiting card it said: To Charlot's violin teacher from Sofie Simonin. The words were erased before Charlot reached Paris. He kissed Madame Simonin's card that often.

On the de las Foresas' fifth floor the mood was glum. Señor de las Foresas was downright offended by the attitude of concert agents. None of them was in need of his violin prodigy.

'Monsieur,' Señor Emmanuelo de las Foresas said to Monsieur Theodor Franz, 'so you won't be rehiring the violin prodigy?'

'Monsieur – have I ever lacked clarity? No – I won't be rehiring *Monsieur* Dupont.'

'So we're released from all contractual obligations?'

'From all of them.'

'That was all I wished to ascertain. Monsieur,' said Señor Emmanuelo de las Foresas, '– agents will fall over themselves to engage the violin prodigy.'

Señor Emmanuelo de las Foresas announced in an advertisement in *Le Figaro* that the violin prodigy Charlot Dupont – our famous little fellow countryman, wrote the newspaper – having concluded his triumphant world tour, had turned down all offers for the time being.*

No-one fell over themselves.

Señor Emmanuelo de las Foresas waited one week, he waited two weeks: not as much as a tour of the provinces. Señor Emmanuelo de las Foresas started doing the rounds with the prodigy. They visited every concert agency. Regrettably no one currently had any use for the prodigy.

Charlot trailed behind Señor Emmanuelo de las Foresas, pale and downcast. He took it all as one big criticism of him.

Madame Simonin's money had been eaten up. Señora de las Foresas wept and began making her familiar trips to the pawnbrokers. Señor Emmanuelo de las Foresas talked about children who drive their parents to an early grave.

Charlot had been taking lessons with a teacher from the conservatoire. The professor grew fond of the tall boy in infant clothing; he said he was making progress. One beautiful day he secured an invitation for Charlot to perform for Pasdeloup.* Charlot felt as if a stone had been lifted from his heart. He thought he was happy for the first time in his life. He rushed home along the boulevard so full of joy that he bumped into people: on Sunday he would play for Monsieur Pasdeloup.

It was as if the de las Foresas family awoke from a deep slumber with one stroke. Señora de las Foresas started to laugh – the de las Foresas children had never heard their mother laugh – but halfway through, her laughter turned into tears. Señora de las Foresas was far too happy. The children began to howl, each at their own pitch, bouncing into one another like wild animals in a cage.

Señor Emmanuelo de las Foresas came home and heard the news. 'That's what I've been saying,' Señor Emmanuelo de las Foresas declared. 'Monsieur Pasdeloup is a man who understands talent.'

At night Charlot slept on a sofa in the dining room. Señora de las Foresas came to him that evening. She placed Charlot's head on her lap and caressed him as if he were a little child. Señora de las Foresas was so happy.

'I hadn't dared hope, I hadn't dared hope – Charlot – I hadn't – '

'Mother … .'

'How they've tormented my boy, how they've tormented him – all those years.'

Señora de las Foresas cradled Charlot's head and looked at him and kissed his hair. 'My good boy.'

Señora de las Foresas talked about the time when Charlot was young, when he was very young, and she taught him to play his first tune. Did he remember it? It was 'Der Schneider Kakadu'.

Oh yes – he remembered. He had been standing by the piano, not yet able to reach the keyboard – he was that small – when he played. But he learned so quickly – he had an ear – after only hearing something twice, he played perfectly, without a single mistake.

But then came the years – they dragged him around – all those countries, her boy.

But now all was well again – it was all good … .

Señora de las Foresas was so happy. 'I hadn't dared hope, I hadn't, my boy. No – I hadn't dared. I thought it was all over for my boy.'

Charlot talked about Madame Simonin, who had played with him, who had said that he had talent. 'Yes – God bless her – God bless her for that.'

'Yes – God bless her for that.' Señora de las Foresas patted Charlot's curly hair; soon Charlot's breathing deepened and he fell asleep.

Señora de las Foresas gently eased her hand from his head and rose. She took the lamp and, for a long time, stood looking at her tall boy, smiling in his sleep. The tears ran down her cheeks. Señora de las Foresas had a tendency to be lachrymose.

Over the next few days Señora de las Foresas argued with her husband. For the first time in years. Usually Señora de las Foresas restricted her role to being the one shouted at and remaining quiet. But now she plucked up courage. Señora de las Foresas wanted a black jacket to be made for Charlot for the concert. Señor Emmanuelo de las Foresas calmed her down with the curling tongs. Señora de las Foresas wept and gave up.

Charlot wore short trousers and a blouse when he drove to Monsieur Pasdeloup. Señor Emmanuelo de las Foresas accompanied his son. Señor de las Foresas entered the venue first; Charlot followed him clumsily, clutching his violin case.

A gentleman came towards them. 'You must be Monsieur Pasdeloup,' Señor de las Foresas said. 'This is the violin prodigy, Charlot Dupont.'

Monsieur Pasdeloup looked straight past Señor Emmanuelo de las Foresas.

'Are you Monsieur Dupont,' he said to Charlot.

'Yes.'

'Monsieur,' he said. 'There must be some mistake. This isn't a fancy dress party. It's a concert. Please go home and change.'

Señor Emmanuelo de las Foresas was about to look personally affronted at Monsieur Pasdeloup. But Monsieur Pasdeloup had already turned his back on them. Señor Emmanuelo de las Foresas spun around and left; Charlot followed him, sobbing, down the stairs. The whole orchestra had been waiting up there.

Señora de las Foresas borrowed a suit from the fourth floor, and Monsieur Charlot Dupont drove back to the concert. This time Señor Emmanuelo de las Foresas did not accompany his son. Señor Emmanuelo de las Foresas was really thoroughly fed up with all these people with no manners.

Monsieur Charlot Dupont delighted, wrote *Le Figaro*.

Charlot Dupont toured the provinces. His stay in every other town got him nowhere.

When he returned to Paris, he applied for a position with an orchestra. Charlot auditioned for the conductor. He wasn't displeased.

'Not bad – not bad … . But the tone is thin.'

'The instrument is so small,' Charlot said.

'Possibly.'

'Your name, Monsieur,' the conductor said.

'Charlot Dupont.'

'Charlot – Dupont – dare I ask – you're not the prodigy, are you?'

'Yes,' Charlot said, 'that's me.'

'Well,' the conductor was somewhat thrown. 'I don't think – there are no places for virtuosi – we … you understand, Monsieur Dupont … we need people who don't mind hard work.'

And he assured Monsieur Dupont that the position was as good as filled.

Charlot Dupont found another impresario.

The Charlot Dupont tour limped through tenth-grade towns. There were empty houses, unpaid bills, confiscated luggage, and long, anxious days. There were fearful messages to the bookseller who sold the tickets. How were the sales going? If they did sell some tickets, it was a blessing if they managed to cover their costs.

Charlot Dupont was mostly very tired.

He had in his repertoire an elegy, 'La folia,' it was called.* Monsieur Dupont played it so that the few sensitive members of the audience would cry. But the critics complained that Charlot Dupont lacked energy and that his tone was threadbare.

At times in these middling towns the first concert would sell out. Subsequent ones were always empty.

Charlot is now twenty years old.

Translated by Charlotte Barslund

5. Her Highness

Her Serene Highness cleared her throat, smiled graciously once more and buried her nose in her bouquet of camellias. The birthday committee curtseyed in a row and backed towards the door, still curtseying.

'Uff – that's made me hot,' said the Court Apothecary's wife. She was as red as a copper pot from emotion and a tight corset.

The Privy Councillor's wife dropped to the floor one last time, straight as a candle in front of the closing door.

'*Mon amie*,' said the Minister's wife to the Privy Councillor's wife as they were putting on their galoshes in the antechamber, 'that woman … .'

'Her Highness has got her way,' said the Privy Councillor's wife, looking over towards the Court Apothecary's wife, who had turned her back and was unbuttoning a couple of buttons in her bodice over in the corner; the Privy Councillor's wife had an expression on her face as if she could smell something unpleasant.

They went downstairs. The Court Apothecary's wife gave the porter a daler.* She had given the footman ten marks. The birthday committee trotted off down the drive with their skirts raised up above their galoshes. The Court Apothecary's wife puffed along in their wake.

'Yes,' she said, 'it was worth the money.' She had paid for the whole bouquet.

The Privy Councillor's wife's skirts flew up indignantly, so that you could see the whole empty length of leg where anatomy had intended a calf.

Her Serene Highness remained standing for a few moments. Then she let the bouquet sink, immensely tired. As she turned round, her eyes fell on her lady in waiting, and Her Highness smiled again. The sight of certain objects always produced gracious smiles from Her Highness's mouth, which did not reach her eyes; they remained tired and grey – and she dismissed her with a wave of her hand.

Princess Maria Carolina went in alone through the apartments.

There were many rooms, all in a row. All the doors were open; white blinds had been pulled down over the windows, and the air in the semi-darkness was as heavy as in a museum.

Princess Maria Carolina stopped in the state rooms and looked around.

The fine furniture was lined up along the walls in stiff ranks, hidden under white covers. All around on consoles and tables were displayed large, dusty, elaborate vases and ancient mantel clocks, which didn't go, but were standing still, dying. Up on the ceilings corpulent rococo ladies were smiling amongst red robes and blue clouds.

Even in the semi-darkness, the splendour was strangely worn and shabby. The gilded mouldings on the wall panels were faded, and in places split. The large mirrors hung discoloured and damaged in their frames *à la Louis quinze.**

Princess Maria Carolina walked over to one of the mirrors; she had never noticed before that its surface was composed of three pieces of glass. She looked in the mirror for a long time. The ducal coat of arms was emblazoned on all corners; it was an old wedding gift from the officials at the residence to a member of her family. She became aware of the reflection in it: you could see through the doors down through all the rooms. There were three candelabras hanging from the ceilings in a row, wrapped up in sheets, like shrunken half-deflated balloons.

On the console there stood a Sèvres vase. The side which faced the mirror was riveted together.

In the next room there hung half a dozen of Princess Maria Carolina's ancestors, the ruling dukes. Occasionally on Sundays the palace castellan asked Her Highness for special permission to show the pictures to some visitors. They were mostly peasants, or schoolchildren accompanied by their teacher. They tiptoed quietly through the rooms, not daring to talk out loud, but whispered quietly and stared wide-eyed and pushed one another. And they gazed reverently at the pictures of their country's rulers and repeated their names with special emphasis, like the names of saints in prayers.

Princess Maria Carolina walked further into the room and looked at her ancestors. They were painted in court dress striking a grand pose, one hand on a jewelled sword-hilt. A couple had a crown lying beside them on a table, on a red velvet cushion. Another had a roll of parchment in his extended hand, like a commander's baton.

Princess Maria Carolina pulled up a blind and studied the pictures for a long time. The paint had recently been refreshed, and the crude colours gleamed. She looked at the faces. They all had the same expression; they stood there in their velvet robes with empty formal faces, stiff and lifeless.

Her Highness sighed. The artists who had painted her forefathers were not masters.

When Her Highness entered her own chamber, she quickly thrust open the large window, as though she needed air. The spring air reached her, warmed by the sun. She sat down and looked out, resting her chin on her hands.

After long rain showers spring had suddenly arrived. The fine fresh greenery was spreading across the lawns, and the buds on the trees were half opened. You could sense the first gentle scent of the chestnut trees and the fresh smell of the warm, ploughed soil.

Her Highness thought she had never seen everything looking so young and bright. The sky was so clear and high it looked endless. It seemed to Maria Carolina that everything was shining, the bushes and the newly green lawns and the trees and the horizon … .

The sparrows were making homes in the elms. And when you breathed in, you could smell the spicy scent of wild redcurrants hanging in bunches. Princess Maria Carolina closed her eyes as if dazzled; and without her being aware of it, nervous tears appeared and ran down over her cheeks.

All that light and life had a disagreeable effect on her, almost as strong as a physical pain. It was as if the spring out there suddenly overwhelmed her. Dizzily she saw the shimmering air through her tears, and the blue lines of the distant hills seemed to billow before her eyes.

The princess stood up and closed the window. She drew the long net curtains and sat down in the darkened room. She did not know herself why she continued to cry. Usually Her Highness only cried on Sundays in church.

She sat there rocking to and fro, with one image constantly in her mind – she had no idea why or where it came from. It was many years since she had thought even once about her uncle, Prince Otto Georg – many years. And now she could see him as if it was only yesterday that she had been a curious child, standing so often on tiptoe behind his chair and staring into Uncle Otto Georg's fire; she could not get his picture out of her mind.

Uncle Otto Georg would place the pieces of wood correctly in the stove, and then carefully strike sparks from his little tinder box and ignite the brushwood under the logs. The flames licked and the flames bored. Uncle stared into it with his chin buried in his hands, with those shining dead eyes.

Maria Carolina dared not speak to Uncle Otto Georg. She knelt silently beside his chair and looked into the fire in the stove. Now and then the silent prince noticed that the child was there; and Maria Carolina could feel Uncle Otto Georg's soft hands gliding slowly over her hair. It was such a soft and gentle movement, back and forth – for a long time. Sometimes Maria Carolina would fall asleep with her head resting on Uncle's chair arm; sometimes she would start to cry.

Uncle Otto Georg would take her head between his hands, and in his strange tired voice, which had only one note, he would say: '*Oui – mon enfant – mon pauvre enfant.*'*

He sat with her head between his hands and looked at her with his dead eyes, and his monotonous voice quavered: '*Oui – mon enfant – mon pauvre enfant … .*'

Then Uncle Otto Georg would get up and, without a sound, wagging his handsome head with its soft blond beard, he would creep across the carpet into the next room. And light a fire in the stove, as cautious as a thief, with his little tinder box, and watch the flames with his glassy eyes.

In the summer Uncle Otto Georg spent the whole day down in the garden with his flowers. How he loved roses. He held their chalices just *so* in his rounded hands and looked silently at the blooms for hours and smiled … .

Maria Carolina came past with her governess. Uncle Otto Georg did not notice. He stood bending his wagging head over the roses, smiling.

The governess paused in her ceaseless examination, curtseyed three times to Prince Otto Georg's back and walked in a little circle around him. Mademoiselle Leterrier was always afraid of Uncle Otto Georg – and Maria Carolina stole past quietly … . They went up onto the terrace.

Mademoiselle Leterrier often gave Maria Carolina lessons on the terrace. From up there you could see the whole residence with its chimneys and red roofs and the church tower and the little river with its two bridges and the red barracks, which was the largest house in the whole town.

The panorama made Mademoiselle Leterrier's teaching easier. She had the vocabulary all around her. The trees and the houses and the red roofs and the smoke from the chimneys rising up through the blue air, and the small clouds in the sky, and the lime trees and the flowers between the tree trunks and stumps, covered in green moss, and the birds singing in the bushes and the gnats buzzing – it was all just vocabulary for Mademoiselle Leterrier.

Vocabulary and points of departure. Mademoiselle Leterrier's teaching depended on points of departure; her method was to base things on real life. On the terrace Mademoiselle Leterrier revelled in points of departure.

A sparrow tumbled down from a branch and gambolled in the dust on the terrace. Mademoiselle Leterrier stopped and looked at the sparrow as if it was one of the seven wonders: '*Ah – le petit oiseau – comme il est beau, le petit oiseau … .*'*

Mademoiselle Leterrier was most curious to know exactly what kind of '*petit oiseau*' it was. Maria Carolina stood there stooping; she looked apathetically at Mademoiselle Leterrier's cheeping wonder.

'Oh – it's a yellow-hammer … as Your Highness knows' (Her Highness knew everything) 'a yellow-hammer.'

Mademoiselle Leterrier was deep into natural history. She ended with the anecdote about Apelles and the birds.* Mademoiselle Leterrier's teaching was rich in anecdotes.

'Your Highness,' said Mademoiselle Leterrier, when Maria Carolina had mumbled one of Lafontaine's Fables for Her Highness the Duchess,* and Her Highness in her drawling French had expressed her satisfaction – 'Your Highness, the art of teaching is the art of interesting.'

For solemn occasions Mademoiselle Leterrier had sayings which she called quotations from Jean-Jacques Rousseau.*

Mademoiselle Leterrier and Maria Carolina walked on along the terrace. Mademoiselle Leterrier had started on botany. She was talking about the structure of leaves.

'Your Highness knows that cells … .'

Mademoiselle Leterrier wandered off into all the things Her Highness knew about cells.

Maria Carolina walked silently beside her governess. She seldom said anything other than 'Yes' and 'No', and she did not say that in any lively way. Her Highness did not betray how much she knew about cells.

Now and again she walked to the edge of the terrace. A loud bell had sounded from down there. It was the bell for break time in the duchess's orphanage.

When Maria Carolina leaned out over the railings a little, she could see down into the orphanage playground. The little children were running around down there in their canvas smocks, laughing and screaming and playing tag … . It sounded joyful.

Maria Carolina stood looking far out over the railings.

Mademoiselle Leterrier found a new point of departure. Wearily, Maria Carolina let go of the railing and followed the governess.

Down below they were singing. Maria Carolina knew the song. It was that game where they all joined hands in a circle, and one of them stood in the middle of the circle, kneeling down with outstretched pinafore, and then another knelt down and then the two of them danced in the circle with the others dancing round, holding hands. 'The farmer wants a wife' sang all the children's voices in chorus.

'Your Highness will ask,' said Mademoiselle Leterrier, who was still on botany. Mademoiselle Leterrier often said: 'Your Highness will ask … .'

It was a formula. Maria Carolina did not ask. She was so tired of points of departure. Mademoiselle Leterrier asked for her. It did not interest her in the slightest. She walked along obediently, saying 'Yes' and 'No', with her oddly old grey face and her dull eyes, beside her governess.

She answered 'Yes' and 'No' in the wrong places. Mademoiselle Leterrier was annoyed. 'Your Highness has no real understanding of nature,' she said.

They were singing down there – how they were singing! Yes, that was the song they were dancing to now:

> The wife wants a child,
> The wife wants a child,
> Ee – ay – alley – o,
> The wife wants a child.

Mademoiselle Leterrier had seen an anthill. Immediately Mademoiselle Leterrier was back at 'Sanssouci'.* It was an old habit of Mademoiselle Leterrier's to think about Sanssouci. Her former pupil had been a member of the house of Hohenzollern, and Mademoiselle Leterrier had constructed her teaching around Frederick the Great.*

Now she had fallen back on her old habit; whatever the point of departure, Mademoiselle Leterrier always returned suddenly to Sanssouci. It was force of habit. But Mademoiselle Leterrier was adroit: the duchess was from the house of Habsburg, so she turned the conversation to Schönbrunn and ended with Maria Theresa.*

When Mademoiselle Leterrier reached Maria Theresa, she paused. The governess and her pupil walked along silently side by side. At most, a lonely phrase interrupted the silence, and Maria Carolina repeated the phrase in her tired voice.

'*La pelouse – Votre altesse le sait … .*'

'*Oui mademoiselle – la pelouse.*'*

Down below, break time was over. The bell rang and the noise of children died away with a busy buzzing.

Mademoiselle Leterrier and Maria Carolina had reached the end of the terrace. The orphanage lay directly below. Maria Carolina saw two small, scared loiterers running across the yard and in through the door … . From the schoolroom you could hear the teacher's voice and the children spelling in chorus through the open windows.

Maria Carolina was stooping over as she listened.

'Your Highness must stand up straight' – Maria Carolina started and straightened up – 'Your Highness has a dreadful posture. Your Highness will have to wear a bandage again … .'

Every six months Maria Carolina was tied to an iron frame for a couple of months in order to correct her posture.

Mademoiselle Leterrier was tired. They sat down on a bench amongst the trees.

The smallest girls from the orphanage came past. They were walking with their foster-mother, chattering from far off in their yellow smocks, in a long line like a flock of little ducklings. They toddled along after their foster-mother in their long smocks, with their white bonnets fastened around their round red faces.

Maria Carolina watched them coming, two by two, their arms around each other's necks, gossiping and squealing as they ran to and fro. As they passed the bench they fell silent, and saluted her with small solemn curtseys, holding out their smocks and staring at her with big round eyes.

And a couple of the smallest ones fell over as they curtseyed, and lay on the ground crying and stumbled up again and curtseyed again, as tears ran down their cheeks … .

Maria Carolina sat on her bench, flushed and embarrassed, and nodded and thanked them.

The little girls had passed by. They were humming together in a clump, getting in one another's way; their voices further down the walk sounded like a song.

Mademoiselle Leterrier looked at her watch. It was time for Her Highness's lesson in dancing and deportment.

Maria Carolina got up and followed her governess. In the rose garden Prince Otto was pottering quietly about amongst his roses in the sunshine. Maria Carolina and Mademoiselle Leterrier walked past him; Her Highness had her dancing lessons in the small ballroom. Her Highness the Duchess supervised Princess Maria Carolina's lessons in dancing and deportment in person. The old teacher was a retired ballet dancer with many toe-pointing inclinations and a stand-up collar.

Princess Maria Carolina was dancing a quadrille with three chairs. The toe-pointer sweated over his collar as he produced a thin tune from a violin. Her Highness was in despair; Princess Maria Carolina was entirely lacking in gracefulness.

'Back – forwards – one, two, three … curtsey … you must *look* at your partner … *so* – *so* – gentleman on the left.' Princess Maria Carolina struggled desperately round amongst her three chairs. The ballet dancer played and marked time with his whole body: '*So* – *so* – three, Your Highness … gentleman on the right – the red ribbon, gentleman on the right' (red and blue ribbons around the chairs aided Maria Carolina's comprehension) – 'two, three, curtsey … .'

The antique dancer leapt about like Harlequin in the pantomime as he fiddled. 'Good – good – one, two, three, gentleman on the left … .'

Maria Carolina curtseyed again to the red ribbon.

'No, no – one, two, three, gentleman on the left … .'

'Those wrists,' Her Highness called out, 'Herr Pestalozzi – her wrists should be flexible!* And what sort of a curtsey is *that*!'

Her Highness the Duchess was on the dance floor. 'Once more … .'

Princess Maria Carolina curtseyed again with a round back.

'What a posture – look at that back … once more … .'

Her Highness hummed the tune. Princess Maria Carolina curtseyed to her three chairs with glassy eyes.

'A dreadful curtsey – *dreadful*.' Her Highness is at her wits' end; the princess is stooping like a water-carrier.

Herr Pestalozzi mops himself with a handkerchief which is as clean as an old make-up rag. Sweat is streaming from Herr Pestalozzi.

Her Highness Princess Maria Carolina is glassy-eyed.

If Mademoiselle Leterrier might venture to suggest … . Mademoiselle Leterrier is making some lace in a corner. Mademoiselle Leterrier is always making lace for her virginal negligés: Princess Ernestine was tied down to her bed at night, so that she could not move. Her Highness Princess Ernestine lay perfectly straight. It had helped Her Highness Princess Ernestine amazingly. It was her arms which were tied … .

Her Highness the Duchess found that a little much. Her Highness Princess Maria Carolina could try walking with a ruler for a couple of hours. Her Highness the Duchess had walked four hours a day with a ruler herself, in her childhood.

The ancient ballet dancer struck up again, and Princess Maria Carolina danced a waltz with a red stool.

Her Highness the Duchess rose to go. She was going to have a painting lesson. Her Highness the Duchess painted. It was always something round and white in a sea of blue. Her Highness presented this white and blue object to bazaars as a prize. In the prize list it specified: Her Highness the Duchess, a painting: water lilies on a lake. All reception rooms in the residence had 'Water Lilies on a Lake'.

Besides, Her Highness the Duchess was hungry. Her Highness the Duchess partook of a meal regularly every hour and a half.

Princess Maria Carolina curtseyed to her mama.

The days passed, one just like the next. Her Highness had lessons, and Her Highness had free time and walked with Mademoiselle. Her Highness was dreadfully awkward and had large red hands.

During her conversation classes Her Highness walked with a ruler.

After dinner Her Highness the Duchess went for a drive. Princess Maria Carolina sat on the back seat and nodded to people. They always drove the same way, down the main drive of the residence and out to the 'Italian castle'. The lady-in-waiting entertained Her Highness the Duchess; the lady-in-waiting knew a story about every person they met.

In the Italian castle the Duchess drank chocolate. Then they returned home.

Princess Maria Carolina was very tired when she went to bed at night, after Mademoiselle Leterrier had tied the gloves around the wrists of her red hands.

Getting enthusiastic in the heat of summer was too much for Mademoiselle Leterrier. She regularly dozed off a little after she had arrived at *cette illustre impératrice* via *Sanssouci.** Maria Carolina moved a little on the bench, gently, in order not to wake her. It was the best time for Maria Carolina, when Mademoiselle Leterrier dozed off a little.

It was so quiet – not a sound in the garden. The green trees of the park and the palace and town lay quietly in the sun. A bee came buzzing up towards the shade of the terrace and then bumbled off again in the warm sun. It was so lovely to sit here in peace, almost as if she were sitting on her own for a while.

She glanced at Mademoiselle Leterrier, nervous at every sound. The orphanage children came past, curtseying; further along the terrace they started laughing and making a noise. On her saint's day Her Highness the Duchess had graciously provided them with a playground up here with swings, a seesaw and a balancing beam.

Mademioselle Leterrier slept on.

Maria Carolina got up softly from the bench and stole along the terrace. When the children shouted loudly, she gave a start and turned round. Maria Carolina watched them playing from behind a tree.

They were standing two by two in a long row with their backs to her. Oh yes, they were playing 'Sur le pont d'Avignon' … . Maria Carolina knew all their games: 'The mulberry bush' and 'The muffin man' and 'Pat-a-cake' and 'Ring o' roses'. How they were running – all round the swings, squealing. 'Catch her – go on, catch her … .' Oh yes, fat little Martha was 'it'.

The little ones were shrieking all around. They played hide-and-seek and stood with their faces against the trees, and yelled when they were found, and toddled off and fell over in the chase and kicked their legs in the air, so that you could see the sturdy pink calves under their skirts.

The older ones got tired. They sat down on the benches in a long row with their arms around one another, rocking to and fro. A couple started to sing. All around they joined in, their bodies swaying. The little ones started singing, repeating the first verse in their piercing high voices. A little golden-haired one had fallen over and was sitting on the ground, crying. She smeared tears and soil around her face as she sang.

Maria Carolina went silently back to her governess.

One day the little girls were alone. They played all the older ones' games but couldn't remember them, and began to quarrel like little cockerels, red up to the roots of their hair, and pouted and sulked.

Maria Carolina stole out from behind her tree. She bent over one little tot who was sniffing and rubbing her eyes. 'Shall I help you?' she said. The little one looked up and stared at her for a minute. Then she pulled away and ran off. The others saw Maria Carolina and began to curtsey and hold their pinafores and retreat backwards towards the trees, bumping into one another.

Maria Carolina stood alone in the middle of the playground. She was flushed. 'Would you like to play?' she said again, and approached a little. The children did not answer. They huddled together with their fingers in their mouths. A couple went on curtseying.

'Don't you want to play,' said Maria Carolina again, more quietly. There was no answer, just some small grunts.

'We're going to play "Pat-a-cake",' said Maria Carolina, coming closer. 'Come on.' She got hold of a little girl's hand: 'You hold on to me,' she said. The little one struggled and started to cry. She burrowed into the clump of children who were standing there scowling and sniffing – it looked as if a general rainstorm was about to break out.

'But – we were going to play "Pat-a-cake",' said Maria Carolina. She took the arm of another; the little one cried as if she had stuck a knife in her neck. Maria Carolina let her go. For a moment she looked at all the children, standing sniffing in a clump. Then she turned round and left.

Mademoiselle Leterrier woke up. They returned home to the palace.

Herr Pestalozzi had no idea what was wrong with Her Highness in her lesson on dancing and deportment; Her Highness suddenly began to weep in the middle of the quadrille, amongst her three chairs, and the weeping would not stop. Maria Carolina pressed her lips together and practised her steps to the accompaniment of Herr Pestalozzi's violin, as the tears ran down her cheeks.

But in the evening, after Mademoiselle Leterrier had tied the gloves around her wrists and had gone out, closing the door, and she had heard her footsteps going away down the corridor, Maria Carolina got up again and knelt on the floor and stretched her arms towards the sky and wept and wept and wept. She prayed to God with her head on the covers. She didn't know what it was, but she felt so boundlessly, so terribly unhappy.

At that time Maria Carolina was around fourteen years old.

Her Highness the Duchess chose two friends for Maria Carolina.

They were a couple of daughters of Privy Councillors with red hair and freckles right down to their necks. They sat on the edge of their chairs, always had clammy hands, said 'Yes' and 'No' and ate like ravens at every meal.

In the evenings they read aloud under the supervision of Mademoiselle Leterrier. They were books from the collection *pour les jeunes filles.** They took turns to read. The two freckled girls did not understand a word. When it was their turn to read, they went at it twenty to the dozen, without pausing for breath, as their freckles glowed. No-one understood a syllable.

Mademoiselle sat making lace, and saying 'Excellent' each time they ran out of breath.

When they played cards the friends always let 'Her Highness' win, and afterwards they could take the rest of the sweets. Maria Carolina treated them with distant friendliness. What interested her most was how much they could fit into their pockets. She really believed there was nothing they couldn't find room for in their pockets.

So time passed.

In the holidays the son and heir came home from cadet school.

His Highness Prince Ernst Georg was a lanky lad who pinched Maria Carolina's arm during dinner so that she was black and blue. On Sundays he sat behind her in church and pummelled the back of her neck with his fists during the sermon. Maria Carolina would have put her hand in the fire for him. She loved him blindly. She was always stiffly correct with him and spoke to him as if she was offended. Prince Ernst Georg teased her by covering her face with kisses. She was blood-red and tearful. Afterwards she sat in a corner admiring him.

'Shut your mouth,' shouted Ernst Georg. Maria Carolina had a habit of sitting with her mouth open while she was admiring.

Maria Carolina was very awkward, and could never work out what to do with her arms, which were long, with extremely red wrists. They hung and dangled as if they were loose.

'Your arms, Your Highness, your arms,' said Mademoiselle Leterrier. And Her Highness started, and her arms stuck out convulsively; her elbows were as sharp as awls.

Her Highness Maria Carolina was depressingly lacking in gracefulness.

Her Highness Maria Carolina was sixteen years old.

She was given her own household. It consisted of a lady-in-waiting, Countess Theodora-Anna-Amalia v. Hartenstein, who took up plenty of room in the official almanac.* She had three entries. Her Highness the Duchess's household:

Countess Theodora-Anna-Amalia von Hartenstein, first maid of honour. Her Highness Princess Maria Carolina's household: Maid of Honour Countess Theodora-Anna-Amalia von Hartenstein, lady-in-waiting. Household at the disposition of foreign princesses: Maid of Honour Countess Theodora-Anna-Amalia von Hartenstein, lady-in-waiting to Her Highness Princess Maria Carolina.

Countess Theodora-Anna-Amalia was round-shouldered and preferred to dress in ivory. Even when she wore a new outfit it looked as if it had been altered.

She stationed herself close to Princess Maria Carolina and said repeatedly: 'Your Highness thinks … .' Countess Theodora-Anna-Amalia von Hartenstein knew exactly what Her Highness thought.

Princess Maria Carolina's absent charms were enveloped in unchanging, tight-fitting pink. With absolute indifference she let everything wash over her.

Her Highness the Duchess wanted to divert her, so Princess Maria Carolina had lessons in watercolour painting.

'Her Highness has anaemia,' said the court physician. 'Her Highness needs exercise.'

Her riding sessions were doubled. Maria Carolina had one friend, and that was her horse. When she had dismounted from the horse in the woods during her rides in order to walk, she could stand still for long periods with her long arms twined around Ajax's neck. She did not speak to the animal, did not give it pet names or caress it. She just stood with her head against the animal's neck, silent and motionless, for a long time. And when she had returned to the palace and the groom led Ajax away, she stood still and watched it, until it finally disappeared through the gate.

She saw Uncle Otto Georg more rarely now. He had become more ill during the past year. Mostly he just sat still, his head rocking. He never spoke, just uttered some strange unarticulated sounds as he sat there; they sounded like owl calls. In the summer he went down to his roses every now and then. Maria Carolina went with him, supporting him. He pottered around the bushes and stroked them and smiled like a child. He became weaker and weaker, and as thin as a rake.

Maria Carolina cried a great deal when he died.

The following year Her Highness the Duchess also passed away. Maria Carolina had an important ceremony to go through and not much time to grieve. She had not known her mother very well anyway.

II

Her Highness Maria Carolina was already an old hand at fulfilling official court functions.

Every year it was the same parties. A ball on New Year's Day, at which His Highness the Duke partnered Princess Maria Carolina in the polonaise. For the quadrille Her Highness the Princess was pleased to invite the same officers every time.

The three winter banquets and the small intimate gathering on Her Highness's own birthday with fireworks and her initials, M. C. with a crown over, in green and yellow, the ducal colours. And the half-dozen small Saturday tea dances in Her Highness's private apartments, where the garrison's dozen officers danced with the young ladies from court circles and practised Herr Pestalozzi's quadrilles, which were performed in costume on His Highness the Duke's birthday.

The yearly bazaar in The Citizens' Association, where Her Highness was presented with a bouquet at the foot of the Town Hall steps, and was towed through the hall by the senior member of the committee (Her Highness could never keep up with the committee members of The Citizens' Association) and sat on a dais of yellow and green (the ducal colours) whilst the court player Herr von Pøllnitz obligingly declaimed 'Die Glocke'.*

Herr von Pøllnitz was the only one in the room who was not word perfect in 'Die Glocke'. He exuded a great deal of pathos, and raised himself on tiptoe at the end of each verse. Herr von Pøllnitz filled out the holes in his memory by rolling out some resonant sounds, which were reminiscent of distant thunder, and swinging his right arm like the sail of a windmill.

When Herr von Pøllnitz had finished – and it lasted longer each year before Herr von Pøllnitz had finished 'Die Glocke' – Her Highness said: 'It is a pleasure … .' She wanted to say more and found nothing to say and was embarrassed by her arms – Her Highness always stood as if she was trying to hide her arms as she spoke – and said again: 'It is a pleasure … it has as always been a great pleasure … .'

Herr von Pøllnitz bowed and puffed like a whale. It took more and more out of Herr von Pøllnitz every year to recite 'Die Glocke', because of the thunder.

After each bazaar Herr von Pøllnitz hoped to be made a knight of the family order. Herr von Pøllnitz had been awarded the medal for art; His Highness the Duke had presented the medal for art to Herr von Pøllnitz on his twenty-fifth anniversary. Herr von Pøllnitz had played Romeo on his twenty-fifth anniversary.

Her Highness walked through the hall and bought something at every stall.

From the mayor's wife she bought ginger biscuits. The mayor's wife baked them herself. 'I eat your ginger biscuits with great enjoyment,' said Her Highness. Every year Her Highness ate the mayor's wife's ginger biscuits with enjoyment. All the housewives in the residence borrowed the recipe for 'Her Highness's ginger biscuits'.

When Her Highness had visited the stalls she inspected the amusements. There was a menagerie. A young teacher from the high school was exhibiting 'a learned pig'. It said 'nuff-nuff' when he tickled its belly. Her Highness Princess Maria Carolina laughed so much that the Countess von Hartenstein started to cough.

Countess Theodora-Anna-Amalia von Hartenstein could never understand how, from time to time – and 'on the strangest occasions, my dear,' she said to Mademoiselle Leterrier, who now resided in the palace wing as a retired lady – Her Highness could permit herself attacks of merriment – '*explosions*, my dear' – so that she almost dissolved in laughter.

'You know, my dear,' said Countess von Hartenstein, 'that is the sorrowful thing; she never does have any grace – and then when she *laughs* … .' Countess von Hartenstein could not sufficiently express her regret.

Countess von Hartenstein, Lady-in-Waiting, laughed only discreetly, behind her handkerchief.

'It is not everyone who has *l'air du trône*,'* said Mademoiselle Leterrier. She was not happy at being a retired lady with no position, to put it mildly.

But Countess von Hartenstein looked at the ceiling. 'My dear, one does not criticize illustrious personages,' said Countess von Hartenstein.

Her Highness had seen the whole bazaar. At the exit the mayor made a speech. That part of the body which is highest when one is chopping firewood was in constant movement when the mayor made a speech.

When the speech had ended, Her Highness stood for a moment trying to find something to say … then she said: 'I thank you … it has been a pleasure …' – and left, always while they were waiting for her to say more.

But Her Highness did not have many words.

On occasion Her Highness hammered in a nail for a shooting club banner or laid a foundation stone. Otherwise day after day passed with no changes. It was always the same.

Now and then, as Her Highness was taking a turn on the terrace and looking over towards the long grey palace, with its lack of style or cheer, with its many small windows and the old cannons which had been drawn up and stood rusting in front of the high steps, and the sentry – a single man who walked to and fro, turned and turned again – Her Highness could feel a kind of tired oppression, as if the whole grey box of a palace were for a moment resting on her breast.

She looked sideways at the Countess von Hartenstein, who was walking along as elegantly as a dancer. And Her Highness walked faster, irritated that she always kept in step. But the Countess von Hartenstein remained in step with Her Highness.

After her walk Princess Maria Carolina returned to her watercolour or her embroidery. The Countess von Hartenstein read aloud from *Revue des deux Mondes.**

In the evening Her Highness sat in her box in the court theatre. Young beginners and former leading men demoted to roles as fathers reeled off Schillerian verses. Her Highness heard it as if over a telephone, half asleep. Every now and then Her Highness briefly touched the tip of her nose with the edge of her fan. The tip of her nose moved as Her Highness concealed a yawn.

Thus time passed, day after day.

And it happened that Her Highness was suddenly surprised to see that the fields were growing green, and the meadows along the river, and that the bushes by the roadside were covered in large buds. 'But can it be spring?' she said.

'Today is only a fortnight until His Highness the Duke's distinguished birthday,' said the Countess von Hartenstein.

'Oh yes, that's true,' said Her Highness. She carried on looking out over the green fields.

III

Her Highness Princess Maria Carolina was of an age to be married.

For several years there were various envoys who visited the court. Three or four princes came along in person.

At dinner Maria Carolina sat next to the distinguished visitor. They both sat embarrassed amongst the discreet excellencies from the royal households, and mumbled inconsequential remarks with animated expressions. Then suddenly they would stop in the midst of their talk and find no more to say, whilst they continued to sit there smiling, leaning towards each other like people about to speak, but unable to think of anything.

The ladies and gentlemen of the court stopped short in their whispered conversations, and like their Highnesses they sat smiling, leaning forwards with interested faces and saying nothing, twisting the knives between their fingers and looking at one another.

His Highness the Duke cleared his throat very loudly several times. Their young Highnesses remained sitting in the same position, smiling at each other, like figures in a waxworks.

That mouth, if only she would keep her mouth shut. The Countess von Hartenstein was as nervous as if it was she who was hoping to get married.

After dinner they drank coffee in the yellow drawing room. The Duke went to his card table to play tarot,* and the ladies and gentlemen of the royal households made themselves inconspicuous in the corners. The Countess von Hartenstein pushed a needle in and out of a piece of canvas and pretended to herself that she was embroidering.

Maria Carolina became very animated. She didn't stop talking, and hung on determinedly to Their Excellencies Kurth and Quaade. There was a question about forestry which interested Her Highness … . Her Highness could not understand … .

The two Excellencies shuffled their feet under the chandelier. Her Highness heard not a word of what they said, but she carried on asking and speaking very loudly and fanning herself with her fan. The visiting Serene Highness twirled his moustache and stared at his boots.

'As I was saying, Your Excellency … .'

Your Excellency was on hot coals – he was the last. His Excellency von Kurth had escaped in a pause with three deep bows.

His Excellency von Quaade came to a decision; he broke off in the middle of a sentence and departed backwards. 'Yes indeed,' he said, 'Your Highness, yes indeed.'

There was a large empty space around Their Highnesses. They sat down at a table and looked at some sketches.

The next morning an expedition had been arranged. Their Highnesses ate lunch in the hunting lodge, and afterwards there was a walk in the woods.

Their attendants disappeared. The two young Highnesses were alone. Maria Carolina clung tightly to her parasol handle and said a few breathless words every now and then as they walked. The visiting Serene Highness left a long winding trail behind him in the muddy ground with his stick.

Eventually they were walking a little apart, in silence. The visiting Serene Highness looked over at Princess Maria Carolina from the side. She was not appealing in profile.

Suddenly they noticed Countess von Hartenstein as they turned the corner of an avenue. His Serene Highness bent hastily over a tree stump and prodded the soil with his stick: well – look at that – there were ants – ants in the stump.

Oh yes … Her Highness really thought as well that there was a colony of ants in the stump. What strange little creatures … .

They both stood there looking down at the stump. Her Highness began to laugh. She had come to think of one of Mademoiselle Leterrier's anecdotes. One from Sanssouci. She recounted it. The visiting Serene Highness laughed and told her about his tutor. Now he was a professor in Old Persian. They both laughed at the word 'Old Persian'.

'And he talked with a lisp as well,' said His Serene Highness.

Their young Highnesses carried on laughing as they walked towards the Countess von Hartenstein.

'Like two children, my dear,' said the Countess von Hartenstein to Mademoiselle Leterrier, 'they were as happy as two children when I surprised them …'

The next day the visiting Serene Highness left.

If Her Highness felt disappointed, she did not burden anyone with her disappointment. She was once more taken in to dinner every day in the smaller dining room by His Highness the Duke; and after dinner, whilst the Countess von Hartenstein read aloud, she embroidered her pearl-encrusted fire-screen for the Citizens' Association's bazaar.

Her Highness sat bent over beneath the lamp and threaded silver pearls onto the fine needle. The light fell on her red wrists and on her face, which was lit up by the glow. Her Highness's cheekbones stood out sharply when the light fell on them like that. Her Highness had begun to look a little pinched.

One evening, when her brother the Prince was visiting, he said – after watching her as she sat there, thin and graceless: 'Maria Carolina, do you think it looks attractive, sitting there threading pearls?'

It was an impulsive remark. Maria Carolina gave a start.

'I think we can send you to Eisenstein right away,'* said the Prince, turning on his heel.

Her Highness Princess Maria Carolina bent a little further forward over the table. Soon after, she quietly collected the pearls together and slowly packed her embroidery away in its papers.

Her Highness retired a little early; she had a bit of a headache. She did look pale. With her parcel of embroidery in her hand, she went over to the Duke's tarot table. He was playing with the Prince.

His Highness the Duke kissed her on the forehead between two tricks. 'Goodnight, my girl,' he said.

'Goodnight.'

The Prince looked up at his sister. She was so pale. 'Are you not well, puss?' he said – it was her pet name from being a child – and he laid his cheek on her hand caressingly. 'Poor thing, I hope you feel better soon.'

Her Highness was very nervous. A couple of tears fell onto the parcel with the Citizens' Association's fire-screen as she walked quickly through the room.

The next morning Her Highness had red eyes as she went out riding with her brother the Prince. They were good friends, just like old times. He teased her, and she was shy and often a bit sulky.

But now and then, when he kissed her on the cheek after dinner with a 'Good dinner, puss,' Her Highness would press herself for a moment against her brother's shoulder, trembling and intense; and the Prince would look after her as she walked over and silently poured coffee and brought it to His Highness the Duke.

Well – the Prince stretched out his attractive legs in hussar's breeches – it can't be that much fun … . He went on watching his sister, who was pouring coffee beside the Countess von Hartenstein: no, you can't say it would be much fun.

His Highness the Prince never stayed at the residence for more than three days at a time. His regiment was stationed in Potsdam.

Her Highness Princess Maria Carolina was once more alone on her rides. She let the new Ajax walk slowly along the forest path. The old Ajax had been shot; he had got so stiff in the legs and was going blind in one eye. So the Prince had shot him, and Maria Carolina had had the old animal buried at the edge of a clearing in the forest, under an oak tree. It was her favourite place to be in the whole forest. But she knew every view and every path in the place. She had spent her happiest hours here.

The forest ranger's children were playing by the fence. Her Highness reined in Ajax and listened to the game. Her Highness was so fond of children. She dismounted and sat down on the edge of the ditch amongst the little ones, and they rode on her knee and laughed and shouted and tried on her riding hat, which came down over their ears.

Maria Carolina could talk to children best. She really wished everyone well with her whole heart – but she could never find the right things to say to all those strangers. Besides, they talked so often about things she knew nothing of. And she never really understood them, but stood there like an outsider, just smiling and feeling shy and embarrassed. But with children it was different. With them she could chatter and laugh. She could sit there on the fence in the midst of the flock for half an hour at a time, as they tumbled over her, sitting on her chest or her stomach, and decorating her riding habit with burrs; the smallest ones rode on her shoulders along the forest path.

The groom waited respectfully amongst the trees, as stiff as a sentry on his horse.

As Her Highness returned home, she stopped by the mill, and the miller's daughter Anna Lise brought her a glass of milk. The old miller's wife with her round, ruddy face appeared in the doorway and curtseyed, and Her Highness drank the milk.

'When is it going to be, then?' asked Her Highness.

'Ah,' the miller's wife curtseyed, 'it takes time to arrange, Your Highness.'

'You know that I'll pay for the trousseau,' said Her Highness, 'as thanks for the milk.'

Anna Lise took back the glass and curtseyed. 'Good health, Your Highness.'

'Yes, God bless you,' said the old woman, and curtseyed again.

'Thank you. Goodbye.' Her Highness rode off. – The mill-wheel clattered as she rode through the forest. Deep amongst the trees a couple of birds were singing. Her Highness reined in Ajax and listened: a woodpecker was busy over there on a nearby tree trunk.

At the end of the path you could see the gate to the palace park with its two broken urns.

Her Highness rode at a walking pace.

The Prince was going travelling in the Orient. His Highness the Duke sold his horses in order to save money. Maria Carolina wore clothes which had been altered to fit. They were her aunts' banqueting dresses from Vienna.

IV

The court had returned from the country and was attending the theatre for the first time. Her Highness was searching for old acquaintances through her opera glasses. She had settled down in her old place in the box, half hidden behind the velvet curtain, and felt so comfortably at home; all the season ticket holders were in their old places in the dress circle. It was all clearly visible now, after the new chandelier had been hung during the course of the summer.

Her Highness heard not a word of *Don Carlos.** Now and then, when she turned her face towards the stage, she could see Herr von Pøllnitz standing on his toes with his hands pressed to his breast. Herr von Pøllnitz was Marquis de Posa* … . Herr von Pøllnitz looked as if he'd put on weight in the holidays again … . Over in the box for ladies-in-waiting the Countess von Hartenstein was already dozing, sitting erect in her chair like a tin soldier.

Her Highness sat there with her opera-glasses to her eyes or her fan half-open in her hand, resting in her lap – and saw and heard nothing. She had no idea what she was thinking about; she just felt how good it was to sit quietly in the corner whilst they carried on performing down there. When there was applause she raised her hands over the balustrade and mechanically clapped her gloved palms silently together a couple of times. She hardly knew that she was doing it.

It was one of Herr von Pøllnitz's 'sorties'. He was sweating like a navvy. Herr von Pøllnitz always sweated when he portrayed strong feelings. Herr von Pøllnitz studied himself in the mirror in the foyer. Herr von Pøllnitz liked looking in the mirror when he was wearing tights. He struck a pose so that he could see the calves of both legs, and smiled into the mirror with a sophisticated courtly smile. Herr von Pøllnitz let Bolingbroke smile like that to Lady Marlborough.*

When he was alone, Herr von Pøllnitz almost dislocated his neck trying to see his back. Herr von Pøllnitz's defect was *there,* behind his back. He was too plump in that part used for sitting on. The director often pointed that out when he was playing heroic roles. Herr von Pøllnitz always looked at the too ample part of his body when he was alone.

He was lost in thought, contemplating his calves … .

Princess Eboli came over to the mirror.* Herr von Pøllnitz woke up.

'My dear friend' – it always sounded as if Herr von Pøllnitz had counted the stars at the very least and was about to announce the result, when he said 'My dear friend' – 'did you see that Her Highness joined in the applause?'

The stage manager was calling Marquis de Posa … .

Her Highness Princess Maria Carolina was still sitting motionless in her corner. His Highness the Duke took his seat behind her. He would sit and run his five splayed fingers continually through his long beard until he fell asleep. He regularly woke up at the sound of the curtain falling with a rattle. Then he would sit forward in the light by the balustrade, leaning over towards the princess. When he was sitting at the front of the box he had the habit of moving his lips as if he was speaking all the time. He never said a word.

Her Highness looked over to the box where the ladies-in-waiting were sitting. Countess von Hartenstein had woken up in the middle of a scene. She was sitting with wide-open eyes, staring down at the stage. Countess von Hartenstein looked like a frightened chicken.

At the same moment she was struck by the peculiar sound of a voice from the stage – it was rough, like an animal's. Her Highness started involuntarily; it was Don Carlos speaking to the queen.

He was ugly, and so thin – with a flat face, with a pair of large, burning eyes … How he waved his long arms about.

> *Sie waren mein – im Angesicht der Welt,*
> *Mir zugesprochen von zwei grossen Thronen,*
> *Mir zuerkannt von Himmel und Natur,*
> *Und Philipp – Philipp hat mir sie geraubt.**

Her Highness bent forward and read Don Carlos' name on the poster: Josef Kaim.* And although she didn't really want to do so, she watched his every expression closely, astonished, leaning forwards a little and without her opera glasses. She hardly heard the words; it was just the voice she went on hearing. And curious, half scared, as if she were bending over some strange insect creeping past her on the ground, she looked down at him.

When he was speaking, he twisted his mouth so that you could see all his teeth; and he leaned forwards with clenched fists, as if he were wrestling madly with invisible, imprisoning bars.

'Cretin,' said His Highness the Duke behind her. He had woken up too.

His Excellency von Kurth was called up to the ducal box in the interval. Maria Carolina greeted him and offered her hand.

'A bit of a rebel, our new leading man, Your Highness,' said His Excellency, bowing.

It seemed to Her Highness that she had been searching for those words. 'Yes,' she said, and saw again how he had looked as he stood before the queen. 'Yes … .'

'Our court theatre is not a menagerie,' said His Highness.

His Excellency von Kurth was taken aback. 'Yes,' he said, 'Your Highness is right, the young man is somewhat excitable … .'

The curtain went up again, and then down. The evening proceeded.

'Time to go home, then,' said His Highness.

'Yes.' Maria Carolina took his arm. They went out through the antechamber and down the stairs.

His Excellency von Kurth and the director were standing in the vestibule. The director bowed and scraped, with a miserable face and his right shoulder raised, as if he were expecting a physical blow to the side of his head.

'Yes, yes,' said His Highness, 'as von Kurth says, a bit of a rebel … .' Her Highness merely smiled.

They walked on outside and down the steps into the fresh air. It had been raining, and there were still a few large drops falling on the stones. A fresh coolness could be felt from the trees in the park.

'Ah, it's been raining,' said Maria Carolina. She felt pleasure at being under the open sky. 'Fold the hood of the carriage down,' she said. 'It's not raining any more.'

The Duke drove off with his footman. Maria Carolina stood waiting on the steps whilst they put down the hood. She stretched out her hand to catch a drop.

'But it's still raining,' said the Countess von Hartenstein. 'There'll be another shower … .' Fräulein von Hartenstein was wearing a hat with real feathers.

'Oh – only a few drops from the trees … .'

They set off, and drove at a quick trot down the avenue and out onto the country road, through the valley. The storm had just finished. The dark clouds were rolled back over the hills like an enormous cloth. The sky was deep blue and full of stars.

The road twisted and turned alongside the river. A light mist was rising from the stream. You could see the dark water between the swaying willow trees.

'Slow down,' said Maria Carolina.

They drove slowly on. The horses shook their heads in their harness, eager to get home. Then they calmed down and slowed to a walk. There was a springlike scent from grass and trees. It was so quiet that you could hear the drops as they fell one by one from the leaves of the willows into the stream.

'How lovely the night is.' Her Highness breathed deeply. She rested her head back on the seat and looked up into the night. A line of a poem occurred to her, then another and another. She didn't know that she knew them off by heart, as they came to her – those beautiful words.

'How lovely the night is,' she said again.

They drove away from the river and up into the hills. Over on the horizon you could see now and then a quick, distant flash of lightning. The spruces and birches on the slopes gave out their scent. In a gatekeeper's lodge deep in the forest a dog leapt up and barked.

Her Highness was sitting in front of her dressing-table mirror. Her maid was plaiting her hair.

The windows were open behind the long net curtains. A couple of insects were flying around the candles. They flew round and round; were caught by the flames and scorched; then round and round again … . Her Highness hit out at them. 'Oh, those creatures,' she said.

It struck her who that man resembled … . Yes. The picture in the Duchess's drawing room, in which Marie Antoinette is led off to prison … . There was a young man with a clenched fist, bowing his head slightly. At the front, on the right … . That was what he looked like.

The two insects buzzed into the candles and fell.

'Oh, close the window,' said Maria Carolina. 'There are so many creepy-crawlies coming in.'

The court had been at the Residence for a month. Day followed day at the same pace.

Her Highness painted watercolours; on some days she received visits; she went on her scheduled walks on the terrace with the Countess von Hartenstein.

Now and again Her Highness met Herr Kaim, the court player. It could not be denied that he was ugly. His flat face was as yellow as a lemon. He also doffed his tall hat very awkwardly.

There came a day in the middle of November, a morning with the clearest light over the park's many colourful trees; the foliage was thinning and fallen leaves already lay like a motley yellow carpet over paths and lawns. Her Highness drank coffee in the upper pavilion with some ladies. They had just stood up to go when Herr Josef Kaim walked past the verandah.

Her Highness was walking down the steps with a couple of ladies. Herr Kaim bowed. Her Highness stopped on the bottom step. 'Herr Kaim,' she said.

'There is an attractive view from up in the pavilion. Perhaps you would like to see it today – whilst it's open?'

Herr Kaim had halted abruptly, with his hat in his hand. 'Many thanks – many thanks, Your Highness.'

'Steindl' – Her Highness turned to her footman – 'could you please show Herr Kaim up to the pavilion. The view is really attractive … .'

'I … I have heard so … Your Highness … .'

Her Highness nodded and walked on with her ladies. The Privy Councillor's wife was still talking about the Queen of Romania.*

'A royal personage who composes verses,' she said. 'And sends *Love Stories* to be *published* … .'

'*Horrible,*' said Mademoiselle Leterrier.

Yes – it was the same voice – abrupt and angry, as if the man was constantly flaring up after an insult.

Her Highness had stopped. She looked out for a moment over the gleaming garden.

'Yes,' she said, 'Queen Elisabeth does write lovely poems.'

The ladies closed their mouths instantly. Mademoiselle Leterrier was first to respond: '*Mais oui,*' she said, '*votre Altesse – des vers étonnants* … .'*

And in the same tone as when she used to find points of departure for Her Highness back then, fifteen years ago, she said again: '*Oui – voilà une madame de Staël sur le thrône* … .'*

The other ladies remained silent, leaving Madame de Staël sitting on her throne. They returned to the palace.

In the afternoons Her Highness would take a drive to the Italian castle with the Countess von Hartenstein. After dinner, when she had poured coffee for His Highness the Duke – His Highness the Duke was much plagued by rheumatism this winter, and his card table had been moved next to the fire – she would drive to the theatre; or she would sit at home in her usual corner in the yellow drawing room.

Her Highness preferred reading to herself this winter. Her Highness was reading Schiller.

She sat leaning forwards, reading with the volume on her lap. She paused frequently, resting her head on her hand and staring at nothing. Nothing could be heard in the room except the gentle slap of the cards on the table as they played, and the old man's cough of the Lord Chamberlain, which he tried to disguise as a discreet and suppressed laugh; it sounded out of place in the silence.

Her Highness let her hand sink, and looked around the room. She could see His Highness the Duke's bent back and the Chamberlain's profile; his head was shaking slightly.

The Countess von Hartenstein was sitting a few yards away. Her black wig was in glaring contrast to her forehead, which was covered in rice powder over her wrinkles.

And Her Highness leant forwards to read again.

'Maria Carolina,' called His Highness.

Maria Carolina got up, closing her book.

'We're ready,' said His Highness.

Maria Carolina walked quietly over to the card table and took her place.

Their Highnesses always played a game of piquet before they retired.

The committee for the Citizens' Association Bazaar requested that Herr Joseph Kaim, the court player, would be so kind as to make a contribution by declaiming something. It was the mayor who had had the idea in a committee meeting one evening after he had had his dinner.

In the ladies' committee meeting at the palace, Her Highness the honorary president was asked for permission to request that Herr Josef Kaim should perform at the bazaar. 'It would perhaps make a change.'

Her Highness was of the opinion that Herr Kaim already had a considerable following.

Herr Kaim the court player was graciously pleased to accept the invitation.

Herr von Pøllnitz the court player had to confess that he did not *understand* the committee.

During this time Herr von Pøllnitz was constantly to be found on the street. You only had to set foot in the street in order to meet Herr von Pøllnitz. 'My dear friend,' he would say, 'can you *comprehend* it?'

No buttonhole was safe from Herr von Pøllnitz. 'For twenty years, my dear friend – twenty years – I have done them the service … .'

'Yes, Herr von Pøllnitz … I'm going this way … .'

'Twenty years …' Herr von Pøllnitz clasped his forehead, and stood still for a moment with his arm outstretched and his fingers spread, with staring eyes: 'My dear friend – oh, you're going that way? I'll come with you.'

Herr von Pøllnitz walked up the street and down the street. 'But there must be some reason,' he said. 'They owe me an explanation … . There must be an explanation … .'

In the evenings, when the public bar in 'The Duke' was closed, Herr von Pøllnitz would take hold of an arm, and hang on to it. 'My dear friend' – Herr von Pøllnitz would stop and peer into his companion's face – 'the thing is, they can't just *say nothing* – there are certain considerations – one has a right to know … .'

Herr von Pøllnitz arrived home at two or three o'clock in the morning.

When Herr von Pøllnitz was at home, he sat still in his chair with his hands on his thighs. From time to time he slowly raised his arm and placed his hand on his toupee. 'That's just it, Mariane,' said Herr von Pøllnitz to his wife, 'if only one could *comprehend* it … .'

Her Highness Princess Maria Carolina had never looked so good. Her Highness was wearing an elegant, slim, grey costume, which suited her remarkably well. Her Highness looked almost attractive as she entered the bazaar with the mayor. Her Highness ascended the steps to the stage and took her place. The singers began to sing.

Herr von Pøllnitz had volunteered to run the tombola.

'My dear Pøllnitz,' Frau von Pøllnitz had said, 'if you will take my advice.'

Herr von Pøllnitz always took his wife's advice. Herr von Pøllnitz was running the tombola with the broad smile of a *bon vivant*.

'It will be fun to hear someone else for once,' said Herr von Pøllnitz to everyone. He was so restless that he was shuffling his feet. 'My dear friend,' he said. 'I have a day off … .'

Herr von Pøllnitz was happy.

Her Highness Princess Maria Carolina was rather unkind to the Citizens' Association's bouquet; during the Choral Association's performance, one petal after another fell by her chair.

Herr von Pøllnitz crossed his arms over by his tombola; Herr Josef Kaim the court player entered in full evening dress. Her Highness Princess Maria Carolina acknowledged him by inclining her head over the Citizens' Association's bouquet.

Herr Josef Kaim declaimed 'The Minstrel's Curse'.* He had sloping shoulders in a pristine new dinner jacket. The effort was such that his shirt rode up and escaped from his waistcoat, so Herr Kaim pulled it down between each verse.

Herr Kaim's performance was rather worse than average.

Frau von Pøllnitz was sitting in a reserved seat. She was wearing a pince-nez, and watching the princess continually. Her Highness sat still with her head bowed. She looked down at the floor, at Herr Kaim's feet, enormous feet in a pair of patent leather shoes with high heels. Feet like *boats* … .

Her Highness was nervous; the Citizens' Association's bouquet suffered. Frau von Pøllnitz was convinced that the ribbons would all be creased up.

He stood *exactly* like Herr von Pøllnitz. His right hand pressed against his breast – a fleshy hand in a pinched white glove – and threw back his head – and how hot he was … . Her Highness looked stiffly down again, at those large feet.

It was done, and Herr Josef Kaim bowed. There was enthusiastic applause in the hall. Herr von Pøllnitz stretched out his arms on a level with his head and applauded loudly.

Her Highness the honorary president stood up quickly. The choir, which was embarking on the final number, stopped, uttering only a stifled squawk. The conductor, who was standing planted with his back to the hall, froze with his hand raised.

Her Highness Princess Maria Carolina had already descended the steps to the dais. The ladies flew to their stalls and whisked away the cloths which were spread out to protect the precious wares. Fräulein von Hartenstein had some difficulty in catching up with Her Highness.

The princess smiled her way hastily along the row of stalls. In stall number two the mayor's wife beamed behind her piles of 'the princess's ginger biscuits'. The princess smiled vaguely at the stall and walked past. The mayor's wife had curtseyed behind the ginger biscuits, and stayed down where she had dropped; Her Highness was buying at the court dentist's wife's stall.

The mayor's wife had brought ten children into the world. On occasions like this she was prone to cramps in her thighs.

Her Highness had never been so animated. She talked for a long time at every single stall, right the way down the hall … .

When Her Highness left, Herr von Pøllnitz took the words 'Three cheers for Her Highness!' right out of the mouth of the mayor. Herr von Pøllnitz was altogether ecstatic. 'My dear friend' – Herr von Pøllnitz embraced Herr Kaim – 'what a voice … what a rendering … I shall include "The Minstrel's Curse" in my repertoire … .'

Later that evening the mayor's wife's ginger biscuits were bought surreptitiously for the buffet.

Herr and Frau von Pøllnitz were walking home.

Herr von Pøllnitz cleared his throat; Frau von Pøllnitz did not hear.

Finally, rubbing his chin – Herr von Pøllnitz rubbed his chin like a huckster at confidential moments, uttering a grunting sound – Herr von Pøllnitz said: 'Hm … well, Mother' –'Mother' was a pet name – 'what do you say, then?'

'What do I say, David – what to?'

'What to?' said Herr von Pøllnitz. 'As if there … what to?'

'Do you mean the young man. It was very nice.'

'My dear Mari- ' Herr von Pøllnitz got no further.

'When you take into account that the young man has no experience at all,' said Frau von Pøllnitz in a kindly way.

Herr von Pøllnitz said nothing. He was hot.

'Pøllnitz,' said Frau von Pøllnitz, 'you should associate with Herr Kaim a little more.'

'Associate – my girl.' Herr von Pøllnitz stood still.

'Yes – he really makes a good impression – still so modest and shy.'

They were home.

Herr von Pøllnitz sat still in his chair for a long time with his hands on his thighs. After that he lay awake for hours. He sighed and puffed and looked across at Frau von Pøllnitz. She pretended to be asleep. Herr von Pøllnitz tossed and turned and struck his head so that his nightcap flew from right to left. Herr von Pøllnitz slept in a nightcap.

The next morning Herr von Pøllnitz took Epsom salts. His stomach could not stand emotional upheavals.

Her Highness Princess Maria Carolina got changed when she came home, and went down into the yellow drawing room. The Countess von Hartenstein read aloud from *Revue des deux mondes.* It was a thesis about European influence in China.

When Her Highness had retired, and the maid was plaiting her hair, Her Highness kept complaining that she was pulling the plait. 'For goodness sake,' – Her Highness was extremely sensitive – 'you're hurting me.'

'But Your Highness … .'

'You still are … .'

'Your Highness … .'

'Oh, let me do it myself.' Her Highness took the hair herself and began to plait it. And a couple of minutes later she let it fall again.

The maid did not understand Her Highness. Silently she plaited the hair and carefully tied it up.

His Highness's rheumatism was very bad. For a couple of weeks Her Highness Princess Maria Carolina did not visit the theatre.

Herr von Pøllnitz was extremely busy; he was promoting social interaction between the members of the court theatre. 'My dear friend,' said Herr von Pøllnitz, 'we never see one another … . My dear fellow, we are comrades, and we live like strangers … . My dear friend – we must see one another … .'

The next Saturday there was a dinner at Herr von Pøllnitz's. Herr Kaim the court player escorted Frau von Pøllnitz in to dinner.

V

Spring arrived, with tingling sun and growth. Her Highness was nervous. The restlessness of the new year affected Her Highness.

'Her Highness has sudden whims,' said the Countess von Hartenstein, 'my dear, she is so unpredictable … .'

The Countess von Hartenstein spent most afternoons with Mademoiselle Leterrier. In recent times Her Highness would often withdraw during the afternoons. She wanted to rest. Her Highness would lock the door, so that the maid had to knock when she arrived to dress Her Highness for dinner.

The Countess von Hartenstein went over to sit with Mademoiselle Leterrier. 'My dear,' she said, 'it's her nerves … . But who it is that suffers *most*, my dear – no-one talks about that … . Her Highness has *whims* – yesterday we *walked* home from the theatre … .'

'*Walked?*'

'Yes, my dear, we walked; Her Highness sent the carriage away … the train of *that* dress has seen better days … .'

The Countess von Hartenstein did not describe how much she had suffered. But she had a way of keeping quiet about her sufferings – 'my dear, I just have to do what I'm told' – so that she looked as if she was slaughtered on a daily basis.

Mademoiselle Leterrier nodded understandingly. '*Mais oui,*' she said, '*c'est l'âge orageux.*'*

'Yes,' said the Countess von Hartenstein; she did not understand what Mademoiselle meant; the Countess von Hartenstein had never had an *âge orageux*.

'*Mais oui – c'est ça,*' repeated Mademoiselle.* *She* knew about it. Mademoiselle Leterrier had a 'nephew', a long, dandified puppy of a law student, who visited her twice a year and regularly emptied her savings book. '*C'est ça,*' said Mademoiselle Leterrier.

The doorbell rings. It is Frau von Pøllnitz. Frau von Pøllnitz has been having French lessons this winter from Mademoiselle Leterrier.

The three ladies talk about the weather, which is so changeable and so bad for His Highness the Duke's rheumatism.

His Highness was dreadfully plagued by rheumatism. He had been unable even to set foot inside the court theatre for the past two months.

Her Highness Princess Maria Carolina took her place on his seat in the darkness. The light from the footlights disturbed her. Her Highness preferred sitting there too, slightly further back and concealed; Her Highness was really sometimes quite frightened in the court theatre these days.

'If he hasn't made the rest of them into rebels as well,' said His Excellency von Kurth. 'It's an infectious madness.'

The Countess von Hartenstein was of the opinion that the great Devrient would be turning in his grave.*

Her Highness just sat there, scared. Josef Kaim was *sweeping* the youngsters on stage along with him. It was not great art. But the heated youngsters set the masterpieces on fire with all the passions. Hatred was utter savagery, and love was a rage. Life was portrayed in the searing flames of licentiousness.

The good people from the Residence sat there in the court theatre feeling as windswept as if they had walked across the Town Hall Square in a storm.

Maria Carolina pressed herself into the corner of her box. She felt a shy astonishment, an uneasy aversion, without knowing against whom she should direct it. So she remained sitting there like a deaf person struggling to hear, and stared at all those people.

Josef Kaim's voice could be heard above all others. At times it could also sound meltingly gentle, flatteringly soft like music – like when Don Carlos spoke to the queen. Her Highness looked down with curiosity at Don Carlos, kneeling to his beloved – at his face which was looking radiantly up into hers, at his lips which moved with gentle words, and his head, which bent as he kissed her hand. And with a strange joy Her Highness dwelt on the picture behind closed eyes.

But the play continued. And Princess Eboli fought wildly for Don Carlos, and Carlos swore enmity to his father with oaths, and Posa went to his death, Posa the Just.

Her Highness was hardly conscious of the words. But she heard the agitated voices as though in a great choir, and she felt a crushing fear, as if something was obstructing the breath and the heartbeats in her breast.

When the curtain had fallen and it was over, she remained seated, staring absently at the curtain as it went dark, and at the safety curtain which slowly descended, a black wall, and clanged heavily onto the floor.

Her Highness stood up, but remained standing at the front of the box, looking out into the empty auditorium in the semi-darkness with the gaping rows of seats.

This winter, Frau von Pøllnitz had a place in the box just opposite the princess, in the dress circle. She put on her coat in the open door to the box. Frau von Pøllnitz was wearing her pince-nez under her veil.

The footman had raised the curtain to the small salon. The princess turned away, walking past him. She drove home.

His Highness the Duke had been waiting for Her Highness for piquet. He was sitting drumming with his knuckles on the card table and looking at his watch every half minute.

'It is eleven o'clock,' said His Highness. He was already holding the cards in his hand.

'Yes, Your Highness.' Maria Carolina took her place, and His Highness dealt the cards. They played in silence, put down and picked up cards and took tricks.

A footman tiptoed across the carpet with the tea service. The Countess von Hartenstein's knitting needles clicked quietly. Their Highnesses continued playing.

When the game was at an end, His Highness picked up the cards.

'It's got late,' he said.

'It's half-past eleven,' said Her Highness. She got up and walked across the floor to a window alcove. For a moment she rested her heavy head against the window sash.

'Your Highness's tea,' said the Countess von Hartenstein.

'Thank you – I'm coming … .'

The company drank tea in silence.

Her Highness Princess Maria Carolina wanted to fetch a book from 'the Duchess's drawing room' before she went to bed. A footman carried a branched candlestick before her.

Her Highness went over to the little shelf and mechanically picked up a book from Her Highness the Duchess's private library. She put it down on the table, and whilst the footman waited with the candlestick held high, she looked at 'Marie Antoinette being taken to prison'.

She studied the faces and the figures with their clenched fists. She looked from the rebels across to the queen's face. She strode onwards, straight and regal, through the mob. Her face was almost radiant in its unassailable calm.

From the picture, Maria Carolina looked around in Her Highness the Duchess's private quarters. It was as if her mother came towards her from every corner … . She could see her sitting *there* on the high-backed sofa from the first Empire, straight-backed and beautiful and calm, with her be-ringed fingers folded in her lap, whilst *she*, a small girl, stood *there* in front of Her Highness the Duchess, in the middle of the floor, whispering one of Lafontaine's fables – and on the chair over there sat Mademoiselle Leterrier, moving her lips to the words of the fable as if she were prompting her.

And when the fable was done, her mother the Duchess leant slightly forwards: 'Good,' she said, 'very good.'

And Maria Carolina curtseyed, whilst her mother the Duchess touched her forehead lightly with her lips. Maria Carolina stepped back. And the Duchess held out her hand for Mademoiselle Leterrier to kiss, as she said again: 'That is very good, Mademoiselle.'

Her Highness could hear her mother the Duchess's voice, clear and always calm, and she looked at the furniture, lined up in orderly fashion, and the vases and the gilded garlands and the pictures hanging symmetrically on the wall panels.

Maria Carolina took a deep breath, as if she had laid down a heavy burden, and turned in order to pick up the book from the table. Her glance fell on Marie Antoinette again. And all her feelings suddenly turned to violent anger against these screaming people … .

Her Highness left 'Her Highness the Duchess's drawing room', and with a wave of her hand, saying nothing, she dismissed her lady in waiting, the Countess von Hartenstein, who was waiting in the yellow drawing room.

But as the maid was plaiting her hair in front of the mirror, her nervous tension returned. She let the maid go, and went to bed. But she tossed and turned, unable to settle and fall asleep. She could constantly hear those passionate voices, as if they were calling to her, and her pulse was racing.

She picked up *Don Carlos* from a little shelf and began to read. She read different passages, and it was the same thing over and over. It was the same words the whole time: 'Love' – 'Human rights' – 'Freedom' – repeated in the same voices.

She stopped reading, and the book sank down onto the covers. Her head was heavy with impotent thoughts. She could not get her head around all those unfamiliar things. She felt her blood throbbing as if in fear.

She read again, and then suddenly stopped. She was sitting up in bed, and the book was resting on her knees; again and again she read the duchess's words to the queen:

Ich bin
Der Meinung, Ihre Majestät, dass es
So Sitte war, den einen Monat hier
Den andern in den Pardo auszuhalten,
Den Winter in der Residenz, so lange
Es Könige in Spanien gegeben … .*

Her Highness let go of the book. She could not see the letters any more; tears filled her eyes and blinded her. She felt an intensely tired and impotent pain – silent and irremediable.

She wept for a long time, and then dried her tears; wearily, she stretched out her hand for the book from Her Highness the Duchess's private library. The maid had placed it on her table.

She opened it. It was the Habsburg family tree. She read page after page, turning over the leaves. There were the same names and the same titles in an endless procession … .

Her Highness Princess Maria Carolina fell into a heavy sleep over the Habsburg family tree.

His Highness the Prince and heir received a large number of sentimental letters of many pages from his sister. He received them in the mornings, and glanced down over the pages whilst he was enjoying his first cigar.

His Highness blew out the blue smoke in smoke rings from under his military moustache. '*Pauvre enfant,*' he said. And with a sigh the Prince stretched out his horse-rider's legs and took a last gulp of his coffee. '*Pauvre enfant.*'

Her Highness Princess Maria Carolina was really unwell. The court physician could not stress enough how important it was to exercise.

Her Highness took long rides in the fresh spring air. Her Highness rode so unpredictably that the footman had to be on the alert the whole time; at one moment she was galloping, at the next walking.

She rode round past the mill. Anne-Lise brought her some milk. Her Highness emptied the glass and kept her horse standing by the door. Abstractedly she watched the foaming wheel.

Suddenly she started, and passed the glass back to Anne-Lise. 'How pale you are,' she said. 'Are you ill?' It struck her how pale and thin Anne-Lise looked.

She did not hear Anna-Lise's answer. She looked again at the foaming water around the wheel. 'It's the spring,' said Her Highness.

Anne-Lise curtseyed to Her Highness, who nodded in farewell.

Her Highness rode over the bridge. Where the path turned she looked back. Anna-Lise was standing on the stone steps, looking after her with her hands over her eyes.

It was the weekly dinner. Their Highnesses and their guests were drinking coffee in the yellow drawing room. Her Highness Princess Maria Carolina was talking to the forest superintendent in a window alcove, about some trees which could be cut down to improve the view.

'Yes – no-one knows the forest as well as Your Highness,' said the superintendent.

'Well, I have ridden there every day since I was a child.' Her Highness looked out into the garden. Herr Kaim the court player was coming up the road with two ladies.

'How mild the air is,' said Her Highness. She had opened the window. 'It's like June.'

She leaned out of the window. You could hear voices from the terrace all the way up here. 'But it's loveliest of all by the forest mill,' she continued, half turning towards the superintendent.

'I know that's what Your Highness thinks,' said the superintendent.

They were silent for a moment. Princess Maria Carolina kept on looking out into the garden.

'You know they have suffered a loss at the mill,' said the superintendent.

Her Highness did not reply at once. – 'Loss?' she then said, as if it had taken a long time for the word to reach her.

'Your Highness may not have heard that Anna-Lise … the young girl who had the honour … .'

'Anna-Lise … what about her?'

'She was found … yesterday morning – I very much regret, Your Highness – in the millstream.'

Her Highness turned around. 'In the stream,' she said.

How they were laughing down there.

'Yes, Your Highness, yesterday.'

'But I saw her the day before yesterday – on my ride.'

'It happened in the evening … the day before yesterday.'

'In the evening,' was all Her Highness said. She could see Anna-Lise standing by her horse, pale and hollow-eyed. 'Does anyone know why?' she asked.

'It's normally an affair of the heart, Your Highness, when a lass of nineteen jumps into a stream.'

Her Highness went quite pale. She could still see Anna-Lise in her mind's eye, thin and wretched. And she thought suddenly of how she had looked over at the foaming mill-wheel and said thoughtlessly: 'It must be the spring.'

And nervously – the whole time she had been hearing that laughter and Josef Kaim's voice – she turned again to the window. 'How they're laughing,' she said. 'Poor girl.'

It seemed to Maria Carolina that she could see neither trees nor terrace nor sky. 'Poor girl,' she said again.

Her Highness dismissed the superintendent with a nod.

The next morning Princess Maria Carolina rode over to the mill. The large, half-rotten wheel was standing still, and the house door and gate were shut. Maria Carolina dismounted and climbed the steps.

She opened the door and went in. The door between the passage and the living room was open. Maria Carolina went in a little way, and stopped. The two old people were sitting on the settle between the windows. They sat still, huddled together. The old miller was shaking his head and sighing.

'There, there, Johan,' said his wife, as if she was comforting a child. 'There, there … .'

Again they sat still, side by side. The mother wiped away her tears with the back of her hand.

Maria Carolina turned around quietly and opened the door to the steps. She rode past the silent mill over the bridge. The banks of the stream were green. The sandy bottom shone in the sun through the calm waters. That was where Anna-Lise had died.

Her Highness galloped away through the forest with her footman.

It was the day after the performance of *Romeo and Juliet.**

Frau von Pøllnitz had a lesson with Mademoiselle Leterrier. The Countess von Hartenstein was there as well. She felt she needed to 'talk to a human being, my dear'.

'Yes, I saw it,' said Frau von Pøllnitz. 'Her Highness left her seat straight after the balcony scene. And she went off alone, with her footman.'

'*Home?*' asked Mademoiselle Leterrier.

'At the palace they saw Her Highness at eleven o'clock, my dear.'

'Eleven o'clock.' Mademoiselle Leterrier dwelt on the words, as if she wanted to force into them all the misdeeds one could commit between the balcony scene and eleven o'clock.

'How did Her Highness appear?' asked Mademoiselle again.

'*I* didn't see her ... ' the Countess von Hartenstein seemed almost crushed – 'Her Highness was without her hat .... '

'It's always Herr Kaim who upsets Her Highness's nerves,' said Frau von Pøllnitz. She had taken off her pince-nez.

Her Highness had been extremely pale as she came out of her box after the balcony scene. The footman, who was sitting in the anteroom to the box, had woken up.

'Come,' said Her Highness.

Her Highness walked down the stairs and out through the vestibule. She had only a veil over her head, and a coat.

She walked through the theatre park, across the avenue and into the palace gardens. She opened the gate to Uncle Otto Georg's rose garden – the bushes were leafless and bare – and walked up onto the terrace. She walked quickly. The footman followed Her Highness at a distance of ten paces, straight-backed and with the same expression as when he was serving at dinner.

Her Highness walked and walked. She had to walk. It seemed to her as if she was crushing something beneath her heel with every step, as she walked and walked. Every now and then she would press her hand against her breast, as if she had difficulty drawing breath. And she started to walk more slowly, then very slowly, with her head bowed and her eyes on the ground. Her Highness's forehead was burning. Maria Carolina was so unused to *thinking*; it was like a severe pain.

She climbed higher, up the steps to the topmost terrace. She walked a few paces and stopped. The evening was lit by a half-moon. The gardens lay beneath her like an indistinct abyss, cut off by the colossus of the palace. You could see the long straight ridge of the roof sharply against the sky and the clouds.

Her Highness stood motionless, looking down on the ducal palace.

The footman had stopped at his distance of ten paces. He stood like a sentry shouldering his weapon.

All thoughts disappeared. Those words – those passionate words, it was as if they had *burst* upon her; the pain – did she know what it was? – which had bored into her like a sudden sting … .

Her Highness saw only the long grey lines of the palace at her feet.

And suddenly, as she was staring at all this greyness, it was as if she could see the image of Uncle Otto Georg before her. She could see him sitting in front of the fire in the blue drawing room, with his thin, pointed face resting in his hands, pale, staring into the flames with his dead eyes. And she could feel Uncle Otto Georg's hands gently smoothing her hair, and she could hear him saying quietly and shakily, as he looked down at her and half smiled: '*Pauvre enfant – pauvre enfant.*'

The footman shifted to the other leg and waited.

Her Highness turned and walked back along the terrace. The large clock on the palace struck many times in the silence.

Suddenly she felt so tired, as she walked down the steps.

The moon had become more visible, and the paths in Uncle Otto Georg's flower garden were quite lit up. Her head was still burning … she felt as if her feet would not carry her any further.

Suddenly she noticed the footman, as he walked past her in order to open the gate; she had quite forgotten him. He stood there in the light with his hat in his hand, in profile, slim and young. Maria Carolina gave a start, and stopped for a moment. The footman turned slightly and raised his eyes a little.

'Close it,' said Her Highness Princess Maria Carolina, and walked past him through the gate.

The footman closed the gate.

Her Highness told her maid to light the candelabra on the mantelpiece. 'Tell His Highness that I am indisposed. You can go. I don't need you.'

The footman was strolling along one of the corridors.

'But where *were* you?' asked the maid.

'On the terrace, miss.'

'And then? Franz, you are unbearable … . What did Her Highness want *there*?'

'We *walked*,' said the footman.

'Walked?'

'Yes – or stood like statues.'

'And looked at the moon – or what?'

'*I* saw no moon, miss … .' The footman caught hold of the maid for a kiss, and then a few more along a darker corridor.

'Idiot,' she said, running away.

The maid returned to Her Highness Princess Maria Carolina's quarters. She was sure that she could hear Her Highness crying in there.

The theatre director was invited to dinner.

The director was talking about the new season and the renewal of engagements.

'Herr Josef Kaim has an offer from Dresden,' said the director. He was sitting opposite Her Highness.

'I suppose he'll be leaving, then,' said His Highness the Duke.

'He does make great demands,' said the director.

His Highness the Duke helped himself to carp.

'*Extremely* great ... .'

Her Highness Princess Maria Carolina was watching with interest a small piece of ice which was floating around in her white wine.

'But Herr Kaim is ... a future talent,' said the director.

'Well, when that future comes' – His Highness laughed – 'he'll be off anyway. Let him go ... he bawls too loudly for me ... .'

The director was silent, looking up from his plate and over at Her Highness.

'Yes ...' she said. 'Herr Kaim is no doubt very talented.' Her Highness was still amused by the little piece of clear ice in her white wine. 'No doubt he will have a bright future ... .'

'Probably ...' it was the director's turn to be served some blue carp – 'that's just the thing.'

'Hm,' said His Highness the Duke, 'there are plenty more where he came from.'

That same evening Herr Josef Kaim the court player had his application for permission to leave the court theatre granted.

Herr David von Pøllnitz forgot to put on his galoshes, he was in such a hurry to get home after the theatre.

Herr von Pøllnitz ate first. Herr von Pøllnitz ate heartily. Every evening he drank three large mugs of tea. Herr von Pøllnitz did not dare to drink beer because of his corporeal encumbrance.

'My dear friend,' said Herr von Pøllnitz. 'Beer – my favourite drink .... But, my dear friend, what does one not do for art?'

Herr von Pøllnitz had drunk two mugs. He began to feel somewhat better. He laid his arms on the table and stared keenly at Frau von Pøllnitz.

'Mariane,' he said. 'Do you *know* what has happened?'

Those who did not know Herr von Pøllnitz would have thought it was something of global significance.

Frau von Pøllnitz said drily: 'No, David.'

'My dear Mariane – ' Herr von Pøllnitz stared into the distance wide-eyed. 'How can one know what is coming?'

Herr von Pøllnitz paused and hit the table with the flat of his hand: 'One can never know, Mariane,' he said.

Herr von Pøllnitz fell into a reverie. 'No, one can never know,' he repeated. 'Why don't you ask what it is?'

'What is it then?' His wife was nervous.

'Herr Kaim has been granted permission to leave.' Herr von Pøllnitz had folded his hands over his plate. He looked at Frau von Pøllnitz and waited.

'*Ass*,' said Frau von Pøllnitz.

'Ass?'

'I said: what an ass,' said Frau von Pøllnitz.

On special occasions Frau von Pøllnitz could find remarkably colourful expressions.

'Have you finished, David?' said Frau von Pøllnitz.

'Yes.' Herr von Pøllnitz stood up, subdued, and pushed his chair under the table. 'A very nice dinner, my dear.'

Herr von Pøllnitz sat still in his armchair in the living room, with his hands resting on his thighs. He patted himself silently in the place where the majority of humanity has a brain.

It was the fourteenth of May, the day before the court theatre season ended.

After dinner Her Highness had left for the hunting lodge in the hills. The Countess von Hartenstein was indisposed. Her Highness was alone. She was sitting by the bay window in the dining room. It had been Her Highness's favourite place since she was a child.

The hill sloped smoothly downwards. The freshly unfurled leaves of the lime trees showed brightly against spruce and pine. Down below you could see the valley with its scattered villages and the fields, whose fences scored dark lines across the view, and the meadows – with here and there a lonely tree wreathed in blue – and the river. Towards evening a cloud of light mist rose from the stream.

The heights in the distance were still shining in the sun. It looked as if they were quite close – whitewashed farms surrounded by tall poplars, which cast enormous shadows over the hills, and the fields, and further up the forest – everything was bathed in reddish light from the sun. The hills and valleys were all of them ducal lands.

The large bell at the lodge gate rang, and Her Highness could hear the lodge-keeper's steps crossing the yard below the bay window. From above she heard the door being opened, and voices.

The lodge-keeper came back across the yard.

'What is it?' asked Maria Carolina.

'It's a group of people, Your Highness, who would like to see the lodge. I said I would ask Your Highness.'

'Of course they can see the lodge,' said Maria Carolina.

She remained standing in the window as the lodge-keeper returned to the gate.

Her Highness took a couple of steps back when she saw Josef Kaim. For a moment she stood by the oak table, pale. Then she walked quickly towards the door.

The visitors were already on the stairs. Her Highness went down a couple of steps and stopped. There were six to eight people – all from the theatre. The ladies curtseyed, and the gentlemen stood there bowing.

Her Highness took hold of the bannister. 'Perhaps I could show you around,' she said.

The visitors stood there shyly; then one of the ladies pulled herself together first and said thank you.

'Perhaps you would like to come this way up the stairs,' said Her Highness.

They came into the dining room. Her Highness knew them from the theatre and spoke to each one by name.

When the players answered, they whispered reverently. After a while they got used to the situation, but their bows were still a little exaggerated, and their expressions of deep interest were wide-eyed. The ladies uttered quiet 'Ah!'s at different pitches before each object.

Josef Kaim wandered off behind the others. He stopped at the windows, and remained standing in the bay window. He had merely answered 'yes' and 'no' to a couple of questions from Her Highness.

Her Highness explained about the bullet-ridden standard which hung from the ceiling. It was a ducal trophy from the Thirty Years' War.

The others went on. Josef Kaim stood with his hands in his jacket pockets, looking up at the standard.

Her Highness told them about the pictures in the gallery. The whole group crowded together in front of a painting of Mary Stuart.*

'Well, she is pretty *average-looking*.' The words flew out of the bald comic's mouth.

'Yes, she was no beauty,' said Her Highness.

Wine was brought up to the dining room. Bottles of Rhine wine in large coolers. Her Highness suggested they should drink a glass to a pleasant summer. The visitors felt very honoured, and trotted off back to the dining room in single file.

The glasses were filled. Her Highness went around clinking glasses. The ladies read the inscriptions on the old German glasses in whispers, and the gentlemen took small sips of the wine, smacking their tongues and glancing ecstatically sideways at one another.

It was a very ordinary house wine.

It began to grow dark. New bottles were placed in the coolers, and the ladies and gentlemen stood around and chatted in whispers. The bald comic told jokes in a low voice, hoping that Her Highness would hear, and then he performed 'his turn': a circular movement through the air with outstretched fingers, which ended with a slap on his round belly. The whole gallery would scream with laughter when he did his turn.

Her Highness had never had much sense for comedy.

She walked over with her glass in her hand past the bay window and into the tower room; the door to the dining room was open. Her Highness gave a little start. 'Are you here,' she said, 'Herr Kaim – you're in here on your own.'

'I was – looking at something,' said Herr Kaim. His short sentences always sounded strangely staccato. Every other time he forgot to say Your Highness.

'I don't believe you've seen our treasures, Herr Kaim,' said Her Highness. They had been standing there silently, and he was about to leave.

'Treasures – Your Highness … .'

Her Highness took a bunch of keys out of a casket to open a little safe in the wall. 'It doesn't want to open,' she said. Eventually she managed it. 'This is our museum.'

Herr Kaim was standing four or five paces away, his head bowed.

Her Highness took a small writing set out of the safe. 'This belonged to Napoleon,' she said, and passed it to him.

He took it and looked at it: 'Oh … did it?' He stood there awkwardly four or five paces away from Her Highness, turning the inkstand in his fingers. Her Highness watched him from the side as he stood looking at the museum piece, holding it in his large hands.

'Did it really?' he said again, and put the writing set down on the table.

Maria Carolina smiled involuntarily as she put Napoleon's inkstand back in its safe.

And as she smiled, she felt the deepest pain she had ever felt in her life.

'Yes,' she said, 'he had it with him in Russia.' She was unaware that she had said anything until she heard the sound of the sentence, which seemed to come back to her from far away.

Her Highness took a small gold staff out of the safe. Josef Kaim felt the jewels which were set in a ring around the staff.

'That is a sceptre,' said Maria Carolina. 'It belonged to Mary Stuart.'

Josef Kaim gave a start. 'Mary Stuart,' he said. He went over to the window with the sceptre in his hand.

It was almost dark, so they could scarcely see each other's faces, even though they were standing close together by the window. Josef Kaim held out the little sceptre in his hand, and carried on looking at it.

From inside the dining room the comic had told a joke again. The others laughed.

'You are leaving us, Herr Kaim,' said Her Highness more quietly, in the way you talk in the dark.

'Yes,' he said, 'for Dresden.' He stood there holding the sceptre. 'Yes,' he said.

What good was that to *her*? He spoke in a deeper voice, with that peculiar dark tone.

Her Highness shivered. 'No,' she said quietly.

Josef Kaim gave Her Highness the sceptre. 'Thank you,' he said. 'Hm – yes – it's a strange thing about such ancient objects … .'

Her Highness trembled as she touched the cool gold of the sceptre. Her face was so pale in the darkness. They were silent for a moment. In the other room the comic must have done his turn again.

'I would like to wish you every success, Herr Kaim,' said Her Highness, as she took a step forward.

Josef Kaim looked up. He had never before heard how melodious Her Highness's voice was.

'I really am' – the tone was still equally mild – 'most grateful to you for this winter … most … .' Her Highness held out her hand, but Herr Kaim did not see it in the semi-darkness. He merely bowed, as Maria Carolina inclined her head.

For a moment, Maria Carolina held on to the wall, before she returned to the dining room to drink a final glass with her guests.

The visitors left. From the path down the hill you could hear their laughter and singing.

'She is ugly,' said Josef Kaim. 'But she has a lovely voice. Such a strangely soft way of speaking – it sounds so genuine … .'

Maria Carolina was standing in the bay window. She had opened the window.

It was night over hill and dale. It was as if the whole of nature was exuding freshness and sweet scents, both forest and earth. Maria Carolina leaned far out of the window.

The lodge-keeper had waited for a moment by the gate; now he closed it and walked back across the yard. Maria Carolina listened to the singing from down below. It grew fainter, and then died away.

The night was quiet again.

Her Highness turned around, alarmed. It felt as if someone was coming up behind her in the room.

It was the standard from the Thirty Years' War, fluttering and slapping against the wall in the draught.

Her Highness drove home through the forest.

Herr von Pøllnitz had a new event to announce over his mugs of tea. 'Just think, Mariane – *Her Highness* showed them round ... .'

'Why weren't *you* there too?' asked Frau von Pøllnitz.

'My dear – who could have known that?'

'You never know *anything*, David,' said Frau von Pøllnitz a little sharply. 'Pass me your cup.'

Herr von Pøllnitz was given his third mug. 'Mariane,' – it sounded like an announcement, and with his hands extended over the table Herr von Pøllnitz made one of his great artistic pauses – 'Mariane,' he said, 'something is *going on* ... .'

'But what?' said Frau von Pøllnitz.

'Yes,' said Herr von Pøllnitz, and paused once more: 'If only one knew.'

Frau von Pøllnitz looked over at her husband. His toupee was crooked.

On May 15th the court theatre ended its season. They performed *Des Meeres und der Liebe Wellen.** Herr Josef Kaim played Leander.*

The review in the Residence's daily newspaper ended as follows: 'Her Highness Princess Maria Carolina was present at the performance until the very end. After the third act Her Highness ordered that the retiring youthful hero and leading man at our court theatre, Herr Josef Kaim, should be presented with a splendid laurel wreath.'

The next day the ducal court departed for its summer residency in the Italianate castle.

The summer passed.

VI

That autumn was a time of celebration.

His Highness Prince Ernst Georg, heir to the Duchy, became engaged to his cousin, Archduchess Elisabeth, and they got married in October. The wedding ceremony took place in Vienna.

His Highness the Duke and Her Highness Princess Maria Carolina arrived in Vienna the day before the wedding.

Archduchess Elisabeth was blonde, as thin as a beanpole and wearing pink. She allowed herself to be kissed twice on the mouth by His Highness the Duke and on both cheeks by Princess Maria Carolina. She smiled incessantly, repeated her French phrases as if they had been learned from a phrase book, and kept her upper lip pulled down in order to conceal a couple of large canine teeth.

After a family dinner with their Imperial Highnesses the archdukal parents, they were sitting in the well-appointed drawing room. His Highness Prince Ernst Georg was entertaining his fiancée, leaning over her embroidery. Princess Maria Carolina was looking at a folder of watercolours just next to them. It pained her to hear the brief remarks of the engaged couple, courteous and meaningless, uttered after long pauses. Maria Carolina studied the watercolours as if through a veil. Her heart was so full and so oppressed.

At coffee, Archduchess Elisabeth had stood for a moment in a window alcove. Maria Carolina went over to her. Archduchess Elisabeth smiled, and they stood for a while side by side, fiddling with the same large plant.

Then Maria Carolina took hold of the Archduchess's hand. 'Do you think ... ' she said in German, breathless and emotional – 'that you'll be happy?'

Archduchess Elisabeth started, looking frightened, and pulled her hand away. '*Mais oui ... cousine ... je suis bien heureuse,*'* she said.

Princess Maria Carolina moved away a little, and for a few moments they stood next to each other, looking silently out into the palace garden.

At ten o'clock the company retired to their apartments.

His Highness the Prince wished them goodnight in His Highness the Duke's apartment.

His Highness had said goodnight to the Duke and turned to Princess Maria Carolina: 'Goodnight, puss,' he said.

'Goodnight.' Princess Maria Carolina laid her hand on his arm. 'Ernst Georg,' she said. The words sounded as if spoken in fear.

The Prince took his sister's hand, and they stood and looked silently at each other for a moment. 'Goodnight, Maria Carolina,' he said.

Princess Maria Carolina turned away. She heard his sword rattling away across the carpet.

His Highness the Duke banged the cards down on the card table. His Highness was waiting for his game of piquet before bedtime. 'Maria Carolina,' called His Highness.

Princess Maria Carolina took her place and His Highness shuffled the cards.

The wedding took place the next day at noon in the Hofburg Chapel. Her Imperial Highness Archduchess Elisabeth went through the pomp and ceremony with a happy smile.

After the wedding breakfast the newly-weds took their leave. The imperial bride was wearing a travelling suit of pale dove grey with a bonnet covered in small rosebuds.

All the company kissed her on the cheeks.

Her Highness Princess Maria Carolina stood in the window looking down into the courtyard of the palace as they were about to drive away.

The Prince led his bride down the steps to the carriage. The Archduchess smiled and greeted the footmen, who were drawn up *en haie.**

Then a couple of large greyhounds ran across the courtyard, barking, and jumped up at the bride. She let go of the Prince's arm and embraced the dogs. They kept on barking, and planted their forepaws right up on her breast. She rested her head on their necks, and stood there with the great beasts.

When the imperial bride took her seat in the carriage, she was crying with her face in her handkerchief.

The horses stamped, and the palace gate was opened and then closed. The noble couple had left.

Around a month afterwards His Highness the Duke was graciously pleased to appoint Her Highness Princess Maria Carolina as Abbess of the Foundation for Unmarried Noblewomen in Eisenstein.*

Her Highness Princess Maria Carolina was welcomed into the Foundation according to ancient custom. Young girls scattered flowers at the railway station with arms so red from the cold that they looked as if they had been scalded. The fire brigade blew their horns and formed a guard of honour.

After the procession there was a service in the foundation's chapel. The old ladies sat stiffly in their habits along the pews. Fräulein von Salzen was led in by the little prioress. Her Grace von Salzen was becoming more and more infirm; now her eyelids had frozen, so that she could hardly open her eyes.

The priest took as his text for the day: 'The Lord lift up his countenance upon you and give you peace'.* During the sermon you could hear old Fräulein von Salzen's 'Ah – yes – ah – yes,' echoing through the chapel.

After the service there was a reception in the conference room. The abbess's chair stood beneath a baldachin emblazoned with the ducal coat of arms. The ladies were admitted to kiss the hand of Her Highness Princess Maria Carolina. The old ladies wobbled forwards one after the other and curtseyed and bowed their heads over Her Highness's hand. She trembled a little as she felt the old, cold lips on her skin.

Her Highness continued to smile as she watched the old spinsters wobbling on their way, their grey heads shaking. She heard old Fräulein von Salzen's repeated 'Ah – yes – ah – yes', and lowered and raised her head, still feeling the touch of the lips on her hand.

The Imperial Countess of Waldeck, the prioress, advanced across the floor to the baldachin. She carried the keys to the foundation on a red cushion.

Her Highness Princess Maria Carolina felt as if the floor was heaving up and down as she leant forward and touched the gilded keys. The prioress received them back, half kneeling. Her long mourning veil flowed down over the cushion and its keys.

'Ah yes – ah yes,' you could hear old Salzen talking quietly to herself through the whole hall.

The fire brigade struck up from down in the courtyard. They were playing the wedding march from *A Midsummer Night's Dream* on seven horns.*

VII

Her Highness was sitting leaning back in her corner with her head resting on her hand; her book had slid down onto the floor. She had not heard the maid opening the door.

Her Highness dropped her hand with a start. It had grown quite dark. 'Is anyone there?' she said.

'It's me, Your Highness,' said the maid.

'Oh, yes' – Her Highness stood up – 'it's quite late. It's high time .... Would you light the candles on the mantelpiece ... I'll be there straight away.'

Her Highness watched the maid's hand near the candles. 'What time is it?' she asked. 'It must be late.'

'Seven o'clock, Your Highness.'

'Seven already? ... Good, I'll be there straight away ... .'

The maid lit the candles, and went.

Her Highness looked in the mirror to see if anyone could see that she'd been crying. For a moment she supported her head with her hand in front of the mirror over the stove, then turned and went out.

Her Highness Princess Maria Carolina was dressed. She was wearing burgundy red with lace.

At half-past eight Their Highnesses drove to the Italian castle for the court ball.

It was the first time Herr and Frau Pøllnitz had attended at court. Herr von Pøllnitz could regard it as certain that he would be appointed theatre director from the 1st of September.

Herr von Pøllnitz had never been so agitated. For the last week he had been bowing in front of all the mirrors with amiable smiles.

He began to get dressed at six o'clock. He had to keep leaving the room; his stomach could not stand such emotional upheaval. Herr von Pøllnitz had diarrhoea.

He was standing in his braces, admiring his legs: 'It is a great mistake that they don't have court dress with knee-breeches,' said Herr von Pøllnitz. 'But it will come – it will come.' Herr von Pøllnitz regarded the bulge of both calves: 'Some time it will – allow us to dream … .'

Herr von Pøllnitz did not explain what he meant. He fell into a reverie.

'Could you just finish dressing, Pøllnitz,' said his wife. She could not get past. Herr von Pøllnitz's corporeal encumbrance was frightfully apparent when he was wearing a shirt and trousers.

Herr and Frau von Pøllnitz got into their carriage.

'Well – now, Mariane – what does one say to Their Highnesses – I wonder …'

'You should just limit yourself to saying as little as possible, David …'

Herr von Pøllnitz sat for a moment. 'Mariane,' he said, 'after two seasons they must give me an honour.'

The company was waiting for Their Highnesses in Prince Ernst Georg's Hall.

The highest ranks were standing in line from door to door. The rest were shuffling behind them like sheep in a fold. The wife of the Court Apothecary was wearing lemon yellow, with a décolleté edged with transparent trimming.

'The Lord knows whether this is decent,' the Court Apothecary's wife had said to the seamstress when she was getting fitted. She would have preferred a lace fichu.

'It is what is worn at court, my lady,' said the seamstress; she brought the trimming to a point behind the Court Apothecary's wife's back.

'That doesn't mean old women have to tart themselves up,' said the Court Apothecary's wife.

The seamstress was so horrified that she stuck a pin in the Court Apothecary's wife. The seamstress would never have used such a vulgar expression.

At the ball the Court Apothecary's wife was showing charms which would have graced the court of King Solomon.* She was standing in Prince Ernst Georg's Hall beside Herr von Pøllnitz. Herr von Pøllnitz confided in the Court Apothecary's wife concerning the matter of his stomach.

'Terribly embarrassing, my dear friend, terribly embarrassing … . And *every* time I have to play a new role … .'

The Court Apothecary's wife had some drops in her pocket. 'I always bring a little bottle with me,' said the Court Apothecary's wife. 'You never know when it might be needed.'

Herr von Pøllnitz took some cholera medicine in a corner.

The Lord Chamberlain banged his staff three times, and the doors opened; Their Highnesses entered with their household. All fell silent, bowing and curtseying as Their Highnesses progressed through the room.

Herr von Pøllnitz was standing in the front rank together with His Excellency von Kurth. Their Highnesses walked past. Herr von Pøllnitz's encumbrance had never been raised so high.

His Highness spoke to His Excellency von Kurth.

'Yes indeed,' said Herr von Pøllnitz.

'Is that you, my good Pøllnitz,' said His Highness the Duke. And the line continued to bow, as if they were bending under a perfumed shower along the path of Their Highnesses.

His Highness the Duke escorted Her Highness Princess Maria Carolina to her place in the green hall.

The ladies in the company were presented to Her Highness the Princess. The Lord Chamberlain waited beside Her Highness. When the audience was over, it pleased Her Highness to engage Lieutenant Colonel Count von Dürchfeld for the first quadrille.

The ball proceeded with the splendour to which we are accustomed at our court, wrote the local paper. It made no mention of one little accident.

Later that evening Her Highness Princess Maria Carolina did Herr von Pøllnitz the Court Player the honour of engaging him for a waltz. Herr von Pøllnitz was so agitated that his toupee slipped askew.

Her Highness Princess Maria Carolina was very gracious towards Herr von Pøllnitz. Her Highness conversed with Herr von Pøllnitz for seventeen minutes. Was it true that Herr von Pøllnitz had taken over the role of King Philip now?

'Yes,' – and Herr von Pøllnitz bowed – 'yes, we're all getting older, Your Highness,' he said.

Her Highness smiled: 'Yes,' she said, and stood for a moment looking out over the room. 'Yes – that's true.'

Her Highness could remember when Herr von Pøllnitz had played Don Carlos. Later on, Herr von Pøllnitz had played Marquis de Posa … .

'Yes … Your Highness does remember … .'

'That was together with that young man – what was his name again? – He was here for such a short time … .'

'Herr Kaim.'

'Yes, that's right … . He appeared to be very talented … . Do you hear anything about him now?'

Herr von Pøllnitz raised his shoulders: 'Your Highness – people *say* that he is a great name – in Berlin.' Herr von Pøllnitz bowed a little clumsily.

One might think that Her Highness's cheeks reddened a little. But perhaps it was just a reflection from the burgundy red dress as she bowed her head. 'Is that so – so he has made a success of it,' said Her Highness. She gave Herr von Pøllnitz her arm for the waltz.

It was then that it happened. Herr von Pøllnitz could not understand it; but it *happened*. Herr von Pøllnitz fell over with Her Highness during the waltz, directly under the candelabra.

'My dear – what can you expect when you dance with a comedian,' said Fräulein von Hartenstein the next morning over coffee with Mademoiselle Leterrier. 'But Her Highness has *ideas* … .'

With a silent glance skywards, the Countess von Hartenstein asked heaven to be her witness. The Countess von Hartenstein was well practised in 'saying nothing' about illustrious personages.

Her Highness had had taken it all in good part. A young adjutant had run over and helped Her Highness up. 'Do help Herr von Pøllnitz,' she said. Herr David von Pøllnitz was waving his legs helplessly in the air like a fat cockchafer which has been turned on its back.

A little later supper was announced. His Highness the Duke drank a toast to 'the health and wellbeing of his daughter, Her Highness Princess Maria Carolina, in this year and in the years to come'.

Herr von Pøllnitz had remained in the ballroom. He was alone, leaning on a pillar and contemplating the scene of the crime.

After supper there was a firework display.

Her Highness Princess Maria Carolina had the balcony doors opened, and went out onto the balcony.

The evening was mild, and the sky above the garden was filled with stars. The rockets rose, whistling, in long arrows of light, and were extinguished. In the canal the waters glistened as if from a falling shower of gold.

Maria Carolina stood leaning on the balustrade, wrapped in her furs. She was looking out over the garden towards the hills when she was roused by the applause. It was the letters M. C. in green and gold, with a crown over them. The M and the C faded away with a few scattered bangs.

The Princess stared at her initials reflected in the canal.

The crown lasted longer, and was still burning. It looked as if it was gliding along the still waters of the canal.

Her Highness Princess Maria Carolina stood watching the image of the crown until it was extinguished, little by little.

Translated by Janet Garton

6. Irene Holm

I

It was announced by the parish clerk's son one Sunday after service at the assembly stone outside the church: Frøken Irene Holm, ballerina from the Royal Theatre, would be offering a course of lessons from November 1st onwards at the inn, comprising comportment, dance and movement, for children and for more advanced learners, both ladies and gentlemen – provided a sufficient number of pupils signed up. Price five kroner per child, discount for brothers and sisters.

Seven pupils signed up. Jens Larsen's three would attend 'at a discount'.

Frøken Irene Holm regarded that as sufficient. She arrived one evening at the end of October and alighted at the inn with her luggage, an old champagne hamper tied up with rope.

She was slight, worn thin, with a forty-year-old girlish face under a leather beret, and old handkerchieves tied round her wrists against arthritis. She spoke very precisely and said: 'Thank you – oh thank you – I can manage, really,' whenever anyone helped her, and stood there looking helpless.

She wanted no more than a cup of tea, and then crept into bed in the box room behind the main bar, her teeth chattering for fear of ghosts.

The following day she emerged with a head full of curls and a close-fitting coat with fur trimmings, which had seen better days. She intended to visit the esteemed parents. Perhaps she might ask for directions. Madam Henriksen came to the front door and pointed out the farms over the fields. Frøken Holm curtseyed down all three steps in gratitude.

'Poor creature,' said Madam Henriksen. She stood in the doorway looking after Frøken Holm, who was walking down towards Jens Larsen's on top of the bank – to protect her footwear. Frøken Holm was shod in goat's leather, with ribbed stockings.

When she had visited the parents – Jens Larsen would pay nine kroner for his three – Frøken Holm looked for lodgings. She took a small whitewashed room at the smithy with a view out across the flat fields. It was furnished with a chest of drawers, a bed and a chair. The champagne hamper was installed in the corner between the chest of drawers and the window.

Frøken Holm moved in. The mornings passed in many processes with curlers and cold tea and a hot crimping iron. When the head of curls was finished, she tidied up, and in the afternoons she crocheted. She sat on her champagne hamper in the corner to catch the last of the daylight. The smith's wife came in and sat on the wooden chair to talk. Frøken Holm listened, smiling, with gracious nods of her curly head.

The smith's wife talked on for an hour or so in the gathering dusk, until it was time to put supper on the table. Frøken Holm rarely remembered what she had said. Apart from dancing and positions and calculating the cost of living – an endless, tedious calculation – the things of this world had some difficulty penetrating Frøken Holm's consciousness. She just sat still on her hamper with her hands in her lap, staring at the narrow strip of light under the door of the smithy.

She didn't go out. When she saw the flat, desolate fields it made her homesick. And also she was frightened of bulls and runaway horses.

When it got later in the evening she heated water on the stove and made some food. Then it was time for the curling papers. When she had undressed as far as her underwear, she did her ballet exercises with the help of the bedpost. She extended her legs so far that she began to sweat.

The smith and his wife were glued to the keyhole. They watched her ballet jumps from behind; the curling papers stuck out from her crown like the spikes of a hedgehog.

Frøken Holm became so engrossed that she began to hum out loud as she swept down to the floor and up, down to the floor and up … .

The smith, his wife and their children squabbled over the keyhole.

When Frøken Holm had finished her practice, she crept into bed. When she was practising she nearly always started thinking about 'when she was at dancing school' … and suddenly she could utter a half-stifled laugh like a schoolgirl as she lay there.

And she fell asleep still thinking about that time – that merry time … .

The rehearsals when they used to prick each other in the legs with pins … and squeal … .

And the evenings – in the dressing rooms … how it all hummed … all the voices … and the stage manager's bell … .

Frøken Holm still woke up at night after dreaming that she had missed an entrance.

II

'Now – one – two – …' Frøken Irene Holm lifted her skirts and stretched out her foot: 'Toes turned out – one – two – three.'

All seven had their toes turned in – with their fingers in their mouths as they jumped. 'Little Jens – toes turned out – one, two, three – bow – one, two, three – and again … .'

Jens Larsen's three bowed and curtseyed with their tongues stuck out stiffly.

'Little Maren *to the right* – one – two – three – ' Maren went to the left … . 'And again – once – two – three – –' Frøken Holm leapt like a colt, so that you could see a long way up the ribbed stockings.

The lessons were in full flow. They danced three times a week in the private room at the inn by the light of two lamps hanging from the roof beam. As they pranced, ancient dust whirled up in the cold room. The seven of them were all over the place like a flock of magpies. Frøken Holm straightened backs and bent arms.

'One – two – three – battement … . One – two – three – battement … .' The seven tumbled down from the battement with legs akimbo.

Frøken Holm got dust in her throat from calling out. They were to dance a waltz, in couples. They stood far apart from one another, awkward and stiff-armed as if they were doing the turns in their sleep. Frøken Holm talked and swung them round.

'Good – turn – four, five – good, turn – little Jette … .'

Frøken Holm followed Jens Larsen's middle one and little Jette, turning them round and round as if spinning a top. 'Good – good – little Jette … .'

Little Jette's mother had come along to watch. The farmers' wives came along with their hat ribbons tied in stiff bows and watched, sitting along the walls, motionless with their hands in their laps, without saying a word to one another.

Frøken Holm addressed them as 'Frue' and smiled at them during the battements.

It was time to dance 'Les Lanciers'. Jens Larsen's three leapt with their boot toes high in the air. 'Lady on the right – good – three steps left, little Jette – good, little Jette … .'

'Les Lanciers' looked like a free-for-all.

The effort of calling and dancing made Frøken Holm groan. She held on to the wall for support – it felt as if her temples were hammering. 'Good – good – little Jette … .'

Her eyes stung from the ancient dust … the seven carried on jumping around in the middle of the floor in the gloom.

When Frøken Holm got home after the dancing lessons she would tie a handkerchief around her curly head. She had a permanent cold. In her leisure hours she sat with her nose over a basin of steaming water to keep the infection at bay.

They found some music for the lessons: Herr Brodersen's violin. Frøken Holm took on a couple of new pupils, an advanced class. They all jumped around to Herr Brodersen's playing – he was otherwise a tailor – so that the dust rose in clouds and the stove danced on its lion's feet.

More observers came along as well. Occasionally the vicar's daughter came, together with the curate. Frøken Holm led the dancing under the two oil lamps with her chest out and her feet arched: '*Point* your toes, children, point your toes, *like this* … .'

Frøken Holm pointed her toes and lifted her skirts.

They had an audience.

Each week Frøken Holm sent her finished crochet work to Copenhagen. Parcels were sorted by the schoolteacher. Each time she had packed or written the address wrongly, so the teacher had to redo it. She stood and watched, nodding slightly like a sixteen-year-old.

The newspapers which had arrived with the post lay on one of the school desks ready to be delivered. One day she asked whether she might see *Berlingske Tidende.** She had been looking at the bundle of papers for a week without daring to ask.

After that she came every day in the lunch break – the schoolteacher recognised her gentle knock with *one* knuckle. 'Come in, little Miss – it's open,' he said.

She went over to the schoolroom and took *Berlingske* out of the bundle. She read the announcements from the theatres, the repertoire and the reviews, of which she understood nothing. But it was about 'all of them over there.'* It took her a long time to get through a column. Her index finger followed each line gracefully.

When she had finished the paper, she walked across the passage and knocked as before.

'Well,' said the schoolteacher, 'was there anything new from town?'

'It's always about them over there,' she said. 'The old days.'

'Poor little mite,' said the teacher, watching her through the window. Frøken Holm went home to her crocheting. 'Poor little mite, she's all in a tizzy about her dancing master,' he said.

There was a ballet which was going to be performed at the theatre, by a new instructor. Frøken Holm knew the cast list off by heart, and the names of all the solo dancers. 'We went to ballet school together,' she said: 'All of us.'

In the evening when the ballet was due to be performed for the first time, she felt feverish, as if she was going to dance herself. She lit the two candles, which had gone grey with age, on either side of the plaster cast of Thorvaldsen's Christ on the chest of drawers,* and sat down on her champagne hamper to stare into the light.

But she *could not* be alone. All the old theatre nerves bubbled up in her. She went in to the smith's rooms, where they were eating supper, and sat down on the chair next to the clock. She talked more in those few hours than she had otherwise done all year. She told them about the theatre and the premières. About the grand solos and the complicated steps.

She hummed and swayed from the waist as she sat there.

The smith was in such high spirits after all this that he started humming an old cavalry song, and said: 'Mother, let's have a punch with this – some of that fine arrack.'*

The punch was brewed, the two candles from the chest of drawers were brought out and put on the table, and they drank and chatted. But in the midst of all the cheer, Frøken Holm suddenly fell silent, with big tears in her eyes. She got up and went to her room.

Sitting on her hamper, she burst into tears and sat there for a long time before she undressed and got into bed. She didn't do her exercises at the bedpost. She kept on thinking the same thing: *he had been at school with her.*

She lay still in bed. Now and again she sighed into the darkness. She shook her head a little on the pillow; the whole time the ballet master's voice was ringing in her ears, harsh and irascible: 'Holm has no élan … Holm has no élan … .' He shouted it so that it echoed through the whole room. She could hear it so clearly – she could *see* the room so clearly.

The extras were exercising in a long row, step after step. Tired, she leant against the wall for a moment – it felt as if her tortured limbs were being severed from her body – and again she heard the ballet master's shrill voice: 'Has Holm no ambition … .'

She could see their sitting room at home. Her mother wheezing in the large chair, and her sister turning the stuttering sewing machine, close to the lamp; she could hear her mother saying in her asthmatic voice: 'Did Anna Stein dance the solo?'

'Yes, mother.'

'I suppose it was "La grande Napolitaine"?'*

'Yes, mother.'

'You two went to school together,' said Mother, looking over at her behind the lamp.

'Yes, mother.'

And she could see Anna Stein in her many-coloured skirt – with the ribbons streaming from her tambourine – so alive and laughing in the footlights in her great solo … .

And suddenly she buried her head in the pillows and sobbed, violently and unstoppably, in impotent and desperate pain … .

It was morning before she fell asleep.

The ballet was a success. Frøken Holm read the reviews in the schoolroom. As she read, a couple of small old woman's tears fell onto *Berlingske*'s paper.

Letters arrived from her sister. They were letters about pawn tickets and poverty. On the days she received such letters Frøken Holm forgot about her crochet work, and sat with her fingers pressed to her temples and the opened letter in her lap. In the end she went round to visit the parents, and asked them, first pale and then reddening, if she could have half of her fee.

That she sent home.

The days passed. Frøken Irene Holm walked to her dancing classes and back again. She took on another group. It was half a dozen young farmers who had got together. They danced three evenings a week in Peter Madsen's front room, next to the forest. Frøken Holm walked two and a half miles in the winter darkness, scared as a hare, haunted by all the old ghost stories from ballet school. She had to walk past a pond surrounded by willows. She stared fixedly at the trees, which reached their great arms out into the darkness. Her heart felt like a cold stone in her breast.

They danced for three hours. (She instructed. She swung round. She danced with the male pupils, so that her cheeks glowed a hectic red.) Then she had to start out for home. Peter Madsen's farm gate was closed. The farm lad came out with her with the light to open the gate. He held the light high for a moment in his hand as she went out into the darkness.

She could hear him behind her wishing her goodnight, and then the scraping of the gate over the cobbles as it closed.

On the first part of the path there was a hedge with bushes which bent over, nodding to her … .

Spring was beginning to appear as Frøken Holm's lessons came to an end. Peter Madsen's group wanted to have an end-of-season party at the inn.

III

The party was very festive with 'Welcome' on a banner over the doorway and a cold table, priced at 2 kroner, with the curate and the vicar's daughter at the head of the table.

Frøken Holm was wearing a dress of barège with trimmings,* and coloured ribbons tied round her head. Her fingers were full of friendship rings from ballet school.

Between the dances she sprayed lavender water on the floor and waved the bottle threateningly at 'the ladies'. Frøken Irene Holm became so young again when there was an end-of-season party.

First they danced the quadrille.

Parents and the old people stood along the walls and in the doorways, each watching for their own, silently impressed. The young ones made their way around the quadrille with faces as stiff as masks, treading as carefully as if they were walking on peas.

Frøken Holm was all encouraging nods and whispered French instructions. Music was by Herr Brodersen and son. Herr Brodersen junior applied himself to the piano, kindly loaned by the vicar.

They began the ballroom dancing, and the mood became more cheerful. The men made free with the punch in the adjoining room, and the 'gentlemen pupils' asked Frøken Holm to dance. She danced with her head on one side, elevated onto her toes, with all the grace of an elderly sixteen-year-old.

After a while the other couples stopped dancing, and Frøken Holm and her partner were left alone on the dance floor. The men appeared in the doorway of the small saloon, and all expressed their muted admiration of Frøken Holm, who arched her feet a little more under her dress and swayed from the hips.

The vicar's daughter found it so funny that she was pinching the curate's arm.

After a mazurka the schoolteacher called 'Bravo!' and everyone clapped. Frøken Holm did a ballerina's curtsey with two fingers to her heart.

It was time to eat, and she arranged a polonaise. Everyone joined in, and the women nudged one another, embarrassed and delighted. The men said: 'Well, Mother – come on then … .' One couple started singing a soldier's refrain and marching in time.

Frøken Holm entered on the schoolteacher's arm and was seated beneath the bust of His Majesty the King.

After people had taken their seats at table the tone became solemn again, and Frøken Holm was the only one who spoke, conversing in cultivated tones as if in a comedy by Scribe.* Gradually the guests' hunger was stilled. The men began to toast one another, clinking their glasses over the table.

The young people were enjoying themselves tremendously down at their end of the table, and it was some time before things were calm enough for the schoolteacher to make his speech. He wanted to propose a toast to Frøken Holm and the nine muses.* He spoke for a long time. Along the table people sat looking down at their plates – slowly their faces took on serious and fixed expressions, like when the Dean was standing in the chancel arch in church – and kneading balls of bread in their fingers.

The speaker arrived at Freya with her two cats,* and went on to call for three cheers for 'the high priestess of art', Frøken Irene Holm. There were three times three 'hurrah!'s, and everyone wanted to drink with Frøken Holm.

Frøken Holm did not understand the speech and was extremely flattered. She stood up and curtseyed, with her glass raised and her arm curved. The powder she had used for the occasion was completely gone after her exertions and the heat, and she had dark red patches on both cheeks.

There was a great hullaballoo. The younger ones began to sing, and the older ones clinked glasses and rose from the table in order to clap one another on the shoulder, laughing, or pat one another on the stomach in the middle of the floor. Their wives began to send them severe glances, worried that their other halves would over-indulge.

And in the midst of the festivities you could hear Frøken Holm, who had become very animated, laughing a girlish laughter just like at dancing school thirty years ago … .

Then the schoolteacher said: Frøken Holm ought to dance.

But she had danced … .

Yes, but dance for them – a solo – *that* would be something … .

Frøken Holm had understood immediately – and a terrible desire seized her: she could *dance.*

But she started to laugh, and repeated it to Peter Madsen's wife: 'Our organist wants me to dance' – as if it was the most ridiculous thing in the world.

The people nearby heard her, and there was a general clamour. 'Yes – you must dance … .'

Frøken Holm blushed to the roots of her hair and exclaimed that the carnival mood was getting almost *too* exalted … . And besides, there was no music … . And besides, you couldn't dance in long skirts … .

One chap shouted across the room: 'You can fasten them up!' – and everyone laughed loudly and started to ask her again.

Well – if the vicar's daughter would play – a tarantella … .

Everyone crowded round the vicar's daughter. She was willing to try. The schoolteacher stood up and tapped his glass: 'Ladies and gentlemen,' he said, 'Frøken Holm will do us the honour of dancing for us.' They shouted 'Hurrah!' again, and began to leave the table.

The curate was black and blue from all the vicar's daughter's pinches.

Frøken Holm and the vicar's daughter went in to try the music. Frøken Holm was feverish, and walked to and fro, stretching her feet. She pointed at the floorboards with their humps and hollows, and said: 'Really, one is not used to dancing in a circus.'

Then she said: 'Well – let the fun begin.' She was quite hoarse with emotion.

'I will enter after the first ten bars,' she said. 'I'll give you a signal.' She went out into the small saloon to wait.

The audience came in and arranged themselves in a half-circle, whispering and curious. The schoolteacher brought in candles from the dining-tables and stood them on the window-sills as a kind of illumination. Then there came a knock on the saloon door.

The vicar's daughter began to play, and everyone looked at the door. After the tenth bar it opened, and everyone clapped: Frøken Holm was dancing with her skirts fastened up with a belt.

It was 'La grande Napolitaine'.

She went up onto her points, and she swung round. The audience watched her feet admiringly, as they moved as rapidly as two drumsticks. There was applause when she balanced on one leg.

She said: 'Quicker' – and began to pirouette again. She smiled and waved and gestured. She danced more and more with her upper body and her arms, it was more and more gesticulation. She couldn't see the audience's faces any more – she opened her mouth – she smiled, showing all her teeth (which were in a dreadful state), – she opened her arms, struck poses, – felt and lived nothing but 'the solo' … .

At last the solo.

It was no longer 'la Napolitaine'. It was Fenella,* Fenella kneeling, Fenella beseeching – the tragic Fenella … .

She didn't know how she had got to her feet, how she had left the room. She had just heard the music suddenly stopping – and *the laughter* – the laughter, as she suddenly saw all those faces … . And she had stood up and extended her arms once more – out of habit – and she had curtseyed, as they shouted … .

In the saloon she stood for a moment by the table … everything was so dark to her, so completely empty.

Then she slowly untied the belt, her hands stiff and strange, smoothed down her skirts and went quietly back in – where they were still clapping. She curtseyed next to the piano, but she did not raise her eyes from the floor.

They were in a hurry to start dancing again.

Frøken Holm went round silently. She began to make her farewells, and her pupils pressed coins into her hands, wrapped up in paper. Peter Madsen's wife helped her on with her coat, and at the last moment the vicar's daughter and the curate came up and offered to see her home.

They walked in silence along the path. The vicar's daughter was unhappy and wanted to apologise, but she didn't know what to say. And the little dancer walked along beside them, silent and pale. Then the curate, pained by the silence, said: 'You must realise, Frøken – these people have no understanding of tragedy – '

Frøken Holm walked on silently. They got to the smithy, and she gave them her hand and curtseyed. The vicar's daughter threw her arms around her and gave her a kiss: 'Goodnight, Frøken,' she said, in a voice that was not quite steady.

She and the curate remained standing on the path until they saw the light lit in the dancer's room.

Frøken Holm took off her barège dress and folded it. Then she took the money out of the papers, counted it and sewed it into a small pocket in her bodice. She held the needle awkwardly as she sat there in front of her lamp.

The next morning her champagne hamper was loaded onto the post wagon. It was a rainy day, and Frøken Holm sat huddled up beneath a broken umbrella; she pulled her legs up under her, so that she was sitting on her basket like a Turk.

As they were setting off – the 'postie' walking beside the wagon, as the old nag had enough to do pulling one passenger – the vicar's daughter came running along the road, hatless. She was carrying a white woven basket. You had to have some food for a journey, she said. She leaned in beneath the umbrella, took Frøken Holm's head in her hands and kissed her twice … .

Then the old dancer burst into tears and took hold of the young girl's hand to kiss it.

The vicar's daughter remained standing in the road looking after the old umbrella until she could see it no more.

Frøken Irene Holm had advertised a 'spring course in modern ballroom dancing' in a nearby district. Six pupils had signed up.

That was where she was going – to carry on with what people call life.

Translated by Janet Garton

7. The Last Ballgown

How cleverly those skilful fingers fly through the clouds of pleats and flounces. And as Antonie sews, her mother and sister Emma lean forward to watch. They all talk, with their faces lit up by the lamp.

Yes – at last there was going to be dancing again – at a proper ball. God knows, it was long enough since the last time. The district seemed almost dead since Pastor Wiberg's family had left. Just the one Christmas party at the mill, with those eternal games of forfeits, always the same – with the well and passing the hat round … and then birthday at the vicarage, where you took your needlework along and listened whilst the governess and Fru Hansen played sonatas as duets.

Otherwise not the smallest thing – not even as much as an open-air dance … . No, the last couple of years had been trying for young girls.

'The last couple of years' were actually eight or ten.

But when the days pass as they do for the widow and her daughters – you don't notice how quickly they pass, and how soon they become years.

When spring arrived, Emma and Antonie would plant their potted plants out in the garden beds, and the two cherry trees on the lawn would be in full flower; the burning question would be whether there were going to be lots of cherries this year. Then the roses would bud, and the buds would flower, and the sisters sat through the long afternoons in the vine-covered arbour near the fence.

Out in the fields they were busy – so much to do; the parish clerk and the miller were already gathering in the hay.

Fancy it being so far on in the summer – ah yes, how time passes … .

The summer passed altogether. The last asters were dashed to the ground by the storm. Emma and Antonie picked rowanberries to decorate the stove through the long winter.

Autumn was not so pleasant. With its eternal rain and fog, so thick that you couldn't even see up as far as the mill. But at least you could always see the road from the window, where Emma and Antonie took turns sitting on the window seat.

They knew every one of the horse teams in the district: the tenant farmer's black ones and the parish clerk's two brown ones and the doctor's gig with Lise. And as they all drove past down on the road, they said almost the same sentences about the same people every day.

It gets close to Christmas – Christmas with all its small secrets and joys – and the New Year arrives: white snow lies gleaming over the fields, the days grow longer and longer … . And then it's spring again … .

Yes, who would believe it? Can it really be coming up for thirty years since the widow with her two small girls moved into that little house – it's exactly twenty-six years.

Emma was eight years old at that time, and little Antonie was just four. They had gone to school in the vicarage with the Wibergs' governess. Then Emma was confirmed, and one fine day Antonie's turn came round as well – 'the little one', and now they were both 'grown up' … .

Those were happy days – back then.

When the students came home for Christmas and summer holidays, it was like one giddy round of balls and picnics in the woods and amateur dramatics and fun.

And it may well be that the hazel walk in the vicarage garden could tell a tale or two; about a kiss, quickly stolen, a couple of words whispered by excited voices, and two hands which had sought each other hesitantly.

Then one winter's day they were down in the vicarage visiting Fru Wiberg, who was quite beside herself with joy and offered them wine and cakes – because they really must drink to *that* … .

At last the vicar's wife told them what it was: 'Such happiness – just think what good news: our Otto has got engaged … and what a match … but little Frøken Emma, do take a cake – oh yes, what a match … Wiberg says that the consul has sixty thousand a year … .'

Emma spilt a little of her wine when they clinked glasses; and she and Antonie did not stay long. They walked quietly homewards side by side, without speaking. But when they reached the crossroads where they were concealed by the fence, Emma sat down on a stone and sobbed quietly.

Antonie knelt down on the frozen earth, took her sister's head in her hands, and she cried as well; she could think of no words of comfort.

Emma sobbed convulsively for a long time; then she controlled herself and stood up.

'Antonie,' she said, 'don't say anything to Mother ... she doesn't need to know ... why should we upset her?'

Antonie bowed her head in silence, and the two sisters walked home.

From that day on, everything was about Antonie – about 'the little one', as she was still always called. It was as if Emma too had become her mother, and every shilling they saved was spent on Antonie alone; they spoke constantly about her future.

Yes, when 'the little one' gets her own home ... and when 'the little one' gets married, they would say. Mother would live with 'the little one', and would be so comfortable and be looked after all day long ... . But Emma would leave home ... as a housekeeper or a teacher for small children (you don't need to know all that much in order to teach little creatures like that spelling and arithmetic).

But during the holidays she would visit.

No, no, she didn't want to live with them all the time ... a man doesn't get married to a whole family ... but in the holidays she would come.

So they spoke and made plans ... and the years passed ... .

Antonie's ballgown was finished. So light and airy it lay on the bed with all its embellishments.

But it was strange that she hadn't had an invitation! They knew for sure that Antonie was to be among the guests. Every afternoon they sat on the window seat watching out for the doctor's young wife to call.

And then finally she did come – just two days before the ball.

Antonie's heart began to beat violently as she saw her coming up the road. The doctor's wife came in and took her coat off and talked twenty to the dozen – about one thing and another – but said nothing about the ball.

Had they heard that the tenant farmer had bought a landau?

Yes, they had seen it from the window.

Really, those people didn't know what to spend their money on next ... .

And the doctor's wife chattered on, whilst the others sat there anxiously, waiting for her to mention the ball.

She was just about to put her coat on again when she suddenly said: 'Oh good heavens, I'm standing here talking and forgetting what I came for ... . You must have heard that the youngsters are going to have a bit of a dance at our place on Saturday – well, God knows they need to get some exercise … and we thought it might amuse you, Frøken Antonie, to come over and watch. Of course, *we* won't be dancing, will we? Those years are behind us. *Our* partners have become too stiff-legged … ' And the doctor's wife laughed.

'Yes, thank you, of course,' said the others, all three of them; 'it would be a pleasure for Antonie … '

The doctor's wife said goodbye, and Mother and Emma saw her to the door.

Antonie remained standing in the middle of the room – it was as if she had simply not understood. Then she went slowly over to the bedroom door and opened it; *there* it lay, so fine and lovely – *her* ballgown.

And with her head on the white counterpane she cried so bitterly, so bitterly – for her youth, which was gone.

Translated by Janet Garton

8. A Lovely Day
A Tale from a Corner of Life

I

Nobody had the slightest idea how it came about.

When General af Varén decided that he absolutely *had* to have Frau Sofie Simonin give a concert in his remote corner of the world, and a telegram had arrived saying the lady would be honoured – in return for a mere 6,000 francs, to be paid into the Bank of Finland – the Etvøses had, of course, been sent out with the lists.

They went out with the lists every time a committee was formed – to raise money for a charity sale or a subscription ball; and every time they would join these committees to organise and run around, even Fru Etvøs. She was a small, shrivelled woman with narrow shoulders and as flat-chested as a board; everything about her was jittery, her head and hands and feet, and also her mouth; her eyes were the only thing that didn't join in all this motion – and they never knew what would come out of her mouth – but her eyes always seemed to burn deep in their sockets with one worry or another.

And the teacher himself, his trousers tight around his skinny legs and exercise books bulging in his pockets – his coat flapping as he ran, his chest out and his head with its mane of hair, pushing forward like a ram about to charge. His mane of hair and his broad chest were pretty much all that was left of the student singer Jakob Etvøs from Helsingfors, once known as The Giant … .

The Etvøses had indeed done the rounds, as previously mentioned, this time with the Sofie Simonin subscription, as they always did, and when she was due to arrive, they were on the platform along with everyone else. Some members of the committee stood rigid as they waited, others shifted their weight from foot to foot; only the General's wife, holding a big welcome bouquet, wore her usual look of sleepy superiority.

And then Frau Simonin had arrived, petite, personable and smiling, and she had nodded and greeted and chatted before driving off in the General's carriage with her 'troupe' – two gentlemen – and Etvøs making up the fourth passenger, taking the General's seat.

God only knows how Etvøs had ended up there. Frau Simonin had merely laughed, as had the gentlemen in her troupe, and the door had slammed shut on Etvøs' woollen scarf. The woollen scarves knitted by Fru Etvøs were the Etvøs family's primary defence against the winter, and they restricted themselves mainly to protecting their throats; the General was left staring after his own departing carriage, he himself having got no further than bowing several times in front of the door.

So during the drive something must have happened, or possibly when they said goodbye. Frau Simonin may well have said, in all innocence: 'So – we'll be dining at yours tomorrow.'

How could she possibly know who was somebody and who was nobody on the committee?

Herr Etvøs stood with his hat in his hand in the hotel entrance long after Frau Simonin had stepped out of the carriage and gone inside. He wasn't entirely sure if he had *understood*.

They wanted to dine at his home tomorrow. They would do him the honour of dining at his home tomorrow.

He still couldn't grasp exactly what the plan was, so he decided to run home, home to Adolfa, home to get it off his chest … because there was also something, something onerous about this honour, Herr Etvøs thought; indeed he was starting to feel terribly hot as he ran.

'But Jakob, but Jakob,' his wife cried out; she was still wearing her short Astrakhan jacket and was struggling with the youngest. It was very difficult for Fru Etvøs to get either dressed or undressed; there was always something that needed doing, or one of their nine children would fall over and cry – right until the end of the day.

Etvøs just flopped down on a chair. He thought that he felt even more breathless once he got inside, where the eight wicker chairs were looking longingly at one another and the wallpaper – Etvøs could see it now – was made up of so many fragments.

'But Jakob, but Jakob – what is it?' His wife stood there fearfully with their youngest on her arm.

'They'll be dining here tomorrow,' Etvøs burst out, like a man who has given up on everything.

'Who are they?' Fru Etvøs asked, still unable to comprehend. No one ever dined in the Etvøs home apart from the nine – and afterwards the maid and Herr Etvøs would eat the leftovers.

'The pianist – Frau Simonin – she intends to dine with us.'

And possibly in an attempt to disperse the now even more oppressive air just a little, Herr Etvøs started speaking in a very loud voice – but in rather stuttering sentences – about the honour, the great honour; they had even been favoured over the General.

Fru Etvøs, however, wasn't listening. At first she had simply sat down while she stared at Etvøs with two utterly terrified eyes. Then she said in a quiet, plaintive tone: 'Oh, but, Jakob, how did that happen? Oh, but, Jakob, how could it have happened?'

That it *had* happened Fru Etvøs didn't doubt for a moment, so used was she to terrible things happening.

Etvøs stopped talking about the honour and wiped his forehead; he didn't know how it had happened either. 'She said she wanted to dine with us,' he merely reiterated, still out of breath.

'And tomorrow, you say?' Fru Etvøs said.

'Yes – dearest.'

As she sat there, Fru Etvøs raked her skinny hands through her thin hair towards her temples. It was her habit when something particularly agonising happened. Over the years she had practically dug trenches into her poor temples, they were so hollow. She dug and she clawed: 'Oh – but, Jakob, *here* – oh, but, Jakob, *here*,' she wailed and threw up her hands.

She looked across the sitting room from wall to wall: there wasn't a single intact item of furniture. Etvøs made no reply; he could see the surroundings were shabby.

A period of silence followed; Fru Etvøs had started pacing up and down.

'Can you get an advance?' she then asked quietly.

'I think so, dearest, I think so, dearest,' and Etvøs gave a start: 'I'll *have* to, I'll *have* to,' he repeated twice.

'But 200 Marks, 200 Marks,' Fru Etvøs said in a voice suggesting that no human power could raise that much money: 'It can't be done for less than 200 Marks … .'

Fru Etvøs had snatched that huge sum out of thin air; the truth was she had no idea how much it would cost. They hadn't entertained since number three of the nine was christened, and that was Etvøs' colleagues for sandwiches.

Fru Etvøs continued to pace up and down. She was already fretting about this latest vicissitude. 'We'll have to invite the whole committee,' she then said in her weary, glum voice.

'Yes, dearest,' replied Etvøs, who had grown very quiet since the advance was mentioned.

Fru Etvøs was thinking: well, the food wasn't the biggest problem, they could hire a cook. But everything else, everything else … even the tablecloths – Fru Etvøs didn't think she had two intact tablecloths.

'So will you go, Jakob,' she said in the same quiet tone, 'to ask for … the money?'

'Yes, dearest,' Etvøs replied. He was actually sweating. An advance was out of the question, and he had no more idea of where the 200 Marks would come from than the most recent arrival of the nine, bawling on the floor.

'Children, children,' the pacing Fru Etvøs hushed them. The other eight were making a noise in the dining room.

'Well, I'll be off then,' Etvøs said and got up; his long legs felt very heavy.

Fru Etvøs paused for a moment. 'Perhaps you could borrow a hundred from Cerlachius,' she said after considerable hesitation.

'The thought had crossed my mind,' Etvøs said. He had thought nothing at all. But now he left to try her suggestion.

Once he had gone, Fru Etvøs let herself fall into the chair he had recently vacated. On the rare occasions during the day that Fru Etvøs managed to sit down, it looked as if she had simply collapsed; her head was buzzing with a myriad of thoughts.

'Oh – no, no, the food isn't the biggest problem – oh, no, the food isn't the biggest problem,' she kept repeating to herself while nodding her head.

'What is it this time?' She shot up from the chair. She had heard a bump from the dining room so loud the wooden house had creaked in its joints. One of the nine had taken a tumble.

'Silla, Silla,' Fru Etvøs summoned the maid. 'Sil – la … .'

'And me, still in my dressing gown,' Fru Etvøs said, touching her hair in a fluster. Fru Etvøs would frequently discover that she was wearing the wrong item of clothing at the wrong time. 'Silla, Silla,' she continued to call out, as she took off her short coat.

Silla appeared with a floor cloth: the youngest children constantly had accidents in the corners.

'Yes, yes,' Fru Etvøs said; everything about her was in motion again, 'now there's something else, now there's something else … .'

Silla was dispatched to the headmaster's wife for the address of the cook.

II

Herr Etvøs had borrowed 100 Marks to be repaid at a later date, as Herr Cerlachius had so kindly put it.

When he came home, the whole house was in uproar. In the hallway all the furniture had been stacked up – it was just as well that each item could support the next. The children were all running around, shrieking, as if the house was a big rollercoaster. In the sitting room Silla was scrubbing the floor with every single one of her petticoats over her head, and her lightly clad backside wiggling, high up in the air, with eager excitement.

Fru Etvøs sat in the sitting room surrounded by table linen. '*Did* you get it?' she asked quickly, looking up at Jakob.

There was a particularly smug air about the teacher, so she knew immediately that he had got something. 'A hundred for today,' he said, quickly sliding five coins across the table.

'Oh – thank God … .'

It came out like a sigh; at least now there was one drop less in her ocean of worries.

'You go on through, Etvøs,' she said, 'after all, you have essays to mark.'

Etvøs was taking up a lot of space; he looked very pleased with himself and was talking about all sorts of people they really ought to invite. 'And we need to put up decorations,' he said, 'it must look festive.' He flung out his long arms in a flamboyant gesture at the yawning walls, as if hanging up invisible paper chains. 'My dear,' he said, 'you can do a great deal with very little.'

'Yes, Etvøs, yes – now why don't you go through?'

There wasn't a single dry patch anywhere on the floor. Silla was washing, there were rivers of suds everywhere, and Emmeline, their eldest, was walking around in leather shoes, wiping down the bigger items of furniture – there were so many forgotten fingerprints on the Etvøses' chattels.

Fru Etvøs had put out their glasses on the table for inspection. It was a pitiful, motley crew; a despairing Fru Etvøs placed her hands in her lap.

'My dear,' Etvøs said, 'we can rent glasses.'

Fru Etvøs could see they would certainly have to. 'Yes,' she said, 'but the expense, Jakob.'

Herr Etvøs left.

Shortly afterwards a dark-clad, exceedingly tall and extraordinarily gaunt creature appeared, whom Fru Etvøs, with much consternation, managed to seat on a chair in the middle of the wet floor. It was the cook, Madam Börner.

She waited in silence, her eyes resting on the lady of the house and her head pushed back in a defensive position, while Fru Etvøs grew increasingly alarmed; she wondered if the woman had taken offence already. It was an easy assumption to make about Madam Börner owing to the peculiar angle of her head; the truth was it was merely an occupational hazard from her profession, where it was important to keep one's face well clear of the frying pan.

'Yes,' Fru Etvøs said, 'it so happens –' she spoke as if apologising for a minor mishap, 'we're having some people round tomorrow ... as it happens ... sixteen,' she added, in a tone of voice suggesting that the worst was now out in the open.

Madame Börner merely nodded. Then she said in a flat, subdued, God-fearing voice with her eyes on the glasses: 'How many courses?' she wanted to know.

'Yes, yes,' Fru Etvøs stuttered, the cook's voice making her even more flustered. She doesn't think it can be done, she told herself. 'Yes, yes,' she said, 'they're very particular people, very particular, Madam Börner.'

'Then it'll be at least six,' Madam Börner responded in the same flat tone of voice. There was something about Madam Börner that made you think she always spoke with her hands clasped in prayer.

'Yes,' replied Fru Etvøs, who hadn't stopped rocking on her chair; she would have agreed even if Madam Börner had said sixteen.

Madam Börner began planning the menu, suggesting dishes and side dishes and 'garnishes' in a voice as if reciting scourges from a book of penitence. It was Madame Börner's condition that had given her this voice: she suffered from chronic stomach ulcers from the constant seasoning of food in her profession, while Fru Etvøs, who understood nothing, as she knew little about cooking apart from plain dishes, kept repeating: 'Yes – as long as it's nice, as long as it's nice ...' and then she suddenly flung her arms almost protectively around the wretched glasses; she thought the cook wouldn't stop looking at them. 'We'll rent the glasses,' she said, quite out of breath.

Madam Börner, however, just carried on in the same minor key, while Fru Etvøs, who had convinced herself that it was their particular situation that dismayed the woman, grew increasingly depressed – also from the many dishes the cook listed – and said in a plaintive voice: 'Yes, it will be difficult, I can see that it will be difficult .... And how much will it cost?' she added and flinched.

Her anxious eyes followed the cook's calloused fingers as they started to move, counting on the table as if practising the scales on a piano.

'Well, I believe we can make an evening of it for 70 Marks,' the cook declared, 'to start with ... .'

Fru Etvøs jumped up, and her fingers found the purse containing the 100 Marks.

'Right,' she said, 'let me give you that immediately,' and she put the gold coins on the table, one after the other – the way connoisseurs handle antiquities – when suddenly the tears welled up in her eyes.

Madam Börner took the coins. 'So where will you be dining?' she said, in the same tone of voice as before.

It was impossible to describe how the cook's constant and quiet anxiety distressed Fru Etvøs. 'Dining?' Every word left her like a gasp. 'Dining? … Well, we'll be dining here.'

'Oh, I see,' said Madam Börner, who might not have heard her, yet looked as if every reply added to the sufferings of Job.*

'Well, you see, well, we were unprepared, it took us by surprise, it was really quite a surprise,' Fru Etvøs said.

Madam Börner asked only to see the kitchen.

Fru Etvøs had fretted in silence about the kitchen for a while – the kitchen wasn't Silla's strongest point, and it would be a lie to say that it was sparkling. 'Yes – the kitchen,' she said, 'of course … .'

She rose from her chair. 'Children, children,' she shushed them, 'children … .'

The nine had eventually congregated on the wet floor and were running around, whooping and getting in one another's way in a distracting manner. They had realised that there was talk of food, a great deal of food.

'Emmeline, light the way,' Fru Etvøs said, 'it's this way, please, this way … yes, we weren't expecting … .'

In the kitchen Silla was drying nappies on four clothes lines.

'Ah, Silla is doing a bit of light laundry,' Fru Etvøs laughed off her embarrassment and began to take down the still damp bits of light laundry in the middle of the kitchen.

'This is the stove?' was all Madam Börner said.

'Yes, light, Emmeline, light … .'

Emmeline held the candle over the ramshackle stand, which was mostly covered with some strange pieces of sackcloth, which Silla referred to as aprons: that was the cooker.

'Four rings,' Madame Börner said, planning her campaign and looking at the furnace with her anxious eyes.

'Yes, it's a little rusty; light, Emmeline; it's a little rusty,' said Fru Etvøs, who was at breaking point. She thought the new arrival could see right into the heart of their poverty, embodied by this unused and badly maintained cooker. 'It's a little rusty … .' The rings on three of the holes were quite red; they only ever cooked on the one ring at the Etvøses'.

'But we do have china,' she blurted out, 'a complete set for eighteen – it's the Kronberg service,' she carried on, clinging to the service, the Kronberg service, utterly crushed in the presence of the rust-red cooker.

'A wedding present,' she said, 'from the House of Kronberg.'

And she launched into talking about the House of Kronberg, where she had lived like a daughter (Fru Etvøs had worked there as a governess when the old Count was alive), and they had travelled – she prattled eagerly and feverishly without stopping as if she wanted to decorate her empty kitchen with the Kronberg ancestors.

'Well, good night then,' said Madam Börner, whose martyrdom the aristocratic Kronberg family didn't seem to alleviate. 'I'll be here tomorrow morning at seven.'

'Good night, – light, Emmeline – light.'

'Good night.'

Emmeline lit the way for Madam Börner. Fru Etvøs herself remained in the cold kitchen – where she sat down on an old butcher's block by the cold fireplace and sobbed.

Someone tiptoed into the gloom. It was Emmeline. She lingered by the side of her crying mother in the darkness. Then she cradled her mother's head.

'Mother,' she whispered, 'why are we even entertaining those strangers?' And then she too began to cry, ever so quietly.

Fru Etvøs removed her hands from her face: 'Hush,' she said, 'I can hear Father.' And they went to join him.

Hearing Etvøs was easy because he shouted through every room as he ran, his trousers flapping around his legs. 'Yes, they are coming, they are coming,' he said, as if he still couldn't believe the miracle. 'I've been up there – *with her*,' he said, and lowered his voice.

'But, Etvøs … .'

'Because they asked me, they asked me, dearest,' Etvøs defended himself. 'But, Adolfa, how she played,' he said suddenly, in a completely different tone of voice, and sat down astride a chair with his salt and pepper mane flopping forwards as if he could still hear the music … .

Etvøs had visited Frau Simonin at her hotel and had sat – surrounded by fur coats and suitcases and a half-eaten meal and boxes – listening to her with eyes like those of a hungry dog.

'Are you perhaps fond of music?' the lady had said in a totally indifferent tone of voice, while her fingers played everything from scales to fragments of Liszt.

He could only nod, his eyes glued to her face.

She laughed as her fingers flew, and the tenor unpacked dresses with trains and spread petticoats over chairs and found slippers wrapped in ribbons from laurel garlands. She slipped into a march and played the finale in order to test her arms after her journey.

'*Hat nichts gelitten*,'* she said contentedly, referring to her Bechstein piano,* and let her hands fall into her lap.

'*Sie lieben das*?'* she said with good-natured indifference and slammed her knees together under her dress, while she turned on the stool and looked at Etvøs – she had quite forgotten about him being there.

A spellbound Etvøs was staring into space between the fur coats and trailing petticoats – as the tears poured down his cheeks.

Fru Etvøs wasn't in the mood for sharing his excitement. She just said: 'The cook was here.'

'Oh,' Etvøs said, and rocked his head from side to side.

'She left with 70 Marks – to start with … .'

At that Etvøs woke up. Then he said: 'Surely we can always get *credit* – in the *big* shops.'

As a rule the family never frequented the big shops – and consequently they owed nothing *there*. That thought had already crossed Fru Etvøs' mind; she believed they could get credit at Jakob Svensson's, and Jakob Svensson stocked almost everything.

'Jakob Svensson also sells wine,' Etvøs said pensively.

'Yes, Jakob,' Fru Etvøs nodded; 'Yes, but it'll still need paying for at some point.' Etvøs was only too aware of it.

'But remember what an honour it is, dearest,' he said, and started pacing up and down: 'We'll be sixteen.'

'Yes,' Fru Etvøs replied; 'if we *have* to invite the headmaster and his wife.'

Etvøs stopped in the middle of the room with his hand outstretched, and said again with the exact same expression in his eyes as before: 'Adolfa – how she played.'

Fru Etvøs had managed to get Etvøs as well as eight of the children to bed.

Etvøs being around made everything more difficult. Either he remembered something or he had an 'idea' every five minutes, and would then start pacing up and down the wet floors as he explored it from every angle.

But now he was in bed and only Emmeline was still up. She was helping clean the china, drying it cautiously and steadily with the pressed lips of an eager child and concentrating eyes that nearly popped out of her head – one plate after another.

'The list, the list – what happened to the list?'

It was the inventory of the cook's 'pots'. It was found in the cupboard and Fru Etvøs stopped and stared at it. These items could probably not be borrowed or rented.

'Mother,' Emmeline said with a pensive, almost secretive expression on her face – there were so many things which she and her mother tended to whisper about and which the others mustn't hear: 'They have lots of cooking pots in Gerda's club.'

But Fru Etvøs didn't hear her. Because tonight it was as if all her thoughts welled up at once in confusion, the forgotten and half-forgotten ones as well as those from long ago. She was reminded of her time with the Kronberg family when they would travel … . And she thought about the winter that followed when she and Etvøs met for the first time, when he was a soloist at all the ballroom concerts … .

'Listen, Mother,' Emmeline said again, 'they have them at the club.' Her anxious thoughts were still preoccupied with the pots.

'Yes, sweetheart,' Fru Etvøs woke up. 'Oh, God,' she said, 'we mustn't forget to put a block under one of the piano legs.' This train of thought came from the ballroom concerts. 'Now you go to bed, Emmeline, you go to bed now.'

Emmeline got up and calmly put everything away. Then she said, standing by her mother's side: 'Mother – do you think the cook is an honest woman?'

'We'll have to hope so,' Fru Etvøs sighed. 'Good night, sweetheart.'

Fru Etvøs got up. She wanted to check if the floor in the sitting room had dried. With a raised candle she stood in the middle of the room, looking from corner to corner.

It had never looked so impoverished to her. The curtains were drawn taut, and still they didn't meet. The chairs were spread out, and still they didn't fill the space, the crocheted covers, which the girls gave her for Christmas – they looked so wretched, so ridiculous … .

Yes – yes – that was the truth of it. Here she had toiled away her life. Here she had given birth to children while, to no avail, she had calculated and breastfed and fretted and given birth again and scrimped, again to no avail; and had another baby, and always 'made do' to no avail – while everything wore out and decayed … .

And Etvøs – he worked as hard as she did: she from one meal to the next, he from one school to the next … . But at least they loved each other. Oh – but did they? She didn't know any more. Surely thinking was a part of loving. And Fru Etvøs felt they only ever toiled, day in and day out, with their debts and with the nine who needed clothing and feeding.

Exhausted, Fru Etvøs turned and went to the bedroom. Etvøs woke up and sat upright in bed. 'Listen,' he said, 'we'll hang her picture above the piano.' A photographic reproduction of Sofie Simonin had been circulated to every household as part of the advertising.

'Yes, Etvøs,' his wife said, and soon he went back to sleep.

Fru Etvøs was sitting on the edge of the bed when Emmeline lifted her head from her pillow. 'Mother,' she whispered in her secretive voice, 'there are 13 Marks in Joakim's piggy bank.'

Thoughts of Joakim's treasure had already crossed Fru Etvøs' mind. 'Yes, yes, child,' she said, 'but you go to sleep now. Good night.'

'Good night.'

Fru Etvøs lay staring into the darkness: there would be no more joining committees or running about with lists – enough was enough. But then again, music was their shared joy … . It would always move them both to streams of tears.

Fru Etvøs was starting to nod off, her eyes half-open. She was a light sleeper; for thirteen years she had listened out for the cradle with one hand over the edge of the bed.

'Inga *could* wear the white dress,' she mused. She had a nagging thought that a few of the nine must be presented at the dessert – as they had done in the Kronberg family.

Then she drifted off.

Emmeline lay still, listening to her breathing. Her heart ached in bitter resentment.

III

The pots from the club had arrived and Madam Börner was in full swing in the kitchen: she moved about her preparations with a particular devotion, like a hospital sister among her sick beds.

Silla chopped and Silla cut. 'They're only going to eat it,' she said, while Madam Börner familiarised herself with her surroundings and gave Silla a comprehensive account of the progression of her illness over the pots.

It was Fru Etvøs who interrupted their steady work. Every five minutes she would come running to ask if the 'goods from Svensson' had arrived.

Etvøs didn't seem to even want to hear about money; he was busy 'decorating'. Fru Etvøs returned to the dining room.

'Mother – are they here yet?' Emmeline whispered.

'Not yet.'

And they sat down again, waiting, close to the window, their hands cold – there was nothing for them to do.

Fru Etvøs went back; she didn't want to ask again so she just wandered about rather noisily, knocking lids off the pots. Madam Börner understood perfectly; she had cooked in so many different houses. 'Where will I find a tip?' she said. 'Because you'll show the boy in here when he arrives, won't you?'

'Oh yes, oh yes,' Fru Etvøs said, and her face lit up while she looked for some loose change. 'Oh, thank you, oh, thank you,' she said, clasping the cook's wrists – she wanted to press her hands; from that moment on the two of them understood each other.

'And what's *worse* is that you lose your sense of taste,' Madam Börner said. She resumed telling Silla about her illness once Fru Etvøs had left.

Fru Etvøs had arranged her dresses – her black silk and the white one – for inspection over a couple of chairs.

'Mother,' Emmeline called out, 'he's here.'

It was the boy with the food. 'This way, this way,' Fru Etvøs said, feeling all of her old fears, while she showed the gangly delivery boy through the dining room; and they both listened out, Emmeline and her, until he *left* – with his tip.

Once the food was safely in the house, Fru Etvøs seemed to liven up. She joined Etvøs to look at the 'decorations' – the photographic reproduction and a couple of odd-looking corner sofas made up of mattresses and packing crates.

'Well, as long as they don't mind … I'm sure everything will be fine, I'm sure everything will be fine … .' She returned to the kitchen and was in the way wherever she stood. 'Well, at least there's plenty to be getting on with,' she said, overjoyed, touching the groceries and holding up the wine bottles with sparkling eyes. 'What an abundance,' she said.

She returned to Etvøs, who was draping the sofas. 'Oh, yes, Etvøs,' she said and sat for a moment looking into space, 'it certainly makes a change.'

'Adolfa,' Etvøs said as he wandered up and down, assessing his efforts: 'It's an *honour* – an unforgettable honour.' He was dripping with sweat.

The doorbell rang and Fru Etvøs went to answer it. It was the daughter of a judge, a sweet, gloved lady who had spent the last twenty years moving about silently in her father's grand official home, acting as the hostess. She had come under the pretext of thanking them for the invitation, with the hidden agenda of offering some form of help. But no sooner had she been seated in the midst of the commotion – Fru Etvøs kept running around a chair: 'It's so untidy, so very untidy,' she said, 'because Etvøs is decorating' – than she silently abandoned her intention. It was better that it was all the same.

Etvøs positioned himself behind her chair to see how his efforts looked from her point of view. 'Well, we do what we can,' he said, happily flicking his mane of hair. From a corner Emmeline watched the judge's daughter suspiciously for as long as she was in the room.

The lady then went to see the china which looked as if it had been lined up for auction on the long table in the Etvøses' dining room. 'Well, it's no trouble at all,' she said, 'when you have everything, as you do.'

She returned home, ashen-faced with horror at the Etvøses' preparations. 'Also for the sake of the whole town,' she said to her father, the judge.

Fru Etvøs had returned to her two dresses. It was decided that Inga would make an appearance at the dessert.

'Emmeline – is she *here*?'

Fru Etvøs was in her underwear, running in and out of the bedroom. Ultimately it ended up being Silla who was sent to the judge's for napkins – they couldn't let Ericsson, the hired waiter, a stranger, fold the Etvøses' serviettes; they didn't lend themselves to such sophisticated shapes.

'Is she here?'

Silla wasn't. She was detained outside every front door by friends who wanted a full and detailed account. 'And they'll be eating tallow,' Silla concluded with derision and ran on; she was referring to the many pieces of candle wax that Madam Börner had artfully carved to support her gastronomic wonders.

'I can see you're in a rush,' called out her friend, who lingered in the doorway. There was always something extraordinarily bouncy about Silla from behind. The cause was a type of half-crinoline she insisted on wearing despite the vagaries of fashion; she was never seen in the street without this highly mobile garment.

'Here she is, Mother,' Emmeline called out from the window.

'Oh – thank God,' sighed Fru Etvøs, who was in the bedroom assessing her black silk dress in the mirror; many of the seams had given way.

Emmeline inspected it as well – in silence, front and back. Then she said in her considerate voice: 'Mother, we could always ink it.'

'Oh, no, oh, no,' Fru Etvøs protested feebly, as she buttoned the buttons around her waist; the corners of a couple of handkerchiefs stuck out from her underwear. When she wore the silk, Fru Etvøs was forced to compensate for her flat chest.

'And your brooch, Mother,' Emmeline reminded her.

The brooch was pinned on. It was a big, ruddy-cheeked, mosaic Cupid, happily pointing his arrow at the observer. Fru Etvøs wore it on all special occasions.

Etvøs flung open the door. 'So – are you ready?' he said, pushing past her to the mirror. 'Yes – if only they were *here*,' he said, 'if only they were all here ... .'

It was Herr Etvøs' sole concern: that not everyone would turn up.

Fru Etvøs was in the dining room; for the hundredth time she arranged the many juniper twigs with which she had filled the Kronberg vases.

A couple of hard knocks were heard on the front door. It was Cerlachius, who said he was just dropping by before putting on his dinner jacket. He clicked his tongue at the strong smell of cooking, and soon made to leave.

'Incidentally, my dear little Fru Etvøs,' he said. 'My man will bring you some bottles. I thought it couldn't do any harm. Börner knows what dishes they go with.'

He had come purely to say this. Cerlachius harboured a deep suspicion of the Etvøses' wine selection.

Fru Etvøs saw him out.

'Mother, wait a moment,' Emmeline said when she returned. She dotted a little ink *there* on the white fabric, in the armhole.

IV

The doorbell had rung. They were *here.*

Every door in the Etvøses' residence was flung open simultaneously as if an earthquake had struck, and all the floors shook.

'Dearest,' Etvøs cried out from the sitting room: 'I believe you need to be in here.' He himself ran out.

'Yes, yes, Etvøs – but Inga …'

It was as if they were all spinning around one another – stunned, for half a minute, like sheep during a thunderstorm.

'Mother,' Emmeline whispered, 'You should let the waiter open the door.'

'Yes – yes, child, but where is he?' Ericsson was in the kitchen, being given numerous instructions by Madam Börner, who had donned a big, tight cap before serving; he appeared eventually and opened the door.

It was Frau Simonin with the troupe. She was always on time; a habit from her concerts, which she also maintained in private homes. She and the two gentlemen filled the whole passage with furs before entering the sitting room, which was empty. Frau Simonin looked about her for a moment.

'Oh, so it's here,' was all she said, addressing the violinist, and she started to stomp up and down the floor rather indelicately in her silk shoes – as if someone else had decided the dinner party would be held at the Etvøses'.

Fru Etvøs burst in – she was under the impression that Etvøs was here; she curtsied twice and was forced to make conversation while the two gentlemen bowed … about 'the honour – the honour' and 'so far north' she stuttered, as she helplessly slid the mosaic Cupid back and forth across her flat chest.

'Yes, we have your picture,' she said in sheer desperation, when Frau Simonin stopped below the photographic reproduction.

'*Ich sehe das*,'* Frau Simonin said very dryly, continuing to pace up and down unashamedly as if trying to keep warm on a railway platform. She was increasingly inclined to regard the Etvøses' sitting room as an insult, and self-restraint wasn't one of her major characteristics.

Fru Etvøs *had* indeed spotted it, almost the moment she herself had entered: the stove had been forgotten – or had she assumed that there would be enough heat from the guests once they all turned up? She didn't know. But the fact was it had been forgotten … .

Etvøs entered, wearing gloves, and bowed – frequently; Fru Etvøs, however, didn't hear a word anyone said, she herself was speaking English with a strange, rather obscure accent, to one of the gentlemen. It was the tenor, a young Norwegian, his hair styled à la Capoul,* whom Frau Simonin had promoted in St Petersburg, and who replied rather nonsensically in his mother tongue.

The other guests had yet to arrive, so they carried on talking. Fru Etvøs heard her husband say: 'Rubinstein.'*

Shortly afterwards they were *both* back in the dining room – with neither of them knowing how it had come about.

'You see,' said Etvøs, who was in a complete state, 'she's a very pleasant lady.'

Fru Etvøs hadn't found her particularly pleasant, but then again, she had not been expecting anything pleasant at all; she stood in front of the table, wringing her hands. 'The fire hasn't been lit,' was all she said. 'But one of us has to be in there,' she burst out, and went back.

'*Was meinen denn eigentlich die Kerls?*'* she heard Frau Simonin say in a loud voice by the window, where she was arguing with the violinist.

The doorbell went; it was the General and his wife.

'They've arrived,' Etvøs said, rushing up and down the dining table, 'they're here now.' He was too scared to go in.

The doorbell continued to ring and more guests arrived – and then more. Etvøs heard voices in the passage.

'It's time to serve the food,' said Fru Etvøs, who had emerged, her face scarlet. Herr Etvøs started busying himself with the wine and said: 'How's it going, Adolfa?'

'Twelve people have arrived so far,' was all she said before she left, this time for the kitchen.

Emmeline, who couldn't bear being with the other children, was in the small dark passage. 'Are the General and his wife here, Mother?' she whispered.

'Yes,' Fru Etvøs replied, as she entered the kitchen.

'We're just waiting for the headmaster and his wife now,' she said quickly.

'And the small choux pastries,' said Madam Börner, whose voice seemed to take on a sharper edge as the time approached for serving up the food.

'They're not *here*?' Fru Etvøs said in a fluster; she didn't know what to do with herself. Something was wrong everywhere, and she returned to the dining room once more and moved stacks of plates and bottles pointlessly on a serving table in the corner.

'But I won't forget Andersson,' she said – Andersson was the treacherous baker – 'the next time, the next time,' she said, as if the Etvøses were hosting another dinner party the following week.

'Mother,' whispered Emmeline, who had followed her and was listening out by the door to the sitting room, 'nobody is talking.'

'No,' said Fru Etvøs, who was sure of it.

'Yes – Frøken Zelchen is now,' Emmeline reported.

'We should have put some paper under it,' Fru Etvøs said, quite distractedly, as she looked at the leg of the serving table, which wobbled.

The door was opened. It was Etvøs. 'We're only waiting for the headmaster and his wife,' he announced, hot and flustered, as if it was news.

'Yes, but please stay in there,' Fru Etvøs said. Emmeline had quietly put some paper under the leg of the serving table.

The door closed once more behind Etvøs, who re-joined Cerlachius and the gentlemen, who, as the waiting time extended, seemed to disappear, as if they were keeping themselves to themselves, with their backs to the party and their faces towards the wall.

'No, I haven't got a clue how it came about either,' said Cerlachius, who was sweating a fair amount on Herr Etvøs' behalf.

'Old friend,' Etvøs said, 'none of us do.'

There followed again a long period of time during which no one spoke except Frøken Zelchen, who continued to carry on a limited conversation with two or three local dignitaries in the middle of the room. The General stayed permanently at the side of Frau Simonin, who was very silent, as immobile as if he was her sentry.

And the little Danish vice-consul, a spindly and virginal person who was tripping about in his small patent leather boots, said, possibly for the tenth time: 'I wonder if she would prefer to speak French.'

Then the headmaster and his wife arrived. That immediately seemed to invigorate the party somewhat – everyone knew they were the last – while the headmaster's wife, an extraordinarily broad woman in bronze-coloured satin with a clearly home-made Point de Laze across her bosom,* walked particularly upright through the sitting room and addressed the General in a measured tone which could be heard across the whole room: 'Perhaps you would like to introduce me?'

Fru Etvøs opened the door to the dining room and they saw that the candles on the table had been lit. The gentlemen stirred to find their ladies and Etvøs clapped his hands. Fru von Linden, a blonde and hefty lady of the rural gentry who almost matched the General in terms of height, rose, with some effort, from one of the Etvøs wicker chairs. 'Well – it'll be fine, God willing,' she said with genuine goodwill, and joined the chairman; Etvøs would, of course, lead the way with Frau Simonin. She was at the centre of the 'troupe' – she had been somewhat appeased at the sound of the gathering's many impressive names, and besides, she was quite used to festive surprises.

'*Na – lustiges Nest*,'* she said in Bavarian with a shrug to the violinist, and entered with Etvøs.

In the doorway, a petite, blonde and sharp-nosed woman with a lorgnette, who steered the vice-consul to the table, literally wedged herself in between Frau Simonin and the General's wife, who was escorted to the table by Count Silfverhjelm of the Customs, and sized up Frau Simonin and her diamond brooches as if she were a lifeless exhibit in a display cabinet.

Fru Etvøs would be seated next to the tenor. But before that she quietly slipped her skinny hand under Frøken Zelchen's arm from behind. 'Thank you,' she whispered. Her eyes shone as if she had a high fever.

The Kronberg treasures wobbled somewhat on the festive table before everyone's legs and trains settled down and the guests were seated in the two slightly uneven rows – the Etvøs chairs being somewhat unequal in height.

Ericsson served the soup with much solemnity.

The door to the sitting room was softly closed behind Fru Etvøs by Emmeline, who intended to drag birch logs through the passage and lay a fire.

A couple of dishes were carried in and out. The locals behaved almost as if they were the invited audience and sat waiting for what was coming next; the troupe ate.

Etvøs was heard saying: 'But you're not drinking, my dear friend, you're not drinking,' and made many errors in foreign tongues, which of course *also* slowed down the conversation, which progressed only in very lame fragments.

Fru Etvøs had beads of sweat on her forehead; she saw everything as through a veil. 'I don't think they're enjoying themselves,' she said in an embarrassed voice, and raised a glass to the headmaster's wife.

'Why, don't you think so?' replied the headmaster's wife, with a friendliness that felt like being stabbed with a dagger.

The troupe had told anecdotes, one each – while everyone stopped eating except for the Zelchens and the General and his wife – but each story was followed by a lengthy period of silence.

'Are they drinking anything? Are they drinking anything over there?' Fru Etvøs then said, echoing her husband. 'Faster, my friend, faster,' she whispered to Ericsson. Ericsson had a tendency to pause during service in order to hear what was being said.

Silla went around with the sauces; she left the door to the small passage open, and thick fumes wafted from Madam Börner's quarters into the room, which was already hot enough as it was, and the faces of the gentlemen quietly turned red.

They also started hearing the children, who were up to God knows what. Fru Etvøs struggled to stay seated with all the noise they were making. 'I wonder if I should get up,' she had started saying to Fru von Linden, when suddenly a thud was heard as if a ram had bashed against the door to the passage.

'Oh – that'll be the children,' Fru Etvøs said, getting up from her seat.

The crash was followed by total silence and so everyone heard Frau Simonin say – it was one of the first things she had said: '*Sie haben Kinder*?'* she said, utterly unruffled.

'Yes, nine,' Etvøs said.

'*Neun.*'

Frau Simonin put down her knife and fork, and looked down at Fru Etvøs with undisguised horror. '*Sie Unglückliche*,'* she exclaimed from the bottom of her heart.

Everyone burst into spontaneous laughter at once, and laughed so heartily they bent over the table, but Frau Simonin, who didn't think there had been anything funny about it, shouted unperturbed into the racket: '*Ja, ich meine das*,'* and they laughed again, even louder than before.

They couldn't stop. Cerlachius, who continued chuckling, said: 'Yes – she might be right about that,' and raised his glass to Etvøs.

The guests laughed once more and began to talk as they laughed. It was as if a weight had been lifted from Fru Etvøs' shoulders. The chairman toasted her and the General, too, raised his glass; her joy had brought the blood to her cheeks.

Frau Simonin slipped off her diamond bracelets and dropped them into a glass; she had reached her pet subject: the reproduction of mankind. Her merry Bavarian dialect drowned out everyone else – she was more than happy to expand on her topic with her lovely arms right across the table. The gentlemen saw only her, with her bust heaving like the sepals of a big, white flower above the lace as she spoke. The General's wife and Frøken Zelchen looked as if they were dispersing a rather strong odour with their solemn fans.

The sharp-nosed woman had, from the moment she joined the table, placed her gloves beside her and armed herself with her lorgnette, as if sitting in the stalls of a theatre.

The headmaster's wife said sternly to her neighbour at dinner, who didn't hear her, that she had expected this of a travelling lady.

'*Gott, dass die Weiber sich dazu hergeben*,'* Frau Simonin carried on, and threw up her hands in horror.

Fru Linden's laughter rivalled that of the gentlemen, and she planted both elbows on the table. 'A happy person,' she said to the chairman, who had pushed up his gold spectacles and was ogling Frau Simonin.

The time had come for Cerlachius' good Burgundy, and everyone toasted Etvøs, who sat beaming with happiness on his chair. 'Thank you, dear friends, thank you, dear friends,' he said, flinging out his hand.

And Fru Etvøs said to the tenor with a tiny, still fearful smile: 'Oh, I don't think she's so bored now,' and when the tenor was convinced that she was not, she said, smiling happily with her mouth wide open: 'Oh, thank God – do you think so, do you think so?'

Silfverhjelm raised his glass knowingly to Cerlachius – he recognised the Burgundy – and the violinist launched into a story which everyone listened to amidst the laughter. At the head of the table, seated between Etvøs and the General, Frau Simonin was as comfortable as if sitting in front of the fireplace.

'*Ja, wer nur jetzt a' gutes Glas Bier hätte*,'* she said, as if that constituted the height of good living.

Etvøs looked at her, somewhat puzzled. 'But we can provide that,' he then said, and rose; he was a little unsteady on his feet as he stood up.

'What? What, Etvøs?' Fru Etvøs called out anxiously from the opposite end.

And the sharp-nosed lady, who hadn't heard it either, asked loudly while craning her neck: 'What does she want?'

'*Ach – a' Glas Bier*,' Frau Simonin said in a supremely reassuring voice. The General's wife's side of the table grew increasingly quiet, the open fans acting almost as a kind of fence.

Etvøs had gone. He left the doors open. 'Do we have any beer?' he said, flustered, while hunting around as if he could find beer on the tables. 'Do we have any beer?'

'What?' Madam Börner said; she was busy with the sweet pudding.

'She wants a beer,' Etvøs said, now frantically rummaging around in his empty pockets. And the others repeated this simple word, quite mesmerised by it, as they, too, started moving around mindlessly.

'Yes – Silla must have some money, mustn't she,' Etvøs said, breaking off suddenly: 'but hurry – hurry,' he said, and ran back inside. Meanwhile Fru Etvøs had got hold of Ericsson. 'Emmeline has money,' she whispered and sent him out. Gustaf Adolf of the Nine ran to get the beer.

The mood seemed to have grown a little quiet again, and Frau Simonin, who had glanced lightly over to the side with the General's wife, who was born Princess Trubetzkoy and who endured her Finnish exile with the facial expression of a potentate suffering a gala performance with a lesser cousin in a language he doesn't comprehend,* switched to French and conveyed to the General's wife a greeting from her Serene Highness the Princess Ghica,* whom she had just met in Paris.

She kept speaking French while she jumped to Romania to talk about Queen Elisabeth – *la charmante femme!* – and her court in Bucharest.*

'They're nothing but a bunch of thieves in that hole,' the violinist said curtly, and launched into an anecdote about the Romanian Lord Chamberlain, who had stolen the bracelet which the Queen intended to present to Frau Simonin. Frau Simonin wasn't listening; she continued to converse with the General's wife, who slowly began to thaw, and asked if the pearl brooch on Frau Simonin's shoulder was part of a collection. It wasn't, it was a present from her Majesty the Queen of Spain: '*Des perles exquises – n'est-ce-pas, madame*.'*

The General's wife took to praising the pearls. And Frau Simonin caught the attention of the violinist – Etvøs had left again to check on the beer. '*Ôtez ça*,' she said,* and he took off the brooch, which was passed around while Frau

Simonin switched back to German and talked about how she had played billiards with his Majesty King Alfonso.*

The brooch went from hand to hand while Frau Simonin continued her account, which positively fizzed with royal names around the Kronberg vases, and everyone listened with happy and shiny faces as if all the courtly sunshine was falling on those who were dining with the celebrity.

One by one they felt the urge to raise their glasses to the host, and there was constant nodding and toasting across the table with thanks and thanks in return – only the headmaster's wife continued to sit unmoved, holding out the brooch at a distance as if it had a foul smell.

'Well, it would be more accurate to say it came from a *prince*,' she said, and passed it on to Fru Etvøs, who held it in her skinny fingers; Fru Etvøs could barely recognise her own life. 'Oh – that this should happen to us,' she said, turning over the pearl brooch in her hand.

'*Mais, madame, vous oubliez votre bock*,'* the General's wife said, and pointed with an affable smile to the newly-arrived bottle, which Frau Simonin hadn't touched.

They had reached the roast, which Ericsson, who had drained the dregs from several glasses on his trips down the short passage, offered around with small, encouraging shoulder pats to familiar faces – Ericsson had a habit of picking certain favourites during service – and then Fru Etvøs suddenly remembered Inga, and had got up discreetly when Etvøs rose unexpectedly, and she sat down as if hammered into the ground.

Etvøs intended to give a speech.

'The master is proposing a toast,' Silla called out in passing; she was carrying the compote, and flung open the door to the bedroom where Emmeline was sitting on the edge of the bed near a candle in a bottle, struggling with the white dress and trying to hide yet another tear with some lace, while a freezing Inga waited in a small petticoat.

'The master is proposing a toast,' Silla could be heard saying again in the kitchen.

Emmeline sat rigid in front of the candle with her hands in her lap – you could hear everything through the open doors.

Etvøs paused for a moment, then he said in a very low voice, and very close to Frau Simonin: 'I just wanted to thank you – thank you, because today you have given us joy and brilliance – and brilliance,' he repeated even more softly, while he stared across the table; then he clammed up, he couldn't think of anything else to say.

A moment of silence ensued. Then everyone called out hurrah nine times, and the gentlemen got up noisily in order to clink glasses with Frau Simonin.

Fru Etvøs sat looking at Frau Simonin, who smiled to all the bowing faces – even the General's wife had stood up in her silk dress.

'How happy you must be,' Fru Etvøs said in a semi-audible voice to the tenor, her gaze lingering on the scene.

'Oh, no,' he just replied slowly, and then he, too, stared into space – but in a different direction.

Inga appeared at the pudding. While she went from lap to lap, Frau Simonin remembered her brooch. It turned out it had ended up with the vice-consul's dining partner and she had been unable to part with it.

They broke up from the table and there were loud 'thank you's from every room where the guests were talking, cheerful and sated, and Etvøs went from embrace to embrace.

'Thank you, my brother,' Silverhjelm said, slapping Etvøs firmly on both shoulder blades.

Fru Etvøs shook hands with every single one of the ladies.

'A lovely day,' Fru Linden said, and squeezed her fingers with her heavy hands before she let herself collapse onto one of Etvøs' seating arrangements. 'Oh, thank God,' she said and let out a long sigh of relief.

Fru Etvøs did the rounds. She didn't hear what any of the ladies said, but she saw them smile and knew that it was positive – while she seemed to glide from circle to circle. With the headmaster's wife were also two ladies who held her hand for a long time as they talked about how well everything had gone. 'And that's not easy, especially when you have to borrow,' the headmaster's wife remarked.

'Oh, *no*,' Fru Etvøs exclaimed and pressed her hand firmly; she was far too happy to sense any kind of sting. She passed Frau Simonin, who had retired slightly towards the windows with her troupe – '*Na, Kinder*,' she was saying, '*schwer mit so verschiedenen Wölfen zu heulen*,'* – and then she went and clasped Cerlachius's hands. She said nothing, she just stood there gazing gratefully at his round, red face.

Much jollity then ensued. The gentlemen consumed a great deal of cognac and the violinist performed dextrous tricks with a saucer in front of a circle of ladies. Silla, who was collecting coffee cups with the laden tray pressed against her stomach, sized up every single person's outfit, and Count Silfverhjelm, escorted by Ericsson, went out to compliment Madam Börner.

All the doors were open and the whole house seemed to morph into one great big party. Furthest in, one could catch a glimpse of Emmeline handing out rations to the eight by the candle in the bottle on the table at the foot of the beds … .

'Now you're happy,' said the short tenor, who was standing next to Fru Etvøs.

'Yes,' she said, and laughed up at his face like a child.

V

Frau Simonin was yawning repeatedly behind her fan.

For a change she had moved near the stove – which was now red hot, thanks to Emmeline – and was standing with a couple of gentlemen, of whom the vice consul was one.

'*Altes Ding*,'* she said in order to escape, pointing at the piano. She struck a couple of keys in passing, and then a few more. '*Sie, Berg*,' she said, now suddenly interested: '*Hören Sie doch, es klingt wie eine Spinette.*'*

She nudged the piano stool and sat down while she continued to play chords.

No one knew how Frøken Blanck, the sharp-nosed woman, had suddenly made it to the front and was sitting two steps in front of everyone else, in a wicker chair with her lorgnette. All fell silent as if by command. Etvøs stood next to his wife. 'Adolfa, Adolfa,' he kept on whispering, while clutching her wrist tightly.

Frau Simonin swiftly launched into a little piece by Haydn. '*Klingt doch lustig? Was?*'* she said when it was over.

No one said anything, and she played again – a little number by Scarlatti.* Fru Etvøs looked as if she were witnessing a biblical vision in the middle of her own sitting room.

Frau Simonin paused, hitting only the odd key or two. '*Singt denn hier Niemand?*'* she said, in a tone of voice as if asking if any in the present company could walk on their hands.

Yes – Herr Etvøs could sing … .

'Herr Etvøs is our local tenor,' the vice consul lisped.

'*Dann singen Sie doch etwas*,'* Frau Simonin said in the exact same tone of voice, as she continued to hit the keys playfully.

Etvøs had turned as white as a sheet. 'It's out of the question,' he said, and wrung his sweaty hands. To sing for her, he could barely utter the words – well – if only he had – if only he had –. But – as he approached the piano – it was all so very old, what he had … .

The guests issued muted objections. Fru Etvøs stood behind her husband's back, tiptoeing like him while moving her lips, forming words that no one heard.

'Well, if he doesn't want to sing,' Fru von Linden said feebly and let her hands flop onto her lap.

'And straight after dinner,' Etvøs said, 'in this heavy air … and who would accompany me?'

'*Ah – ich*,'* said Frau Simonin, in the same tone of voice as before.

'Sing *Alfredo*,'* Fru Etvøs said, still standing right behind her husband, and so moved that she could barely utter the words.

'Yes, yes,' said Etvøs, who couldn't see the sheet music, 'but where is it?'

Fru Etvøs had left. She had gone to get lozenges and some tepid water so he could rinse out his mouth.

'But in this air,' Etvøs said, 'and with a fire burning in the stove … .'

He thought about opening a window in the dining room, and in his confusion he ran through every room into the bedroom. 'Who on earth lit the fire?' he shouted. 'We're suffocating in there.'

'I did, Father,' Emmeline said.

'Oh – why do you always have to do things that nobody has asked you to do.'

Etvøs moved away from the mirror where he had smartened himself up like an actor in the wings. 'You always do that,' he said, and then he left.

Emmeline made no reply. Slowly her eyes began to sting, then she wept very quietly, sitting in the corner by her bed – she had experienced so many emotions these last twenty-four hours.

Fru Etvøs appeared with the tepid water. 'Oh, Emmeline,' she said by way of apology. 'But Father is going to sing.'

He had already begun, and Fru Etvøs stayed where she was. They both listened, mother and daughter, their heads bowed, without moving.

'He's in good voice,' Fru Etvøs whispered with a smile, and they listened again.

'This is the place,' Fru Etvøs said, clutching Emmeline's arm. It was a passage where Jakob Etvøs often struggled with a note from the chest. 'Yes, he's in good voice,' she repeated, and smiled. The tricky spot had been navigated.

When Etvøs stopped, everyone applauded, and Fru Etvøs, now quivering from excitement, let go of Emmeline as if wanting to return to the noise as quickly as possible; she opened the door and stepped into the light. Etvøs was beaming and said: 'Well – when you have an accompanist like that,' and started rummaging around for more sheet music.

'*Er hat ja gelernt*,'* the violinist said, approaching Fru Etvøs.

'Yes – my husband has had training,' she said.

Only Silfverhjelm said to Cerlachius: 'Well – music is not my thing,' and returned to the dining room where Emmeline had sneaked in; she *had* to see her father.

Etvøs had started singing again – he was facing the guests, his face purple, his body swaying, expelling the worn notes, louder and louder, with a beaming face, completely carried away, while Frau Simonin little by little became quite mechanical – with her head tilted – and simply let her hands travel up and down, up and down the keyboard.

The tenor felt the need to hide. He sought out Etvøs' study, where a lamp was burning quietly. Behind the door, however, he bumped into Fru Etvøs, who was also hiding and peering through the crack, nodding her head, at her singing husband.

The tenor was taken aback and wanted to say something – an adjective about the singer, but didn't have time before Fru Etvøs suddenly stood up and pulled him down on a chair and started to talk – to him, a total stranger, a nobody, about their situation, their narrow existence, their lives, so tiny, so tiny, she said. 'And nothing ever changes,' she said, 'all those long years.' She repeated the words as if talking to herself, and she looked at him again, her face close to his; she carried on talking, feverishly and hurriedly telling him about their youth, that she had travelled – 'out there, out there,' she said; and about Etvøs, what he wanted, what he had hoped. 'To break out – because he had ambitions,' she said and bashed her splayed hands like two tired hammers against her knees.

'And yet here we are,' she said, suddenly staring into his face with eyes that saw nothing: 'Here … .' She pushed the door shut – in the other room Etvøs continued to sing, he sang one aria after another; all the gentlemen had moved to the dining room now – and she continued pinning down the tenor with her stream of words, leaning towards him, clutching his hands: 'Then it turns into longing, you understand, a desperate longing, you see, while we sit here year after year … .'

Suddenly the tears began pouring from her eyes, and she sobbed quietly and continuously, her face turned to his all the time.

The small tenor hadn't moved; he couldn't think of anything to say and so said only with a half bow: 'Yes, I understand, of course, I understand … that it's stifling here, ma'am.'

In the sitting room Etvøs had stopped singing, and everyone began talking at once. Suddenly Fru Etvøs opened the door again. 'I believe they're done,' she said, trying to compose herself; the tenor just bowed and left without a word. Etvøs had gone to the dining room where everyone was clapping; he made a sweeping gesture towards the headmaster and Cerlachius.

'Well, it helps if you have the voice, of course,' he said, gesturing to his throat.

Then he returned to the sitting room and the ladies gathered around him to compliment him. 'No, indeed,' he said, 'I haven't forgotten it all; it comes back when I get excited.'

Then he was suddenly distracted and stared into space until he broke free from the circle with an abrupt: 'Excuse me.' He had spotted the violinist, who had yet to comment. He made a beeline for him with many odd nods of his head, and struck up a conversation about the art of singing; he didn't know how professionals like him viewed his voice. And halfway through he said with a brief little nod of the head – softly – colleague to colleague, so to speak: 'Well – how was it?'

At first the violinist just looked at him – his mind was no longer on Etvøs' exertions – then he said: 'Well, it's an exceedingly tenacious voice.'

Etvøs' face lit up. 'It is, isn't it?' he said, sounding terribly pleased, and nodded: 'At least I know a thing or two about singing,' he said, and spoke at length about how *he* viewed his own voice.

The General's wife had already put on her cape in order to leave, and Frau Simonin rose from the stool, a little too quickly. '*Ja – gehen wir*,'* she said with a hard tug on her gloves.

All the ladies were getting ready to leave as Fru Etvøs entered from her husband's study. 'So soon,' she said, 'but why so soon … . It was all over so soon,' she said, shaking hand after hand.

'Well, you must be *very* tired,' Fru Linden said, placing her hands on her shoulders.

'No, no, oh, no,' Fru Etvøs kept saying, while she shook her head and clasped every single hand as if she didn't want to let it go. 'But it's not so late after all!' she said to the headmaster's wife.

The door to the hall was open and she saw, as if through a fog, the ladies disappearing one after another into their big coats … .

The gentlemen, however, were less keen to leave; they were still drinking, they proposed a toast to her and she joined them briefly for a drink – until they, too, were gone, and all she could hear was them stumbling about in the front hall.

It was Cerlachius' voice. 'Well, we have drained *that* festive cup,' he said.

And the front door slammed shut. Fru Etvøs could hear their voices far down the street, until eventually they too faded away.

She wandered about for a long time as if still listening out for the absent noise; the wicker chairs stood abandoned, the table was covered with half-empty glasses. She extinguished the candles in the candlesticks one after the other – an old prudent habit – so only the lamp was left burning and the place grew gloomy again. Then she suddenly collapsed and started crying again, resting her head on the old piano.

Silla roused her. Madam Börner was waiting to say goodbye.

Fru Etvøs went to the kitchen, where Madam Börner sat buttoned up by the water bucket. She thanked her many, many times, she said, her voice still wobbly from crying.

'Then again it was the *big* wedding menu,' Madam Börner said, without moving.

'But there's no rush, is there,' Fru Etvøs said, sitting down on the butcher's block and taking the cook's hands as well. 'Surely we can talk for a little while,' she said, 'it's not that late yet … .'

But Madam Börner was in a hurry, she didn't cook in people's houses for the fun of it – not with *her* condition. And she had children, seven children, and Börner, he wasn't reliable. And it was worse on the days she was out. Madam Börner talked monotonously, her eyes fixed on her lap.

Fru Etvøs barely heard her, she just said with her face close to the cook's, shaking her head, recognising this litany of misery: 'I know, I know,' she said like a chorus, and kept nodding her head as if accompanying it.

But then she woke up and said: 'But haven't you had any? You haven't had any food – to take home. I'm sure you have plenty of mouths who would like to taste … .' And she started wrapping up one thing after another, putting the leftovers in a basket.

Then Madam Börner left and the kitchen, too, was empty.

The guests walked home through the streets. The headmaster's wife clutched her husband's arm rather hard.

'She was lovely, Louise,' the headmaster said, stopping under a streetlight.

'She was *naked*, Kalle,' was all his wife said.

The headmaster walked on, defeated, in silence.

When she opened their front door, the headmaster's wife said in a definitive tone of voice while turning the key hard in the lock: 'Cerlachius paid for it.'

The sharp-nosed Frøken Blanck was escorted home by the Danish vice-consul, who on the return journey was full of French adjectives.

'That's what I'm saying,' Frøken Blanck stated, 'she's not respectable.'

The General's wife had long since returned home and was taking the flowers out of her hair in front of her mirror. When she loosened the last flower, she said, shrugging as she turned to the General: '*C'est bonnet blanc et blanc bonnet.*'*

Frau Simonin was resting in her hotel room in a dressing gown. She spent a long time contemplating the toes of her slippers; tomorrow she would be dining with the General.

Then she clicked her heels and said in a resigned tone of voice: '*Na – am End, sie haben ihr Geld bezahlt.*'*

Etvøs had accompanied the tenor, who preferred to walk, to his hotel. He was still on the art of singing and wanted to know how the professionals treated their instrument. He stopped on every tenth step.

When they finally parted at the hotel entrance, Etvøs glanced at the singer and said: 'Do you think it's too late to make a break?' And when the tenor clearly didn't catch his drift, he said: 'Could I build on this, I mean?' and pointed quickly to his throat.

'But why?' the tenor said, turning scarlet.

Etvøs continued walking up and down the street for a long time.

When he finally came home, he was still in ecstasy, but eventually everyone managed to get to bed.

Her father was already asleep when Emmeline half-sat up on her mattress. 'Mother,' she whispered.

'Yes.'

'I heard Frøken von Zelchen say something.'

'What?' her mother whispered.

'That it was a very good day, she said so to her father.'

'When did you hear that?' Fru Etvøs whispered back.

'I crept down to the entrance as they were leaving,' Emmeline said.

Fru Etvøs smiled as she lay there: 'Good night, child.'

'Good night.'

Three days later Frau Simonin left in the morning. She was giving concerts in Russia. Seventeen concerts in twenty-one days, one programme. The first would take place in Kiev. Other towns would follow – she didn't know their names.

Fru Etvøs was there to see her off with a couple of roses in foil – poor, pale specimens with just five petals that will barely open on a grave at Christmas.

Etvøs didn't have time, of course – he was on his way to school. But in one of the streets intersected by the railway, a tall figure stood swinging his hat.

It was Etvøs with two of the nine who were running to school. The wind caught their long, woollen scarves, which flapped like three grey pennants.

Translated by Charlotte Barslund

9. Frøken Caja

I

The hum of the departing lodgers had died away at last, and the door on the third floor banged open and shut. The twittering of the 'social butterflies' could be heard from the foot of the stairs.

And now there would be an hour's peace in the sitting room.

Fru Canth was sitting in her favourite spot on the sofa below her mother's portrait. She would nod off and then wake up, the ribbons of her cap billowing softly all the while.

Frøken Caja simply slept – hard, straight up and down on her chair behind the urn. Her mouth was open and her breathing loud as if she was toiling even in sleep. Suddenly her breathing stilled and she half-woke up as if someone had summoned her, only to go back to sleep almost immediately.

Fru Canth had woken up fully – she never dozed for very long – and began walking up and down the floor as she hummed to herself. She had a habit of humming – no one recognised the fragments of the old songs – while her feet touched the floor as lightly as if she were dancing and she lifted up her dress at the back as if it had an old-fashioned train.

She continued to swish back and forth past Frøken Caja. Her humming grew louder and louder – her daughter's boorish sleep irritated her – in an attempt to wake her. From Frøken Caja, however, came only mumbling in the twilight, and then her loud breathing resumed; once she sat down, Frøken Caja slept like a day labourer.

Fru Canth could endure her sleeping no longer. 'The urn needs taking out, surely?' she said with a loud and impatient voice in that harsh tone none but her daughter heard.

Frøken Caja shot up and shook her coarse hair; the lamps had been lit – it was time to get the fire going in the Captain's room.

Without a word she took the urn – her busy schedule waking in her brain once more – and left. It was as if she passed through every single door on this floor at once, and her voice rang out: 'Eugenia, Eugenia,' through the passage. She stressed the 'ge' syllable with a particularly high-pitched tone.

Eugenia, the sole maid, who spent her life in down-at-heel dancing shoes, either sleeping – she had a weakness for resting on the edge of the beds she was meant to be making – or styling her fringe with a pair of curling tongs, emerged at an exceedingly sedate pace from her room and managed to send a couple of mumbled but most eloquent reassurances after Frøken Caja, who was already heading down the third floor stairs, from where her journey through the building could be heard.

The social butterflies, still wearing their coats, were kneeling on the kitchen table next to one another in order to see the bridal carriage – there was a wedding feast in the middle building of Thorup's Function Rooms – and they jumped down from the table when they heard her.

The Sundby sisters lived life on the edge in general: they rented the third floor bathroom for only forty kroner per month, meals included – for both of them.* And even so, Lissy still had to practise for the Conservatoire on the sitting room piano for three hours every day.

Frøken Caja, however, didn't see them; she just marched down the passage where Kattrup, a student, flung open his door on hearing her so that 'she could at least smell the heat' on her way to the Captain's room.

She laid the fire, turned down the bed, set out a candle – all of it mechanically, swiftly, and without a thought. Frøken Caja's thoughts always focused on whatever she might get done next. On her way back up, she turned down another couple of beds.

In the passage she bumped into Frøken Emmy: 'I was going to open the door,' she whispered in a frightened voice. Once it grew dark, the Sundby sisters had a passion for opening the door. Every time someone rang the bell, they would both come running like a couple of excited sparrows and show in any ladies or gentlemen. At twilight the ringing of the bell made the third floor resemble a telephone exchange.

Frøken Caja was back on the fourth floor. Kattrup closed his door, and Emmy had returned to the kitchen table, where Lissy was already kneeling once more with her face pressed again the windowpane over the café curtain.

Frøken Caja lit the hanging lamp and the squat lamp on the dining table where the napkins lay scattered across the tablecloth. 'I'm going now,' she called into the sitting room in a sharp voice, picking up in passing a couple of forgotten plates on the Saturday tablecloth where Herr Lerche had eaten late.

'Will you be taking the jumpers?' Fru Canth called back through the door, but there was no response. The three Hatting brothers stormed through the dining room on their way to their private tutor. 'Do you think you could walk *quietly*, Constantin?' Frøken Caja said, as she came towards them with the plates.

None of the three college schoolboys replied; the last one merely slammed the door to the passage shut, causing the lamps to smoke. The Hatting brothers had a habit of rushing out of their stuffy cage like three hunting dogs chasing their prey.

'Will you be taking the jumpers?' Fru Canth called out again.

A hard 'yes' rang out from the passage, and Fru Canth let go of her alpaca shawl, a shawl in shades of brown in which she constantly wrapped and then unwrapped herself and which when distracted she would forget about and leave behind on a chair, in order to fetch the jumpers from her bedroom, a neat chamber full of white drapes and with a couple of old silver candlesticks gleaming in front of the mirror. Fru Canth's room was the only place on the Canthian floors where anything truly shone.

Fru Canth took out the jumpers – woollen ones which she knitted to be sold in a shop – from a drawer and wrapped them in paper. Her fingers, however, were relentlessly clumsy, and the bundle refused to stay closed.

'Right – that'll do,' said Caja, who had followed on behind her, as she took the misshapen bundle from her hands.

She went to the bathroom, which was also her room, where her clothes hung on nails hammered into the wall covered by a sheet, and a small mountain of bed linen was piled high in a corner. She tossed the jumpers into a drawer, which she locked, before she put on her outdoor clothes. A long coat whose pleat for the missing bustle flapped in a strangely sexless manner at the back, and a leather beret pulled right down over her hair. She slipped on her lined gloves as she hurried down the passage – her wrists were bony like those of a man.

A few more shouts of: 'Eugenia – Eugenia' were heard before the door to the passage slammed shut. In the entrance Frøken Caja was nearly run over by the bridal carriage as it pulled up, ringing its bells.

Frøken Caja, however, neither saw nor heard anything. She was busy doing sums from the moment she left the house; the Canthian cashbox had to cover so many, many expenses, and it was a Saturday shop, which meant shopping for two whole days.

Upstairs, peace seemed to have descended on the rooms at last.

Fru Canth had lit the candles in the silver candlesticks and was meandering around humming and busying herself with numerous combs and sponges and brushes – she could spend hours doing that; then she would buff her nails and smooth her hair while she chatted to anyone who entered the sitting room. Everyone had something they wanted to confide in her, as she skipped around putting on and abandoning her shawl and hearing only half of what was said.

Fru von Casse-Muckadell had entered and, as she came in, had straightened a couple of the chairs – the sitting-room chairs looked permanently as if strangers had departed in haste – before she sat down at the table and took out her cards. Fru von Casse-Muckadell, a round and stout body, whose limbs seemed still to remember past caresses, played a game of patience for each young person at the boarding house in order to foretell their luck in love and marriage, all the while looking knowingly at the cards with a red, lascivious mouth, and would at times stir in her seat as if she was overheating and needed to move; she saw everything so clearly in the cards.

The Sundby sisters could be heard from the dining room, where they filled the space with words which poured from their tiny, fish-like mouths in an unbroken stream – one had the feeling, said Spørck, a medical student, that the Sundby sisters' flow of words never passed through their brains at all: about who they had seen and who had been let in and out and who they thought was the bride, while they constantly interrupted their outpourings with an:

'Isn't that right, Iss?'

'Isn't that right, Im?'

addressed to the other; then they went at it again, fidgeting and jerking all the while as if this stage of their precious youth was about cramming in as many movements per minute as possible.

Fru von Casse-Muckadell paused over her cards, reared her head, and with her hands, which were still as pretty as a couple of fat little white cats, on her round knees, said: 'Who came for Sparre?' as she quickly tilted the lampshade in order to see.

'The lady with the brown hat, of course – as usual,' Emmy said. 'And I refuse to shake hands with him any longer,' she said, pressing her lips shut. The Sundby sisters had a habit of protesting against certain irregularities in the third floor's manner of living by temporarily suspending handshakes after meals.

'Yes, that's her,' Fru von Casse said, appearing to caress her own hands in her lap.

'What's that?' asked Fru Canth, who had emerged from the bedroom, and who only followed half of what was going on.

'She wore cashmere,' said Lissy, referring to the bride. And Fru Canth asked: 'Do you think there will be dancing?'

That was her main concern: she so loved hearing happy music through the house.

Lissy replied – the Sundby sisters' replies were always loosely connected to the point: 'Yes – they all wore high-necked dresses'; and Fru von Casse remarked dryly from her patience: 'Brides should always wear a high neck.'

'But why?' 'But why?' the Sundby sisters exclaimed in unison, craning their necks – they tended to do so whenever they asked questions.

'Because it's wiser,' Fru von Casse said, briefly fixing them with her grey eyes.

'Well,' said Fru Canth, who had settled on the sofa once more: 'I do like to see a pretty neck.'

The Sundby sisters fell silent as if someone had walked over their graves. Then they both laughed, a brief, baffled laughter; and Emmy went to the piano to steal half an hour while Frøken Caja was out.

When Emmy had been playing for a little while, Arnljot Oulie entered through the dining room, and said good evening in Norwegian. His gait was a little hunched, as if his young body was too heavy, even for him, and he sat down quietly in a corner, shielding his eyes with his hand. He could sit like that for hours, listening, during Frøken Emmy's rather jumpy music.

Emmy continued playing while the door to the passage opened and closed, and a head popped round and disappeared. Regularly, every five minutes, someone or other wanted to see what was going on in the sitting room.

'It's getting a little cold, my girl,' Fru Canth said to Lissy, who got up and went to the stove. Due to the frequent opening of doors, there was always a temperature approaching that of a snowy square in the Canthian communal rooms.

Fru von Casse-Muckadell had gathered up her cards and shivered. 'It's your turn, Herr Oulie,' she said, aiming two glittering eyes at the Norwegian.

Oulie's hand swept down from his forehead. 'Yes,' he said and got up – it was as if he had to pull himself together for the tiniest action, even to move or merely ask a question. 'Yes,' he said, and seemed to snatch himself out of his deep reverie: 'Do please tell me something about life.'

And Lissy, who was crocheting a decorative border – the undergarments of the Sundby sisters would surely end up consisting of nothing but decorative borders – said (it was her speciality to utter such unexpected and quite bizarre sentences): 'Oh, God, yes, Fru von Casse, the things you must know about life.'

Fru Canth had gone to the dining room where, humming softly to herself, she wandered around brushing crumbs from the table and onto the floor with the flat of her hand. Then she meandered into the kitchen, where Eugenia was washing her hands in the sink – she invariably used Frøken Caja's shopping hour for a more extensive personal grooming session, which included gallons of hair oil. Fru Canth wandered back and forth between the kitchen and the larder, where every now and then she would help herself to some leftovers; she tended to snack between meals.

Eugenia rinsed the soap off a scaly arm and started to complain about Frøken Caja: 'But Frøken Caja really should be ashamed of herself for how people talk in this house,' she concluded and tipped the water out of the basin.

Fru Canth listened: 'But you know what Frøken Caja is like, Eugenia.'

Fru Canth was the mediator in the house, and sided with everyone against Caja.

'And who do you think, Fru Canth, has to pitch in on the third floor,' Eugenia said. 'It's not easy – with the new men, what they put me through.'

The three college boys had come home and announced in rough bass voices that they had been invited round to a friend's to play cards.

'Very well,' Fru Canth said, 'but then you'd better go before Caja comes back.'

Frøken Caja walked swiftly, without hearing, without seeing, down the street. The bright flow of lively people on the pavement slipped past her unnoticed.

At the fishmonger's a couple of maids, their cotton petticoats hoisted up, were haggling with the assistant, Herr Hansen, who was walking about in a pair of wooden clogs on a floor swimming in water.

One of the girls gathered up her petticoats so high that one could see up her black stockings and, addressing Frøken Caja with a smile, said: 'But perhaps this lady would like to go first?' Frøken Caja made no reply; she just stood there silent and away from the windows with her big purse in her hand.

And the other one said: 'Or perhaps the lady would prefer to wait.'

Frøken Caja just stayed put; she was used to ignoring people and having to wait. Every servant girl in the neighbourhood regarded it as their official duty to harass her as much as possible.

'Well, Hansen,' the girl said, and swung her backside demonstratively round towards Frøken Caja: 'go on, knock off those few øre . . . . After all, we're the sort of customers who only eat the fresh ones . . . .'

The assistant caught in his net a fish wriggling in the running water in the aquarium below the window.

The girls departed with much giggling, and Hansen, who went to his counter, said casually in the direction of Frøken Caja: 'The older ones are over there.'

Frøken Caja went to a basin in the corner where six to eight dying codfish lay in the somewhat stagnant water. Frøken Caja studied them, and Hansen, who was wandering about with his hands in his pockets as if no one else was about, said: 'Well, that's all there is . . . . And we're out of fish mince.'

Hr. Hansen himself manufactured the fish mince from the dying specimens.

In a low voice Frøken Caja mentioned a price.

'Yes, you can have them,' said Hansen, who even over his shoulder was looking at the dead goods with contempt.

Frøken Caja, who did everything slowly, deliberating or recalculating the sums yet again, took out the coins from her purse as if every single one of them was tied to the bottom with a piece of string.

She returned to the street – to the lady who sold game, who stood big and broad with her white apron over her mighty chest, behind a marble counter, conversing with a customer about a masked ball in 'The Association.' She greeted Caja with a quick, compassionate nod – similar to the one she reserved for Madam Jørgensen, who rented her attic room in return for 'cleaning the shop' – and gestured lightly to the corner where four or five hens with very limp and much-handled necks lay on the marble counter. They looked as if they had been dead for three days.

Frøken Caja looked at the anaemic poultry; but they had only just had chicken for dinner – only just had chicken. Two deep furrows appeared in Frøken Caja's brow: varying the menu – that was the tricky part … . And incidentally, the word 'varying' was mostly superfluous, as pretty much every meal in the Canthian boarding house tasted the same – it left the same flat taste in the mouth.

She prodded the hens for a long time with the same expression on her face. Then she said in a muffled voice – she had placed a few coins, half-hidden, behind the hens, and nodded towards the shopkeeper – 'Well, then – the usual,' she said, walking past the other customer and up the steps to leave. Frøken Caja had a particularly shy and timid manner in shops.

The customer turned to look after her.

'Yes,' the shopkeeper said, 'they always come from the pension in the evening' (the shopkeeper pronounced the first syllable like the writing tool) 'and pick up what's left over. It's not what you'd want, but how else can you feed starving students, Fru Michelsen, for 60 kroner per month?'

Frøken Caja had concluded the boarding-house's shopping. On Kultorvet she stopped at a small florist. And with a sudden brusque tone as if she were offended, she said to the little woman behind the counter: 'Some snowdrops.'

She got them, and at the last minute added a bunch of violets. Then she returned home.

II

Fru Canth was walking up and down the sitting room in a state of excitement when Frøken Caja returned.

'Oh, Caja, guess who's here?' she said, her hands fluttering.

'Who?' Caja said impatiently, and stopped. She knew that her mother had a habit of inviting the world and his wife and then, when people arrived, acting surprised – to her – as if the visitors had turned up of their own accord.

'Grøntoft – would you believe it,' Fru Canth said.

'Grøntoft? Who? Which Grøntoft?' Caja said, still impatient, but with a sudden catch in her voice.

'Why Vilhelm Grøntoft, Caja, our Grøntoft … .'

'What does he want?' Caja asked; she had turned away.

'Why, he wants to stay here … . So there we were just going about our daily business when someone rings the bell and the Sundby sisters run to answer it, and I hear a voice asking for Fru and Frøken Canth … and the door is flung open – he hasn't changed a bit, I'm telling you – and there he is, imagine – of course, I recognised him immediately – with three big suitcases … and he says that his wife will be joining him.'

'Oh.' Caja opened the door to the passage and saw the suitcases. 'Well, they can't stay there blocking everyone's way,' she said in a quick, angry tone.

And Fru Canth said – to get it over with: 'Caja, the boys are out.'

But Frøken Caja was no longer listening. She had gone, closing the door behind her. She entered her room just as speedily. *There*, however, she sat in the darkness on the lid that covered the bath tub; she didn't seem to hear a couple of prolonged 'Frøken Cajas' echo through the house.

She took off her coat and picked up the comb and brush that lived on the windowsill. Then she put them down again and stopped in her tracks as she suddenly caught sight of the bride in the function room, the white bride, and the groom and the guests, sitting in the glow of the lights. She gazed – almost in wonder – at the two of them, and at the others, the guests, happy, along the table … .

Most days it was almost as if she saw nothing at all, but merely toiled and toiled. But today she *saw*: they were celebrating a wedding … she, the woman in white, was the bride.

Frøken Caja stayed where she was. She sensed that it was such a long time since she had last thought about other people. The couple were celebrating their wedding … she, the woman in white, was the bride.

She heard her name being called again, and she left quietly.

Eugenia had left the waste water bucket in the middle of the floor and was busy admiring herself in front of the boys' mirror – there wasn't a single looking glass in the house which didn't reflect Eugenia's slightly puffy physiognomy several times a day; she didn't even turn around. She thought it was Fru Canth making her journey from the kitchen.

Frøken Caja was holding the snowdrops in her hand, but hid them hastily on the sideboard in the corner on hearing Grøntoft's voice.

No, his voice hadn't changed. And then he came towards her.

'Oh, you're a funny one' – and he took both her hands and shook them with the same handshake as before, his particular handshake: 'I come here to visit you, and you fail to show … .'

He spoke in his confident, happy voice as if they had parted only yesterday.

All she said was: 'How tanned you are.'

'Yes – and better looking,' he laughed.

They entered the sitting room. Grøntoft talked and asked questions and laughed. Fru von Casse-Muckadell beamed: she would appear to know all about the ladies in Peru and thereabouts.

The Sundby sisters sat with their arms around each other's waists – a pose they favoured when there were guests. And Arnljot Oulie stayed in his corner, quiet, with his gentle, faraway smile.

Frøken Caja moved restlessly from chair to chair – with an expression similar to Arnljot's – and went in and out, tidying away a dirty glass, turning a chipped vase as if subconsciously trying to make everything look nicer.

Grøntoft was still talking: 'Remember that?'

'Remember that, Frøken Caja?' he called out after her every other minute through the doors. 'That winter when the Royal Theatre opened* – what fun we had sneaking about in the darkness on the second balcony … . Remember that, remember that, Frøken Caja?'

'Well, it was your treat … .'

Grøntoft sat astride his chair, completely lost in youthful memories.

'And do you remember – when we made a winter garden in my room and had a party … three old Christmas trees in pots in the corners.'

How Grøntoft laughed, seconded by the Sundby sisters.

Frøken Caja slowly smoothed the tablecloth – the clean tablecloth she had put out – with absent-minded hands.

'And Frøken Caja – when you put cognac in the duck ragout to give it flavour – and no one could eat it – remember that?' Again they all laughed. Fru Canth, however, said: 'Now, now, Grøntoft, you used to like strong flavours.'

Frøken Caja had gone. Because there was nothing for dinner, nothing to put on the table. Eugenia would have to go shopping. But Frøken Caja couldn't find her and forgot, as she walked through the rooms, that she was looking for her.

How he was laughing in there.

When someone came up behind her, Frøken Caja spun around as if startled. It was Arnljot Oulie, who turned his bright face towards her. 'Frøken,' he said in his soft language: 'Herr Grøntoft can have my room tonight until you sort things out tomorrow. I can sleep just as well on the sofa.'

Frøken Caja clasped his hand. 'Thank you, you're always so kind,' she said, as the tears suddenly welled up in her eyes.

Oulie's gaze too – he didn't know why – looked almost veiled, as he continued to stand there staring at Frøken Caja's figure moving about in the gloomy kitchen.

Eugenia flung open the door to the kitchen stairs. She had been dawdling on the landing, chatting to the fifth floor, a lady in red jersey, who traded in bed linen and rented out attic rooms. Oulie went back in; he didn't enjoy Frøken Caja's and Eugenia's exchanges.

Frøken Caja, however, said only that *this and that* needed buying. Eugenia's eyes widened as she stared at the purse. The money spilled out across the table.

Doors started opening and closing rapidly again. The third floor was already heading upstairs for supper.

'Doctor' Spørck was the first to arrive. 'Bless me,' he said when he saw the clean tablecloth, to Kattrup, who turned up for all meals in slippers, a habit from the rural vicarage where every family member celebrated mealtimes in embroidered footwear: 'Well, how about some clean sheets as well … .'

Sørensen, a theologian, found the least threadbare napkin. It was his daily ritual before the lodgers filled their bellies.

Eugenia had no idea what had got into Frøken Caja. 'Would you believe it?' she called out in passing to Tea on the first floor: 'She has loosened the purse strings.' She started running again. Eugenia had an inimitable way of shaking her petticoats which hinted at a complete absence of further undergarments.

Frøken Caja went in and out, setting the table. She closed the door to the sitting room; the gentleman from the third floor always made so many jokes about the table-setting.

Fru von Casse-Muckadell had abandoned her playing cards, and the Sundby sisters had gone down to tidy themselves up; they powdered their faces for mealtimes with a ball of cotton wool.

In the sitting room Grøntoft was alone with Fru Canth. He was holding both her hands. 'So how are you really?' he said.

'Ah well, ah well,' Fru Canth said, shaking her fine old head. 'You know what Caja is like. But I mustn't complain,' she said, gazing into his face with her big eyes.

In the dining room Spørck closed the door to the kitchen passage with a bang. He was starting to wonder if he would get any dinner at all.

Fru von Casse-Muckadell, who invariably grew very ceremonial just before mealtimes, waited majestically with a bottle of malt beer and her napkin in a silver ring. She took out her watch and said: 'It's nine o'clock.'

Frøken Caja, however, was still in the kitchen. 'She's cooking a hot meal,' Eugenia announced, as if this remarkable activity explained everything; she practically threw the urn on the table.

Fru von Casse installed herself. The Sundby sisters had to practically put their hands behind them in order to avoid touching Sparre, who finally turned up – with red and tired eyes. Fru von Casse shifted slightly in her chair, as if still bent over the cards. She wanted to have a word with Sparre and looked at him with playful eyes. 'So where have you been?' she asked him.

Grøntoft opened the door from the sitting room. 'But what's keeping Frøken Caja?' he wondered out loud. 'Right,' he then said, 'so this is where we'll be eating.'

'Well, my name is Grøntoft,' he added, bowing to the present company. 'But where is Frøken Caja?' he said again, and asked for directions to the kitchen. 'Frøken Caja,' he called out into the passage: 'Isn't it time to feed the animals?'

She was standing by the cooker, and turned around as if trying to hide the frying pan. 'Yes, it is,' she said.

Grøntoft looked around at the gloomy, squeezed-in kitchen, at the larder with the many small leftovers stored on saucers, and the butter dish where you always seemed to be scraping out the last little bits. 'It looks as if nothing has changed,' he said. And he lingered for a long time.

Frøken Caja said nothing. But an emotion seemed to cross her face – in front of the small, oil-saving lamp.

III

At long last everyone was ready to sit down for dinner – except that chaos ensued when Grøntoft insisted on sitting near the urn rather than at the head of the table. 'I insist on having my old seat,' he said, moving his plate himself. 'We used to always grab the best bites down at this end of the table.'

There was a certain amount of commotion around the table, and Frøken Caja – Arnljot Oulie had never seen her with such moist eyes – moved serving dishes and side plates quite feverishly. It was a fact that the rations diminished in size on the Canthian table once you approached the far end; in front of the Sundby sisters you would often find a plate with a very solitary object.

'There,' Grøntoft said. 'Now we're all settled.' Everyone had been seated. Frøken Caja picked up a small bowl from the sideboard. Grøntoft took it: 'Why, you have even made remoulade,' he said.

'Yes – but I'm not sure about it, I hope it meets with your approval … because …' Frøken Caja suddenly went scarlet, 'it's so long since I last made some … .'

'Excellent, excellent, brilliant,' said Grøntoft, who had already started eating. 'And then, when everyone has had their tea, we'll put an extra ration in the pot – as we always used to … .'

'How well you remember everything,' Caja said. Her voice sounded so quiet.

'Well,' said Grøntoft, placing the palms of his hands on the table; 'it was jolly nice at this end of the table in the old days.'

Up at the other end there was animated conversation.

Spørck and Sparre were being particularly medical, telling hospital stories – that was their speciality at mealtimes – which could make the hairs on the heads of old consultants stand on end. A young author of the modern school talked about the rape of children, so that the widowed Fru Hassing, who had two offspring of the female sex in a boarding house in Lyngby, trembled with outrage, and Fru von Casse, who appeared to be caressing Sparre incessantly with her eyes, stuck out her chin over her bottle of malt.

Kattrup talked to old Fru Canth about Darwin. Miscellaneous ideas, scandals and questions crossed the Canthian boarding house like the wind blowing dust across Frue Plads.* Fru Canth listened with wide and eager eyes. 'Yes, yes,' she said, 'I'm very fond of modern thinking – it seems to help me understand many more things about us humans.'

Grøntoft was sated now, and wanted some tea. He laughed at his and Frøken Caja's distorted images in the urn – as if reflected by a convex mirror. Frøken Caja, too, looked at her face while she poured his tea. 'Yes,' she said, 'that's what I look like.'

She sat for a moment. Fru Canth's voice – as light and fresh as that of a young girl – reached them, and Frøken Caja raised her head from the urn. 'But don't you think,' she said, 'that my mother is unchanged?'

'Yes,' Grøntoft looked in the same direction, 'unchanged.'

And, suddenly moved, he placed his hand on Frøken Caja's, which was resting on the edge of the tray – her fingers were so hard and coarse.

At that moment music could be heard from the function rooms. 'They're about to dance,' cried out the Sundby sisters.

'Now we'll have music,' Fru Canth said.

The Sundby sisters made numerous small, childish dance movements, as if they could barely stay still in their chairs. Downstairs they were now dancing so the whole house trembled.

'Do you know, Grøntoft, it brings life to the house,' Fru Canth called out down the table to him.

At once the conversation across the whole table turned to weddings. The Sundby sisters embraced the topic enthusiastically. The proximity of the function rooms seemed to give them permission to constantly inhabit the feverish atmosphere of a wedding. 'Though *I* wouldn't like to have my wedding on a Saturday,' Lissy declared.

'But why?' Spørck cut in, looking straight at her. The 'butterflies' had a habit of blurting out extremely odd statements that offered a remarkable insight into the foundation, so to speak, of their considerable innocence.

'But, God, Iss,' Emmy said, 'wouldn't it be lovely if the first day was a Sunday.'

Fru von Casse said: 'Oh – surely any day of the week will do,' and she sized up with knowing eyes the row of gentlemen, right down to Arnljot Oulie. The widowed Fru Hassing, however, would never in all eternity get married on a Friday.

At the Grøntoft end the conversation was quieter. He was speaking about his wife and child – with a soft and lingering voice, as if caressing them as he spoke. 'You should see her,' he said, 'so good and fine and no taller than' – he indicated his wife's height with his hand – 'so fine and petite,' he repeated, and smiled as if visualising her.

Frøken Caja said nothing, and the urn concealed her face.

Arnljot Oulie, who always looked mostly at Frøken Caja at the table, turned his bright face towards her and said: 'You really ought to eat something, Frøken.'

Absentmindedly, she took the dish he was offering her and put it down untouched. Then she suddenly looked up and said softly – with the same gaze as earlier in the kitchen: 'Thank you, Herr Oulie.'

Grøntoft continued talking about his home and his wife and his son.

Frøken Caja listened in silence with her hands in her lap. 'What's his name?' she suddenly asked, slowly and in a voice that came from far away.

'Georg,' Grøntoft said with a smile. And she echoed the name.

Around the table they were still on the subject of weddings. Fru Hassing talked about Tycho-Brahe days,* and Fru Canth said: 'Well, I think it's lovely to sit here thinking about all the happiness that seems to spread from that house to us.'

Frøken Emmy wanted to be wed in a village church.

Fru Hassing announced that she had her heart set on Taarbæk Chapel.

Fru Canth said: 'Perhaps we should get down?'

And they left the table while Fru Hassing said in a soft voice: 'Because there, birds fly under the roof.'

Grøntoft took Frøken Caja's hand and shook it. 'Yes, Frøken Caja,' he said, 'happiness does exist, but first you have to catch it and then never let it go.'

Frøken Caja's hand lay immobile in his.

'How cold your hands are,' he said, taking her other hand.

She just turned away. Sparre and Spørck played L'hombre.* Then they needed water brought in for a toddy. And perhaps the Captain had come back and might want something.

Grøntoft looked at Arnljot Oulie – he, too, followed the constantly busy Caja with his eyes – and said in a mild tone: 'I believe you're fond of Frøken Caja, Oulie.'

'Yes,' Oulie said in his soft mother tongue: 'because she's unhappy.' They both fell silent for a moment. Frøken Caja continued to walk in and out.

Then Arnljot Oulie asked Grøntoft if he could show him his room.

The Sundby sisters were looking out through the window. Downstairs the bride was being danced out of the ranks of single ladies.

IV

Downstairs the dancing continued to make the whole house shake.

The three college brothers had come back, and whenever a door was opened you could hear them arguing; they had been sent a basket of apples from the farm back home, which they had shared out equally and hidden in their respective drawers. And now the youngest boy's apples were gone.

In the sitting room the women, married as well as unmarried, wandered around with their needlework without settling.

'It's not properly warm,' Grøntoft said, joining Fru Canth.

'No, Caja, it's *never* properly warm here,' Fru Canth said.

'Over there we're used to heat,' Grøntoft said. 'It can get so hot that it's oppressive.'

He resumed telling them about South America – about the big rivers with rainforest along the banks from where the continent's native beasts of prey would stare with yellow eyes at the steamers. He talked about the silence in the mighty forests where the lianas hung like green nets and the sun would set with a glow as if it was at the bottom of the sea. He spoke of tropical nights with twinkling stars resting silently over the sea.

Fru von Casse-Muckadell had long since returned to her cards. The jungle held no interest for her.

Fru Canth, however, continued to ask questions. Suddenly she looked across to Frøken Caja, who was sitting on Oulie's old seat by the window, listening. 'Why, Caja, you're still awake,' she said.

In the evenings Frøken Caja tended to nod off in a corner.

'Well, it's easy to stay awake here,' Grøntoft said, and laughed. The door never stayed closed for more than ten minutes. Kattrup, who was sitting over by Spørck's L'hombre, got up to join them and sat down with his plump legs stretched out across the floor.

Then one of the college boys shouted for oil for a lamp. Frøken Caja had to get up and see to it. Grøntoft grew rather distracted by all this coming and going. 'What lively people,' he remarked.

'Yes,' Fru Canth replied, humming, 'but you get used to it.' She started wandering up and down, as was her wont. 'And it livens things up,' she said.

Fru Canth started walking in and out of her bedroom in order to hint that it might be time to call it a night. Downstairs they were dancing ever more happily, and they could hear their footsteps. On the third floor the door to the passage had been opened for air, and the noise from the card game travelled up through the house.

The Sundby sisters, who were watching from the dining room window, called into the sitting room: 'The bride is leaving.' Fru Hassing got up from her chair.

Fru Canth bumped into a figure by the window in her dark bedroom. 'Is that you?' she said. It was Caja. She was watching the bride drive off. 'Yes, Mother.'

She moved away from the window as if she had been caught stealing.

'And they've left,' the Sundby sisters exclaimed, quite out of breath. 'Oh, God, Fru Muckadell,' one of them said to Fru von Casse, who was finally ready to abandon her playing cards: 'See if the cards foretell happiness, please.'

'Why don't you sit down for a moment, Frøken Caja,' said Grøntoft, who had also entered the dining room to see the bride drive off, and was standing by the window.

'Oh, yes,' she replied and stopped. 'But Saturday nights are tricky.'

Grøntoft looked at her – the glow from the lamp fell across her face. How she had aged, and her face had turned stiff or hard as if it were made of wood. 'Oh,' he said, suddenly moved, 'I imagine they're all the same.'

Frøken Caja didn't answer him immediately. 'Yes,' she then said, as though she hadn't heard him until now: 'We have two floors now.'

They sat for a while. Then Frøken Caja said: 'It must be so beautiful.'

'Where?'

'Over there … where you live.'

'Yes,' he replied. 'But – what's the situation here?' he wanted to know. 'Do you have room for us?'

He really was serious. He had come to live here, he and his wife. Because they would be staying in Denmark for five months.

Frøken Caja said: 'Let's talk about it in the morning,' and got up.

Suddenly Grøntoft started to laugh. 'But, God, do you remember, Frøken Caja, that night we were at Casino and I persuaded you to go on the ice rink on Kongens Nytorv,* and you slipped and landed – right in the middle of the square – hard on that body part which we've been blessed to sit on.'

Frøken Caja laughed in short, dry gasps, as people who are not in the habit of laughing do: 'Ah, ha – and it hurt so much that I could barely sit down on the omnibus… .'

Fru Canth joined them. She had suddenly remembered her jumpers and wanted to know about the money.

Frøken Caja burst into spontaneous laughter once again. 'Of course, Mother,' she said, putting a few coins into the palm of her mother's hand, and carried on laughing.

'So she's still knitting jumpers?' Grøntoft asked.

'Yes.' And they both laughed.

'What are you laughing at? What are you laughing at?' Fru Canth demanded to know.

'At the old days,' Grøntoft said.

Caja's whole face seemed to light up. 'Yes, at the old days,' she laughed.

She was unaware that she was humming – in a small pure voice that surely couldn't live inside her wooden personality – as she walked down the stairs, passing the open doors which, as from a tavern, allowed noise and tobacco smoke to spill out into the passage, and entered the kitchen.

'Why hallo, Herr Oulie,' she said. Arnljot Oulie was sitting with his hands wrapped around his knees on the kitchen table, occupying the Sundby sisters' usual spot. 'What are you doing here?'

'I'm watching life go by,' he said, taking his eyes off the dancers.

'You should join in with it, Oulie,' Caja said cheerfully.

Arnljot Oulie sat for a while. '*I don't dare*,' he then said slowly, in a subdued voice.

Frøken Caja entered Oulie's room. Grøntoft's duffel bag was there – so handsome and fine. She looked at all his travelling clothes, the case with his sticks, the folded travelling blankets, and she smiled: he must be rich.

On the table next to the bed was a picture. She picked it up: it was her, his wife. She looked at her face, her figure, it was fine and delicate. She measured every line. She had no idea that she could still suffer like this.

She heard one of the L'hombre players run up the stairs, yelling her name. But she stayed where she was. Then Sparre shouted for her again, and she put the picture down – and like a shadow she walked past Arnljot, who was day-dreaming with his head resting on his knees.

She heard Sparre fling open the door upstairs. 'When is that water coming?' he shouted. And she walked up the stairs. She met the card player in the doorway and the man, who was hot from toddy and punch, shouted again, right into her face, as if yelling at a servant: 'When is that water coming?'

Frøken Caja went scarlet – she spotted Grøntoft in the middle of the room – and mortified, outraged and tormented, she snapped back in a shrill and embittered voice: 'When you ask for it nicely.' And she slammed the door to the passage shut as Sparre left.

Grøntoft was white with anger. 'In my day we weren't so rude,' he said to Fru Hassing, who sensed a row brewing and was standing, eagerly anticipating it, and shifting from foot to foot.

'Oh,' she responded in that uniquely concerned tone of voice in which malice shines through: 'But lodgers these days have so many places to choose from … . And then,' she added, looking knowingly at the door closing behind Caja, 'there's so much noise in this house. That also puts people off.'

Caja returned with water for the toddy. Grøntoft followed her with his eyes. And when she came back, he said: 'Surely that man will be told to leave?'

A grimace that was meant to be a smile crossed Caja's face. 'Why?' she said. She carried on walking: she wasn't thinking about Sparre any more. She had forgotten him already.

Grøntoft kept watching her as she moved around between all those strangers: putting a candle on the piano for Fru Casse, and a small lamp out for Fru Hassing. In the sitting room the lodgers sat scattered about; the author had arrived and was talking, still in his coat and with his hat in his hand, and Fru von Casse was dozing. It was as if they were waiting for a train at a railway station.

Finally they broke up and everyone got a candle or lamp. The Sundby sisters rushed downstairs ahead of the author.

'Good night then, Frøken Caja,' Grøntoft said.

'Good night.' He left.

Frøken Caja put the chairs back in their place, while Fru Canth prepared to go to bed. She lifted up her dress and hummed. Caja's eyes followed her.

Then she suddenly went up and flung her arms around her mother, and kissed her.

'Caja,' her mother snapped, and quickly freed herself: 'You're always so rough.'

Caja released her mother. For a moment she felt a dull pain, and it was as if all the tears she hadn't had time to weep were now surging in her chest.

Then she noticed Oulie, who was waiting in a corner, and quietly and automatically she started making up his bed on the sofa.

'Good night, Frøken,' he said.

She barely heard his voice. 'Good night.'

Then, as she passed the sideboard, she saw the flowers. She had meant to put them in his room. But now it was too late. He was bound to be asleep. It was too late.

She took the snowdrops and the violets and said: 'I'm just going to put the flowers by Mother's chair.' And quietly she placed them next to her mother's seat in the sitting room.

She went to her own room and made her bed mechanically with bedlinen from the pile in the corner. She opened drawers and closed them. She smiled once when she saw the jumpers. 'Oh, for so many years Mother has believed that … .' And they had all ended up as rags.

She heard Grøntoft: 'Do you remember – do you remember, Frøken Caja.' And his laughter, his merry laughter.

She lay in the darkness, but she didn't sleep. She could hear every sound in the house as she lay there. Doors were quietly opened and closed. She could tell from the knocking on the water pipes how the waiters were calling for the maids on the different floors.* Rapid footsteps on the back stairs while the door to the backyard rattled. There were fumblings in the many attic rooms.

Frøken Caja lay immobile in the darkness for a long time – then she sat up in the bed with her head in her hands. The last wedding guests were about to go home.

They were also awake in the third floor bathroom. 'Iss' had curled up by the window in her white linen. These eternal weddings were quietly making the Sundby sisters very hot indeed. And Frøken Lissy stared down into the bright room for a long time … . Then she tiptoed quietly over to Emmy, who was snoozing.

The L'hombre players were breaking up. Perched on the edge of his bed, Kattrup added up his winnings. There was enough money for three billiards games tomorrow, and coffee.

Grøntoft was still with the Captain, whom he had met on the stairs. Captain Jensen was a good friend of his older brother, and had invited him in for a grog. They talked about the past and the present. Their conversation also touched on the boarding house.

'Yes,' Grøntoft said, looking into the lamp. 'Frøken Caja was actually quite pretty once … . And she had such a good voice,' he said, still with his gaze on the lamp.

The Captain looked archly at the 'South American' for a long time. He thought he must be joking.

V

The Canthian boarding house was stirring. Eugenia was making her way through the dining room with several worn-down brooms. She made a great deal of noise – although Arnljot was still asleep on the sofa. Eugenia wasn't created to be very considerate in the morning.

She left all the doors open and opened the sitting-room windows. Arnljot Oulie got up from the sofa and wandered, homeless, in the draught, while Eugenia spilt coke over all the floors as she struggled with the cold stove.

Frøken Caja was in the kitchen, battling with the urn which was billowing smoke.

No one spoke.

Eugenia pulled the bedlinen off the sofa and onto the floor and fell asleep, standing there, until a sudden 'Eugenia,' cut through the air, as Frøken Caja brought in the urn.

Fru Hassing arrived and opened the door to the hall; she was going out for a walk. She was wearing a grey dressing gown and a Charlotte Corday cap whose volume hid the preparations for today's hairstyle.*

She began putting on her outdoor clothes while asking Arnljot Oulie in an exceedingly amicable voice how he had slept. 'One's head ends up a little high,' she said in the same cheerful tone: 'but then again, you're so accommodating.'

Perhaps she had expected a word from Frøken Caja, but none came; Caja just walked quietly in and out.

Suddenly the author, Herr Feddersen, arrived, dressed to the nines with a walking stick with a silver knob. He needed a button reattached to his glove.

'Oh God, Herr Feddersen, are *you* up?' said Fru Hassing, launching immediately into some bizarre movements like those of an elderly hen that senses the rooster is about to crow. Herr Feddersen muttered something about having to consider his health.

It was very odd, but at irregular intervals – every week or two – Herr Feddersen would rise for a morning walk before anyone else in the boarding house had even stirred.

Once the button had been successfully reattached, Fru Hassing followed his path across the street, concealed behind a curtain. She thought so: he was going to Ørsteds Park.*

The third floor was becoming lively. Heads popped out of doors, people called for water – there tended to be a considerable water shortage in the Canthian boarding house, as if water was sold by the pound. In the midst of the commotion Kattrup lay, fat and happy, in his bed with the door wide open.

Spørck needed soap and extended a long, bare arm out through a gap in the door.

Fru von Casse and the Sundby sisters had arrived for tea. All had wraps or scarves tied around their necks.

Frøken Caja poured and served. She looked like a shadow as she walked from one place to the next in the dim light by the sideboard, while Fru von Casse proclaimed once more that she had to have draught-excluders on her windows. She had felt the draught right under her duvet.

'Yes,' was all Caja said from the gloom.

The door to the bedroom opened. It was Fru Canth. She was always so lively, like a bird flying the nest. She would talk and chat and would always have had a dream – the most incredible things.

'I dreamt about eggs,' Lissy said.

Emmy had dreamt that she was picking roses on her parents' grave.

'Caja,' Fru Canth said: 'You're forgetting everything.' Fru von Casse was waiting for her second cup of tea.

'Yes, Mother,' Caja said, and brought it.

The Sundby sisters continued to discuss their dreams.

There was a very loud shout from a door on the third floor, and Frøken Caja went downstairs. The kitchen was full of buckets of dirty water and old footwear. Eugenia kept worn-down brooms in a corner. The door to Spørck's rather bare room was open.

Frøken Caja saw it all. It was just like her, a picture of her toil.

Sparre shouted again. This time it was about his boots. And Frøken Caja went to fetch them.

Kattrup appeared in his undergarments to brush his black clothes in the kitchen. He didn't even notice her. The third floor mostly treated Frøken Caja as if she were a non-person.

Frøken Caja came and went. She opened windows, she tidied up a room. Then she heard Grøntoft's door open, and he came down the corridor. She was in Kattrup's room and hastened to close the door. But he had spotted her and entered. 'Good morning, Frøken Caja,' he said, clasping her cold, raw hands.

'Good morning.'

He looked about him: the bed had yet to be made, many torn books lay on the pine table, the jute curtains were flapping their pelmets in the draught. 'Proper student digs,' Grøntoft said.

'Yes,' Caja replied. And spontaneously she uttered her sole thought, the final decision she had reached while walking about in the dawn light among all the lodgers. She said in an urgent voice: 'Don't stay here. This isn't for you. You should live – better … .'

Grøntoft said, but without conviction – because the same thought had indeed crossed his mind last night and again this morning – his wife couldn't live *here*: 'Isn't this a good place to live?'

Frøken Caja said: 'Oh, no – we've had to … lower our standards … the competition is so strong. This isn't a place,' she said, turning away, 'for travellers.'

Grøntoft made no reply, he only asked where in that case he should go. She gave him the address and prices and said: 'You should go there once you've had your breakfast.'

She lingered for a moment after he had gone. It was as if all her thoughts stopped and there was silence, the blood in her heart was stilled.

Then she went upstairs.

Grøntoft was sitting with old Fru Canth, who was still eating and chatting. Fru Hassing had returned from her walk, and the Sundby sisters and Fru von Casse formed a circle around her by the window. Rather flushed, the widow described her observations: 'It was obviously a date – and with a *new* one,' she said. 'A small, nimble thing – in a red hat … One can tell by the way he rushes off in the morning – and it's always to Ørsteds Park.'

'Hm,' Fru von Casse said, and smiled for a long time, 'it *starts* in the morning.'

The Sundby sisters were puce with indignation, and carried on asking questions. The four ladies huddled even more closely. From time to time you could catch the odd word.

'She's an actress,' Fru Hassing would bet her life on *that*.

Grøntoft had moved away from Fru Canth. He was looking towards the ladies, gossiping with their heads close together. Over at the table the College boys were arguing. It never grew truly light– from the one window – and every face looked grey.

Fru Canth sat alone at the end of the table with her fine old face turned to the light, animated and free as if she drew life from all the commotion.

Frøken Caja brought Fru Hassing her boiled milk.

Grøntoft had gone.

He had stood up as if shaking off a burden, and then had taken her hand. 'Well, I'll be off then,' he said, 'as there's no room here.'

Frøken Caja had merely smiled. She could find no words. Silently she went down to Arnljot's room and slowly started packing Grøntoft's belongings, piece by piece. She closed the duffel bag and set it aside.

Arnljot entered. 'It's only me, Frøken,' he said.

Frøken Caja began to shake her head and made to leave. Suddenly Arnljot clasped her hands as if he could feel everything she was suffering. 'Oh, Frøken,' he said, almost with tears in his voice.

Caja stopped, and a glimpse of light crossed her face as she leaned against Arnljot's shoulder for less than a second. 'Oulie,' she said, 'if only you could be happy.'

She let him go. Her voice had sounded as gentle as a caress … .

Frøken Caja had gone. Arnljot stood by the window. As he looked across the houses and the people, the day out there seemed grey and heavy.

Frøken Caja went upstairs. Loud chatter could be heard from the first floor landing. The Sundby sisters were getting ready for church.

Upstairs, Fru von Casse-Muckadell could be heard having words with Eugenia. When Fru von Casse-Muckadell spoke to her inferiors, one could still tell from the tone of her voice that – through three marriages – she had married her way up from milkmaid to the nobility.

The church bells started to ring. Both pavements were packed: they ran *here* and they ran *there*. Some people were carrying hymn books in their hands.

Suddenly tears burst from Arnljot Oulie's eyes, and overcome by a deep, indescribable pain, he wept – wept on the threshold of life.

Translated by Charlotte Barslund

10. Les Quatre Diables

I

The stage manager's bell sounded. Slowly the audience returned to its seats,* whilst the trampling in the gallery, the chattering in the stalls, the shouts of the boys selling oranges drowned out the music – and at last even the languid occupants of the boxes settled down to wait.

The next number was 'Les quatre diables'. That was apparent from the outstretched safety net.

Fritz and Adolph ran out of the dressing rooms along the artistes' passage; calling out, with their grey cloaks flapping around their legs, they ran along the passage and knocked on Aimée and Louise's door.

The two sisters were waiting, feverish as well, in their long white silken capes, which shrouded them completely – whilst the dresser, with her poke bonnet all crooked, screeched continuously, running around in a flurry with powder, arm make-up and crushed resin for their hands.

'Come on,' shouted Adolphe. 'It's time.'

But they carried on running around one another a moment longer, aimlessly, gripped by the fever which overcomes all artistes when they feel their legs sheathed in tights. The dresser shouted loudest.

It was only Aimée who calmly stretched her arms out of the long sleeves towards Fritz. And hurriedly, without looking at her or saying anything, he brushed a powder puff mechanically up and down the outstretched arms, as he usually did.

'Come on,' shouted Adolphe again.

They all went out, holding hands, and waited. They stood ready by the entrance and heard the first strains of 'The Waltz of Love',* the music for their act.

Fritz and Adolphe dropped their cloaks to the ground, so that they stood there gleaming in their rose-pink costumes, a rose so pale that it was almost white. You could see every muscle; their bodies appeared as if naked.

The music played on.

In the stables all was empty and quiet. A couple of grooms were inspecting the collection boxes in a leisurely fashion, lifting the heavy copper coins suspiciously.

The opening bars rang out, and 'The Four Devils' entered the ring. They could hear the applause only as a muffled roaring, and could not make out any faces. It was as if every fibre in their bodies was already vibrating with tension.

Then Adolphe and Fritz quickly loosened Louise and Aimée's wide capes, which dropped to the sand, and the sisters stood there in the fire of a hundred pairs of opera-glasses, naked but for their black costumes – like two black girls with white faces.

They all swung themselves up to the net, and then climbed further, one white, one black, one white, one black, like four eager animals, with all the opera-glasses trained on them.

They reached the trapezes and began to work. They seemed to fly naked between the jingling swings with their shiny brass bars. They embraced one another, they caught one another, they encouraged one another with shouts; it was as if those white and black bodies were linking together and releasing, linking together and releasing, full of love in an arousing nakedness. And all the while the waltz of love played on with its sleepy, languorous rhythm, and the women's trailing hair, as they flew through the air, fell undulating around their exposed blackness – like a satin cape.

They never paused. Now they were working at two levels, Adolphe and Louise higher up.

The applause rose up towards them like a confused murmur, whilst the artistes in their box (where the dresser was always at the front, heated, her rose-festooned poke bonnet still crooked, leading the clapping with her bare, slapping hands) followed 'the Devils' with their opera-glasses, studying the finer points of their costumes, whose daring was famous in the artistes' world.

'Oui, oui, their hips are naked …'

'The refinement is that you can see their thighs,' several people in the artistes' box shouted.

The plump first rider from 'The Sixteenth-Century Tournament', Mademoiselle Rosa, lowered her opera-glasses dejectedly.*

'No, she's not wearing a corset,' she said, sweating in her own restrictive armour-plating.

They went on working. The electric light changed to blue and yellow as they flew through the air. Fritz yelled; hanging by the legs, he caught Aimée in his arms. Then they rested, sitting side by side on the same trapeze.

Above them they could hear Louise's and Adolphe's shouts. Her breast heaving, Aimée drew attention to Louise's work: 'Voyez donc, voyez,' she called.*

Louise was caught by Adolphe's legs.

But Fritz made no reply. Mechanically drying his hands on the little cloth which was hanging there, he was staring down towards the barrier in front of the boxes, which stretched out beneath them, lit up and full of life like the rippling edge of a brightly-coloured flowerbed. And suddenly Aimée too was silent, staring in the same direction, until Fritz said, as if tearing himself away: 'We're on,' and she seemed to wake with a start.

They dried their hands on the cloth once more, and then launched themselves outwards until they hung by their arms, as if to test the strength of their muscles. Then they began swinging again. They measured the distance between the trapezes as if their souls were in their eyes.

At the same moment they both yelled: 'Du courage!'* – and Fritz flew off backwards towards the furthest trapeze, whilst Louise and Adolphe from above uttered a long-drawn-out cry, as if encouraging an animal.

Their big number began. They both launched themselves backwards with hoarse cries, flew past each other, grabbed the bar. They did it again, with renewed cries. And from above, from the rotunda, whilst Louise and Adolphe spun like two unstoppable wheels on their swings, there fell suddenly a rain of glittering gold like a golden cloud of dust, sinking slowly and brilliantly through the white glare of the electric lamps.

For a moment it looked as though the devils were flying through a gleaming shoal of gold, as the dust slowly sank down, spotting their nakedness with a thousand sparkling spangles.

And all at once they dropped, one by one, headlong through the gleaming shower and down into the safety net – and the music ceased.

They had to take their bows again and again.

Dazed, they supported one another, as if they felt suddenly dizzy. They went out and came in again. Finally the applause died down.

Groaning, they ran to the dressing rooms, and Adolphe and Fritz threw themselves down onto a mattress on the floor, at full length, wrapped in blankets. They lay there for a while, barely conscious. Then they stood up and got changed.

Adolphe looked through his mirror at Fritz, who was dressed in an equerry's outfit: 'Are you going to give a hand?' he asked.

And Fritz said sullenly: 'The manager asked me to.' He went over to the others who were acting as equerries at the entrance, and who, like him, were dead tired and stealthily taking turns to lean their exhausted bodies against the walls for a moment.

After the performance, the troupe gathered in the restaurant. The 'Devils' sat at the same table, silent like the others. At a couple of tables they were starting to play cards – still without speaking. All you could hear was the sound of the money being pushed across the table.

The two waiters stood in front of the buffet, waiting, watching all the silent people apathetically. Sluggish, with their legs stretched out in front of them and their arms hanging down slackly, as if they were dislocated, the artistes sat along the wall.

The waiters began to turn down the gas.

Adolphe shoved some money over beside one of the beer tankards and got up. 'Come on,' he said. 'Time to go.' And the three others followed.

The streets were already deserted. They could hear no other sound than their own footsteps, as they walked home two by two, just as they worked. They reached their house and parted in the dark passage on the first floor with a muted 'Good night'.

Aimée remained standing on the landing in the darkness until Fritz and Adolphe had reached the second floor and their door had closed.

The two sisters went in and began undressing without a word. But after she'd got into bed, Louise began to chatter about the other acts, about who had been in the boxes, about the regular patrons; she knew all the faces.

Aimée was still sitting on the edge of her bed, half undressed, not moving. Louise's conversation became more intermittent. Finally she fell asleep.

But after a while she woke up again and sat up in bed. Aimée was still sitting in the same spot. 'Aren't you coming to bed?' asked Louise.

Hastily Aimée switched off the light. 'Yes, I am now,' she said, getting up.

But once in bed she couldn't sleep. She thought about only *one* thing: that Fritz never met her eyes any more whilst he was powdering her arms … .

Upstairs, Fritz and Adolphe were in bed. But Fritz was tossing on his bed as if in agony: *Was* it him, and what was it she wanted, that woman in the box? Did she *want* him? Why would she otherwise be looking at him all the time? Why would she otherwise be brushing past him so closely? *Was* it him?

He had no other thought than that woman. No other from morning till night. Only her. He circled around the same question like an animal in its cage: did she really *want* to, that woman in the box? And he was continually aware of the perfume from her clothes, as she came down and walked past him. Always close past *him*, when he was standing there as an equerry.

But *was* it him then? And what was it she wanted?

He tossed and turned in torment, and again and again he said out into the darkness, as if the words fascinated him: '*Femme du monde*,'* again and again, under his breath.

And all the questions began over again: what if it was him, what if it was him?

... Aimée had got out of bed again. Silently she crept across the floor. In the darkness her fingers searched in the drawer for her rosary, and found it ....

In the house all was still.

II

'The Devils' had been practising.

Adolphe got angry in the dressing room because Fritz, as he saw it, was breaking their contract with his constant work as an equerry, even though 'the Devils' were excused.

But Fritz made no answer. Every evening he put on the equerry's costume and stationed himself by the entrance to the boxes and waited for 'the lady from the box' to come down the stairs on her husband's arm and walk past him – she often visited the stables now during the last act – and then he followed them.

She spoke with the stable lads, she patted the horses, she read aloud the names which were nailed up over the stalls. Fritz followed.

She didn't speak to him. But she was doing everything *for* him, he *knew* that; and by means of a thousand small movements – by the straightening of a back, the extending of an arm, the flash of a glance they both displayed themselves secretly for the other, and each of them as it were examined the other, although they were continually at a distance – the same distance, as they hesitated and yet were bound together, as if their shared desire had imprisoned them in a strange double snare, which had trapped them both.

Fritz followed.

She laughed, she walked to and fro, she caressed the dogs.

Fritz simply followed. She led and he followed.

He did not seem to be looking at her. But his eyes dwelt on the hem of her dress or on her outstretched hand, with the stare of a wild animal which is being tamed, a stare which wonders and hates and feels itself to be powerless, all at the same time.

One evening she came up to him. He looked up, and she said: 'Are you frightened of me?'

He was silent for a moment. Then: 'I don't know,' he answered, in a low, harsh voice.

And she found nothing more to say, confused and almost afraid (a fear which made her suddenly serious) of the gaze charged with desire which she felt focussed on her feet.

She turned and walked away, with a little laugh which sounded irritating in her own ears.

The next evening Fritz did not dress as an equerry. He had said to himself that he would avoid her, he had vowed not to see her. He shared that special fear common to all artistes of women as a destructive force. He regarded them as mystical enemies who lay in wait, born to covet his strength. And on the rare occasions that he surrendered – suddenly, gripped by an irresistible instinct – it was with a kind of desperation, with a vindictive hatred of the woman who, he felt, was stealing a part of his body, his precious working tool, the very stuff of his existence.

And he was doubly afraid of this lady from the box. The very thought of her tortured his slow mind, which was not used to thinking. And with a suspicious fear he spied on every movement by this stranger from another race, as if she wished him some secret harm, something he knew he could not escape.

He didn't want to see her any more – no, he didn't want to see her.

It was easy to keep his vow, because she did not appear. For two days, for three – she did not come. The fourth evening Fritz appeared as an equerry again. But she did not come. Not that evening. Not the next.

The whole day long he thought fearfully about 'when she comes'; and in the evenings he felt a dull anger, a brutal but silent rage because she did not come.

So, she had been making a fool of him. So, she had only been mocking him. She, *that vixen,* she. But he would take his revenge, he would find her … . And he saw himself thrashing her, trampling her underfoot, hurting her, so that she bent double, so that she curled up, so that she was half-dead from the attack.

He lay there at night for hours in silent fury. And his desire grew with desperate greed during his first sleepless nights.

Then on the ninth day she came.

From the trapeze he saw her face – it was as if he could see with a different sense than purely with his eyes – and with a sudden leap, as if with a boy's glee, he hurled his slim, beautiful body into the air, hanging by his outstretched arms.

His whole face shone with a brilliant smile, as he swung himself up once more. He spoke to Aimée, he rocked his blond head slowly to the rhythm of the waltz; and he grasped Aimée's hand as he had not done for many days.

'Enfin – du courage,' he called out.*

It sounded like a cry of triumph.

And later, when he entered the stables in his equerry's costume and saw her, he was again mute and hostile, watching her hatefully with the same glance which did not dare to look directly into her eyes.

But after the performance, in the restaurant, he suddenly became merry again – almost wild. He laughed and performed tricks. He played with cups and tankards, and balanced his silk hat on its edge on the end of his stick.

The other artistes joined in the fun. Tom the clown fetched his concertina and played, straddling the chairs with his long legs.

There was a terrific hubbub. Everyone did tricks. Mr. Fillis balanced a huge cone on his nose, and two or three clowns cackled as if they were in the middle of a chicken run.

But Fritz shouted loudest of all, standing on a table, juggling with two glass globes which he had unscrewed from the hanging lights; his pale face shining, he yelled into the furore: 'Adolphe, tiens.'*

Adolphe, standing on the next table, caught the globe.

The artistes were clambering up and down, some on tables, some on chairs. The clowns cackled, the concertina twisted.

'Fritz, tiens.' The globes flew through the air again, over the heads of the clowns. Fritz caught one and turned suddenly: 'Aimée, tiens.'

He tossed it towards her, and Aimée stood up. But she was too late, and the globe fell and was smashed.

Fritz laughed, looking at the splintered glass from his table. 'That means good luck,' he said, and laughed; suddenly he stood still and smiled up into the light of the lamps.

Aimée had turned back. Pale, she sat down again by the wall.

The hubbub continued. It was nearly midnight. The waiters turned down the gas. But the artistes did not stop; they just turned up the volume in the gloom. From all parts of the room you could hear a deafening cackling and crowing; on the table under the lamps Fritz was walking on his hands.

He was the last to leave – he was as riotous as if he was drunk.

They all wandered down the alley in a crowd. Once in the artistes' quarter they went their separate ways. There were many strange noises in the darkness as they made their farewells.

Then finally it was quiet, and the Four Devils walked on, silent and side by side as usual. No more was said. But Fritz could not keep still. He twirled his best hat around once more on the end of his stick.

They reached the house, and said goodnight.

Once in their room, Fritz opened two windows wide and began to whistle loudly out into the street.

'You're mad,' said Adolphe. 'What the devil is the matter with you?'

Fritz just laughed. '*Il fait si beau temps*,'* was all he said, and he carried on whistling.

Down below Aimée had also opened the window. Louise, who was getting undressed, called to her to close it, but Aimée just stood there, staring out into the narrow street.

For so long she had not understood – not why his eyes had become so empty when he looked at her, not why his voice had seemed to become tired when he spoke to her, not why his ears were half closed when *she* spoke. It was as if they weren't together any more, even when they were sitting close … .

And he didn't powder her arms any more.

That was yesterday. He had come in, hurried and impatient as he did these days. And she stretched out her arms towards him, and he just stared at them, unthinking, not registering. 'Powder yourself then,' he said crossly and went off. And slowly, without understanding, she powdered one arm, then the other.

Oh no, oh no – she had never known that it was possible to suffer like this.

Aimée leaned her head on the window frame, and tears began to run down her cheeks. Now she knew it all. Now she understood … .

Suddenly she raised her head again; all at once she could hear Fritz, who had begun to hum loudly. It was 'The Waltz of Love'.

Louder and louder he hummed; now he was singing. How gladly he was singing, how happily. Every note hurt her, and yet she stayed there; it was as if this song brought back everything, their whole lives.

How well she remembered – how well, from the very first day … .

Louise called to her again, and she shut the window mechanically. But she did not go to bed, merely sat down silently in the corner in the dark.

How well she remembered – everything.

III

How clearly Aimée could still see them as they arrived that first day, Fritz and Adolphe – when they were to be 'taken on' by 'Father' Cecchi.

It was in the morning, and Aimée and Louise were still in bed.

And the boys had been standing in the corner, their heads hanging – they were wearing striped sailor's trousers in the middle of winter, and Fritz had a straw hat. They were undressed, and Father Cecchi felt them and twisted their legs and tapped their chests until they cried, whilst the old woman who had brought them just stood there with her mouth twitching, a still, shrunken figure – only the black flowers on her hat trembled a little. She didn't ask about anything. She just looked at the boys, following them with her eyes – as they were terrorized, naked, under Cecchi's hands … .

Aimée and Louise were also watching from their bed. Father Cecchi carried on feeling them and cursing, and the boys' fearful eyes pleaded for their lives.

Then they were taken on.

The old woman said nothing, didn't touch the boys, didn't say goodbye. It was as if the whole time, while the flowers in her hat trembled, she had been looking for something – something she didn't find. And she went out of the door in the same way, slowly, uncertainly, and it closed behind her.

Fritz screamed – just once, a long child's scream, as if he had been stabbed … .

Then both of them, he and Adolphe, went back to their corner and sat down with their chins on their knees and their clenched fists braced on the ground – silent, both of them.

Father Cecchi ordered them into the kitchen to peel potatoes. Aimée and Louise were hustled in after them. They sat silent around the bucket, all four of them.

Louise asked: 'Where do you come from?'

But the boys didn't answer. They just pinched their lips together and looked down.

After a while, Aimée whispered: 'What about your mother?'

But they still didn't answer, just sat there with their breasts heaving, as if they were sobbing inside. And all you could hear was the sound of the potatoes plopping into the water as they were peeled.

'Is she dead?' whispered Louise then.

But the boys still did not answer, and the two girls just looked silently from one to the other; then suddenly Aimée began to cry quietly, and after her Louise.

The next day the boys began to 'work'. They learned the Chinese Dance and the Peasant Dance. After three weeks all four of them began to perform.

When they were going to dance they stood in the wings in pairs, Aimée with Fritz and Louise with Adolphe; with staring eyes and moistening their lips with their tongues in fear, they listened to the music of the orchestra.

'Pull your shirt down,' said Aimée, who was so feverish she could hardly stand still herself, and she pulled at Fritz's shirt, which was crooked.

'*Commencez*,'* came from Father Cecchi in the other wings. The curtain had gone up; it was their entrance.

They didn't see the footlights, they didn't see the audience. With terrified smiles they went through their prescribed steps, counting the beats and moving their lips, their eyes fixed stiffly on Cecchi, who was stamping his feet over in the wings.

'To the left,' whispered Aimée to Fritz, who could never remember; she was sweating in fear for both of them, and had to remember for both of them.

As a group they resembled the wax figures which dance on top of barrel organs.

The audience clapped and called them back on stage. Oranges were thrown onto the stage. They picked them up, smiling in gratitude; they had to surrender them to Cecchi, who enjoyed them at night, when he was playing cards with Watson the agent, with his cognac and water. Father Cecchi played all night long with the agent, back home in their lodgings.

The children woke up when they quarrelled and watched them wide-eyed from their beds, before they fell asleep again, dead tired.

Time passed.

The 'Cecchi troupe' became attached to the circus, and all four had to learn all the acts. They began rehearsals at half-past eight. Teeth chattering, they got changed and started work in the half-light of the circus. Louise and Aimée walked the tightrope, balancing with two flags, whilst Father Cecchi instructed them, sitting astride the barrier.

Then the horse was brought out, and Fritz was to leap onto its back.

Father Cecchi issued orders, armed with a long whip. Fritz jumped and jumped. He couldn't do it. He fell against the barrier. He fell against the horse. The whip curled out and struck his legs, leaving long stripes.

Father Cecchi carried on instructing. Battling with his tears, the boy jumped and jumped. Once again he couldn't get up, but fell. The old sores on his body were opened up and bled so that there were bloodstains on his old tights.

Father Cecchi just shouted again: '*Encore – encore*.'

Breathless, half sobbing between breaths, Fritz jumped, his face twisted in pain.

The whip struck him, and he said desperately: 'I can't'; but he had to carry on.

The horse got a double flick of the whip and galloped faster with the sobbing boy, whose limbs were trembling with pain. 'I can't,' he shouted in torment.

The artistes were watching mutely from the stalls and the boxes.

'*Encore*,' called Cecchi; Fritz leapt again.

Pale, her lips white, hidden in the corner of a box, Aimée watched him, frightened and full of bitterness.

But Father Cecchi did not stop. It went on for an hour, an hour and a quarter. Fritz's body was just one continual sore. He fell again, fell again, kicked the sand in pain, fell again.

No, it would not work. And he was dismissed with an oath.

Aimée ran out of the box; moaning in pain, Fritz hid himself like an animal behind a stack of hoops. Breathlessly, his fists clenched, he uttered scraps of imprecations, a stream of words from the gutter, stable-boys' curses in all languages – in impotent rage.

Aimée sat next to him, silent. Her white lips were trembling. For a long time they sat in the dark behind the hoops. Fritz's head fell against the wall and he slept in painful exhaustion, whilst Aimée sat there white-faced and motionless, as if she were watching over his sleep.

The years passed. They were grown up.

Father Cecchi was dead. He had been kicked to death by a horse.

But they stayed together. Things went up and down. They performed at large venues and did not refuse the small ones.

How clearly Aimée could see that whitewashed provincial Pantheon where they performed that winter.* It was so icy cold. Before the performance two coal braziers were carried in, and the whole circus filled with smoke, so that you could hardly breathe.

Out in the stables the artistes stretched out their bare arms over a pot of coals, blue with cold, and the clowns jumped up and down on the bare earth in their canvas shoes, trying to keep warm.

The Cecchi troupe covered all specialities. They danced, and Fritz was Aimée's partner. Aimée did acrobatics on horseback, and Fritz was the groom who tightened the girths.

The troupe toiled; they made up half the programme. But it was not enough. Week after week one of the horses disappeared from the stables to provide food for the others. Those artistes who had money left the circus, and those who had to stay went hungry – until finally it was all over, and they had to close.

Horses, costumes, everything was taken. The officers of the law had arrived, and cleaned the place out … .

It was the evening of the day when it had all happened. The few artistes who were still around were sitting in the dark arena, mute and wretched. They could not leave. They had nowhere to go. In the stables next to a food trough the director was sitting in front of the empty stalls and crying, as he muttered polyglot oaths over and over again.

It was completely silent, completely dead. Only the dogs – the authorities had forgotten them – lay mournfully, with watchful eyes, on a pile of scattered straw.

The Cecchi troupe went into the restaurant. All was deserted. The manager had closed his buffet and packed away his glasses. Dusty tables and chairs were strewn around.

The four sat silently in a corner. They had come from the post office. It was their daily trip. They collected letters from agents – rejection after rejection. It was Fritz who opened them. The others daren't even ask.

He opened letter after letter and read slowly, almost suspiciously – and then put each letter down. The others looked at him, silent and dispirited. Then he said: 'Nothing.'

And they sat still once more in front of the miserable letters, which had brought nothing.

Then Fritz said: 'This won't do. We'll have to have a speciality.'

Adolphe shrugged: 'There are enough people doing everything,' he said scornfully. 'Say something new.'

'You can make money with trapeze acts,' said Fritz in a low voice.

The others were silent, and Fritz said again: 'We could work up under the dome.'

It was silent again, and then Adolphe said almost angrily: 'I suppose *you've* insured life and limb?'

Fritz made no answer. It was warmer now, and all was perfectly silent for a moment.

'We could always split up,' said Adolphe hoarsely and almost inaudibly.

They had all had the same thought and been afraid of thinking it. Now it had been said, and Adolphe added, looking straight ahead in the dark and deserted shelter: 'We can't keep on starving together, can we?' He spoke in a tone of suppressed anger, like people do when the cupboard is bare; but Fritz remained silent and motionless, staring at the floor.

They got up and went out in silence. In all the passages it was cold and dark.

As they were walking along close together, Aimée said in a voice so soft that Fritz could hardly make it out: 'Fritz, I'll learn the trapeze.'

Fritz stopped. 'I knew it,' he said, taking her hand.

Louise and Adolphe said nothing.

They decided to stay there, in town. Fritz pawned the last of their rings. Adolphe just carried on writing to agents. But Fritz and Aimée were working.

They had hung up their trapezes in the Pantheon, and they began to practise every day. They transferred some of their floor acrobatics to the trapeze, and for hours at a time, dripping with sweat, they tortured their bodies. Fritz's commands rang out as the minutes passed. Afterwards they rested side by side on the same trapeze, with exhausted smiles.

They began to get used to the work, and started on the Hanlon Volta jumps.* They attempted to jump between the swings, and fell headfirst into the safety net.

But they carried on, with encouraging shouts: '*En avant*.'

'*Ça va*.'*

Fritz succeeded, Aimée fell.

They carried on.

Their souls were in their eyes, they tensed their muscles like springs; their voices sounded like muffled battle cries: they succeeded.

Each followed the other with their eyes, enthralled, in a fever: '*En avant – du courage.*'

Aimée had done it; her muscles trembled as she hung from the furthest trapeze. She tried again, and did it again. They felt suddenly joyful. It was as if they were drunk on the strength of their own bodies. They flew past each other, and then rested again, dripping with sweat, smiling – hand in hand.

Full of joy, they praised each other's bodies, caressed the muscles which bore them up, looking at each other with sparkling eyes. '*Ça va, ça va*,' they shouted, laughing.

They began to make the jumps more difficult. They worked out new tricks. They practised and calculated. They were absorbed by the acrobatics with the eagerness of inventors, discussing them, planning new variations. Fritz didn't sleep any more; the thought of the work kept him awake at nights.

In the morning, before daybreak, he would wake Aimée, knocking on her door. And waiting outside whilst she got dressed, he was already outlining his plans, explaining things to her – shouting loudly, whilst she answered, as keen as he was, filling the house with her happy voice.

Louise sat up in bed, rubbing her eyes. She had started to come to the rehearsals. She was carried away by the speed of their work; she called to them and applauded them. They answered her from above; the arena echoed, full of their joyous voices.

Only Adolphe sat silently in a corner by the stables.

He had come in one day and sat down to watch. No-one spoke to him.

The practice was finished; they had no energy left, and fell heavily down into the safety net.

Fritz leapt to the ground and carefully lifted Aimée out of the net; happy, he held her for a moment in his outstretched arms, like a child.

They got changed and went over to a small café to eat. They began to talk about the future, about where they could find an engagement, about the wages they could earn, about the name they would use – about the success which awaited them.

That quiet pair became talkative, they laughed, they were building the future. Fritz was constantly working out new routines. 'If only we dared,' he would say, burning with eagerness, 'if only we dared.'

And Aimée answered, gazing at him: 'Why not? If that's what you want.'

Something in her voice moved Fritz. 'You are courageous,' he said all at once, looking at her; her eyes were blazing at him. And they both sat there leaning their heads against the wall, dreaming, staring into the distance for a long time.

One day they made their first attempt at the final jump – the one they were agreed would be their particular speciality. They succeeded, flying backwards to grasp the trapezes.

They heard a shout from below. It was Adolphe. With his face turned upwards and his eyes shining, he shouted up his applause so that it echoed. 'Bravo, bravo,' he yelled, full of admiration.

And they began to talk to one another, all four of them, Louise as well, from up above and down below, asking and explaining.

That day they all ate together, and the next day as well. They talked about the routines, as if they were all involved. Fritz said: 'Yes – if all four of us could become an act.'

And he started to explain, unfolding his new plan, describing all the evolutions, whilst Adolphe sat silent, and Louise dared not answer.

But the next day, as Adolphe was standing there looking down at the ground and moving his legs to and fro, he said: 'Are you practising this afternoon?'

No, they weren't going to.

'You know,' said Adolphe, 'we're just wasting our time here, and our muscles are getting stiff … .'

That afternoon Adolphe and Louise started practising. The other two came along to watch. They shouted encouragement and advice.

Fritz sat there cheerfully, playing with Aimée's hand. '*Ça va, ça va*,' they both called from below.

Up in the air, Louise and Adolphe flew boldly between the swings.

They had finished their training. Their act was ready to perform. They called themselves 'The Four Devils', and got costumes designed and sewn in Berlin.

They made their debut in Breslau. Then they toured from town to town. Wherever they went, their success was assured.

Aimée had undressed and got into bed; sleepless, she stared up into the darkness. How clearly she could see it all, from the very first day. Their whole lives they had lived together – their whole lives side by side.

And now she had come along, *she*, this stranger – and at the thought, the little acrobat could only grit her teeth in impotent, despairing, purely physical fury – in order to ruin him.

What did she want with him, *she* with her eyes like a cat? What did she want with him, with her smile like a tart? What did she want with him, offering herself like a whore? To ruin him, to steal from him, to take away his strength.

Aimée bit her sheets, pounded her pillow, could find no rest for her feverish hands. In her thoughts she could not find enough powerless curses, not enough angry, coarse, furious accusations – until she burst into tears again, and once again felt that deadening pain which invaded her night and day, night and day.

IV

Fritz lay with his eyes closed, resting his head in his lover's lap. Slowly and yet more slowly the tips of her nails glided lightly through his blond hair.

Fritz stayed still with his eyes closed and his head lying lightly in her lap: so it was really him, Fritz Schmidt from the back alleys of Frankfurt, him, the boy without a father, whose mother had jumped into the river one day when she was drunk, and whose grandmother had sold him – him and his brother – for twenty marks … .

So it was really him, Fritz Schmidt called Cecchi of the 'Devils' who had become her lover, hers, 'the lady from the box'. It was *his* neck which lay against her knee. It was *his* arm which could reach around her waist. It was *his* throat where her lips now rested. *Him,* Fritz Cecchi of the 'Devils'.

And he half-opened his eyes and looked with the same uncomprehending but intoxicated wonder at her fine hand, so soft, which no work had deformed; her nails, pink and curved, which he loved to gaze at in devoted astonishment, one by one … .

Yes – her hand was gently stroking his forehead.

And it was he who was able to breathe in the scent of her body close to him, of her clothes, made of materials which were like clouds – how his hands loved to caress them … .

It was him she waited for at night by the high gate, shivering as she waited as if from the cold. It was him she led through the little garden of the mansion, clinging to his body in every bit of shelter … .

It was him whose lips she called her 'flower', whose arms she called her 'transgression' … .

Yes – what strange words she used: *his* lips a 'flower', *his* arms a 'transgression' … .

Fritz Cecchi smiled, and closed his eyes again. His lover saw his smile, and bent her head over him again and softly moved her lips over his face.

Fritz carried on smiling, absorbed by the same wonder. 'But this is strange,' he said quietly; and he went on saying in the same tone: 'But this is strange', as he gently shook his head.

'What?' she asked.

'This,' was all he answered, and he lay still beneath her kisses as if he was afraid of wakening from a dream. He smiled constantly; his thoughts continually repeated her name, with continually renewed amazement at her name

– one of the great names which was heard throughout Europe and which had reached his ears like a legend.

And slowly he opened his eyes again and looked at her, and got hold of her ears with both hands and laughed like a lad as he pinched them – harder, hard; even that he dared to do – even that.

He half sat up and leaned his head against her shoulder. Still with the same smile, he looked round the room. Everything was a wonder to him, everything that was hers: the thousand fragile knick-knacks scattered over the bizarre pieces of furniture on flimsy legs; sometimes he hardly dared touch them, he – the juggler – would pick them up so carefully, as if they would shatter in his fingers; sometimes, arrogantly (*he* was master here, he, Fritz Schmidt), he would play ball with an ornamental table or balance a whole cabinet, as she laughed and laughed.

The paintings were unfamiliar to him, the pictures of ancestors in seventeenth-century dress with ceremonial swords and gloved hands. There were moments when he could suddenly laugh right into their faces, merrily, like a street urchin – laugh irrepressibly, whilst he, Fritz Schmidt, was sitting there with her, their descendant, on his lap.

And he went on laughing and laughing – why, she couldn't understand. Finally she asked: 'But why are you laughing?'

'Yes, yes,' he answered, and went on: 'Because this is comical,' – and laughed right into the portraits' noble '*Gesichter*'.*

But most often the room would merely increase his strange wonder – as it did right now, and he felt a peculiar, half-happy, half-shy amazement – that *he* was *here*. That he was master here.

For he felt like a master; she was *his*. He owned her. In his uncivilized brain there brooded all those thoughts about man's absolute ownership of females, which he makes complete by inseminating them – he, the active one who takes the initiative, he who, in the devouring rage of his passion, can crush them beneath his thighs.

But all of these primitive male notions of Fritz's – gloating over taming and punishing and exploiting at will – they all evaporated, helpless and powerless in the face of his constantly renewed mute wonder at her: her slightest word, which had a different ring and a different fall; her slightest movement, which was of a different kind; her body, every part of it, which was of a different, unfamiliar beauty, tender and undeveloped. And he became humble and fearful, and suddenly opened his closed eyes in order to make sure that it was no dream, slowly caressing her fine, slim fingers; yes, it was true.

… So he lay now, whilst her hands went on gliding, more and more lingeringly, through his hair, and his breathing gradually quickened, whilst he lay there as if sleeping.

Suddenly he opened his eyes: 'But what do you want with me?' he asked.

'Oh, stupid man,' she whispered, with her mouth close to his cheek: 'You stupid man.'

She went on whispering, near to his ear – and the sound of her voice excited him more than caresses: 'Stupid man, you stupid man … ' – as if she was lulling into ecstasy this beautiful apathetic body, which she had to seduce each day all over again.

'Stupid man, you stupid man.'

But this evening she did not rouse him. He simply sat up, still smiling, and, sitting beside her and laying her head on his breast while he looked at her, he said with infinite tenderness: 'Could you sleep here?' And he rocked her in his arms like a child.

Until they both laughed, eye to eye.

'You stupid man.'

Then his eyes lit up, and he seized her; quickly and wordlessly he bore her before him on outstretched arms, across the living room and – in.

Only the pale blue hanging lamp watched silently, like a sleepy eye.

It was almost dawn when they parted. But in all the corners on the stairs, and in the garden in front of the silent house – elegant and chaste with its curtained windows – they greedily prolonged the hours of their rendezvous, as she continued to whisper the same three words, which had become a kind of refrain for their love (a love whose innermost soul was instinct): 'You stupid man.'

Then Fritz tore himself away, and the gate closed after him. But she called him back, and he turned back once more. Once more he took her in his arms, and suddenly he laughed – standing beside her in front of the huge mansion. And as if their thoughts had met, she laughed too – up towards the house of her ancestors.

And he began to ask – curious, enjoying a strange feeling of triumph – about each one of the stone coats of arms over the windows, each one of the inscriptions over the portals, as she answered and laughed and laughed.

They were the country's proudest names. He didn't know them, but she told stories about all of them. They were stories of honour. They were stories of wars. They were stories of victors on the field of battle.

And he laughed.

There were shields which had protected the throne. There were emblems which had led to the chair of St. Peter itself.*

And as if aroused by the very indignity, her caresses became more heated, seeming coarse and almost blasphemous here in the coming dawn, whilst she continued to tell her stories, as if with dismissive scorn she were tearing down, word by word, the shields of her ancestral home, and grinding them into the filth of her love.

'And that?' he asked, pointing at the coats of arms. 'And *that*?'

She carried on. It was centuries of history. Here thrones were raised, and royal seats were thrown down. *That* one was an emperor's friend. *That* one had slain a king.

And she carried on talking – whispering, with snarling mockery, leaning against her acrobat's shoulder, abandoning herself to the feeling of profanation.

He too became intoxicated.

It was as if they both could see, *here* before their eyes, ruination itself; and they savoured it – savoured minute by minute the fall of this grand house – with its weapons, portals, shields, memorial tablets, spires – which was despoiled and came crashing down as a result of their passion, their merciless passion.

Then she tore herself away and fled down the passage. One last time she turned in the little door, and as she waved at him, she blew a kiss – a final mockery – towards the grand coat of arms over the front gable, and laughed.

Fritz walked home. It was as if he had wings under his feet. He could still feel all her caresses.

Around him the large town was waking up. Carts rolled through the streets. They carried all the treasures of the flower market – violas, early roses, auricolas, wallflowers.

Fritz was singing. In a low voice he sang a verse from an operetta:

Amour, amour,
oh, bel oiseau,
chante, chante,
*chante toujours.**

The carts kept rolling past him. The whole street was filled with the scent of flowers. The flower sellers, sitting on their boxes, wrapped up in large shawls, turned round on their perches and smiled at him.

He went on singing:

Amour, amour,
oh, bel oiseau,
chante, chante,
chante toujours …

In their own street it was still quiet and half in darkness behind the tall houses. Fritz walked more slowly. He was still singing, as he looked up and down their house.

Suddenly he started – he thought he had seen a face behind the window-pane.

Pale, holding her breath, Aimée was listening behind her door. Yes, it was him.

Amour, amour,
oh, bel oiseau,
chante, chante,
chante toujours.

The door upstairs closed, and all was silent.

White as a sleepwalker and with her hands pressed against her breast, Aimée went in and got into bed. Motionless, she stared up at the grey day, a new day.

V

It was late when Fritz Cecchi woke up, and little by little he remembered everything, dully, whilst he looked uncertainly at Adolphe, who was standing in the middle of the room rubbing his naked body with a wet towel.

'You're awake then,' said Adolphe scornfully.

'Yes,' was all Fritz answered, as he carried on watching his brother.

'Perhaps you'll get up now,' said Adolphe in the same tone.

'Yes,' said Fritz; but he just went on staring at his brother's strong, untouched body, in which all the muscles were alive and rippling, and he felt a dull rage, the bitter and miserable resentment of the conquered.

And as he went on staring at his brother, and suddenly lifted his own arms and felt them strengthless, and then tensed his leg muscles against the end of the bed and felt them feeble – it was as if he was choked by a shameful and wild bitterness against himself, against his body, against his desire and against her: the thief, the robber, the destroyer – *her.*

His anger had no thoughts. He knew only one thing: he could beat her to death in his madness. To death with his clenched fists. To death, inch by inch. To death as she screamed and she laughed. To death, so that she gasped no more. To death under his heel and his foot.

He raised his arms again and clasped his hands together, and he felt again how his strengthless muscles failed, whilst he gritted his teeth in fury.

Adolphe went out, banging the door behind him.

Then Fritz jumped up, and began to examine his naked body. He attempted his exercises, but was unable to complete them. He tried some parterre work, but couldn't do it. His tired limbs just trembled in protest.

He tried again. He hit himself, then tried again. He pinched himself with his nails. It was useless. He could do nothing.

He beat his head on the wall and tried again. It was useless.

And he sat down slackly in front of the large mirror, and studied one after the other the muscles in his inert and relaxed body.

So it was true: they took everything. Health, strength, the power of your muscles. So it was true: everything was ravaged, work, status, renown. Yes, that was how it was.

And it would be the same with him as with the others, and it would soon be over.

The same thing would happen to him as it did to 'The Stars', who dragged two tarts from town to town, who slept with them and whom they beat up – until they were finally locked up in a madhouse.

The same thing would happen to him as to Charles, the juggler, who had an affair with the chanteuse Adelina – his limbs became as flabby as a drunkard's. Then he hanged himself in a tree. Or Hubert, who rode at markets, or Paul, who was ringmaster in a tent. Yes, they trashed their own bodies.

Once more he stood up. But he *would not* give in. And he started working again, straining every muscle, calling up all his strength, urging on every fibre of his body.

He managed it.

And suddenly he got dressed. He just threw on his clothes, scarcely tidying himself, and went out. He wanted to rehearse – to rehearse in the circus, on the trapeze.

Adolphe, Aimée and Louise were already at work, hanging on the trapezes in their grey blouses.

Fritz got changed and began to train on the ground. He walked on his hands, balancing on the right, then the left, his whole body trembling. The others watched silently from their swings.

Then he swung himself up into the net, abruptly and quickly, and climbed up to the trapeze above Aimée. He dropped to catch himself by his hands, so that his slender body was stretched out, and started to work.

Aimée just sat there. With heavy, sleepless eyes she stared fixedly at that creature she loved, that *man* she loved, who had come from a night of love with another.

Year after year they had lived body to body. She measured him with her eyes: his neck, which had carried her, his arms, which had caught her, his loins, which she had embraced … . And the training of their craft, the awareness of their skills increased her agony.

Mute, overcome by dreadful suffering – a physical pain which she alone could feel – she watched Fritz working with staring eyes.

But Fritz roused her. 'Why don't you get going,' he shouted harshly.

'OK.'

She gave a start, and stood up mechanically on the trapeze. For just a second their eyes met. Then suddenly Fritz saw her white face, her wide-open eyes, her stiff, inflexible body, and he understood everything. And in the same moment he felt a wild and unconquerable loathing for this woman's body, a disgust, a revulsion at its touch – the body of another woman who loved him. An insuperable, an icy loathing – like hatred.

'Begin!' yelled Adolphe.

'Why don't you begin?' called Louise.

But still they hesitated.

Then they flew towards each other and met. Pale, they took stock of each other and let go again. He caught her, but she fell. They began again, but then he plunged down.

They tried once more, staring into each other's eyes. Each moment seemed to make them paler – and then both fell, Fritz first.

Louise and Adolphe laughed out loud from their trapezes. Adolphe shouted: 'You are having a good day today, aren't you?'

Louise yelled: 'Someone has put the evil eye on him.' And again they laughed from up on their trapezes.

The two up there carried on, and failed again: Aimée let go, and Fritz told her off from down in the safety net.

And all at once they were all quarrelling, bitter and heated, their voices high-pitched and loud, whilst Aimée alone sat still with the same wide-open eyes, pale even after all the effort of training.

Again Fritz swung himself up, and again they started work. They both yelled, and they both pushed off. They flew towards each other, and it was as if the same rage awoke in both of them at the same moment. They caught each other with a scream, and entwined savagely.

It was not work any longer. It was a battle. They were not meeting any more, they were not catching or embracing. They were simply wrestling, gripping each other like animals. The two bodies hurled into the air seemed to be engaged in a trial of strength, in a desperate fight. They did not pause. They issued no more words of command. Senseless in their brutal and unstoppable hatred, it was as if they were tumbling through the air in a fearful confrontation, horrified at themselves.

Then all at once Aimée plunged down with a scream – she lay in the net for a moment as if lifeless.

Fritz swung himself up onto his trapeze with clenched teeth; as pale as a mask, he looked down at the defeated woman.

He stood up on his trapeze and said: 'She can't work any more. We have to change over – she can take the top trapeze and Louise can work down here.'

He spoke roughly, as if he was the one in charge. No-one answered, but Louise began slowly to slide down from the dome to Aimée's trapeze.

Aimée said nothing. Like an animal on its knees, she had only half stood up in the net. Then she slowly climbed up the long rope towards the dome. And they started again.

But Fritz's strength was exhausted. His fury had worn him out. His arms couldn't hold him, and he fell. His knees were shaking, and he dropped Louise.

'What's wrong with you?' called Adolphe. 'You must be ill. You'll have to go up in the dome, this won't work.'

Fritz made no answer; he just sat with head bowed, as if he'd been punched. Then he said – muttering through compressed lips: 'OK, perhaps we can swap over – for today.'

He got down from the net and went out. The knuckles of his clenched fists were white. He thought he could hear the stable lads whispering his name, and walked past them ashamed, like a dog.

In the dressing room he threw himself down on the mattress. He couldn't feel his body any more. Only his eyes smarted.

But he could not keep still. He began to practise again. In the same way that you prod an aching tooth, or inflame a boil by pressing on it with your fingers, he kept on urging his apathetic limbs: could he do *that*, could he do *that* – he kept on trying feverishly. He could do nothing; once again he threw himself down, and once again he made the effort. And the struggle of repeated attempts wore him out even more, to no avail.

So the day passed. He didn't leave the circus. He slunk around the circus ring like a man with a guilty conscience around the scene of the crime.

In the evening he worked in the dome with Louise.

He fought like a madman against his limbs, which would not obey him. Desperately, he exerted his trembling joints. He managed it – once, then once more, a third time. He flew backwards, he flew forwards, he rested again.

He could see nothing – not the dome, not the boxes, not Adolphe. Only the trapeze – the one he had to reach, and Louise swinging in front of him.

Then he let go, flung his arms out with a shriek towards Louise's legs – it felt as if the rushing of his blood would explode his fearful brain – and fell, down into the wildly swinging net.

There was silence in the huge enclosure – silence as if people thought him dead.

Then Fritz half lifted his upper body. He didn't know where he was. Then he came to himself, and with a dreadful effort he made out the circus ring and the net and the black rim of people, the boxes and – *her*. And overwhelmed by despair and humiliation rather than by the pain of the fall, he suddenly raised his clasped hands, and then sank down again.

The other three had stopped and called to one another in confusion. In a flash Adolphe had dropped down the hanging rope. He and two of the grooms lifted Fritz out of the net and supported him between them, so that it looked as if he was walking on his own.

Only then did Aimée slowly slide down the rope. She walked off as if she were blind; she could see nothing.

Two artistes were standing by the entrance. 'He can be grateful for that net,' said one.

'*Na*,' answered the other, '*er wäre schon "kalt" geworden*.'*

Aimée came to with a start – she heard those words. And as if she was looking at them for the first time, she took in with a single glance the net and ropes and trapezes – those high, extremely high trapezes.

One of the artistes followed her glance. '*Auch schändlich hoch*,' he said.*

Aimée just nodded – really slowly … .

It was quiet again, and the performance continued. In the dressing room, Fritz had got up off his mattress and was sitting in front of his mirror. He was not injured, just stunned by the fall.

Adolphe got changed, and they were silent for a long time.

Then Adolphe said: 'You must see that we can't go on like this?'

Fritz did not answer. He sat there, pale, and did not look away from his own face in the mirror.

Adolphe was finished, and they heard Louise knocking on the door of the dressing room. 'Are you ready?' asked Adolphe. 'They're waiting.'

Fritz took his ticking watch down from the mirror, and they went out to where the two sisters were waiting without speaking. Silently they walked home – Fritz alongside Louise.

Humiliation was burning in his soul, as if he had a wound in his chest.

VI

Fritz and Adolphe had gone to bed long ago, and Adolphe was sleeping, inert, his mouth open, as acrobats sleep when their bodies relax into heavy repose. But Fritz didn't fall asleep; stretched out on his back, he lay sleepless in torpid despair.

So it had happened. So it had already happened. He could not work any longer.

He circled round and round the same thought: so now he could not work any longer. And slowly and listlessly he unravelled how it had happened – day by day, and night by night. Calmly and dully he saw it all again: the blue room and the raised bed and himself and her; the yellow drawing room with the withdrawing area behind the screen and the portraits and himself and her; the staircase where the lamp went out and himself and her … . And the garden, where he had turned back.

And now it was all over. Now he was harvesting the fruits. He knew it. His thoughts continued along the same sluggish path. But if he was ruined, he could ruin her too. He could.

He could go over there one night and let himself in. And when he was there – with her, in her bed (and again his thoughts stopped, and he saw the blue chamber and himself and her) – he could, he would ring the bell, summon the household, summon her husband, the servants, the maids, all of them, so that they could see her – *her.*

Yes, he could. And she would be naked, she would be exposed (as he saw her now), shameless and dishonoured. Yes, he would. And suddenly, seeing it all in his mind once more, he said: 'Yes, I'll do it now.'

All possibility of rest disappeared. Yes – why should he not do it now? Now, when the plan was fresh, his anger immediate, his thoughts strong? Yes, he would do it now.

And hurriedly, without lighting a lamp, he began to rummage for his clothes, putting them on without a sound, in order not to disturb – with the constant image before him: himself and her in the blue room, in the middle of the blue room himself and her: *there* it would happen.

He bumped into a chair in his haste, and then was suddenly still, sitting on his bed, afraid that Adolphe might wake up. He must not wake up.

Then he carried on dressing, noiselessly, holding his breath. He *wanted* to go – he *had* to go – now.

He trampled too hard on the floor and had to stop again … .

Adolphe turned over in bed and muttered: 'What the hell's going on?' he said. 'Where are you going?'

Fritz made no answer. Half-dressed, he threw himself under the bedclothes to hide – suddenly trembling like a thief caught in the act. And shortly afterwards, when he heard Adolphe's breathing once more, he began again, still lying in bed, to put on his clothes; trembling still, and fearful as if he were stealing his own clothes – and *all too aware of why he really wanted to go there.*

He was on his feet. He felt his way forwards, smiling each time he avoided an obstacle, creeping along the wall – scarcely breathing; crafty as a drunkard who sneaks out a bottle unseen. And he opened and closed the door and made his way out and down, still creeping … . And he knew that he was as shameless as a dog. And he said to himself: so I won't be able to work tomorrow. And he knew: now I am seeking out ruination. And he ran – ran all the faster, along the walls of houses, in the shadows … .

Back home no-one had heard him – except Aimée. She was the one who followed him – gliding down the stairs, out of the house, across to the other side of the street … . Like two shadows chasing each other, they kept pace noiselessly through the silent streets.

Then Fritz reached the mansion and the little gate: now he was inside, and his footsteps died away. Hidden in a gateway, Aimée stood in front of the mansion's windows. She watched a light moving past the windows on the first floor. She watched two shadows against the lace curtains. There they were.

The light moved again, she saw the shadows again – then the light went out … . Only a glimmer of blue showed behind the last window. *There* they were – *there*, behind those windows.

With baited breath, tormented by jealousy, Aimée stared at those windows: all the pictures filled her mind at once, torturing her. All the pictures, the final agony of the one who has been abandoned – and which came into the mind of the little acrobat, even though she was chaste – it was as if they were being drawn by hand on those windows, where he was, where *they* were.

And her whole life, which had been lived in self-sacrifice; her whole existence, which had been one of mild devotion; everything she had thought, every tender thought of him; all she had aimed at, every plan made together; it all sank into the ground before those pictures – the pictures of those two bodies. Her whole life, piece by piece, memory by memory, thought by thought – it was all broken apart, swallowed up, laid in ruins, and vanished away because of one thing: desire. Desire, born of the sexual drive – that triumphant sexual drive. Nothing remained: not her devotion, not her tenderness, not her self-sacrifice – nothing … misery reduced it to its simplest form, rejection made it depraved, it shrank back to its original form: *desire*, triumphant desire, annihilating desire.

The hours passed.

It was as if Aimée could suffer no more. As if in sleep she watched that pale blue glimmer, apathetic.

Then the gate opened and closed again. It was him.

And in a new, desperate stab of agony Aimée saw him, grey in the growing dawn, walking slowly past.

VII

'Aimée,' said Louise sharply, as if to wake her up: 'are you asleep?'

Aimée merely lifted her arm – strangely slowly – and fastened up her long hair.

'You would think so,' said Louise.

And Aimée sat motionless once more in front of her image in the mirror; it was as if two sleepwalkers were staring at each other with their eyes open. Slowly she put on her blouse and got up and went out – with the same strange look in her eyes, as if she were following a hidden vision, and with the step of an automaton, as if the soul had fallen asleep in her body. Louise followed her, and they both went out into the dark arena where Fritz was already waiting on the trapeze.

It seemed as if Aimée had never worked so securely as she did now; with a mechanical rhythm she caught and released and flew.

She was working with Fritz again, and it was as if her calm was infectious; like the lifeless cogs of a machine they came together, parted and came together again. And again they rested on opposing trapezes.

It was as if Aimée could see only *one* thing, all the time only *one* thing in the whole of that great space: his body. That vital body, that moving breast, that breathing mouth, the blood vessels which throbbed warmly – it could become still and cold.

Still and quite cold.

Those bulging muscles; those hands which seized her; the neck which was the fount of life – would all become still and cold. The arms motionless, the muscles like stone and the forehead cold, the throat dead, the breast high and still. And the hand, when you lifted it up, would just fall heavily. Arm and leg and hand – dead.

They were working again. They flew, they met. Every touch spurred her on: so warm to touch and would become so cold, so trembling and would be so still.

She thought no more about why. She thought no more about her. The only thing she saw was the image of the dead man – *that* she saw. *Him,* cold and still.

And like a madman following a secret mania, she became crafty and devious. Like a morphinist seeking to sate his desire, she became endlessly inventive. She developed the stamina of a monomaniac with but a single thought.

She sought out Fritz, whom she had been avoiding for a long time.

When rehearsals were finished she started work alone. She transferred all the stunts from the lower trapezes to the ones under the dome. She called down to Fritz, keeping him behind in the ring by asking his advice – flatteringly, like an apprentice asking the master.

She dared do anything. She was playing with death. Foolhardy, she spurred him on. She was watching over his uncertainty. She was seeking help from the powerlessness he was trying to hide. She attempted preposterous moves, calling: 'We need to show what we're capable of. We can't let them fly higher.'

She incited him. He made suggestions. Then he climbed the swaying rope up to the trapezes where she was. It was as if she *flew* before him between the rattling trapezes. She swung from trapeze to trapeze over the yawning abyss.

Then – fuelled by an irresistible force – he started to imitate her, as she incited him with shouts. It was as if he had a feverish strength in his violently straining body, as if he were wrestling for one final time with his final strength.

She yelled: *'Ça va – ça va.'*

He swung forwards and caught: *'Ça va – ça va.'*

The artistes who were going in and out stopped in the arena and watched them.

He got even more worked up. He dared do everything she dared. From trapeze to trapeze she flew – wild, with her hair streaming, in front of him, in front of him, as if she were showing him the way.

They met and caught each other. Her body was cold, as if a pair of marble arms were seizing his heated and trembling body.

Then she stopped, while he carried on. Curled up, she sat on her swing, driving him on with low, almost growling calls – as she sat there in the darkness, watching him. Fritz groaned and stretched out towards the dangling rope; then it looked as if he plunged down and away into the great blackness. Aimée remained sitting on her swing. She heard him fall with a thud into the net. Then his footsteps on the floor of the arena – footsteps which died away.

It was quite dark. There was only a dim light from the cupola. The whole of that great space was silent. Still Aimée sat there, curled up on the trapeze between the net and the ropes. Then she stood up. The hand-holds and swings and ropes rattled gently.

She was lifting things, trying them out. Like a shadow Aimée was absorbed in the darkness – busy as in a workshop.

The brass knobs on the swings shone like cats' eyes.

Otherwise it was dark.

The ropes from the trapezes slapped gently.

Otherwise it was quiet.

For a long time Aimée pottered around under the dome.

Then there came a loud shout from down in the darkness of the arena.

It was Fritz calling: 'Aimée, Aimée.'

'Yes, coming,' was the reply.

Aimée took hold of the long rope. Slowly she slid down, hovering silently for a moment over the waiting man. 'I'm coming,' she said again, and joined him.

VIII

There was going to be a benefit performance for 'The Four Devils'.

It was the evening before – after the performance. The public were making their way home from the circus.

Adolphe knocked on Aimée and Louise's door, and they all went out through the passage.

None of them spoke, as they sat down quietly at their normal table in the restaurant. The tankards arrived and they drank in silence. It was as if Aimée was making even the slightest movement – down to the way she picked up her glass – calculatedly, and so slowly, as if she were measuring everything, however small.

It was noisy in the restaurant. Bib and Bob were celebrating their birthday, and a number of artistes had joined them at their table. One was performing conjuring tricks, and Trip the clown was pretending to be Rigolo the donkey, wiggling his backside.

The 'Devils' remained sitting in their corner.

The ballet dancers who had been waiting along the walls disappeared quietly – picked up by men in a hurry. At a side table the agents were playing cards.

The clowns carried on making a noise. One of them was playing an ocarina, and was answered by half a dozen 'cri-cris'.* Tom the clown gave his colleague Bob a present of a cabbage filled with snuff, and began to sniff and sneeze, sniff and sneeze without ceasing, whilst the 'cri-cris' shrilled. Standing on the table, Trip the clown was still pretending to be Rigolo the donkey, wiggling his backside.

The 'Devils' were still sitting there.

The 'poster man' came in with his glue-pot and bag, and pasted the programme for the next day up on two boards. It bore the name of '*Les quatre diables*' three times.

Adolphe got up and went across to read it. He asked one of the agents to translate it, and the agent got up from the card table and slowly translated from the foreign language, as Adolphe listened:

'With the assurance that we shall exert ourselves to the utmost for our benefit performance, your humble servants

Les quatre diables.'

Adolphe nodded as he followed the foreign text word for word. Then he returned to the table and stared at the poster with its huge print, assessing it with a satisfied expression. Then he said: 'Nice letters.'

And Louise and Fritz got up as well and went over to look at it, one after the other.

The 'cri-cris' shrieked as if to burst everyone's eardrums. Tom the clown was making music by blowing through small whistling instruments inserted into his nostrils.

Aimée had stood up as well. She stood quietly behind Fritz and Louise, as the agent kept on translating the same words:

'your humble servants

Les quatre diables.'

Louise laughed, mocking the unfamiliar language, and they began to make fun of the letters, of the sounds which the agent pronounced for them, of the peculiar words, pulling faces, both Louise and Fritz; the same sentence: 'your humble servants … .'

It sounded so comical that the others joined in; they all began – clowns and acrobats and girls – to laugh and shout and pull faces, loudly, each one in their own language, whilst the whole scene was drowning in laughter – the same words, in one great, loud, distorted chorus:

'your humble servants

Les quatre diables.'

The 'cri-cris' shrilled. High in the air on two tables, Trip frantically wiggled Rigolo's backside.

Then Aimée laughed too, loud and long – and last, as the noise gradually died down.

The 'Devils' returned to their places. Adolphe took out some money and placed it beside their tankards. Then the three of them stood up – but Fritz remained seated. He was not going home.

'Good night,' said Adolphe and Louise.

'Good night,' was all Fritz answered, not moving.

Aimée stood there; for a moment she looked at him, weighing him up as if she was suffering once more at the thought of this night, the last one.

'*A demain,* Aimée,'* he said.

Slowly she looked away: 'Good night.'

She went out into the long passageway. It was dark. The poster man's lamp was standing on the ground, and in its gleam the yellow paper of the poster shone out at her. The two others were waiting outside. She followed them, alone.

It was dead and silent between the tall houses.

Aimée looked up at the masses of stone, with their windows, their eyes – the eyes of strangers. The sky was high and clear. Aimée looked at the stars, which they said were worlds, other worlds. And again her gaze travelled over the houses and doors and windows and lights, and the street cobbles – as if each thing was a remarkable wonder – as if she were seeing them now for the first and only time.

'Aimée,' called Louise.

'Yes, I'm coming.'

And again she stared at those rows of houses, silent and dark and shut in – stone house after stone house – where her footsteps died away … . Behind her the blaring 'cri-cris' shrieked, and she heard the laughter of the clowns.

'Aimée,' called Louise again.

'Yes.'

Aimée caught up with them. They were standing there arm in arm, with a lamp shining into their faces, waiting for her.

Louise bent her head back and breathed out gently into the air:

'For God's sake!' she said. 'What's taking you so long?'

Leaning on Adolphe's arm, standing there in the light from the lamp, she looked down that dead and unfamiliar street they had just left, and which was disappearing into the gloom behind her. 'It is pleasant,' she said, 'a street like that.'

And as she started laughing once more, making fun of those three highly comical words: 'your humble servants', casting a last glance down the cold street: 'I wonder what that one's called?'

'Oh,' said Adolphe, 'we pass through so many alleyways.'

And they went on their way – through the next rows of houses.

Fritz had remained at the table. The others, over at the clown's table, offered him a drink. But he just shook his head. And one of the clowns shouted – making everyone laugh – 'He's got better things to do … Good night.'

The others raised their glasses and went on laughing: Bib and Bob had made a fishing rod and were fishing all the artistes' hats down off the hooks.

Fritz got up and went towards the doors of the restaurant, which were standing open to the street, and sat down at a table out on the pavement under a couple of laurel trees.

An endless ennui, a nameless revulsion descended on him. He saw the whispering couples walking to and fro, pressing against each other. They were billing and cooing in the shadows, smiling lovingly at each other. The women were wiggling their hips and the men arching their backs, strutting for one another like animals in the fields who want to mate … .

Suddenly Fritz laughed, abruptly and briefly. He was thinking about Tim the clown, the one they called the dog master – yes, he had been right.

And Fritz saw him in his mind's eye. Tim with a face as still and regular and melancholy as a statue, his lips curved and red and fine and sad – like a woman's lips. Fritz could see him at home in his lodgings, the big room where he had built a house for his dogs – a house with two floors, where all the dogs lived in tiers. They lay there, the animals, each in its own room, still, with their heads protruding out of the holes, just staring, their eyes as melancholy as Tim's.

And Tim sat there in their midst.

It was such a quiescent gathering. All the dogs were castrated.

Tim had got hold of a new dog that day. And when Fritz went up there, it was lying bloody and maimed on a blanket. Then Tim looked down at the wounded dog with his expressionless eyes, and said: 'Now that animal is more human than humans themselves.'

Yes, Tim had been right: animals were people. There *was* no difference between this world's creatures: we are all born in a pool of blood and die in a pool of vomit. And those moments of existence when we are *alive* are bestial – bestial just like the beginning and the end.

Fritz sat there watching those couples walking past, cooing, and he was overwhelmed by a pent-up, corrosive rage against those strutters, those coquettes, those hypocrites. Animals, that's what they were – animals on the hunt for food. Losers, that's what they were – losers, as we all are.

We groomed ourselves, we took care of ourselves, we worked with thousandfold effort. We sacrificed days, years, the whole of our youth, our strength, our inventiveness – in order to become 'people', people who were esteemed by others. Until one day we see: everything is in vain.

The animal has stirred – the animal within, the animal which is us – and then what is left? what remains? of the person, *the man* … .

Fritz laughed. And involuntarily he ran his hands over his body, cherished for a whole lifetime, destroyed in three months.

An artiste came out through the door. He waited for a moment and then his wife joined him, and they waddled off along the pavement. Fritz looked after them, and went on laughing.

Then there were the ones who got married, mated for life, eating their daily bread and serving the cause of procreation. Did they not lose their bodies too? Like fat drones they swelled up and acquired big bellies from their ordered lives. And raised children to carry on doing the same.

Losers – losers.

Fritz sat there, watching the passing couples. They were becoming more intimate. The hunters became more insistent. They sought refuge in the shadows, and bargained more bluntly.

Inside, the clowns were rampaging. The 'cri-cris' shrilled. They echoed over all the heads, into all the faces, reaching all the couples – like a triumphal song of idiocy.

Fritz stood up. He threw a coin onto the table. Then he left.

Inside the restaurant, the hullabaloo increased. They bawled, they shrieked and they laughed. It was Trip who began to sing. And whistling, blowing, cackling, they all joined in; with clowns' grimaces, with gestures from the ring, with twisted mouths they sang:

Amour, amour,
oh, bel oiseau,
chante, chante,
toujours.

Outside on the pavement the couples stopped by the doors and by the window, and laughed, supporting each other. Then, two by two, they hummed the clowns' tune. Disappearing into the darkness, you could hear them humming:

Amour, amour,
oh, bel oiseau,
chante, chante,
toujours.

Fritz had reached the square. Inside he could see the crazy clowns, outside the loving couples, whose heads moved, gently following the rhythm.

And suddenly the acrobat began to laugh; leaning against a lamp-post, he laughed and laughed – wildly, madly, uncontrollably. A representative of the forces of order came along and stared at this gentleman in a top hat, who was causing a public nuisance. But the gentleman just carried on laughing so much that he shook.

Then the guardian of public order started to laugh as well, just like that. And inside they went on singing:

Amour, amour,
oh, bel oiseau,
chante, chante,
toujours.

Fritz turned away.

He went – to *her.*

IX

Once more the applause rang out, and Louise came forward again.

Then the grooms started to pull the large net together. It sounded like a main sail being hoisted, as the music went quiet.

'Herr Fritz and Mademoiselle Aimée will perform the *salto mortale* without a net.'

A couple of stable boys raked the sand of the arena with large rakes. Then all was ready. The grooms lined up like a guard of honour, as the 'waltz of love' sounded again.

Fritz and Aimée came out, hand in hand. They bowed in acknowledgement of the flowers which had been thrown in. Then they swung themselves up by the long dangling ropes. Thousands of eyes followed them.

Now they were up there. For a second they rested there side by side.

A shudder went through the crowd as Fritz let go and flew – a shudder which seemed to run through a single body.

But never had they been more secure in their work. In the breathless silence you could hear their hands grasping firmly on to the rattling trapezes. Fritz flew forwards – then backwards. Aimée's eyes were fixed on him – large and shining dully, like a couple of lamps which will soon be extinguished.

The waltz sounded louder, and the play of the swings became more violent. The nervous applause sounded breathless.

Now Aimée let her hair down, as if she wanted to shroud herself in a dark cape; she stood on the trapeze in front of Fritz, waiting. The big jumps began. They flew, they leapt. Their words of command sounded like birds' cries over the waltz, and it was as if all thoughts had become confused.

'*Aimée, du courage.*'

He flew again.

'*Enfin, du courage.*'

He grasped her again.

Aimée saw nothing but him – a body which seemed to her to shine. The applause increased again: it echoed! The waltz grew louder; it was jubilant.

Aimée was conscious only of suddenly lifting her hand, as, swinging out wide from the moving trapeze, she released the fastening which secured it.

And Fritz flew forwards.

She saw nothing more.

There was no scream.

As his body fell, there came a sound like that of a sandbag hitting the ground in the arena.

For a thousandth of a second Aimée sat still on her trapeze. She did not know before now that death was voluptuous … then she let go, screamed and fell.

Now it was quiet in the circus.

As if all restraints had snapped, hundreds had fled in horror. Men leapt over the barriers and ran, women crowded together at the exits and fled. No-one waited, everything was in motion. The screams of the women rang out as if they had been stabbed.

Three doctors appeared and knelt down by the bodies … . Then it had gone silent. The artistes crept around in their dressing rooms without getting changed, as if they wanted to hide themselves away. You could hear every sound, and every sound was shocking.

A stable boy came up to the waiting doctor, whispering, and they lifted up the bodies and laid them in the same tarpaulin. Silently they carried them out – out through the passage and the stables, where the horses were moving nervously in their stalls. The artistes followed like an endless funeral procession – clad in the many costumes of the pantomime.

The large hearse was waiting.

It was Adolphe who climbed up and placed them inside in the darkness – both of them, first Aimée and then his brother, side by side. Then the door was closed.

Another scream could be heard, and a woman ran out and clung to the black carriage. It was Louise, who was slowly dragged away … .

A waiter from the restaurant ran through the long deserted passageway – scared as if frightened by ghosts under the bright lights.

He shouted for a doctor. There was a lady in the restaurant who was having a fit.

One of the three doctors attended and they called for her carriage. It drew up – with its splendid coats of arms on the doors, and the 'lady from the box' was escorted out, leaning on the doctor.

Her carriage had to wait for a while. It was the hearse which was blocking the street.

Then the carriage was allowed through, and drove on.

In the alley there was light and bustle. Two young men had stopped under a street-lamp. With merry, enquiring eyes they looked out over the large market. Two others came up and told them about the 'incident'.

Someone swore, and there was an explanation with many gestures. Then the two news-bearers went on their way.

The two other gentlemen remained standing there.

One of them banged his stick on the cobbles. 'Well,' he said, '*mon dieu – pauvres diables*.'

And shortly after they began to hum once more, looking out over the merry crowd:

Amour, amour
oh, bel oiseau
chante, chante,
chante toujours.

Translated by Janet Garton

11. A Tale of Happiness

It was Easter.

At the manor house they had made it through to the evening of Easter Sunday. The entire household was dying of piety and boredom.

In a corner of the billiard room a gaming table had been set up, and the Master of the Royal Hunt was playing a dutiful Easter Sunday game of L'hombre with his estate manager, the local doctor and the vicar.*

No one spoke.

The estate manager sat over the L'hombre as if humbly delivering an account of the sale of tenant farms. The Master would occasionally mutter curses behind his moustache, and stretch out his legs so far that he kicked the vicar. It was the Master's greatest joy to extract money from his employee through gaming; but today the estate manager won.

A short distance from the gaming table the son of the house, a lieutenant, stood watching with his hands stuffed into his trouser pockets. He had been standing there, immobile, for almost an hour. Except when he yawned – then he would he hide his noble mouth with a white hand.

Finally he turned on his hussar's heel and went down to the first floor.

In the hall the footman, a young man with very slim hands who at the Master's dinner parties gave the impression of being the most well-bred of the guests – his mother was a washerwoman, but the young man would hint to his fellow servants that he was the fruit of an illegitimate liaison which, on his father's side, gave him a fine lineage – was sleeping, sitting straight up and down on a high-backed chair. On hearing the lieutenant's footsteps, he shot up with a sudden subservient expression in his eyes as he bowed.

'Were you asleep?' said Lieutenant Georg.

The young man muttered something, but the lieutenant merely said: 'Can't say I blame you,' and went in.

In the sitting room the guests were slumped in big armchairs, while the conversation limped along. The lieutenant, too, flopped down in a corner. 'Well, this is fun,' he said, and then there was silence once more.

'Why don't we play a game of cards?' somebody drawled at last from one of the armchairs.

It was Lieutenant Knuth, a small, albino dragoon, who spat out every word he said between his front teeth, and who had broken his collarbone three times in as many Eremitage races.*

The son of the house yawned. 'We can't play cards the whole bloody day,' he said. They had played all afternoon behind closed curtains in a turret room.

'No,' someone said from another corner. It was Lieutenant Vedel, the tallest lieutenant in the Hussar Regiment, who, when he had nothing better to do, would stare in amazement at the length of his own legs. He rarely had anything better to do.

A short silence followed, until Feddersen, a civil servant from the Ministry, who had long been absorbed in the admiration of his own English silk waistcoat, said in the same drawl as the others: 'What's the staff doing?'

'They're *asleep*,' said the son of the house.

Lieutenant Knuth blinked and said: 'Bloody odd thing that, peasants are like dogs; they can sleep at any time.'

'Yet still they sin,'* said Feddersen. 'Both the scullery maids are pregnant.'

No one could be bothered to smile, but, as if the word 'sin' had inadvertently prompted thoughts of the vicar, Knuth said: 'Why did the Master propose a toast to the vicar at dinner?'

'He always does at Easter,' said the son of the house.

'Ah,' the lieutenant said, 'so that's why we got the Sillery to drink -- you usually serve Mumm.'*

The Master only saw the vicar with his daughter – the other 'indispensables', the manor house's term for officials, were invited without their ladies – on the first day of Easter, Pentecost and Christmas.

On those three days he would escort the vicar's daughter in to dinner, and would give a speech in praise of the spiritual adviser of the house – he used the word 'spiritual adviser' on those three occasions – who 'had so loyally shared the vicissitudes of his house in bad times as in good'.

'It's tradition,' said the son of the house, who had heard his father's speech ever since he was a boy.

Then Vedel suddenly burst out: 'Well, it's much worse in Copenhagen.'

In the conservatory Frøken Alice, the daughter of the house, was looking at albums with the vicar's daughter. The vicar's daughter was a forty-year-old withered spinster whose life was spent setting up Associations, and whose most recent achievement was a subsection of the Peace Association,* which counted seven members, of whom five were civil servants.

Whenever the vicar's daughter spoke, she always sounded as if she was addressing a general assembly. At the manor house, where she had turned up for ten years in a row in the same grey silk dress, tailored as a kind of reform dress,* she limited herself to being silently envious, as well as collecting association subscriptions in return for receipts which she brought along in a sewing bag.

Opposite the two ladies Berner, a Groom of the Chamber, sat gazing at the face of Frøken Alice, without knowing it. His eyes were so soft, almost misty.

Frøken Alice looked up from the album. 'What's on your mind, Berner?' she said.

Berner was startled. 'Nothing at all,' he said.

A moment later his eyes returned once more to Frøken Alice's face, as she sat there in her satin dress, under the red glow of the lamp, leaning forward. Frøken Alice, however, just laughed and turned over another leaf. 'Yes,' she said, 'that's my aunt, Duchess Denti.'

The vicar's daughter looked at the picture and thought: she's the one who drinks.

Suddenly the son of the house called out through the sitting room: 'Berner, what time is it?'

Berner was startled once more, and turned to the white Empire clock. 'It's only nine o'clock,' he said.

'"Only" is good,' said the son of the house.

'Yes,' said the vicar's daughter, who – as was her wont – immediately found reason to feel offended. 'Our carriage is booked for ten o'clock.'

The footman had organised a carriage for the vicar.

On the three occasions when the manor house entertained the vicar and his associated company, it was invariably from five to ten o'clock.

'They provide their hospitality by the hour,' the vicar's daughter would say, and yet she arrived nevertheless on the dot in the carriage year after year.

'Berner,' Frøken Alice said, 'say something.'

Startled yet again, Berner simply grew even more flustered. 'I'm *thinking*.'

Frøken Alice's laughter echoed beneath the vaulted ceiling, until she suddenly broke off. 'That's my cousin,' she said, returning to the album, and the vicar's daughter, whose lips continued to tighten – the vicar's daughter had a moustache – thought: he's the one who got the dairy maid in trouble.

Leafing through albums at the manor house was for the vicar's daughter as good as savouring a *Chronique scandaleuse.** She absolutely loved it.

In the sitting room the guests had started discussing politics and the forthcoming parliamentary election. A radical was standing in the garrison town, and the prospects of 'the right side' – as Herr Feddersen phrased it, with an expression he had taken from an opposition newspaper – were doubtful.

'Yes,' Knuth said, scrunching up his nose in pensive wrinkles. 'The turner' – the radical was a wood turner – 'has caught the public mood.'

The son of the house, however, said: 'As far as I can see, it makes no bloody difference, because the Government has his Majesty's confidence.'*

'Indeed,' Feddersen said. He was suddenly speaking in quite a loud voice.

And the political conversation ebbed away after 'confidence'.

Shortly afterwards tea was served, and the lieutenants got up from their chairs. Then a loud cry could be heard from the window: 'Bloody hell – what's that I see? It's snowing.'

Everyone livened up and rushed to the window, while the son of the house dashed out of the sitting room and headed up the stairs to the billiard room where the four older men were still playing.

'Master!' his son cried out, 'it's snowing!'

'Have you gone mad?' the Master said.

'Oh, but it jolly well is,' his son insisted, 'and on the 20th of April.'

The men rose from the table and went to the windows, which the Master opened. Indeed – it was snowing; dense, soft snow was falling silently onto the white courtyard of the manor house.

The Master stood with his mouth hanging open. Then he said – forgetting all about his spiritual adviser: 'Well, the almanac's gone to the devil!'

From the courtyard below they could now hear animated laughter; it was Frøken Alice running into the white snow. 'Come on, Berner, come on, Berner!' she shouted, and all the young men immediately spilled out from the broad steps and into the courtyard.

'Alice, Alice,' the Master called out, still by the window: 'Alice … she's not wearing a hat … '

But Frøken Alice didn't hear him. Holding up the train of her dress with one hand, she stood in the centre of the courtyard as the snowballs began to fly.

'Take that,' said Vedel, aiming a missive right at Herr Feddersen's neck.

Frøken Alice dropped the train of her dress as the snowballs whizzed around her and the gentlemen whooped with laughter. '*There*,' she said, hurling a ball at Vedel. It hit him right in the face.

'*There*,' he shouted back at her, and a ball zoomed past her ear. 'Thank you!' as she jumped out of the way. The snow stuck to her hair.

The son of the house raced down the steps to join in. He shouted the loudest. From upstairs the Master could still be heard fretting, while the lieutenants laughed and the snowballs splattered.

'Look at Berner,' Alice called out, 'look at Berner.' She had covered Berner completely with snow, masses of snow, which she scooped up with her bare hands. 'Fight back, fight back,' she urged him.

Berner didn't stir. He just stood in front of her, an immobile snowman, all white, in the middle of the snow, and allowed himself to be covered – without saying a word.

'Fight back,' she urged him again.

But Berner didn't move. '*No*,' was all he said, and slowly he wiped his eyes with his hand in order to see her as she stood there, laughing, with snow in her hair, red and white, with her hands raised. And Frøken Alice suddenly stopped laughing, until she was hit by a snowball from her brother. '*Take that*,' he called out, as it smashed into her forehead.

The lieutenants were doing battle, scooping up snow with their bare hands. No one could see a thing any more, but they all laughed, their eyes blinded.

'Georg, Georg,' Frøken Alice called out to her brother: 'Let's have some champagne now.'

'Yes, absolutely,' Georg replied.

The Master called out from the window once more, but no one heard him. They ran around in the snowfall, all white. Berner was always wherever Frøken Alice was – and didn't know it.

No one noticed the vicar's carriage pull up in front of the door and drive off shortly afterwards. But suddenly Frøken Alice heard the old chassis rumble across the bridge and exclaimed in horror – her arms dropping to her sides: 'The vicar and his daughter have gone.'

Gone they were indeed.

The vicar's daughter had said: 'Please don't disturb the young people', as she climbed into the carriage. She had worn the same expression on her face as when she chaired the local branch of the Association Against the Legal Protection of Immorality.*

The vicar said nothing for a long time. The vicar had a great deal of respect for his daughter. Eventually he spoke up: 'Kathrine, they really were very kind.'

Kathrine allowed a few seconds to pass. 'Yes,' she then said. 'And it's good that it's over.'

She sat for a moment before she resumed speaking. '*Interests*,' she said, 'are not something one should look for at the manor house.' The word 'interests' encapsulated the whole of Frøken Kathrine's life.

Inside the carriage the vicar and his clerical company reached their home in silence.

'The champagne is here,' Georg called out.

The footman carried two coolers down the broad steps, while everyone cheered 'bravo' so the courtyard echoed.

'Set them down on the fountain,' Alice said, 'and escort me to the table.' They laughed as it continued to snow, and the corks popped as they sat down on the edge of the fountain.

'Damned comfortable here,' Knuth said, knocking back the contents of his glass.

They drank and they laughed. They looked like five snow figures as they sat there, covered in snow, with the white column behind them, on the white edge.

'Yes,' Alice said, turning her face upwards so the snowflakes landed on it, 'it's damned wonderful.'

Frøken Alice would occasionally swear when she was happy. 'Oh,' she said, 'it's awful when the vicar's daughter hears me – she takes revenge by immediately signing me up for a new society.'

'Your good health, Berner,' she said.

And in a completely different voice, looking him right in the eye, she said softly: 'You know, Berner, you're the only one who isn't ridiculous.'

Suddenly they heard a muffled tolling like that of the bell. It was the Master, who, without a hat, had appeared on the steps and was banging the gong. 'Now will you come in?' he demanded. And he banged it again. 'Will you come in?'

'Yes, we're coming,' Frøken Alice called out, and in she ran – through another door, the gentlemen behind her. They walked through the long corridor on the ground floor, the lieutenants first, with Berner and Feddersen following them.

Feddersen was twirling his moustache. 'Berner,' he said, offering no further explanation for his words: 'Berner, my good man, you're truly mad.'

Berner didn't ask why.

'But you're too modest,' Feddersen concluded. 'That's the secret.' Feddersen fell silent for a while. Then he said: 'One would think you weren't even aware that you had been given "God's gift".'

Berner, who never listened at all when speaking to men, and when he spoke to women mostly just *looked*, said in a distracted voice: 'God's gift?'

Feddersen nodded. 'Yes, my friend.'

Frøken Alice was standing by the big window in the sitting room. She had opened it and was looking out at the snowfall. 'Georg,' she said, 'if it carries on snowing like this tomorrow, we'll have to take the sleighs to the ball.'

Georg took the cigarette out of the corner of his mouth. 'Are you out of your mind,' he said, 'do you really think there'll be a proper snowstorm at

Easter? And we definitely won't be going in the sleighs because they all need fixing. They're with the blacksmith.'

The guests had retired to their rooms.

Axel Berner was standing by his window,* staring blankly at the falling snow, without seeing anything at all. His entire soul was consumed by one single, frightening question.

Frøken Alice was still in the sitting room. She sat down in front of the piano and smiled into the air for a long time. Then she hit a key and started to play.

Rubinstein's Gallop could be heard throughout the room beneath the vaulted ceiling.* The footman opened the door.

'The Master wishes to know for how long the young lady intends to continue playing?'

But Frøken Alice just nodded. 'You may go to bed, Hansen,' was all she said, as she played on.

Herr Hansen put out all the lamps in the house and made his way to his room. He placed one of the table lamps from the conservatory behind the headboard of his bed and started to undress. Herr Hansen was in the habit of reading in bed, and when he had put on a Chinese silk shirt – the young man wore Lieutenant Georg's discarded linen – he devoted himself to reading.

His Easter reading was *Bel-Ami* ... Guy de Maupassant was his favourite author of all time.*

Knuth and Vedel were still up. They were lingering over a bottle of Madeira.

'Damn fine girl,' Knuth said.

'Yes,' Vedel mumbled.

'She's yet another one that got away,' Knuth said.

'True,' Vedel mumbled.

For a while both lieutenants looked pensive.

Then Vedel said: 'And what do you make of Berner?'

'Well,' Knuth replied, 'he doesn't say an awful lot.'

They sat for a while longer until Vedel said – perhaps it was a response: 'But do you know something, I've started to think that what it's really about is looking at the girls. It's the eyes that count .... And besides,' he added, 'there aren't *enough* girls.'

'Yes,' Knuth replied. 'Of that sort, you mean.'

And then they suddenly started talking about a wire-haired German pointer.

The whole manor house was asleep.

Outside the snow continued to fall.

Lieutenant Georg stretched out in bed with a yawn.

Herr Hansen brought him his tea. 'How's the weather?' the lieutenant wanted to know.

Herr Hansen, who looked sleepy – the young man didn't undertake his full ablutions until after he had carried out his morning duties – bowed and said: 'It's snowing, Herr Lieutenant.'

'What the hell … open the curtains.' The lieutenant sat bolt upright in his bed. 'Yes, bless me, it is still snowing.'

It could not be denied. There was snow everywhere – deep drifts of snow. 'And we're supposed to go to Vedby,' the lieutenant said.

Herr Hansen left, and the lieutenant continued to sit upright in his bed without moving. 'Well, the Master will be pleased,' he said. He was thinking of the paternal rye crop.

'*Bien*,' he said, 'there'll be no drill for the time being', and turned to the wall to sleep away a little more of the holiday.

When he woke up again and rang the bell, Herr Hansen turned up with water for shaving. During a three-month stay in Copenhagen, Herr Hansen had been trained in modern table setting as well as shaving, and he handled the razor as if driving a plough through a fallow field.

While Herr Hansen wielded the razor, the lieutenant didn't dare utter a word, but when Hansen paused, he asked: 'Is anyone up?'

'Frøken Alice has gone to see the blacksmith,' Hansen said.

'What the devil does she want with him, … oh, it's bound to be about the sleighs … but she hasn't a hope of getting them, so she could have saved herself the trouble. And where is Berner?'

Herr Hansen bowed with the razor in his hand. 'I believe he went with the young lady,' he said.

Herr Hansen resumed driving the plough. Not a muscle had moved in his face. Herr Hansen had turned into one of those people who can think a great deal without revealing it.

Frøken Alice and Berner were leaving the forge. They had found it closed, and Frøken Alice had said it was no use trying the blacksmith at home. 'His wife is religious, you see,' she said, and laughed.

Berner didn't seem to be listening to what she was saying. He just walked by her side with his head half-bowed and smiling – all the time. His lips pursed so softly when he smiled.

Frøken Alice continued to talk about the blacksmith and the pious folk and the ball in Vedby. After a while she realised that even she didn't know what she was saying.

'Well, that was the blacksmith,' she then said very suddenly, making no sense at all.

And she, too, fell silent while their footsteps carried on so close to one another in the snow.

The church bells started to sound and the snow fell lightly.

'Berner,' she said, 'it's so very nice to be quiet with you.'

They carried on walking and the bells carried on tolling. Churchgoers passed them, three old women shuffled past, as did clusters of the pious. Religious people had such a strange gait, it was as if they were constantly creeping around corners.

Alice laughed at them – she seemed to laugh the whole time.

But then her mood changed abruptly.

'Come on, Berner,' she said, 'let's visit the churchyard, it's so beautiful.'

The branches of every tree were weighed down by snow, and they walked up to the church on a cleared path between two white banks.

'Listen, Berner,' Alice said – and she lowered her voice even more: 'Let's go inside.'

The congregation filled the church completely. They sat bowed, men and women, on the hard pews. The candles on the altar burned tall and straight.

Alice and Berner stood behind the rear pew. Side by side, they too bowed their heads. Around them they could hear the congregation singing.

Then the vicar emerged on the pulpit. 'Let's go,' Alice said.

They left through the porch and stepped out into the snow. 'Let's stay here,' Alice said. 'The church bells sound so lovely here.'

They were on a mound near the wall. In front of them lay the white landscape with softly falling snow. The church bells were muffled by the snow-filled air.

'It's so beautiful.'

'Yes.'

They stayed where they were. Inside the church, the singing resumed:

Fair is creation,
Fairer God's heaven,
Blest is the marching pilgrim throng.
Onward through lovely
Regions of beauty
Go we to Paradise with song.*

They stayed where they were, and Alice turned her face to the churchyard. You could barely make out the height of the graves under the snow. The crosses and the gravestones were all white, and their names had been erased.

Frøken Alice gazed far beyond the graves. 'Yes,' she said, 'so now they rest *here*. But how many of them ever lived? Berner, nobility is a nonsense. There are only two kinds of people: those who know how to live – and everyone else.'

Berner's eyes met hers – where a gentle sparkle shone. Then suddenly he looked away and said: 'But who is happier?'

'The others will *never* be happy,' Alice insisted. And with that she broke off. 'Come,' she said.

Berner walked behind her. He loved it. The curve of it. The line of her back. No, no one, no one walked like her.

They reached the gate and Frøken Alice turned around. 'Are you there, Berner?'

But Berner had made his way towards a beggar by the wall. He had slipped a large coin into his hand. Alice laughed happily. 'You're so kind, Berner,' she said. 'But' – and she laughed again – 'you don't want to.'

'Want what?'

Frøken Alice carried on laughing, then she suddenly she swung her arm through the air as if brandishing a whip. 'I'm saying,' she said, 'that I want to go to the ball.'

When they came back, Herr Hansen was sounding the gong for lunch, and the manor house courtyard echoed to the sound.

'Hurry up, Berner, hurry up.'

Crossing the bridge to the manor house proved quite a challenge, because the wind had increased. Georg was in the dining room by an open window. 'Where the bloody hell have you been?' he shouted out.

'We went to church,' Alice shouted back.

'That's a lie,' the lieutenant said, and slammed the window shut.

Frøken Alice ran through the hall and into the dining room. 'Where's the Master?' she said, looking around, flushed from the running and the storm. It was not until now that she snatched her hat from her unravelling hair.

The three lieutenants were having their coffee. 'Well,' Georg said. 'You're only two hours late.' You could set your watch by the Master's mealtimes. 'It's half past one.'

'And I'm so hungry I could eat a horse,' Frøken Alice said, as she started eating, while Hansen, without hurrying the pace of service, went through the various stages of lunch – without hearing and without seeing.

'So,' said Lieutenant Georg, 'the ball is off then.'

'At least we're spared that,' Knuth said.

'Want to bet?' said Alice, who was still eating.

Georg's head turned instantly. 'Are you betting for money?' he said as his eyes lit up. Robbing his sister of her annuity from Vallø through betting was one of Lieutenant Georg's ways of 'maintaining his lifestyle.'*

'Yes,' Alice said, 'a hundred kroner.' And then she added, as she stared into space in the dining room: 'Today is a special day.'

'Eat up, Berner,' she suddenly exclaimed. Berner had quite forgotten the meat on his plate. Frøken Alice for her part wolfed down her food. Happiness always stimulated her appetite.

The two visiting lieutenants couldn't take their eyes off her, when suddenly Alice leapt up – with the haste of happy people. 'Right, I'm off to see the Master,' she said.

And Georg called out: 'He's not that mad,' after her as she ran. Alice was about to close the door behind her. 'Just you wait and see,' she said.

The two visiting lieutenants and Feddersen retired to the sitting room, each of them gnawing at a Havana cigar. They were silent for a long time. Then Knuth said: 'Yes, it would be quite wonderful … .' He fell silent for a while, before he spoke again in the voice of someone who is completely besotted: 'First, a late supper … then make it last by sitting very quietly, chatting … . And later – .' The lieutenant didn't complete his sentence, but continued to nod repeatedly.

Vedel, however, said: 'My friend, there's no use in dreaming.'

'No,' Knuth said.

Feddersen, who was running an ivory-backed brush over his moustache, said: 'Women with a healthy appetite always have substance!'

'They do,' Vedel said, and nodded as if he had made a sudden discovery. 'They make excellent wives.'

The Master was in the library. It was lined with bookcases, filled with books from previous centuries which no one in the last century had read. A special section contained Parisian novels of a dubious nature from the 1840s, which had been acquired by the Master's father. The Master himself had no interest in literature. He hoped to reform the business side of the estate through intensive sheep breeding, and so his only reading material was sheep breeding journals in the three major European languages. He reviewed these periodicals stretched out in a leather-covered armchair and wearing his slippers.

Frøken Alice knocked forcefully – for reasons of diplomacy: the Master would invariably be deeply offended should he be caught napping – and entered.

'I'm reading,' the Master said.

'Yes, Papa,' she said. She drummed her fingers on the windowpane, against which the snow was blowing. 'Hm,' she then said abruptly, as if concluding a matter that had been decided through a lengthy conversation: 'So we'll take the brown horses to spare the black ones.'

The Master looked up from his sheep periodical immediately. He hadn't expected even that much consideration; in fact, the Master wasn't used to either of his children sparing him or his property. 'Right,' he said – and his voice sounded very loud – 'so you have *indeed* lost your mind. You can't see your hand in front of your face out there.'

The Master looked down again. 'Besides, I'm reading,' he said again.

Alice was already out of the door and back in the sitting room like a single gust of wind. 'So we're taking the brown ones,' she said – she was standing in the middle of the room. 'And we're leaving at seven!'

Twilight was already encroaching on the sitting room; the old portraits faded and slipped out of sight, while the palm trees around them rose like mighty shadows. The lieutenants were quietly discussing whether to put on their uniforms, and Alice was softly playing Rubinstein's "Der Asra".*

'Well, tonight,' she said, 'you're in uniform. Tonight is a gala!'

It sounded like a fanfare.

Vedel saluted her in front of the piano. 'A gala in honour of the Queen!' he said.

'Knuth,' Alice said, 'what date is it today?'

'The twenty-first … .'

'The twenty-first,' Alice echoed in a lingering voice, as if humming it.

But when the lieutenants and Feddersen had left, Berner said quietly from the window: 'It's my mother's birthday today.'

Alice made no reply, but her eyes suddenly filled with tears in the darkness; he had spoken so tenderly. 'She died very young?' she said, after a pause.

'Yes – and yet she was so happy.'

They fell silent, and the twilight of the room enveloped them both.

'But now it's time to get changed,' Frøken Alice then said.

'*Yes*,' Berner said.

Alice lingered for a moment by a bouquet of flowers in one of the big vases. 'This is for you, Berner,' she said, 'for your buttonhole.' She had picked a daisy. 'Here,' she said, and she followed his hand as it took it: 'yet it's the humblest of all the flowers … .'

She had many candles lit in her dressing room, which was very large and very full of plants.

'The white one,' she said immediately. She stood in front of her mirror, gazing into it. She looked like someone who has decided to give a very lovely present to a person she is deeply fond of.

Her lady's maid paused for a moment at the order for 'the white one'. When the dresses had arrived from Copenhagen in March and were laid out for inspection – incidentally Frøken Alice made her inspections quickly – on seeing the white dress, she had said: 'Yes, we'll save that … for a proper party.' And yet she hadn't worn it in town at the ballet with the English Minister.

Silver daisies had been embroidered onto the white dress and the fabric was moiré.

Frøken Alice sang all the time as she was washed and dressed. While the water was poured over her and she was sponged with Eau de Lubin,* while her hair was brushed, her long, long hair .... 'Shiny, I want it shiny,' she said to the maid, who held it up like a shimmering garland in her hand. But once it had been brushed, she put it up herself. It had never seen curling tongs. It sat, in the end, like a crown. She didn't look in the mirror. Standing in the middle of the room with her head held high and her chest out, she let her maid button the daisy dress – while she smiled.

'And then roses,' she said.

'The gardener doesn't have any,' her maid said.

'He *must* have,' Alice insisted. And her maid went off to check.

There was a knock. It was Georg.

He was taken aback as one is when one encounters something very beautiful, and he said, as he sat down on a chair: 'You look jolly nice today.'

Alice just walked up and down between the many, many candles, and over by a what-not she took something from a box. 'You'll lose, Georg – here you go,' she said, handing him a crisp new hundred-kroner note.

'I'm not going to lose,' the lieutenant drawled, yet there was gratitude in his voice. 'That's new,' he said after a pause.

Frøken Alice stopped in front of the mirror. For the first time. 'Yes,' she said. And soon afterwards, as she gazed into the mirror, she added – and possibly she was talking about something quite different: 'Whatever you give away must be beautiful.'

Georg stayed and they talked until the gong sounded. Then he left, and her maid came back. 'The gardener says there are no roses.'

'Nonsense,' Alice said. 'I'll have to go there myself.'

She walked down the passage; in the hall she met Berner. 'Berner,' she said, 'you're coming with me. I'm going to the greenhouse.'

Then she suddenly looked down at her silk shoes. 'Ane Marie, Ane Marie,' she called out, 'I need a pair of clogs!' She got the clogs and she and Berner left through the conservatory. 'Good Heavens,' she said, 'give me your arm. I'm going to keel over on these stilts.' And on Berner's arm she ran through the snow towards the greenhouse, her clogs clattering.

'Turn on the light, Eriksen,' she said as she entered the greenhouse. And Eriksen, the head gardener, a bespectacled man who always looked anxious and had a suspicious expression on his face as if people were constantly trying to take something from him, flicked the electric switch. The broad palms stood proud beneath the bright white light.

Alice hopped out of her clogs. 'It's wonderful here, isn't it?'

She walked beneath the big trees. Berner followed quietly. It was as if he could only see her train, which flowed over the gravel.

'Why, here are the roses,' she said. She had stopped. 'Those ones!' she said.

Herr Eriksen just cut them – a little aggressively – and the red roses fell. Frøken Alice had intended them for the grave of her mother, Eriksen knew.

Alice carried on smiling. 'Thank you, Eriksen,' she said.

She left the greenhouse, and all the way back she spoke about her mother, of whom the roses reminded her. 'She was the finest person I've known,' she said, 'so sweet and fine – and you can't imagine a more beautiful singing voice.'

In the hall she stopped for a moment and pinned the roses to her dress, holding them in place with a diamond pin.

'Hm,' she said, – and her face took on a gentle expression, like when you think of your best friend. 'Papa may take me in to the table now.'

Berner opened the door to the sitting room and Frøken Alice entered.

'Yes,' she said and laughed – there was something flustered about the lieutenants as they leapt up: 'I look pretty tonight – thank God.'

Feddersen entered the dining room by the side of lieutenant Knuth. 'She's as lovely as happiness,' he said.

'Yes,' said Knuth, who had paid more attention to the details, and who was a man of a somewhat envious nature. 'You could say that again.'

Hansen served the soup with his well-manicured hands.

'Well, once people go mad, they stay that way.'

It was the Master who concluded the meal by raising a glass of Madeira: 'Cheers, children, and enjoy yourselves!'

'Thank you, Master,' Alice said, and – while looking at him – she suddenly leaned towards her father and kissed him on both cheeks. 'Oh – Papa,' she said in a tender voice.

They rose from the table and entered the sitting room.

Herr Hansen announced the carriages were ready, and everyone said: 'Time to wrap up!'

'Yes, by God, we need wrapping up,' said Georg, 'it's a bitter cold.'

Every fur at the manor house was snatched from its pegs – travelling furs and walking furs and driving furs all mixed up together.

'Feddersen, Feddersen,' said Alice, whose head was sticking out of an abundance of white pelt: 'That monstrosity hasn't been in use for twenty years!' Feddersen wriggled and sneezed inside an enormous grey travelling fur which had been heavily sprinkled with pepper.

'Bloody hell,' Georg said, 'that's cayenne … .'

And everyone started to sneeze and laugh, while Herr Feddersen continued his fight to get out of the fur, and no one was willing to lend him a hand because the pepper stank. They all sneezed and shouted until Alice flung open the door and said: 'To the carriages!'

'Right,' said Georg as he emerged out onto the steps. 'Now that's what I call a stiff wind!'

The storm seized them as if hoping to sweep them off the steps.

'Larsen,' Alice shouted, 'do you think we'll make it?'

'No, Frøken,' the coachman said.

'Well, that's a bore,' was all Alice said, as she jumped inside the carriage.

Feddersen sat down, as did Berner, opposite Alice and Knuth. Vedel and Georg were in the other carriage.

'Right then, time to go?' the first coachman said in an unruffled voice. Herr Hansen merely nodded, and the first carriage started moving.

'Well,' said the coachman on the second carriage to Lieutenant Georg: 'At least they made it across the moat.'

The storm shook the carriage as if trying to throw the next generation of the family right into the moat. 'Yes, just about, what a performance,' Georg said, slamming the carriage door shut.

The front carriage joined the main road, and the storm came at it from the side and rocked the carriage like a ship. 'We're all at sea!' Feddersen said.

Alice hummed with every gust of wind. One moment they were moving and the next they had stopped; the horses were blinded and could not get through.

Knuth was quite cross. 'I feel sorry for the animals,' he said.

'But we *must* get there,' said Alice, who normally treated every beast on the estate like her personal favourite; she stopped humming.

There was a new gust of wind and the carriage practically jumped. 'Look out for the second carriage!' Alice cried out.

'I can't open the window,' said Knuth.

It was so dark inside the carriage that they could barely see one another's faces. Only Berner was sitting with his head strangely reclined, immobile and silent in his corner, with the same sparkling eyes turned to the spot where Alice's white furs were shining.

'Of course you can, of course you can, we *want* to see that carriage,' Frøken Alice insisted. Frøken Alice *wanted* to see that carriage, and Knuth managed to push the window down.

'What is it?'

There was another jolt, and the carriage keeled over. It landed very comfortably – in the middle of a snowdrift, on its side.

'Good God!' shouted Alice, who had Feddersen's fur as well as Feddersen himself on top of her – into the darkness of the carriage where everyone was struggling on top of one another. And in the same moment she said, suddenly quite out of breath: 'Where's Berner?' As if he had been injured. 'Where's Berner?'

By the time Feddersen and Knuth crawled out, Berner had already got her up and out of the carriage.

'Well,' Alice said, 'just look at the four of us!'

The storm was howling and the snow was blowing.

'Larsen, Larsen, what do we do now?'

'Go home, I suppose,' said Larsen, who was busy with the horses.

'Yes, Larsen,' Alice shouted, still laughing: 'But will we be able to?'

'Who knows,' Larsen replied.

The gentlemen had to help with the carriage. Georg and Vedel joined them, and everyone toiled, shouted and laughed, in the middle of the snow.

'This really is a fine mess,' said Georg.

They managed to push the carriage upright and calm the horses down. Knuth stood patting them as if they were his own animals back home in Odense. Alice just laughed. 'It looks as if we'll be dancing at home,' she said. 'Because we must have a ball – on the twenty-first.'

Georg was pouring out shots of snaps from a hip flask in the middle of the road. 'Well, the family has gone mad at last,' he said.

The coachmen had a quiet discussion before they returned to their boxes.

The Master, who was snoozing in the library over a copy of the district council's minutes, was roused from his slumber on hearing the carriages roll across the bridge to the manor house. 'Right,' he said, 'they must have damned well turned over!'

He ran out of the library towards Herr Hansen, who bowed with the same expression of unfailing politeness, and said: 'Yes, Master, I think the company is coming back!'

'So I hear,' the Master said. 'I fear that Alice might have broken her leg.'

It was his sole concern. He was already down the stairs. Frøken Alice, however, was standing calmly in the hall below the bronze chandelier where seventeen wax candles were burning – glowing in her white furs.

'Good evening, Papa!' she called out. 'It looks as if we'll be dancing at home.'

The Master stopped running. He was just delighted to see her in one piece. 'Well, I did tell you,' he said, 'but there's no stopping madness.'

The Master might have intended to say more – his mouth was still open – but Frøken Alice just clapped her hands. 'Take your furs off, gentlemen!' she called out, 'we have work to do.'

She was gone through the sitting room like a storm. First she had to talk to Sørensen. Sørensen was a very broad and damask-clad lady who wore a brown wig and a set of shiny false teeth, which seemed pressed together over every ancestral secret. She had run the house for twenty years without any of the gentry hearing her utter ten words. If she had any passions, she hid them well. She quietly collected gold items on the side. Her speciality was brooches.

Frøken Alice found Sørensen crocheting by the table in her room, which was agreeably warm and offered many places for rest in the corners.

'Sørensen, dear?' she began – and she thought at that same moment: heavens, it really is very cosy here – 'Dear Sørensen, I'm sorry for disturbing you … .'

Frøken Sørensen looked as if the situation did indeed call for an apology. Frøken Sørensen was not used to being disturbed at unexpected times.

'But,' Alice said, 'we need to light the chandeliers. Do we have any candles?'

'Which chandeliers?' Frøken Sørensen wanted to know.

'In the great hall, dear Sørensen … . And we'll need sandwiches and wine and lots of things – we're going to have a ball.'

Frøken Sørensen had got up. She said only a single word: 'Fine,' and began to move about in her laced-up fabric boots. Her feet were weak, as a result of standing too much when making sandwiches.

Alice ran ahead of her into the pantry, a vast room with cupboards whose contents could feed an army. She opened the cupboards and pulled out drawers; there were great big heaps of prunes and plums and figs and chocolates. 'Ah,' she said, 'what an abundance.'

'It's what there usually is,' Sørensen said.

'Hansen, Hansen,' Frøken Alice called out, 'tell the staff to get dressed, because the dancing starts at nine o'clock.'

Herr Hansen stopped in the middle of the butler's pantry. 'Staff,' he said, 'the staff, Frøken?'

'Yes,' Alice said, 'the maids and the hands, all of them – at nine o'clock, they have one hour … .' Alice laughed. 'Don't you understand,' she said, 'we're having the harvest ball at Easter.' Frøken Alice had already left.

Herr Hansen and Sørensen didn't exchange even a single glance. But from the dining room Alice called out: 'And, Sørensen, please light the stoves.'

She ran back to the sitting room, holding the daisy train in her hand. 'Right, gentlemen,' – the lieutenants had now been freed from their wrapping – 'time to move.'

'Move – what?' Georg said.

'The piano,' Alice said, dropping her train.

The lieutenants just laughed as if they hadn't understood, but Alice clapped her hands: 'Yes, the piano, gentlemen … . We'll get some of the hands to help. We'll be dancing in the great hall.'

She summoned Hansen so that he could fetch some members of staff, and she herself began to move vases and busts, while the lieutenants continued to laugh.

The Master was standing in the midst of all the confusion. 'What the hell?' he said.

But Alice just ran up to him – holding two knick-knacks from the piano, one in each hand – and uttered a long, smiling: 'Boo,' into his face.

Four hands arrived. They waited inside the door, standing straight up and down, four pairs of blue socks. Their faces gave nothing away.

'Let's get to work,' Alice said. And the four hands began to move the piano.

'Go on, help them,' Alice ordered the lieutenants. And so the three lieutenants had to help. Feddersen held a candlestick.

'*Berner*,' Alice said, 'you're daydreaming.'

Berner just stood there smiling, like someone who has been given the moon as a present and is gazing at it in his outstretched hand.

'Feddersen,' Alice said, 'give Berner the candlestick.' Berner took it with a start.

'There, Berner will light the way for us,' Alice said.

The four hands struggled to lug the piano up the stairs. Alice led the way, her white train flowing like a silver stream down the steps, while at the top Berner was holding the candlestick.

'We'll put it here,' Alice said. They had reached the great hall.

Fires were already burning in the big stoves, and the flickering glow made the old portraits on the high oak panels look as if they had come alive. Alice ran into the middle of the great hall, where two footmen were lighting the fifty candles in the bronze chandeliers.

'Yes,' she said, 'isn't it wonderful here.'

'*You're* wonderful,' Feddersen said.

'And that's just the frame,' Alice said. Feddersen looked at her for a moment. 'Yes, Feddersen, – for the picture.'

Suddenly she changed her tone. 'But do all the staff really know there's going to be a ball, I wonder,' she said.

The staff did indeed know. Torrents of suds were flowing in the hands' quarters, and petticoats flew around the maids as they scrubbed their upper bodies.

'Georg,' Alice said, 'go fetch Lars the Fiddler. I want him and his son to play their violins. They fiddle so hard you can't hear yourself think. Right, gentlemen, let's have a glass of champagne.'

Alice went downstairs followed by the lieutenants. Knuth made up the rear with Feddersen.

'It's jolly strange,' Knuth said.

'What is?'

'All of it,' Knuth drawled.

But Feddersen continued to walk downstairs, as a sudden expression of pain seemed to flit across his face, which was otherwise quite immobile. 'My dear fellow,' he said, 'envy is an undesirable quality.'

'Right,' said Knuth, who had no idea what the civil servant meant.

'But,' said Feddersen, having stopped on the landing: 'He, who has a closet, ought perhaps to go in there and pray that something like that can last.'*

Knuth said nothing more. He didn't normally think that Feddersen ever gave himself away.

'But,' Feddersen said, 'a ball is a ball … .'

The penny suddenly dropped for Knuth. 'And life is just life,' he said.

In the sitting room Herr Hansen had already put out the coolers.

Lieutenant Georg stopped in front of a side table where they were standing: 'It's like a never-ending communion this Easter,' he said.

However, Alice, who had sized up the fluted glasses, turned to Herr Hansen. 'No, champagne coupes,' she insisted. And she extended her arm as if already raising a coupe.

She crossed the floor to her favourite spot below the big palm trees. There the lamps were low, and the shadows cast by the trees fell across the ceiling like a mighty vaulted tent.

'Feddersen,' she said – Herr Hansen was discreetly popping the champagne corks – 'Feddersen – it's time for the guitar.'

The lieutenants had sat down; there was an odd distance between them and a great deal of space in front of Alice, because the piano was no longer there.

'Yes,' said Knuth, whose Eremitage collarbone was silently aching quite considerably from the effort with the piano: 'A bit of guitar would be nice.'

'Sing us a song,' Vedel said. Lieutenant Vedel, too, needed a rest. He wasn't used to this, and got rather tired of balls which were in preparation for too long before the actual activity commenced.

Berner was sitting in his corner, but Feddersen had fetched the guitar from the bay window. Alice raised her head. 'Right, you man without a face,' she said – that was her nickname for Feddersen; she always said that the day Herr Feddersen had decided to hide his face, he had borrowed one from a fashion magazine – : 'Go on, sing. We're listening.'

Feddersen paused for a moment. He had fixed his suddenly moist eyes on a lamp. Then he sang while his hands, accompanying, moved around the instrument:

> COME, rosy day!
> Come quick—I pray—
> I am so glad when I thee see!
> Because my Fair,
> Who is so dear,
> Is rosy-red and white like thee.
>
> She lives, I think,
> On heavenly drink
> Dawn-dew, which Hebe pours for her;
> Else—when I sip

At her soft lip
How smells it of ambrosia?

She is so fair
None can compare;
And, oh, her slender waist divine!
Her sparkling eyes
Set in the skies
The morning stars would far outshine!*

Feddersen stopped. He looked down once more and, for a moment, the room was silent.

Then Lieutenant Georg said: 'Who is the poet?'

Herr Feddersen didn't reply immediately – then he mentioned a name.

'That chap knows what he's talking about,' said Georg.

Lieutenant Vedel had stretched his long legs a little too far out with only a slight lack of grace.

No one knew if Frøken Alice had been listening. She was resting her head against the back of her high chair and the silvery mesh over the lamp cast a veiled glow over her upturned face.

Then she suddenly raised her head. 'And yet,' she said, 'it's strange how little the poets know about how deeply a person can love … . But,' – and she leapt up without warning – 'the staff will need apple dumplings. People like that never think it's a party unless they get their apple dumplings.'

She rang the bell for Herr Hansen, and quickly gave the order about the apple dumplings. 'The apprentices will have to make them,' she said, 'they'll have to take turns dancing and cooking. The staff must have their apple dumplings.'

The apprentices were three daughters of various shopkeepers who spent their time tightly corseted and utterly homeless while they were trained under Sørensen's watchful eye, and secretly paid a mere 340 kroner per year to the same Frøken Sørensen for doing her work.

'And they'll need wine,' Alice said.

'It would be better to give them punch,' Georg said.

Alice didn't care. She just shook her head. '*Chères bêtes*,'* she said, 'how wonderful it is to be rich.' She snatched up a glass. The rose-tinted champagne sloshed around in the shallow coupe.

'Here's to the ball,' the lieutenants called out; and they drained their glasses.

'Yes,' Alice said, 'the staff will be here soon.'

Without intending to and without knowing it, Berner stepped forwards and took Frøken Alice's arm. 'Thank you, Berner,' she said. And she smiled. The other men had to walk some distance behind her, because her train was long and she didn't lift it up.

The entrance hall was crammed with people from the estate. 'Good evening, everyone,' Alice said. 'Do come up, do come up.'

Some of the hands and the maids started making their way up the stairs. They crept up them in such a strange fashion, as if they only knew how to climb them in their stockinged feet. Two housemaids stood on the landing and curtsied.

'Come on, up you go, up you go,' Alice insisted. 'Liven things up, lieutenants,' she whispered. 'That should be easy for experienced men such as yourselves.'

The lieutenants – whose own knees were buckling somewhat with shyness – began asking the ladies to dance, and marched with them into the great hall, where Feddersen was already at the piano playing in a trio with the cottager and his son, who were wearing white socks.

'A march, a march,' demanded Alice, who was leading with Berner, while the hands and the maids crowded around the doorway, until six Swedes with very broad shoulders entered, each with a girl, with the familiarity of men who have been here before.

'Quite right, quite right,' Alice cried out.

'He knows only one march,' Feddersen said, as she passed the piano.

'Well, let's hear it then,' Alice said, and laughed.

It was Crown Prince Frederik's honorary march.* The cottager and his son went at the march just like when they made up the whole orchestra for the autumn visit of the travelling fair. Eventually everyone was paired off – coachmen with housemaids – and they began to process in a long line, their faces solemn as if they were walking around the Christmas tree at a charitable Christmas event.

But Alice led the way. 'There, Berner,' she said. 'Now it's time for us to change our partners.'

She let go of his arm and curtsied to Lars the coachman. 'You, Larsen.' She went onto the floor with the coachman. She danced round once with Larsen. Then she went on to the next man and the next man again. That was an agricultural student, who blushed like a peony and sweated through his gloves. She ended up with a cottager.

And it was Frøken Alice who led them all through the great hall, and everyone followed her – the lieutenants and the hands and the Swedes. The two footmen started serving wine, and the maids, who were not used to strong drink, grew red-faced and wiped the sweat off their cheeks with the sleeves of their dresses. Tongues were loosened, and the hands downed their glasses and hid them in the window niches, while Vedel found himself a tightly-corseted apprentice, who danced close to his padded uniform with the secret desire for abandonment that characterises provincials.

But Alice danced at the front, her train in her hand, her back straight and her head held high, mostly as if she was following her own swift beat.

The Master arrived.

His face glowed red as he went around and took wine with his staff – the Master always walked with a peculiar gait, as if he was wearing knee-high boots. 'Well,' he kept on saying, 'they're clearly mad – but as long as they're enjoying themselves … .'

The three Swedes had managed to push three of the maids into a corner, where as they conversed, they emphasized their well-endowed Swedish manliness through explicit and somewhat provocative postures.

The Master had stopped in another corner; he was looking for his daughter, his eyes shining. 'Yes,' he then said, – he had to say something and the person nearest to him was an old cottager – 'she's a big girl now.'

The cottager was Per Eriksen. 'Yes,' he said slowly, 'Frøken Alice seems to have grown up.'

Per Eriksen was the oldest of the cottagers. His temperament was gloomy, and he could recall every accident at the manor house in the past seventy years – right back to the time when the Master's aunt hanged herself from the stove pipe.

'Yes, those were the days,' Per Eriksen would conclude, whenever he had told his story about the aunt yet again.

Twenty couples on the floor swung around one another.

'Faster, faster,' Alice cried out. And Feddersen bashed away at the keys. She was standing next to Berner between the windows. 'You see,' she said, 'now that's what I call a ball.'

The noise rose, and the sound of the dancers' footsteps across the oak floor dissolved in laughter and chatter.

Lieutenant Georg, who attracted every member of the female sex under forty, was sweating profusely from executing his social responsibilities.

'But where's the estate manager?' Alice said. They had forgotten the estate manager. Hansen was dispatched to fetch him and his family.

'But they'll be in bed by now, God help me,' the Master said.

'Well, then they'll just have to get up,' said Alice, and laughed. 'No one shall sleep tonight.'

Standing next to Berner, she looked across the dancers, who seemed like one moving body in the glow from the bronze chandeliers. In the corners the cottagers were quietly drinking port, as if knocking back shots of schnapps.

A smile flitted across the face of Frøken Alice. 'My friend,' she said, turning to Feddersen, whose dark eyes suddenly looked up from the keys and rested for a moment on hers: 'Play a waltz, please. A slow waltz.'

A slow waltz was too much for the cottager and his son. They took a break with glasses between their knees, their faces puffy as if they were in the final section of a Roman bath.

'I really ought to dance with Sørensen,' said the Master, who had reached the piano.

But Feddersen wasn't listening.

The waltz had begun. Everyone on the floor suddenly stopped, and a space was freed up as if the crowd had been swept away.

'Berner,' Alice said, 'it's our turn now.'

They were the only couple on the floor. Her straight body swayed softly in his arms as they slowly danced. No one joined them.

The notes from the piano, which rang out alone, accompanied them from far away, while the glow from the wax candles in the chandeliers, which had flickered during the tumult, burned steadily once more. They carried on dancing. Neither of them spoke.

Alice saw only Berner's soft mouth with its trembling lips. 'Axel,' she said, and repeated his name twice.

The waltz ended.

'And now a gallop,' Alice called out. She walked past the piano on Berner's arm. And when the commotion resumed once more and the lieutenants were all dancing, she said, laughing right into his face: 'Go on, Berner, say it.'

But Berner didn't speak. His face was still turned to hers like a nature worshipper's towards the sun.

Suddenly Alice's eyes sparkled. 'Berner, you're impossible,' she said.

And with that she ran to the piano, pushed Feddersen aside, and took his seat. And in the midst of the chaos where all voices merged, she sang:

Daisy, Daisy,
Give me your answer, do!
I'm half crazy,
All for the love of you!
It won't be a stylish marriage,
I can't afford a carriage,
But you'll look sweet upon the seat
Of a bicycle made for two!*

Berner had gone to stand by her side. His whole face seemed to light up with a sudden glow. And without knowing it, in an act of recklessness and sudden elation, he quickly pushed her away and sang himself – he had never known that he could sing:

Daisy, Daisy,
Give me your answer, do!
I'm half crazy,
All for the love of you!
It won't be a stylish marriage,
I can't afford a carriage,
But you'll look sweet upon the seat
Of a bicycle made for two!

He didn't quite make it to the end. Hand in hand they stood for a moment in front of the piano. Neither of them spoke.

'Come, Berner,' said Alice.

Slowly they walked towards a balcony door, and Berner opened it.

'Close it, Axel,' said Alice.

It was quiet on the balcony. No noise penetrated the sturdy door. They stood there for a long time, shoulder by shoulder.

'Alice, how I love you.'

His sparkling eyes shone into her face while she, all white, stood on the white balcony. 'How I love you.'

They stood like this for a long time, and they were silent for a long time. Their caresses were without end. 'How I love you.'

The snow-clad landscape stretched out in front of them like a bridal bed. Above them the stars twinkled silently.

'Have you seen the stars, Axel,' Alice said. 'Look, they're shining for us.'

But Berner kept on whispering, kept on saying, trembling faintly as if he was *born* to say, as if he *could* say only those four words: 'How I love you.'

Inside the great hall, the estate manager and his family had arrived. It consisted of two surly women, mother and daughter, whose clothes reeked of stale Eau de Cologne and drooped like clothes kept in the wardrobe for too long. The two ladies curtsied as they came towards Alice.

'What a party, and so unexpected,' the mother said.

'No,' Alice replied, and suddenly burst out laughing: 'It has been planned and anticipated for *quite* some time.'

There was dancing all across the great hall.

Alice stood quietly on Berner's arm.

'Axel,' she said, 'let there be joy for all around our joy.'

Translated by Charlotte Barslund

12. The Ravens

For the third time the hired help, Madam Jensen, broke off her task of taking out and polishing the glasses and made her way to the kitchen. Whenever she helped out, Madam Jensen possessed an appetite which every three-quarters of an hour would cause her to seek solace in food. She was especially fond of sauces, which she would scrape off the saucepans with a knife when the kitchen maids were done with them.

Hidden behind the chimney, she was interrupted in this activity when the bell was rung – angrily and twice.

'The monster is here,' said the housekeeper, who was peeling celeriac, 'let her in.'

Madam Jensen walked through the apartment in a peculiar way, as though sailing in her excess of petticoats. The bell rang again before she reached the door and was able to open it.

Frøken Sejer was waiting on the landing. 'Did the bell fail to ring?' she demanded to know, jutting out her ape-like lips, before turning to the boy from the wine merchant's, who was struggling with a basket of bottles.

'In there, little friend, in there, little friend,' she said, as she wiggled all ten fingers restlessly in front of her. Enveloped in grey and saggy gloves, they resembled the talons of a bird. The boy from the wine merchant's set down in his basket in the hall, where he lingered while Frøken Sejer looked at him with a tiny glint in her eyes.

'Right, well, goodbye, little friend,' she said, and turning to the hired help, Madam Jensen, she added: 'You can see him out,' as she herself went inside. The pearls on her short jacket jingled as she walked through the rooms and into the kitchen. Her grey eyes, which were still sharp although they had a tendency to water, took in every dish in a single sweep.

'Someone has been scraping the saucepans,' she said, and laughed with two short snorts, which sounded like a nasty cough.

'I accompanied the wine,' – Frøken Sejer continued to chortle, while her crooked shoulder shot up and down under the flapping pearls, 'I'm no fool, and I won't have them swapping the wine behind my back.'

The housekeeper made no reply; she just carried on peeling.

'Now bring me my father's labels,' Frøken Sejer said, 'and some paste.'

Frøken Sejer returned to the dining room, where Madam Jensen had resumed wiping down the china. She placed the unlabelled bottles on the table, and while her crooked shoulder rose and fell like the back of an arching cat, she began sticking her father the late Counsellor's old and yellowing château labels onto the bottles.

'It enhances the taste no end, my dear,' she said, as she glued on the labels and got sticky paste on her shaking fingers. 'The wine is from Greece,' she said, 'the Greeks have always understood wine.'

She busied herself with the labels, looking like someone shuffling a dirty pack of playing cards, until she suddenly jerked up her head and said: 'Have you had something to eat, Jensen?'

Madam Jensen muttered in reply.

Frøken Sejer rocked her head gently back and forth. 'Then you need something now. No one starves in this house, little friend. Let me get you something.'

And she rushed off with odd little leaps like a frog.

'There now,' she said, and set down a plate of food on the table in front of Madam Jensen, who ate quickly, half-turned away like someone who has a habit of swallowing their food in secret.

Frøken Sejer watched every single one of her movements as if observing a fly in a bell jar. 'Yes, we can't do without food. It gives you strength,' she said, never once taking her eyes off Madam Jensen. 'And you don't always have a plate in front of you.'

'Where is she off gallivanting now?' she said out of the blue. 'She' was the paid companion.

'Frøken Holm is out,' Madam Jensen replied.

'Hm, she's happy to take my bread and my money,' Frøken Sejer said, and as she looked at Jensen's plate, she added in a falsetto voice: 'There's still a little left. Jensen must clear her plate.'

Madam Jensen ate the remaining food with the same urgency; all the while the two women watched each other with eyes like two fencers through their masks.

'Thank you very much, Frøken Sejer,' Madam Jensen said, and took the plate away.

The housekeeper had come in to fetch a serving dish from the sideboard, and Frøken Sejer turned to her. 'Hm, no wonder Jensen stinks, given how she stuffs herself. But in this house we *must* be good hosts.'

Frøken Sejer had finished with the bottles. 'How pretty they look,' she said, admiring the false labels. 'Put them by the stove to dry.'

The housekeeper did so before she left.

When Frøken Sejer was alone once more, she got up and ran quickly up and down in front of the bottles three or four times, while the fire in the stove cast flickers over her as she ran – in front of her brew.

Madam Jensen returned and resumed her work, while Frøken Sejer sat in an armchair. 'Yes,' she said, 'eighteen guests is a lot. And yet one would so like to entertain many more.'

'But it's family,' Madam Jensen said.

'Yes,' Frøken Sejer said, and in the help's tone there had been something that caused her to glance quickly at Jensen's face. 'Blood is thicker than water.'

'Yes,' Madam Jensen said. After a pause she added: 'Would you like me to get out the bowls with the silver feet?'

'No, thank you, little friend,' Frøken Sejer replied, and suddenly started to play with her fingers once more. 'They're too much hassle.'

Madam Jensen watched the jumping fingers.

'You would just have to polish them again, little friend,' Frøken Sejer said with a nod to the help.

The bell rang again. The two Meyer nieces with red bonnets over their blonde hair had arrived. They waltzed in as if showing up at their favourite café, and kissed Frøken Sejer almost simultaneously.

'Gosh,' they said, 'darling Aunt Viktoria, we practically ran all the way here to see if we could help with anything.'

'How kind of you,' Frøken Sejer said. 'Sit down, children.'

And turning to Madam Jensen, she said: 'Don't forget the little bowls for the flowers. There'll be violets.'

'Violets,' one of the red bonnets exclaimed. 'Aunt, you are pushing the boat out.'

'Yes,' the other added quickly, 'and your home grows ever lovelier.'

'Children,' Frøken Sejer said, 'an old lady does whatever she can for the young. There are so many calls on my small capital.'

'Yes,' said one niece, who had eyed up everything, down to the last fork, 'you certainly know how to delight others, Aunt.'

'What else is there?' said Frøken Sejer, looking pointedly from one to the other.

But then she suddenly remembered something. Something she had seen the other day at the house of Frøken Svane, a wealthy and single friend; some absolutely darling little lamps, which would look so pretty on the table:

'Young people are so very fond of light,' she said, and the next moment she added, 'and it helps you see people's faces.'

A grimace which no one noticed flitted across the face of Madam Jensen while Frøken Sejer continued: 'Perhaps you could buy some for me, twelve please, seeing as you're going into town? Jensen, fetch my casket.'

Jensen went to the front sitting room and picked up the casket, a kind of money box where Frøken Sejer kept her valuables. Frøken Sejer opened it, and started piling up banknotes on the table with her wrinkled hands, whose fingernails were yellow and exceptionally hard.

Suddenly she caught the eye of her elder niece probing the many little hideaways in the casket, and she said: 'Yes, looking at money is nice.'

'Yes, indeed it is,' said Frøken Lucie, the younger of her nieces, and reached her hand into her damask bag as if gripping it, 'so is having it.'

'But the young prefer gold,' Frøken Sejer said, and flashed her godmother smile – she had served as godmother for the whole family, and her christening presents were her late father's old spoons and forks, into which she had new names engraved. 'Here's gold, children, for the lamps. Gold always looks so pleasing on the counter.'

She handed her older niece, Frøken Emilie, a gold coin – the cold metal seemed to tickle her niece right through her gloves – and reiterated: 'So get me twelve,' when the bell rang once more. It was the boy with the flowers.

The two red bonnets opened his basket and discovered an abundance of violets.

'But there's enough to decorate *two* tables,' Frøken Emilie exclaimed.

'And a little corsage for each of you as well,' said Frøken Sejer, and it was as if her yellow nails pierced the buttonholes like needles as she attached a small bouquet of violets to her nieces' coats.

'Right,' she said and smiled again, 'food and flowers go together, and there's going to be so much food for you all, children. Jensen, what are we having again? You know an old lady can't remember a thing.'

Madam Jensen started reeling off the menu in a tone of voice as if firing every dish at the nieces like bullets from a loaded rifle.

'So, that should fill you up,' said Frøken Sejer, whose own voice was very soft.

The nieces had taken all the violets out of the basket, and Frøken Sejer said: 'Hm, I know flowers wilt quickly. But as long they bring joy for a moment.'

The nieces kissed her goodbye, and Frøken Sejer said: 'You're freezing, little Emilie, your lips are so cold. Goodbye, children, and don't forget the lamps.'

The front door had barely closed before Frøken Emilie said, and her voice was practically squawking: 'Where *does* she get it from? Can you tell me that?'

Frøken Lucie replied: 'She takes money *out* of the bank. I've been telling you for ages. I've seen her run in and out of the savings bank umpteen times.'

Her older sister let the street door slam shut with a bang. 'And now we have to buy her lamps,' she said, 'the sort of tat that will undoubtedly fetch a tidy sum at auction.'

The two sisters walked on, lifting up their petticoats with both hands.

At the square, the younger said: 'I need to buy a stamp,' and started crossing the street, heading for a kiosk.

'Beware of kiosks, sister dear,' Frøken Emilie said.*

'Why, are messenger boys any better?' retorted Lucie, and carried on.

Her sister Emilie stopped in front of a mirror in a florist's shop, leaning slightly to one side because of her damask bag, which seemed full of several particularly heavy objects, such as keys for the entrance door and a pair of curling tongs.

The two red bonnets proceeded along the pavement, and ran into the arms of a petite and chubby lady, who exclaimed: 'Darling girls, fancy meeting you here.'

'Are you in town?'

'Yes.' The petite woman, who was a vicar's wife from the country, had a habit of shaking her head so vigorously it was a wonder it didn't fall off. 'I only arrived yesterday and I'm running around, my lovelies, all over town – seeing as everyone in the family wants to see me.'

The red bonnets told her about the lamps they had been sent off to buy, and the vicar's wife joined them, although first she needed to stop by an uncle who would simply have to pay for her return journey. 'Because we live on nothing but bull calves at the vicarage,' she said. 'And we only see actual money on the days we get tithes.'

Whenever one heard Fru Lund speak, it was tempting to believe that there was nothing edible at her vicarage at all apart from pork belly, salted herring and new-born calves.

Once they were inside the lamp shop and standing holding the small porcelain objects, Fru Lund said: 'And that money only lasts for a fortnight. But,' she added, 'seeing as Aunt Viktoria is having a dinner party, then I'll go over there and invite myself.'

They went their separate ways from the steps to the shop. When Fru Lund had gone, the elder Meyer sister said: 'I bet she manages to wheedle another twenty kroner for herself *there*, over coffee. There's no mistaking Emma when she's on a mission.'

Once her nieces had left, Frøken Sejer returned to her armchair. She soon fell asleep. As she sat there, with her head in her tall cap slumped towards her chest and her misshapen left shoulder pressed up against the chair back, she looked like a strange, broken toy as she dozed.

She didn't wake up when the bell went once more.

Madam Jensen opened the door, then paused for a moment in front of Frøken Sejer – giving her a look as if observing a cadaver in a ditch – before she woke her up.

'There's a gentleman here who wants a word with you, Frøken Sejer,' she said loudly.

Frøken Sejer awoke with a start. 'What?' she said, still half-asleep and, shaking her head, she added quickly: 'Yes, the mind wanders. Who is it?'

'The one with the curly hair,' said Madam Jensen, and left.

Frøken Sejer ran to her bedroom and, in front of the mirror, quickly straightened her cap, her wig, her blouse, and the whole carapace which was her body.

The housekeeper, who had heard the door to Frøken Sejer's bedroom being opened from the kitchen, asked Madam Jensen: 'Who's she tarting herself up for?'

'For him, the dandy,' Madam Jensen replied.

'Oh,' the housekeeper said, 'well, that'll be fun. I wonder what he'll take away this time.'

'Is there anything left to take?' Madam Jensen wondered out loud, and pursed her lips.

Skipping and jumping, Frøken Sejer ran to the furthest sitting room, where a young and very slim man with unusually white and soft hands got up from a chair.

'Hallo, you handsome devil,' Frøken Sejer said, and quickly drew the portières across both closed doors.

The companion, Frøken Holm, entered through the front door and walked, pale and upright, down the passage. 'Where's Frøken Sejer?' she asked in a voice which carefully maintained the same stress on each syllable.

And Madam Jensen, looking her right in the eye, replied: 'She, too, has business to attend to.'

Frøken Holm went to the dining room, and started taking tablecloths and napkins out of a cupboard.

Just under an hour passed before Frøken Sejer, whose quivering face was now beaming, drew back the portières and saw the young, blond man out herself.

'I'll see you soon, you handsome devil,' she said, 'you're always so helpful.'

'I regard it as a pleasure, as you well know,' the young man said in a very soft voice.

And he was seen out.

Frøken Sejer fluttered into the dining room, fingers, hands and feet twice as busy as usual. 'Ah,' she said when she saw Frøken Holm, 'you're back.'

'Yes,' the lady's companion replied.

Frøken Sejer laughed. 'Is it the day for your nephew, my dear?' she said in a very kind voice.

'It was my free time,' replied Frøken Holm, whose face remained inscrutable.

The bell went yet again, and this time it was Fru Lund, whose jolly, youthful laughter soon filled the whole hall. 'Dear Aunt Viktoria, I'm in town as you see, I only arrived yesterday and I hear you're giving a dinner party. Of course I'll be there and take my place. *I* can always squeeze in.'

Fru Lund sat down, and started chatting in her happy voice about her vicar husband and the five children and the vicarage, where pretty much everything was falling apart.

'Ah,' she suddenly exclaimed, 'I see you're busy with the tablecloths. Hello, dear Frøken Holm. Whereas we, little Aunt, have to wash and wash our ten so they're practically in shreds. Let me have one of yours, Aunt, would you?' she said, slapping her pretty hand on the table. 'You're always so kind towards a poor relative.'

Frøken Sejer, whose behaviour towards Fru Lund was strangely changed, as if she were faced with someone whom she secretly respected, chuckled and said: 'Do we have one, Frøken Holm?'

But Fru Lund jumped up from her chair and went to the linen cupboard herself. 'Dear Aunt Vik, it must be one of the older ones, of course,' and she dived into the tablecloths, while her aunt said with a smile: 'I'm sure, Emma my friend, that you'll find something you can use.'

Fru Lund continued to rummage around. 'Here's one,' she said, 'you wouldn't want to use this in your fine house anyway, and, Heavens, in my home, dear Aunt, it will be the best we have. We'll put it out when the bishop visits.'

Frøken Sejer said: 'Well, you take that one. It's always nice to be able to help. I'll have it sent to you,' she added.

'Dear Aunt Vik, I'll take it myself. It's the least I can do, I'm certainly not too grand for that. Little Frøken Holm, do you have a newspaper?'

Fru Lund was given the newspaper; she wrapped up the tablecloth and secured the parcel with a piece of twine. 'You have to take what you can get,' she said, and laughed right into her aunt's face.

'That's right, my girl,' Frøken Sejer replied.

'But now I must leave,' Fru Lund said. 'Goodness, I won't get to Uncle's in time unless I take the tram.'

A flash crossed Frøken Sejer's face. 'So you're seeing *him* too, little friend,' she said.

'Why of course, Aunt Vik,' Fru Lund laughed, 'one wouldn't want to disappoint any of one's relatives.'

She searched all her pockets, but couldn't find as much as a ten øre coin. 'You'll have to give me money for the tram,' she said.

When Fru Lund had gone, Frøken Sejer returned to her armchair. 'What a lovely girl,' she said and, looking at her companion, she added: 'and so direct.'

Madam Jensen and Frøken Holm had started putting the cloth on the table when Frøken Sejer's personal physician arrived.

Frøken Sejer was sitting in the sitting room when Madam Jensen announced briefly: 'It's the doctor.'

Frøken Sejer practically leapt up and flew towards the doctor: 'Little Doctor, why have you walked up all those stairs to visit a healthy person? Especially as you're still coming to my little dinner party, I hope. But do sit down, sit down.'

The doctor, whose beard was white and whose face was very narrow and composed, said: 'I just wanted to see you during the preparations. I've already told you that you over-exert yourself, you have a tendency, if I may say so, to take on a little too much.' The doctor hesitated for a moment, before adding: 'For someone with your constitution.'

'Too much,' said Frøken Sejer, whose eyes were flitting about, 'my dear Doctor, you just have to keep going.'

'Yes,' the doctor said, still looking hard at her, 'until one day you are forced to stop.'

Frøken Sejer's fingers clutched the armrests on the chairs, while the doctor continued in the same tone of voice: 'And this changeable weather causes much sickness among us old people.'

Frøken Sejer's eyes continued to flit about restlessly. 'There will be nineteen of us, Doctor,' she said out of the blue, 'seeing as little Emma is also in town. She just left with a tablecloth.'

The doctor didn't change his tone, as he said: 'Yes, the family is gathering.' He rose, adding: 'But at least I've been here.'

Frøken Sejer's hand was shaking as he took it.

'But is something the matter?' Frøken Sejer, from under whose wig a trickle of sweat was running right down the middle of her forehead, burst out, 'I'd rather you tell me now.'

The doctor took his hand away. 'Just be careful, but then again you already know that.'

'Yes, Doctor,' said Frøken Sejer, whose chest was wheezing and wheezing, 'but I so want to delight the young people.'

A barely perceptible smile crossed the doctor's face. 'I'll see you later,' was all he said.

'And you, Doctor, will be seated next to me at the table,' Frøken Sejer said, and laughed.

'And I trust you take champagne against the attacks?' the doctor asked in the doorway.

'Whenever it's necessary, little Doctor,' Frøken Sejer replied.

The doctor took his leave.

When he had gone, Frøken Sejer remained standing in the middle of the room and started grinding her false teeth. And suddenly she started running again with outstretched arms through the living room, while the two corner mirrors reflected her figure, back and forth, back and forth – as though she were engaged in a secret duel with herself.

Then she returned to the dining room, where Madam Jensen's eyes sought out her face like two evil ice picks, while Frøken Holm, who had started to arrange the violets on the table, also raised her head for a moment.

'Oh, that dear doctor,' Frøken Sejer said, 'I know he only came by to hear the menu.'

No one responded. Frøken Sejer continued onwards to the kitchen. 'Make sure you serve the hares,' she said, 'so there'll be enough for two lunches.'

And suddenly her shrill voice could be heard through the passage: 'Jensen, little friend, make sure you don't forget half the saddle in the pot – like you did the other day.'

There was no reply from the dining room, and Frøken Sejer went to her bedroom. Whenever she got dressed, she would lock the doors. She rummaged around in wardrobes and drawers for a long time before finding lace, a shawl and a wine-coloured dress. Lastly she took out her party wig and placed it on the candlestick next to her vanity mirror.

She was about to sit down, when she suddenly flung a shawl over her partial nudity, and with hands that started to shake – Frøken Sejer often exhibited this kind of nervous trembling when sitting in front of her mirror – she tore off the old wig and put the new one onto her bald head, hastily and without looking at the glass. The black wig sat awry, and she adjusted it with fumbling fingers until she got the parting, whose corpse-like pallor seemed to laugh in the midst of all the black, centred in the middle of her forehead.

Then she looked in the mirror again, and styled the side sections of the wig, which protruded from the temples like two horns.

Once she had done her hair, she poured water into a glass and quickly took out her teeth, causing her face to collapse suddenly like an empty nutcracker. She cleaned her dentures, which were very heavy, before reinserting them. The two white rows in her mouth looked as if they could still bite.

The doorbell rang constantly, and Frøken Sejer shouted through the door without opening it: 'What is it?'

Frøken Holm replied from the other side: 'It's the boy from the patisserie.'

'Has he brought the crackers?'

'Yes, he has.'

'Have Jensen bring them in here,' Frøken Sejer called out, and threw a shawl over her distorted shoulder. Madam Jensen was the only person who ever got to see Frøken Sejer when she was getting dressed. It was also possible that Frøken Sejer was summoning her in order to disturb her further in her duties.

Madam Jensen brought in a basket filled with colourful crackers, and Frøken Sejer rocked back and forth happily under her wig. 'Yes,' she said with a smile, 'they're the right ones. They always amuse the children.'

The right crackers were from a French patisserie, and contained exceptionally indecent verses.

'Put them out,' Frøken Sejer said, 'it's always such fun for the young people.'

Frøken Holm arranged the French crackers in a glass bowl, while the corners of her closed mouth twitched.

Madam Jensen had retired to the larder with two saucepans for company.

At the last moment a gardener arrived, and filled the sitting room corners with some dented palm trees and other plants, which bore visible traces of having been transported on a cart and displayed repeatedly.

Frøken Sejer, who had emerged with a turban covering her wig and a cashmere shawl with many tassels and folded many times over her back, said: 'Little man, I've told you I don't want the rubbish you've been carting around for a year.'

'I swear these plants are brand new, Frøken Sejer,' the gardener replied, as he continued to set out his plants with the damaged bits facing the wall. 'They just get a few knocks in chapels and other such occasions.'

Frøken Sejer turned abruptly, and started reorganising the table settings in the dining room. 'You must distribute the seating cards,' she said to Frøken Holm, 'that suits such white, virginal hands.'

In the doorway stood a very tall and exceedingly well-groomed gentleman, with black hair that fell in waves either side of his centre parting. 'I'm the waiter,' he announced with a bow.

Frøken Sejer sized him up with shining grey eyes from the tips of his shoes and upwards, and the waiter, who was studying his slim, neatly manicured hands, asked where he could change.

'Little Adonis,' Frøken Sejer replied, while continuing to inspect him, 'you may go and see the housekeeper.'

'Thank you, Madam,' the waiter said, with another bow.

'Miss, Miss,' Frøken Sejer chuckled: 'I'm one of *those*, Adonis, who has kept her liberty. Off you go.'

The waiter left through the passage to the kitchen, and spoke to the housekeeper in the same soft, polite tone until he was shown into the butler's pantry, which contained nothing except Frøken Sejer's commode.

The young man returned – he was enjoying a kind of holiday from a restaurant on Kongens Nytorv – wearing a black tail coat with all the trimmings. He was practically dressed for a ball.

While the young man started to arrange the bottles on the buffet, Frøken Sejer said to Frøken Holm with a slight shiver: 'Such white fingers holding a dish always delight the young girls.'

She had gone into the furthest sitting room when the bell rang again. It was Fru Emma Lund from the vicarage, who laughed on entering, as she flung both arms around her aunt. 'Sweet Aunt Vik,' she said, 'don't you think I look pretty? I've borrowed the plum-coloured blouse from Clara.'

Frøken Sejer said: 'Emma, dearest, you really should keep it. It looks as if it were made for you.'

'Nah,' Fru Lund said, 'Clara would never agree to that. The Rubows aren't like you.'

'No,' Frøken Sejer said, and she suddenly burst into a smile, 'they prefer to accumulate.'

Fru Lund said that she just had to have a look at the table, and went into the dining room, where she managed to make herself a quick corsage of flowers from the table.

When she returned to the living room, it was almost full of people.

Herr Bernhard Meyer, a barrister, was speaking to Fru von Hahn about accidents on the icy roads, and Fru Madderson, his housekeeper, who wore her canary yellow hair over a face that had retained a relative innocence over the course of several trusted positions with affluent widowers, sat down next to Frøken Sejer and said: 'Thank you, thank you, it's so kind of you to include me.'

Frøken Emilie Meyer went up to Fru Lund. 'I see,' she said, 'that you have already helped yourself to a bouquet of flowers. Well, it's not as if there's a shortage of them.'

'It's remarkable,' Herr Meyer said, still on the topic of accidents, icy roads and trams, 'it's remarkable that people never learn to take out insurance. Especially these days where you can take out insurance against practically anything.'

Frøken Sejer immediately started to laugh – she looked like a strange Buddha figure as she sat there in her cashmere: 'Yes, you're right about that. But people never learn.'

However, Fru von Hahn said: 'But my Augusta never takes the tram because of the sort of people you meet there. Besides, there's always a draught.'

And when Frøken Sejer said something about trams not going right past Fru von Hahn's door in Oehlenschlægersgade anyway,* Fru von Hahn replied: 'Viktoria, dear, walking does Augusta good, it promotes a straight back.'

Fru Lund had practically fallen into the arms of William Ask, the author. 'Yes, my dear man,' she said, 'Here I am at last; you know, you really must offer complimentary tickets to us poor wretches from the countryside.'

As William Ask was screwing his rather pale and weary face into a suitable expression, Fru Bella Schou, a slim, dark lady, who in her marriage to Herr Schou, a barrister, had been living the life of a widow for ten years, arrived enveloped in silk.

She apologised for turning up before her husband: 'But you know, Aunt, how busy he is. He asked me to tell you not to delay dinner because of him.'

'Yes,' Fru von Hahn said, 'your poor husband, Bella, he'll wear himself out.'

Frøken Lucie whispered under her breath to Herr Ask: 'Herr Schou hasn't shared a carriage with his wife for an eternity'; while Herr Willy Hauch, a young man from a wholesale business, who seemed English and was polished to a shine all over, said: 'I'm late, I know. But I had an errand at a kiosk.'

Frøken Lucie laughed as she looked her slim cousin right in the eye: 'What kind of kiosk do you frequent?'

Herr Willy widened his slate blue eyes: 'Perhaps the same as you.'

Cousin Lucie continued to laugh, and said: 'Incidentally, how you stay so slim is beyond me. By God, Willy, I'm always tempted to fling my arms around you.'

Her cousin parted his lips so she could see all his white teeth below his tiny moustache. 'You're welcome to do that,' he said, 'but worsted is very cool to the touch.'

Herr Meyer was conversing with Fru Bella Schou – he invariably stooped, as if his trusty nose wished to inhale the person to whom he was speaking: 'Yes,' he said, 'times are difficult even for those people in my profession who are prepared to get into the construction business.'

Suddenly he turned to Frøken Sejer and said: 'I don't suppose you have any money in property?'

Frøken Sejer – who was talking to Frøken von Hahn about the waiter, and saying: 'It's always nice for young eyes to have such an erect posture to look at,' – responded to Herr Meyer: 'Little friend, surely you already know that, you who are so knowledgeable about all my affairs.'

Frøken Holm, who had started to walk around with the seating plan, had reached Herr William Ask, who raised his very dark eyes and said: 'And how are you, Frøken Holm?'

'As I always am,' Frøken Holm replied, handing a card to Herr Willy, who, when she had gone, said: 'By God, you're right, there's something about that girl.'

Herr Ask smiled. 'But not something for you,' he stated.

Herr Willy swayed his exceedingly supple body: 'Are you sure about that? When you start at fourteen, you soon turn thirty-eight.'

'And that's what you did?'

'I guess one should follow the natural order,' Herr Willy replied, pushing his shoulders back and hooking his thumbs into the pockets of his waistcoat in order to enhance his figure.

Everyone was chatting, while Fru Madderson – still on the subject of the construction business – said: 'Well, Herr Meyer always confines himself to strictly legal matters. Herr Meyer says the profession can only be tarnished by speculation. And he keeps well out of it.'

'He does,' Frøken Sejer said, and added in a somewhat louder voice: 'So did he get to administer Fru Jacobson's estate?'

Fru Madderson believed so. And Frøken Sejer called out at the top of her voice: 'Congratulations, Bernhard. Then again, you have been frequenting that house a great deal these last few years.'

Fru von Hahn approached Herr Sejer, a civil servant, and said: 'By God, we really must put a stop to this. She's bought plants today as well. It's like being in a greenhouse.'

But Frøken Emilie, who was passing, said: 'They're hired. I've checked.'

Fru von Hahn replied: 'Even so, I'll have a word with the physician – after dinner. Because this is abnormal.'

'But first we're getting plenty to eat,' Frøken Lucie said. 'God help me, you'd think she wanted to choke us with her food.'

'Who says she doesn't,' said Herr Sejer, studying his patent leather boots.

Willy, who was passing, said: 'And besides, it's not as if it's all coming her way'.

Herr Meyer seemed to flex his knees strangely in front of the physician, who had just arrived, while Minna and Ottilia Hauch were still in the hall. They had sent the waiter away, as they always required many combs before they made their appearance, and many little kerchiefs needed removing by Frøken Ottilia, who was invariably dressed in mourning after a prematurely deceased fiancé, and still displayed ample décolletage.

'Right,' said Herr Schou, as he flung open the door: 'We can sit down for dinner. The parrots have arrived.'

The Hauch sisters entered and greeted Frøken Sejer. 'Dear Viktoria,' Frøken Minna said, 'I always look forward to coming to your home, even when I'm weary of the season.'

Frøken Sejer said: 'Well, you'll have to squeeze in, because our lovely Emma has arrived from the country.'

'My dearest aunt,' said Frøken Ottilia, 'that will only enhance the mood.'

The gentlemen started seeking out their ladies, and looking about him, Herr Schou said: 'Oh, is my wife here?' He then proceeded to escort Frøken Lucie in to dinner.

Everyone entered the dining room, where they marvelled at the violets and the tiny lamps – then they took their seats, and the waiter served the soup.

'Yes,' Frøken Sejer said, 'my dearest children, it's a tight squeeze, but I think it's cosy – and such fun for the young.'

Frøken Lucie, who had immediately eyed up the waiter, said to Willy: 'Oh, another vision of delight, I see. Heaven knows where the old witch gets them from.'

Willy, who was studying the Madeira, said: 'I guess that's her secret. Incidentally, she has a reputation for paying well.'

Sniffing first to the right and then to the left as he sat down between the two Hauch sisters, Herr Meyer said: 'I hope I'm not bothering the ladies,' while Herr William Ask turned to Fru Bella Schou, saying: 'Yes, it certainly is a tight squeeze,' and the lady replied with a smile which contorted the mask that was her face: 'Oh, I don't notice it.'

'Then again, one never notices what doesn't matter,' Herr Ask replied.

Fru Schou looked up. 'So what do you see in this room?' she said.

'A flock of birds,' Herr Ask replied.

'Eat up, children, eat up,' Frøken Sejer called out across the table, and as she raised her glass in a toast, she said: 'And the old lady welcomes you all.'

She looked down the table to where, tilting her canary head towards Herr Sejer, Fru Madderson was talking about her 'little songs': 'Oh, it's really nothing. But if they please Herr Meyer … when he's tired, in the evenings.'

Frøken Sejer called down to Fru von Hahn: 'Little friend, the shellfish are safe for you to eat. They're from Limfjorden.'*

Fru von Hahn, who looked as if she was choking on every single shellfish, said: 'Thank you, Viktoria, I know you don't cut corners,' and she started abruptly to discuss mortality in the capital with the physician. 'I tell you, Doctor, we genuinely saw no less than seven hearses on our way here, Augusta and I. It was a frightening sight.'

The doctor conceded that mortality was high.

'Yes,' Fru von Hahn said, 'and they say that it's the elderly in particular who are snatched away so suddenly.'

Fru Lund said: 'Yes, disease is everywhere. Back home, Lund had five funerals in one week. But for us that's only a good thing.'

Frøken Sejer was constantly rearranging her glasses, eager to toast Willy; while Herr Sejer and Frøken von Hahn also started discussing disease, mortality and epidemics, so that human frailty rose like a dense fog over the plates.

'Cheers, Willy, cheers, Willy,' Frøken Sejer shouted down the table, as she raised her glass.

'Cheers, Aunt Viktoria,' Willy said, 'I do believe the family gets its breeding from you.'

Frøken Sejer laughed and wagged her head. 'Only the red blood, my lad,' she said, and her watery eyes shone as her voice was lost in a coughing fit.

Frøken van Hahn had recently sung in a choir at the funeral of a female friend. It had really been exceedingly emotional and beautiful.

Fru von Hahn, who was studying the waiter's hands with approval as he poured the wine with the late Counsellor's labels, announced that a church funeral was ultimately far more solemn – if you could afford one. Chapels tended to smell like sitting rooms with too many plants.

'You're spilling it,' the doctor said to Frøken Sejer, whose hand had shaken when she toasted Willy.

Frøken Sejer looked up at the doctor: 'Drink up, little Doctor,' she said, 'it's the real thing.'

And she continued to stare at his face as the doctor was forced to swallow the bitter Greek drink.

The re-labelled bottles had reached the Hauch sisters, who took to reminiscing at the sight of the yellowing paper. 'We were so very much younger, of course,' Frøken Minna said, 'but *that* was a house on the *right* corner – a proper old patrician residence.'

Frøken Ottilia pulled her shoulders back to display her décolletage, and said: 'Oh, yes, as I remember it from my school days, that nice old Counsellor would stand on the threshold every Tuesday and Saturday and watch the maid polishing the finials on the banister.'

'Yes,' said Frøken Minna, 'there was something so atmospheric about those old brass finials.'

'And then the balls,' Frøken Minna continued, 'there was nothing quite as festive as the Counsellor's wax candles.'

'Heavens above,' Frøken Lucie said to Herr Schou, 'if it isn't Aunt Minna, confessing to dancing by the light of altar candles.'

'It's always the quiet ones,' Herr Schou said, 'but at least the lady is older than this wine.'

Herr Sejer said: 'Yes, the old house had style.'

Frøken Sejer chuckled, while her ancient limbs started twitching under the table – one never knew if these movements were caused by a secret lust for life or a kind of spasm. 'Yes, those floors were made for dancing.'

Fru von Hahn said kindly down the table: 'Now I always remember you, Viktoria, in the rose-coloured dress.'

'How time flies,' said Frøken Minna, as if she had been reminded of something.

'But that property was sold too soon,' Herr Meyer said. 'People never wait for the upswing … these days people are in such a rush to do business.'

'No,' Fru Madderson burst out, her thoughts still on the dances, 'there's nothing as graceful as waltzing,' while the Hauch sisters started talking about a property they owned in Nørrebrogade.

'Yes, that's right, you have that,' Herr Meyer interjected. He must have exceedingly flexible ears, because the moment someone mentioned property, his ears would prick up like those of a rabbit.

'And my sister and I often talk about selling it. There's an issue with rent in the area. And it's agony for us when tenants have to be thrown out. But the law is the law. Then again the property has been in the family for God knows how many years. And, of course, one never has any help with these matters.'

'But there are competent people around,' said Herr Meyer, 'whose very mission is to assist with such straightforward cases. Such sales are perfectly legal.'

When Herr Meyer talked about the profession and the law, his eyes would dart repeatedly in the direction of Herr Schou.

'God, yes,' said Frøken Ottilia, feeling Herr Meyer inching a hair's breadth closer, 'a lady can always trust you, Herr Meyer.'

Herr Schou, whose entire face was flushed, something that probably had less to do with Frøken Sejer's wine and more with some large tablets he was constantly swallowing after retrieving them from the pockets of his waistcoat – suddenly enquired across the table: 'Where's the property?'

Frøken Minna mentioned the location in a rather hushed voice.

'That's marvellous,' Herr Schou said, 'because there is talk of a development in that very area. With turrets, linoleum and water closets. People expect such things these days. Better still,' he went on, 'if you can also give them some rural air. The planning sketches become more attractive the closer you get to Hellerup.'*

'Yes,' Frøken Minna said, 'these days, so much more is done to house those less fortunate.'

'The lower-middle-classes,' Herr Schou said, 'that's the future. They're the ones we need to get to stick their hands in their modest pockets.'

Frøken Sejer, who was rocking back and forth happily under her wig, said: 'Yes, little Albert. You have inherited my father's head for business.'

Willy addressed Frøken Emilie: 'Hm, yes, I'm sure the old man was another fraudster.'

'God, Willy, didn't you know? He was the one with all those houses along "Aaen."'*

'Is that right,' Willy said, 'I've always suspected that we emerged from a swamp.'

Frøken Sejer, who continued to rock back and forth in a self-satisfied manner, said to Herr Schou: 'But you young ones, thank God, you understand everything so much better.'

'Yes,' Herr Meyer said sharply, 'well, I'm not an expert on matters of construction. I have no time for *anyone* in the profession who operates with borrowed money. According to my principles, one should always stay clear of it. But then again, I belong to the older generation.'

'Indeed, Herr Meyer,' said Fru Madderson across the violets.

Herr Meyer bent a little deeper over Frøken Ottilia and her iris-powdered décolletage, and said in a soft voice: 'But then again, I dare say I've had many ladies among my clientele.'

'Yes,' Frøken Ottilia said, 'that's perfectly understandable.'

'What's important, of course, is trust,' said Herr Meyer, suddenly seeming to fold his entire body together in an excess of modesty. 'And then,' he added, 'that you know how to handle your clientele with care.'

Not long afterwards he started discussing building plots with the two sisters.

Fru von Hahn, however, had moved from church funerals versus chapel funerals to discussing vicars: 'I do love Stelberg ... especially his little reminders. When he asks at the church door with such gentle eyes if one isn't in need of sustenance at God's table. Oh, it feels as if he has a little message for every single one of his parishioners.'

'Who do you favour?' she said, turning suddenly to Fru Bella Schou.

'I never go to church,' Fru Schou said.

'Oh,' Fru Hahn said, 'well, I suppose some people's consciences are clear.'

William Ask leaned forwards and said: 'Does the lady really believe that the pew is a place for washing consciences clean?'

Fru von Hahn made no reply, and Fru Lund said with a laugh: 'Others go there for spiritual guidance,' while Fru Madderson added: 'I do like a poetic sermon.'

Frøken von Hahn, who was helping herself to the hare and who, because she ate with her elbows close to her sides, got her hands near the waiter a little too often, said: 'For me, there's much truth to be found in the Mission.'*

Herr Schou, who was talking to Herr Sejer, said: 'Yes, a new neighbourhood gains greatly from the addition of a new church.'

The doctor replied to a question from Fru von Hahn: 'A clergyman can be very helpful at a sickbed.'

And down at the other end of the table Herr Sejer said: 'It's my belief that the state can't manage without the Church. It does moderate behaviour to *some* extent.'

Frøken Sejer, who had a secret fear of clergymen, or perhaps more specifically of the black, funereal cassocks which concealed them, addressed Fru Lund: 'Emma, my girl, how long will Jacob stay in that parish?'

'Twenty years,' Fru Lund said, 'with that bishop I don't think we'll ever get out of there.'

'True,' said Herr Sejer, 'all appointments are being frustrated these days.* Soon they'll be appointing district councillors from the peat bogs, and overlooking entire government departments. The days when experience and seniority counted are long gone.'

The conversation on appointments spread and surged like a wave.

Glancing at Herr Sejer, Herr Meyer said: 'One even hears talk of dismissals in the departments.'

Almost at the same time Fru von Hahn said: 'My dear cousin, the right is as bad as the left when it comes to such sinecures. Poor Hahn sat on his sand dune as a customs controller for twenty-three years.'

Frøken Sejer, whose face was glowing while one hand moved on the table as if she were kneading dough, was addressing Fru Hahn: 'Little friend,' she said, 'you're letting all that lovely compote pass you by.'

Fru Lund exclaimed: 'Yes, Aunt Vik, you're drowning us in compote.'

'It's so easy to come by these days,' Frøken Sejer said, 'and it always appeals to young tongues.'

Turning suddenly to Fru von Hahn, she added: 'But then again, your dear Johan hadn't passed any exams.'

They continued talking about appointments, while Herr Schou, who was still on the subject of housing, said: 'It's no use, Doctor. Development is the fastest route. If you understand materials, a level-headed investor can be sure of a six per cent return. And you can buy the support of the press for the price of a lunch.'

Herr Meyer said: 'True, but some businesses require wine.'

'Indeed,' Herr Schou responded, 'you get *that* in probate – from the heirs.'

Herr Sejer, who was still on appointments in the civil service, said vehemently to Fru von Hahn: 'I do believe exams are necessary as proof of ability.'

Fru von Hahn responded: 'I don't know if office jobs provide practical experience.'

'You certainly need brains to get one,' said Herr Sejer, whose words were coming thick and fast.

'Aren't quick fingers enough?' replied the lady, whose voice had a tendency to shrillness.

'The mechanics of government,' and Herr Sejer turned down the corners of his mouth, 'are a little difficult for ladies to understand.'

Frøken Sejer said gently, as if to mediate: 'Yes, there are many nooks and crannies, my friend, in those old buildings.'

'And many little sources of income on the side,' Fru von Hahn added, still in the same tone of voice.

'Just as well, Therese,' Frøken Sejer said in the same voice as before, 'because we all have to make a living.'

'Dear Willy,' said Frøken Lucie Meyer, who was talking about her father's probates, 'didn't you know, Emilie gets one per cent when father is executor.'

And, turning to Fru Madderson, she said: 'And how much do *you* get?'

Fru Madderson smiled and said: 'Frøken Lucie will have her little joke.'

Herr Schou drowned them all out in a battle against the doctor, who insisted that it couldn't be denied that mortality was high in the new housing blocks.

'The statistics contradict you,' Herr Schou shouted, 'but you only have this from the newspapers, which stick their noses into everything without ever having been asked.'

'And find some juicy morsels,' Herr Meyer said.

Fru Lund, whose cheeks had grown very hot during the ongoing talk of the bishop, said: 'And it might have been all right, if one wasn't stuck with the widow. God, I could happily strangle her.'

Frøken Sejer sat with sparkling eyes in the midst of the cacophony. In her cashmere shawl and with her lips tightly pursed, she looked like an old sibyl. 'Oh,' she said, 'how lovely it is to be surrounded by so much life.'

She trailed her restless fingers across the tablecloth as if carving runes in the damask.

Fru Bella Schou, who was conversing with William Ask, who preserved his politely mournful expression, said: 'Yes, my closet is beautiful. One must have somewhere in the house which is a little bit one's own. For my part, I occasionally need a room with no telephone, at the very least.'

William Ask said: 'There are those who can't do without that constant ringing.'

Fru Bella smiled faintly. 'That's true,' she said. 'But it is and always will be a nuisance when one is trying to read.'

'Yes,' said William, 'I know; you're one of the few people who buy books in this country.'

The expression on Fru Bella's face didn't change. 'The dead are company for the dead,' she said. And, perhaps in order to stop herself, she added: 'I wonder why the lovely bowls with the silver feet haven't been put out on the table?'

Fru von Hahn had heard her words, and her eyes quickly scanned the table. 'Why, Viktoria,' she said, 'you've bought new bowls.'

Frøken Sejer laughed. 'Yes, the old treasures are hidden away. There'll be no more broken in my time, my girl.'

Frøken Holm, who was being entertained by Willy, whose slate blue eyes said more than his lips, looked up immediately.

'What are you looking at, Frøken Holm?' he wanted to know.

'I was looking at your aunt,' Frøken Holm said.

'I do believe,' Willy said, 'the old girl cheers up whenever the family argues.'

Frøken Lucie Meyer was talking about literature and female authors. She said: 'I think they're more courageous than the men.'

Willy pursed his very soft lips, and threw a glance at Lucie: 'What do you mean by courageous?' he said.

'Ugh, you're intolerable,' and without meaning anything at all, she added: 'Willy has always thought being pretty is enough.'

'No,' her cousin said, 'I think, unfortunately, that being well-dressed is enough.'

Fru Madderson laughed and said: 'I do think that books by ladies are a little scary.'

'Why is that, Fru Madderson?' Willy said.

'Heavens, Herr Willy,' Fru Madderson said, 'one can never be sure of one's discreet little secrets these days.'

They continued to discuss literature until, addressing Herr Ask, Willy said: 'Have you ever *seen* a woman?'

'Yes,' and William smiled, 'a few.'

'Well, I never have,' Willy said.

The conversation about literature spread out and reached the theatre.

Fru von Hahn expressed the opinion that one could never truly feel safe anywhere these days: 'I won't even send Augusta to the Royal Theatre, except for Heiberg and the ballets.'*

'Yes,' Frøken Ottilia said, 'at least we always have Bournonville. There's nothing as lovely as *The Bridal Procession in Hardanger*.'*

Frøken Ottilia had lowered her voice; *The Bridal Procession in Hardanger* was a memory she had shared with her late fiancé.

Herr Sejer expressed the view that those gentlemen wrote with no respect for anything. 'One barely knows if one dare even expect common decency any more.'

While Herr Schou pouted, and said: 'Literature exists for my wife. But I'm the one who has to foot the bills.'

The doctor raised his glass to Fru Bella and said: 'Perhaps modern literature has proved useful after all. Except it seems – to a doctor – at times as if its characters were conceived in hallucinations.'

The waiter set out plates for the ice cream, and Fru von Hahn suddenly whispered to her daughter: 'Augusta, these aren't the china ones either.'

Frøken von Hahn didn't hear her. The waiter was struggling somewhat to free himself from her tautly pulled-back shoulders.

Frøken Minna Hauch, who had just stated that one would never see a dancer like Scharff again,* joined in the literature debate and opined that this

I. P. Jacobsen was now found in the homes of many families – as a confirmation present.*

'Yes,' Frøken Ottilia said, 'we have even made a present of him ourselves. But then again the two volumes do make a suitable gift.'

Herr Meyer leaned towards Herr Ask: 'Then again, perhaps it's a little awkward,' he said, 'to talk about books when an honoured author is present.'

William pursed his lips a little: 'Herr Meyer, I never bring my books to a party.'

'Oh, Herr Ask,' Fru Madderson said, 'I've just read one of your books aloud to Herr Meyer. We always read from eight till ten.'

Herr Sejer opined that reading aloud had now disappeared from family life for perfectly obvious reasons. 'Because you surely can't skip every second page,' he said.

Fru Lund, however, called out: 'I don't care. There's nothing I look forward to more than new library books. In a vicarage, dear friends, you really do need a bit of variety.'

And she started recounting in detail a very indecent novel. Frøken Sejer wagged her head and raised her hand like an ear trumpet.

'Gosh, Aunt Vik,' Frøken Lucie said, 'at least one knows that in novels every man has three wives.'

'What's Lucie saying?' Frøken Sejer said, leaning across the table.

'Or every wife three husbands, Aunt,' Frøken Lucie called out.

Frøken Sejer's laughter echoed through the room. 'What a remarkable child,' she said. 'Yes, Doctor, girls like her dance through life.'

Frøken von Hahn's thirty-two-year-old face smiled the smile of a seventeen-year-old girl: 'If I didn't know better, sweet Aunt Viktoria, I'd be tempted to think you're trying to corrupt us all.'

'Not you, little Augusta,' Aunt Viktoria replied, with a nod to her.

Herr Meyer's face had turned puce: 'Well, in my home, my daughters don't learn such things.'

Herr Schou laughed out loud and said: 'So you're not present when books are being read aloud, Lucie?'

'No,' Lucie said, 'I read in bed.'

'I only read books from Buda-Pest,' Willy said.

Herr Sejer switched the conversation very abruptly via Buda-Pest to travelling, tours and spa trips; while Fru Madderson exclaimed in respect of books from Pest: 'And they're illustrated as well,' and Frøken Sejer could be heard shouting: 'In what language are they written?'

Fru von Hahn, who supported the travel conversation, observed that Franzensbad was really very pretty, and Frøken Ottilia Hauch said – and blushed scarlet after having said it: 'Well, of course I used to go there every summer while *he* was alive.'

The waiter brought the ice cream. It was in the shape of a giant hen shielding its chickens under its wings. Cries of admiration erupted.

'Oh, look, it's speckled,' Frøken Minna exclaimed.

'Yes, by Jove, if it isn't ice cream parfait,' Herr Schou exclaimed.

'You can see every single feather,' said Fru Madderson.

But Fru Lund laughed louder than anyone: 'Aunt Vik, Aunt Vik, it's already in my mouth, I can taste it on my tongue.'

Fru von Hahn, however, who went to carve, cut it so violently with a spoon that she severed an entire wing in one swoop.

Then Herr Meyer suddenly stood up and tapped his glass.

'The executor intends to speak,' said Herr Schou in a stage whisper, while Frøken Sejer's face lit up and her eyes gleamed – a little steely – at her friend Herr Meyer.

Herr Meyer, who was standing so that everyone could see that a hunched back ran in the family, said that he knew very well that Aunt Viktoria wasn't fond of speeches, 'least of all in her own honour'. 'But once an idea comes into your head,' Herr Meyer said, 'then you are but … but its … slave. I'm no orator. I just wanted –,' and he gestured with his slightly crooked right hand towards the ice cream, 'merely to highlight this image, and I'm sure that everyone understands me. Thank you, Aunt Viktoria.'

Herr Meyer stood for a moment, a little emotional, leaning over the image and his thought, while Fru Lund and Fru Madderson ran to Frøken Sejer, who nodded. 'Why, thank you, thank you,' she said to everyone who clinked their glasses with hers. 'This old aunt shields those she can.'

'Yes, you're always so symbolic, Herr Meyer,' Fru Madderson said.

They clinked their glasses. Willy and the young ladies banged their spoons in unison against their plates, while Fru von Hahn whispered with a sneer to Herr Sejer: 'Why didn't you say something? Why is it always Meyer?'

Frøken Sejer watched them all as they returned to their seats.

'Well, children,' Frøken Sejer said, 'you may now slaughter the hen.'

She gestured to Frøken Holm, who got the hint.

The hen had now reached Fru Lund, who stabbed at it violently. 'Oh, no, it's breaking up,' she said.

'Oh, that such a beautiful sight,' Fru Madderson said, 'must be ruined.'

Fru Lund, who had helped herself to half the breast, said: 'Gosh, I really couldn't help myself, there was nothing I could do. The bird is hollow.'

'Yes,' said Frøken Sejer, whose eyes were still darting across the table like the eyes of a reptile, 'there's nothing inside it; once it's gone, it's gone.'

'*Indeed*,' Fru von Hahn said.

The hired help, Madam Jensen, who over her many petticoats was wearing a huge white apron with lace, entered with three champagne coolers from which gleaming silver necks stuck out.

There was a near riot, as all the young people clapped their hands. Herr Meyer's face froze like a mask, and Fru Madderson, who had happily smiled and clapped her hands along with the youngsters, stiffened immediately with the very same expression on her face as that of Herr Meyer.

Fru von Hahn had turned ashen. 'Why, this is a drinking bout,' she said, completely failing to hide her quivering voice, 'one is tempted to think, Viktoria, that this is a wake.'

'Is that what you think, little Therese,' Frøken Sejer replied.

Herr Sejer drummed all ten fingers on the table, while Fru Lund said: 'Oh, but nothing quenches the thirst like champagne. We only had it when we christened number one.'

Frøken Lucie said in a stage whisper: 'Never mind, we might as well have some fun while she's still alive.'

Frøken Sejer suddenly grew very still. She was craning her neck – as if to see everyone's faces better – and with her outstretched fingers resting on the table, she looked like a giant spider spinning its web. 'Once opened, the champagne won't keep,' she said.

Herr Schou, whom the waiter had now reached, asked quietly: 'What brand is it?'

'Mumm, Herr Schou,' the waiter replied.

'Well, then she really has lost her marbles,' said Herr Schou.

'It tickles my mouth,' said Frøken Lucie, and took another sip.

'How?' Herr Schou wanted to know.

'Oh, you know exactly what I mean.'

The first cracker exploded around the table. It was Willy, pulling his with Fru Madderson. The verse landed in the middle of the table, and the young people fought to read it out loud.

'Let Willy,' Frøken Sejer cried out, 'he has such a clear voice.'

'Yes, let Willy,' Frøken Emilie shrieked, 'he knows a little French.'

But Frøken Lucie had already pulled a cracker with Herr Schou. 'Ugh, how rude,' she said, while Herr Willy read Fru Madderson's verse out loud; it was a saying from Montmartre, which could make a stable boy blush – while everyone laughed.*

'Augusta,' Fru von Hahn said. But Frøken von Hahn was already pulling a cracker with Herr Sejer.

'Listen, Willy,' Fru Lund shouted, swinging a cracker over her head: 'I'll save them for … for our local teacher.'

But Herr Willy, who pulled one first with Fru Lund and then with Fru Madderson, carried on reading aloud one verse after another, while everyone laughed and clapped their hands.

'Oh, Herr Willy, I've burned my fingers,' Fru Madderson squealed, fluttering her fingers coquettishly in the air.

Willy carried on reading: '*Encore un baiser qui ne tire à rien …* '* when he suddenly stopped. 'No, that's too vulgar,' he said, but his red lips seemed to sparkle with pleasure.

'What's he saying?' Frøken Sejer wanted to know; she had dropped her cashmere shawl and was sitting with her hands stretched out like an old witch warming herself by the fire.

'Give it here,' Frøken Lucie demanded, snatching the verse from Willy, and then, turning bright red, she read it together with Herr Schou, whose moustache caressed her cheek like a sergeant's might his lady during a slow waltz in a dance hall.

No one could hear themselves think while more crackers were pulled, and all the young people read the verses out loud, leaned back, laughed – and mingled.

'No,' said Willy, leaping up, 'I have the floor,' and he shouted down all the others: '*Amour, amour, oh, chose difficile …* .'*

'Let's have it,' Fru Lund said, 'I'm collecting them.'

'I can't hear a thing,' shouted Frøken Sejer, rocking back and forth on her oak dining chair.

'Bless me, Herr Willy,' Fru Madderson could be heard exclaiming, while Frøken Ottilia was almost bursting out of her décolletage in youthful eagerness.

'*Amour, amour, oh, chose difficile …*'

'Perhaps it's time to leave the table,' said Fru von Hahn, who wasn't used to French patisserie verses on her sand dune.

'You do have the most wonderful ideas,' Herr Sejer said, and pulled a third cracker with Frøken Emilie, who, when Herr Sejer reviewed his female acquaintances with the future in mind, still seemed to him to possess a reassuring solidity.

Next to Herr Schou, Frøken Lucie laughed until she got hiccups. Danish cries mingled with French verses. Fru Madderson reached across the table to show Herr Meyer her poor burned finger, while in the middle of the floor Fru Lund was play-fighting with Willy, who had jumped up on a chair.

'Would you like one?' said the waiter, who was still circulating with the bowl of crackers, addressing Frøken von Hahn.

'What fun they're having,' said Frøken Sejer, with tears of laughter in her eyes, 'Oh, Doctor, laughter really is the best medicine.'

Frøken Lucie had almost fallen into the arms of Herr Schou, while Frøken Minna said to Herr Meyer: 'Yes, it's wonderful, isn't it, when the young can enjoy themselves with the family.'

'You don't want a cracker?' Herr William Ask asked Fru Bella Schou.

And when she shook her head, William said: 'The power of money, Fru Schou, isn't the only power in life.'

'No,' Fru Schou replied quietly, 'there are other regions where you can get even more lost.'

Willy suddenly jumped down from his chair. 'Your turn,' he called out to Frøken Holm, who was sitting next to him, and offered her a cracker while his shining eyes looked deep into hers.

'Thank you, Herr Willy,' she replied, 'but I don't know nearly enough French.'

'Little friend,' Frøken Sejer called out, 'fear not, you won't get your fingers burned.'

'Except once bitten, twice shy,' Frøken Lucie quipped. 'How about the two of us,' she said, holding out a cracker to Willy.

Amour, amour, oh, bel oiseau … .*

There were no more crackers. The doctor got the last one, which proved to be empty.

'Even a pastry chef,' he said, 'knows that verses are wasted on the old.'

During a brief lull the waiter brought the finger bowls and the guests rinsed their fingertips.

'Well, I hope you enjoyed your dinner, says the old lady,' Frøken Sejer said, and got up with help from the doctor.

'I do think there ought to be a law against this,' Fru von Hahn said, as she passed Herr Sejer.

Herr Willy lingered behind in the dining room, his hands stuffed into his pockets as he surveyed the battlefield with playful eyes. 'Well, Lauritzen,' he said to the waiter, 'there are as many different night cafés as there are kinds of families.' He paused. 'So you don't have a permanent position right now?'

'No, not at the moment,' the waiter said, as he polished his nails with a napkin.

'Well,' Herr Willy said as he turned, 'I'm sure you'll manage anyway.'

'I have many strings to my bow,' Herr Lauritzen replied, his face expressionless.

In the middle of the sitting room Fru Lund was totting up her verses. 'I have seventeen,' she said.

The guests thanked Frøken Sejer for the dinner, while Fru Madderson whispered to Fru Lund: 'I hope I'll get a chance to read them undisturbed while the others are having coffee.'

'Thank you for the dinner,' Herr Schou said, then he kissed his wife on her cheek, barely brushing it.

While the waiter served the coffee, Herr Meyer brought up a divorce case. 'One wonders if people have any conscience these days,' he said, 'in this specific instance there are five children.'

The divorce, which had become notorious, rippled through the rooms and the doctor said: 'Yes, divorce is becoming another of our society's sacraments.'

'Pooh,' Frøken Lucie said, 'Otherwise why get married in the first place, as I see it.'

But Herr Meyer, looking right into the face of Herr Sejer, said: 'But where does all this immorality come from? It's ravaging families.'

Herr Sejer shrugged: 'It's the death of principles, Herr Meyer.'

Frøken Sejer, who was sitting with her coffee cup as if reading the grounds, said: 'There, there, children; for my part, I am pleased that people have more freedom.'

'Why, Frøken Sejer?' Herr Ask enquired.

Frøken Sejer, peering at him up and down, responded: 'Little friend, one should never talk to a writer.'

'But,' she added, 'I think it's nice that people drive faster now. When I was young – yes, children, it was a long time ago – they used to hold a kind of sack race in Tivoli. Some boys would run with sacks over their heads. People were more childish then. But it was hilarious to watch them fall over.'

'I believe they still hold those sack races,' William said.

Frøken Sejer smiled. 'Well, I wouldn't know. I only visit the concert hall these days, though that's nice enough. – Drink up, children dear,' she said, gesturing to the many liqueur bottles.

Herr Schou approached the waiter, who was waiting to fill the glasses, and said in a stage whisper: 'What kind of rotgut is this, Lauritzen?'

'I refer you to the labels, Herr Schou,' the waiter said, with a bow.

'It's time for the old folk to have a game of cards,' said Frøken Sejer. 'Please would you set up the tables, Frøken Holm?'

Frøken Holm left without saying a word, walked through the rooms and started getting the tables ready.

'What does Aunt Vik want with that wishy-washy, irritating person?' Fru Lund wondered out loud, once Frøken Holm was out of earshot.

'Dearest,' Frøken Emilie replied, 'it's always convenient to employ someone with troubles of their own. You know she has a kid somewhere in Lyngby.'

'Oh, poor creature,' Fru Lund said, 'imagine having children, and out of wedlock too.'

'Extramarital births are also on the decline,' said Herr Willy, who had joined them.

Fru Lund laughed. 'Is that down to your virtue, Willy?' she said.

'It certainly wouldn't make any difference if I were to marry,' Willy replied, and turned on his heel.

'No,' Fru Lund said, 'one shouldn't have a Willy in the family.'

'Ah,' Lucie interjected, 'other men aren't much better. You wouldn't believe what you hear at a ball.'

'And what you *say*,' Willy called out from his corner, where he was leaning against the table, kicking his heels.

'Augusta,' said Fru von Hahn, who had waylaid her daughter behind a cupboard: 'I'm telling you, it's like I've been saying. She's actually selling off her possessions. Otherwise why were those bowls not on the table? However, I'm sure that as you wander around, you can sneak a peek at the china cupboard, so we can get proof. I'm definitely talking to the doctor while she plays cards. But the problem is, of course, that the family won't present a united front.'

Frøken von Hahn paused for a moment, then she said: 'You should speak to Cousin Schou first, Mama.'

'Why?'

'Because he would have to be her guardian,' Frøken Augusta said.

'Child, it's remarkable,' her mother said, 'how practical you always are.'

'Well, that's how you brought me up, Mama,' her daughter replied, 'seeing as we have never had anything but rags.'

Mother and daughter went their separate ways.

Frøken Augusta went to the dining room, where Madam Jensen was slurping down the cream from the ice cream plates with a soup spoon by the sideboard, while Frøken Holm was gathering up the caramelised almonds from the crackers, which had been discarded around the table – and both of them froze the moment she entered.

Frøken Augusta said she was convinced that she had left her gloves in here, and started wandering around the table, searching closely as if looking for a sewing needle.

Madam Jensen didn't move and Frøken Holm had left.

Frøken von Hahn had reached the large cupboard. 'Oh,' she said, 'those enchanting old locks. How wonderful they would be on a dressing table.' She started touching the old locks and the keys.

In the furthest living room, the Hauch sisters, Fru Madderson and Frøken Sejer had sat down for a game of cards.

'It's so nice,' Frøken Sejer said, easing her deformed back, 'so very nice to handle the cards. Doesn't it always feel, children, as if you're mixing something with your fingers?'

The other gaming table was vacant.

'Do you fancy a game, Doctor?' called out Fru von Hahn from the doorway to the other living room – she had decided to start with the doctor: 'Otherwise I would very much like to talk to you, Doctor – just a quick word.'

'Well, I was thinking of playing,' the doctor replied.

'It'll only take a minute,' Fru von Hahn said.

The lady stepped aside for the doctor, and they went into the other sitting room, where she invited the doctor to sit down on a sofa.

'Oh,' Fru Lund said, 'have they started playing cards? Then I had better get in there and make sure Aunt Vik lets me have her winnings.'

And Fru Lund left, with Willy in tow.

'My dear Doctor,' Fru von Hahn began, 'I'm so very sorry. But Cousin Sejer and I are really very worried these days – about Viktoria's well-being, given how she is.'

'How, Fru von Hahn?' the doctor said, and looked at her.

Fru von Hahn made an involuntary movement with her head, almost like a jockey about to take a hurdle. 'My dear Doctor,' she said again, then suddenly called out to her cousin: 'Cousin Sejer, come over here,' before addressing the doctor once more: 'Surely this can't be normal, my dear Doctor.'

'No,' Herr Sejer joined in, 'and we all suffer, if I dare say so, because we have to watch it. Quite apart from her squandering her wealth.'

'Little Augusta,' Fru von Hahn said to her daughter, who had just arrived: 'Close the portière.'

Frøken von Hahn whispered to her mother: 'Mama, they're not there. Neither the bowls nor the china.'

'Didn't I tell you so,' Fru von Hahn declared.

The doctor, who was still watching her, said: 'But in what way do you think Frøken Sejer is abnormal?'

'Abnormal,' said Fru von Hahn, whose face was ashen, 'abnormal? Well, we must seek Meyer's counsel now. After all, he knows the law.'

Herr Meyer joined them, followed by his daughter, Frøken Emilie, who perched on the edge of the sofa.

'Dear Meyer,' Fru von Hahn said, 'we're discussing poor Viktoria. I know that you agree with me that she would be much better off in an institution.'

Herr Meyer was rubbing his hands incessantly. 'Yes,' he said, 'Doctor, I'm afraid there are signs …. But it would have to be a clinic.'

'Dearest Meyer,' the lady interrupted, 'clinics wouldn't offer us any security. And Viktoria is no longer of sound mind.'

'But,' the doctor said, 'how does this manifest itself? Surely there would be symptoms ….'

'Symptoms!' Frøken Emilie burst out on the edge of the sofa; her face had taken on her father's expression completely, 'there are plenty of symptoms.'

'But one wouldn't reel them off in Viktoria's own house,' Fru von Hahn said.

'A clinic would be best,' Herr Meyer said, 'so as to keep up appearances. And there can be no talk of guardianship in this family.'

'Why not?' Fru von Hahn wanted to know.

'Aunt Therese, do you want to cause a scandal in the family?' Frøken Emilie said, pivoting swiftly and falling in line with her father.

The doctor had leaned back with an expression on his face as if devoting himself to his favourite occupation, which was taking x-ray photographs.* 'But,' he said with a bemused smile, 'I thought guardianship was the desired goal?'

'Doctor,' Herr Meyer said, 'that can simply not be done in a family which enjoys respect and – and furthermore is in the public eye.'

'And what's worse,' Fru von Hahn said to Herr Meyer, 'Schou would become her guardian as he's her closest relative… . And any "trust" might be undermined.'

Herr Meyer's face grew white, as Herr Sejer said: 'Well, gentlemen, it certainly can't go on as it is. For the sake of the family. Tell me something, Meyer, what does she live on? She must be eating into her capital.'

Herr Meyer said: 'As her executor –'

'I don't think,' said Fru von Hahn, who was quivering, 'that mad people can appoint legal executors –'

'What exactly are you saying?' Herr Meyer was practically shouting.

'What I am saying,' the lady replied, looking straight into his birdlike face. She paused for a moment, then changed her tone: 'Now I've always found that the direct route is the best. And an institution and guardianship have become necessary… . I know what I'm talking about.'

'Schou,' she called out.

Herr Schou didn't hear her. He had cornered Herr William Ask and was holding forth about a concession to build a railway line to Amager. One of his friends was trying to get it.

'One has to respect that,' said Herr Schou, whose eyes were a little glassy, but whose tongue was still agile: 'He has put the money on the table. Who does that these days, my dear fellow, where everybody relies on the banks? Money straight on the table. One has to respect that.'

'Schou!' Fru von Hahn summoned him once more.

'Yes,' Herr Schou said, steadying himself against a table as he came towards them.

Eagerly Fru von Hahn resumed her account, until Herr Schou said: 'Well, I don't care either way. But what do you think, Doctor?'

The doctor made no reply. Fru von Hahn, however, interjected: 'But what do *you* think? After all, you would become her guardian?'

'I think nothing at all,' Schou said. 'Now *inheriting* her would be nice. Not because there'll be a lot. But being an heir strengthens your position on the market.'

'And that sums up his entire business strategy,' said Herr Meyer, and turned away.

'What are you talking about in there?' Frøken Sejer called out from the gaming table.

Herr Schou laughed. 'We're talking about you, Aunt,' he said.

'That must be why I'm in luck,' Frøken Sejer called out in response.

At the gaming table they had reached the end of the second rubber, and started totting up the points while Fru von Hahn said: 'Well, a decision must be made.'

The doctor paused for a moment before he said: 'The family could always seek advice from a specialist. In these cases specialists will often find a way out. Incidentally, I don't think you'll succeed.'

He fell silent once more, then he said: 'Frøken Sejer can hardly be described as being a danger to her surroundings.'

The Hauch sisters, who had played together as a pair, were handing over money to Frøken Sejer. Frøken Sejer, however, had no change. She had only three twenty-kroner coins in front of her on the table.

'Aunt Vik, your winnings are mine,' Fru Lund said, and she ran to get change for one of the twenty-kroner coins from the doctor, who came back with her.

'I can't cope with the sight of gold,' Willy said.

'Why ever not, Herr Willy?' Fru Madderson said.

'I think everyone my age,' Willy said, 'has a thief inside them.'

The doctor suddenly looked at him: 'True,' he said, 'there's a small nugget of madness in many young brains.'

Willy stretched his slim body: 'Yes, Doctor, we're playing highwaymen in the woods.'

'Oh no,' Frøken Lucie exclaimed, 'how can you say that, Willy.'

'So,' Frøken Minna smiled, 'what do you get up to in the woods, Lucie?'

Herr Willy laughed: 'She builds cabins,' he said.

'Hm, hm,' Frøken Sejer said, shaking herself, 'no one makes jokes like Willy.'

'And,' Frøken Ottilia said, 'he is so very kind to his mother.'

'Yes,' Willy said, 'I only see her twice a year. Even though she's the one who brought me into this world.'

'Ugh,' said Fru Madderson, and shuddered as though she were cold, 'that's shocking. You're not serious, are you?'

'Oh, little Fru Meyer, Fru Madderson, I meant to say,' Frøken Sejer said, 'I'm sure you'll survive hearing that.'

After a pause lasting several seconds, William Ask said: 'It's a shame, Willy, that you didn't become a poet. One might have learned the truth from someone like you.'

'I wonder,' Willy replied.

'Hm, yes,' said Frøken Sejer, 'that boy has a brilliant mind. – You two can share it,' she went on, splitting her winnings between Fru Lund and Willy. 'Everyone has their family favourites.'

'Is it time for tea?' she called out to Frøken Holm, who went to the kitchen, where she found Herr Lauritzen alone with the housekeeper.

Once Frøken Holm had left, Herr Lauritzen said: 'Isn't this a rather difficult house?'

The housekeeper shook her head: 'No,' she said, 'I prefer houses where everyone has problems of their own.'

'What do you mean?'

'Then you can join in the charade,' the housekeeper said, placing the teapot on the tray.

While Herr Lauritzen served the tea, Frøken Sejer said: 'Please, Fru Madderson, would you sing one of your little songs.'

Fru Madderson replied: 'Oh, it's nothing very much. But I'm happy to oblige.'

Fru Madderson started flicking through the music album, while everyone, now a little tired, drank their tea.

Fru Madderson began to sing:

> I sat beside the streamlet,
> I watched the water flow,
> As we together watched it
> One little year ago;
> The soft rain pattered on the leaves,
> The April grass was wet,
> Ah! Folly to remember –
> 'Tis wiser to forget.*

Fru Madderson's voice faded away while they heard Frøken Minna say: 'A little singing is always so lovely. It's not the same without it, in my opinion.'

'Yes, it adds to the mood,' said Frøken Ottilia, whose eyes had opened at the sound of her sister's organ, 'and then Fru Madderson sings so beautifully. It's remarkable that she has kept her voice at her age.'

Herr Meyer, who was listening on a chair and following the beat with his head, said: 'Yes, it's a talent, a rare, rare talent. She was *born* for the stage.'

Herr Schou, who was standing next to Herr Sejer, said, and he was half-laughing: 'Yes, take Meyer, for instance. Every man has his own folly.'

But Fru Madderson turned as she started the prelude to the second verse, and said: 'I never sing as well as I sing at home, Herr Schou.'

> The nightingales made vocal
> June's palace paved with gold;
> I watched the rose you gave me
> Its warm red heart unfold;
> But breath of rose and bird's song
> Were fraught with wild regret.

'Tis madness to remember –
'Tis wiser to forget.

While Fru Madderson sang, Herr Sejer said in response to Herr Schou's words about folly: 'I've never understood that relationship, and I must say that I don't approve of that lady being included in the family.'

'Oh, no,' Schou said, 'we've got enough dirty laundry as it is.'

He went over to the Hauch sisters and said: 'So tell me about this property?'

And he sat down between them.

'Well,' Frøken Minna said, 'I confess that we would prefer to sell. And we have already spoken to Meyer,' – she glanced across to Herr Meyer, who continued to listen with his eyes closed – 'but he's a little hard for a lady to understand, him being such a fine lawyer.'

'Is that right?' Schou said.

'He goes on about stamps and seals and things like that,' Frøken Ottilia said.

'Yes,' Schou said, and grimaced, 'the more he obfuscates, the more he can bill.'

'So we would rather talk to you, Albert,' Frøken Minna said.

'Yes,' Schou said, 'with me it's cash up front. And my clerk deals with the formalities.'

'What are you talking about?' Frøken Sejer called out through the music.

Whenever music was being played, Frøken Sejer's hearing improved as if she were holding seven ear trumpets at once.

'We so rarely get to see Albert,' Frøken Ottilia said to her.

'And yet he's always so helpful,' Frøken Sejer remarked, 'and quick.'

Herr Meyer appeared to surface at the sound of Frøken Sejer's voice.

'Yes, Meyer,' she said to him, as he suddenly stood up, 'it's nice to have a little music, Meyer, my friend.'

And Frøken Minna said quickly to Herr Schou: 'Right then, Albert, we'll come to you – both of us. The fact is we'll never get as much in interest as we can get in rental income.'

Schou twirled his moustache: 'Oh, yes you can,' he said, 'and I'm sure everything will be fine once we find the right buyer for the place. They're never the trickiest properties to shift.'

Frøken Emilie emerged from behind a curtain and quickly joined her father, while Fru Madderson was still singing:

I stood among the gold corn,
Alas! No more, I knew,
To gather gleaner's measure
Of the love that fell from you.

For me, no gracious harvest –
Would God we ne'er had met!
'Tis hard, Love, to remember, but
'Tis harder to forget.

'Hm,' Frøken Emilie said to him, 'so Schou will be selling the Hauch sisters' property. Then again, you can't be everywhere at once.'

Herr Meyer suddenly lowered his head twice like an angry ram: 'What would you know about that?' he hissed. And he spun around to the piano and said in a very loud voice: 'The lady has sung enough.'

'Yes, Herr Meyer,' Fru Madderson said, and her hands fell limply from the keys.

'*Thank you*,' called out Willy from the other sitting room, where Fru Bella Schou was sitting in a corner looking at albums.

William joined her. 'Ugh,' he said, 'she sings like an artificial canary.'

'Because that's what she is,' Willy said.

'I wasn't listening,' Fru Bella said, 'I've been in here looking through the albums.'

'Family photographs?' William asked.

'Yes,' Fru Bella said, 'it's strange how all the faces look alike – right from when people were young.'

'Yes,' he said.

'Though there is one difference,' Willy said, 'the hunchback on the others has grown inwards.'

William Ask laughed: 'Yes, Frøken Viktoria might very well be the most innocent of them all.'

'But,' Fru Bella wondered out loud, as she gazed into the air, 'where does all the money come from?'

'From the late Counsellor,' Willy said, 'and now we have the third generation.'

Without warning Fru Bella burst out laughing: 'And you, Willy, are the gentleman of the family.'

Willy swayed back and forth a little. 'Why, Bella,' he said, 'can't you ever consider falling in love with me, just a little bit?'

'Oh, Willy,' Fru Bella replied, still laughing, 'that has never crossed my mind.'

'Besides,' she added, 'I don't think it would do me any good at all. Willy, you only ever think about the one you have yet to have, but all the ones you have notched up, you never spare a thought.'

'It's the times we live in, I suppose,' replied Willy, whose eyes had suddenly grown mournful.

'It's greed,' Fru Bella said.

The waiter announced that the Hauch sisters' carriage had arrived.

'Oh, so soon,' Frøken Ottilia said, and the two sisters began taking their leave with many little nods.

Fru von Hahn was standing between Herr Sejer and Herr Meyer. 'Well,' she said, 'so we made no further progress today either. Then again, Cousin Sejer, one can't trust you.'

Inspecting his fingernails, Herr Sejer answered: 'A man in my position, Therese, never crosses the line.'

Fru von Hahn laughed: 'But you can forget about there being any estate left to administer, Meyer. I don't mind saying it outright: she's selling off anything of value.'

Herr Meyer's jaw dropped. 'What's that you're saying?' he said.

'I'm saying,' Fru von Hahn replied, 'that she's flogging off absolutely everything. Didn't you notice that we ate off stoneware?'

'Now that you mention it, kind lady,' Herr Meyer said, looking as if the cogs in the wheels of his brain were finally starting to turn. 'But why … why?' he said, shaking his head, 'why would she do that?'

'To bankrupt the estate, Meyer,' replied Fru von Hahn, in whose hair two ostrich feathers were swaying like two pennants.

'How very odd – because Fru Madderson told me the same thing. Yes, yes,' Herr Meyer went on, as a sudden flash of admiration flitted across his puzzled face, 'that's female intuition, as I always say, female intuition … . But on the other hand, one has to consider the situation,' he said in a different tone, 'how would she go about it? After all, she can't personally … .'

'It's obviously that blond man who is always here,' Frøken Emilie interjected, 'who takes care of it for her.'

'Who?' her father said.

'Who's he?' came from Fru von Hahn.

'I don't know him. But I have seen him with parcels many times – on the stairs.'

'But how, Emilie?'

'Well,' Frøken Emilie replied, 'I occasionally stop to button my boots in the entrance.'

Herr Meyer glanced at his daughter. 'Yes, but seeing that the doctor is refusing,' he said.

'Surely there are others,' Fru von Hahn said, 'fortunately specialists have a deeper knowledge – even if they are more expensive.'

Herr Sejer said, still studying his fingernails: 'Therese is right, of course – ultimately.'

Herr Meyer, who continued to look as if he was having an epiphany, said: 'Well then, an institution is the only option. One has to intervene, I suppose, regardless of how regrettable it is for all of us.'

And as Herr Schou strolled past, he spun around quickly and said in a hearty tone of voice: 'We two colleagues haven't had a chance to chat very much tonight.' And he slapped his colleague on the shoulder with his crooked hand.

'What did he look like?' said Frøken von Hahn in a stage whisper to Frøken Emilie.

'Who?'

'The man you saw on the stairs, the blond one.'

Frøken Emilie described him.

'Then I recognise him,' Frøken von Hahn said, 'from the street, I think.'

'You do?' Frøken Emilie laughed briefly. 'Well, I don't doubt that. You always have your eyes about you – in that respect.'

The Hauch sisters had finished taking their leave and embraced Frøken Sejer. 'Oh, Viktoria, I almost forgot. The floral bedspread. Ottilia and I would like to borrow it to copy the pattern, if you don't mind. The old patterns are starting to come back into fashion, you know.'

'Did I get the last one back?' Frøken Sejer wondered out loud. 'Well, get Holm to fetch it for you.'

The Hauch sisters were gone.

'Hm,' said Frøken Sejer, when the door had closed behind them, 'how sweet, Minna never tires of decorating Ottilia's maiden bower.'

'Albert,' she added in a loud voice, 'have you seen the Hauch sisters' new manservant? He has a very fine body. They got him from the Hussars.'

Herr Schou, who was talking to Herr Meyer and had reached the point of guardianship, said: 'I don't care a fig either way. It won't affect me.'

'True,' Herr Meyer said. 'And the authorities can always appoint a guardian.'

Fru von Hahn had suddenly settled down next to Frøken Sejer, and was asking where she bought her game, because she had never had a hare like that anywhere.

'But you serve such lovely sauces, Therese,' Frøken Sejer said.

'God, Viktoria, how can you compare them to yours?'

In the other sitting room Fru Lund and the Meyer sisters were rereading the cracker verses under much somewhat risqué laughter.

William Ask and Willy were sitting on a sofa. 'Oh,' Willy said, 'why do I bother coming here to watch the sparrows peck at the crumbs? I don't even come away with as much as two ten-kroner notes so I can have a proper dinner tonight.'

The author proffered him a weary smile. 'I can give you some money,' he said, and took two bank notes from the pocket of his waistcoat.

'It's a blasted shame,' Willy said, taking them with his ringed hand and stuffing them into the pocket of his dinner jacket, 'but I can't be at home either.'

'Why not?'

'Well,' Willy said, 'because I might lie down and cry.'

And when William raised his head and looked at him, Willy added – and his face was suddenly full of all those wrinkles which the next thirty years would add to it: 'Yes, because what is there, man?'

The doctor, who had spent the last hour in a rocking chair where he had been studying *Berlingske Tidende*, passed them.* 'Tell me, why don't you want to *do* anything, young man?' he said, addressing Willy.

'What is there to do?' Willy said.

'Be a link in the chain,' the doctor replied, 'but, my young friend, that's exactly what young people refuse to do.'

The doctor walked on, and went to say goodbye to Frøken Sejer, who was still sitting next to Fru von Hahn.

'My dear Doctor, your eyes look a little tired,' Fru von Hahn said.

'Perhaps so,' the doctor replied, 'and yet, Fru von Hahn, I'm neither deaf nor blind. – Goodbye, Frøken Sejer,' and the doctor bowed, 'and remember that I'm still watching over you.'

Fru von Hahn's face grew very white at that, but she said vehemently: 'As you do over so many others.'

'Hm,' the doctor replied, as Fru von Hahn's yellowing face suddenly turned scarlet under his gaze, 'a personal physician doesn't count for much these days. He can just about … keep the wolf from the door.'

'Yes,' Frøken Sejer said, 'you're good to have around,' and she suddenly smiled, '*if* one should need you.'

Fru von Hahn had turned her head abruptly and was staring at her cousin. But Frøken Sejer just got up. 'Goodbye, little Doctor, goodbye. And thank you for coming.' And she escorted him to the door.

Fru von Hahn shot up, quick as a flash, and joined Herr Meyer, who had finished his conversation with Herr Schou, his fellow lawyer.

'Well,' she said, and emitted a desiccated laughter: 'Did you get the guardianship?'

Without waiting for an answer, she walked back to Frøken Sejer and said: 'It must be wonderful to be able to afford a personal physician. A personal physician always adds style to a house.'

'Yes,' Frøken Sejer said, 'little Therese, the doctor is so reassuring.'

The waiter announced that Herr Schou's carriage was here, and Fru Emma Lund said to Fru Bella: 'Dear Bella, might I ride with you? It would at least take me some of the way.'

'Dear Emma, of course you may,' replied Fru Bella, who went to say goodbye to William Ask and Herr Willy.

'We'll leave together,' Willy said, 'I think it's finally time for the birds to tuck their heads under their wings.'

Herr and Fru Schou, Willy and Ask went to the hall, where the Schous' fur-clad servant placed a matt-black coat around Fru Schou.

Fru Lund, too, emerged and took her short coat, while Herr Schou turned around and said: 'Is *Madame* ready?'

They all walked down the stairs, Fru Bella and William leading the way.

When they were one landing ahead of the others, Fru Bella said: 'My friend, the worst thing is that it never ends.'

'How do you mean?' Ask said.

Fru Bella hesitated, then said: 'Tomorrow *we're* giving a dinner party. My husband's business associates.'

'Yes,' William said, 'doing business is often combined with meals these days.'

'*Some* businesses are,' Fru Bella said.

Everyone had reached the entrance, and Fru Lund was the first to step inside the waiting carriage.

'I think I'll take a stroll with Ask,' said Herr Schou, once his wife was seated in the carriage. And, turning to his servant, he added: 'No need to wait up for me, Hans.'

Without saying anything, Fru Bella wrapped herself in her matt-black coat as if it were a shroud. 'Good night,' she said with a bow of her head.

The carriage departed.

Willy had stepped outside the entrance and jumped onto an electric tram by the time Herr Schou and Ask reached the pavement.* Inside the tram Willy was lit up by the yellow light.

'He's a handsome man,' Herr Schou remarked.

'Yes, that light flatters him,' said William, who was following him with his eyes.

Inside the tram Willy turned around and suddenly spotted Herr Lauritzen, who was wearing a collar protector of black moiré silk. 'Fancy meeting you here, Lauritzen,' Willy said, 'we've caught the same tram.'

'So it would appear, Herr Hauch,' Lauritzen replied with a nod.

Herr Schou and William Ask walked further down the street in silence.

Then Schou breathed in lightly and said: 'It's good to get some fresh air. Believe me, my good friend, the brain can get a little foggy nowadays.'

'I can imagine,' Ask said, 'it's no easy matter to rebuild a whole city … by speculation.'

'Change it fundamentally, you mean,' Schou said. He walked on in silence. 'Do you happen to know,' he then said, 'that I used to be a writer? I even published an anthology of short stories under a pseudonym when I was twenty-three. Now I make up prospectuses. – Well,' he added after a pause, 'perhaps we have too many writers in general – in business as well. Too many of us are fighting over the same crumbs. Too many people going after the same money – and hunting in the same city.'

Schou laughed into the air: 'Quite a tight squeeze over at Aunt Viktoria's, didn't you think?'

'Yes, a little tight. But,' said Ask, 'as long as you go after the small profits with everything you have?'

'They're too small,' Schou replied, 'and I believe every word in the language has already been misused in the prospectuses.'

He walked on a little further, before turning to William: 'Listen, I've had an idea, how about you writing a prospectus for some property on Strandvejen?'

Ask made no reply.

'We'll pay you well,' Herr Schou said, 'and surely you, too, have days when you're low on funds?'

'Yes.' Herr Ask let out a sigh from the bottom of his heart.

He hasn't said no – so I might ask him one day, Herr Schou thought to himself.

And on they walked.

At Frøken Sejer's only close family remained, and Fru von Hahn and her daughter rose to take their leave.

Once the two ladies were outside in the street, Fru von Hahn said: 'And the Hauch sisters running off with a bedspread, and Emma taking the winnings.'

Frøken von Hahn walked on a little further before she said in a very dry voice: 'I do wonder, Mama, whether they're not the smartest ones.'

The Meyer family was still in the living room. Frøken Sejer kept herself awake by letting her feet dance under the table, while her hands jumped about on the tablecloth.

Herr Meyer, whose face had taken on an expression in the last hour as if he could smell smoke – and on whose nose rested a pair of gold lorgnettes he normally only wore during very confidential depositions – was watching Frøken Sejer's restless hands.

'You're anxious tonight,' he observed.

'Me, Meyer my friend, not in the least.'

'Yes, you are,' Herr Meyer insisted, 'I can tell from your hands.'

'Little friend, I get that from my father,' Frøken Sejer replied, suddenly looking at him. 'My dear father would always sit with his fingers on the tablecloth as if writing in a ledger.'

'You have a habit of doing sums on the tablecloth too, Father,' said Frøken Lucie, who was unaware of the link between 'restless hands' and 'institution'.

Fru Madderson dozed in an armchair until everyone was finally ready to leave, and Frøken Sejer was alone.

She opened every door in the apartment and ran back and forth through the whole house like a jumping jack. She kept her fists clenched. 'I'm going to bed now,' she called out through the whole house. And she went into her bedroom and locked the door.

She sat down on a chair, took off her wig and removed her dentures. She never slept with her dentures in her mouth for fear of choking on them. Then she wrapped herself in dozens of shawls and scarves and handkerchiefs – turning into a colourful and lumpy bundle to which someone had loosely attached a head.

She crawled into bed, then rang the button by the headboard.

Frøken Holm entered with a glass filled with a steaming liquid.

'That does me good,' said Frøken Sejer, and drank: 'And at least I know it's not poison.'

She carried on drinking while Frøken Holm waited, motionless, by the bed.

'Well, little friend,' Frøken Sejer said, 'that was a lovely day … very enjoyable.'

Suddenly she emitted a loud, shrill laugh: 'Yes, an *annuity* is a wonderful thing,' she said, 'what a great invention. Then you can treat your family for as long as you live.'

Frøken Holm made no reply.

But then, as if in a sudden rage, Frøken Sejer raised up her disabled body with the aid of a rope.

'Yes,' she said so loudly that her voice cracked and grew hoarse: 'What did life ever give to *me*? I want to see them *all* dance until they weep at my grave. – You may leave,' she said, and slumped back onto her pillows.

Frøken Holm extinguished the lamps in the house one by one. Then she went to her own room. Standing in front of her table, she took out the caramelised almonds – the almonds she had stolen for her son.

Translated by Charlotte Barslund

13. 'Barchan is Dead'

We were sitting outside a villa after dinner, on the terrace.

The day had been extremely hot. And now, towards evening, the air was heavy – so heavy and sultry that even the smoke from our cigarettes was lazy, seeming to dissolve only with much effort. The two poplars stood in front of us on the grass in the gathering gloom, motionless and identical – like two burnt-out torches, high above the thuja bushes.

Ivan Ivanovich's face was turned towards the garden. Without moving, he was resting his chin on the cold marble balustrade. When I turned my head – as if to escape from the scent of the thujas, which was permeating the air – I could see that he was very pale.

We had not spoken for a long time.

I turned my head away again.

And merely in order to say something, from a vague need to speak and hear my own voice in that oppressive air and in the half-darkness, I said: 'You're very quiet, Ivan Ivanovich.'

Ivan Ivanovich did not move. Still resting his chin on the marble support, he said in a low voice: 'The air is so heavy. On evenings like this it is difficult to dismiss one's memories.'

'What memories are those?' I asked.

'The memory,' answered Ivan Ivanovich – his eyes in that white face looked wide open in the half-darkness, and he suddenly said in a completely different voice which I had never heard before, a voice which seemed to force its way out of his breast: 'The memory that I am a murderer.'

I had turned my whole body towards him, and in that sultry evening I felt a shiver down my spine. 'Have you gone mad, Ivan Ivanovich?' I said, trying to laugh and then stopping again.

'The memory that I am a murderer,' repeated Ivan Ivanovich.

For a moment I felt as if I ought to leap up and grab hold of the man, because I believed in all seriousness that he had gone mad, insane, just like that, because of the heat, the thunder in the air, or some such thing.

But Ivan Ivanovich said, without moving in the slightest: 'I have never told anyone of this. I want to tell you.'

'Ivan Ivanovich,' I said, 'that is an insane thing to say.' (And I was half conscious of checking on the bell by the door – to see how far away it was.)

'Just listen and see if it's insane,' said Ivan Ivanovich: 'Sit there and listen to me. It's a long story.'

And in a muffled voice, but very clearly, strangely, piercingly clearly, the way you narrate a story you have repeated to yourself a thousand times without ceasing – Ivan Ivanovich told me about it, sitting in the same position the whole time, as if confessing to an invisible face just there in the air in front of him.

'This was five years ago. It was in St Petersburg. At that time I was living close to the Finland railway station.* You need to know that, because that is the reason that Waldheim so often called in on me in the mornings to drink tea. He lived in the country from Saturday to Monday, on the other side of the border, the Finnish border,* and so, when he came from the station in the morning, he came up to see me and drink tea before going to the Ministry. He worked in the Ministry of the Interior. He had had a very successful career, even though I had thought him a pretty empty and unexceptional person. But he was very handsome … .'

Ivan Ivanovich was silent for a moment, stretching out his hands in front of him on the marble edge. On that grey marble those two hands looked as if they were dead, or modelled in clay.

'It was Monday morning when he arrived. I was still in bed. I can remember it all extremely clearly. The sun was shining, it was a cheerful and pleasant morning. Then Waldheim comes in and we shake hands, and as he sits down by the bed, he says, in the way that people do: "Well, is there any news?"

"Any news?" I answer.

And for my whole life I shall ask myself how it was possible, how and why it happened, how it occurred to me – how it flew into my mind, even though the second before I had had no thought of it – how the words came out of my mouth – the words: "Any news? Barchan is dead."

"Barchan is dead," I said. Why? How did that occur to me? Barchan, a mutual friend, was blooming. Only ten hours ago he and I had eaten dinner together. Feodor Alexeyevich Barchan was full of life, as healthy as you and me – yet despite that I said straight out, boom! without hesitating, right in the man's face: "Barchan is dead."

Immediately Waldheim leapt up and then sat down again, as if he was falling.

"Barchan," he cried out, "what did you say – Barchan. Barchan is dead."

And his whole face was altered .... You know, I would never have believed that that empty, polished, unremarkable face could take on such an expression of horror or agonized pain as it did then. And astonished and curious about this new face, this new man who was suddenly standing before me, I repeated (urged on by curiosity, I am now convinced of that): "Yes, Barchan is dead."

I didn't take my eyes from the man's face.

He had got up again and was standing as if to attention right by my bed, with his feet together. "But how did he die? How? Barchan, is Barchan dead? I dined with him only three days ago ... .'"

Ivan Ivanovich passed his left hand across his forehead – and this hand still looked as if it were dead – whilst he stared straight ahead at nothing, as he went on:

'Tell me, was I hypnotized at that moment by that face, just next to my bed? Was I speaking in a trance from which I could not break free? Or was it – yes, was it perhaps a purely artistic desire, an irresistible impulse to study grief which impelled me? Or – have you noticed that deep down inside all of us there smoulders a secret cruelty, a prickling and evil cruelty directed precisely towards those we are most fond of, which can suddenly blaze up, and we plunge the stiletto we always carry in our sleeves straight into their flesh, and twist and twist, unable to stop. We have to, we *have* to cause them pain. Was that it? Was that what made me carry on speaking? You see, I began at once to tell the story – at great length, with all the details, the whole picture – of *how* Barchan had died ... .

How he had fallen over in Pushkinskaya Street,* late at night, as we were walking home, in a sudden seizure, face down, full length, on the cobbles – just outside Princess Ustupoff's house, yes, it was right by the princess's front gate.

In the meantime Waldheim had sat down again, with his face in his hands, repeating the same words over and over again: "Barchan – Barchan dead ... but I dined with him three days ago ... ."

And I carried on (without being able to stop, caught up in my own lies, tormented by my own stream of words, by my own *fiction* about the living Barchan's death), I carried on: about Barchan's face ... how his left eye had closed because of the seizure, and only the right one could see; it followed me, squinting, terrified, as I tried to lift him up, and couldn't manage it … whilst Barchan's single eye, which had become bloodshot, followed me, followed me the whole time … .

Suddenly Waldheim got up out of his chair, and his hands fell away from his face, hanging loosely down; I could see (yes, I did notice it) that his left eye was closed, the eyelid had covered it … only the right one could see, as he said: "No, don't tell me any more … say no more … ."

And without another word he turned and left – walked across the floor … like a reeling man, a man who is drunk, who can't stand on his own feet, he walked across the floor and out.

And I did not hold him back.

I remember it very clearly: as I lay there in bed, I thought of only one thing – how amused Barchan will be. And as I got dressed and stood in front of my mirror, I said to myself: "So Waldheim really is human. I hadn't actually believed it, although it is true that I am very fond of him … ."

And I went off to work.'

Ivan Ivanovich was silent.

A large insect flew past us, a large, hairy insect, which I quickly waved away with my hand.

Ivan Ivanovich had bowed his head and placed one hand over the other. It was odd, but as he sat there like that, bent over, with one wrist laid on top of the other, he looked as if he were a man in chains.

'Ivan Ivanovich,' I said, 'don't tell me any more. All this is just fantasy, and you shouldn't encourage fantasies but dismiss them … .'

Ivan Ivanovich shook his head gently and said: 'I *must* tell the story.' And he began to speak once more, very slowly at first, as it were with laboured steps, as a man walks when he knows he has to go over a cliff.

'The next morning – I must have slept late, because when my doorbell rang loudly, time after time, and then yet again, I saw – how one remembers all those things one doesn't register and yet afterwards somehow knows – I saw (as the ringing went on) that my housekeeper had already brought in my tea, and that the new issue of *Severnyj Vestnik* was lying on the chair beside my bed.* I opened it. Volynsky had written an essay about "Beauty" – a long essay.* I began to cut the pages with the edge of my teaspoon.'

'But who was it ringing? Who on earth was it?'

'It came in bursts, urgent prolonged bursts – prolonged, like a telegram boy ringing in the middle of the night. And suddenly I thought (you know, I wonder if Barchan had already partly transferred to me, communicated to me his message and his thoughts, his thoughts through the locked door?): it was exactly like that when the telegram boy rang the night – or rather the early morning – when he brought the telegram from Tula that my mother was dead … .

And I ran out … .

There he stood, Barchan – there he stood, leaning on the doorframe, and although he could see me with both eyes, he carried on ringing with his left hand, like a madman, like a maniac … .

And instantly gripped by an inexplicable terror – as if his terror had infected me, or as if I already knew what it was – I said: "But Barchan, Barchan my friend – what is it?" My teeth were chattering in my mouth.

He made no answer, just went in. You know, he is very tall, far too tall and skinny, so that when you see him you think that some empty clothes have been thrown over a skeleton – that's how he looks. With a long neck and a thin face.

"Barchan, Barchan … ."

He had sat down just by the door, his arms swinging between his legs, swinging like two pendulums … and he said nothing … .

"Barchan – what is it? Barchan – say something – what is it?"

I grasped him by the right shoulder, and when I had done so, I already knew what he was going to say … knew … what had happened … .'

Ivan Ivanovich turned his head towards me with a jerk, and his wide-open eyes stared directly into my face – I have never seen such a look in anyone's eyes.

'Yes, I *knew* it: Waldheim was dead. And as if Barchan had guessed that I knew, that I knew what he had not yet said, not told me, he said, whilst still swinging his arms meaninglessly and idiotically between his legs: "Yes, isn't it dreadful … it's so dreadful."'

Ivan Ivanovich had turned his head away again, and with his hands clasped in front of him, he sat there as before, speaking slowly: 'What is it that happens in a person at such a moment, and *how can you know what you don't know?*

But at once I became completely calm. I have often said to myself that there is only one time in my life that I have felt so calm. It was in the Caucasus – do you know the Caucasus? – during an avalanche which suddenly made my horses panic … and my life depended on the sinews in my hands … . That's how calm I became, whilst the thought ran through my head: "How much does Barchan know? He knows that Waldheim is dead – but does he know any more? *What* does he know?"

And I said to myself: "You must defend yourself against Barchan. You must be on the alert for Barchan."

But out loud I said (and my voice sounded as cold as if I were speaking to an accused man – yes, it was really as if I were accusing him): "But how did he die?"

Barchan answered: "He died just now. He's dead."

"But what do you *know* about his death, Feodor Alexeyevich?" I said, in the same voice as before.

"But I saw it. I saw it" – and suddenly Barchan clasped the back of his head with both hands – "Ivan Ivanovich, it is the most terrible thing I ever saw … ."

Suddenly Feodor Alexeyevich Barchan stood up, and staring into thin air, he said: "But who can explain it? Who can explain it … Ivan Ivanovich … it is the most terrible thing I ever saw … yes, yes" – and he began to walk up and down the room – "I shall tell you about it. Let me tell you the whole story."

He stopped right over in the corner … oh, I could paint him, him and every one of his movements, as he stood there … whilst I thought: "Yes, let him tell the story, let Feodor Alexeyevich tell what he knows, and mind you don't give yourself away."

Out loud I said: "Yes, tell me the whole story."

Barchan remained standing in the corner. He looked like a painting by Repin* as he stood there talking: "It was last night, when I had eaten. I don't know why it suddenly occurred to me to go and call on Marian Mikhailovich.* But I had not seen him for four days … yes, that's right, it was exactly four days since we dined together at Bartov's. He was in high spirits, and talked all the time about it soon being time to get married … Yes, that's what he was talking about, and I could see that Anna Petrovna was quite pale, and could hardly lift her glass to her lips."

Suddenly Barchan turned towards me, and, as if seized by a new terror, he said: "Ivan Ivanovich, how – who is going to, how are we going to tell Anna Petrovna about this?"

I answered: "We must of course send a message to her husband. What do we know of the relationship between Anna Petrovna and Marian Mikhailovich … ?"

"No, no," answered Barchan, "but we do know … ."

I slammed my hand down on the couch where I was sitting, as if on a bar: "But Feodor Alexeyevich, just tell me and let's make an end of this."

"Yes," said Barchan, shaking his head, "it's true, I haven't told you about it yet. – Well then, I went up there last night. Marian Mikhailovich wasn't at home, and didn't come. So I sat down to read. It was *Severnyj Vestnik*. It was lying on the table. It had just arrived and the pages weren't cut. It was an essay by Volynsky I read … ."

"Yes," I said, interrupting him with a lie (and saying to myself at the same moment: "How clever you are – but now you must be alert, for now it's coming") – "I have read it."

But Barchan did not hear. He was still standing *there* in the corner and seemed to be addressing the room: "In the end I got tired and lay down on the couch – on the couch in the bedroom – there's a couch just under the window … you lie directly facing the door. The lamp – a large lamp – I had placed on the wash-stand. I must have fallen asleep."

Barchan was silent. In the corner where he was standing, his face was as grey as a stone … yes, that is just how Repin painted Ivan the Terrible, staring into the face of his half-stifled son.*

"And then?" I asked.

Feodor Alexeyevich took out his handkerchief and wiped his long, thin fingers, before he answered: "When I woke up – I didn't believe I was awake … Ivan Ivanovich … Dante has not seen any face like the one I saw* – like Waldheim, who was standing there, just in front of me, at the foot of the couch, white, distorted, with his mouth drawn down – you could see his teeth, all his lower teeth, that's what his mouth looked like, twisted and drawn down … .

I wanted to call out, but couldn't. I said to myself 'You're dreaming' – and yet I could see Waldheim – and it *was* him – it was Waldheim, and foam was running out of his twisted mouth. And without being able to move, without being able to lift a hand, I said to myself: 'Marian Mikhailovich has gone mad … if you are awake, Marian Mikhailovich has gone mad.'

Then all at once – and I didn't scream – he grabs the lamp and lifts it up and makes as if to throw it at me, and falls … ."

Suddenly Barchan was speaking more calmly:

"He fell, Ivan Ivanovich, with the lamp in his hand – it was smashed – forwards, full length, full length, with his face down, straight out, flat on the floor – face down, face down – like this" – and in a frightful impulse to mimic it, Feodor Alexeyevich made a movement as if to let himself fall – "whilst I jumped up and wanted to ring for help and didn't do so. Now, now, I said to myself, calm down, you know Marian Mikhailovich suffers from epilepsy; and I wanted to lift him up, but I couldn't … then he turned his head himself, and I saw his face … Ivan Ivanovich, his left eye was closed, the eyelid drooping – only the right one could see, and was staring up at me, bloodshot – just the one eye … .

I couldn't stand it. I had to get him up … . And then suddenly – all at once he leapt up himself and came at me and struggled with me, lying on top of me he struggled with me like a man possessed, like a savage – battled as if he was battling against a ghost … . He was lying on top of me – on top of me … we were lying just outside the living room door … . He had his fingers around my neck as if he wanted to strangle me, or rather not me, but a ghost – because his one eye, that dreadful bloodshot eye, was looking at a ghost … .

And all at once I said to myself: *you're* the one who is terrifying him. But how was it possible, Ivan Ivanovich, that I, I could terrify Marian Mikhailovich like that? I, his best friend – we were childhood friends, we've known each other for twenty-six years – yes, twenty-six years up to now."

Barchan had come towards me. "How is it possible? How had it become possible?" he said, staring into my face.

"My dear Feodor Alexeyevich," I said, without taking my eyes from him (although cold sweat was running from my neck down over the lining of my shirt): "this is your nerves playing tricks on you. Do calm down. Waldheim died a natural death" (yes, that's what I said, those words: *a natural death*) – "he has succumbed to a seizure."

"Yes, a seizure, *because he saw me* – at the sight of me," said Barchan, still staring into my face, until he suddenly began to walk up and down again feverishly. "I know it, it was I who terrified him. When I had torn myself away and lifted him up – his body had become stiff, quite stiff, as stiff as if he were already dead – and laid him down on the bed, I could see it in that eye, that open, dreadful, half-dead eye, which followed me around: that it was me who terrified him. But why, why, Ivan Ivanovich, why?"

Barchan turned his face to me once more.

"Did he speak?" I asked (and at the same moment I thought to myself: a spectre speaks so clearly).

"No," said Barchan, stopping in the middle of the floor. "His tongue was paralyzed … oh, Ivan Ivanovich" – and Barchan covered his face with his hands – "if only he had spoken … ."

I could have laughed, indeed I felt an unreasonable, an irresistible desire to laugh – at Barchan, at Waldheim, yes at the dead man himself – I don't know whether it was from relief or despair … .

"He just lay there," Barchan continued, "with his eye fixed on me – mute, with that one eye boring into me, mute, as I sat by his bed. I wanted to go, but didn't. I said to myself: 'You're the one who is killing him,' and I didn't go … ."

Barchan turned again, and his voice sounded as tired as if he had journeyed through a whole life. "Ivan Ivanovich," he said, "how can you become a murderer against your will?" With the same breath he said: "He died at 5 o'clock."

It was silent.

I just said to myself – *nothing* else, and thought of nothing else: "Barchan knows nothing. No-one knows anything. No-one will find out anything. You are saved."

And I said to Barchan very calmly: "You should drink a cup of tea, Barchan." And I went into my bedroom and brought out the tea tray and poured tea.

Whilst Feodor Alexeyevich drank, he said: "We'll have to tell his parents too."

Then I must suddenly have grimaced ("his parents"), because Barchan said, looking at me: "Yes, isn't it terrible?"

I answered: "Marian Mikhailovich has died from a stroke; of course that is very sad."

Barchan merely repeated in the same tone: "We must tell his parents" – and he went towards the writing desk. Then he said: "No, I can't," and his arms fell to his sides. "Ivan Ivanovich, can you do it?"

And *I* wrote the telegram – I have never written so clearly in all my life – never.

For five years I have dreamed of those letters. They are pieces from a game, which I have to arrange into words, and I can't arrange them; and they grow larger and fall upon me, fall like trees with outstretched branches, which pin me down and wound me. In other dreams they are sea creatures, crayfish which scuttle towards me, giant crayfish which scuttle over my blanket, dragging their tails, and grip my throat with their slimy claws, their horrible ice-cold claws … .'

Ivan Ivanovich stopped talking. Drops of sweat were running down his temples.

'When you're awake, you can protect yourself,' he said. 'Why can your will-power not control your dreams too?'

Ivan Ivanovich was silent. He sat there for a long time without moving his outstretched hands.

I did not know what to say to him.

In the garden all was quiet. The shadows of the thujas had grown darker, and the two poplars stood in front of us in the night, motionless and like two swords – whilst the car horns, somewhere far away out there, sounded like the frightened screams of hunted animals at night.

Ivan Ivanovich spoke again, in a different voice. 'I left Russia,' he said, looking out into the darkness. 'I live here now – and I shall never go home.'

I got up and put my hand on the Russian's shoulder: 'Come, Ivan Ivanovich. Come, let us go in and light the lamps.'

Translated by Janet Garton

Auto-biographical Writings

14. An Artists' Tour of Bornholm

We scoured the map of our native Denmark for some out-of-the-way locales where Herman Bang had yet to perform readings.* They were not easy to find.

It appeared that the choice lay between Thy and Bornholm. We decided upon Bornholm owing to its natural beauty.

The troupe was arranged to perform concerts. Its members consisted of a tenor, father of nine and pottery maker, a pianist with a testimonial from the conservatoire indicating she was 'splendidly suited to the role of schoolmistress', and yours truly.* The Impresario, an actor who made a living offering dance lessons, was charged with making the local arrangements.

We set off with the greatest of expectations.

Upon our arrival in Rønne we learned that we were to appear that evening in the lesser hall of the Dannebrog, the local dance establishment. The Impresario had deemed 'the lesser hall' suitable. 'Rønne needs to sell out for the sake of the other locales,' he said (the other locales being the towns of Hasle, Allinge, Svaneke and Nexø – we omitted the village of Aakirkeby): 'and, gentlemen, circumstances are limited … .'

We agreed to the lesser hall; it had a capacity of one hundred persons. And we made enquiries with the local bookseller as to whether he believed the mood was 'promising'.

He believed so. But all the same, there were 'a good many tickets remaining'. If truth be told, twelve tickets had been booked. The dance teacher spent the afternoon ingratiating himself with the parents of his students; at the request of the troupe he judiciously sent them complimentary tickets with a liberal hand.

In the evening we discovered that he did not exactly dance among the *beau monde*. The tenor, stationed by the keyhole of the artists' room, declared that we would have to adjust the programme. He did not want to close the concert.

Nevertheless we held out some hope: a crowd was gathering at the box-office window. We were not yet aware that a crowd always formed at box-office windows on Bornholm. It is due to the slowness with which people remove the coins from their pockets. They conduct business at the box office in the same manner as at the shop when they are looking at cotton fabric. First they enquire about the prices. These are provided. Then they consider the matter carefully for a while, before taking their leave. You believe them to have abandoned all thought of the amusement in question, but they absent themselves only to pull out their money painstakingly in a corner. While this is taking place, the space nearest the box office remains empty. Other prospective buyers wait quietly for the one who arrived first. When this first person has finally completed the transaction – the native of Bornholm has a distinctively tender and reluctant way of parting with every coin – he questions the box-office clerk about the programme. He does so exhaustively, as though he intends to memorise it. It later turns out that he has the printed version in his pocket.

Finally he withdraws. It's the next person's turn.

The concert was scheduled for 7.30. We started at a quarter past eight. The tenor opened with *La donna è mobile.** As per the altered programme, the pianist concluded with a waltz by Chopin. The tenor, swathed in numerous scarves, had already gone home.

When the rest of the troupe arrived at the hotel, the chambermaid passed on kind regards from our fellow artist: he had paid his bill and taken the steamboat. He had packed his suitcase and returned to his pots.

The rest of the troupe wished to continue. The next stop was Hasle.

The supply of art on Bornholm is undertaken by landau, on a pleasant ride from town to town. The carriage now had more than ample room for the troupe: the Impresario had remained in Rønne 'owing to the limited circumstances'. At the remaining stops, ticket sales could easily be seen to by our coachman, who went by the name of Andreas.

We arrived in Hasle a little after midday. I enquired at the rather rustic guest house about the bookseller. I never learned whether there was one. But our business manager was a cobbler. 'He had dealings with the hall', which was some kind of chapel.

We sought out the cobbler, who was a splendid man. We asked about the prospects. Well, he wasn't sure, Hasle was a difficult town. But of course he had been beating the drum – yesterday.

We thought that perhaps he ought to be beating it today as well. He'd had the same thought; because the expenses were rather high. Four kroner for the hall alone – including lighting. The lighting consisted of four dim lights strung across a wire.

We asked whether it might be possible to view the hall. Yes, it certainly would be. Though he, the cobbler, was the *manager* (that was his title) of the hall, the bank teller had the key.

So we went to ask the bank teller. We had to trek through the entire town. When we met him, we were given the key, and he said: 'Yes, I suppose the worst part is that you'll probably need a piano?'

'Yes, we certainly will, half the programme has piano music.'

'Hmm,' the bank teller had suspected as much. 'I suppose the worst part is that there is no piano.'

We began to realise that there were particular complications in regard to performing concerts in Hasle.

However the bank teller believed – since everyone was so terribly helpful – that we might be able to borrow one, since the local merchant had a piano. The troupe resolved to walk to the local merchant's. And his wife was very obliging; we could by all means have the piano, but the worst part was that it hadn't been tuned in years. For it was difficult to get piano tuners to come to Hasle.

We had expected as much. The pianist said that she would perform with it untuned.

We walked back.

Along the way we fell into the clutches of an art lover. She claimed to have 'encountered me through the family' ten years ago, and she was bursting with anticipation at my arrival. For a week she had spoken of, indeed thought of nothing but our concert. And now – imagine – she couldn't come, nobody could come. It was Tuesday, and of all the days – imagine – it was sewing circle Tuesday.

Naturally I regretted that fact, and enquired whether this circle had many members?

The whole town, the art lover said.

I came to the quiet realisation that Hasle was one of those places where for reasons of frugality, the community limits itself, so to speak, to dispatching lookouts to attend artistic events. You send out two, three, four scouts to attend the festive occasion and report back to the families. And then for the next fortnight, you talk about the festivities as though you had personally bestowed upon them the honour of your presence.

To the art lover, the wife of a minor official, I issued two complimentary tickets.

The cobbler was waiting for us at the hotel. He asked how it had gone. We replied that it had gone according to expectations. He hoped so, and asked if we had heard the drum. It had sounded. And, as it happens, the cobbler had faith in his comrades. They would come.

At eight o'clock, the coachman, Andreas, sat alone in the empty chapel with a plate in front of him, in which he intended to collect the coins of the Hasle public. He sat undisturbed for a long time. Little by little, however, a few bashful men sauntered inside and sat on a bench by the door. I understood them to be the cobbler's comrades. He didn't have many.

'The community' was represented by the art lover and the town clerk's assistant, who in his official capacity had received a complimentary ticket.

We shook the dust from our feet and left our reputation in the hands of Hasle.

Our next stop was Allinge. We arrived as the drummer was beating with his sticks. He announced the Herman Bang concert, whereupon a drumroll ensued. Then the man started again, and we stopped the carriage in order to listen. It was an announcement that Anders Olsen's widow would be serving up fresh pork sausages that night. The widow must have thought that her pork sausages might as well be included, seeing as the people of Allinge already had their boots on.

The performance was held at the hotel. The artists waited in their room. The coachman, Andreas, who was once again stationed at his plate, ran incessantly back and forth to the window. He leaned out, as though about to launch himself onto the cobblestones below. I asked whether he would be so kind as to calm down and remain by his plate.

His reply was that he was beckoning his acquaintances in. He maintained that he had already waved in seven.

And the landlord's wife, who was in quite the state, as though she herself were going to perform on the upright piano – which had not exactly been tuned yesterday, either – walked back and forth saying: 'Yes, you must let Andreas carry on – he's a good boy – Andreas was born and bred in Allinge.'

Andreas continued beckoning from the window. It helped a little. The takings were twenty-seven kroner for Allinge. After the concert, a petite lady introduced herself to me. She was around fifty, with corkscrew curls all over, and wearing a grey jersey with a red belt. Her black skirt was exceptionally short and revealed a small pair of feet set in goatskin. She introduced herself as Fru Nielsen and thanked me through many tears. I realised that the lady was a competitor of our Impresario – she gave dance lessons.

I had read my story about the dancer, 'Irene Holm.'

We departed for Svaneke.

We were recommended to an art-loving family, the head of which was going to perform a violin solo at the concert. We found the family fully engrossed in preparations for a party in support of the troops. The head of the family was sketching decorations, which his six daughters of all ages filled in

with bright paint. There was not one spot that wasn't covered in colourful, patriotic symbols.

On the marital beds – the doors were left open during all the activity – there rested Denmark's tutelary spirit in life-size.* She was dressed in so much red that it looked as though she was bleeding.

The lady of the house offered us refreshments in the midst of the preparations. She explained that the decorations were not without some use. Firstly, they adorned the bazaar:

'And people here in Svaneke,' she said, 'do enjoy something pleasing to the eye.' And later they were raffled off.

'It certainly is something to have on a wall, at any rate,' she said.

The head of the family abandoned his decorating and moved on to the next art form: he wanted to rehearse his solo.

The lady expressed her apprehension about our visit. It was because of the party in support of the troops, which was also right now. And people didn't have money for all sorts. And there was so much happening in Svaneke.

On a placard in the street I had just read that Professor Epstein junior had entertained with his 'mystical magic' around New Year – it was now May.

But as for the daughters, they were confident. The daughters – these young ladies had all now donned tarlatan hats – had faith in their friends. And they had many friends.

I asked whether one could be so bold as to offer them a couple of complimentary tickets.

They wouldn't say no.

We went to rehearse the violin solo.

The festive hall at the hotel was decorated with spruce garlands and Danish flags along with a bust of His Majesty King Kristian IX. The proprietor of the hotel asked me to reduce the quantity of numbered seats. People in Svaneke preferred to sit in the unnumbered ones.

The concert began with the violin solo. Half the town was gathered outside the windows of the hall. It was a little annoying, because the town clerk kept sending a rather boisterous police officer outside to bring the rabble to order – which caused some disruption. In addition these outsiders were joining in, and voiced their displeasure when they were unable to hear. And 'Gravesen's Ball' is a long number when you're restricted to following the performance in mime.*

Apart from that, the concert was a success and the deficit considerable.

Nexø was our final stop. Our Impresario, who stayed in the town for his dance lessons, declared that it was sold out. He had made enquiries with the parents.

It was sold out – packed with people in full dress and ladies in concert hats. The town is about ten miles from Svaneke, and it was as if we had arrived in a completely different world. People sat in numbered seats and were in the mood for a concert.

The fire brigade was posted in the courtyard, and I asked if it was the custom here for more or less the entire crew to turn out for festivities. Their chief answered me by saying that it was to keep the lads under control. They were prone to trying to watch for free. So the firemen kept watch on the stairs.

The concert began with a number from Chopin, before it was vehemently interrupted by a dog. The audience was indignant and chased the dog through all the rows. It sounded like an entire pack.

In a hole in the ceiling above, six female faces appeared. It was the female staff of the hotel, observing the concert from the attic. Eventually these ladies grew weary of the entertainment and started to talk very loudly. There were a couple of Swedes among them, and their conversation sounded very shrill. They scrutinised the entire audience critically.

There was a good deal of restlessness, and a gentleman ran into the hall. It was the town clerk's assistant, who had orders to clear the hole to the attic in the name of the law. Loud shrieking was heard (the entertainment temporarily paused) and a general exodus of slippers across the ceiling.

Then the clerk returned.

We continued … .

At the last moment we decided to try Rønne again, knowing full well that after a concert you could catch the steamship.

We booked the Dannebrog's main hall and sought support from a male voice quartet, whose fee was ten kroner – to be paid in advance.* The quartet had been drinking beer until about eight o'clock, when their leader inquired whether they might be able to begin. We did have a steamship to catch, after all.

I saw no reason to wait.

Seventeen people were sitting in the hall, and the coach driver, Andreas.

The quartet began with Bellman.* The young female pianist, who was somewhat less accustomed to the vicissitudes of fortune, was crying, out of sight behind an old curtain.

I kept myself entertained by talking to the ticket collector. He told me how packed Rønne was when there were amateur dramatics on.

'They're good,' the man said, 'they're experienced – they perform every fortnight.'

I stood counting the kroner as a parish clerk does his Whitsun collection: it was meagre, very meagre.

'Above the stage it says "Not merely for pleasure",' the ticket collector said.*

I'd heard of that.

A couple more fifty-øre coins dropped into the slot, and the ticket collector and I added and totalled. 'Yes, it's a loss,' the ticket collector said.

'It is indeed,' I said.

The quartet had finished. The pianist started on Chopin.

Then that evening too came to an end.

We went aboard on empty stomachs. The travel budget did not make allowances for avoidable expenses.

The steamship was packed. People wanted to see the artists.

We had finished our tour of Bornholm.

Translated by Paul Russell Garrett

15. Expelled from Germany

I had, without posing any danger to society, been staying at a hotel for six weeks when, on the first of January, I moved into a private residence, and the misfortunes began.*

My landlady's registration form had fallen into the hands of Berlin's imperial state police.

One fine morning, a young and rather well-dressed individual turned up at my door, asking me rather too intimate questions about my work activities and my various private affairs, and I was somewhat taken aback. When I meekly expressed my astonishment, he respectfully presented a small badge and told me it was perfectly reasonable for the police to take a little interest in recently arrived foreigners such as myself.

He asked me, still exceedingly amiable – it was a formality, just a formality – to simply jot down on a small piece of paper for whom I wrote.

For whom I wrote? Well, the man certainly couldn't know how long the list would be. I made a note of – Danish newspapers, Swedish newspapers, German newspapers .... .

The pleasant man asked in a friendly manner whether I also wrote for Norwegian newspapers. I replied in the affirmative and added a Kristiania newspaper to the list.*

The kindly individual asked: whether that might be the only Norwegian newspaper.

No, I replied, there was also another.

'I see … .'

It was impossible to tell whether that was of any particular interest to the gloved man. Though he did ask, as a matter of form – after all, it was just 'a formality' – to add the name of that newspaper as well. Which I did, writing: *Bergens Tidende*.*

The splendid fellow expressed his thanks. He needed no further newspapers. He uttered a few words about 'what hard work it must be', and pocketed the piece of paper; that would be sufficient.

He was very agreeable, as I said, though he did not offer his hand when he left.

Two days later, when I returned from the theatre, my landlady notified me that a strange man had paid me a visit; he had insisted on waiting and had done so for three hours.

But I had been to the Deutsches Theater,* where they preferred not to cut Schiller short, and I had seen *Don Carlos*,* so in the end it had been too much for the strange man, and he had taken his leave.

The next morning, I was woken from a deep slumber. The peculiar gentleman had returned. I suggested he might be so kind as to return at a more civilised hour. I was sleeping now. But the landlady said that would not do. For she believed he was with the police.

I sat up in bed. 'With the police? What the deuce does he want?' I asked.

Well, the landlady, who was rather frightened, said I would surely discover that when I came out – for the peculiar man was waiting. He would not leave. He would wait.

Quite right – the gentleman was waiting. He asked me – and he certainly wasn't as polite as the man from the other day – to remain calm about the matter; but I was required to report to the police station. To the central station.

I said I would be there within the hour. But he stated that he was to accompany me – and straight away. I would not exactly say I was pleased with the situation, as I got dressed in the bedroom while he waited in a chair, legs crossed, in my sitting room.

When we got down to the front door, he asked me whether I might like to take a hansom.

'Yes, please.'

Would I prefer first or second class.

We got a first-class carriage, and the dogged gentleman sat down next to me.

I asked what exactly it was that I had done. And the man replied: 'You mustn't ask. It doesn't concern me.'

So I arrived at the central station rather uncertain as to the nature of my offence.

I passed through many corridors and many rooms – my man was at my side; past many public officials at many desks – the man was at my side.

Finally, I entered a room where I was instructed to wait. It was a holding cell for vagrants. On a wooden bench there were already a couple of fellows who did not exactly appear beyond reproach. The gentleman from the hansom left me in the care of the room supervisor and withdrew.

I asked again why exactly I was here. And the new gentleman repeated: 'You mustn't ask. It doesn't concern me.'

I spent the next hour measuring the floor, during which time more and more vagrants kept arriving, until the air was no longer very pleasant.

Finally, I asked how long I might have to wait?

The new gentleman replied that there was no way to know.

And I waited again – for half an hour.

Then the gentleman from the hansom returned and led me off. 'Now you will find out,' he said.

I felt already as if I were a Russian being sent to Siberia.

I was led into another room and waited once again – in front of a counter. Behind the counter there must have been twenty gentlemen at work, each in front of his own ledger.

One of these gentlemen suddenly appeared in front of me holding a large document. I could see that there was something printed on it. The gentleman asked me to confirm that I was Herman Bang, and when I did so, he read out my deportation order. I was to be expelled from the Kingdom of Prussia.

I took the liberty to enquire in a low voice as to the reason. The gentleman simply continued reading. I was to leave Berlin within twenty-four hours, and if after that time I was found in the kingdom, I would be imprisoned and then transported to the border.

When the declamation was over, I again asked the reason. The gentleman with the document replied gruffly: 'Please sign here.'

'No reasons are given here.'

I suspect that I had to sign 'for the record', as it were.

I drew attention to the fact that I was not some journeyman joiner, and that my deportation would cause quite a stir. The gentleman with the paper seemed quite unperturbed as to the stir. He handed me the pen and said: 'Ah, it won't be all that bad.'

I signed, after being allowed forty-eight hours to make preparations for my departure.

During the entire scene, none of the nineteen others had so much as raised their eyes from their desks. Prussian officials do not listen to that which does not concern them. I once visited a government department in St Petersburg. In the corridors, there would be a couple of officials at every turn, standing and talking. There were a hundred people who wanted to oblige us, and nobody who knew a thing. The one official hardly seemed able to locate the other. Every time we entered a new room, everyone looked up and flocked around us to supply us with information.

An older gentleman, who was an office manager or something, left his office and conducted me through half the building. He asked me about the geographical conditions of Denmark and detained me in the cold corridors for over an hour. He was an amateur geographer. He took off some sort of cap from his head and, swinging it in the air over and over, said: 'People really ought to know the world they inhabit.'

At the police station in Berlin, things proceed rather differently than they do in St. Petersburg. A Prussian public official guards his ledger like a sentry, and a Brandenburg sentry guards his door and his alone; and he is forbidden to talk.

After being given the expulsion order, I drove out to the ambassador, who promised to do his utmost, or at the very least, he would discover the reason.

We discovered the reason: it was lamentable. And Count Herbert von Bismarck himself had laid it on the table before the ambassador, in the form of a column in a Bergen newspaper.*

After that all objections had to cease; the article spoke for itself. Even I saw no reason to complain. Moreover the feuilleton had been forwarded to them by the consul in Bergen, and had – in its rightful place and properly docketed – already been waiting for some time at the Ministry of Foreign Affairs alongside mountains of other Nordic documents. For all manner of printed matter is painstakingly collected in Berlin.

Astonishingly painstakingly, according to those who are familiar with it.

A year after my expulsion, in connection with some very outspoken statements at a couple of political meetings back home – statements that were quoted in the newspapers – I wrote that perhaps people ought to speak a little quieter here at home.* Because only a wall stood between us and Germany, and 'walls can have ears'. The remark was widely derided. If people had known who had spoken it, perhaps they would not have laughed so loudly.

My sole hope was that my expulsion might pass off quietly. I did not find the occasion particularly opportune to cause a spectacle. I knew that *Bergens Tidende* would reach Berlin sooner or later – in translation.*

All I wanted was to find out whether I might stay in the rest of Germany without further incident. Count Herbert von Bismarck was confident that I could. And so I decided to travel to Meiningen.* I paid a farewell visit to *Berliner Tageblatt*.*

One last time I walked up the stairs to the office of the world-renowned newspaper. Arthur Levysohn had been instrumental in getting me to come to Berlin.* He had followed my work at home and believed there would be a place for me in Berlin. I was to write for the paper's theatre column. My first articles had already been published.

Now there was nothing to be done other than say goodbye. I took my hat – and left.

On that last night a Danish friend and I drove up Unter den Linden. Beautiful and vast it lay before us, with its vibrant stream of people – one of the great thoroughfares of the world.

My Danish friend stood up in the carriage. He looked wistfully down at the Brandenburg Gate with its triumphal chariot; everything was bathed in light, everything, people and palaces.

'Beautiful, splendid city,' he said. And for a long time we sat silently.

Beautiful, splendid city.

Yes, here was the great big world, and now Herr HB had to go home to his own little corner, to a new corner. He departed the following morning.

It is not exactly easy to get to Meiningen. You change trains a number of times until finally you're on a single-track railway on a train with one passenger car and one freight wagon. On that train you lumber along steadily. You really get the sense of being shunted onto one of the side-tracks of the world.

But in Meiningen it would be nice and peaceful. What had befallen me was well known, but everyone acted as if they did not know.

The days followed their course. The court actors went to rehearsals, and from rehearsals they went to the hotel to drink their beer. Their promenades were the highlight of the day. People watched them move throughout the city. This Residenz city only has one street, where all the doors of the court purveyors are rusting silently on their hinges.*

At night, the city was at the theatre.* The Duke led the way in his box, and the people listened. They knew the repertoire by heart and enjoyed themselves immensely.

It could be well into the night before you made it home. There are a lot of costume changes in Meiningen.

The good Thüringians wandered home amidst a cheerful buzz. They savoured the troupe's world renown as if it were their own. Their favourite piece was *William Tell.** In that play, Geheimrat Schiller makes such a din that it sounds as though an avalanche was thundering down across the stage.*

'*Gott, gott*', the good citizens said, '*heute hat er denn brav gedonnert.*'*

They were also pleased with *A Blood Wedding.** For that occasion, the garrison was deployed to encircle the theatre. In the palace park, on an agreed signal, they fired to the sound of loud howling.

On the stage, Frau Olga Lorentz observed the ravaged Paris from a window.* The spectacle in the castle park was *St Bartholomew's Day Massacre.*

Every Sunday all the young people in the duchy arrived under banners. They marched to the theatre like Grundtvigians to a shooting competition.*

There were also concerts, such as Hans von Bülow's farewell concert.* Hans von Bülow was of course the renowned conductor of the Meiningen Court Orchestra, though whilst in this position, he was not always in exact agreement with His Highness. On the contrary, he often had opinions of his own, which he was in the habit of expressing rather loudly.

Now the splendid conductor had openly criticised His Highness from the podium at a concert in Cologne and boldly allowed his criticism to be reported. His application to resign was therefore most graciously granted.

He was now to conduct a farewell concert. The entire town was shivering in anticipation of the concert. Herr von Bülow was not expected to go easy on his audience at parting.

Herr von Bülow appeared on his rostrum at ten minutes before seven. It was evident that on this evening, he wished to start on the dot; for His Highness was from time to time delayed by a single minute.

But on this night Duke Georg had checked his pocket watch just as precisely as Dr von Bülow, and he entered his box at one minute before seven. Herr von Bülow pretended not to see. He observed the other members of the audience like a Prussian drill sergeant inspecting his unit.

The attitude of the audience was such that the departing conductor did not feel called upon to make a statement.

His Highness applauded sincerely.

One fine day I received a newspaper from Hamburg. It contained an article from a Copenhagen correspondent.* I was the subject of the correspondence. I dare say that not a single unpleasantness that has been uttered about this subject in the corner of a Danish café was omitted from this depiction. Everything had been painstakingly included, even the misfortunes that had befallen the deceased members of my family.

To those who believed all this, I surely must have appeared a dangerous character. And why would someone in a foreign country not believe it, if someone in my own country could write it?

As soon as I read it, I thought: 'Now you'll be expelled from here, too.' Which in fact I was – exceedingly swiftly.

A couple of days later a summons arrived. I was to report to the mayor. He wished to see me at eight o'clock the following morning. German public officials are given to doing everything first thing in the morning.

I duly reported, and saw at once that the document was in order. It lay completed next to the mayor. It turned out that I was to be expelled from the town of Meiningen with the familiar twenty-four hours' notice.

I stated that it would be impossible for me to leave so quickly. The mayor opined that it wasn't that far to the border of the duchy, which of course it wasn't. However, I did, I said, have to travel a little further than Gotha.*

I went to the chief minister. He was a plain, good-natured man, who often sat in the parlour of the hotel at dusk with his tankard.

I now went to pay him a visit at the ministry, which looked most of all like some kind of large freight office. The minister was sitting in his living room – the chairs were upholstered with horsehair – in front of an old bureau. I presented my case to him and asked the reason for my expulsion. In Berlin they had told me that I would be able to stay in Meiningen without any problems.

The minister said: 'I don't know the reasons. *Wir haben nur Befehl aus Berlin.*'* And lowering his voice almost imperceptibly, he said: 'Here we can do nothing.'

The old man got up and turned to the window, as if he were suddenly overcome with emotion. And after a brief silence he said: 'Here too there are parents whose sons fell at Langensalza.'*

However, he did extend me two days – and we parted with a handshake.

Despite that, the very next morning a police officer – I believe the Residenz has two – appeared at my bedside to remind me on behalf of the mayor of my departure. I was now feared as a spark of revolution in the duchy.

When I left, the police officer was present on the platform – in plain clothes. I departed for Munich. I had been advised to choose to reside in a kingdom.*

I arrived in Munich in the evening. I went to a hotel where I had been accustomed to staying for many years. The next morning I was woken by the hall porter, who was exceedingly agitated. The police had been to ask where I was residing. Already, I thought, realising that Munich was hardly suitable for any kind of lengthy asylum. I arranged my departure for that afternoon. I was certain that there was no time to waste.

First I went out to see Henrik Ibsen,* who looked so strangely homeless among all that rented furniture, at which some family portraits on the wall were staring with confused or curiously astonished eyes. The master shook his grey head during my story, saying over and over: 'You don't say – you really don't say.'

At two o'clock I took the fast train eastward. I thought it best to retreat from the Hohenzollerns and seek out the Habsburg Monarchy.* I settled in Vienna.

For four or five months I lived completely undisturbed. One of the few people I knew there was the Danish envoy, whom I – like all Danes, I'm sure – remember with the greatest affection.

I'd moved out to Hernals and lived there quite alone.* I literally went weeks without seeing another person, but worked and worked on *Katinka*.* My landlady was a widow with six children, and the entire lot of them lived in a kitchen with an adjoining pantry.

It struck me that of late, there was a constant stream of men staying in this pantry. The landlady told me they were suitors. Her husband was barely cold in his grave, and she was frenetically replying to the matrimonial columns of all the newspapers.

She said: 'What can a woman do, all on her own?'

For a long time she claimed that the gentlemen in the pantry were suitors, as already mentioned. But one fine day she informed me in confidence that they were 'detectives': they questioned her about me on a daily basis.

I asked whatever they might want with me.

Well, she didn't know that. But they looked at my papers when I wasn't home.

I supposed that they weren't able to read them?

No, they were not. But they kept asking whether I went out at night, and whether any Russians came.

I realised that I was now well on my way to becoming an out-and-out nihilist. I informed the envoy, and he went to the police chief. And sure enough – I was assumed to be a person of dubious character. Enquiries were made as to what I had done. But as to that, I received no information. Only that they believed my presence in Vienna was entirely superfluous. In addition the chief shrouded himself in a cloud of secrets.

The Austrian police in general enjoy having their secrets. They still work in the tradition of Prince von Metternich.*

To these police officers, naturally, I must have been a juicy titbit. People could happily invent anything here, for the precise reason that there was nothing.

Morning and night the landlady submitted her reports in the pantry. I stumbled across detectives at my front door.

The landlady was flouring her own cake. She claimed that she had stored her rent in the chest of drawers in my room. The rent was now missing. 'I know perfectly well,' she said to me in a gentle and heartfelt tone, 'that no one else has been in my room.' She would hate to involve the police in the matter. 'I'm sure the gentleman has enough – more than enough already … .'

The look on her face expressed understanding sympathy for all that I must 'have'. But she was a poor housewife, who had to have her rent.

I understood that, she had to have her rent. It was twenty Gulden.* My purse was lightened by that many notes.

And a couple of days later I travelled to Prague. It was believed that I would be less bothersome in the provinces.

I rented a flat in a suburb, and on Saturday evening I moved in. On Sunday morning a constable rang the bell. Whether I was Herr such and such?

Yes (I'd heard the story before), I was Herr such and such.

So here was a summons, the man said. I had no cause to doubt it, and accepted the document.

I went to respond to the summons. At last I had fallen into the hands of a couple of public officials who knew their duty, and took it seriously. Here they had no intention of letting an offender die in his sins.*

For the time being, I was made to wait on the accused's bench for an hour. I sat between two gentlemen who were arrested for begging. When I was finally called forward, I understood that now I had come to the right people. These two gentlemen were not ones to let a secret pass them by. They were far too fond of secrets to do that. And they were as insightful as magistrates in an operetta. They treated me as if I was destined for the gallows, and started by claiming that I had falsified my passport.

The public official in charge, whose nose was very red, proclaimed importantly that they knew who I was.

I responded meekly that they seemed to know more than I did.

The one in charge implored me to save my wisecracks; a report had been received.

I asked what was written in that report.

The one in charge said only that the report was from Vienna. He pronounced the name of this town as if, in the middle of Kärntner Ring, I had killed a significant proportion of my unfortunate family.*

I said, I understood that it must have come from Vienna.

The public official smiled and said with particularly strong emphasis: 'So you understand that, do you?'

The younger official entered my confession into a ledger.

I understood that I was now completely dubious. Nevertheless, I assured them of my innocence.

'Sir,' the official said, 'innocent persons do not have reports made against them. We know who you are.'

The younger official indicated with a nod that he, at any rate, knew me intimately. But it was clear that, even if they knew me, they did not know my secret. And they wanted to know it. They would find out.

I was interrogated for an hour and three quarters. By then the two gentlemen had filled seven folio pages with confessions, and I was considered a hardened criminal. The older gentleman told me so in words that left no doubt as to his sincerity. And as I left, he said that I would be hearing from him.

And I did: for a week, there was a police constable at my door every morning. Every other day I received a summons. The yellow papers were familiar to everyone in the house. I have to admit that the inmates of the house were not exactly crowding round to make my acquaintance.

It was right at the height of summer. The sun scorched the courtrooms. The two officials sweated blood in pious and excited zeal; never before have I heard public officials be so foul-mouthed.

One day I received a summons from the police chief himself. I now accepted everything that happened without any emotion. I had grown accustomed to waiting at the counter.

I was led in to see a rather distinguished-looking gentleman, who treated me as if I were a Polish Jew hawking doormats. I was informed that once again a report had been received from Vienna.

I replied that I couldn't understand what there was to report.

He stated harshly that 'reports would not be made unless I had done something.'

I asked wearily – despairingly – because it was probably the thousandth time now – what I had done wrong. And the man replied: 'If we knew that, Herr What's-your-name, we wouldn't be interrogating you, would we.'

I didn't tell the man that he was going round in circles. I said absolutely nothing. It would have been pointless. But I can vividly imagine that it is in moments such as these that arrested individuals make up crimes just in order to get it over with.

The police prefect sent me off, having recommended caution.

In addition, the house I stayed in was festooned with detectives. Particular interest was directed to discovering whether I received nocturnal visitors. I received no visitors, neither night nor day.

Friends in Vienna advised me to return home, because 'Austrian police officers are intractable once they get something into their heads. The police there, they usually stick to their guns.'

I had to give them that.

But nevertheless I didn't want to travel home until I could do it with *Stucco* in my pocket.* So I stayed on for another year. The police paid me constant attention. But as to the content of 'the reports', they never informed me about that.

They must have had their reasons.

Well, be that as it may – they were persistent, you had to give them that.

Translated by Paul Russell Garrett

16. A Christmas Eve on Foreign Soil

'Snow,' I shouted, drawing the sitting room curtains back.

'No – damn it,' the painter shouted from his bedroom, as he jumped out of bed and dashed to the window, not exactly fully dressed.

'By God, it is snowing,' he said.

There was a lot of snow: drifts of it in the street, mounds of it in front of the gates. Great quantities of snow. Snow and more snow.

'Well then, the trains are going to get stuck,' the painter said.

'That they will,' I said.

'They'll never make it through the mountains,' he said.

'No,' I replied, observing the rooftops. The snow had settled like massifs on the rooftops.

'Well,' the painter said, 'there are four more days until Christmas.'

'And I'm sure they'll send the post by sled.'

The sleds helped to console us.

We were in Prague.* Living in a suburb, four gentlemen – a painter and myself on the second floor, and a pianist and a law graduate on the third. 'Die Hausmeisterin' made soup for the four of us and served it in earthenware bowls.* The four of us were equally well-off. On the third floor they confessed their poverty, while on the second floor, great efforts were made to conceal it.

That's also why as far back as November – it's good to do such things in good time – the second floor had invited the third floor down for Christmas Eve.

We then began to prepare for the party. When abroad, one gradually gets accustomed to all sorts. Editors aren't always so swift to print what you write. Some of it goes in the rejection pile and some of it goes in on Mondays. And if the editors do eventually print it, they're not exactly expedient in dispatching the fees. Postal orders arrive sporadically and somewhat late in the month. As for publishers, they are not much better.

When you're abroad, you are – well, it can also apply here at home for that matter – on the outside, and it's as though the entire world has to be reminded first, reminded firmly.

So you have to hedge your bets in good time. We had done that.

I was writing regular columns for five countries.* For a month I had not spared a single one of them. I had feasted on the Christmas snow while November's fogs lay densely over Hradčany,* and I had sounded the festive bells for all the family magazines I could get hold of.

Nor was there any other journalistic pursuit I had neglected. Politics and social commentary flowed abundantly from my pen. In journals I had been serious and in the less serious magazines I had attempted to be jocose. Journalists grow accustomed to a little versatility over the years.

For a German family magazine, whose editor expressed his programme in the words: 'Esteemed sir, our magazine appeals to the heart' – I had delivered novellas.* One of them bore the title: 'A Village Ophelia,' a title that deserved success in a country where there is such respect and reverence for the great works.*

The painter had not been idle either. His market was Berlin, and his speciality was studio portraits of gypsies. Never had I seen such black hair and such big eyes. He painted one per day. There wasn't a single art gallery in Berlin whose walls were not adorned with his gypsies. The closer it got to Christmas, the smaller the portraits became, and the bigger the frames.

'That's how they damn well want them,' the painter said: 'then they're more suitable as presents.'

He painted himself to death. All the beauties looked alike. 'But it doesn't matter,' he said, 'so long as you're careful to disperse them sufficiently.' He dispersed them, as I said, across all of Berlin.

But of course a painter's métier is always uncertain. The most certain part is the cost of the frames. Those you have to pay for in advance. Only then can you exhibit the pictures, which isn't always the same thing as selling them straight away.

We knew that. And that's why I was even crueller to my magazines. Still we were happy. Most of mine were published, so we were at the stage where we were anticipating the postal orders.

Day after day passed, but nothing arrived. Even the editor's assistant, who ordinarily keeps the books, is busy on his own behalf leading up to the festive season, so he hardly has the time to pore over postal orders.

The fifteenth arrived: no fees. The eighteenth arrived: still no postal orders. As for the art dealers, they remained alarmingly quiet.

We started to slack off a little in our work, both the painter and I. During the day we walked the streets window shopping, thinking of what we would buy for our guests. For it had to be a proper Christmas with a tree and presents.

The nineteenth drew to a close with the post passing the second floor by.

That evening the painter said: 'Wouldn't it be just great if it snowed and the trains couldn't run.'

'Yes,' I said slowly. I had already thought of snow. I'd grown accustomed to thinking the worst. Now on the morning of the twenty-first there were snowdrifts. It was poor comfort, knowing that I had expected it.

We consoled ourselves – to start with – that the snowfall was local. The papers, however, announced that not since 1830 had so much snow fallen across the entire country. Traffic had come to a complete standstill across central Europe.

The days that followed were not exactly cheerful. We were not very talkative. I cursed the editorial staff, as if they had also arranged the snowfall. We began to realise that we would have to rein in our expectations.

'Presents are out of the question,' the painter said.

The fact is that for weeks – because adults become children when you are so to speak on your own on foreign soil – we had deliberated about the presents. Before long there was not an object that we had not considered giving.

'No,' I said, 'they are out of the question.'

'But listen,' the painter said: 'the fact is it might be better like that. It was a bit pretentious – when the others had nothing to give. And they damn well have nothing to give … .'

I hoped not.

All the while it continued to snow, and it was the day before Christmas Eve. All we had was a Gulden and a few Kreutzer.* The painter went around checking old waistcoat pockets, as was his wont in very critical, moneyless moments. He found nothing. He had probably already been there.

Old Veith, the husband of die Hausmeisterin who waited on us, would tiptoe uncertainly around in his felt shoes, and was never done with his table arrangements. Old Veith walked on the balls of his feet and raised his knees with every step, as though he was still doing his knee bends.

When he wasn't waiting on us, he tied loose ends. Die Hausmeisterin worked with two seamstresses for a shirt factory. The machines took care of the long seams. Der Hausmeister tied the loose ends. This womanly occupation had over time given him certain hand gestures, as if he was for ever pulling the needle out of a piece of canvas.

Now he was walking around sheepishly, raising his knees, scenting our worries and wanting to say something but without managing to, until he stood in the doorway, rubbing against the frame as though he were giving himself a shake.

'About the tree,' he said finally, turning copper-red, the poor fellow: 'I'd been thinking – my wife had been thinking' (it was always my wife who did the thinking) ' –whether I, whether we mightn't buy the tree – because I'm a local, and foreigners such as yourselves, foreigners – you'll just – you'll end up paying twice as much ... .'

The old man could say no more, and was as red as dripping blood. We understood that he wanted to help us with the tree.

'And I'm putting my foot down,' he said: 'so that's that.' He'd grown bolder. He sensed that we had accepted his offer.

We were silent for a long time after he left.

'Well, the post could come tomorrow,' the painter said.

'Yes …,' I said.

I doubt either of us was expecting post at this point.

Out on the stairs, there was laughing and singing. It was from the third floor – our guests for tomorrow. They were already in festive spirits.

On the second floor there wasn't much sleep that night. At seven o'clock in the morning we heard the postman. We hadn't expected anything different: now he walked slowly past our door.

Nothing, nothing.

We didn't say anything to each other. And we heard the postman stomp back down – such stupid, mechanical stomping – and then Hausmeister tiptoeing back inside in his felt shoes. He'd never before walked so quietly.

'Well, we might as well get up and celebrate Christmas.' With what's in our coffers – one Gulden.

When we got up, we smelled spruce: in the entrance hall stood the tree. It was probably cut from the edge of the woods, for it looked as if it had been ravaged by many a fierce storm.

'Poor old chap,' the painter said, thinking of Veith. We stood looking at the crooked shoot. We didn't know where we would find anything to hang on it.

Old Veith arrived. He cocked his head and said: 'It's a fine tree, really fine. That's how it is when you're a local.'

'Yes, it really is fine,' we said, our voices a little thick.

It was placed on the sitting room table. There it stood in all its nakedness.

There was a ring at the door, and we all gave a start. The postman had just left and we thought: maybe the post has come after all.

It was our guests from the third floor. They wished us good morning – they were beaming from ear to ear – and asked us when they should come.

I said: 'Yes – eight o'clock.' And the painter invited them in. But they declined, not wanting to disturb our preparations ... .

That was rich, talking about preparations.

The painter said: 'Well, we have to do something.'

'Yes,' I answered, with no bright ideas.

The painter said: 'We could put cotton on the branches.'

'Yes,' I answered, 'but we also need candles.'

'Well,' he said thoughtfully, 'we could use wax tapers.'

'Yes,' I said.

Neither of us mentioned food. We knew the food was the most desperate part. Because we had wanted to celebrate Danish style, with goose and crackling – and that's what we had told our guests. All the way back in November.

Hausmeister kept coming in and out, his eyes shifting from one of us to the other. We were getting a bit tired of him. It wasn't the kind of situation you wanted to share with strangers.

'You have a lot of time on your hands today, Veith,' the painter said.

We had just as much time. We just sat, each in our own chair, staring at the crooked tree.

'Yes,' Veith said, almost stammering: 'today ... there's no sewing today… Mutter is cooking Christmas dinner,' he managed to say. And suddenly he burst out into a torrent of words: 'That's what she's doing, she's cooking carp – blue carp, that's what she's cooking ... . Of course, that's what everyone here eats this evening' – and he laughed in embarrassment – 'including the finest … in sour sauce with prunes ... yes ... that's what she's cooking ... . And as it happens, she cooks in all sorts of ways ... from back when we worked in the canteen ... . You know we cook ... from back then ... and it's lovely jellied ... .'

Hausmeister got all jumbled up.

'Yes,' the painter said (we didn't hear half of it): 'they say it's good jellied.'

Hausmeister made another attempt: 'Yes – well, it was just that ... it was just that my wife was thinking, that you might like to try carp ... and feel ... that you were in Bohemia ... that's what we were thinking ... Mutter,' he said rather breathlessly, 'really has woken us up tonight.'

I'm fairly certain that both the painter and I had tears in our eyes. We understood it all: there was no sewing because Hausmeisterin was cooking – cooking for us – foreigners.

'Yes, thank you. That really could be a lot of fun ... a lot of fun to celebrate Christmas Bohemian-style,' we said. And we thought: fortunately the guests *are* Bohemians. I wasn't really sure whether carp with prune sauce was as agreeable to foreigners.

Veith beamed and raced in and out. He was like a victor on the field of battle. The door to the caretaker's room was left open. The smell of cooking and baking filled the entire house. The painter took our Gulden and went out and bought wax tapers.

Veith bustled about, knees raised. He started to talk about how his son-in-law was a conductor ... a conductor for the railway. For the northern railway.

Yes, I knew that.

As it happened, there were good positions there at the northern railway ... because the spas ... those spa guests didn't spare a Gulden when they wanted to have a compartment all to themselves ... .

'No,' I said, 'of course they didn't.'

'No, they don't,' he said. 'And they also have a cooperative,' he said suddenly.

'A cooperative?' I asked. I wasn't particularly interested.

'Yes – and they get everything – they have the best wine there ... from Opava, you know ... the best wine, pure wine ... they get it for thirty Kreutzer ... .'

He turned away. 'Yes,' he said, 'we have a few bottles ... if ... .'

It ended up with us also getting wine – for thirty Kreutzer per kerosene bottle from the railway conductors' cooperative.

The painter returned home and I told him. 'Well,' he said: 'it sounds as if dinner is going to be a group effort.'

'Oh yes,' was my only answer; actually we were only contributing the cotton wool – and the wax tapers.

Some gold thread was picked out of an old riding cloak, which figured among the painter's things; that was used instead of tinsel for the tree.

Veith continued running up and down and in and out. He was so loud and he had such good intentions. He brought glasses and he brought bottles; we had to taste the conductors' wine. 'Yes,' Hausmeister said, 'it's the real deal.'

He clinked glasses. 'My daughter takes this to fortify herself every time she goes into labour,' he said.

We laughed – for the first time – and emptied our glasses.

The painter spread the cotton wool across the branches and hung tinsel on top. It looked a little pitiful. 'What the hell,' the painter said, 'you can't see it that closely with the wax tapers.'

He was right.

I didn't know why, but Hausmeister insisted on us coming down to the cellar. We had to see the carp, he said, and Mutter had also been baking.

We thought we had better go down, so we followed the old man.

Down in the cellar Frau Hausmeister had moved the sewing machines into the corner and a freshly-scrubbed table to the middle of the floor. She was cooking and frying up a storm, leaving her in a cloud of steam.

Hausmeister tiptoed off and closed the door behind him.

'Yes,' his wife said, laughing with her round ruddy face: 'it is a change ... but the holidays do have to be celebrated.'

She kept talking about that for quite a while, until all at once she said in an angry tone: 'But Veith is an old fool' – and suddenly came over and stuck a ten-Gulden note in my fingers; 'because there are still things to be bought from the shops,' she said in the same angry tone: 'and we don't have time for it here. You'd best hurry along now.'

We both went over and took her by the hand. 'Yes,' she said, preoccupied: 'I'm making two kinds of carp now ... so you can choose ... because with the blue one ... .' She went on about her fish, and wouldn't hear of anything else.

We went back upstairs – with the note we had been given. It was starting to get dark. The tree with its white cotton was in the living room. Old Veith was setting the table.

We had to spend the Hausmeisterin's ten Gulden. We decided to get candles instead of wax tapers and some more tinsel to decorate all the cotton wool. We bought as prudently as paupers who have neared the bottom of their purse.

When we came out of the shop, the painter said: 'Oh hell, listen, we'd best save a little ... there are more days to come ... and who knows when we'll next have money.' It was probably the only time in his life the painter had thought of tomorrow. But these had been tough days.

I thought we had best spend all the money for the Veiths' sake: they were so happy, as if it was their own Christmas tree.

When we returned home, it was twilight. The painter started to tell me about Christmas in his home town in the March of Brandenburg.* At four o'clock on Christmas morning the children were woken, and would walk through the streets to church holding large wax tapers.

'How we guarded those candles, so that they wouldn't go out,' he said; 'and how carefully we walked, looking at the flame with big round eyes ... . Then we sang the Christmas hymns when we'd reached the church.'

He continued telling me about his home and about his childhood. I probably only heard about half of it, busy as I was thinking of my own home.

The painter talked about Christmas – last Christmas, when he was in Berlin, poor and alone. He went into the street, he said, and stood in front of the gates of the large barracks. He waited for the moment when the soldiers, who were on home leave, came out in droves. Off they stomped, carrying bundles, long rows of them, toward the railway station – all the young lads, going home, each to his home. Then he walked around the streets and squares, which were soon deserted. And finally he was the only one in the long, broad streets, slipping past the row of houses like a shadow.

I remained silent. Then out of nowhere I said: 'Listen, do you think we might get any telegrams?'

'Well, do you have anyone who might send you a telegram?'

'Ah, yes,' I said, thinking: at one time there were many.

'Well, I don't have anyone,' the painter said. And we were quiet for a while.

Veith roused us. He arrived with two lit candles in a couple of old plated candlesticks. He said that the table needed some light. It was also getting near the time when our guests were expected.

The pair of candles shone upon the table. It made a very tolerable impression.

All the Veiths' dishes were put to use. They were bought, as Veith put it, 'just in case', and all appeared to have led an eventful existence. The tablecloth was bountiful, at least, it reached the floor on all sides and was as coarse as one of their matrimonial sheets.

The guests rang. They were dressed to the nines, and beaming.

We exchanged Christmas greetings with them – I had my heart in my mouth – and told them that it would be a Bohemian Christmas after all – out of regard for Frau Veith's culinary skills.

Veith opened the dining room with a '*Gesegnete Mahlzeit*'; and we went in to the carp.*

At first it was a little quiet, the Bohemians ate and we hosts sat mostly, looking somewhat absent-mindedly at the multifarious plates. Old Veith seemed to be in a state of ecstasy. He brought in dishes so big, as though he were still at the canteen, and had half a division to feed. With each new dish he brought in, his face shone, as though he was opening the door to a Christmas tree for a bunch of children.

He passed the carp around – there was carp in sour sauce and carp in sweet – and he prattled on: 'Yes, yes, I'm sure Herr Pianist knows it is Czech food from the way it's served ... yes, yes, carp is food for the holidays ... from when we were small ... .'

He pressed us incessantly to eat his blue fish. The prune sauce was his favourite.

'It did seem as if they liked the prune sauce, the troops, in sixty-six* ... But oh, all things considered, oh, how the Prussians ate ... .'

It was in sixty-six that Herr Veith had provided food for the soldiers. And, holding his dish of fish, he starts telling a long story about all that the Prussians could eat: 'You had a Gulden per day per man, but you had to take care. Because those fellows ate whatever they saw.'

But Veith had his methods; when they arrived at their quarters, they were, understandably, as hungry as ravenous wolves. 'But then,' Veith says, with his finger to his nose, while screwing up his eyes: 'if you just let them stuff themselves as much as they could – so that they damn well gorged themselves on the first day ... then over the days to come, their appetites were far more delicate ... .'

Veith laughs loudly; that trick is his lifetime achievement. And the rest of us have to laugh along – we've heard the story some twenty times.

'Yes, yes,' Veith says, 'but they were patient and as kind as children... . They gave Mutter a hand, as if they were her own sons ... and peeled their own potatoes. But in the ranks' – he concludes – 'they certainly were disciplined there.'

Veith stares ahead so happily, as if he was once again getting a Gulden per head from the hostile Prussian ranks. Then he calls me out to the bedroom. 'It's a bit quiet,' he says: 'keep pouring ... .'

'The wine is fine. It's good stuff.'

The litre bottles of railway wine are passed around, it's as sweet as mulled wine. Even more fish is brought in, and the atmosphere begins to get livelier.

The pianist talks about Christmas back home in Most, back when they were still well-off and his father was alive.* His father was a tanner. When the morning of Christmas Eve arrived, two large tubs of carp were set up in the entrance, and his mother dished out the blue fish to all the poor who turned up.

'That's how it is, you know, in small towns,' he says, 'you share the wealth.'

The painter and I look at each other; we want to drink with Old Veith. First he wipes his mouth on his shirt sleeves – he's dressed for the occasion, wearing a black waistcoat and with gleaming white shirt sleeves – before he clinks glasses with both of us.

The pianist continues talking about life back home in Most: how all the workers and all the boys were served dinner in the evening.

The law graduate, whose father is a district judge in a small town, stops eating and gazes far back in time at *his* Christmas: 'Yes,' he says: 'we were sixteen children ... .' As if that says it all. And he bows his gaunt neck, which still seems to bear witness to all the hunger of the child of a public official.

The litre bottles are passed round and everyone is talking. Die Hausmeisterin has slipped up from the cellar to listen in from the bedroom through a crack. The painter gets her to come in and everyone clinks glasses with her.

She stood in her stockinged feet with folded hands. 'Yes,' she said: 'it's lovely to have young people here.' And she stood staring happily, eyes shining, at the table with the carp and the two candles.

We got up from the table and the painter went in to light the tree. It was really glittering, with its cotton wool and tinsel from the riding cloak. But the four of us grew a little quiet again, until the pianist suggested we should sing.

He led the singing. But it wasn't quite right. We tried song after song, while the tree shone silently. But we didn't know any of the same songs. And so the singing petered out. We continued eating by the tree. Veith brought in so many dishes; then there were pastries and then there were preserves. And it was good there was so much food, because the conversation was a little sluggish, until in the end we all sat quietly, the four of us.

In the dining room I heard tiptoeing. It was Mutter Veith, who had come back up. She stood quietly in there, a little away from the door, looking at the crooked tree with wide eyes … .

Our guests had left. The painter and I sat near the base of the spruce tree, with its candles snuffed out.

Veith went into the dining room and made himself busy. We hadn't heard him come in, but then I heard the scraping of a chair, and turned to see that he had something on his mind. Then finally he said, in a rather unsteady voice: 'Yes, you must forgive us – we weren't able to do any better.'

The painter and I had tears in our eyes.

Veith had left, and we sat quietly for some time.

Then the painter started telling me about other Christmas Days and other Christmas parties. He told me about a Christmas party in Munich – a heathen party with rich and beautiful women and wine and wit and a massive rose tree instead of a spruce. And he told me – in a completely unsentimental tone, though perhaps tinged with melancholy – about his friend, who was the life of the party back then. He was some kind of poet who suddenly appeared on the scene in Munich as an energetic twenty-two-year-old. He had some talent and a lot of energy. He had a gentle voice and a sentimental delivery, which suited the poems he recited everywhere.

There was one year where he was the toast of the entire city – perhaps only because in that moment there was no one else to toast. It was a year like out of a legend, so full of fortune and favour. He took it, I think, for granted. And in fact he was rather unpretentious, and he also shared his good fortune with others. But the public's intoxication was short-lived, while its rancour and its apathy lingered. It always goes that way when an audience has let itself be caught unawares.

"The audience had been roused, my dear friend, and it has never forgiven the man. He has now written far more talented work than back then – even a book, which I think is good … but he remains an outsider. And is kept away from all enterprises. It's as if those in charge were afraid of getting stung by him or even just by his name. He'll never come back. As if a circle has formed and he's on the outside.'

'And does he take it to heart?' I asked.

'To heart!' the painter said. 'What do you think? There probably was a time … . Now I think he has set himself other goals – more internal, if I may put it like that. The satirical magazines still run stories devoted to him now and again; haven't you noticed how they continue to peck stubbornly at a "subject" ten years after it loses its relevance, and it's only when they go quiet that you've really died. They still regard him as a self-promoter, but he shuns society now, I think – he keeps to the shadows and only wishes to be left alone, to be able to sit in peace.

'But perhaps,' the painter said pensively, 'he suffers a little from time to time from … the fact that so many of his gifts are wasted. That might torment him. Bavaria, you see, is a small country. And he may say to himself that in a small country there are always only a few talented people – so perhaps there ought to have been some use for him – even for him, a job to elevate the life that's lived, the life of his own day, which links with others down through the decades. From time to time he probably says with sadness that even he could have been used there. Because he really had some dynamism to him, and I also think some selflessness – some of that desire that drives a person to act for the benefit of all, that desire that creates society's leaders, the big and the small. He had some of that. And it's possible that once in a while, when he measures the others and himself – the others who took his place to gain the positions and the influence – he thinks to himself that they only have the power in order to feel and possess it, whereas he would have owned it … in order to wield it.

'But it doesn't do any good. And anyway the others can do everything just as well as he can – back in Munich. There is nothing so stupid as believing that I of all people can carry any greater weight than others. What one other person can't do, can be done by two others – and it is done.'

The painter went quiet for a moment. Then he said: 'How clearly I remember the last Christmas we spent together. After dinner we sat down in front of the fire in his sitting room. He still had his positions back then, though it was as if things had begun to grow dim around him … . We sat in silence. Then suddenly he said: "You look as if you're listening." "Listening – I – no, what would I be listening for?"

"What do I know?" he said. "It just looked that way."

Little by little the tree was lit. And the doorbell began to chime. There was present after present, flowers and more flowers. The entire room was filled.

Later that night we were sitting again in front of the fire. I looked around the bedecked room.

"Listen," I said: "I *was* listening earlier."

"Yes, I could see that … . For what?"

"For the doorbell," I said, pointing round the room: "I'd hate for someone to have forgotten you tonight."

He laughed – then smiled a little wistfully … .'

'Good Lord,' the painter said, 'what do you say to that? It's during such moments you notice that you were once stupid enough to allow yourself to be the toast of the town.'

The painter went quiet and again we sat in silence.

He said: 'You're not saying much.'

'No –'

'You're welcome to try ... .'

'Ah,' I said, 'I am also thinking, perhaps, that it's strange how things go up and down in life – mostly down, as with your friend.'

'Yes,' the painter said. He continued: 'Do you know what I'm thinking: I should like to paint Mutter Veith, as she stood there by the two candles saying her piece: "It's lovely to have young people here." Good Lord, those poor old things, those kind old things.'

The painter got up and retired for the night.

I sat for a while in front of the extinguished tree. It was quite dark in the sitting room. Out in the hallway someone was moving around very quietly. It was old Veith, checking to see whether we had retired.

I struck a match and lit the candles.

The gold trim on the Veiths' coffee cups was gleaming. They were fancy cups with lots of inscriptions. In the dining room, plates had been placed over all the leftover carp to protect it. I said to myself: it will be carp again tomorrow.

I knew Fru Veith would want the left-overs to be eaten.

In the building at the back there was a bakery. Through the windows I could see the workers in front of their long troughs. They probably didn't get to celebrate Christmas at all.

But a city needs its bread.

The next morning the postal orders arrived. They really had got stuck up in the mountain passes. And money even arrived for the painter. There were art lovers who had taken pity on his gypsies.

'That's the thing,' he said: 'you damn well have to know how to choose the appropriate format.'

He gathered the postal orders in a fan and looked at them. 'You know,' he said: 'if you just keep your nose to the grindstone – then it all comes good.'

'A little late sometimes,' I said. And we both laughed.

But we ate out for a few days and left the carp and the conductor's wine to the Veiths.

The world can be so ungrateful.

Translated by Paul Russell Garrett

17. By Ship Across the Atlantic

Fritsche brings my tea.

Scarely have I lifted my head from the pillow before I say: 'Fritsche, how old are you?'

Fritsche gives a little start as he puts the tea down. 'Fifty-five,' he says.

'Hm, and how long have you been at sea?'

'Twenty-three years,' answers Fritsche.

'So you must have started as a steward.'

Fritsche regains his usual expression. Fritsche's expression is always a worried one. His legs are lively enough; they run about. But his expression is as still and concerned as that of a night nurse, and he talks like a parish clerk who is showing you round the cathedral.

'Oh yes, my wife died, as I explained, Herr Bang, and I was left with two children – and so I started on the ships. And that's how it is at sea, sir, once you're there, you stay there ... I've been with this company now for thirteen years ... .'

'That's a long time,' I say.

Fritsche's voice changes a little, although he keeps his hands clasped.

'But times are bad,' he says, ' there are too many lines.* So the better-off public has too many choices. And because there's competition the companies keep reducing the prices, you see, sir, so that there are many travellers today who can't actually afford it.'

'That is true,' I say, laughing out loud.*

'And it'll get worse,' says Fritsche, and his head nods, to and fro, to and fro, like the clapper of a church bell; 'much worse. – But,' he goes on, and his head stops suddenly: 'we do have our pleasures too. We have the bowling alley down there – it's fun in the bowling alley … .'

'Bowling alley – here?' I say, sitting up in bed so that I notice how the ship is vibrating.

'No, in Genoa … there are two, you see, Herr Bang, but I always go to Friedrich's. Because he's an old colleague. We have a good time there, when we stop over in Genoa – in the bowling alley.'*

'Now Herr von Tschirnitz is ringing,' and Fritsche turns suddenly.

'He's been doing that for some time,' I say. The morning is Herr von Tschirnitz's most troublesome time; manicures and parting the hair behind his head are a little difficult for an impatient man out on the ocean.

'*Feiner Herr, feiner Herr*,'* says Fritsche, and his lively legs are already over by the door.

'But it will get rougher, Herr Bang,' – and his voice takes on its parish clerk's tone again – 'it will get rougher today.'

Herr Fritsche has gone.

The vibrating of the floor has become more nervous, more trembling, as I walk along the passageway, and if I hold on to the walls, they are vibrating too. The deck steward is standing by one of the stairs. 'It's getting rougher,' he says.

He is solid and somewhat gruff, with a backside like a Rostock skipper.

In the dining room the chief steward hands me the day's first orange. He has the bearing and appearance of an officer from the reserve, and manicured hands. I think of Fritsche and ask suddenly: 'Do you have children?'

'Yes, two.'

'And yet you are so rarely in Hamburg.'

'Last year,' answers the chief steward, with the same smile, 'I had four weeks' holiday.'

From the windows of the dining room you can see the blue-grey waves rising higher. It feels as if the ship were crouching down and then stretching out and leaping in one bound over the waves.

But when I arrive downstairs in the hairdressing salon, everything is in confusion. The water has broken in because the hatch was not closed. The maître, who is as fat and red-faced as a pub landlord from west Jutland, is so furious that he is shaking:

'There – what did I say? Close down the hatches, I said – *Donnerwetter*!* When I was on my first trip – this is the fifteenth year I've been on board, sir – on my first trip I was as sick as a cat … but I did what I had to and threw up like a bucket … .'

His assistant does not answer. He has thin fingers, like a clerk in a bailiff's office, and melancholy eyes beneath his fiery red eyebrows. He is from Neu-Brandenburg.*

'Do you know Neu-Brandenburg?' he asked yesterday. 'It's so lovely in Neu-Brandenburg. It's in the middle of the forest. A little town, right in the middle of the forest.' That's where his sweetheart lives too, and he's working on a ship in order to be able to settle down earlier.

'Yes, of course, Frøken, of course,' says the maître suddenly behind us.

It is Mrs Prower's maid, who has handed a greying, curly lady's wig in through the door and asked if it can be ready for five o'clock tea.

The maître holds the battered wig aloft. 'What a way to make a living!' he says, laughing over his whole landlord's face; he's forgotten all about the flood.

Herr von Tschirnitz hurtles in through the door like a storm. 'What the devil!' he says, throwing his lieutenant's legs up onto a chair, as he takes in the chaos: 'Did the sharks try to swallow your jars?'

'Good morning, Lieutenant,' says the assistant in his quiet, consumptive voice. 'This morning the water was *so* high in the corridor. A wave had broken open the iron doors. The weather is fierce.'

'Yes,' says the lieutenant, 'it's the devil's own job, doing your hair in weather like this.'

'Are you going on deck?' he asks me.

'Yes, when I've visited the doctor.'

In the doorway I say hello to the man from the north, who sits down, exhausted, to submit to the maître's razor.

The doctor is busy with his cotton wool and his jars, which are rattling in their cupboards. 'People don't think that a ship's doctor has anything to do,' he says. 'We have four hospitals, with no patients as yet. But this morning a man hit his head badly – a passenger from steerage. He went out on deck and was swept off his feet by a wave. But no-one gives any thought to how powerful the water is – it's dreadfully powerful in weather like this.'

'Yes, dreadfully,' I repeat, almost without thinking, seeing the long waves in my mind's eye. And we are both silent, as the multitude of cupboards in that large room groan to the movements of the ship.

'The barometer is falling,' says the doctor, passing me my medicine.

But when I emerge into the passage, von Tschirnitz is in the middle of a conversation with the head cook. The head cook is wearing a kerchief around his neck and the resigned expression of all cooks whose intestines are protesting against the many different sauces.

'My dear sir,' he is saying to Herr von Tschirnitz, 'cooking on board ship is something quite different – quite different … . If you put a land cook into my kitchen, sir; I have ten cooks where a land cook would not find room for two.

But the art is to buy the right provisions and then be able to vary the menu for the guests with the ingredients you have.'

'Quite right,' von Tschirnitz nods.

'We have five different menus,' the head cook goes on: 'first class, second class, the officers' mess … .'

'Yes,' says von Tschirnitz, 'it really demands a lot of skill.'

And the head cook, whose face has brightened up at the word 'skill', nods and says: 'It is quite different.' And he returns to his five different menus.

The chief steward has joined us, and says, smiling: 'It will be quite another matter on the "Imperator".* There there will be seven hundred passengers eating in the dining room.'

We go up onto the deck, where people are walking up and down, wrapped up in capes and plaids. Madame is feeding seagulls with bread from a large basket.

Herr von Tschirnitz stands for a moment looking at the circling birds – they look like white flowers over the blueish water. 'There are a lot of them,' he says. 'That means a storm.'

We stop by the railings in front of the dining room, in the midst of a small crowd of people, and look down at the steerage deck. They are all outside down there, now the sun is shining.

There are women in colourful skirts, elderly and crooked, who are gossiping unconcerned, arm in arm, just as if they were in a church square in Poland; there are Ukrainians in brightly-coloured embroidery, who are still staggering after getting drunk for the last time on Europe's spirits, and young Jews in gaudy summer clothes, which can't keep their limbs from freezing; and peasants who won't let go of their bundles, but drag them along, holding on to them as if they were toiling along a country road; and young girls – where can their path be leading? – staring out across the sea, freezing in their grey shawls; and a couple of young lads, drunk already so early in the morning, yelling for their food over by the linen stores; and children; and two old men in coats belted with rope, sitting on a couple of hawsers as if they had sunk down together on a stone at a crossroads.

And whilst we are still staring down at this marketplace, the young merchant from Lima suddenly says, in a voice trembling with indignation – an indignation which conceals feelings he perhaps won't admit to himself: 'Just remember – these are the happiest days of their lives.'

The man from the north, who is standing next to him, raises his head and looks at him.

The crowd down there has gone. The storm is increasing. It makes a deep sound – or perhaps a more distant one, distant as if it came from too far away and never completely reaches us. And the waves have grown wider – as wide if they were hurling themselves forward in order to catch the tumbling ship.

And the ship shakes its masts like a noble creature its mane.

'I'm going to change for lunch,' says von Tschirnitz. He does that every day. 'Come down with me to those damned cabin trunks.'

Fritsche has to come along to show us the way. We walk down the many flights of stairs, then finally climb down iron ladders to a low-ceilinged room, meeting kitchen boys lugging rubbish and laundry boys lugging clothes. There are inscriptions in iron on the walls, and they are in Italian.

'Ah – ha,' says Tschirnitz, and pulls a face; 'there'll be crowds down here all right, when the ship lands at Genoa.' But Fritsche is already over by the trunks, where von Tschirnitz's twenty-seven outfits are strewn about.

When we get up to the promenade deck we meet Mr Evans, who is taking a walk.

'Just look at that American,' says von Tschirnitz; 'he's jumping about on deck in a rising storm as if he was running a marathon on a country road … . But America – have you been there?'

'No, Tschirnitz.'

'Hm. But America,' he says – God knows what thoughts are running through his mind – 'America is not a place for people with clean nails, you know. – But by Jove, I'd better go and see how the Count is.'

And he's gone like a flash. The Count is his uncle, whose estate he will inherit, and for whose sake he has left the army in order to accompany him on twenty safaris every year to the four corners of the earth.

As we are about to descend the small stairs, one of the engineers is perched on the steps, putting up a steel-wire barrier. 'What's going on?' I ask.

'The stairs are a bit too steep,' answers the man politely.

But Tschirnitz, who has come back, (the Count is eating in his cabin) pushes the netting aside: 'It's all right to use them for now, surely,' he says, and we go down.

The vibrations in the floor have transferred to the white walls, which are shaking as if in painful spasms.

Everyone is at table, and they are on the second course. Madame has a ravenous appetite, since she has been riding for two hours on an artificial horse in the gym. The Berliner, who knows everything and can explain everything and does so very loudly, is talking about the enormous rise in the price of caviar. Twenty years ago you could get an acceptable caviar for four marks – and now, gentlemen, it is impossible to find edible caviar for sixteen marks – in Berlin.

'That's right,' says the banker from Austria, whose slightly excessive number of diamond rings are gleaming around his fork.

'And why, why is that, gentlemen?' the Berliner goes on. 'The general standard of living has increased. Everyone wants to eat caviar. In the end a connoisseur won't be able to get hold of a decent product, not even for gold.'

'Yes,' says the worthy gentleman from Krefeld (his face is quite overgrown with beard, but he has such kind eyes behind his glasses), 'we in Krefeld have to get so many things sent from Cologne.'

A lady raises her head. 'Is it raining?' she asks me.

'No, ma'am, I think it's the storm.'

Madame, who is still talking about the artificial horse, intends to use her round-the-world trip as a dieting cure. There is nothing, absolutely nothing, which is as slimming as the ocean.

Everyone talks about dieting, sanatoriums and round-the-world trips. The young postgraduate has spent the autumn reading many books about India. '*Man muss es doch, nicht wahr*?' he says. '*Man muss doch was wissen.** – But,' he concludes, 'altogether, travelling is fun.'

The dining room's glass lampshades are rattling as if under pelting rain, whilst the chairs we are sitting on are swaying.

Madame has turned her head. 'Why have all the lamps been lit?'

'I think the waves make it dark, Madame.'

And suddenly Madame looks out through the window: the waves are towering up like living mountains around all the dining-room windows. '*Grand Dieu*,'* and Madame lets her orange fall onto her plate, whilst the young engineer from Havana, with a stare like an imprisoned bird of prey, devours her pale face with his eyes.

The young lady who asked about rain says suddenly: 'A man on steerage deck almost got his head smashed to pieces.'

'My dear lady,' says Tschirnitz, who never joins in conversations at table, 'it sometimes happens that the waves smash a ship to pieces.'

People leave the table, as the Berliner explains that he has chosen South America for his holiday trip after all. South America, gentlemen, is the up-and-coming land of German industry, so one can combine the useful with the enjoyable, you see?

Mr Evans is standing in the middle of the room, staring up at the creaking glass shade. 'Now it's hailing,' he says, laughing up at the glass roof.

Herr von Tschirnitz and I have gone over to the middle window. The ship is lifting its shuddering stern, crashing into the rising waves and being raised up and shrouded in water. It's like standing on dry land in a white cloud of dynamite, as mountains are blown up.

'It's beautiful.'

'Yes, beautiful.'

The bow rises and falls, crashes into new mountains and is shrouded in new clouds, whilst the rising storm sounds like distant thunder – the thunder of a gun salute over the wide plains of the ocean.

'Come.'

We walk along the corridor, where a group of young cooks have gathered on a corner after lunch. They're talking about 'Imperator', of which they've seen a model in Hamburg, about its cold stores and enormous kitchens and the lifts for serving food, and the pens for transporting poultry.

But we walk past them and up the swaying stairs. The passengers are dozing in deckchairs, wrapped up in blankets. The Count is asleep in the midst of them, his mouth open. To Herr von Tschirnitz's delight his uncle sleeps the whole time, except when he is on the scent of game whilst out hunting.

'They're sleeping,' says Tschirnitz to the doctor, who is passing. 'It's the air.'

'Yes, that's what people say.'

'And what do *you* say?'

'People sleep because they're anxious,' answers the doctor. '*Everyone*, even the ones who don't know it, is anxious inside on a journey like this – they feel feverish, and so they sleep … . But,' says the doctor, looking ahead over the sea, 'they'll soon be woken up now.'

'Moltke', 17 January 1912.

II

The sky has become grey and lowering – a grey interspersed with streaks of white, as if silent white bolts of lightning were piercing through the clouds.

The deck steward is standing by the stairs with his hands in his pockets and the Rostock stern turned towards us. 'Getting rough, gentlemen,' he says. 'It's coming.'

As we move forward, it feels as if the ship is fearful; it doesn't want to advance but has to, and the crash of waves sounds like long blows, answered by the anxious groaning of the hull.

We peer into the second-class cabin. Women and young girls are knitting and sewing as if they were respectable middle-class wives from Pomerania, and young men are playing tig on the lurching stairs, as cheerful as schoolboys in break-time.

'Those people have employment,' says Tschirnitz; 'they know where they're going.'

I'm standing alone in the stern of the ship; the water towers up into grey mountains behind us, and from their tops the sea froth pours out like waterfalls which are split and splintered. And suddenly the mighty propellor is lifted clear of the water, beating powerlessly at the empty air, with a thunderous noise as if it were a hundred propellors, and then plunges into the sea again.

'Where did you get to?' shouts Tschirnitz, who appears at the side of a young man. 'And how long have you been playing on ships?' he asks the young man.

'This is my first trip.'

'Hm,' says Tschirnitz, and then, measuring up the slim young thoroughbred at his side as you measure a horse at a parade, he adds suddenly: 'You'll be popular with the girls in the West Indies.'

The slim musician smiles out at the foaming waters. 'That's why I'm going there,' he says.

The flocks of seagulls are increasing over our heads; they are screaming, though we can't hear it for the screaming of the ocean. But the ship's groaning sounds like sighs beneath our feet. 'Come.'

It is deserted on deck, as darkness slowly falls, and the large ventilators raise their red jaws silently towards the coming night.

'Come then.'

'Yes.'

I can't stand still any more; I'm thrown forward by the lurching of the ship.

'So come then.'

'Yes.' And I'm thrown backwards.

The ladies' saloon is empty. The trio of musicians is playing on its own. Only Mrs Prower is sitting motionless in her corner with her book, in her white ermine, beneath her curly wig, whilst in the corner the young Spaniard is reclining on a sofa – stretched out like a young animal.

The head steward offers us tea. In his agreeable voice, which sounds like that of the leading actor in a comedy of manners, he says: 'In November the voyage was very rough. The water smashed the railings – as you can see, gentlemen, they are made of iron – and there was only this much left of the for'ard mast … .'

Through the windows of the saloon we can see the ship's bows, like the palpitating breast of a half-bolting steed. 'And we, gentlemen, we didn't see our berths for two days and nights.'

The chairs we are sitting in are shaking, with a trembling which transfers itself to our bodies, and the thundering of the lifted propellor in the air almost drowns out the noise of the storm.

'But the passengers, gentlemen, they hardly noticed anything … passengers always find it difficult to judge the real danger … if there *is* any danger, I mean.'

'And it's important not to upset the honoured passengers.'

An officer runs down the library steps from the bridge and out through the vestibule, and suddenly the violinist grabs the white railing with both hands, and the music ceases.

'What are they playing?'

'"*Tristesses d'amour*",' I answer.*

At a sign from the head steward the other stewards suddenly pull the shutters across all the windows, with a sound as if an iron curtain is falling; the officer runs back through the vestibule with rubber boots on, towards the streaming water from the bridge. At the clatter of the shutters the Spaniard has sat up, looking around in confusion like a man just woken from sleep; he laughs and carries on laughing … . Behind the shutters the storm sneaks in; it is as if a sheet were being dragged continually around the walls of the cabin.

'Stop that, for God's sake,' Hugo Tschirnitz calls over to the Spaniard, who is still laughing, unable to stop.

The man from the north, who has joined us, has got the steward to fetch *The Transatlantic Daily,* and is reading the Marconi telegrams.* The King and Queen of England have decided to cut short their visit to India.

But von Tschirnitz has got up: 'I can't stand this chair shaking.' And he adds more calmly: 'Let's go and bathe.'

The Spaniard is standing out in the vestibule, and says, like someone who is still not fully awake: 'I really think the weather has got worse … .'

'But the water in the tubs is choppy,' says the bathing attendant.

'That doesn't matter.'

And I am admitted.

The racket tumbles around the iron walls of the bathing chamber like a drunken giant: the noise of the sea and the noise of the storm and the noise of the ship. Now the propeller is lifted again; it's as if you were imprisoned, shut in a cell with the hurricane itself. And the tub with the slopping water shakes beneath your naked body.

'The storm is increasing,' says the steward.

'Yes.'

The dinner bell booms out and is drowned out again; we must get changed. Hugo von Tschirnitz and I fasten back our doors, which are directly opposite each other. Through the door opening I can see von Tschirnitz in his mirror. Brushes and bottles escape from your hands, you can't get your clothes on.

'What's that, what's that?' Tschirnitz calls out suddenly. The steamship's horn has sounded … and again, and again; hoarse like a groan, the groan of a human being through the storm.

'What's that, what's that?' calls Tschirnitz.

'The fog must be thickening.' And the horn sounds again.

'Fog?' calls Tschirnitz; I can see him in front of his mirror.

And the horn carries on, reluctantly, as if it were tired and could not do any more and did not want to, but carries on, bleating into the storm. Whilst Tschirnitz and I, each in front of our own mirror – we know we can see each other – are rubbing cream into our nails … .

In the doorway to the dining room we meet the Count, who is greeting everyone, just as sprightly as if he was greeting a hunting party on his estate in Poland.

'What was that?' says Tschirnitz, sitting down.

Mr Prower answers: 'It's snowing heavily.'

There is champagne on the table, and the red lamps are lit, and everyone is talking … .

Mr Prower is describing his business in Chicago, his huge business in Chicago – every morning he buys for three million, and every day he produces for three million.

But at Madame's end of the table (Madame is wearing white) they are talking about 'Imperator'; there are said to be gardens on deck, and there is a ballroom and a theatre.

The dining-room lamps are chinking as though they were about to burst under sheets of ice, and the stewards have to cling on to the white columns. The floor is trembling, and so are the chairs beneath us and the walls around us and the ceiling above us, and all the painted pictures.

'The reserve capital, my dear sir, the reserve capital is twenty-five million, the reserve capital alone … . And our turnover' – Mr Prower's voice becomes more vehement, almost metallic in its tone – 'our turnover is in excess of a billion and a half … .'

'And there are to be lifts on "Imperator", lifts between all the floors … and a billiard room. Ebony … .'

'Yes,' says the Berliner: 'and a new system, a new scientific system, so that the ship will never be able to sink.'

'Never. They have proved it.'

Madame stops talking for a moment, as the Spaniard stares at her face.

'And no bunks, just beds, suspended beds, so that you don't notice the movements of the ship.'

The horn sounds again through the noise, like a scream. Madame has crossed herself. 'What is it they're playing?' she asks, turning her deathly-white face.

'"*Le Comte de Luxembourg*", Madame.'* And Tschirnitz's plate is hurled away beneath his fork.

But all at once they are talking about women, and the postgraduate maintains that the ladies of Copenhagen are the loveliest of all. But the young Austrian smiles: 'Oh no, oh no, nothing can compare with the women in the West Indies – the way they carry their heads, the women in Havana …'

The Count keeps ordering more champagne, whilst drinking soda water himself, and talking about the Wailing Wall in Jerusalem.

'All Spanish women carry their heads proudly … and their busts, their busts … but they fade early.'

'A billion and a half, and 9 percent profit.'

A couple of glasses smash on the floor.

'What was that?'

'A glass.'

All are talking, and 'Imperator' and the stream of gold get mixed up together. Others talk of homes in the south and the north. The pastoral scenes on the lampshade are dancing to the buffeting of the storm.

'No, I'm from Thüringen,' says the doctor, 'a long way into the country. And I studied in Jena – wonderful days.'

Madame, who hears that, talks about her villa in Biarritz. 'It is so lovely in Biarritz, and close to Spain. I was brought up in Spain.'

'Madame,' says the young Spaniard, bowing his head, 'you should see Havana.'

'No, Ma'am, I am from Denmark,' I answer Mrs Prower, who has asked, and who is peeling an apple, her fingers shaking slightly.

And Mrs Prower, who has noticed my glance, says: 'I am a seasoned traveller … it's just this foghorn, which … my sister lost her life at sea.'

I stand up.

'Are you going?' Tschirnitz asks at once, and makes to follow me, but stays.

In the vestibule the bookseller is standing close to the door. Behind the strong mahogany doors the wind and the ocean sound like a wild whirring of windmill sails, and he starts to talk to me in a strange voice, as if he had a cold. Once, off South America, he had experienced a storm where everything fused into one, sky and sea fused into one, and the ladies had already put on their life jackets.

'But there was no panic,' he said. 'I believe, sir, that … I mean, civilised society provides a kind of protection against such things.'

'Possibly.'

The bookseller stands there for a while, then says shortly after: 'But I do have … I have so much of value onboard … .'

'Of value?'

'Yes, the books, sir. Forty thousand marks worth of books.'

'That's a lot of books. Goodnight.'

Down by his corner the head cook is standing freezing, with his kerchief around his neck, leaning against the vibrating wall.

'Good evening, chef.'

'Good evening.'

I stand there.

'But,' says the cook suddenly. 'There's no actual danger.' And suddenly I notice that his hands are folded.

I walk on, and by the stairs to the ladies' saloon I meet Mrs Prower, accompanied by Mr Prower and Mr Evans. They are off for their whist. By the bright light of the candelabra their American faces look like masks.

The two ship's boys have their arms round each other's shoulders and are staring through a hatch into the sea, which is nothing but white foam. Far away, behind the doctor's passageway, the steerage passengers are moving about like unclear, swaying shadows.

When I enter the passage to my cabin, the man from the north is standing in the open door on the leeside. 'You're here!' I say, 'I haven't seen you all day. You weren't at lunch or dinner.'

The man from the north raises his eyes. 'Well, I have been here. I know both the storm and the people.' He stands there staring out into the darkness: 'But tonight the ocean is angry.'

And suddenly he looks me in the face, and with a wry grimace he says: '*Felicissime notte, signore.*'*

In the passage Fritsche is plodding around with several jugs of water. 'It's terrible weather, really terrible weather,' he says, 'but I said it would be. When I can feel it here – here in my knuckles – then I know it's coming …'

Fritsche is shaking as he plods. 'Well, good night, sir,' he says, shutting my cabin door.

I sit down and am trying to read when there is a knock on my door.

'Who is it?'

'It's me – Hugo.'

Herr von Tschirnitz comes in, stumbling over the threshold.

'May I sit here for a while,' he says.

'Yes, with pleasure.'

'But I can't talk.'

'Nor can I.'

And we sit there on the trembling sofa, silent, side by side, in front of the large mirror – in front of our own trembling reflections.

Translated by Janet Garton

Portrait

18. Sarah Bernhardt

I

Sarah Bernhardt is the living embodiment of contradictions.

She is a pessimistic non-believer who surrounds herself with all the symbols of superstition. She is a cosmopolitan who lets a Joan of Arc write for her for the glorification of patriotism. She is indomitable in her zest for life, and she sleeps with her coffin by her bed. Millions pass through her fingers, yet she lives in golden poverty. She complains of constant illness, yet she roams the world extravagantly with the strength of a giant.

This is the costume of contradictions in which Sarah Bernhardt, an experienced huntress in pursuit of the extraordinary, has draped herself for twenty-five years, in order to keep the world engaged for twenty-five years.

It is a costume, for it is an exaggeration of her nature. But it has only been able to keep the world engaged because it is her nature. And her nature – extraordinary and rich in contradictions, tired and lustful, sensation-seeking and satiated, invincible and infirm – is the very image of the world's nature.

Sarah Bernhardt once sculpted a model of a sphinx and gave the mysterious being her own face. She did it with proud impertinence and rightly so.

For the 'mysterious being' of any period is always the Zeitgeist of that period. That temperament is born of a thousand things. The reasons for its emergence are hundredfold. It colours everything, and it shapes what our eyes see. It spreads and is transmitted through the air and our breath. It gives our thoughts their tempo and our speech its rhythm. It clothes our ideas in its skin. It is our true destiny, and the atmosphere in which our minds breathe.

But the temperament of our particular time in female form is called Sarah Bernhardt: the sphinx wears her face.

The world only welcomed this insufferable exhibitionist unto itself because it was also with us that she yelled on the marketplaces of Melbourne.* If millions have gaped for twenty years through a thousand panes at the face of the vagrant, they have done it because they were staring at something of themselves when they gaped at the features of the self-publicist.

This is her power over the world's mind.

II

The days when Sarah Bernhardt was the obedient daughter of the house of Molière are long gone.* It now sounds like a myth, that this unpredictable creature once belonged to a framework like others, and obeyed writers like others.

In any case that time is now long past, and she will no longer obey, but must be obeyed. From a ship's mast she scatters Victor Hugo's verses to the winds of the seven seas,* but only rarely does she make his figures come to life. And Racine is set aside by an art that will no longer have a master ruling over it.*

Sarah Bernhardt is no longer tied to any theatre; she commands her own troupe, while the Sardous write roles for her that do not constrain her,* but serve only to flatter her personality. The actress dictates to her writers – herself.

Fédora was the first of these dictated roles. And as bad as it is, it became perhaps her best. For in that at least we are able to read what should have been written, and what Sarah Bernhardt longed to play.

The spirit of *Fédora* is found in two simple cries to the same man: '*Je vous haïs – je t'aime*.'* The love that hates, and the hate that is love – that is the theme of the role. And is that not the mark of potency, of all the painful contradictions of the feelings we own?

Here there was room for all the contradictions of the soul, which turns passions that examine themselves and never understand themselves, into agonising conflict. Here rancour was desire and desire was disgust. Here happiness was despair and despair was jubilation. Here Proteus, perpetually morphing into his opposite, was presented in the form of female passion.*

Or rather, could have been presented. Because *Fédora* is written for the Sarah Bernhardt who is her own exaggeration, and it is written by Sardou.

The fact is that it is written by Sardou, which means that it is a melodrama, whose impoverished art is called ingenuity; the fact is that it is played by the exaggerated Madame Bernhardt, which means that it pursues the actress around the outermost periphery of her being, and the fact is that the entire drama becomes a huge 'tumult' in four acts.

Fédora comes from Russia. The nihilistic tsardom is her native country. From there Sardou directs a broad current for Sarah Bernhardt's nature, because pessimism is the core of her spirit. It is the fount of her pleasures, which aim at forgetfulness, and of her strength, which is concentrated willpower. It feeds her weakness, which is hollow despondency, and her loathing, which craves pleasure: she drinks everything down to the dregs, for she knows she is drinking from a skull.

The existence of Fédora, who loves the one she hates, and longs simultaneously for blood and for embraces, is based on a heedless lack of moderation. But life itself, which grinds down sick souls in the undertow of a thousand contradictions in and around us in order to throw us into the skeleton arms of death, which is eternal annihilation – that seems to Sarah Bernhardt just as heedless as is Fédora's existence. That is why she lets her Fédora seek out annihilation in an exasperated rage, raging at the nothingness in everything she is forsaking.

Extreme pessimism, that transforms into a clinging fever, runs throughout the play. Its primary content is the ultimate feeling of pessimism, the worm of its spirit, the skeleton in its house: fear.

Fédora is the play of fear. It begins in fear, and fear is its driving force.

The moral fears belong to us and besiege us. They encircle us, and never do their evil eyes stray from us. They live within us and they multiply around us. They are fed by all of the contradictions within us, and they are nourished by all the contradictions between our feelings. They are the backlash of our thoughtless pleasures, and they are the nightmare that haunts our relaxation.

In *Fédora*, Sarah Bernhardt plays all of that tormenting fear, and the horror of that fear. She is so tormented by the fear of life that in the end, the fear of death does not enter her mind.

So then Sarah Bernhardt can fling the very essence of pessimism into Sardou's melodrama, which takes her entire person into its service – which is what she wanted.

III

Sarah Bernhardt, who is the exaggeration of the Zeitgeist of her time, speaks and lives as Fédora speaks and lives. Fédora comes to life for us every time the person of Madame Bernhardt herself comes fully alive behind the transparent shell that Sardou has created around her very nature.

But not every evening does it happen exactly that way, nor can it. That is precisely the danger with all these roles, everything which is most extreme in your nature gushes out in a thin stream. You do not reach your highest potential three hundred nights in a row, and nor can you. You cannot access the utmost extremities of your temperament three hundred times.

So on some of the great many evenings, Madame Bernhardt can only rather mechanically imitate herself. She offers her nature as a pure automaton.

On such evenings Fédora resembles Sarah Bernhardt the way a heartfelt prayer resembles a reeled-off rosary, and the entire thing seems to be a blasphemy against a great human being. At the same time she has made herself into a cartoon, so even the Yanks can understand it – and behind the cartoon she is as though dead and gone.

Because Sarah Bernhardt, like no one else, can be seized by the thoughtlessness of the virtuoso, a terrible illness that afflicts wandering artists and torments them, whilst irresistibly commanding them. During the perpetual excitements of their existence, their thoughts fade away in the midst of the very execution of their art. In listless apathy they become sleepwalkers and only awaken many scenes later, after their thoughts have been off on their own.

Sarah Bernhardt can go around like that for long evenings. On these evenings, her technique is victorious to a certain extent. Because anyone who has seen her in the same role day after day will know that every scream is exactly the same, every tone has the same pitch, every look has the same expression. Her body is so well practised and so obedient, that it even obeys the soul when it is dozing. It is admirable and it is agonizing. You get the feeling that the person walking and standing and screaming before your very eyes, is in China or in New Zealand or maybe just in Basel – but here, here is the only place she is not.

On such evenings you feel a deep compassion. Towards Adelaide Ristori you could have felt an agonizing sympathy owing to her age, at which her genius was no longer able to do everything she wanted it to.* But for Sarah Bernhardt on some evenings you feel an even greater pain, at all the absent-mindedness during which she imitates her living self whilst dead.

There are still days, however, when Madame Bernhardt lives.

These are celebrations of art.

IV

And the impression Sarah Bernhardt's art is capable of generating in our minds is involuntarily enhanced by all those memories from her life which are so closely associated with her. The legends about her lust for life are vividly recalled for those who listen intently in front of the artist.

There is one scene in *Fédora* that seems symbolic. It is the first scene in which the Russian appears. She arrives at a rendezvous, expecting her beloved. She waits impatiently. She keeps a close eye on the passage of time, the minutes, the slow seconds. Uneasily she roves around the walls of the room like a trapped beast of prey, which finds a strange delight in feeling the bars of the cage against her haunches.

This feverish impatience that is driven round and round in passionate tension – she is the very Sarah Bernhardt that the world sees as an eternal wanderer: a huntress seeking gold and all that is new. Because the hunt for gold also drives her.* As the clinking of gold sounds through the *Comédie Humaine*,* it also resounds like a fever chord through Sarah Bernhardt's art.

That is what increases her excitement. It makes the strong weak and the sick appear healthy. It is the master of the hunt, and it spurs her on ardently.

But she is happy to go along. Because in her perpetual travels, where her nerves only find respite – brief respite – in perpetually new horizons, she is burning for the excitement of constant change. She believes in finding new respite on a constantly new earth. Weary of one, she hopes for the next.

These new worlds tempt her like fresh hopes: the sight of the seas will satisfy her, the boundless seas. The prairies will calm her, the prairies, the limitlessness. On the uncharted islands of the oceans, where no one has set foot, her spirit will find rest.

And as the new worlds disappoint with the deceitful hopes of perpetual roaming, then different art forms entice her – or enticed her: confined within the cage of one art, she breaks down the barriers between the arts and sates her restlessness by practising all of them. The restless days have forty-eight hours that need to be filled. That is why she mixes colours and becomes a painter. That is why she masters clay and conjures up images in stone.

In marble she depicts Ophelia, Hamlet's beloved, the ill-fated bride of the Zeitgeist, and in bronze she casts a group of laughing monkeys – in indecent mockery of mankind.

V

In a final fit of despair, Sarah Bernhardt commissions *Pierrot Assassin*, so as to deride both life and art with a final grimace. *

To dress up your despair as a Pierrot in mourning and let it sob out its misery over the gauzy-skirted body of a Columbine; to make a tragedy of a pantomime and to turn the burlesque into a tragedy; to make a corpse drunk so that it wakes and comes to life again, and to thumb one's nose at death – that was probably the pessimistic juggler's final game.

Pierrot Assassin is *la grande tragédienne* mocking tragedy, and *Pierrot Assassin* is also mankind's ultimate reckoning with existence. The pantomime is the most despondent art form of pessimism – it is the dance of hopelessness. Before the eyes of the world Sarah Bernhardt's art raises a grieving Pierrot as a symbol.

And yet life still has beauty, and existence contains happiness. Sarah Bernhardt knows this. And there are times when she is seized by a tender desire to depict this happiness. Happiness for those who are troubled lies in stillness. Minds find repose in the softest gentleness, and delicate chastity is the dream of fortune.

Valérie becomes her role.* It is her innocence on which Sarah Bernhardt bestows the light of heaven.

VI

We have run through all the contrasts of this art. We have stretched from pole to pole in the vast secretive world we call our own feelings.

Behind all the disintegration, we encounter in this art, like in no other – unless Josef Kainz can be mentioned in the same breath – our own faces.*

Sarah Bernhardt has roamed through the world of our time like a mysterious presence. As a mysterious presence, she has captivated the minds of hundreds of thousands. As the mysterious presence, she has triumphed like no other. Because this mysterious presence was the incarnation of our time.

That is why Sarah Bernhardt was understood everywhere she went – she who can hold aloft a grieving Pierrot over the head of our time upon the shield of art.

Translated by Paul Russell Garrett

Journalism

19. A Poor Folks' Inn

The candles on our Christmas tree were snuffed out.

How happy the children had been! Little Hans had stood completely still with all five fingers stuffed into his mouth, staring at the tree, unmoving; his light blue eyes had grown twice as large as normal, twice as large and sparkling. We had danced around the tree and sung the old songs, those which turn us into happy children again. We had been happy giving and pleased to receive, unwrapped parcels and plundered the tree; we had smiled and laughed, admired and thanked. How Viggo had shouted with glee when he got his trumpet, and Jenny settled down at once to read about 'The Steadfast Tin Soldier' and 'The Old Woman'.* The tree glittered, the oranges hung on its branches like golden fruit, the large sugar angels with yellow wings swung from the topmost branches, fastened with red ribbons; the dark sugar pretzels full of sweet liqueur glinted and glowed as they caught the light. And right at the very top there was a large star. All around children's laughter and song.

Now the candles were snuffed out.

We walked down the street, which was deserted. A couple of hours ago it had been full of people: men with parcels and men with baskets, lads with spruce trees and poor women with branches, errand boys who ran into one another and cursed crossly as they hurried past, gentlemen hurrying home from the office and ladies on their way to church. And the shops were crowded, people jostled one another at the counter and hardly had time to collect their change; they completely forgot to try and bargain – even elderly ladies made up their minds quickly. People bumped into one another and said 'Merry Christmas!' instead of 'Excuse me'; they laughed, they pushed, they shouted. The poor shop assistant was completely befuddled; he wrapped up a fan for someone who had asked for a box of cigars. Then out into the street again. A quick 'Happy Holiday!' to a friend running past, a contented humming; you pat your pockets, wondering if you've forgotten anything, catch yourself joining in with a street urchin's whistling, then hurry onwards. Yes, what a hurry everyone is in; and yet you don't really get angry when a bustling passer-by shoves you roughly into the gutter. You just accept it; there is something strangely egalitarian about Christmas, you never feel like punching anyone.

But now the streets were deserted. The lighted windows all along the street in the darkness looked just like the happy homes' gleaming and sparkling eyes. And I do mean home, for *that* is the best of all gifts on Christmas Eve, that it succeeds for a short time in creating a *home* for every family. For some people the Christmas hymn set in Bethlehem has become a pleasant myth, which they value only as an ancient fiction; yet the gospel of salvation is still obscurely alive in them all. It flickers like the reflection of their childhood's candles, it rings out in their souls like the echo of a sentimental song they have half forgotten … .

But what can one say about *this* Christmas celebration? You yourself are a mother who has decorated the Christmas tree, whilst looking forward to the children's joy and happiness; you are a father who has perhaps grumbled in the morning that the whole thing was simply designed to swallow up money, but who now in the evening, whilst the tree is shining with Christmas lights, are so ridiculously improvident that you would gladly have paid more than double in order to see all this jubilation; you are a child or relative of one of these happy homes, made twice as light and joyful by Christmas, the homely celebration. How could I tell *you* anything new about all this, which you know so well?

I knew that I could not do that, and that is precisely why we were walking through the deserted streets, slipping in melting snow and slush, with water slopping into our boots – out to visit the Christmas celebrations not of the happy people, but of the homeless ones.

One Christmas Eve a few years ago a couple of young people went out into the streets and alleyways and collected all the poor children they could find. They brought them into a warm hall where there were long tables all set, and where they were given food and drink. And they had a Christmas tree as well, a large and beautiful tree, the like of which most of them had no doubt never seen. It was a beautiful thought and a beautiful deed; but there are more homeless people than those you can find in the street, and even with the best will in the world, you can't light Christmas candles for them all.

And there are homeless people of various kinds. There are single old people with no family or friends; you can call them homeless because you know that their lonely room even on Christmas Eve cannot be called a home. Or you can meet a single old man sitting sleepily and grumpily in the corner of a café or an oyster bar – he is in the same sense homeless. Then there are others who are homeless in a literal sense, people who don't know when they get up where they will be lying down that evening, who own nothing and have no permanent abode, whose life is one of random odd jobs; you might call them life's journeymen, except that they very often have neither knapsack nor bundle. It was *their* Christmas I was looking for.

You come across them when you leave the theatre in the evening, begging on Kongens Nytorv.* You will often have heard their reiterated plea: 'Please, sir, some money for lodgings' … 'Please, sir, spare some change for a bed'. If they'd been born in Naples these people would be vagabonds; here we call them dossers. They have no profession, and their desires do not extend beyond getting hold of what they need for today and a bed for the night. They help in the market and offer their services at the customs-house; some get work in warehouses, but it is always by the day, and those who had work yesterday have less than nothing today. Therefore, when evening comes, they have to go out and beg for the 25 øre it costs to stay at the 'lodging house' where they sleep.* The proprietor does not give credit. Have you ever been in one of those lodging houses? Or do you perhaps still believe those old tales imported from London about standing room only, where you sleep with your arms hanging over a stretched rope? The rooms of our lodging houses are carefully inspected by our sanitary police, and you won't find any horrors there – just as little, of course, as you would find any particular comfort. A few large rooms, where the volume of air is precisely measured, and along the walls some beds, the number of which the police determine according to this volume. By the door the regulations are pinned to a wooden board; these inform you amongst other things that the sheets will be changed at least once a month. That sounds fairly normal – but on the other hand you must remember that a month has thirty nights, and that every bed during these thirty nights most often has thirty different occupants. In addition there are both duvets and mattresses on the beds, as well as two pillows, which according to the proprietor are quite difficult to keep track of. 'Those pillows,' he said, 'are constantly on the move … a couple of times a week I have to go over to the police station to collect them.' And in order to become the owner of such a berth for a single night an odd-job man has to pay 35, 25 or 15 øre, depending on the bed; for there are differences in the beds and thus also in the prices. It is these 25 øre which he is often reduced to getting hold of during the evening on Kongens Nytorv, or wherever the opportunity arises at night – for there are many vagrants amongst them, and night after night the police pick up a good catch amongst the shifting occupants of the lodging houses. Homelessness begets recklessness – that is an old saying.

On the morning when I had said I would call – it's always a good idea to make an appointment in advance – I was received by the proprietor in a friendly fashion. 'I would like to see something of Christmas Eve amongst the really poor,' I said to him, 'Christmas for the homeless, as it were.' 'You're welcome, but there are no homeless people here: this is their home.' Then he explained that from seven o'clock until ten he treated his regular customers to roast pork, beer and brandy. He was expecting two hundred and fifty, both old and young. It sounded promising.

So we went along at nine o'clock.

'They're eating in the taproom,' says mine host's wife, who is in the kitchen, heaping mountains of potatoes onto various dishes.

Inside the taproom there is a dreadful stink. The air is heavy with tobacco smoke – the kind of tobacco smoked by these people – the fumes of brandy, the smell of the large pork roasts, the odour of chewing tobacco, the exhalations and sweat of these seventy people who are sitting squashed together around the horseshoe-shaped table. The stifling air hits me. To start with I make vain attempts to see clearly. There is a fog lying over everything like a thick, ubiquitous fug, a veil over objects and people. The little Christmas tree with the large elf is shining sleepily through the foul-smelling fog. Not much is said, they are *eating*; it's not every day that you get roast pork and fried potatoes.

After a while you get used to the air. You can quickly learn to breathe in any atmosphere, and your eyes adjust to be able to see. How greedily they are eating; they cut the meat into large, wide strips, dip it in the mustard and ram it with their forks into their open mouths, then their teeth close on it. In between the occasional exclamation or the occasional curse you can hear a kind of ceaseless accompaniment of mumbling chewing. After a while you can make out faces through the fug.

Bearded physiognomies, young and old, smooth and wrinkled features; most are broad-shouldered and muscular, some with bare arms. The chap over there with a baker's cap and a blond moustache has rolled up his shirt sleeves – he's wearing a shirt – in order to be more at ease. The muscles on his arms are thickly bunched, and his hands are large, fleshy and sinewy. He's started on his third portion, the proprietor tells me. Now he takes off his cap; he has thick, fairish, wavy hair with a centre parting. 'I'm a butcher by trade,' he later tells one of my companions. You can see that from his arms and his parting.* Beside him sits a chubby fellow with puffy cheeks and very pale blue eyes which look dull and colourless. He's already had enough; people who drink as much as that are rarely hungry. Now he's leaning on the wall, yawning. Soon he falls alseep, his upper body swaying forwards towards the table, to the right towards the butcher, to the left towards Petersen, then he gets a push and falls back against the wall, snoring. Petersen is a thickset man, somewhat bent by the weight of years, with swimming eyes, the whites streaked with orange, a pinched mouth, a sharp nose … . I'll keep an eye on him.

Now someone starts bawling a song. 'There is a Lovely Land' – performed by a mixed choir.* Bellows, screams, howls – howls to music. Everyone sings in his own key, almost to his own tune. The little black-bearded fellow at the end of the table throws himself into his neighbour's arms, and hugging each other in a long embrace, they both lie back shouting into each other's faces. People stamp to the non-existent rhythm, and those who can't sing, whistle, or beat a drum with the shaft of their knife on their overturned plate. Down at the other end of the table people are sitting on one another's laps, marking the beat by slapping one another's thighs. Then someone shouts and kicks up a din, they stop in mid-verse and start all at once on 'The Girls of South Jutland', and stop again in the third verse.* The butcher starts up with 'The Brave Soldier',* and jabs his sleeping neighbour in the stomach so that he wakes up, stands up and then falls over with a prolonged squeal, which is accompanied by the butcher's bellowing, muffled like the call of a foghorn.

People get up from the tables and help to clear away. Now you can see them properly. The room resembles one of the dismantled stalls on Helliggeiststræde,* from which the clothes have come to life and are walking around like a frail covering over some strange-looking figures. They find seats all around, and we order a round. The proprietor puts bottles of beer on the table, glasses for us. The noise grows louder. On the floor in front of the bar three or four guys are dancing a stamping folk dance; a few disappear into a corner to sleep; a few more gather around us, watching us curiously, perhaps a little fearfully. Well-dressed gentlemen are something threatening for them, they remind them too much of police officers … . But the beer reassures them, and once they have made sure who they have before them, they flock round to tell their stories – or perhaps one should say, *a* story. They have had a lot of practice at that, and they are good actors. They speak in subdued voices, they snivel, they tell about undeserved misfortune and unexpected burdens … . But their stories sound so disingenuous.

Petersen has sat down just next to me. He pulls out some references. The first one is dated 49. Then he was a private in the volunteer brigade, otherwise a grocer's assistant. After that he becomes a corporal, comes home from the war, then becomes a grocer's assistant again. A few years pass. The next date is 59. I ask him what happened during those years. He looks sideways at me, then says artlessly: 'I don't remember.' There are years in everyone's life that one would rather forget, times one does not remember because one doesn't want to, and because one actually remembers them all too well. After this interval we meet him as a judge's clerk on – Bornholm. He gets good references for diligence and ability, and can be relied on in legal matters; however, he quickly moves on again to something new, becoming a bookseller's assistant, guard at an exhibition, usher at Alhambra, watchman on St. Nicholas' Tower, grocer.* Then again a dead period, where the otherwise so eloquent papers are silent, but where the man starts talking volubly and persuasively. If it were not for that lowering sideways look, you could be tempted to believe him – but instead you ask what he's doing now. 'He lives here.' You look at his faded overcoat, which is carefully brushed, at his hands, which are small and as clean as they can be without the use of soap, at his sharp features, which could be attractive if they were not spoilt by that glance, which is directed down, away, never straight at the person he is talking to. 'Would you like a krone?' I ask. He looks up quickly, with something like a glint in his lowering eyes. Then he grabs my knee hard, convulsively, and whispers quietly: 'Thank you, but don't say anything to the others. You understand, it is hard for a man like me … .' I let a krone slide into his hand. If the others saw it, he would not have much enjoyment from his money. He would have to buy a round, and he is aware of that.

On out the floor a friendly fight is going on.

A small, squat fellow elbows me in the side and says he would like a confidential word with me. He pulls me over to the doorway. 'What's this about?' I ask. 'What do you want with me?' – 'I just wanted to warn you about the others, sir. It's humbug, sir – pure humbug, the lot of them.' – 'Yes, I am aware of that,' I answer. 'Would you like 50 øre,' I add quickly, as I see him stretching out his hand with a suggestive gesture. 'Thank you, sir, I am a bit short for tonight. But the others – that's just humbug.' We go in again. The good man spends the money on a beer, and then summons one of my friends after the other out to the doorway in order to tell them the same truth – about the others.

I get into conversation with 'the graduate'. He speaks Latin, talks about Carl Ploug and his 'Atellaner' sketches, about the men of the thirties when they were young.* He talks about philosophy too. 'Yes, Nielsen is an able tutor,' he says. I don't inform him that Rasmus Nielsen is now an elderly professor.* For him, he is still the able tutor. There is something terrible about this fossilized survivor from the thirties. And yet he is an authority in his circle, and when he speaks, the others are silent. They listen with reverence to his fragments of Hebrew, shout 'Bravo!' when he tells his old jokes, and treat him to a coffee with brandy when they have anything to treat with. He tells me about the time he had both himself and his wife painted in oils. It is long ago, but it inspires respect, especially when you are a former student who used to belong to 'the upper ranks'.

What a strange concept 'the upper ranks' is to these people. The upper ranks means everything which is up on the surface, everything which can keep afloat without sinking.

There's an old mechanic here as well; he used to play the violin in Korup's Garden,* and studied and researched in order to devise a 'perpetuum mobile', pondered and calculated how he could invent a flying machine which could carry a person. Now he's sitting here sawing at the old violin, which in its better days played in Korup's Garden, but now has only two strings, which are made of unravelled twine … .

Out on the floor they are still dancing the folk dance. A large chap in an unbuttoned blue jacket, who tells us that he has one reason to be happy – he has no shirt – is swinging round with a fair-haired lad of eighteen or nineteen, who is singing and whistling and stamping, and frequently taking a long draught from a champagne bottle standing on the bar. I couldn't see any other than champagne bottles in there.

'They're the only ones which don't break here,' said the proprietor.

So this is where Veuve Cliquot's empty bottles finish up. What tales these bottles could tell us! Stories of carefree, joyful hours in the houses of rich men, cheerful meals, celebratory parties. People have poured from them into slim, cut-glass goblets, where the wine has sparkled like playful pearls; smiling women's lips have drunk their animating wine, they have given birth to enthusiasm and to fleeting desire, whose only fruit was a momentary touch, a single lingering glance, a silent and searching pleasure. Longing has been awoken by their grapes, and lust and blushing happiness. People have drunk from them during stirring fanfares, have emptied them to the soft tones of a waltz, at balls, at masked carnivals, during the turmoil of sleepless nights; the wine has eased the grief of some, and increased the joy of others … .

And now they're standing here filled with thin beer. A poet who saw them would be able to write a poem about them, a poem as varied and colourful as the chance events of life itself.

Or is there perhaps nothing chance about life? I merely ask, I look at these champagne bottles whose silver paper is half peeled off, and I ask. But you must answer either yes or no. Here it is a matter of all or nothing.

But how stifling this fug is. The fat-cheeked man is snoring dreadfully. The butcher begins to bawl another song. Down at the other end of the room they are singing psalms; they mix one up with another, stop in the middle of the verse to make a joke, get going again, only to be drowned out by 'Dummepeter'.* Petersen has sunk into melancholy observation; he has finished his story, which he has told to all four of us.

New people come over all the time to tell us stories and beg. The proprietor offers us a glass of punch, it's unlucky to leave without drinking something.* That reminds me that it really is Christmas. I had forgotten both Christmas and the pork roast … . Yes, it would be an idea to get out into clearer air, and in any case it has got really late, far into the night. We must go home.

Over in the corner by the stove the graduate is dispensing wisdom, the old mechanic is sawing at his fiddle with the twine strings, the butcher is singing for the seventh time the first four lines of 'The Girls of South Jutland' .... How the fug and the odours are concentrated in that low space. They're singing dreadfully out of tune. Psalms don't sound good when they're sung out of tune ....

We're out in the street again. It is deserted, empty and dark. The melting snow whips into our faces, lies on our cheeks like wet clumps, forms a film in front of our eyes. We tramp off, as from inside the lodging house the bass voice of the butcher resounds. I can see a face in the window, it's Petersen. I recognise the sharp nose. He nods to us. Then there is a loud crash.

'A good thing we left,' says one of the company. 'Now they're knocking over the tables.'

Back home there is disorder in all the rooms.* The Christmas tree has been moved into a corner; the candles have burned down and dripped on all the branches. Here and there hang the remains of some pink tissue paper; it's a cake which has been forgotten. I go over to the window. Right opposite is the church, lit up by a flickering light, tall, majestic and calm. The noisy waves of human misery could break for a long time against this immovable mass of stone. And at the top of the narrow spire shines out the cross.

Translated by Janet Garton

20. 'Magasin du Nord'

There is a secret behind the work of a writer of occasional pieces: it must always look as if he stumbles over his subjects in the street – look like it, because that's not what he does.

The work of such a writer does not consist of reading, studying or thinking a great deal – all he has to do is constantly to see a great deal. If Albert Wolff in his best days seemed to stumble over his subjects, that was only because he had seen so much that he was able to do that.*

And what a writer of occasional pieces has to be able to see, above all else, is what we all see and what no-one sees: things which are so familiar to us that we bump into them every day, and which we have never bothered to listen to anything about, because we hear about them every day – in short, things which are closest to us and which we therefore don't know.

What you then see, you must describe truthfully. There are many reasons to prefer truthfulness when you are reporting, amongst others that in the long run it is absolutely the most interesting. And when you believe you have something to report, you must not keep quiet about it because, for example, no-one has written about such things before, or because you would upset some prejudice or other, or because what you report will provoke censure. As far as I am concerned, I would never envy an author who has never been an object of censure, because he must have been of extremely minor importance.

My articles over the last winter have drawn their subjects from the most widely differing areas. My intention has been to print reports here about a bit of everything, and especially about such things as are not discussed elsewhere, either because they are quite correctly viewed as bagatelles which are not worthy subjects for a serious man, or because, as stated above, they are so close that we can't see them.

When I have written about 'Holger Danske' and about 'A Dolls' Shop', about 'Børre-Lorenzen's Fashion Bazaar', about 'How We Bury Our Dead' and about 'The Gutter Press', it has been with the same intention every time.* I have wanted to tell my readers what they could very easily see for themselves, but never notice, because it is too ridiculously easy to see it. When I have written about a dolls' shop, it has been in order to explain what modern-day children play with; when I have described a fashion bazaar, it was in order that everyone could see how modern-day women dress. I have written it because I thought it was useful for people to see such things in print; there are so many things which look strangely garish when you see them in print.

And I shall continue to write in this way, continue without worrying about the fact that thoughtless people, who are incapable of seeing, and who always believe that 'there must be something behind it' whenever they don't understand, get the idea of insisting that I am writing about a certain business because I have a personal interest in writing about that particular firm. Anyone who thinks about it will at once understand that the reason I write is simply that I wish to inform readers about such bagatelles as only a writer of occasional pieces can discuss, and that it is the same disinterested impulse which makes me write about a dolls' shop as about 'Holger Danske'. Or would it occur to anyone to believe that I wrote about Christmas Eve for the homeless for the sake of the glass of punch which the host forced me to drink, and which made me feel more ill than any glass of punch has ever done?* Hardly – but in any case, I just let people talk and carry on reporting. This is really the only way I can avenge myself on the censure of the thoughtless.

If I have decided to preface my comments about Magasin du Nord today with these remarks, addressed to many people and to none (for who would readily admit to being thoughtless?) the reason is not that there is any special occasion to do so precisely today – Magasin du Nord is too prestigious an enterprise for there to be any suspicion that a presentation of it constitutes an advertisement – but because my visit to Vett & Wessel will be my final one this year,* and I wished to take this opportunity to respond to the insinuations I have received after people have read my recent articles.

'It must be wonderful to walk around here knowing that you have a share in all this,' I said to the firm's youngest director on our tour of the building, as we walked up the broad carpeted staircase in the large central hall of the premises.

He smiled. What I had just uttered was one of those exclamations which escape from us involuntarily, against our will, and which precisely for that reason can convey an unvarnished compliment, since they express uncensored thoughts, which emerge exactly as they are thought, without being decked out with a barrage of words to embellish or obscure them.

What I had felt on this tour was real admiration, I admit it gladly. I am always helplessly captivated when I am brought face to face with a will, with an energy which is driving forwards; and it has taken a great deal of willpower to create Magasin du Nord, talent and willpower.

Or is there anyone who doubts that it takes energy to build up this business brick by brick over ten years? to expand into new terrain year after year? to advance day by day, under trading conditions which would cripple any other business, until you now employ a staff as numerous as the population of a small market town, and daily see thousands of shoppers in your emporium?

And yet the business, with its 20 heads of department, 20 clerks and 8 female cashiers, has grown from modest beginnings.

It all started in Aarhus in 1867 with a draper's shop. At that time it was a small business; now they have their own extremely elegant building in Aarhus too, and Vett & Wessel's premises are one of the sights which waiters at the Royal Hotel insistently recommend that you should visit.* And you go along, mainly, it seems to me, to get the thing over with; you get a little tired of constantly seeing the same name which pursues you everywhere, on the advertising hoardings along railway lines, in all the provincial newspapers and all the main streets of market towns. You can't get away from it. But that is understandable; Magasin du Nord has 15 branches, of which 14 are in Danish towns. You can find the firm in Aalborg and Stege, in Odense and Grenaa, in Nakskov and – nine other places. All these independent businesses have their own space on Kongens Nytorv, down to the left on the lower ground floor. Dark, high-ceilinged rooms full of the same discreet bustle as all the rest of the establishment. Amongst others, there are six people there who spend their time day in, day out, all year round sorting samples to be sent to the provinces. So you can imagine how many are employed in ordering, sorting and packing the 40,000 parcels and packing cases which leave this place in the course of a year. And these 40,000 parcels themselves are only a minuscule part of the total which are sent out. In addition, in 1879 no fewer than 125,000 parcels were distributed to customers outside the towns, and of those there were around 15,000 in the last three weeks before Christmas – which are not even as busy as the months of the big sales, where those in the know assure me that the daily volume of trade can amount to 20,000 kroner. But it is true that Magasin du Nord employs 22 men and boys daily to dispatch and deliver this endless stream of parcels; they run three omnibuses – those well-known, gaudy vehicles, exact copies of the vehicles of the great department stores in

Paris, which make all the omnibuses owned by Brama Life Elixir seem pale in comparison* – and 9 wagons, open and closed. Does that not sound 'Parisian'? With so many people packing, much can be achieved. It also has to be said that the customs duty paid every year by Magasin du Nord adds up to a greater amount than is collected in customs dues by a whole town such as Veile!

But let us stay with the provincial stores. One of the firm's directors is in charge of all these branches, and travels constantly to the respective towns. 'You have to divide responsibility,' my guide informs me. 'One of us has taken over the provinces, two of us are here, and the fourth is permanently in France, stationed in Paris. It is essential to be on the spot, because what counts for us is speed and low prices – we have to get hold of everything as quickly as possible and as cheaply as possible, and for that we need a permanent representative close to the large fashionable department stores.'

As we wandered through the establishment, it became clear to me how essential this Parisian residence is. It is a necessary consequence of the principles which have created this business's reputation. Only by being able to buy things in person the whole time, by being physically present, can you in a lucky moment snap up these splendid tapestries, whose glorious shades of colour are reminiscent of beautiful water-colour paintings, and which can now be sold at such a reasonable price; only then can you barter for those amazing Indian rugs, for which you would pay a great deal in a curiosity shop as rarities, but of which Magasin du Nord right now can offer a few dozen at around 10 kroner apiece. The firm's director in Paris keeps an eagle eye on everything, and buys everything which suits conditions here at home; his residence benefits both the general public, which wants to buy cheaply, and the white-bearded gentleman from Skåne, who whilst I am watching decides to buy a Brussels carpet for 3000 kroner.

A propos Skåne! Here as everywhere else it is Swedes who buy the expensive things. With the exception of three or four families, there is no-one in Denmark who understands luxury; they are satisfied with being comfortable. But in order to be 'comfy' you don't need green satin falling in heavy folds, interwoven with bouquets of flowers in gold thread. Denmark prefers corduroy door curtains and dark carpets. The Swedish aristocracy, on the other hand, understands how to use its riches; even if those riches are great, its debts are often even greater. Such people are welcome customers in a store where you can buy a single chair seat for the master's desk chair for 100 kroner, or a hat for the lady of the house – yellow, decorated with yellow feathers and mauve velvet, the exact likeness of one which was ordered from Paris for one of our own high-ranking ladies – for 120 kroner, or light-coloured summer costumes for the little bébés and Henri II outfits for the eighteen-year-old miss.* All of this you can really buy in Magasin du Nord – all of this and much, much more.

In 1870 – today you must forgive me for indulging, even more than usual, in leaps which strain the patience of my readers, but it is only possible to describe this establishment if you as it were spin anecdotes around it – the firm moved to Copenhagen, and the motherhouse in Aarhus became merely a branch. It was on the ground floor on the left that it began, first just as a wholesaler in linens, then later as a retailer. Then they moved from sheets and towels to complete bedding – the whole department which now occupies the left ground floor, where you are struck by spontaneous alarm about overpopulation as you pass by the display of innumerable cradles, all waiting for their hopeful occupants. 'This is where we began,' says my companion. And I look around in the relatively insignificant area which is – excuse the wordplay – the cradle of Magasin du Nord.

But this space soon became too small. So one tenant after another had to decamp; room had to be made for carpets, furnishing materials, lingerie – they took over the whole of the ground floor, they doubled the selection of the lines the business stocked, the warehouse space had to be extended, the departments enlarged. It is not a small area you need for a carpet department in which the yearly sale is 95,000 square yards of carpeting. Do you understand what that number means? What that number tells us, if I have calculated correctly, is that every year they could cover around a quarter of Nørrefælled with the carpets they sell. Nørrefælled is 90 acres of land, and an acre of land measures 6600 square yards – so you can work it out yourself. Or would it be easier to understand if I illustrate the sale by saying that every year they sell 150 miles of carpeting in Hôtel du Nord?*

And linens also take up room. They need space for the 25,000 pairs of curtains which pass through every year, and the 200,000 handkerchiefs which are spread across the country from here.

As I said, the space became too small, and one fine day the first floor had to be vacated as well. It was in 1878 that Magasin du Nord took on its present form. They acquired new specialities. The upholstery workshop, which now employs 25 craftsmen, was set up; they opened a department for gentlemen's underwear, a most impressive one for ladies' lingerie, a growing trade in children's clothes, in ladies' outfits, in French hats, in flowers, in sewing articles, in perfumes, in – well, come and see for yourself. You can't buy boots in Hôtel du Nord; otherwise I believe you can find what is needful!

As the business now stands, it is comparable to the great Parisian department stores. The principle is the same: everything gathered under one roof, and therefore a modest profit with the help of a very large turnover. Here the two things belong together; convenience and cheapness go hand in hand for the customer. But the secret of this enormous machine, which looks like a chaotic mixture of everything conceivable, is that all twenty departments work independently. Here there is not a shelf of socks, but a separate business, in which every year they sell a bagatelle of 10,000 dozen – 120,000 pairs of socks – and the hosiery department is separate from the rest. The manager of the hosiery department is a specialist in hosiery, just as the manager of the carpet department has studied in the French factories.

We go into the ladies' outfitters. What remarkable hats! Here is a hat made of sateen, mauve with pale mauve feathers and a cascade of lilac flowers, there is a bonnet, richly decorated with black pearls and pale pink roses, the edge finished with broad lace made of gold thread; otherwise it is pansies which are in evidence everywhere. There is a large clothes basket in one corner which is full to the brim with artificial grasses, fastened together in thick bundles – that is a small part of this spring's fashions.

In the lower room there is a young lady leaning over a matt silk dress with ruffles and flounces of satin trimming a four-foot long train of imitation Brussels lace. It is her wedding dress. Magasin du Nord has provided her whole trousseau, and its upholsterers have furnished her apartment. The Jensen Brothers' joiners' workshop, which is in a side building, has made her furniture.

In fact this department is the latest one. Formerly they only sold woollen dress material by the yard; they didn't want to take on sewing as well. They really had enough to do with the material itself. Just to keep up with the measuring and dispatch took 25 ladies, who were stationed in the secretive Holy of Holies, from where two hundred seamstresses daily collected the cut lengths, and where there was No Admittance for Shop Assistants. Only department managers had the right to open those firmly closed doors.

But then circumstances forced them to start stocking ready-made outfits. Now the carpeted rooms in which the 32 ladies employed by this department are busily engaged make up one of the most important areas of the business – and across town there are 4-500 seamtresses working away daily in order to satisfy the demands of all those ladies who wish to be modern for a modest outlay. For here as elsewhere a small profit on each article is the watchword.

It is without doubt this watchword which has created the impressive enterprise which today provides work for 1400 people, in addition to 100 workers employed in the firm's factories in Nørrebro,* substantial damask and linen weaving mills, which are further linked to a bleaching yard which provides bread for around fifty people.

We have sauntered from room to room. Everywhere I have been struck by the sheer volume, the enormous quantities of everything. All of this disproves the continually repeated refrain about our limited capabilities, because this is huge. There are endless rolls of white curtain material and of tape, heaps of flowers, gigantic piles of carpets, mountains of damask, oceans of duvets, masses of beds, model gowns by the dozen and fashionable hats by the box-load – you have the feeling that in this retail establishment everything is counted in quantities of three-score and sold by the gross. It is so encouraging to register this, and then to go to the window and see that the horse is still standing there – frail though it may be – and that you are still in Copenhagen.*

Finally I see the restaurant. For the moment they only serve lunch in here, but the restaurant manager, who has a permanent position, is said to be discussing with the firm a plan to extend the catering to all meals.

'Now there's no more to see,' says my companion. And I was on the point of thanking him for that; it is quite exhausting to visit Magasin du Nord.

In the face of an enterprise such as this, the journalist has a difficult task. The amount of material is overwhelming; you can't put these large halls into novelistic shape. You struggle with numbers which a normal person – and I permit myself to count myself amongst the normal people – finds it difficult to breathe life into, you can't go into details, you want to give an impression of everything and thus can't give a complete idea of anything, you drown in sheer volume, you don't know where to start to be able to encompass the whole. So what you write becomes mostly just anecdotes, you abandon a complete description and take refuge in passing thoughts.

It is asking too much to be able to convey a picture of all this.

I have not tried to do so. I have merely jotted down a few things here and there, just as they occurred to me whilst I was writing. And I will have achieved my aim if, when you have read these lines, you have the same impression as I did myself, and have conceived real respect for the energy which has created Magasin du Nord, this great republic with its 1400 inhabitants.

Translated by Janet Garton

21. 'The House with the Happy Faces'

There is no Biblical quotation over the door, no Christ figure to indicate an institution. The red house stands on its own in the middle of the plot of land which in the villa district would be called a garden. If you walk past, you can see at the wide windows on the ground floor a crowd of chattering children, often with their heads close together. You can see the back of the necks of some of them, a couple of outstretched arms of others; the ones at the front have their foreheads pressed against the windows. Upstairs, all the windows are open all day long; they must be very fond of fresh air in that house.

You hurry on, you are frozen and sleepy, and now you're going to be late for work on top of everything. The tram left while you were buttoning your overcoat, and you're always irritable in the mornings.

But if, as you hurry past, your glance falls on the chattering children behind the window, it may be that you pause for a moment, and if the person walking past is a father or a mother, they might think of the happiness of being a parent. And then perhaps the picture will stay with that person all day; he feels tired, he lifts his head for a moment from his books and lays down his pen, and as he leans back in his chair or slowly lets his hand slide down over his forehead, he will see behind his closed eyes the crowd of smiling mouths behind that wide window, round arms reaching out, children's necks … .

And the vision will be as dear to him as a fragment of a gentle melody, which comes singing to us and soothes us without our wishing for it.

From that time on he can't forget that house; he stops for a moment and nods to the happy faces, and he often sends an involuntary thought to 'the home with the smiling children'.

It was as if they grew out of the earth itself.

Large and small, boys and girls, the girls wearing cotton dresses and threadbare shawls through which the wind blew, frozen. With chattering teeth they would stretch out their frozen hands towards you, some would shout, others appeal: 'Papers!' – 'Papers!'*

You would meet them at every other step; some were cripples, and all were freezing – you practically fell over them. 'Papers!' – 'Papers!' It wasn't very long before their calls became an annoyance, and it was upsetting as well. It had started in a small way: a few boys had begun to sell newspapers on the streets, and that was convenient, you got the news directly, and you could always find a couple of øre in your waistcoat pocket … . But now it had got out of hand; the street was swarming with yelling children, standing in doorways, emerging from every corner – it was too much, it became a public nuisance, something had to be done, you couldn't hear for all that clamour.

Apart from that, it put you in a bad mood; all the streets and alleyways sent out their children, blue with cold, onto the squares beneath the gaslights – it was pitiful to see. And how easily they could come to harm! All those cripples, tiny children who could barely walk, all that starving misery … . It was indefensible – for the sake of the traffic.

The police drove away the swarm, the children were obstructing the traffic, their shouts were painful to the ears, even their silent pleas were irritating: a blue arm reaching out, a couple of begging eyes in a thin face. You can't let the poorhouse flood the squares like that, it looks so bad. So they chased away the childish misery.

Østergade was clear again; they drove the children home, into the darker streets and narrower passages, where misery holds court in the back rooms and in attics in crumbling shacks. But the authorities see to it that the lamps shine less clearly there, and there is no light from large shops. So you don't see it so well.

Sometimes it is comforting to keep it in semi-darkness like that.

But even since then, and despite the police and the authorities, it has been possible to meet such children in harsh winters, driven by need. They keep to the shadows, pressed up against doorways and walls, away from the gas lamps. They dare not shout any more, they simply hold out the matches or the lottery tickets in their cold hands and whimper or entreat quietly: 'A lottery ticket – a shilling – a shilling for luck, gen'l'man.'

We know very well that destitution exists, but to see it laid bare like that every day – no, it is not amusing, and besides it does no good.

So the guardians of public order tell the children to go home.

And where do they go?

We know that well enough: up to the cold rooms under the roof which we read about in ladies' novels, dark back rooms about which we have all heard so often. We know them. Perhaps – but it is easy to forget about poverty, it rarely appeals to our senses, and often it is more wretched in life than it is in novels.

So let us take a look at where these children go when they are chased away. What I shall describe is what I have seen, not read, seen all around in those streets which the authorities keep in semi-darkness, and where the semi-darkness is comforting.

There are children who crawl up rickety ladders, right up under the roof. It is called an attic apartment – it is a nest under the roof slates, where you keep out the cold with rags and wisps of straw and scraps of clothing; but the rain pours down from the slates into pools on the floor, so that the straw where Mother is lying gets wet. Because this is 'Mother', this half-naked creature who has to suckle that screaming bundle of rags lying hidden under the straw at her flabby breast. Now at least she can have a covering for her body, when the lass comes home with the shawl.

And others call home those large 'coffin houses', where water seeps in through the thin walls, and which shake when there is a storm outside. The room is empty, unemployment has stripped it – unemployment and despair. Over by the table on the only chair, which *he* takes for himself, he sits dead drunk with the half-empty bottle: he can't provide bread, and he sees his children starving. So he is warming his despair a little. All around in the corners the children are sitting on the floor; they dare not whimper or sigh, they just sit absolutely still, utterly forlorn as children are when they're starving … . Is all this trivial? Have you heard it so often?

Oh – there are other stories which you hear just as often, happier stories about happier people, brighter pictures. Those you are eager to hear. But to these you close your ears, and say to the person who wants to tell them at an inconvenient time: 'Go away, we've heard it so often!' But sometimes you just *have* to hear.

There are children who, when they are driven home, steal into the streets of vice, where rent is cheap – right up under the roof. There it is not comfortable enough for vice, so there it is cheap for the completely destitute. And sometimes the woman in the attic is just their foster-mother – their mother lives down below,* and they don't know their father – and neither does she! Some go home to sickness, others to drunkenness, some to blows, others to tears – but they all go home to misery.

However, at times it happens that the child selling the lottery tickets answers the authorities that it has nowhere to go. That child belongs to society, which is its only mother. But society has to employ foster-mothers, and the foster-mothers should preferably be cheap.

That is why you sometimes have to pity homeless children.

It is always dreadful to come face to face with destitution, always dreadful to be in the presence of barefaced vice. You feel your heart wrung, you can scarcely breathe; but to see *children* suffering, childhood starved, their early years sinking down beyond hope of rescue into hopeless ruin, that is the most dreadful thing of all. When the depravity is old, you admit your helplessness; if misery has grey hair, you console yourself that those days will not last for ever.

But destitute *children!* Children who grow up in the gutter, who are nourished by filth and breathe a poisoned air – when faced with them, you are shocked, you cannot accept the misfortune. The life you measure for them stretches over years which seem to be without end, a grey eternity of unrelieved woe.

But it is precisely for that reason that compassion – although it will unfortunately always be less powerful than misery – is at present focused on children. They are our neighbours, and it is for their sake we must act; if we are happy, we should make them just as happy as we are, and if we are unhappy, make them happier than us. The children can be saved. However decisive heredity is, however determining *blood* can be, the way their lives develop is more important than both, and nowhere can the compassion which confronts misfortune have greater prospects of success than here.

That is why our age, which attempts in a thousand ways to heal the wounds inflicted by society, has nowhere put in a greater effort than here. Children's homes, orphanages, workplaces, shelters have all in different ways been working towards the same goal: to provide society with a well-adjusted individual by pulling an unhealthy shoot out of its wretched circumstances as early as possible. And the disappointments which attend all acts of compassion have been fewer here than in other areas.

It is this compassion, which gathers up the children, which has created a home for the homeless in the red house with the happy faces. The house with the happy children – *a foster-mother's flock!*

If you were to tell the story of this house, it would – as so often – be the tale of a woman's sacrifices, quiet tasks carried out in a hidden corner, growing in silence – which is why no-one has demanded thanks, why no-one has been named. But perhaps that is precisely why it has grown.

And perhaps you would be able to learn from this story. For to demonstrate willpower every day, to battle with the small things every day, to make small sacrifices every day – that perhaps demands more courage than being a hero on one occasion. The stories of heroes are recorded, those of quiet existences are preserved in individual hearts.

But this story does not belong to us. The principal of Vodrofsvej's Children's Home says merely: 'The time before I got the home.'* What sacrifices these words conceal, from the long years when she alone, with her own means, which were not great, brought up 'the first fourteen' – about that, both she and history are silent. 'The time before I got the home' is now so long ago, and perhaps half-forgotten – except by the fourteen, some of whom are still at the home.

Fourteen or fifteen years ago the principal took in some poor children, brought them up and saved them from destitution – that is the simple beginning. And slowly the number of children increased. Their foster mother could not manage the task alone, and private individuals joined together to help. You could see the fruitful results: the children were plucked from early misery – some were motherless, some fatherless, and for some their parents were a curse – here they found clean air, blossomed and grew healthy. People are always helpful when results speak for themselves. And here it was red cheeks and childish happiness which spoke.

This was the beginning of the Vodrofsvej's Children's Home, where five years ago they were bringing up 25 children and now have 62. On a summer's evening, when the workers are on their way home from the mill directly opposite, they sometimes stop and watch the children playing in the garden. 'You certainly have a lot of children,' they say to the principal.

The children are playing hide-and-seek or tag. The area is not large – a patch of earth like a dinner-plate, just as small as the house, which is built for 80 and usually houses more than 70 little ones – but they are merry nonetheless. They hide, they shout 'coming', the smallest play with the dog, the oldest sit whispering on the bench beneath the hawthorn .... Then there's a call from 'Mother', and at once they all flock around her. She says goodnight to each one and tells them to sleep well, and big and small go inside.

There's a hubbub in the dormitory. There the beds stand close together – rather too many beds and rather too little air – with white sheets and red blankets, the smallest so small that they look like dolls' beds. They get undressed sitting on the wooden bench at the foot, they sit there shouting and kicking their little pink legs whilst they put their night clothes on, and the older ones try to hush them, but they can't calm down. Just as children have always been able to chatter when it's time for bed. They play until they fall asleep, then they drift off with a smile.

The smallest – two-year-old toddlers, who lie there reaching out their arms to kiss 'Mother' – are laid on the table to be washed. Then they scream and wriggle and won't lie still; but eventually they are dried with a cloth and bundled up. Then they get their nightshirts on, and off to bed.

The principal walks through the dormitories, stopping now and then and raising her light. They're already asleep; with their heads to one side and their hands folded on top of the sheet, they lie there, bed after bed. Upstairs is where the older ones sleep. There's a buzzing up there; some of them are fourteen-year-old girls, and at that age there's always a lot to whisper about, chattering quietly from bed to bed. But they have been up since five o'clock, and they are tired. Slowly the words become fewer and the pauses longer; the whispering dies away with a 'goodnight'.

The children's home is asleep.

At five o'clock the older ones are woken up, and a couple of hours later the little ones wake. They wake with a cry, just like birds shaking their feathers with a chirrup, and when they've had their *øllebrød*,* the day's work begins.

And the day's work is greatly varied throughout the red house. The children's home is not rich, it has to rely on the help of good people, and good people have so many causes to support; and even if it were richer than it is, it would be necessary to work. *Everyone works,* that is the principle. They teach even the smallest to make themselves useful, and those who feel useful are not far from being happy.

That is why everyone has something to do, a task to perform in the home. The smallest unpick rags. They sit along low benches in the workroom with their rags and unpick so busily, so busily; they know that what they unpick will be turned into both dresses and stockings. And *that* is a help. One of the older ones is supervising – one of the fourteen from 'before the home', the house's best supports – sometimes she tells stories, sometimes she sings to them. And they learn to knit too. Their small fingers can hardly hold the knitting needles, and it costs a few tears to drop so many stitches – but in the end they learn that too, and then they proceed into the next class in the next room, where they learn spelling and reading and geography. By then the children are already big, they are – six years old.

In the next room are the big ones – not the biggest, for they are down in the laundry cellar wringing out clothes – but the twelve to thirteen-year-old girls. They are studying with a teacher. First they have been up to tidy the dormitories and scrub the floors. 'We do it ourselves,' says the principal, 'it is so lovely to be able to do things yourself – and you can save on servants' wages too.' And in the children's home they don't sweep the dirt into the corners, they prefer to sweep it clean and wash the floors every day. There is such a lack of room that it's really necessary to air it all out. Then when they're finished upstairs, the big ones put their good dresses on and go down to school.

The biggest ones work in the kitchen. It's a large kitchen. Along all the walls the pewter bowls are hanging in rows, shining here in the half-darkness, and on the shelves the plates are stacked up, plate after plate, a shining legion. 'The pans will soon be too small,' says one of the big girls, pointing to some enormous casseroles. It's a vast undertaking.

Today they're going to have *sød suppe.** Chunks of apples are floating on top of the pan.

There's a lot to do in the kitchen. From here they have not only to feed the home's 62 mouths, but also make food for the women's refuge, hearty food for the sick women – and everything is done calmly and quietly, without a fuss. It is from a room on the ground floor that this peaceful activity, which never seems to be hurried and always has the time to pause, spreads throughout the whole house: the principal watches over it all, and one of the ladies assisting was no doubt speaking the truth when she said: 'The secret of it is that the mistress is everywhere.'

At 3 o'clock they eat. They clear things away and open up to get some fresh air – for they have to remain in the same rooms, there are no others, and even here the rooms are merely rented – set the tables and put out the food. The older ones help the younger ones, who wear bibs and burn themselves on the fruit soup and can't cut their meat. Then all those sweet mouths clamour and babble. But if they don't eat nicely, they get a tap on the fingers.

After the meal the older ones read.

In the evening they play. In between they also do housekeeping tasks, darning, sewing and patching. Or they have some extra work, like cleaning raisins. It's the younger ones who are set to cleaning the raisins. When the crate arrives, it is brought into the workroom, and the little ones are set to work. They know they must not eat – and they don't.

The older ones too have a responsible task. In their free hours they collect contributions; they go round to all the home's benefactors and pick up their monthly payments. Often every child is carrying a hundred kroner by the time they come home, but it has never happened that so much as a shilling has disappeared.

'For children outside the home,' says the principal, 'there are plenty of ways in which they are introduced to the realities of life. My children are not tempted by that – yet they cannot stay here inside the home, and when they leave, they go out into the world. They have to be educated about it.'

So she sits the little ones down in front of the crate of raisins. 'They have to know about life – I talk to them about it. When the oldest ones leave here, there is nothing they do not know. I tell them everything, so that they can choose.'

Do you not think that 'real' mothers could learn from this foster-mother? Mothers for whom ignorance is the same as innocence, who let their children guess instead of being informed, and who have so much distrust of their own flesh and blood that they refuse to acknowledge the existence of temptations, as if there would not come a day when that blood, unfortunately, will speak? The foster-mother knows life better than that.

On Sundays they have a day of rest in the home. The older ones go to church – those who have deserved it. 'Those who have been lazy during the week don't come along; to hear the Word of God is a reward.'

In the home itself there no services, no idle prayers. Here children learn not to stay in bed in the mornings because they would like to say The Lord's Prayer 'one more time'. They are not taught to 'enter into their closet' in order to be with God,* or to kneel in order to worship. What they are taught is that God is everywhere where they do their duty with love, and that if you pray as you work, you are serving God at the same time as you are petitioning and thanking. To work – for each one to take up their task in quietness – that is this home's motto.

To glide into the great mechanism without fuss, and there to labour quietly to the best of one's ability – that is what the homeless children learn in this house, where the small ones unpick rags and the bigger ones wash floors; and perhaps that is the teaching which is best designed to create satisfaction in the future. Satisfaction is not happiness, but it is at least the closest substitute for it.

So pass the days in the red house with the happy faces.

'So where do these children come from?' I asked.

Strangely enough, the principal told me about the time of the paper-sellers. 'And the children are still there, even though the police make sure they don't obstruct the traffic. Some we gather up ourselves, and rescue from misery, but others are brought in by their parents – a father who has lost his wife or a widow who has no bread. – There are always enough unfortunate ones!'

I asked how old the children were.

'All ages – we just take them and put them in a bath at once.'

I had seen everything, and got up to go, thanking her for all I had seen, which had pleased me greatly.

'Yes,' said the principal, 'it is a blessed activity. There is only one thing which is sad: the home is full, this house is so small, and we are only renting it … . Yesterday a widow brought us a lame child, I had to turn her away and shut the door.'

'But what about the money which is raised by the bazaar – if you could afford your own house … .'

'Oh, don't say that, I daren't even admit to myself that I am hoping for that!'

But those of us who could each bring our mite, could we not turn this hope into a reality?* If for no other reason, then so that many can see that there is always a blessing on a quiet duty faithfully performed, if for no other reason, then in order to honour a single one of the many 'unsung heroes', whose story is never written – except in grateful hearts.

And more than this: for the sake of the work itself, for the sake of the house in which motherless children have found a mother, homeless ones a home.

But the enterprise will succeed. You never speak in vain about this house – however inadequately you do so – never in vain to any mother's heart; never in vain about this life's work to any woman who has made sacrifices in her life. And there are many mothers and many quietly labouring women.

Translated by Janet Garton

22. Visiting the Poor Before Christmas

We walked along an old walkway;* the floor was unstable, and the boards wobbled beneath us. We had to bend our heads and almost crawl – there were grey cloths hung up over some old ship's rope to dry. They obstructed our passage.

From behind the filthy windows of both wings, the faces of women and children were staring at us with that half-shy, half-greedy look so characteristic of wretchedness, which had followed us from hundreds of faces on the whole of this dreadful pilgrimage.

'They're washing ready for Christmas,' said the police officer; he stooped down to pass beneath some much-mended rags, which around here would pass for a skirt.

We fell down a couple of steps into a dark corner, and reached the stairs – or rather a peculiar kind of ladder leading up and down, with worn and sticky steps. On each landing was a grey, dirty post, quite damp, like everything in these houses, put there as a marker for those who would tumble down this ladder with no bannister in the darkness.

'It must be difficult to climb up here when they're drunk,' said H., the third member of the company.

The police officer remarked drily: 'That's why they fall.'

We continued down the stairs and out through an alleyway, where an open drain made passage difficult. 'In summer there's a terrible stink here,' said the police officer.

'The most difficult thing must be to get them out when they're dead,' says H., stretching out his arm to measure the alleyway.

'Ah, they bring them down here to put them in their coffins … .'

'I see … yes, I can understand that.'

We were out on the street. The police officer took out his notebook and consulted it. 'Let's go to the next ones,' he said. We both followed in silence. He talked. And what he told us about was 'the interiors,' which were as scary as the houses themselves. I was only half listening; his account was like an unclear and muffled accompaniment to my paralysed thoughts. We reached the end of the street, and I was roused by the silence; he had stopped talking.

My head felt empty, just like when you come round from a faint, and I noticed that H., who was walking on the other side of the police officer, was whistling a waltz. But when I looked across at his face, which was pale and grey despite the coldness of the winter day which should have given it colour, I could see that his whistling seemed to be covering the same emotion as my silence: horror.

The police officer began again. 'We have only four or five left now,' he said. He looked up and paused; we had reached the corner. 'But … perhaps you're already tired, you look a bit pale round the gills… .'

I made no answer. H. muttered something about not being used to it.

'I can well understand that. Even we old hands can feel a bit strange doing these visits – usually when the weather is gloomier. You've seen it in sunshine, after all.'

'In sunshine?'

'Yes, just imagine when it's raining, then it's night-time all day long in these holes – then the wretched people stagger around falling over their own legs in the murk … .'

I understood him, and in an instant I could see all those images, which were dimly visible in my thoughts, appearing even darker and more comfortless in the sleet of rainy days, or in the gloom of foggy days. Wretched people staggering around in the darkness and falling over their own legs.

'Well,' I said, 'thank God it was sunny!' We said goodbye there on the corner.

H. and I wandered down a couple of narrow streets and emerged onto Østergade, where it was promenade time.* Here the cold did bring colour; round cheeks were red, and figures were sprightly – hurrying along at speed in order to stay warm. Flocks of people were doing their Christmas week window shopping, and both pavements were full. Ladies in figure-hugging coats with smiling faces peeping out of fur collars and tulle veils, gentlemen in furs and gentlemen in cloaks. And over the whole scene the sunshine of the December day.

I stared at the faces, at the varying colours of the costumes, at the happiness in all those smiles. It was like waking up from a dream, a heavy stupor. But on waking you felt strange and disconnected.

We didn't speak, neither H. nor I. For a moment we paused next to the king on horseback.* Then he seemed to give himself a shake. 'Goodbye then,' he said.

'Goodbye.'

'Listen, you know what – I'm going in to have a steak. I feel so odd – almost empty, just as if I've been to a funeral.'

He shook hands and sauntered over towards the Hotel d'Angleterre.* But when I met him again yesterday, he said: 'You know what – that's the last time I'm going on that police visit .... I still haven't got over it.'

'No, it wasn't much fun.'

'So we might just as well stop seeing it,' he said. 'It doesn't make it any better.'

'No, not much!'

'We might just as well stop seeing it,' said H. Perhaps that's true, because it is no fun; when you have seen what we three saw that day, then you know what wretchedness looks like, and its face is scary. It's no fun, because once you've seen that terrible face, you can't forget it in a hurry, and there may well be several months during which words like want and misery, hunger and starvation really make you think; where every letter in those words is a face which is seared in your memory, every sound a dissonance which torments your ear – where we are a little less thoughtless than usual. And thoughtlessness is a blessing.

And when you *have* seen it, it is perhaps best to keep silent about what you have seen; talking about it does no good, and you get no thanks for doing so. What you have seen is unbelievable, and even if a genius – who was at once deeply humane and completely unsentimental – were to paint this unbelievable scene, he would be met with disbelief, still more if one of us did so. And since all that poverty which we saw on our pilgrimage is inescapable in this happy society, why should we talk about it, when no-one will believe us, and no-one will thank us? Who is asking for it? Does anyone want to be scared by staring into the face of death? Hardly.

Despite that, if I have decided to tell you something of these visits today it is not to titillate, not to play with the cloth which is laid over the features of the dead, or to lift a corner of it and then let it fall again frivolously, as if in play. This is no frivolity on my part.

But these people are starving. That is why I shall speak out, and I must beg the society in which these wretches suffer from hunger every single day, to be merciful and feed them properly, just for one day.

To this end I ask not the exalted Muses, who no doubt are busy dancing with the Graces on Olympus,* but my own memory to come to my aid, so that I can describe a little of what I saw, and simply that. Here it is not possible to exaggerate, it is scarcely possible to measure. For what I saw was without colour, and to describe it there are no words.

We writers are irresponsible. Why do we so often play with words, play lightheartedly with effects like hunger and misery – with the result that when we finally come face to face with wretchedness in all its nakedness, we are empty of words and at a loss for pictures?

That is why *you* must read a deeper tone, a more serious note into these same old words, because I am unable to create a new language in order to write about this horror. And one more thing. Do not say that what I am describing is exaggerated. What we saw was worse than all the words, even if imagination can give them colour, and if readers hide behind the excuse of exaggeration, they are hiding from the truth.

So to the first house.

The yard was an alleyway. On one side a hovel which you would think was a shed, a tumbledown half-timbered shack with crooked and ill-fitting doors, windows covered in stuck-on paper, empty panes stuffed with rags.

These rags surprised me as I walked past. But perhaps the shed was used as a workshop.

On the other side was a housing block with a raised ground floor above the cellars. Five doors, each with a flight of steps up to the entrance. They were freezing, those five flights, which led up to such bareness. And the house itself, in its ramshackle state, was freezing too, seeming to hug itself, shivering.

'Here,' said the police officer, 'the second steps. This is a good place.'

We knocked on the front door, but there was no answer. The police officer took hold of the handle and opened it. We came into the kitchen. A small room with an empty fireplace; it was surprising that it was so smoky, since the fireplace was bare. A table beneath a filthy window – a table over which someone had wiped grimy, cold remains, which now lay like a grey mould over the boards, like dust over the deserted kitchen. On the shelf above the door were a couple of flowerpots.

H. opened the cupboard under the table. I'm not sure whether the substance he took out might once have been one of the loaves distributed by poor relief. Nothing else.

But how to convey the coldness in that room, the bareness, the emptiness? It was hunger's antechamber, that room.

Behind it lay the living room. Construct four walls, cold and dirty in their bareness, lay in your imagination a floor as grimy as the table in the empty kitchen. Fill this room, whose ceiling is split so that the rain comes through, with the smell of poverty – a stinking dankness. Then you will know what this room looked like.

In one corner stood a bed with some bundles of rags, a colourless grey heap, tatters of what were once blankets and items of clothing; on the floor two chairs, cane chairs with broken seats. On a hook by the door hung a skirt. A pawnbroker would have given it back, smiling and shaking his head. But no doubt that was why it hung there.

That was how it looked. On the floor lay the youngest child, bundled up in a grey shawl. Two others crept in behind the door, snivelling. I don't know whether they hid because they were naked – but that is hardly likely; they can have had little experience of what it meant to wear rags which could cover them.

The police officer pulled out one of the children. It was frightfully thin – that appalling skinniness of a starving child. Its cheeks were hollow and blueish, its eyes large, but deepset in its skull and apathetic. Its gaze was fearful, older than its years. Hunger gives children a peculiar expression of precociousness. And the skin which was stretched over those thin bones, which was as yellow as bronze on all of them, was covered in sores. There were sores on its arms and legs, and nasty weeping sores around its nose.

'Hunger,' said the police officer. 'They're hungry.'

'I had no idea it looked like that,' I said. And there must have been a shudder in my voice, because our guide looked up. 'These are the most fortunate ones,' he said.

He let go of the child's arm and turned to go. We were already out in the passage.

'I'm glad it's not me that has to write about it,' he said.

'Why?'

'You won't find the words in Molbech,' he said.*

There was a rope hanging down from the ceiling. The benevolent landlord had hung it there in order to save the lives of those who paid 10 kroner a month for the attic, and who had to climb up the ladder. The steps swayed a little.

It was completely dark up there. The police officer staggered slightly, bumped into something wooden, then knocked. A grunt could be heard from inside. Then we opened a door made of a few planks nailed together, and entered. I drew back a bit.

'Do we have to go in?' I asked.

It was the air which forced me back. You could *taste* the foulness. It was a stench of emanations from the sick, of rotten food, of filth; you need to be born in this air to be able to breathe it.

When you had got used to the darkness, you could make out in the gloom a table with a vast array of broken crockery, smashed plant pots, and unidentifiable fragments; and on all these pieces there were the half-rotten remains of food for the destitute. It was these remains which stank.

By the window stood a chest of drawers with the drawers open; they were crammed with indeterminate scraps of rags, all covered in grime. The bed coverings had been plundered by hunger, and what was left was some nondescript material and decomposing remnants of straw.

But why are all words so misused that no expression can convey to you how dreadful this boil-encrusted nakedness was, no expression can paint a picture of the stinking contents of these drawers, of the disgusting mess on this table? There was not a patch on this floor which had not become a dung-heap of rags and filth, not a patch. In the walls were holes with colonies of lice.

In the middle of the floor, like Job, lay a half-grown figure.* He was the only son of a widow, and an idiot. When he saw us he made the jerking movements of St. Vitus' dance,* with that spasmodic, lalling laughter with which idiots greet you. He half rose and tried to speak, babbling incomprehensibly like a drunkard who can't control his mouth properly. The only covering he had was an old skirt.

The idiot carried on with his mumbling laughter, whilst digging and rummaging around in the scraps on the floor. It was as if wretchedness had taken on the figure of a ghastly jumping jack, pulling faces at himself.

We didn't want to see any more of this house, *didn't want to*. 'Just a little more,' said the police officer, and after we had clambered down the steps, he opened the door to the shed. There were people living in this shed.

I cannot describe what it looked like. The inhabitants, who speak the same language as us, would call these random sticks tables, beds and chairs; personally I can find no name for these bits and pieces, which were permeated by mould and damp and stank of muck and putrefaction.

Sleeping places which were wet straw covered by stinking blankets, tables which could only remain standing by leaning against the walls, themselves as rotten as the tables. It was all freezing filth.

One of the flats was empty. The woman was dead. The other day one of the neighbours had come over to the station. They were worried that Madam Lund would stop breathing, he said – she was lying there gasping dreadfully, he said.

When the police arrived, they were all standing around idly, the people from the house, their mouths open listlessly, doing nothing. The neighbour had gone in and found Madam Lund lying on the floor, having convulsions. Then the others had arrived to watch. Now they thought she might be gone.

'And gone she was,' said the police officer.

'What did she die of?' I asked.

'Oh,' – H. shrugged – 'it's perfectly reasonable that these people die.'

Yes – perfectly reasonable. What is more curious is that they live.

As we walked down the street, our guide told us stories about the police, many of them amusing. They suited our mood just like bad jokes at a funeral feast.

'Of course these are the dregs,' he said. 'But there's one good thing about it. This population is so stable that we know them from one generation to the next. That makes our work easier.'

'And your surveillance,' said H.

'Just like in ancient Egypt,' I said without thinking.

'That's right,' said the police officer. 'They stay where they are.'

These words were more terrible than everything we had seen. Dante's inscription over the proletarian hell.*

So on we went. We saw another house, then a third and a fourth, but what we saw was the same pictures. The only thing which gave this misery any nuances was the degree of vice which accompanied it. Misery is a Janus head, and its twin face is called vice.*

We were climbing up to the top of a house, where you had to ascend by ladder. And through all the floors we were assailed by the odour of drunkenness, which was mingled with the stench of filth and damp, an evil-smelling mould which made taking a breath an effort.

In some houses they were shy, they opened doors a fraction and stared out through cracks, they followed us with the hungry eyes of the starving from windows and doorways.

Here they were aggressive. We were met by the impotent whining and wailing laments of drunkards. A large women stood barring our way. She forced us to look at her child's head – it was covered in sores, and to examine her own fingers – they were swollen. The child was less than a year old. The police officer tried to get past. But she remained standing there, and in the midst of her whining she kept on repeating more and more loudly: 'Are we getting anything to eat? Are we getting anything to eat?'

The police officer pushed her aside, shoving her despite the fact that she was pregnant, and finally we got past and continued up another floor. But from inside the room we heard again, more loudly: 'Is he giving us anything to eat?'

'How old is the child?' I asked.

'Oh,' – for the first time there was a quickly suppressed emotion in our guide's voice – 'You're right, children here are just as dreadful a misfortune as drunkenness.'

In the attic they didn't want to open the door. We could hear moaning from inside. In the end the wife came out. She was practically naked, just holding a ripped nightshirt together with her hands. The skirt gaped over her stomach.

She was already incoherent this early in the morning, and her excuses that she hadn't cleaned were drowned out by the drivelling tearfulness of alcoholism. She dried the tears from her streaming eyes with swollen fingers. The sweaty puffiness of the drinker had inflated this carcass.

We needed to examine the roof, said our guide, and eventually we were allowed in.

You need courage to observe her lodger, sitting on a stool in the corner under the skylight and rocking stupidly with his mouth open, his lips covered in sores like everything else in this frightful house; you need courage to observe the two children, rolling about naked in the box which contained these four at night: the woman, her lodger and her daughter's children – you force yourself to look at it, but cannot bear to describe it. Memories like this can't be put into words, horror at the thought paralyses the pen in your hand.

'Those children live on brandy,' said the police officer.

They were squatting down on the bed, blue with cold, staring at us. Only hunger can stare so enviously and so apathetically. What their eyes were envying was not our clothes, not our happiness, nothing but the flesh on our bones … .

Thus in house after house we saw drunkenness coupled with wretchedness.

And each time our guide showed us fresh misery, he said: 'But this is how it must be. No help is possible here.'

We saw cellars, damp rooms in which the air was poisoned by noxious smells, where water ran down the walls, where day was night.

In one room there were nine people sleeping every night. I shall explain how. In one corner was a double bed in which lay the man and his wife, and at their feet a ten-year-old daughter and a toddler. On some straw in a corner we saw two horse blankets, which made a couch for four. The ninth was in a cradle. That was how they found room; how they got enough air I have no idea.

Three of the children were over ten years old.

There were other places where, for the sake of decency, rooms were divided by rags which could give the illusion of a screen; but immorality was rife in this crowded proximity. Everywhere there were cradles, even in the most barren home, everywhere there were children. Helpless, miserable nakedness had brought them forth into misery.

Misery here means hunger. For these people know nothing and understand nothing. Any sense of morality is stifled in their first years, and they have their own concept of conscience, which is different from ours. Their society has its own laws, and they don't understand ours; hunger is their law!

Look at their lives! They came into the world in this room, where their mother gave birth without help; 'another mouth to feed' is their baptismal blessing. There are half a dozen mouths to start with, and the husband has 'no steady work'. If the mother has milk, she suckles the child, and if not, it probably dies – which is the most fortunate outcome. Otherwise it grows. Around it, it sees drunkenness and poverty, its enemy is hunger and its only clear desire is one day to get enough to eat.

When you're starving, you become lethargic.

'I feel most sorry for the poor little girls,' our guide says. 'Most of them have only one way to go.'

'But that means at least they can eat,' says H.

'Yes,' – he pauses – 'for a while, at least.'

'Well, then they are admitted to Ladegården – and *that* must be a blessing.'*

He made no answer.

'But no help is possible here,' he said then.

'Take the children away from them,' I said.

He shook his head. 'Yes,' he said, 'if you could … .'

We saw other houses in which the men struggled and toiled, and the women, skinny and wearing hardly any clothes, took care of their children, whose rags their hands had not tired of patching; here misery was at least clean.

We saw dwellings where vice was richer than misery, where there were still remnants of prosperity, and where indifference was greater than poverty. Then again others, which malnutrition had paralysed with sickness and hunger had punished with sores … but everywhere was the same terrible story: the battle for bread.

And our guide constantly repeated the same phrase: 'Feed them'. For him these people had become one single starving mouth which had to be fed. 'Feed them! – Give them bread!'

'And tomorrow?'

'They'll be starving again – but some people have to starve.'

I must stop, yet I know that I have not given you a picture – not at all.

The words are choked in my throat by the atmosphere of this helpless misery. But – and this is my comfort – here it is not a matter of my words, which are poor, or my brush, which cannot paint a Hogarth canvas;* all I have to convey is an entreaty, which I put forward for the hungry, from those who hunger to those who have food.

What we saw on that pilgrimage I cannot paint; but if there is in my words just an inkling of that awful pity, of that feeling which has left me incapable of pictures, incapable of images, incapable of finding colours to paint the colourless – then you will understand from my inability that what we saw was dreadful. And if you understand that, then you will know that this misery can be expressed in one word: hunger. And for just one day you will feed these people who are crying out for bread.

Don't forget that the most vivid moments in the lives of these wretches are probably those moments in which they hate 'the fortunate ones', in which their resentment becomes envy of the fact that *we can eat our fill.* They do not realise that the lives of the 'fortunate ones' – and this is where justice asserts itself – may not be any happier, and that the souls of those who are not consumed by the fight for bread are fighting other battles and have other griefs.

To starve is their suffering, and to eat their fill is their highest pleasure. Their life is simplified.

But precisely because of that we can, by feeding them for a single day, make them happier for an hour – perhaps happier than we ourselves, who are feeding them.

Wherever we went, they begged us for bread – bread for the children, at least.

'For Christmas Eve,' said our guide everywhere we went, liberally distributing meal tickets for the Christmas Party for the Children of the Poor.

Let them eat their fill on this one day, those thousands who otherwise starve. Let every one of us who can, send their mite.

'You see,' said the police officer, 'here you can create happiness with a bowl of rice pudding. You can't do that everywhere.'

No – not everywhere.

Translated by Janet Garton

23. On 'Thingvalla'

I

NIGHT

A wind had sprung up. It had arrived together with the flaming sunset out in the west. Now the skies were lowering and dark.

'Thingvalla' was making slow progress, with engines labouring heavily.* There was no noise from the waves. The sea rolled peacefully in a powerful rhythm. The waters rose up, then sank back, gliding smoothly, wave after wave.

On deck it had become quite quiet. Down below the engines throbbed. From the glass roof of the engine room a flickering light shone out, falling across the ghost-like funnel, then uncertainly further over the deck, throwing a gleam across a few bowed heads which were leaning together, whispering, on the roof of the cargo hold. The sound of footsteps on the bridge was monotonous.

We walked up and down silently. Our conversation had come to a stop, first drifting into chat and monosyllables and then ceasing altogether. No doubt we were each lost in our own thoughts.

'But what you say is right,' said the young merchant from New York, 'these young people with no profession will have a hard time. They'll be splitting rocks, sweeping the streets or dying of hunger.' He stopped by the cabin door:

'But most of them aren't worth any more than that, and America is a convenient cemetery to bury them in. I'll say goodnight, my dear sir; remember to look at things realistically. Even on an emigrant ship they are all very ordinary, and there really are amazingly few novels here – unless you write them yourself. Good night!'

'Good night.'

Round behind the coiled ropes there was an excellent place, completely sheltered. There you could sit comfortably and not feel the wind.

Amazingly few novels, he had said, and no doubt he was right. He knew how things stood, he had crossed the Atlantic five times, and I had seen so little of the sea … .

And yet. As the sea rolled lazily out there, and the smoke seemed to unfold like a coiling grass snake against the low sky, I saw once more, involuntarily, all those faces – one by one, picture by picture … .

First the departure. It was quite early. Baskets, canvas bags and boxes were piled up. All around, people were sitting on chests and wooden planks, keeping an eye on their own things. One family was already eating lunch. The children were crowding around the open wooden chest where Father was slicing bread; Mother had a child at her breast.

I asked them to keep an eye on my suitcase; you couldn't go on board yet. Then I got into conversation with them.

The man is a driver. – And now he had decided to emigrate? – Yes, they thought it would be for the best. – So he had some money to get them started? – No, they had nothing to speak of, but *she* had a brother … .

It was the man who had spoken, soberly, a little dispirited. The woman was rocking the child. She had been sitting bent over so that I couldn't see her face; now she raised it. The words came out like an explosion. 'Can we live on 12 kroner a week with *them*?' She looked over at the children, then at me. There was something nervously restrained in her tone, something indescribably dry, which struck me. A glint in those pale grey eyes, hollowed out under the red eyelids, something which was burning like a fever.

Then she held the child closer, and without looking at me she said quietly: 'If you have enough to eat, you don't leave your own country … .'

Yes, that New Yorker was right. It is perfectly ordinary, and you would have to be an author to make a novel out of that, out of this broad-shouldered, despondent peasant, out of the wife and the five children. Their life has nothing to do with novels, it's too trivial for that.

Yet there was once a time when she was young. Perhaps she had even been pretty, back then when her cheekbones didn't stand out so sharply. Then she married the driver, had a child, and the following year another one, and yet another the year after that. *That* is very ordinary. And gradually, as there were more mouths to feed, the food became scarce, and their cottage no bigger. And another child arrived, and another, and then they began to go hungry. That is just as ordinary. And now she had got *tired* of being hungry. Most people just put up with it, but that glint in her eye revealed that she was not one of them. That was why they were now making the crossing to try their luck.

She must have had a little more willpower than most. Where would you expect people like that to get willpower from? They are born in low rooms with poor air, they till the soil like their fathers before them. Apart from that they learn a couple of psalms and a little Bible history. When they are young they have a few dreams, but they don't range far. Love means having a sweetheart and then taking a wife. God is what they talk about in church, and children are what you have to work to feed. That is their life.

So it is difficult to say what they would use willpower for, or where they would get it from.

But she had grown tired. Tired of patching up the children and labouring all day long for a pittance, in order to spend the night thinking about the next trivial worry, tired of that lethargic man driving his horses, tired of seeing misery increasing slowly but surely. She had not just closed her eyes. For the affliction of grey trivialities falls over these people like snow, steadily and silently, like snow falls in the winter, as day by day the food becomes scarcer, the marriage more bitter, the burden heavier – but it all happens so stealthily, so soporifically. And they become more and more apathetic as they toil.

But now she has pulled up short and determined to leave this existence … .

No, there is no novel here!

We had boarded the ship. The constable was keeping an eye on the gangplank; you were not allowed to go back on shore. On land there was a restless throng, the staring of a thousand eyes. On board ship people were crowding along the railings. They stood there leaning on the railings, a long row of heads. How motionless they were, those faces! Just now and then their mouths quivered slightly. And the look in those gazing eyes was one of utter emptiness.

Music was playing behind them on the deck. A couple of tipsy fellows joined in, and the song seemed to steal along the row. But then it died away again.

People wanted to stand quietly. And if they were startled by a hurrah or two, there was only a brief shock which ran through the people along the railings.

Then the ship began to move. On land people crowded together more closely, they started to shout farewell, and all at once everyone's hats and handkerchiefs were flying in the air.

On board ship they seemed to wake up. And from all mouths as one there issued something you might call a cheer. It sounded like a scream. In that scream, which was mixed with the shouts from land, rising raggedly and intensely, there was a mixture of the pain of those departing and the good wishes of those staying behind.

It was a short shout.

A strange restlessness passed through the people on the quayside, like through those who crowd together to watch a fire. From on board people waved. And then they scattered, and everyone looked for their own corner. There were not very many who were talking whilst 'Thingvalla' steamed past the quayside.

There is a young man who has been standing by the ropes the whole time, staring unmoving over the heads of all those on shore. He is still standing there. The captain tells me that he is one of those who are being sent away. There are twenty of them on board.

What does it mean to be sent away? To have done something wrong, and in the opinion of the family to be beyond saving. That is what it means to be sent away. They have tried everything. Now the family has to abandon the individual, in order to save their good name. They provide travel money, references and their blessing. Then give a sigh of relief … and bring up the next generation in the same way as this one. It is no-one's fault.

At the start they engaged a wet-nurse to feed the boy, a wet-nurse they didn't know, but who had three children, although she was unmarried; later they found a nursemaid to look after him. Father had his business, Mother had her visits and her housekeeping. At school the boy learnt his lessons and learnt about immorality; the home left everything to the teachers, and the teachers left everything to the home. It was a most honourable house: they had their vicar, their country seat and made an honest living. Of course they called it a home.

When the young man is sixteen, he starts work in an office. What has he learnt? A great deal: French, German, English and physics. In addition a good portion of worldly wisdom. Ah, yes – there's a lot of whispering at school desks, and it is not always the finest stories. Who pays any attention to what feeds the boy's imagination?

Then there is what they read as well. Who keeps an eye on that? Does the teacher, who lends Musset to fifteen-year-old lads?* Or Paul de Kock to even younger ones?* Their anaemic imagination burrows into these books, and it is a dangerous labyrinth. Perhaps they have their own experiences too. So much can happen in a home.

And yet, after this education most of them become good citizens like their fathers. Of course, they are never young, and they never really achieve anything either. They become sceptics, and their morals are doubtful – but all in all, they create good foundations for future society.

On the other hand, you must admit that such an education can make them into hotheads. Not people who become criminals or anything like that, but people who do stupid things. Perhaps they are precisely the ones who could have been the most gifted. But they have been given neither ideas to live for nor any solid ground to stand on. So they throw their energy and their passion into the first aberration that comes their way, and now that they are leaving, it is not because they have known any great passions, but simply because their senses have been alive.

And then they have stolen money from the till.

But is *that* a novel? Such a mundane thing is not a novel. The fact that youngsters are not given anything to believe in, that no-one keeps their minds pure, that there is silence instead of speech, that schools leave everything to the home and that home is just a house in which you live; that a son goes off the rails – is that a novel?

The young man is still standing there – but suddenly he lets go of the ropes and swings his hat, as he utters a long roar. Others join him, and from land they are answered by new hurrahs, a final greeting.

'Thingvalla' labours on. In the sky the flames are extinguished and the clouds are scudding.

In the cabin I had a chat with a young girl. Young, that is to say twenty-eight years old, and here that is called old. She was a teacher. She had had a place on some large estates, but now she had had enough of that and was leaving, all alone, and without references.

There might be a novel behind that. It is not everyone who would decide to travel to America after becoming a teacher and studying at Frøken Zahle's school.* Something must have happened. There could be unhappy love behind it, a broken heart, a crushed hope. But to be honest, she didn't look as if that was the case. Her forehead was uncreased, her mouth with its thin lips just a little tight. Only a poet would be able to read storms and misfortune into her features.

More than anything she looked a bit tired.

You don't need a novel in order to drive such an existence into exile. She is poor, with no family, and she is not pretty. She has not got married and knows she never will. Such a grey, monotonous, constant grind of a life, which ends in an institution, such a sad, lonely wandering along a dusty path, is that so attractive? What is provided for her heart? for her feelings? for her needs? To become an old maid with knitting needles and a lapdog and a few faded dreams for company?

Perhaps she has been unable to live off dreams, this narrow fasting-place for our abilities, starvation rations for our lives. Perhaps in her existence too there has been a disappointment which has made her see its emptiness, perhaps she has suffered, and *she* has been strong enough to refuse to swallow this disappointment like opium to send her to sleep. Now she is leaving.

But nevertheless – this is no novel. There are so many twenty-eight-year-old governesses, and they all have their novels, bottled like old potpourri. The only difference is that they are more sensible, they accept their lot, they warm up their old dreams every day and don't make too many demands on life. They stay at home; it is only the hotheads who leave. Or it may be that those who set sail are the most sensible of all. There is a great shortage of wives amongst the Scandinavians over there. If an unmarried girl arrives in a district they travel a hundred and fifty miles to see her, and most often propose at once .... That is what will probably happen to the teacher – and it can be very pleasant to make a good marriage – but it is not what you would call romantic.

I get up from my place and walk over to the entrance to steerage.

The air down there is stifling. I descend a couple of steps quietly, stop and look in. It is the upper deck. Men are sleeping, women and children lying on the bunks in the semi-darkness. Here and there a head pokes over the side in the light. Further in, lamplight falls right across a bunk. It is the driver's.

The wife is sitting up, rocking the baby, and the husband is sleeping with two boys next to him. Undressed as they are, half-hidden by an ocean of blankets, clothes and pieces of material which are spilling out everywhere, they look like ragged tramps ....

Further away, the stairs down look like a dark abyss.

I go up again. I don't want to see any more. Daylight will bring brighter colours, I will wait for day.

And the night will soon be over. Out in the east the lowest clouds are turning pink, and the twilight is drawing back across the sea like a curtain opening.

'Thingvalla' steams on to meet the day with its crowd of seekers after happiness.

II

DAY

People were rubbing their eyes on board 'Thingvalla'. All around in the steerage bunks they were a little dazed, waking up to find themselves lying all twisted up, after having slept restlessly. They were rubbing their eyes and trying to collect their thoughts.

The day before had been so confused. The farewells from home, the last glance, then once out in the sound the speeches and the cheers and the band playing and the national songs – the whole arrangement resembled a leisure cruise. They had not had any time to think how they felt or to collect themselves. They had simply joined in and shouted hurrah and made a noise; it may well be that there were things they wanted to drown out. Then the mood had become so strangely animated on the surface, with everyone attempting to show that *he* was a hell of a guy, and regarded the whole thing as just an everyday event ... . They concealed themselves from one another and played hide-and-seek behind the merriment.

The night was a little restless, as I said; outside the sea was rolling heavily, and in the hold people tossed to and fro for some time before falling asleep. They didn't talk very much, but each one lay listening to his neighbour's sighs, and no doubt stole the chance to relieve his feelings now and then by taking some deep breaths.

The first twenty-four hours had not been normal. But now it was morning, and now the journey was properly underway. So people made themselves comfortable, they settled down, they resigned themselves to their fate.

Yesterday they had just accepted things the way they were, been happy about everything and shouted hurrah and found everything to be delightful, simply because they had to say something, even though they felt indifferent about it all and didn't really give it any thought. But now they thought about the fact that they would be living here for a fortnight, and that a fortnight is a long time. So they began first of all to find fault, and then to improve matters according to taste.

The floor of the steerage hold was full of open chests and boxes; people set out their pans on the lids, hung small mirrors up on the walls of their bunks – in short, they composed their surroundings. Some brushed their clothes or took them out of the suitcase to examine them, and to check for the hundredth time that they had everything, that nothing had been forgotten. And while that was going on they got dressed or busied themselves in nightwear or coloured skirts or coarse shirts, with their braces hanging down loose and unbuttoned. Mothers hung clothes on the railings to dry, or rocked their children, or crouched down and suckled them on the edge of the bunk.

What a swarm of children! They're crawling between blankets and pillows on the bunks, they're rummaging in chests and boxes. There is not a single dark head amongst them, nothing but blondness, that pale dirty yellow of peasants, bleached by the sun and coarsened by the weather. And they're all yelling in chorus, in both Swedish and Danish.

So the steerage quarters on 'Thingvalla' look lively enough. In the middle the broad square opening with the stairs up to light and air. Between its beams and the bunks there is a wide passage which goes all the way round, where the children and the grown-ups are competing to make the most noise; along the walls are the bunks. The bunks are set up one above the other; they resemble the shelves for storing cheese on large estates, like broad trays with a raised edge – the kind that is used in hospitals for laying out corpses. But here there are duvets and blankets instead of a single sheet.

There are emigrant ships in which each bunk has its own canvas partition; that is not the case here. 'Thingvalla' was originally designed to transport goods, so it is somewhat primitive; the families live in something resembling borderless communism, where one territory merges into the next, and divisions are not strictly observed. I talk to my American merchant about that.

The New Yorker has certainly seen ships bound for America in which each family even had its own – admittedly tiny – cabin, a little cave which you had to yourself and where you could be alone. 'But you see,' he said, 'they're experimenting to see how it goes with "Thingvalla". So it may be that there are one or two things which are lacking – but believe me, there is much to make up for that. Emigrants who cross on a Danish ship have a guarantee of being decently treated – because if they're not, they immediately complain to Copenhagen, and they know where to find the company and make a public fuss. So they *have* to be treated decently if the company is going to survive. But if they emigrate from Hamburg, and find something to complain about on the way over – well, then their complaints might just as well be called crying in the wilderness.'

'But aren't the Hamburg lines pretty good?'

'Admirable – some are even exceptionally good – but there can be irregularities, and it's always good to have some recourse. It is possible to come across pretty much slave-like conditions on board an emigrant ship.'

We go down to the next deck: this is where the young women are. A couple of them, who are running around bare-legged and with not very many clothes on, scream and disappear into their bunks; others are brushing their hair or making themselves smart in front of their opened chests, which in this section are neat, and painted with black letters on a yellow background. They give names and dates and years, and the whole thing is shining with fresh paint.

One girl's chest is pink, with a wreath of roses around her name, which is painted in white. She took refuge in her bunk when we arrived, and in her haste she left the chest standing open. On top there is a real cashmere shawl, an album with many flourishes and three false plaits. Perhaps she is one of those who are going to get married.

Furthest down, still down the same staircase with air and light coming from the same square hole, which from up on deck just looks like the entrance to a cargo hold, there are the young single men. Here it does not look so cosy, and here the chests are not painted. The inhabitants are sitting around enjoying their morning pipes or skinning herrings, large fat herrings, which are served in tubs by the cabin boys.

'It's the best remedy for seasickness,' says the young doctor who has become my guide. The doctor has just passed his medical exams, and is crossing the Atlantic in order to see Niagara. That is quite understandable, and it is no wonder that the post of doctor on board the 'Thingvalla' is a popular one; you get

400 kroner and free passage for the pleasure. It is of course inevitable that there can be times out in mid-Atlantic when the pleasure is not an unmitigated one.

'Do they get plenty of herrings every day?' I ask the cabin boy.

'Oh yes – they get a tub full.'

'And they're allowed to eat as many as they want?'

'Yes – until they run out.'

The steward comes down the stairs with a large kettle. It's tea. There is a sudden stir, and people come forward with pewter saucepans and mugs. The sea air gives you an appetite. Butter is brought in on a large platter and placed beside the bread in the middle of the room. Sugar too is served *ad libitum*. Each one helps himself, and it is not small portions which are consumed down here in the men's quarters. From out of their chests they take sausages, glistening in greasy paper, and dry cheese which they cut into slices. It is lunch time.

'And they get all that for 120 kroner,' says the doctor, as he climbs up the stairs again. 'Crossing, accommodation, food and all – you can't complain that it's expensive.'

We go into the 'hospital'. It's not very large, this hospital. Four bunks with good bedding in a small room with a door out to the first-class deck. Behind the sail there are four more bunks for women.

'It's quite good,' said the doctor, 'so long as no-one is ill.'

'But if there was an epidemic on board, it would not be so pleasant.'

'That's true enough – and in that case I doubt I would see Niagara. But who builds emigrant ships for epidemics! Most of the sickness on board is constipation. Absolutely everyone gets constipated on board an emigrant ship, whether they're in first class or in steerage. Goodness knows why that should be!'

'So there are 600 passengers?' I ask.

'That's right. Well, the last 200 will come on board today in Norway. Then we'll have a full complement.'

'And the hospital has eight bunks?'

'Ah,' – it's the New Yorker who has joined us – 'Here he is again then. Has his pessimism now filled the whole of "Thingvalla" with smallpox patients and consequent deaths and burials? He is completely incorrigible, Doctor, completely incorrigible. Do you think that just because of remote possibilities they should turn half the ship into a sick-bay waiting for an epidemic? That would really be a practical idea.'

'Well no, not exactly – but it is good to be prepared … .'

'Tell me, what arrangements do you think they've made about the boats?'

'The boats?'

'Yes, the lifeboats, my dear sir.'

'Surely that is a legal requirement.'

'Ye-es, but fortunately the law is sensible, and realises that if there were going to be *enough* lifeboats, we wouldn't have room on board for anything else. There, Doctor, look at him now, how shocked he looks.'

Over in the kitchen they are roasting and frying ready for dinner. It is soup day in steerage. A large bowl of soup for each of the 400 who are already on board demands a large pot and a large piece of meat in the pot.

'They use half a cow at a time,' says the doctor. 'Just think of feeding a small market town back home from one kitchen – and a floating one as well, where you can't send the maid off to market – and you'll have some idea of what the steward here has to think about.'

'What else do they have as well as soup?'

'A bit of meat and some bread.' The steward slices a piece to demonstrate. They certainly don't go hungry on 'Thingvalla'.

'And the other days – what do they get for dinner?'

'Gruel and fish; peas, cabbage and soup again, for as long as the fresh meat lasts. After that we just have to make do.'

'With salt preserves?'

'Yes, in the main. Although in first class the meat will hopefully last. That's why we have the pigs and chickens.'

I had seen the pigs and chickens. The poor animals had been seasick, and were grunting and clucking and did not look very appetizing.

Over in first class they were eating lunch.

The group were in relaxed morning toilette, dressing gowns, housecoats, and the ladies' hair was a little disordered. Obviously people were no longer self-conscious together; they were all merging into one family.

Lunch was plentiful, a cold table with all the delicacies of Copenhagen. Appetites were good.

Had anyone been seasick?

No-one at all. It was so calm on board. Everyone had slept well.

A couple of girls were pouring coffee. The ladies got out their crochet work, the gentlemen their books. A couple of them had not brought anything to read, so they made use of the captain's large encyclopaedia.

Up on deck people are beginning to get together. They have got to know one another this morning, and now they are obviously sitting down in groups of new acquaintances. The girls and women are industrious. They are knitting and sewing, and have got out their workboxes and bags. The men and boys are strolling around, or lying down on their backs or their stomachs.

There's a circle of youngsters over there: a few young girls in raincoats have pitched camp on some ropes, and at their feet three or four of the lads who are being 'sent away' have installed themselves. They are laughing so that you can hear them over the whole deck. Over in the shade of the cabin some older men are lying down reading, sweating with concentration. They are studying phrase books.

When you stand on the bridge you can see over the whole deck. The sun rises higher and higher, and its rays begin to bake the deck and its inhabitants; they look for shade under opened umbrellas or behind the engine room. It looks like a general siesta. There is something peaceful and restful about this sunlit deck and its small groups of citizens.

'It all looks idyllic, don't you think?' said the captain.

'Perhaps more like a kind of ceasefire. The troops are resting on neutral ground.'

'An army resting before battle – that's not bad,' says the doctor. He has been away to bandage a sprained finger.

'What happened to that woman?'

'Oh, she fell on the stairs. These stairs are not easy to negotiate.'

The morning passes, with the same groups still on deck, the same peaceful stillness amongst those who have nothing urgent to do, the same sun. The men are stretched out comfortably, asleep with their hands over their faces, the women constantly working.

Most of these four hundred are peasants, thick-set, sinewy fellows, blond wives, freckled and thin. The few townies keep to themselves. Most of them are strangely dressed: the young people in light overcoats and promenade hats and small shoes with high heels, the younger girls in raincoats and light hats, flimsy, already dishevelled. They look as if they're on a Whitsun trip to Møn.*

There are others too who are joining 'the Atlantic adventure'. They have affected sailor costume, large straw hats and long boots, and the young ladies have bound up their skirts and fastened scarves around their heads. They are the youngsters, and those who want to get married. They are playing at travelling to America.

Poor things – they are the ones you have to feel sorry for. The others, those with broad backs and sober dispositions, the skilled labourers, they will no doubt struggle and work hard – and be no happier than they were at home; but these, the luxury goods or sixpenny trinkets from life's bazaar – they will probably be smashed to pieces.

In the meantime all the youngsters are behaving like thoughtless soldiers: they laugh and joke until the drum starts to beat.

We guests will soon leave the table. We are already a long way up through the blue mountains and strange-shaped rocks of Kristiania Fjord, and we are now having our last meal on board 'Thingvalla'.

'So how has this crowd been recruited?' I ask.

'The agents recruit them.'

'Round them up, you mean,' I suggest.

'Not at all,' answers one of the company. 'These days that is not necessary. The desire to emigrate has reached epidemic proportions once again.'

'And why is that?'

'It's difficult to say. One single letter can start a fever in a village, or in a whole parish. They become restless and set off, family after family. You may well say it is a madness – but it's a madness which opens the veins of society, and that is a good thing.'*

'And you mustn't forget,' says the captain, who is carving the roast beef in slices which are excessive even for a giant's appetite, 'that out of the four hundred we have on board, about a hundred are being sent for by their families, who have made a new life over there and are now paying for their relatives to travel. That is the best section of the passengers.'

One of us praises the bread. 'It's been baked by our own baker – just a little chap.'

'Is he emigrating?'

'Yes; we had over fifty people applying for the place. They get free passage, and there's supposed to be a shortage of bakers right now. – Let us drink a toast to "Thingvalla", gentlemen, and to the new ships and the future.'

'And to *their* future,' says the New Yorker, pointing out to the deck, where the emigrants are gathered quietly in their ceasefire under the June sun.

'Yes – to *their* future!'

There was a moment's pause. No doubt each of us had his own thoughts and hopes as he drank that glass of good Burgundy.

When we left the table we shook many hands and were given many greetings to pass on. More than one eye glistened during those greetings, and more than one handshake was heartier and firmer than the kind one normally exchanges with a stranger. I bring those greetings here – from one stranger to another, I send them to all the families and all the friends who are following 'Thingvalla''s travels in their thoughts.

Up on deck people crowded together, waving and shouting. We were slowly approaching the quayside in Kristiania.

'Thingvalla' lay at anchor in the fjord until evening. Towards sunset we watched it from the balcony of Viktoria Hotel,* raising anchor and steaming out into the fjord. It was perfectly still, and the smoke from its funnel remained like a dark cloud in the clear summer night for a long time after the ship itself had disappeared behind the mountains. Then the smoke disappeared too.

Out on the islands people were already beginning to light fires in the clear evening. It was Midsummer Eve.

Translated by Janet Garton

24. The Fire

I shall try to write as calmly as possible. But when I raise my eyes, I can see a ceaseless fiery rain of sparks falling just outside my windows, and the constant cracks from the burning palace reach my ears like cracks from an exchange of gunfire.* I am writing with shaking hand and feverish head. Much of what I write will overlap with others, but that is unavoidable.

The message was brought to me at half-past six. There was a disturbance in the street, and as I dashed out, people were gathering in doorways and outside houses; I was greeted by a subdued fear, as if before an approaching earthquake. The sky was ablaze, and you could already see the flood of light, like a purple stream punctuated with dark smoke. By the cathedral the sparks were falling like rain. But still no-one knew where the fire was. People were shouting 'Christiansborg'. As I was running, whilst the flames rose red above a side street, I heard a long, female cry. It was a young girl, who fell forwards to the ground.

Then from Høibro Square I saw the flames shooting out of the palace roof. From the windows up here you could see tongues licking along the whole ridge. I went down and pushed my way once more through the crowd; people were silent and dejected. No-one spoke to anyone else. Women were crying and wailing. The fiery rain was as violent as if it was being thrown out of a crater; blown by the increasing gale, the sparks fell like a fiery snowstorm over

Thorvaldsen's Museum,* over the church, over the house where I had been and the canal.*

I walked through St. Jørgen's Gate. The confusion was indescribable. You could hear repeated shouts for water, yells to save the collection of paintings. There was utter chaos. The pumps were working hard as soon as there was any water, but there was none. The fiery rain was falling so thickly over the palace square that sparks landed on your clothes.

The continual crackling of flames sounds like salvoes of bullets. People are running pellmell into one another in order to save the most ridiculous things. I hurried up to the picture collection. By the windows the fire is so fierce that it can singe your hair. The light from outside is the only light in the gallery. People are storming in and out, tearing the paintings from the walls and throwing them on the floor in order to break the frames apart.

Opposite across the square the colonnade is gleaming like an Attic temple at sunset. We run around with a few dim lights in order to choose between the paintings, but it is impossible. The shutters are pulled open, so that we can see as much as possible; we pull down the pictures at random. I get hold of some small Dutch paintings, someone else grabs them out of my hands, and we go on in order to find others. Jerichau's statue of Ophelia is caught by the gleam,* and seems to come alive in the flood of light. The figure is prized from its plinth, which resembles a coffin when it is turned over. That is how it is carried away. The ceaseless booming betrays the fact that the fire is becoming more intense. 'The Panther Hunter' is carried down.* Calls of 'Hurry, hurry!' resound constantly through the gloom.

There is no panic here. Only a busily bustling nightmare. I go down the stairs. People are crowding up all the time. They throw the paintings down and go up again. There were paintings high up near the ceiling which could not be saved. One single figure was suddenly illuminated in the gloom by the gleam of the flames.

I went over to the other side of the gateway, up into the parliament building. It was deserted. A fireman ran past, shouting: 'There's no *water* here!' The corridors were awash with streaming water. I met no-one. Smoke began to fill the corridors, and it was completely black. I pushed my way through to the parliament chamber and inside it. In the ceiling there was a hole through which the flames were flickering down with licking tongues. And the whole time those little cracks of the fire up above, and right over me those small convivial flames caressing the cornices. It didn't look as if anything had been saved. Books and manuscripts were strewn on the tables and across the floor. You might almost think there had been a stormy meeting, which had degenerated into fisticuffs.

A man came running along the corridor with the intention of saving something or other. It was official documents, locked in a money chest which was so heavy that you couldn't drag it along. Two men tried to break it open. It was impossible. In one of the adjoining rooms an astral lamp was burning quietly in the middle of a coffee table. It looked homely.

The corridors were black with smoke and soot. I heard some long shouts of command as people fled – and I had to get out. Immediately after that the ceiling collapsed. I ran across the palace square. It was positively hailing balls of fire and red-hot rubble. Between the columns it was pelting as if with bullets. There was scarcely any shelter between the pillars. The square was emptied. It was abandoned to this destruction without hope of rescue.

I made my way over to the parliament building again, to the opposite entrance. In the foremost room the flames were boring like small sharp-nosed bullets through a white door. It looked as if it was being shot at and perforated, until in the end it looked like a bottle-stand. I walked past the door and out into a dark corridor. I took careful note of the way, in order not to get lost. But until my dying day I will hear that ceaseless crackling of flames above my head. And the rumble as of a mighty trapdoor crashing down over my head. I reached a staircase. The flames had attacked it from below, and the charred landing hung in front of me, covered by a seething swarm of sparks. There was a terrible beauty about that fragment of a staircase hanging in the midst of the flames. Beneath it was a bonfire.

I took it all in with one single glance.

Behind me I heard a crash; it was the door to the chamber which fell. In one second there was a burning profusion of fire – a brightly shining colour, victorious and exulting. The two or three of us there fell back, shouting to a couple who were arriving that there was danger, and it was too late. Streams of useless water were flowing over our feet.

Two of us forced our way in at a different point. There were some rickety back stairs, and water everywhere; an empty hosepipe was slumped in the middle of the mess. This staircase was dreadful. We met some firemen, who were shouting for water: water, water, or all is lost. Strong men were wringing their hands, cursing. There was no leadership. 'Tell them we must have water' – 'There's no more we can do.' People were rushing down to get water. We passed an iron door which was red-hot. During the fire I saw three such iron doors, and no-one had dampened them down.

This door had buckled under the force of the fire. It was warmer than in a baker's oven, a stinging, unimaginable heat. We forced our way further up. A fireman was on watch at the top. We were almost at the roof, and from nearby we could hear the roar of the flames. The six or seven faces I could see were white, despite the red glow.

Suddenly there was a shout of 'Get back!' and a burning beam fell past us. After that it was quite dark. I don't know what happened then. There were voices shouting 'Stop! Stop! It's burning beneath us.' But the cries were indistinct, and we did not stop. We rushed on in the pitch blackness and fell over the hoses which lay forgotten on the stairs. The smoke filled the room with a choking and impenetrable mass. Such seconds, when you hear the shrieks of fleeing firemen you can't see, together with the boiling of the flames along the landing you have just left – such seconds last for eternity.

We slipped in water and got up again; I pressed my handkerchief to my mouth and went on. So we got down. Then there were some terrifying bangs. They said it was the banqueting hall which had fallen in. From inside the building a long howl sounded.

I come across a soldier. His face looks scorched by the fire. He is wandering around like an automaton, swinging his arms aimlessly.

'Was that the banqueting hall?'

'Yes. I was just outside. They shouted for us to get out – three men were left inside. Then the roof fell in. They were just *there,* all three – so far away' – and he stretched out his arm, trembling – '*so* far. The three of them were buried at once – gone, underneath it. I could see the arm of the third one and got hold of it … . Ah – how he screamed, how he screamed … and then gone … we couldn't hold him … .'

I go in to the enclosed square again. The flames are leaping out of the first-floor windows. Then that dreadful crackling rose to the sound of an enormous storm. There was a frightful din from the fire, like the pounding of the sea itself. And in the midst of this witches' dance of fire the booming crashes of walls falling in.

In the parliament wing the bare walls were standing with gaping window openings, like open throats in to the merry yellow fire. So much fire.

We went back to the riding yard. The confusion was indescribable. The military are arriving in hordes, but no-one is in command. They are dragging furniture, cushions, bedclothes and knick-knacks out of the audience chamber. I see one soldier running past with a basket full of empty bottles, another with a single embroidered cushion. People are screaming and smashing windows out or in. There are no ladders and there is no water.

Then those of us standing in the yard saw a weak gleam of light just by a window above the archives of the High Court. It looked as if someone had placed a lamp covered by a shade just next to this window. The gleam did not fade; it was quite weak, but alarming. We shouted that it was burning, that it had caught hold just by this window. No-one heard. I saw a man urgently beseeching a superior officer to investigate whether it was on fire just there. Nothing was done. And for almost ten minutes we could see that weak lamplight – until with a sudden crack the windows exploded, and flames leapt out around the frame.

Then everyone began to shout. There were hundreds of people behind these rooms. In the chamber next door they broke the window, and shouted down. There were soldiers and civilians. We couldn't hear what they were shouting apart from: Fire! We saw them trying to call out to us … impossible. They waved and threw out long strips of carpet. It was no good.

There was a shout for ladders. There were none. Those which did arrive were not long enough to reach. One man climbed along the mezzanine and smashed a window in with an axe. And the people up there were still shouting something we could not understand. I had not felt afraid before, but now I was deadly afraid for those people who were running aimlessly to and fro up there, yelling something no-one could hear out into thin air and then running in again.

An old sergeant of the guards said: 'They're running wild up there … . Times like this, when people lose their heads … they don't know where there's a way in or a way out.'

Then they came out, leaping down from the mezzanine, crowding down the dark stairs. Hagar and Ishmael were dragged out in the midst of the throng and overturned in the mud.*

I was standing under the pillars, and heard once more that crackling which told me that the fire was up above me. Then flames leapt out from both sides and met. The palace was lost.

The whole of the inner courtyard seemed to be on fire. The heat was scorching our cheeks. I saw the king in the midst of a group with his two sons.* His face was horrified and pale, just like a stiff mask. He was kneading his fingers mechanically. I heard that he had given the order to blow up the gateway to the chapel. Everywhere people were calling for Zeltner.* He was nowhere to be seen. And down in the cellars the gas was still burning. They couldn't turn it off, no-one knew where the mains were. *So the gas went on burning in the midst of the burning palace.*

Everything was confusion. A Navy commander gives the order to chop down, break down, the wing over by the museum, the portals, everything. The crowd hurls itself against a gateway, which gives way with a crash under the pressure, and a scream rises from all throats.

I have never seen a sight like it. It looked as if those people wanted to tear down the walls with their fingernails. They get hold of hammers, axes, beams as weapons; they throw themselves against the walls, which remain desperately standing. We emerge into the churchyard, where everything is still dark. But thick plumes of smoke are streaming out of the windows. And always that dreadful roaring in your ears.

We went down into the cellar again. The inhabitants are rescuing their belongings by gaslight. When we come up, the storm is loosening burning rubble, which is falling around us. People are driving off with large artillery carts filled with a variety of things; the whole of this side of the palace is still dark. The whole church roof is covered in sparks like a layer of phosphorus.

We got out through the church gateway and walked the length of the palace. It was a blizzard of fire. It looked like glowing sticks of rockets shooting through the air; it was so brilliantly lit up that the gaslights looked like small tallow candles.

The whole of Gammelholm was illuminated by the gleam.* The statue of Frederik VII was silhouetted in front of the blaze.* I don't know how to describe it other than by saying that the fire was *whistling* around us. People were throwing books out of all the windows. The ones up above were yelling and tipping out masses of books, which we down below threw onto the lawns. Water was flowing everywhere. People sprang over the chain fence around King Frederik's statue and threw books up onto the plinth. In the midst of it all there was a simple wooden bed standing in the square. I found a book lying just under the burning wall. It bore the king's coat of arms. It was *Souvenirs intimes de Napoleon III.**

It was as if the air itself was blazing. Everything shone with fire. But the flames themselves were more yellowish-white, more 'playful' than the glowing air.

We walked into the library courtyard. Everything was on fire. Thorvaldsen's room was untouched as yet. There was fire on both sides. The gleam of the flames from the burning folding door lit up the frieze on the door opposite. You could see every figure in the glare. Then the curtains whirled up in the flames like rags, and the room was enveloped in fire … .

A corps of cadets dashed through the courtyard. Their clothes were singed. They had done a heroic job.

Whilst I have been writing, I have heard the distant roar of the fire – the window glass crashed and splintered as the chapel gateway was blown up. I have written with this fire continually before my eyes, with a stream of sparks over the house where I am writing. Now all that remains of the royal palace is the heavy walls with a hundred windows like flashing eyes. It looks dreadfully like a cyclops' house, built by a giant who is lighting up his enormous hall with a fearful bonfire.

The day which is dawning will reveal a charred, jagged ruin. That *was* Christiansborg.

Translated by Janet Garton

25. Letter from Herman Bang

On my travels again. Once more breathing in the dust from railways and seeing towns and steppes and forests from the speeding train. Once more pounding hotel stairs and giving tips to waiters for indiscriminate politeness and staying in the splendour of a caravanserai, cheek by jowl with shabbiness. Living in the atmosphere of strangers' indifference; seeing new things every day, which you leave twenty-four hours later and never have the time to grow fond of … .

In short: travelling.

Running through museums; leafing through catalogue pages and glancing fleetingly at masterpieces; gaping at a Raphael and walking indifferently past a Rembrandt; digesting dust and comments from the guides; gathering material in order to compose nonsense. Crossing off the beauties of nature in your Baedeker;* gawping at a moon over a mountain summit; lying on damp sheets; nodding over classical tragedies in a private box; ruining your stomach drinking water from ten different places; stuffing yourself mentally with indigestible things; becoming indifferent to everyone and everything. – In short: travelling.

Seeing a hundred streets which all look the same; eating the same food every day with different names; listening to a Murillo being insulted by idiocies in every language; seeing the same spruce trees covering the sides of twenty mountains; suffering under the Fahrbachs of fifty orchestras;* being pursued by Sabine women through fifteen towns.*

In short: travelling.

Travelling again. A brief tour. You find the time to write a couple of diary pages in the evening by the light of the hotel's traditional two candles.

Here are those random pages.

Hamburg.

The clamour from Jungfernstieg dies away.*

During the day the noise rises up towards my windows like a heavy shower, like the sea, which is calming down after a storm.

Now the Alster is resting quietly, and the gleaming boats are no longer thrusting out from under the Lombard Bridge, bringing disturbance along the quays. Silently dreams the beautiful Alster, with a hundred rippling cascades of gold, the reflections of lights from the banks.

The thousand steam engines are quiet, no longer drawing hissing and smoky breath. No longer can you hear the noise of the winches or the cranes down at the harbour, or the swearing and singing of the sailors. In the alleyways the young ruffians have stopped fighting. And around the stock exchange, where during the day you can hear the bartering of a thousand voices, all is silent.

Hamburg is sleeping, or seeming to do so.

Silently dreams the beautiful Alster, with rippling golden cascades over the water.

There are those who let themselves be photographed more often than Sarah Bernhardt:* the German Kaiser's family. No other family in the world demands so much loyalty on every street corner. There is no secret in their most private existence which they have not allowed the photographers' black box to reveal; there is no pose they have not struck in front of the aperture.

It is inconceivable that these people have time for anything else,* or can carry out any duties other than to pose for photographers. When you see the dozens of portraits of the Kaiser, you say to yourself that William the Conqueror must rule in the free time allocated to him by the photographers;* and when you think of how many hours the Prince of Bismarck has had to spend in front of painters, sculptors and photographers, you ask yourself in amazement how on earth that man has found the extra time – to create an empire.*

Just to stay with this picture for a minute. First the Kaiser. At his advanced age he seems to have a weakness for idylls. He lets himself be snapped on lonely forest benches with an ecstatic expression; or he dandles Germany's future – Prince Wilhelm's little son – on his knee with a prophetic smile;* or he appears by the cradle of the same future, leaning tenderly over it beside the delighted Princess Victoria (the child himself is bawling, as he has the sun directly in his face);* or he is the central figure in a forest scene which portrays the four generations from himself down to the aforementioned youngest German hopeful; or he is drinking regularly from the well in Bad Ems,* surrounded by visitors to the spa … .

Now he is old. Just look at this latest 'new edition'. He has become a trembling old man, William the Conqueror, hobbling along with his stick in that informal portrait. His military bearing has deserted him. Everyone knows that face, suited to a lower-ranking officer, which had no expression except fierceness. The Kaiser has it no longer. Now there is nothing other than age, the obliteration of senility, and in the midst of all this ruin the military moustache, which hangs limply and incongruously on features to which it no longer belongs.

How little intelligence there is in all these Hohenzollern faces.

Look at the Crown Prince. He resembles a cavalry officer who is good at swinging a sword, and who otherwise has no pretensions, because he knows very well that he is incapable of doing anything else. Fate seems to have predestined this man to take command in a guardroom; but as chance would have it, he has been picked out as heir to a throne. When he was brought up, his future kingdom was expected to be Prussia. A country whose kings passed the time drilling soldiers and hunting, and to whom it never occurred to aim at a grander place on the world stage. Until that day when the century's Mephisto chose one of those kings as his Faust and made him into a Kaiser – one day in Versailles.*

And that same day the Crown Prince's existence was turned upside down. He had learned how to be King of Prussia – who has since taught him how to be Kaiser?

His son is Prince Wilhelm. You can see that he is the third generation. All too clearly. Wadding has not succeeded here in creating the traditional Hohenzollern breadth. He adopts warlike poses with an uninterested smile, and his face, which is more distinguished than those of his grandfather and father, expresses nothing other than cold and disarming indifference.

It retains this expression in all situations. If you place Prince Wilhelm at the cradle of his firstborn, he will let himself be arranged with immobile features; if you present him in a fond handshake with Crown Prince Rudolf, his countenance expresses at most an empty astonishment;* if you introduce him to his future empire with his consort on his arm, he looks as solicitous as if the same lady were no more than empty air.

His little son has a mouth which extends as far as his ears. Such is his physiognomy, and it is difficult to read. But it may be that it is superfluous to try to make it out. It will be a long time until it is his turn, and thrones are no longer so secure. They have become strangely rickety in our days, and at times they fall on the heads of those who are waiting to mount them.

The supports which prop up Germany's imperial throne have also grown old. It is said that when Elizabeth of England became old, she always drove through London's streets with blinds drawn. She did not wish people to see her weakness and stop fearing her. Perhaps Germany's men of power should follow the example of the Queen of England. For these faces, which once at least expressed strength, are now merely stiffened old men's faces, which almost inspire pity.

How much effort has it not cost this Moltke to summon up this mask of calm and energy, suitable for a battle general.* Every fibre of his parchment face must have trembled before he succeeded.

Even the man himself – the iron man – the Chancellor – Bismarck. He who has so often threatened with his weakness, flirted with his feebleness – he is the best preserved of all. But in his cold face the expression of brutality has given way to an expression of bitterness. The lines around his mouth have become almost tormented. Is it possible that he, the Chancellor, who grew strong by despising other people, has arrived at the day when he feels the weight of the loneliness which has grown up around him because he too often showed his scorn to others?

Yet natures like his are always alone. They can find no-one of equal worth, and nothing which in the long run is worth loving. The mediocrity of others forces them into a painful loneliness. And they suffer in this loneliness. For their deepest secret is a deep, never admitted sensitivity. If you pry into the hearts of these men of iron you will find there a sentimental longing, an almost sickly softness … . Sickly because this feeling is hidden from the light, and they daily deny its existence.

Those men who founded the empire have grown more than old, they have grown weak. Germany will be inherited by Prince Wilhelm, with his face of an Uhlan lieutenant.* These features gaze out, empty and uninterested, at the gawping curiosity outside the windows. And with a feeling of antipathy one turns away from the Prince and looks once more at those three: the Kaiser, Bismarck and Moltke – who have grown so old.

Follow Elizabeth's example, you leaders of Germany. It is not wise to allow the people to stare at your weakness at close quarters. What you need is respect, not pity.

In no town are people so uniform as in Hamburg – the men, at least. The ladies attempt to stress their individuality by making a painstaking use of all the colours of the rainbow.

The gentlemen make no such attempt. Our Lord created one Hamburger, and all the others formed themselves in the same image. They acquired a slim-fitting brown-checked jacket, a pair of blue trousers and a pair of buttoned boots with pointy toes. They let their moustaches grow, parted their hair on the left, purchased a light brown hat – and young Hamburg was born. The young gentleman who arrives at the office at 9 o'clock, writes numbers in large ledgers until 2 o'clock, promenades along Jungfernstieg until 4 o'clock, eats dinner for 90 pfennigs, writes again in the large ledgers until 8 o'clock – and then goes to bed after having drunk beer for two hours.

Since their employment is the same, their appearance becomes the same.

In other towns there are people who study, people who live off the money of others, people who beat recruits, people who do nothing. In Hamburg there is only one kind of people: people who do accounts.

Hamburgers have cold and precise eyes. Even when they are promenading along Jungfernstieg, you can see that with their inner gaze they are reading a folio page of double-entry book-keeping.

In addition they are said to be brutal, and women are mathematical sums which they – apparently – quickly work out. They know that the bottom line is always the same, and they hate unnecessary inconvenience.

Translated by Janet Garton

26. The Chinese

About a month ago, down in Taubenstrasse in Berlin,* an enormous sign was erected, on which some strange symbols from tea chests were painted in striking triangles around some fantastic pictures of irons. That sign – and the three Chinese in the basement underneath the sign – were the beginning of the 'Chinese invasion'. That is, if one is to believe those panic-stricken columnists and half-educated popular authors – that whole flock who, ever since the day when that Chinese ironing sign was erected, have filled newspapers and journals and brochures with noisy superlatives about the 'swarm of rats from the East'.

For the time being the whole thing amounts to no more nor less than a sign, with the accompanying three washerwomen, or rather washermen, because with the Chinese it is always the male sex which washes. But those who claim that this single sign with its triangles is the beginning of a Biblical flood of Chinese, point out that these industrious ants always start by washing. It was as washerwomen they first infiltrated America; it was as washermen they began on the Sandwich Islands.* As innocent, harmless 'washerwomen', who scrubbed all the washing they were given until it fell to pieces – and otherwise slept on straw beside their tubs, lived on a couple of handfuls of cooked rice a day, never hurt a fly, and yet over the course of twenty years had stripped fruitful California like a swarm of grasshoppers, had depopulated the blissful Sandwich Islands amd threatened to plant the seeds of a frightful revolution over the whole of North America, a terrible civil war in the battle for bread .... All that, they say, began with these washerwomen.

That is why all the German newspapers are calling the population to arms, and appealing to all patriotic housewives to lock their linen cupboards. They warn the housewives of what is in store for their linen, their good, costly linen: do they have any idea of how these Chinese wash? They have scrubbed every honest sheet in California into rags, they have ripped every decent shirt in Chicago with their washing. And can respectable ears bear to hear about their ironing? They put water in their mouths and spit it out onto the starched cloth before ironing it. That is what the newspapers tell the housewives.

And they warn the husbands about all the dreadful destruction which is to come when these Chinese have finished with the linen cupboards; when they worm their way into the country's workforce; when they start to labour in the factories like an army of machines with hands and brains; when, after having stolen the secrets of maufacture from Europe, they form huge consortiums, which flood the market with their production of shoes, linenware, hats – of a thousand things with which Europeans are unable to compete, seeing as European workers don't agree to sleep fifty to a room, don't live on air and a few portions of rice, cannot retreat from the requirements of a human being to the needs of an animal – just as surely as you can never make Europeans into Chinese.

These panic-stricken journalists explain all this and more to housewives and husbands, and achieve – possibly nothing at all. Because these good Chinese people in Taubenstrasse do their laundry so cheaply, after all. And who would not be glad to save ten øre on each starched shirt, at a time when money is in short supply, and when the shirt front is equally clean? It is likely that the Chinese will get plenty of laundry, and there will be many divine basement ironing parlours, just as there already are many genuine tea outlets, and after the ironing parlours will follow shoe factories, and after the shoe factories, hat factories – because the shoes are cheap, just as the laundry was cheap, and the hats will be cheap, just as the shoes were a giveaway. And people are looking for bargains in our competitive age.

Well, what of it? Is it such a misfortune if there is the same law for the 'sons of heaven' as for those of earth,* and if these busy bees make and sell their shoes and hats as cheaply as they do? America has outstripped Europe in productivity, just as Germany has again outstripped France and England – or is about to do so; now the Chinese are outstripping America and beginning in a small way to set up laundries for the Germans. It is simply a matter of dog eats dog in the great open marketplace.

Nevertheless, one does have misgivings about it.

For it is certainly true that the Chinese have plundered California. Whatever they earn, they take home with them; they are happy living abroad, but they all take the proceeds back home in order to die at home. They were brought in by factory owners and large landowners, who wanted to profit from their work. They invaded all areas of work and wiped out all competition. Emboldened by their success, they pushed further and further towards the East. Laws, prohibitions, deportations – nothing stopped them. As with certain migratory animals, who follow their instincts to undertake a predetermined migration over water, over walls, and through death without pausing, this great migration seems to be unstoppable. And for as far as it reaches, it seems undeniable that the land is ruined for the 'white working man'; no-one can prevail against this foreign doggedness and these modest living requirements. Across the whole of prosperous America, the hundreds of thousands of Chinese are already regarded as the deadly enemies of the country's welfare.

All of this is true enough: this Chinese question, prompted by three washerwomen – who are men – is not simply a bubble which has been blown up by journalists on the hunt for material. But how can it be solved and how can it be prevented? Will there not in Europe, as in America, be large employers who will be pleased to solve the whole 'labour question' by taking on this extraordinarily cheap workforce, who know nothing of strikes, who know nothing of demands, nothing of equal rights – but merely labour, labour, labour, like the machines themselves? And if such employers exist, who is going to forbid them to employ the workers they wish to?

But then – then we are in California.

Or is it possible that in this best of all worlds – where everything is changing, and yet there is nothing new under the sun – the rest of the earth will build a wall against China, as China once built its wall against us? And if we want to – *can* we build walls strong enough to hold against these 450 – four hundred and fifty! – million souls, who dig like rats, who toil like ants, who cannot be held back by water or by mountains?

It is possible that it is not only our linen cupboards we should be locking and bolting.

Bernhard Hoff*

Translated by Janet Garton

27. Smart

Nowadays, our market towns have also acquired their 'men-about-town'.

In appearance, they are exactly like those of Copenhagen – as alike as two peas in a pod. They are English-suited, patent-leather-booted, grey-gloved and à-l'Anglaise-coiffured.* In their manner they are just as true to the ideal as in their apparel. Their shoulders are relaxed, they speak through their teeth and affect an air of lethargy which is only interrupted by those moments when it is suddenly important to show how smart they are.

For these gentlemen from the market towns are smart, just as are their colleagues in Copenhagen.

They are young men, whose aim it is to expand the businesses they have inherited or purchased with the speed expected nowadays. A small and steady income is not enough, either for their customs or for their ambitions. That is why they prefer a lightening coup, and they transform their enterprises as swiftly as possible into impressive-sounding stock companies, in which they themselves become directors – a most up-to-date title – and often own all the shares as well.

But despite all these 'European' efforts, our towns will nevertheless remain neither more nor less than Danish market towns, and the arena is not extensive enough for a huge profit or a grandiose coup.

One day, when our young businessman has built himself a villa on the fjord, has provided himself with horse and carriage and a dinner service with the arms of the town and his monogram, he falls off his own roof and breaks his neck – unless he has also provided himself with a railway ticket in advance of the catastrophe and has gone travelling, accompanied by all his English valises.

However things turn out for him, his example does not deter others. His colleagues carry on.

Amongst them there are also lawyers. Their type is equally stylish and correct. In their apparel they pay scrupulous attention to the shifting demands of the time of day. They owe their careers to an elegant slimness and a speedy dispatch of all business. The citizens of the town gladly and confidently entrust their properties and their cash to those slim white hands.

They even gain easy admission to the country estates on the basis of their wordly-wise scepticism, their pleasing voices and their perfect table manners. They count the landed gentry among their clients, and they get a seat on the boards of the local banks. At the same time they arrange small dinners; they are leading lights in the private entertainments of the bourgeoisie, and employ twice as large an office staff as they need. Every week they spend a day and a night in Copenhagen.

During all these activities, money runs particularly quickly through their slim fingers, and they take the cash sometimes from one of their coffers and sometimes from another. They are so busy that they don't even have the time to check which coffer they are actually using – until that fateful hour arrives when all the coffers are empty, and they discover that the contents of the money chests were not always strictly speaking their own.

On that day they follow the example of the businessmen, and arrange to get themselves a passport – either for a long voyage in this world or for a voyage over into the next world. They have lived fast, and they disappear even faster.

In order to be followed by the next ones. For the prototype does not die out.

Translated by Janet Garton

28. An Event

The Danish Automobile Association has been founded.*

This is an important, a decisive event, which ought to be greeted with unfeigned joy by all those who appreciate practical advances in our country. It ought also to be welcomed by all those who are patriotic enough to feel satisfaction every time our little motherland can take first place in the advancement of the human race.

The importance of the automobile for transport is preoccupying many minds over the whole world. But even in France, the home of motor clubs,* they have not got much further than driving races and using motor trucks in their large factory complexes.

The Danish Association has been created with a clearer and broader vision. In our country it is the post which will be carried by motor vehicles, and it is the stagecoach routes which will be replaced by automobile routes.

I would be bold enough to claim that the consequences of this upheaval are incalculable.

When I recently wrote in my series of articles 'Around the Country' in *København*, in connection with the Hornbæk railway line,* about the certain and imminent victory of automobile routes, I had – strange as it may sound, this is actually true – no idea that the Danish Association was so close to being launched. It was simply the sight of a road built for automobiles, combined with my long experience of travelling around our flat country, which gave rise to my firm conviction that automobiles are a method of transport which is perfectly suited to this land. Roads for automobiles make perfect sense in the eyes of all of those who are accustomed to travelling across country.

Perhaps we should make a start on some of our smaller islands. Langeland, Mors, Møen, Taasinge, Ærø, Samsø – all would vie for the attention of the new association.

But perhaps the greatest and most fruitful opportunities would be in our moorland districts.* Here the speed of progress would be inestimably quickened with the help of the automobile.

Now we must hope for two things.

The first is that the cautious – far too cautious – automobile law must either be changed rapidly,* or that its interpretation must be flexibly adapted to the demands of the transport network.

The other thing we must hope for is that no more small railways will be constructed until the new association's activities have clarified how far automobiles will be practicable. In my opinion, small private railway lines will no longer be required in the time of motor vehicles, and they will soon be outdated.

Here I am thinking, for example, of the railway on Bornholm.* This railway line passes through a completely flat terrain. Over this terrain it is only thirty kilometres long. On this stretch of thirty kilometres it has fifteen stations and stops in addition to the two terminuses. That means that along the track seventeen station buildings or shelters have been built, and each one of these requires its own staff or attendants. The amount of traffic has not been able to sustain all these expenses. The Bornholm railway is operating with a deficit which no-one expects to be eliminated.

All this waste of money could have been avoided with an automobile route constructed along the excellent country roads – and if they used automobiles, travellers would have made their journeys far more quickly.

Then there's a railway like the Hornbæk line. Whatever other people might say, for me it would be a great mistake in this time of upheaval to push for or insist upon the construction of this branch line, with its multitude of stops. If there is anywhere where we ought to wait a little and see what happens, it is here.

Yet one single mistake will count for nothing in the face of the massive movement which the Danish Automobile Association will speedily set in motion.

Translated by Janet Garton

29. In a Flash

Berlin.*

Just one hour ago, or perhaps not even that, immediately outside my house – literally just outside the front door – I was witness to the most frightful, the most ghastly event, for all its quietness, which my eyes have ever seen … .

I am on my way home and just about to open the front door when I hear the blare of a car just a few feet away, in the street to my right – and then again, the sound of a horn; and I see a lady, a tall slim lady, running out – across the street, running a few steps and stopping, then running again, straight into the car.

Right in front of the car – right into the car.

And she is caught and thrown and the car surges over her – over her neck. Over her neck with one wheel, as if she had been executed … .

Her body lay in the middle of the road, with its neck severed, in a pool of blood.

Her face was turned upwards. With eyes open, it looked like the face of a wax doll.

And when people came running, calling out, horrified and confused, and lifted her up – she was stone dead – she looked like one of those mannequins exhibited in shop windows.

The car had stopped.

The chauffeur helped to lay the dead woman inside the car. The covers were filled with blood, which ran down over the running board … .

I have never seen anything as shocking as this running out and then being dead – in a flash.

Translated by Janet Garton

Epilogue

30. Herman Bang on America

Just at the close of editing we received a letter from Herman Bang, written five days before his death. As well as promising us future contributions and pictures, he gives an account, through editor Emil Opffer, of his impressions of New York.**

New York, 23 Jan. 1912

Immediately upon his arrival here in America yesterday, Herr Bang had vanished, and we spent the entire day phoning New York's hotels and express companies in search of him.

Finally we tracked him down, but it wasn't easy. The difficulty was increased by the fact that for Herr Bang, the telephone has not yet been invented. To date he has never succeeded in holding a telephone receiver to his ear, and there will be seven Sundays in a week before that happens.

We found him at Hotel Astor, right in the heart of New York. He had arrived in the night on the German steamer 'Moltke', completely unexpected, and that was why the many friends Herman Bang has across the world, and which he also has in New York, weren't able to meet him at the quayside.

It's been eight years since we last saw him. His hair is not as smooth or as thick, his face has become a little fuller, but the ravishing smile, the unforgettable sparkle in his eyes, the booming laughter like a walrus baying in the polar night, are all exactly as they were in the good old days, and in his attire, he's as fastidious and eccentric as ever.

We immediately took him underground, swooshing off at ninety miles per hour on New York's Subway Express, and here, as everywhere, Herr Bang was a magnet for people's gaze. The small, dapper gentleman with the gold-knobbed cane, the sea-lion-golden travel coat and the road-grey hat is immediately conspicuous among these Americans, who set such store by looking alike, one piece of dry straw identical to the next. Herr Bang is himself everywhere, and nowhere does he seem more peculiar than in America, where people walk around daily with a perpetually beardless, stereotyped business physiognomy. Everyone exactly alike.

'You were delayed by two days, Herr Bang?' we asked, with the windows of the express rattling.

'Storm,' Herr Bang replied, telegram-style. 'We got caught in a snowstorm that was out of this world. I had told the captain that I so wanted to see a storm, and we were provided with one. I was sitting in the bath when it was at its fiercest, and there was a noise as though a drunken giant was tumbling about between the metal walls. And up above the siren wailed. I entered the dining hall ... everyone was drinking champagne, and everyone was talking of a hurricane. When the weather settled, I said to the captain: "Was that really a proper storm?" With a smile he said: "It seems Herr Bang won't be satisfied until the ship is turned upside down!"'

We left the subway, and moments later we stood on the 22nd floor of the Singer Building's tall tower. Far below us the white smoke drifted across the landscape over to the other state, New Jersey, from which we are separated by the river so diligently utilised by all of Europe's emigrant steamers, the Hudson.

'Well, Herr Bang,' we said, after he had polished off a couple of Havana cigarettes, 'what do you think of New York!'

'It seems to me,' says Herr Bang, whose composure New York does not appear to ruffle, 'that New York's streetscape doesn't differ significantly from that of Europe's big cities ... nowhere near as different as the prevailing view in Europe. Tracks above and below the ground for example are not at all startling to someone who has lived in Berlin in the last few years. The speed or feverishness is if anything greater in Berlin. And the public's attitude and nature seems practically the same to me.

'I think Americans are most "American" when they are travelling. On "Moltke" the American passengers played at being American far more than they do the moment they've set foot on dry land.

'Naturally, the buildings are taller. So immensely tall. But just as in the Alps you cannot measure the height of the Alps, so you can't measure the colossal height of the buildings, and it's incredible how quickly the eyes grow accustomed to them. Only when you are on the rooftops or on a bridge do the gigantic buildings tower up almost like in a fairy tale.

'As far as the hotels are concerned, they're so full of technical wonders that they are rather difficult to live in. There are so many buttons to press that handling such complicated devices requires an enormous amount of practice, and it is easy for the uninitiated to set an electric fan in motion when you intend to switch on an electric light. Edison, who has supplied his countrymen with so many comforts, causes the foreigner, on the other hand, many onerous surprises.* If, for example, you understand the mechanism of the bath, the mechanism is undoubtedly ideal. But if you don't understand the hundreds of taps, it's simply impossible to have a bath.

'As for the service in American hotels, I am sure that is also ideal ... for those who have become accustomed to it. For a European, it's the exact opposite. In order to make everything as practical as possible, the service is divided into so many departments that everything becomes as impractical as possible. For example, a waiter who brings my tea cannot fill my inkpot, because filling inkpots is the work of another department. And the lady who makes my bed can by no means supply me with towels. For hanging up towels is the responsibility of a different lady entirely. So practical arrangements for non-Americans turn out to be fraught with equally many difficulties.

'But naturally: you know that you find yourself in the most practical country on the planet. If you had not been aware of that fact, you would think the exact opposite.

'As it happens,' – Herr Bang continues – 'I am here on an all too brief stopover. In India the impressions, even the briefest, will strike the consciousness and the nerves with the full force of the exotic.* They don't do that here. – And any statement about such hastily viewed things easily becomes stupid and ridiculous. Some powerful impressions of beauty remain. The river at night with the colossuses along its shores, all lit up, the giant bridges spanning the water ... I'm sure that can never be forgotten. That sight enriches the soul. It is always the one big impression that is worth the travails of the long roads and the journey. New York at night is worth the passage across the ocean.'

It's clear that Herr Bang is not overly burdened with pleasant impressions upon his arrival, but perhaps the impressions will be improved before February the sixth, when he sets off from San Francisco for Japan. Because America improves on closer acquaintance.

In only a few hours Herman Bang can describe more than even the storyteller from Baghdad can in an entire week. His mind is a gem shop, and each small story is a pearl. It's no wonder that his stay here in New York has been a celebration for us, his friends, who already knew of this most entertaining storyteller out of all of the two-and-three-quarter million Danes. A few random notes on what he told us while here in New York:

'You think my hair is growing thin. Bald, you think. But that has happened in the past four months, travelling through Norway – Sweden – Russia. It was such an arduous journey. And there on the top, that is from where the French gendarme slashed me with his sabre. However did that happen? Well, let me tell you: there was some student unrest in Paris,* and it was terribly bad, so bad that 30,000 men were bivouacked in Luxembourg Gardens. At night there was a dreadful racket on the other side of the Seine, and I ran across the bridge to see what it was. The Parisians possess great technical skills in staging a revolution, and now the masses, by pressing together into one great phalanx, had toppled two kiosks and a tram, which they doused in petrol and set alight. Just then the Brigade Centrale arrived, galloping into the square. The Brigade Centrale is the worst uniformed gang France possesses, and it is only set loose when something particularly bad is underway. Forced to fan out, the masses were pressed toward the Palais de Justice, as I was crossing the square. It was in front of Notre Dame that it happened. All at once, a gendarme is shouting at me: "Ma-r-r-r-ch!" "Yes sir," I answered in French, "I'm going, I'm going!" Naturally I should just not have replied, but simply run away, for all of a sudden the gendarme flashed his sabre through the air and it struck me right on my head. There I lay, bleeding, slumped in the dust. I arrived at the hospital unconscious, and it wasn't until the next morning that I awoke. They thought I would die. I was told that when I was wounded I shouted: "*M'ont tué!*"* But I have no personal recollection of that.'

'Where am I going to spend my birthday, April 20th? In India. "The night will be spent in the compartment," it says in my programme. Besides, I never notice whether it's my birthday or not, and Christmas Eve is the worst day I know. I do decorate the Christmas tree for all those back home, but ... .'

'Were the reviews kind to you in Russia?'

'Oh, yes, but the press over there is very bold. The review from the official government newspaper in Moscow, *Novoye Vremya*, opened with these words: "A typical morphinist, everyone said when the curtain went up."* I really am no morphinist, but even if that was so, it really does not do to write like that. And all the papers wrote: "Herr Bang is badly cross-eyed." A friend of mine read the review out loud to me from one of the papers, and I commented: "Doesn't it also say there that I'm cross-eyed?" "Yes," my friend answered, "I'm coming to that." Ha-ha!! Each country to their own. In Russia they wrote that I was cross-eyed, in Sweden the papers all wrote about my gloves. Yes, is that not strange. But listen to this: in Hamburg there was one paper that tore me to shreds, before ending with these words: "One thing we must admit: Herr Bang still has beautiful legs!" Ha-ha!!'

'You ask me about Russia.* Let me tell you about a distinctive feature from that country. When I crossed the border, four loathsome customs officers entered the compartment and started rummaging through my hand luggage. Everything was turned inside out in the most merciless fashion. And then they asked me if I had a revolver. I had no revolver. It was nine o'clock in the evening before we arrived in St. Petersburg. Here my three *large* suitcases were meant to be inspected, but they weren't even opened. There could have been 3000 revolvers inside. My hand luggage was searched in the most meticulous way, my suitcases not at all. But this is Russia: no logic, no principles!'

'One thing I'll never forget from Russia: the Kremlin. If you haven't seen the Kremlin, you haven't seen Russia.'

'I had an amusing incident over there. In Moscow I received a letter from a female student. She wrote: "You don't know how beloved you are in Russia . . You don't know how often we talk about you and discuss your ideas." There I had to laugh – ha-ha!! – because the truth of course is that there isn't a spark of an idea in my books. Fortunately.'

'During my stay in St. Petersburg, I heard Russia's greatest singer. Chaliapin, he's called.* He's infinitely bigger than Caruso.* Such a great actor I'd never seen before. And as a singer, he is staggering.'

'In Moscow I saw the Moscow Art Theatre,* where great importance was placed on the tiniest details. *Hamlet* had been rehearsed for a year, and yet they'd only just completed the read-throughs. To prepare for *Julius Caesar*, on three occasions they had hired special trains and transported even the extras down to Rome, so that they could familiarise themselves with the Capitol. Isn't that tremendous?'

'You want to know about the journey I once made from Denmark to Paris to see my rooms in Rue de Rivoli?* Yes, I was working on *Mikaël*,* and part of the story took place in my former home. I had to experience the smell of the rooms, before I could finish writing it.'

'Where did I write *Katinka*?* At a kitchen table in Vienna. There were so many bedbugs. Oh, I was so poor back then. Then one day a messenger arrived from the ambassador, Count Knuth, catching me unawares at the kitchen table. Count Knuth had been a good friend of my grandfather, the great Doctor Bang. "But this will just not do, Herr Bang," the messenger said. They offered to support me in various ways, but I moved to Prague, where I stayed for two years.'

'Have I been translated into English? No. Though *The White House* has been published in England, and the only review I saw went like this: "Denmark must truly be a strange land, and Danish literature a mysterious literature, if a book like *The White House* can be published. This is not a book. This is a kindergarten."* Ha-ha!! Once, though, I was close to getting my foot in the door. My Dutch connection had written to me, saying that an English publisher wanted to visit me in Copenhagen, and he told me to demand a proper price. One morning at nine o'clock there was a ring at my door, and the servant announced a stranger. "What the hell is the man thinking," I replied. "I haven't even had a bath. Tell him to come back at twelve."

I expected him at twelve. Soon it was one, two. At four o'clock I drove to Hotel d'Angleterre. Quite rightly there had been an English publisher. He had come directly from London early that morning to pay me a visit, but he had already set off back to London, in full fury. So now, for the time being, I have to content myself with the other eight languages in which my books are published.'

'You ask me about my meeting with the famous French painter, Claude Monet.* Yes, it was at a spa in Norway. One day Monet said to me: "Herr Bang, you're a very modest man. I've lived with you for weeks now, and you haven't said anything about being a great novelist. I have ordered *Tine* from Paris.* They call me the greatest impressionist among painters. I call you the only impressionist among authors." You will understand that my heart was pounding, moved by these words from such an outstanding man. Incidentally I have made use of his outward appearance for the artist in *Mikaël*. An altogether remarkable man … imagine, he had thirteen children. A Frenchman with thirteen children. Yes, it sounds unbelievable. Ha-ha!!'

This is but a small selection of what Herr Bang told us. But alas, when it comes to some of the most interesting things, he said to us: you must never print that! Every journalist knows the pain entailed in keeping a truly good anecdote to oneself. But discretion is a journalist's most sacred duty!

Translated by Paul Russell Garrett

Notes

Short Stories

A Poet's Wife

First published as 'En Digters Hustru. En Studie af Herman Bang' in *Nutiden i Billeder og Text*, 29.2.1880, 7.3.1880, 14.3.1880.

Republished in book form in *Tunge Melodier*, 1880.

The Mistress

First published as 'En gammel Veninde' in *Nationaltidende*, 30.7.1882. Republished in book form in *Præster*, 1883.

p. 36 *Pollux:* Castor and Pollux were twin half-brothers in Greek and Roman mythology, sons of Leda and Zeus, and who later became the star constellation Gemini.

Franz Pander

First published in *Excentriske Noveller*, 1885.

p. 41 *Kleine Dammstrasse:* a street in Hamburg.

p. 42 *Jungfernstieg:* a street in the centre of Hamburg with shops and restaurants.

Neuer Wall: an exclusive shopping street in Hamburg.

p. 44 *Der Bub' wird Glück haben:* That lad will do well.

Schön – eine dritte Stellung im Restaurant vacant: Right – there's a vacancy for a third-class waiter in the restaurant.

Na – ein netter Zugvogel – nicht?: Well, that's a fine bird of passage, don't you think? (Has a sexual connotation: a young man of loose morals.)

p. 45 *Louis – wie du bist – Louis*: Louis – how you're behaving – Louis. In German, 'Louis' can also suggest a pimp.

p. 50 *Ganymede:* a handsome Phrygian youth in Greek mythology. Zeus fell in love with him and carried him off to Olympus disguised as an eagle, where he served as Zeus' cup-bearer.

p. 51 *Carl Schulze's Theatre:* a popular theatre on Langenreihe, now Reeperbahn, in Hamburg. From 1865 it was known as Carl Schulze's Theatre.

Aber – es hat keinen Werth: But there's no point.

Gänsemarkt: a square in the centre of Hamburg.

Charlot Dupont

First published in *Excentriske Noveller*, 1885.

p. 53 *Palais du Trocadéro:* this was built for the 1878 World Fair in Paris, and later used as a concert hall.

Herr Kakadu der Schneider: the song 'Ich bin der Schneider Kakadu' ('I am Kakadu the Tailor') originates from Wenzel Müller's 1794 comic operetta *Die Schwestern von Prag* (*The Sisters From Prague*), and was the basis

for Beethoven's popular Kakadu variations.
Napoleon after Leipzig: presumably a reference to a painting by the Belgian artist Antoine Wiertz, which Herman Bang saw in the art museum in Leipzig and described in an article in *Nationaltidende* 21.8.1881.
Adelina Patti: an Italian soprano (1843-1919), the most famous and best paid soprano of the period.

p. 54 *an Erard piano:* Sébastien Érard was a French instrument maker who specialised in the production of pianos and harps, and pioneered the modern piano.

p. 55 *all shop-bought:* it was normal during this period for those who could afford it to commission made-to-measure garments.

p. 56 *Sarasate:* Pablo de Sarasate (1844-1908) was a Spanish violin virtuoso.

p. 58 *Baku:* the largest city on the shores of the Caspian Sea – in other words, the furthest point of a broadly European culture.
Charlot Dupont made Patti money: the meaning here is a little unclear, but it may mean that he made as much money as Adelina Patti.

p. 59 *broken the bank in Baden:* the casino in the southern German resort of Baden-Baden was famous.

p. 60 *Miss Tisbyrs:* possibly a reference to the American soprano Emma Thursby (1845-1931), who undertook a European tour in 1878-82.

p. 63 *the Radetzky March:* a march composed by Johann Strauss Sr. (1804-49) and dedicated to Field Marshal Joseph Radetzky von Radetz.
Pesth: an old spelling for Pest which, with Buda on the west bank, forms the capital of Hungary.

p. 64 *Pauvre enfant – mon pauvre enfant:* Poor child – my poor child.

p. 75 *Le Figaro:* popular French newspaper, founded in 1854.
Pasdeloup: Jules Etienne Pasdeloup (1819-99) was a French conductor who arranged popular concerts in Paris.

p. 77 *La Folia:* a Portuguese dance (*folia* means madness).

Her Highness

First published in *Stille Eksistenser,* 1886.

p. 79 *a daler:* silver coin used in the German states and the Habsburg empire.

p. 80 à *la Louis quinze:* in the style of Louis XV (i.e. rococo).

p. 82 *Oui – mon enfant – mon pauvre enfant:* Yes – my child – my poor child.

p. 83 *Ah – le petit oiseau – comme il est beau, le petit oiseau:* Oh, the little bird – how pretty it is, the little bird.
Apelles and the birds: Apelles was a renowned painter of ancient Greece. Here it seems he may be confused with the Greek painter Zeuxis, whose paintings were so realistic that it was said that birds tried to eat the grapes he had painted.
Lafontaine's Fables: the fables of the French author Jean de la Fontaine (1621-95) were published in several collections in 1668-94. They were translated into many languages and often used for teaching.
quotations from Jean-Jacques Rousseau: Jean-Jacques Rousseau (1712-78)

was a French author and philosopher. The implication here is that these are quotations from *Emile* (1762), as a tract on an ideal education.

p. 84 *back at 'Sanssouci':* the summer residence of Frederick the Great (1712-86) in Potsdam, near Berlin, built in 1745-47.

the house of Hohenzollern: a German royal house, from 1701 kings of Prussia and in 1871-1918 Emperors of Germany.

Schönbrunn: a royal summer residence near Vienna.

Maria Theresa: daughter of the Holy Roman Emperor Charles VI, Maria Theresa (1717-80) was the only female Empress of the Habsburg dominions, ruling from 1740 to 1780.

La pelouse – Votre altesse le sait … . Oui mademoiselle – la pelouse: The lawn – as Your Highness knows … . Yes, mademoiselle – the lawn.

p. 86 *Herr Pestalozzi:* probably named after the Swiss pedagogue Johann Heinrich Pestalozzi (1746-1827), who favoured natural Rousseau-inspired teaching methods.

p. 87 *cette illustre impératrice:* this distinguished Empress (presumably Maria Theresa).

p. 89 *pour les jeunes filles:* for young ladies. There were several series of improving books for girls published during this period.

the official almanac: a register of the highest ranks of the nobility.

p. 91 *die Glocke:* 'Das Lied von der Glocke' ('The Song of the Bell', 1800), a long poem by the German poet Friedrich von Schiller (1759-1805).

p. 92 *l'air du trône:* a regal air.

p. 93 *Revue des deux Mondes:* a highbrow French journal, covering literature, culture and current affairs.

p. 94 *tarot:* an old card game played with a tarot pack of 78 cards.

p. 95 *Eisenstein:* presumably a fictional town name.

p. 97 *Don Carlos: Dom Carlos. Infant von Spanien* (1787), a play by Friedrich von Schiller.

Marquis de Posa: friend of Don Carlos, a freedom fighter.

let Bolingbroke smile like that to Lady Marlborough: characters in *Le verre d'eau* (*The Glass of Water,* 1840), a comedy by the popular French playwright Eugène Scribe (1791-1861).

p. 98 *Princess Eboli:* a royal lady-in-waiting in *Don Carlos.*

Sie waren mein – im Angesicht der Welt, / Mir zugesprochen von zwei grossen Thronen, / Mir zuerkannt von Himmel und Natur, / Und Philipp – Philipp hat mir sie geraubt: You were mine in the eyes of the world, / promised to me by two great thrones, / acknowledged mine by heaven and nature, / and Philipp – Philipp stole you from me.

Josef Kaim: the character is based on the young Austrian actor Josef Kainz (1858-1910), whom Bang greatly admired.

p. 101 *the Queen of Romania:* Elisabeth Ottilie Louise (1843-1916), Queen of Romania; she wrote a number of books in German under the pseudonym Carmen Sylva.

Mais oui, … votre Altesse – des vers étonnants …: But yes, Your Highness – astonishing verses.

Oui – voilà une madame de Staël sur le thrône ...: Yes – a veritable Madame de Staël on the throne. Madame de Staël (1766-1817) was a celebrated French-Swiss author. She was also a supporter of the French revolution and thus, to Mademoiselle Leterrier, an example not to be emulated.

p. 103 *The Minstrel's Curse:* 'Des Sängers Fluch', a poem from the collection *Gedichte* (*Poems,* 1815), by the German poet Ludwig Uhland (1787-1862).

p. 106 *Mais oui, ... c'est l'âge orageux:* Oh yes, it's a turbulent age.

Mais oui – c'est ça: Oh yes, that's what it is.

the great Devrient: Ludwig Devrient (1784-1832) was a famous German actor at theatres in Breslau and Berlin.

p. 109 *Ich bin / Der Meinung, Ihre Majestät, dass es / So Sitte war, den einen Monat hier / Den andern in den Pardo auszuhalten, / Den Winter in der Residenz, so lange / Es Könige in Spanien gegeben ...:* I am of the opinion, Your Majesty, that it was the custom to spend one month here and the next in Pardo, and the winter in the Residence, for as long as there have been kings in Spain ... . A speech by the Duchess Olivarez to the Queen in Schiller's *Don Carlos,* Act I, Scene 3.

p. 112 *Romeo and Juliet:* Shakespeare's play from 1597.

p. 116 *Mary Stuart:* i.e. Mary Queen of Scots, 1542-67; her dramatic life has attracted great interest from artists and authors, including Schiller's drama *Maria Stuart* (1800).

p. 119 *Des Meeres und der Liebe Wellen: Waves of the Sea and of Love* (1831), a tragedy by the Austrian writer Franz Grillparzer (1791-1872).

Leander: the Greek myth of Hero and Leander is a tragic love story which was the subject of Grillparzer's play.

p. 120 *Mais oui ... cousine ... je suis bien heureuse:* But yes, cousin, I am very happy.

en haie: in two rows facing one another.

p. 121 *the Foundation for Unmarried Noblewomen:* a foundation set up to provide a home for ladies of the aristocracy who did not have a realistic chance of getting married.

The Lord lift up his countenance upon you and give you peace: the third part of the Aaronic blessing, often used as a benediction at the end of a church service.

p. 122 *A Midsummer Night's Dream:* a reference to Mendelssohn's incidental music, 'Here comes the bride' – a piece entirely unsuitable to the occasion.

p. 123 *the court of King Solomon:* King Solomon's splendid court in Jerusalem is described in the Bible (I Kings, 7).

Irene Holm

First published as 'De Glemte. Novelletter. I. Danserinde Frøken Irene Holm' in *Nordstjernen,* 21.11.1886. Republished in book form in *Under Aaget,* 1890.

p. 130 *Berlingske Tidende:* a major Copenhagen newspaper, first published in 1749, and daily from 1841.

'all of them over there': i.e. in Copenhagen. From the description of the landscape, the events of the story take place in Jutland.

p. 131 *the plaster cast of Thorvaldsen's Christ:* a copy of the sculpture of Christ from 1821 by Bertel Thorvaldsen (1770-1844). The original is in Vor Frue Kirke, Copenhagen's cathedral.

arrack: an Indonesian spirit made from the fermented sap of coconut flowers or sugarcane, with added grain or fruit. The punch would be a combination of arrack, black tea, sugar, lemon and water. It was often served warm.

La grande Napolitaine: a solo from Act III of the ballet *Napoli* (1842) by the Danish choreographer August Bournonville (1805-79).

p. 133 *barège:* a sheer gauze fabric made from wool.

as if in a comedy by Scribe: Eugène Scribe (1791-1861) was a prolific French author of comedies which were extremely popular on the Scandinavian stage.

p. 134 *the nine muses:* goddesses of the arts in Greek mythology.

Freya with her two cats: goddess of love and fruitfulness in Nordic mythology. Her chariot was drawn by two cats.

p. 135 *Fenella:* heroine of the opera *La Muette de Portici* (*The Mute Girl of Portici,* 1828) by D.F.E. Auber (1782-1871) and Eugène Scribe. Fenella drowns herself after her lover has been murdered. At the première in Copenhagen in 1830 the solo was danced by Johanne Luise Heiberg (1812-90). Herman Bang wrote an article about the opera in *Nationaltidende* 6.5.1883.

The Last Ballgown

First published as 'De Glemte. Novelletter af Herman Bang. II. Den sidste Balkjole' in *Nordstjernen,* 9.10.1887.

A Lovely Day

First published as 'En dejlig Dag. Fortælling fra en Krog i Livet', in *Tilskueren,* September 1889 and January 1890. Republished in book form in *Under Aaget,* 1890.

p. 147 *the sufferings of Job:* refers to the Book of Job in the Old Testament, which recounts the sufferings inflicted on Job by God.

p. 148 *Hat nichts gelitten:* Got here unscathed.

her Bechstein piano: produced by the German manufacturer Karl Bechstein (1826-1900).

Sie lieben das?: You like that?

p. 154 *Ich sehe das:* So I see.

his hair styled à la Capoul: the hairstyle of the popular French tenor Victor

Capoul (1839-1924), with a centre parting and hair brushed forward on both sides, was copied by other performers. Herman Bang knew Victor Capoul.

p. 155 *Rubinstein:* Anton Rubinstein (1829-94) was a Russian composer and pianist.

Was meinen denn eigentlich die Kerls?: What do you two think about this, then?

p. 156 *Point de Laze:* needlepoint lace.

Na – lustiges Nest: Well – a merry gathering.

p. 157 *Sie haben Kinder?:* You have children?

p. 158 *Sie Unglückliche:* You poor thing.

Ja, ich meine das: No, I mean it.

Gott, dass die Weiber sich dazu hergeben: God, that women put up with it.

p. 159 *Ja, wer nur jetzt a' gutes Glas Bier hätte:* Oh, what I wouldn't give for a good glass of beer.

Princess Trubetzkoy … Finnish exile: the Trubetzkoys were an aristocratic Russian family, and the idea of the Princess having to live in Finland, away from fashionable St. Petersburg, might be seen as a joke on the part of the author at the expense of this unfashionable area of small-town Denmark.

her Serene Highness the Princess Ghica: the Ghicas were a Romanian noble family, many of whom lived in France because of conflicts with the Turkish authorities. This reference is presumably to Elena Ghica (1828-88), who wrote a number of historical works under the pseudonym Dora d'Istria.

Queen Elisabeth: Queen Elisabeth Ottilie Louise of Romania (1843-1916); she became queen after Romanian independence was recognised in 1878 and her husband became King Carol of Romania. She wrote a number of popular books under the pseudonym Carmen Sylva.

Des perles exquises – n'est-ce-pas, madame: Exquisite pearls, don't you think, madame?

Ôtez ça: Take this off.

p. 160 *his Majesty King Alfonso:* Alfonso XII (1857-85), King of Spain.

Mais, madame, vous oubliez votre bock: But madame, you're forgetting your beer.

p. 161 *Na, Kinder, … schwer mit so verschiedenen Wölfen zu heulen:* Well, childdren, it's not easy to howl with such different wolves.

p. 162 *Altes Ding:* Old thing.

Sie, Berg … Hören Sie doch, es klingt wie eine Spinette: Listen, Berg, it sounds like a spinette.

Klingt doch lustig? Was?: Sounds jolly, doesn't it?

Scarlatti: Domenico Scarlatti (1685-1757), an Italian composer of several hundred keyboard sonatas.

Singt denn hier Niemand?: Can't anyone here sing?

Dann singen Sie doch etwas: Sing something, then.

Ah – ich: Oh, I would.

Alfredo: one of the arias of the lyrical tenor Alfredo in the opera *La Traviata* (1853), by the Italian composer Guiseppe Verdi (1813-1901).

p. 163 *Er hat ja gelernt:* Why, he has a trained voice.

p. 165 *Ja – gehen wir:* Right – let's go.

p. 166 *C'est bonnet blanc et blanc bonnet:* That was a lot of fuss about nothing.

Na – am End, sie haben ihr Geld bezahlt: Well – ultimately, they've paid for it.

Frøken Caja

First published in *Under Aaget,* 1890.

p. 170 *they rented the third floor bathroom:* the Sundby sisters actually live in one of the bathrooms here – and Frøken Caja herself lives in another one. It would be cheaper than renting a room to themselves.

p. 177 *when the Royal Theatre opened:* the new building of the Royal Theatre in Copenhagen was opened in 1874.

p. 180 *Frue Plads:* a large central square in Copenhagen, location of the Cathedral and the University.

p. 181 *Tycho-Brahe days:* i.e. unlucky days; called – for no particular rea- son, it seems – after the Danish astronomer Tycho Brahe (1546-1601).

L'hombre: a popular Spanish card game.

p. 183 *Casino … Kongens Nytorv:* Casino was a popular theatre in Copenhagen, which opened in 1848. Kongens Nytorv is a large square on which the Royal Theatre stands.

p. 186 *the knocking on the water pipes:* knocking on the exposed water pipes was a way of sending messages from floor to floor in old houses.

p. 187 *Charlotte Corday cap:* Charlotte Corday (1768-93) was an important figure in the French Revolution, who was guillotined in 1793 for the assassination of the Jacobin leader Jean-Paul Marat (1743-93) in his bath. She is often depicted with a voluminous head covering, loosely secured with a ribbon.

Ørsteds Park: named after the Danish physicist H.C. Ørsted (1777-1851), who discovered electromagnetism. The park was a favourite meeting-place for lovers.

Les Quatre Diables

First published as a feuilleton in *København,* 24.8.1890 – 17.9.1890. Republished as *Les Quatre Diables. Excentrisk Novelle,* 1890. Later versions of the story have the title *De fire djævle* (The Four Devils).

p. 191 *the audience returned to its seats:* this story is set in a circus. The Circus in Copenhagen was a permanent structure, with dressing rooms, restaurants and stables.

p. 192 *The Waltz of Love:* this may be one of a set of piano works by Valdemar Fini Henriques (1867-1904) called 'Silhouettes', op. 38. No 13 is called 'Waltz of Love'.

The Sixteenth-Century Tournament: circus performances usually consisted of two parts, the first with various artistic numbers and the second often a dramatic pantomime like this one, with a historical or fabulous theme.

p. 193 *Voyez donc, voyez:* Watch, watch.
Du courage: Good luck! (lit: courage!)

p. 195 *Femme du monde*: a woman of the world (i.e. high society).

p. 196 *Enfin – du courage:* Right – good luck!

p. 197 *Adolphe, tiens:* Adolphe, catch!
Il fait si beau temps: The weather's so lovely.

p. 199 *Commencez:* Begin.

p. 201 *that whitewashed provincial Pantheon:* the original Pantheon is a round building in Rome, built as a temple. This may be a reference to entertainment venues such as the Pantheon in Odense, which opened in the 1850s.

p. 202 *Hanlon Volta jumps:* the Hanlon Volta troupe was a contemporary English-American group of artistes, known for their daring aerial acrobatics. When they performed in New York in August 1890, one of the artistes fell, but was not killed.
En avant ... Ça va: Go on ... that's it.

p. 206 *Gesichter:* faces.

p. 207 *the chair of St Peter itself:* i.e. the Pope in Rome.

p. 208 *Amour, amour, / oh, bel oiseau, / chante, chante, / chante toujours:* Love, love, oh beautiful bird, sing, sing, sing always. The text was presumably composed by Bang, perhaps on the model of 'Habanera' ('*L'amour est un oiseau rebelle*') from Act I of Bizet's *Carmen* (1875).

p. 213 *Na, ... er wäre schon "kalt" geworden:* Yes, otherwise he would already be cold (i.e. dead).
Auch schändlich hoch: It's outrageously high as well.

p. 218 *cri-cris:* the sound made by crickets, here probably produced by a primitive instrument made from a walnut shell with a membrane stretched over it, on which you can drum with fingernails.

p. 219 *A demain, Aimée:* Until tomorrow, Aimée.

A Tale Of Happiness

First published as 'Den hvide Paaske' in *Hver 8. Dag. Illustreret Familieblad,* 23.10.1898 – 4.12.1898. Republished in *Liv og Død,* 1899.

p. 225 *L'hombre:* a popular Spanish card game.

p. 226 *Eremitage races:* the Eremitage is a hunting lodge built for Christian VI in the forest park of Dyrehaven, where he could host royal banquets. From 1885 there was a yearly steeplechase in the grounds for the officers of the hussars and the artillery regiment.
Yet still they sin: a reference to the Danish proverb 'He who sleeps does not sin'. See also Martin Luther: 'whoever sleeps long, does not sin'.
that's why we got the Sillery to drink -- you usually serve Mumm: both are champagnes. Sillery is named after the town of the same name near Reims, and Mumm is a well-known vintage champagne. At that time Sillery was cheaper than Mumm.

p. 227 *Peace Association:* the Danish Peace Association was founded in 1882 by Fredrik Bayer to promote Danish neutrality.
a kind of reform dress: a loose-fitting dress favoured by agitators for women's rights, in protest at the tightly-corseted fashions which could damage women's health.

p. 228 *a Chronique scandaleuse*: a scandalous tale (usually concerning the nobility or the court).
the Government has his Majesty's confidence: probably a reference to the Conservative administration of H.E. Hørring (1842-1909). King Christian IX supported the right-wing government long after it lost public support, and did not accept a Liberal government until 1901.

p. 229 *Association Against the Legal Protection of Immorality:* this association was formed in 1878 in opposition to the regulation of prostitution in Copenhagen, which allowed women to work as prostitutes so long as they had regular medical inspections.

p. 231 *Axel Berner:* Bang's naming of his characters is inconsistent here (as occasionally elsewhere). He changes Berner's name to George at the end of the story. We have taken the liberty of retaining the name Axel in order not to confuse the character with Alice's brother Georg.
Rubinstein's Gallop: the Russian pianist and composer Anton Rubinstein (1829-94) composed several gallops (lively ballroom dances).
Bel-Ami ... Guy de Maupassant: Bel-Ami (1885) is a novel by the French author Guy de Maupassant (1850-93). It was translated into Danish as *Smukke-Ven!* by Oscar Madsen (1866-1902) and published in 1891. Madsen was prosecuted for pornography, and the second edition from 1898 was heavily censored. Bang is referring to the first edition here.

p. 233 *Fair is creation:* the hymn 'Dejlig er Jorden' was composed by the poet and novelist B.S. Ingemann (1789-1862) and is one of the most popular Danish hymns. This translation is by J.C. Aaberg (1877-1970).

p. 234 *her annuity from Vallø:* Vallø was a foundation for unmarried gentlewomen, founded in 1737 in Vallø castle, near Køge. Unmarried women could live here and receive an annual pension.

p. 236 *Rubinstein's "Der Asra":* see note to p. 155. 'Der Asra' is the last of six musical pieces written to texts by the German poet Heinrich Heine (1797-1856), *Sechs Lieder von Heine für eine Singstimme mit Pianoforte,* ca. 1856.

p. 237 *Eau de Lubin:* a famous French perfume from the house of Pierre François Lubin, established in Paris in 1798.

p. 242 *He, who has a closet:* a reference to the New Testament, Matthew 6,6: 'But thou, when thou prayest, enter into thy closet ... .'

p. 244 *Come, rosy day:* the original song here ('Der er mange Glæder...') is of unknown origin (probably by Bang himself). This translation uses a love song of Henri IV, with similar sentiments.
Chères bêtes: Dear (dumb) animals.

p. 245 *Crown Prince Frederik's honorary march:* there are a number of marches dedicated to Frederik VIII (1843-1912), who became king in 1906. It is unclear which one this is.

p. 247 *Daisy, Daisy, Give me your answer, do!:* the original song, 'Hønsefødder og Gulerødder', is a well-known Danish nursery rhyme. 'Daisy, Daisy' is from a popular song, 'Daisy Bell', written in 1892 by Harry Dacre (1857-1922).

The Ravens

First published in *Ravnene. To Fortællinger,* 1902.

p. 253 *Beware of kiosks:* there are several references in this story to kiosks being dubious places; the implication is that they might provide opportunities for casual meetings or trysts.

p. 260 *Oehlenschlægersgade:* a street in Vesterbro, at that time a working-class quarter of Copenhagen.

p. 262 *Limfjorden:* a shallow part of the sea which separates the North Jutlandic Island from the rest of the Jutland peninsula. It is notable for its tasty mussels and oysters.

p. 264 *Hellerup:* now a suburb of Copenhagen, it was still fairly rural in the nineteenth century, but was developed for housing from 1887.

all those houses along 'Aaen': i.e. Ladegårdsåen, in the late nineteenth century a polluted river running between the lakes in Copenhagen. In the twentieth century it was covered over.

p. 265 *the Mission:* Indre Mission was an evangelical Christian movement founded in Denmark in 1861. It was based on Lutheranism and had a strict pietist morality.

p. 266 *all appointments are being frustrated these days:* a reference to 'Systemskiftet', the system change which occurred in 1901, when parliamentary rule was introduced in Denmark and the King could no longer appoint a minority government. The privileges of the nobility were reduced.

p. 268 *Heiberg and the ballets:* Johan Ludvig Heiberg (1791-1860) was a popular dramatist.

Bournonville ... The Bridal Procession in Hardanger: August Bournonville (1805-79) was a ballet dancer and choreographer at the Royal Theatre 1830-77. *The Bridal Procession in Hardanger* was a ballet he composed to music by H.S. Paulli (1810-91), which was first performed in 1853.

Scharff: Harald Anton Scharff (1836-1912) was a ballet dancer at the Royal Theatre 1856-71.

p. 269 *this I. P. Jacobsen:* Jens Peter Jacobsen (1847-85) was an author regarded by some as rather radical, whose collected works were published in two volumes in 1888.

p. 271 *a saying from Montmartre:* a district in Paris which was a centre for brothels and variety shows around 1900.

p. 272 *Encore un baiser qui ne tire à rien:* Yet another kiss which leads nowhere.

Amour, amour, oh, chose difficile: Love, love, oh, a difficult thing.

p. 273 *Amour, amour, oh, bel oiseau:* Love, love, oh, beautiful bird.

p. 276 *taking x-ray photographs:* a topical reference in 1902, as Wilhelm Conrad Röntgen (1845-1923) had just been awarded the Nobel Prize for his discovery of electromagnetic radiation.

p. 279 *'Tis wiser to forget:* the original has a song by Christian Winther (1796-1876). We have used a similar song by Charles Hamilton Aïdé (1826-1906), 'Remember or Forget', from 1830.

p. 284 *Berlingske Tidende*: see note to 'Irene Holm', p. 130.

p. 285 *an electric tram:* electric trams were introduced to Copenhagen in the 1890s, replacing steam-powered tramways.

'Barchan Is Dead'

First published as 'Barchan er død' in *Hjemmets Noveller,* 15.9.1907. Republished in *Sælsomme Fortællinger,* 1907.

p. 290 *the Finland railway station:* the Finland station in St. Petersburg was below the River Neva, which flows through the city.
the Finnish border: at that time the border of the Grand Duchy of Finland, which was part of the Russian Empire, was around 30 kilometres north-west of St. Petersburg.

p. 291 *in Pushkinskaya Street:* a side street to Nevsky Prospect, the main street of St. Petersburg, close to the Moscow railway station.

p. 292 *Severnyj Vestnik:* The Northern Messenger, a literary journal published in St. Petersburg in 1885-98. It was an organ for Russian Symbolism and the fin-de-siècle movement.
Volynsky had written an essay about "Beauty": Akim Lvovich Volynsky, pseudonym for Khaim Leybovich Flekser (1863-1926), was a Russian literary critic and historian, and editor of *Severnyj Vestnik* 1891-98.

p. 294 *He looked like a painting by Repin:* Ilya Repin (1844-1930) was one of the most prominent artists of Russian Realism in the 1870s and 1880s, and often used theatrical effects in his paintings.
Marian Mikhailovich: i.e. Waldheim.

p. 295 *how Repin painted Ivan the Terrible, staring into the face of his half-stifled son:* Repin's painting 'Ivan the Terrible and his son Ivan on 16th November 1581' is from 1885. It depicts the killing of Ivan Ivanovich by his father Ivan IV in a fit of rage, and the father's expression of horror made the painting famous.
Dante has not seen any face like the one I saw: Dante Alighieri (1265-1321) wrote *The Divine Comedy* in ca. 1307-21. The first part describes Dante's horrified journey through Inferno.

Autobiographical Writings

An Artists' Tour of Bornholm

First published in *Ti Aar*, 1891.

p. 301 *where Herman Bang had yet to perform readings:* Bang frequently made tours both in Denmark and abroad in order to read from his works. This tour took place in May 1889.

Its members consisted of: the other members of the troupe were a concert singer called Jachimo Tagnerelli and a young pianist who had recently finished her studies at the conservatoire.

p. 302 *La donna è mobile*: the Duke of Mantua's cynical aria from Act III of the opera *Rigoletto* (1851) by Guiseppe Verdi (1813-1901).

p. 305 *Denmark's tutelary spirit in life-size:* i.e. a female figure representing the country.

'Gravesen's Ball': Bang was reading a chapter from his novel *Stuk* (1887): Part 2, Chapter II.

p. 306 *the Dannebrog's main hall:* a building in Borgergade in Rønne, built in 1887 by the Conservative voters' association. Dannebrog is the Danish flag.

Bellman: the Swedish poet Carl Michael Bellman (1740-95), whose songs and ballads were extremely popular all over Scandinavia in the nineteenth century.

'*Not merely for pleasure*': 'Ej blot til Lyst', the inscription over the proscenium of the Royal Theatre in Copenhagen, formulated by Chr. Fr. Jacobi (1759-1810). Rønne Theatre, the oldest Danish provincial theatre, had the same inscription.

Expelled From Germany

First published in *Ti Aar*, 1891.

p. 309 *the misfortunes began:* Bang travelled to Berlin in December 1885 in order to write. On 13 January 1886 he was issued with an expulsion order because of a letter he had written in *Bergens Tidende* on 1 October 1885, which was less than complimentary to the German Kaiser and his family. The letter is printed in this volume as 'Letter from Herman Bang' (pp. 407-11). He travelled on to Meiningen in Germany, but was expelled again, and the same thing happened in Vienna. In July 1886 he finished up in Prague.

a Kristiania newspaper: i.e. *Kristiania Dagblad*, founded in 1864. The capital of Norway was called Kristiania until 1925.

p. 310 *Bergens Tidende:* a liberal Norwegian newspaper.

the Deutsches Theater: the theatre was in Schumannstrasse 13, in the centre of Berlin.

Don Carlos: see note to 'Her Highness', p.97.

p. 312 *Count Herbert von Bismarck:* Herbert von Bismarck (1849-1904) was a

German politician, the son of the German Chancellor Otto von Bismarck.
perhaps people ought to speak a little quieter: Bang's article was printed in the Danish liberal newspaper *Politiken* 14.12.1886.
I knew that Bergens Tidende would reach Berlin: after this affair, both Bang and the newspaper expressed themselves cautiously for a while. He still wrote for the paper, but for some time his contributions were signed 'Armand'.
Meiningen: a theatrical and cultural centre in south Thüringen, where Bang stayed from 15 January to 19 February 1886.
Berliner Tageblatt: a leading German newspaper 1872-1939.
Arthur Levysohn: (1841-1908), the chief editor of the newspaper.
p. 313 *This Residenz city:* a Residenzstadt was a city where a sovereign ruler resided.
At night, the city was at the theatre: the theatre at the Elisabethenburg castle prospered in the years after 1866, when the 'theatre duke' Georg II of Sachsen-Meiningen (1826-1914) took charge of it and established a permanent company of actors. The troupe toured Europe and North America in 1874-90, and became pioneers of Naturalism.
William Tell: Schiller's play *Wilhelm Tell* was from 1804.
Geheimrat Schiller: 'Geheimrat' was an honorary title often conferred on prominent authors. Schiller was not actually a Geheimrat, though Goethe was.
'Gott, gott … heute hat er denn brav gedonnert': Good, good … today he thundered well.
A Blood Wedding: it is not certain which work this was, but it is most likely *La reine Margot* (1847), a play by Alexandre Dumas the Elder (1802-70), based on the author's novel of the same title. It deals with the massacre of the Huguenots in Paris 23-24.8.1572 in connection with the wedding of the future king Henri IV and Marguerite de Valois.
Frau Olga Lorentz: Olga Lorenz (1854-1920) was a German actress who belonged to the Meininger ensemble.
like Grundtvigians to a shooting competition: in the 1880s in Denmark various left-wing groups who opposed the right-wing Estrup government formed rifle clubs. Among them were the supporters of the politician and religious leader N.F.S. Grundtvig (1783-1872).
p. 314 *Hans von Bülow's farewell concert:* Hans von Bülow (1830-94) was a world-famous German conductor and pianist, in charge of the court orchestra in Meiningen 1880-85. Bang wrote about his farewell concert in *Politiken* 8.2.1886 under the name of Bernhard Hoff.
an article from a Copenhagen correspondent: a Danish lawyer named H.W. Boldt (of whom no more is known) published an article viciously attacking Bang in *Hamburger Nachrichten* 3.2.1886.
Gotha: a German town west of Erfurt.
p. 315 *Wir haben nur Befehl aus Berlin:* we have simply received orders from Berlin.
whose sons fell at Langensalza: Bad Langensalza was a town 30 kilometres

north-west of Erfurt. During the war of 1866 between Prussia and Austria, the King of Hannover inflicted an unexpected defeat on the Prussian troops here on 27 June. This humiliation was not forgiven in Berlin even twenty years later.
to choose to reside in a kingdom: Munich was at that time the capital of the kingdom of Bavaria.
I went out to see Henrik Ibsen: Henrik Ibsen (1828-1906) spent the years 1864-91 living abroad, mainly in Dresden, Rome and Munich. Bang visited him with the intention of returning later to the Meininger Theatre and introducing his plays there, but Ibsen was less than enthusiastic. Bang wrote about their meeting in 'Personlige Erindringer om Henrik Ibsen' in *Det ny Aarhundrede*, July and August 1906.
retreat from the Hohenzollerns and seek out the Habsburg Monarchy: the Hohenzollerns were the Kings of Prussia, and the Habsburgs were the rulers of the Austro-Hungarian Empire.
Hernals: a district in north-eastern Vienna.
Katinka: i.e. 'Ved Vejen', a long novella published in *Stille Eksistenser*, 1886.

p. 316 *the tradition of Prince von Metternich:* Klemens von Metternich (1773-1859) was an Austrian foreign minister, who had a great influence on European politics in the early nineteenth century. He was known for his decisive repression of any opposition.
twenty Gulden: originally a gold coin, since the middle of the seventeenth century it also existed in silver. It was the currency of the Austro-Hungarian empire until 1892.

p. 317 *letting an offender die in his sins:* a Biblical reference (Numbers 27,3).
in the middle of Kärntner Ring: a section of Vienna's ring road.

p. 318 *Stucco:* i.e. *Stuk* (1887), a novel which was largely written during Bang's stay in Prague.

A Christmas Eve on Foreign Soil

First published in *Ti Aar*, 1891.

p. 319 *We were in Prague:* Bang spent Christmas 1886 in a flat in a suburb of Prague with his friend, the young Berlin actor Max Eisfeld, a pseudonym for Max Appel (1863-1935). Because of the bad weather, several payments were delayed, including the weekly advance from his publisher. From Bang's letters it is clear that his Christmas was actually much more miserable than he describes it here.
'Die Hausmeisterin': the landlady.

p. 320 *regular columns for five countries:* i.e. Denmark, Finland, Norway, Sweden and Germany.
Hradčany: the castle district of Prague.
a German family magazine: i.e. *Schorers Familienblatt*, a respected German weekly magazine.
'A Village Ophelia': the original story, 'Landsbyens Ofelia', was printed in *Nordstjernen* 8.1.1888.

p. 321 *a Gulden and a few Kreutzer:* silver coins. In the Austro-Hungarian Empire there were 100 Kreuzer to the Gulden in 1857-92.

p. 325 *in the March of Brandenburg:* a Prussian province.

p. 326 *'Gesegnete Mahlzeit'*: bless this meal!

the troops, in sixty-six: i.e. in the war between Prussia and Austria in 1866.

p. 327 *Most:* a town in Bohemia, northwest of Prague.

By Ship Across the Atlantic

Published as 'En Rejse om Jorden. Atlanterhavsbaaden I-II', in *København* 16-17. 2.1912.

p. 331 *there are too many lines:* in January 1912 Bang was travelling to America on the 'Moltke', a ship of the Hamburg-America line, which made the trip between 1902 and 1915.

p. 332 *'That is true,' I say, laughing out loud:* the reason for Bang's amusement is that he was one of the passengers who couldn't really afford to travel. He was hoping to make money on his tour of America, but met one financial disaster after another.

when we stop over in Genoa: the Hamburg-America line stopped at the Italian port of Genoa to take on provisions and more passengers, before embarking on the crossing.

'Feiner Herr, feiner Herr': a fine gentleman.

Donnerwetter!: a mild oath.

p. 333 *Neu-Brandenburg*: a town in Mecklenburg, north-east Germany.

p. 334 *on the "Imperator":* the new ship of the Hamburg-America line, which was launched in 1913, could accommodate 3512 passengers, and on its maiden voyage reached New York in five days and fifteen hours.

p. 336 *'Man muss es doch, nicht wahr? … Man muss doch was wissen':* You have to, though, don't you? You have to know something.

Grand Dieu: Good Lord.

p. 338 *'Tristesses d'amour':* the sorrows of love (an unidentified piece of music).

p. 339 *The Transatlantic Daily … the Marconi telegrams:* the *Transatlantic Daily* may have been an internal ship's paper for the Hamburg-America line. Guglielmo Marconi (1874-1937) was the inventor of the wireless telegraph system. In 1901 he established the first wireless connection between Britain and America.

p. 340 *"Le Comte de Luxembourg":* an operetta from 1909 by the Austro-Hungarian composer Franz Lehár (1870-1948).

p. 342 *'Felicissime notte, signore':* I wish you a very good night, sir.

Portrait

Sarah Bernhardt

Published in *Teatret*, 1892, pp. 267-279. Sarah Bernhardt (1844-1923), originally Henriette-Rosine Bernard, was the greatest French actress of the later nineteenth century.

p. 346 *the marketplaces of Melbourne:* Bernhardt performed in Melbourne, Australia, in May 1891.

the obedient daughter of the house of Molière: Sarah Bernhardt began her acting career at the Comédie Française, France's national theatre, where comedies by Jean-Baptiste Poquelin (1622-73), known by his stage name Molière, were staple fare.

she scatters Victor Hugo's verses: Bernhardt was rumoured to have had an affair with the writer Victor Hugo (1802-85), and starred amongst other things in his verse play *Ruy Blas* (1838).

Racine is set aside: Jean Racine (1639-99) was one of the two great tragedians of seventeenth-century France. Bernhardt was famed for her performances as the protagonist of his play *Phèdre* (1677).

the Sardous write roles for her: Victorien Sardou (1831-1908) was a prolific French dramatist, one of the creators of the well-made play. He wrote several plays with Bernhardt in mind, including *Fédora* (1882).

'*Je vous haïs – je t'aime*': I hate you – I love you.

Proteus: in Greek mythology Proteus was a sea-god, whose nature was changeable like that of the sea. He could foretell the future, but would change his shape to avoid doing so, and answered only to those who could capture him.

p. 348 *Adelaide Ristori:* an Italian tragedienne (1822-1906). She was 84 when she died, but had retired from the stage in 1885 at the age of 63.

p. 349 *the hunt for gold also drives her:* Bernhardt insisted on being paid in gold coins.

the Comédie Humaine: the French novelist Honoré de Balzac (1799-1850) wrote a long series of novels portraying French society from the French Revolution (1789) to 1848. He called the series 'La Comédie Humaine'; a definitive edition was published in 24 volumes between 1869 and 1876.

Sarah Bernhardt commissions Pierrot Assassin*:* a reference to the play *Pierrot Assassin* (Pierrot the Murderer, 1883), by Jean Richepin (1849-1926), in which Bernhardt appeared together with Gabrielle Réjane (1856-1920), about whom Bang wrote enthusiastically. Bernhardt was photographed in costume in 1883 by the famous French photographer Nadar (Gaspard-Félix Tournachon (1820-1910)).

p. 350 *Valérie becomes her role:* the French dramatist Eugéne Scribe (1791-1861) wrote a large number of plays, mainly comedies, which perfected the formula of the well-made play. His first successful comedy, *Valérie,* had its première at the Théâtre Français in 1822. Bernhardt first played the role while at the Comédie Française in 1862-64.

Josef Kainz can be mentioned: Josef Kainz (1858-1910) was an Austrian actor who was revered as one of the greatest actors of the German-speaking theatre, and whom Bang much admired. He wrote many reviews of his work, and published a book entitled *Josef Kainz* in German in 1910.

Journalism

A Poor Folks' Inn

Published in *Nationaltidende* 28/12/1879.

p. 353 *to read about 'The Steadfast Tin Soldier' and 'The Old Woman':* 'Den standhaftige tinsoldat' (The Steadfast Tin Soldier, 1838) is a fairytale by Hans Christian Andersen. 'The Old Woman' may refer to a nursery rhyme by Adolf Curdts from 1867, 'Katten og Kællingen, sloges om Vællingen' (The Cat and the Old Woman Fought for the Gruel).

p. 355 *begging on Kongens Nytorv:* it was common to find beggars sitting on the benches on Kongens Nytorv in Copenhagen, around the equestrian statue of Christian V.

the 'lodging house' where they sleep: the lodging house was called 'Holger Danske' in Farvergade. It offered lodgings for people of no fixed abode.

p. 356 *You can see that from his arms and his parting:* a centre parting was part of the clichéed image of a butcher.

p. 357 *'There is a Lovely Land':* i.e. 'Der er et yndigt Land', a song by Adam Oehlenschläger (1779-1850) which later became the Danish national anthem.

'The Girls of South Jutland': a poem by Holger Drachmann (1846-1908) from his documentary work *Derovre fra Grænsen* (From Over by the Border, 1877).

'The Brave Soldier': a song from 1848 about the Thirty Years War by Peter Faber (1810-77).

one of the dismantled stalls on Helliggeiststræde: there was a row of stalls on Helliggeiststræde where you could buy material, second-hand goods etc. The stalls had doors but no windows.

p. 358 *usher at Alhambra, watchman on St. Nicholas' Tower:* the Alhambra was a large entertainment complex built on Frederiksberg Allé by Georg Carstensen (1812-57), who was also one of the developers of the Tivoli Gardens. The tower of St. Nicholas' Church was used as a lookout station for fires until 1892.

Carl Ploug and his 'Attellaner' sketches: the Danish politician and journalist Carl Ploug (1813-94) wrote a series of satirical dramatic sketches in the 1830s and 40s called *Atellaner*, under the pseudonym of Poul Rytter.

Rasmus Nielsen is now an elderly professor: Rasmus Nielsen (1809-84) was a distinguished professor of philosophy, best known for his influential and popular books and lectures.

p. 359 *he used to play the violin in Korup's Garden:* a beer garden in Frederiksberg.

'Dummepeter': i.e. 'stupid Peter', a character from a popular song from the 1870s by Wilhelm Rautzau (1832-97).
it's unlucky to leave without drinking something: a reference to a popular superstition that you bring bad luck to a house at Christmas if you leave without eating or drinking.

p. 360 *there is disorder in all the rooms*: this last paragraph was later deleted by Bang in the subsequent publication of this piece in *Herhjemme og Derude* (At Home and Abroad, 1881) - perhaps an attempt to make the text appear more spontaneous, whereas in fact it was a more considered version.

'Magasin Du Nord'

Published in *Nationaltidende* 23.5.1880.

p. 361 *Albert Wolff in his best days:* the Franco-German journalist Albert Wolff (1835-91) specialized in conversation pieces about art and theatre for *Figaro* and *Evénement.*

p. 362 *When I have written about 'Holger Danske' ... :* all the pieces Bang mentions were articles he published in *Nationaltidende* in 1879 and 1880.
I wrote about Christmas Eve for the homeless: see previous article.
Magasin du Nord ... Vett & Wessel: the trade magnates Theodor Wessel (1842-1905) and Emil Vett (1843-1911) opened a draper's shop in 1871 in the Hotel du Grand Nord, Kongens Nytorv 13-15. The shop grew to occupy an ever larger part of the hotel, and the company adopted the name 'Magasin du Nord' after it in 1879 – though it was still known locally as 'Wessel and Vett' for many years. By 1889 it had taken over the entire hotel; the building was demolished in 1893 and rebuilt in its present form. It is still called 'Magasin du Nord'.

p. 363 *waiters at the Royal Hotel:* the Royal Hotel, Ved Stranden 18, was where *Nationaltidende* has its premises.

p. 364 *all the omnibuses owned by Brama Life Elixir:* the elixir was produced by the firm Mansfeldt-Büllner, which occupied the Turkish-style 'Villa Hasa' on Strandvejen. These 'omnibuses' were for the transport of goods, not people.
Henri II outfits for the eighteen-year-old miss: originally a sixteenth-century vogue influenced by the Renaissance, characterized by simplicity, straight lines and geometric figures. It was extremely fashionable for girls around 1880.

p. 365 *150 miles of carpeting:* these are approximate figures reckoned from Danish measurements (Alen, Tønder and Danish miles (= ca. 7.5 km.)).

p. 366 *the firm's factories in Nørrebro:* in 1876 the two owners founded a textile manufacturer in Nørrebro, Vett, Wessel & Fiala, which later moved to Østerbro where it also produced textiles for furniture.

p. 367 *the horse is still standing there:* the equestrian statue of Christian V on Kongens Nytorv.

'The House With The Happy Faces'

Published in *Nationaltidende* 31.10.1880.

p. 370 *'Papers!' – 'Papers!'*: the children would be selling popular pamphlets, such as ballads, handbills, religious tracts etc.

p. 371 *their mother lives down below:* the inference is that she is a prostitute.

p. 373 *The principal of Vodrofsvej's Children's Home:* after 1864 children's homes began to be distinguished from older 'houses of correction' and to spread across the country. Nearly all of them were funded by private benefactors. The home on Vodrofsvej 20 was opened in 1874, and the principal was the pioneering Josephine Schneider (1820-87). Josephine Schneider's House is still caring for children.

p. 374 *øllebrød:* i.e. a sweet soup made from dried scraps of rye bread and low-alcohol beer.

p. 375 *sød suppe:* i.e. a fruit soup, made with both fresh and dried fruit.

p. 376 *to 'enter into their closet':* a Biblical reference: 'But thou, when thou prayest, enter into thy closet ... .' Matthew 6,6.

those of us who could each bring our mite: a reference to the Biblical parable of the widow's mite, Mark 12, 41-44.

Visiting the Poor Before Christmas

Published in *Nationaltidende* 19.12.1880 as 'Rundt fra Krogene. II. Nogle Fattigbesøg før Jul'. Republished as 'En Fattigmandsknejpe' in *Herhjemme og Derude*, 1881.

p. 379 *We walked along an old walkway:* the property Bang was visiting here is what was known as the 'Jewish House' at Overgaden oven Vandet 4 in Christianshavn. It was pulled down in 1890.

p. 380 *it was promenade time:* it was customary for the leisured classes to take a walk in the afternoon in fashionable Østergade – to see and be seen.

p. 381 *next to the king on horseback:* the equestrian statue of Christian V on Kongens Nytorv.

the Hotel d'Angleterre: a deluxe hotel on Kongens Nytorv.

p. 382 *the exalted Muses, who no doubt are busy dancing with the Graces on Olympus:* the Muses were the nine inspirational goddesses of literature, science and the arts in ancient Greece, and the three Graces attended feasts and dances. Mount Olympus was the home of the Greek Gods.

p. 383 *'You won't find the words in Molbech': Dansk Ordbog* (1833, 1859 ff.), the Danish dictionary written by Professor of Literature Christian Molbech (1783-1857), was the most authoritative dictionary of the day.

p. 384 *like Job:* in the Bible, Job suffered many torments in order to prove the strength of his faith. See The Book of Job in *The Old Testament.*

St. Vitus' dance: an alternative name for the movement disorder Sydenham's chorea, often used as a synonym for epilepsy.

p. 385 *Dante's inscription over the proletarian hell:* 'Abandon hope, all ye who enter here'; this sentence is inscribed above the gates of Hell in *The Divine Comedy* (1317) by Dante Alighieri (1265-1321).

Misery is a Janus head: the Roman God Janus was depicted with two faces, facing forwards and backwards. He was the god of entrances and exits, and guarded gates and doorways.

p. 387 *they are admitted to Ladegården:* the building lay on the present Åboulevard, and was until 1908 Copenhagen's main poorhouse and workhouse. It had a section for women who had once been prostitutes and were now destitute.

paint a Hogarth canvas: William Hogarth (1697-1764) was an English painter and printmaker, whose satirical paintings highlighted the misery of the poor in eighteenth-century England.

On 'Thingvalla'

Published in *Nationaltidende* 3.7.1881 and 10.7.1881.

p. 389 *'Thingvalla':* the emigrant ship 'Thingvalla' belonged to a steamship company of the same name, and had a widespread network of agents whose job it was to persuade people to emigrate to America. In 1880 there were 4,418 people who emigrated from Denmark, mostly to North America. Bang travelled with the ship from Copenhagen to Kristiania (Oslo) on 22.6.1881.

p. 392 *lends Musset to fifteen-year-old lads:* the French author Alfred de Musset (1810-57) was one of the young Herman Bang's favourite writers. His autobiographical novel *La confession d'un enfant du siècle* (1836) tells of his celebrated love affair with George Sand, and was one of the works which inspired Bang's novel *Haabløse Slægter* (Hopeless Generations, 1880).

Paul de Kock: Paul-Henri de Kock (1819-92) was a French author of salacious novels which were not considered suitable reading for young boys.

p. 393 *studying at Frøken Zahle's school:* Natalie Zahle (1827-1913) was a pioneer of girls' education in Denmark. In 1851 she opened a training college for women teachers, and in 1869 a course for primary school teachers.

p. 399 *a Whitsun trip to Møn:* Møn is an island just off the southern tip of Zealand, a popular tourist destination.

p. 400 *a madness which opens the veins of society:* blood-letting was in use by the medical profession up to the end of the nineteenth century. It was incorrectly assumed to be a cure for a variety of ailments.

Viktoria Hotel: a hotel in central Kristiania with a view out over the fjord.

The Fire

Published in *Nationaltidende* 4.10.1884.

p. 401 *the burning palace:* the Christiansborg palace was first built by Christian VI in the 1730s and 40s as a royal residence. After burning down in 1794, it was rebuilt. On 3 October 1884 it burnt down again; Bang was on the spot and recorded events more or less as they happened. Work on the new palace did not start until 1906, and it was finished in 1928.

p. 402 *Thorvaldsen's Museum:* the museum is the oldest in Copenhagen, and was opened in 1848 to house the sculptures of Bertil Thorvaldsen (1770-1844). It is close to Christiansborg.

over the house where I had been: Bang wrote his report in the offices of *Nationaltidende* at Ved Stranden 18, just across the canal from Christiansborg.

Jerichau's statue of Ophelia is caught by the gleam: the sculptor Jens Adolf Jerichau (1816-83) was represented by several works in the Christiansborg collection; one of them was his 'Ophelia'.

'The Panther Hunter' is carried down: a major work by Jerichau from 1845, which was rescued with only slight damage.

p. 405 *Hagar and Ishmael were dragged out:* in *The Old Testament*, Hagar was a slave who bore Abraham's son Ishmael. There are several paintings and sculptures with this motif.

the king ... with his two sons: Christian IX with the princes Hans and Valdemar.

people were calling for Zeltner: the architect Johan Theodor Zeltner (1822-1904) was the palace steward.

p. 406 *Gammelholm:* literally 'The Old Island', a residential area in the city centre bounded by several canals.

The statue of Frederik VII: at that time there was an area of grass in front of the palace, where the equestrian statue of Frederik VII by Herman Vilhelm Bissen (1798-1868) was erected in 1873.

Souvenirs intimes de Napoleon III: presumably Henry de Kock: *Souvenirs et notes intimes de Napoleon III à Wilhelmshoehe* (Paris 1871).

Letter From Herman Bang

Published in *Bergens Tidende* 1.10.1885 as 'Breve fra Herman Bang III'.

p. 407 *your Baedeker:* Karl Baedeker (1801-1859) was a German publisher who pioneered the production of worldwide travel guides; the name was later used as a shorthand for any kind of travel guide.

the Fahrbachs of fifty orchestras: a reference to Philipp Fahrbach Sr. (1815-85) and his son, Philipp Fahrbach Jr. (1843-94), both orchestra conductors and prolific composers of dance music.

being pursued by Sabine women: probably a reference to the play *Der Raub der Sabinerinnen* (The Rape of the Sabine Women, 1884) by Franz and Paul von Schönthan.

p. 408 *Jungfernstieg:* the most prestigious boulevard in Hamburg.

Sarah Bernhardt: world-famous actress (1844-1923); see Bang's portrait of her (pp. 345-50).

It is inconceivable that these people have time for anything else: Bang's irreverent portrait of the Kaiser and his family caused such outrage that it led to his expulsion from the country; see 'Expelled From Germany' (pp. 309-18).

William the Conqueror: a reference to Kaiser Wilhelm I (1797-1888), ironically suggesting a comparison with William I of Normandy and England.

the Prince of Bismarck: Otto von Bismarck (1815-98). 'Prince' is a title of the German nobility.

Germany's future – Prince Wilhelm's little son: when Wilhelm I died in 1888, his oldest son Frederick (1831-88) became Kaiser Frederick III. He died almost at once, and was succeeded by his son Wilhelm (1859-1941), who became Kaiser Wilhelm II, and ruled until he was forced to abdicate in 1918. The reference to 'Germany's future' is to his oldest son Wilhelm (1882-1951), who never became Kaiser.

the delighted Princess Viktoria: the wife of Wilhelm II was Augusta Victoria, Princess of Schleswig-Holstein (1858-1921).

p. 409 *the well in Bad Ems:* one of Germany's most famous bathing resorts in the nineteenth century; Kaiser Wilhelm I had his summer residence there, as did several other European monarchs and artists.

the century's Mephisto chose one of those kings as his Faust: a reference to the play *Faust* (1808) by Johann Wolfgang von Goethe (1749-1832). Mephistopheles is an evil spirit to whom Faust sells his soul. In Bang's reference Mephisto is Otto von Bismarck, who had a central role in proclaiming Wilhelm I as German Kaiser in Versailles in 1871.

Crown Prince Rudolf: Rudolf, Crown Prince of Austria (1858-89), was the son of Emperor Franz Joseph I and Elisabeth of Bavaria. He was heir apparent to the Imperial throne of the Austro-Hungarian Empire from birth. In 1889, he died in a suicide pact with his mistress, Mary Freiin von Vetsera, at the Mayerling hunting lodge.

p. 410 *How much effort has it not cost this Moltke:* Count Helmuth Karl Bernhard von Moltke (1800-91) was a Prussian field marshal and chief of staff of the Prussian Army for thirty years, regarded as the creator of a more modern method of directing armies in the field. He commanded troops during the Second Schleswig War, the Austro-Prussian War and the Franco-Prussian War.

face of an Uhlan lieutenant: the Uhlans were originally Polish-Lithuanian light cavalry units armed with lance, sabre, and pistols.

The Chinese

Published in *Politiken* 21.2.1887.

p. 413 *down in Taubenstrasse in Berlin:* Taubenstrasse is a street in central Berlin which has many imposing nineteenth-century buildings.

the Sandwich Islands: the name that the explorer James Cook chose for what are now known as the Hawaiian Islands.

p. 414 *the 'sons of heaven':* the Chinese Emperor was the son of heaven, and his subjects were also the sons of heaven.

p. 415 *Bernhard Hoff:* the name of one of the main characters in Bang's novel *Haabløse Slægter* (Hopeless Generations, 1880). Bang often used it as a pseudonym.

Smart

Published in *København* 22.1.1903.

p. 417 *à-l'Anglaise-coiffured:* i.e. they comb their hair in the English fashion.

An Event

Published in *København* 1.9.1904.

p. 419 *The Danish Automobile Association:* Dansk Automobilselskab, which was founded in 1904.

France, the home of motor clubs: the first automobile club was the Automobile Club de France, formed in 1895 in Paris.

I recently wrote in my series of articles 'Around the Country' in København, in connection with the Hornbæk railway line: Bang's article, entitled 'Hornbæk-Banen', was published in *København* 16.8.1904. The construction of the Hornbæk railway line was completed in May 1906.

p. 420 *in our moorland districts:* i.e. in Jutland.

the cautious – far too cautious – automobile law: the first Danish automobile law was formulated in 1903, and imposed a speed limit of 15 km an hour in towns.

the railway on Bornholm: the railway was inaugurated in December 1900.

In A Flash

Published in *København* 4.9.1907.

p. 421 *Berlin:* Bang spent two years in Berlin from July 1907 onwards, after being hounded by the Danish press because of his homosexuality.

Epilogue

Herman Bang On America

Published in *Illustreret Tidende* 4.2.1912.

p. 425 *a letter from Herman Bang:* this letter is included in this volume as 'By Ship Across the Atlantic', pp. 331-42.

an account, through editor Emil Opffer: Emil Opffer (1863-1924) was a Danish journalist and newspaper editor who emigrated to America in 1905, where he continued to edit various newspapers. His interview was accompanied by a picture of Herman Bang with the caption 'Died on 28 January in Ogden, Utah'.

p. 427 *Edison:* Thomas Alva Edison (1847-1931) was an American inventor who developed many devices to do with electric power generation and mass communication.

the full force of the exotic: after crossing America, Bang had planned to continue his tour further to the Far East, including Japan and India.

p. 428 *there was some student unrest in Paris:* Bang was living in Paris in 1893 when there was some rioting in the Latin Quarter, regarding a lawsuit

against some models who had attended a ball wearing costumes which were considered too risqué.
"*M'ont tué!*": they've killed me!
The review from ... Novoye Vremya: it has not been possible to locate this review.

p. 429 *You ask me about Russia:* Bang's international tour commenced with a trip through Finland to Russia at the end of 1911, then back to Hamburg to take ship for New York.
Chaliapin: Feodor Chaliapin (1873-1938) was a Russian opera singer with a deep and expressive bass voice.
Caruso: Enrico Caruso (1873-1921) was an internationally popular Italian operatic tenor.
the Moscow Art Theatre: founded in 1898 by the seminal Russian theatre director Konstantin Stanislavski (1863-1938).
my rooms in Rue de Rivoli: it has not been possible to find the date of this journey.
I was working on Mikaël*:* Bang's novel *Mikaël,* a tragic homosexual love story, was published in 1904.
Katinka: published as 'Ved Vejen' in *Stille Eksistenser*, 1886.

p. 430 The White House *has been published in England ... the only review I saw:* it has not been possible to find any mention of this translation or the review.
my meeting with ... Claude Monet: Bang met Claude Monet (1840-1926) in Norway in 1895.
I have ordered Tine *from Paris:* Bang's novel *Tine* (1889) was translated into French by Maurice Prozor (1848-1928) and published in 1895.

DORRIT WILLUMSEN

Bang:
A Novel about the Danish Writer

(translated by Marina Allemano)

29 January 1912. In a train compartment in Ogden, Utah, a Danish author was found unconscious. The 54-year-old Herman Bang was en route from New York to San Francisco as part of a round-the-world reading tour. It was a poignant end for a man whose life had been spent on the move. Having fled his birthplace on the island of Als ahead of the Prussian advance of 1864, he was later hounded out of Copenhagen, Berlin, Vienna and Prague by homophobic laws and hostility to his uncompromising social critique as journalist, novelist, actor and dramaturge. Dorrit Willumsen re-works Bang's life story in a series of compelling flashbacks that unfold during his last fateful train ride across the USA. Along the way, we are transported to an audience in St Petersburg with the Dowager Empress Maria Feodorovna, to a lovers' nest in a flea-ridden Prague boarding house, to the newsrooms and variety theatres of fin-de-siècle Copenhagen, and to a Norwegian mountainside, where Claude Monet has come to paint snow and lauds Bang's writing as literary impressionism.

A pioneering journalist, author and dramatist, Herman Bang (1857-1912) was a key figure in Scandinavia's Modern Breakthrough. His major works include *Haabløse Slægter* (Hopeless Generations, 1880), *Stuk* (Stucco, 1887) and *Tine* (Tina, 1889).

Dorrit Willumsen's *Bang* was awarded the Nordic Council Literature Prize, 1997.

ISBN 9781909408340
UK £15.95
(Paperback, 398 pages)

KIRSTEN THORUP

The God of Chance

(translated by Janet Garton)

The God of Chance focuses on the relationship between Ana, a high-flying Danish career woman from the international finance sector whose work is her life, and the young teenager Mariama, two women whose circumstances are completely different. Ana first meets Mariama selling snacks on a beach in Gambia, and the girl gradually becomes a substitute for the family she has never had. The novel moves to Copenhagen and then to London as Ana brings Mariama to Europe to be educated; the girl finds the cultural shock and living with Ana intensely difficult, whilst Ana's obsession with her leads to her own carefully controlled life descending into chaos. The story depicts the gulf between European affluence and Third World poverty; it explores our dependence on money, our need to be in control in every situation, and the problematic relationship between sponsor or donor and recipient. The scene moves from colourful depictions of life in a luxury hotel in Africa, cheek by jowl with desperate poverty, to elite designer flats in Copenhagen, and finally the bustling multicultural community on the streets of London.

This novel from 2011 is by the prize-winning Danish author Kirsten Thorup. Her most well-known works are her series of four novels about little Jonna from the provinces, which are also about growing up into the rapidly-changing Danish society of the late twentieth century; and *Bonsai* (2000), an unflinching account of the scourge of Aids and its devastating effect on an ordinary family.

ISBN 9781909408036
UK £13.95
(Paperback, 302 pages)

SELMA LAGERLÖF

Lagerlöf in English

Selma Lagerlöf (1858-1940) was born on a farm in Värmland, trained as a teacher and became, in her life-time, Sweden's most widely translated author ever. Novels such as *Gösta Berlings saga* (1891; *Gösta Berling's Saga*) and *Jerusalem* (1901- 02) helped regenerate Swedish literature, and the school textbook about Nils Holgersson who traverses Sweden on the back of a goose has become familiar the world over. Two very different trilogies, the Löwensköld trilogy (1925-28) and the Mårbacka trilogy (1922-32), the latter often taken to be autobiographical, give some idea of the range and power of Lagerlöf's writing. Several of her texts inspired innovative films, among them *Herr Arnes pengar* (*Sir Arne's Treasure*), directed by Mauritz Stiller (1919) and based on *Herr Arnes penningar* (1903; *Lord Arne's Silver*), and *Körkarlen* (*The Phantom Carriage*), directed by Victor Sjöström (1921) and based on Lagerlöf's *Körkarlen* (1912). She was awarded the Nobel Prize for Literature, as the first woman ever, in 1909, and elected to the Swedish Academy, again as the first woman, in 1914. Having been able to buy back the farm of Mårbacka, which her family had lost as the result of bankruptcy, Lagerlöf spent the last three decades of her life combining her writing with the responsibilities of running a sizeable estate. Her work has been translated into close to 50 languages.

A Manor House Tale, translated by Peter Graves
Lord Arne's Silver, translated by Sarah Death
The Phantom Carriage, translated by Peter Graves
The Löwensköld Ring, translated by Linda Schenck
Charlotte Löwensköld, translated by Linda Schenck
Anna Svärd, translated by Linda Schenck
Nils Holgersson's Wonderful Journey Through Sweden, translated by Peter Graves
Mårbacka, translated by Sarah Death

www.ingramcontent.com/pod-product-compliance
Lightning Source LLC
Chambersburg PA
CBHW060607310726
48982CB00008B/1260/J

* 9 7 8 1 9 0 9 4 0 8 6 8 5 *